The Sodmire Rats

James Copp

Published by New Generation Publishing in 2015

Copyright © James Copp 2015

First Edition

The author asserts the moral right under the Copyright, Designs and Patents Act 1988 to be identified as the author of this work.

All Rights reserved. No part of this publication may be reproduced, stored in a retrieval system or transmitted, in any form or by any means without the prior consent of the author, nor be otherwise circulated in any form of binding or cover other than that which it is published and without a similar condition being imposed on the subsequent purchaser.

www.newgeneration-publishing.com

Contents

1: SAM JOHNSON … 1
2: TITUS ANDRONICUS PLEBIUS … 10
3: PICKFIGHT THE ACOLYTE … 23
4: NIGEL QUENTIN ADAMS … 31
5: CLIVE MINNOWFIELD … 40
6: LADY KITTY … 53
7: VICKY AND BETH … 64
8: AMY JOHNSON … 77
9: BONCE MANGLE … 87
10: BOBBY AND LOUISE … 102
11: RICHARD CHOAT … 110
12: VINNY TRASHMAN … 121
13: SIR RICHARD … 137
14: NOBBLER BATES … 148
15: BOADICEA … 156
16: CHARLOTTE PIECE … 167
17: TOM HERTZ … 178
18: PERCE PRATT … 189
19: ROOTS PENGARDON … 198
20: LANCE AND GAVIN … 203
21: TOBY BANNISTER … 213
22: JACK STRAWBRIDGE … 221
23: JO CORNWALL … 232
24: SIMON HAWKER … 243
25: WPC GWEN EVERS … 252
26: NELL AND THE DRAGON … 260
27: MORRIS AND NORA … 271
28: DOCTOR SPIEGEL … 280

29: JACKIE CHOAT	295
30: LA DEMOISELLE SAUVAGE	306
31: ROBBIE THE MECHANIC	317
32: MAGIC MERV	327
33: HUBERT AND HORACE	336
34: BRUNO THE BEAR	351
35: GRANDDAD AND GREAT UNCLE BERT	360
36: NURSE BLOSSOM	368
37: DOLLY KILLJOY	379
38: GARETH AND THE WHALE	388
39: MR. AND MRS. KITE	401
40: MR. LIVINGSTONE	413
41: COCO THE CHIMP	427
42: SERGEANT ARTHUR	437
43: J. C. KINSMAN	451
44: ERNIE STAMPEASY	462
45: LIEUTENANT CALLIOPE	474
46: HENRY KITE	482

1

SAM JOHNSON

It is not generally appreciated, even amongst the sorts of people, often characterized as geeks, nerds and scientists, who display an unhealthy interest in such things, that temporal displacement, or time travel as it has become popularly known, can cause the human brain to snap instantaneously into a particularly stubborn form of short-term memory loss that renders the displacee, or time traveller, temporarily unaware of what has happened to them. It is also not widely appreciated that this effect can be especially pronounced when the displacement is initiated accidentally and/ or without the prior knowledge of the individual experiencing it.

It was not so surprising, then, that when Henry Kite was transported without warning almost two thousand years backwards in time, his brain failed at first to keep pace with his body, causing him to labour for several hours after the event under the mistaken impression that the date was still Monday, 27 April AD 1987, and not Tuesday, 20 June AD 61, as was actually the case. It was even less surprising, perhaps, given that self-denial is also a familiar side effect of involuntary displacement, that it took Mr. Kite rather longer than a few hours to come to terms with the fact that the whole thing was his own stupid fault.

(Extract from *The Incompetent Displacee: An Essay on Accidental Time Travel* by Professor W. I. C. Kinsman BSc, MSc, PhD, FRITD.).

When Henry Kite found himself standing in the middle of Stonehenge wearing nothing but a singed bath towel and a look of astonishment, his first thought was that he had fallen victim to Sam Johnson's idea of a practical joke. It was a reasonable enough assumption for him to make, too, given that the last thing he remembered doing before coming to his senses on Salisbury Plain, was sinking to his knees after Sam had hit him on the side of the head with a pool cue. At the time, he had assumed that the contact between cue and skull was accidental. Now, he wasn't so sure.

Henry's second thought, if you discount the bit about his skull and the pool cue and a self-pitying and somewhat obscure 'Why does it always happen to me?' was that his predicament had something to do with a stag night: and that, since he was the one standing alone and half-naked by moonlight, any such event must have been organized in his honour. Not that honour, he told himself bitterly as he trembled with a mixture of chill air and growing resentment, was something he thought he was likely to feel a lot more of during what looked like being a long and embarrassing journey home from Wiltshire to Essex without his car, his clothes, his shoes, his credit cards or anything resembling money.

'F-f-friends!' he stammered, through teeth clenched tightly against the cool night air. 'Who needs the b-bastards anyway?'

He shook his head irritably at the thought that Sam was probably tucked up in bed at home in Chelmsford, while he had been left to gaze down at his dimly seen toes curling with icy discomfort on the damp ground.

'How'd he do it, though?' he asked them. 'That's what I w-wanna know. And where's that burning smell coming from?' He sniffed the air, his arm, and the back of a hand. 'Like someone set fire to the cat . . .?'

Another thought struck him as he turned to frown up at the ghostly bulk of a nearby standing stone. 'Doesn't make any kind of sense, though, does it?' he asked it. 'I mean I haven't even got a g-girlfriend, never mind a f-f-fiancée.'

He pursed his lips sadly and tried not to think too hard about the disaster that had for so long been masquerading as his love life. He had more important things to worry about, he told himself, than his habitual failure with women. Things like how Sam had spirited him the one hundred miles, or whatever it was, from Essex to Wiltshire in the middle of the night and without him noticing. And, more important than that, why it was that he seemed to have regained consciousness standing up, and not, as might have been expected had he been battered into unconsciousness with a pool cue, lying on the ground. Healthy people did not, he decided against a rising tide of panic, lapse into and then out of unconsciousness so rapidly that they couldn't manage to fall to the ground in between times. Or at least, not as far as he knew they didn't: unless, perhaps, they had suffered in the process some serious malfunctioning of the central nervous system, like an aneurism or an embolism (whatever they were), or some other equally fatal-sounding ailment that might reduce his mental capacities to those of a root vegetable in the twinkling of an eye and without him noticing that either. The thought that he might be caught in the throes of some rapidly advancing senility made his scalp tingle and his anal sphincter clench and unclench in what felt uncomfortably like the prelude to a soiling of what would have been his underpants had he been fortunate enough to have been wearing any. And as if that wasn't bad enough, most unsettling of all, given that there was nothing obviously erotic about freezing from the feet up in a damp field at dead of night without so much as a porno mag for company, was the fact that he had a passably respectable erection: an occurrence which, under other circumstances, might have been a cause for modest rejoicing, but which, in his current situation, had him wondering uncomfortably if he had developed, albeit unwittingly until now, a liking for getting his rocks off while skulking half-naked around ancient monuments by moonlight.

Suddenly, he felt a powerful urge to wave his arms above his head, and to flee screaming into the night. He was still trying to decide which point of the compass would offer least resistance to his craven flight when the howling started. It seemed to be coming from the shadows beneath the massive standing stones immediately in front of him. But rather than being paralyzed into immobility by it, he smiled knowingly to himself and shook his head in grudging admiration for what he took to be yet further proof of Sam's infantile fascination with the art of making other people, particularly those he numbered amongst his closest friends, look and feel stupid in public.

Everything seemed to fall into place for him then as he imagined his erstwhile best friend, a can of beer in one hand and an enormous spliff in the other, sitting in front of the sound system that always seemed to occupy most of his untidy flat, copying tracks from a BBC sound effects album entitled *The Scariest Animal Noises of All Time Ever*, or something equally puerile, for the specific purpose of terrifying him, Henry, out of his wits.

'Well, we'll see about that, won't we?' he snarled as he marched towards the howling in search of Sam and the sound system he fully expected to find hidden somewhere in the surrounding darkness.

'All right!' he shouted, 'you can come on out now, you *bastard*!'

But he was wrong: Sam knew nothing of his predicament. This was the late Iron Age, and Sam, and sound systems, and BBC sound effects albums hadn't been invented yet: wouldn't be invented for another two thousand years, in fact. Or to put it another way, the howling was real and so were the wolves that were doing it: two uncomfortable facts that became all too obvious to Henry a moment later when half a dozen huge bristling bodies came stalking towards him out of the shadows, tongues lolling, teeth glistening and hard eyes glittering hungrily at him in the suddenly unfriendly moonlight.

To say that his reaction to the appearance of the hunting pack was athletic would be to seriously understate the facts. The knowing sneer vanished instantly from his face, and a fraction of a second later, without any clear recollection of how he had managed it, he found himself lying flat on his belly fifteen feet up in the air clinging for dear life by chipped fingernails to the lintel at the top of one of Stonehenge's giant stone trilithons. A nanosecond after that, peering down into the gloom from this newfound place of safety, he was about to congratulate himself on his hitherto unsuspected athleticism when his brain remembered that the top of his head had been cracked hard against the underside of the stone lintel on its way up from the ground, and lapsed into a sudden and blissful unconsciousness.

Almost three hours passed before he came back to his senses, by which time the sun had risen, dull red, through the early morning mists shrouding the horizon behind him, and the air had became noticeably warmer than it was when he passed out. The world looked a much friendlier place, too: not least because the wolves had finally given up waiting for him to come down and had gone off in search of a more easily accessible breakfast elsewhere. In fact, so brief had been his encounter with the terrifying creatures that he could almost have convinced himself that they hadn't existed. Almost, but not quite: his precarious position on top of the country's most celebrated ancient monument, wrapped in a singed bath towel and with no explanation, other than terror, for what he was doing there, saw to that.

But the more he tried to make sense of what was happening to him, the less sense any of it seemed to make. The most logical explanation seemed to be that he was dreaming. But the cool morning breeze on his face, the pain in the top of his head, and the clamminess of the cold stone pressing against his naked chest were far too real to be mere figments of his imagination. And if *they* were real there was a better than even chance that the wolves had been real, too: escaped, perhaps, from some zoo or circus or biological research institution nearby. Of course, the fact that he hadn't heard about any such escape could mean that it hadn't happened. But it could also mean that it had happened so recently that the country's media hadn't had time to catch up with the story. Either way, he couldn't rid himself of a nagging suspicion that the look in the eyes of the wolves had been so quintessentially primeval that they couldn't possibly have belonged to any zoo, circus or research institution that existed outside of a horror movie.

'And that isn't the worst of it,' he muttered as he gazed uneasily at the surrounding countryside. 'What the hell have they done to Stonehenge?'

It was true that there weren't enough trees out there to qualify as a wood, much less a forest – just a few scrubby silver birch with the odd gorse bush scattered between them – but the point was that trees, no matter how few and how stunted they might be, should not be growing all around the country's most important archaeological site. And while he was prepared to believe that a few escaped wolves could have gone unnoticed by the country's media, he was absolutely certain that if someone had tried to turn Stonehenge into an arboretum it would have been splashed across the front page of every newspaper in the land.

'The place is a World Heritage Site for God's sake!' he blurted. 'You can't go planting trees all over the bloody thing and expect no-one to notice!'

Then there was the visitors' centre and the main road that ran past it from London to Cornwall, or wherever it went. He couldn't even begin to imagine how someone had got rid of them.

He shook his head, and decided that the best thing he could do was go back to sleep and wait until everything got back to normal. He gave a long, ragged sigh, lowered his head onto his forearms, closed his eyes and hoped against hope that he would wake sooner rather than later to find himself at home in his nice warm bed with Spike lying across his legs purring contentedly. He sighed again, and was just starting to drift into something that might easily have resembled sleep when he heard, or thought he heard, a voice calling to him from somewhere below his hiding place.

'Hey, buddy,' it seemed to say, drifting upwards in a hissing stage whisper, 'how the hells did you get up there anyhow?'

He opened his eyes and listened intently. But all he could hear were the sighing of the breeze and a bird singing somewhere high above his head.

He listened for a second or two longer, then pursed his lips, closed his eyes and rested his head back down on his forearms.

A moment later, he heard the voice again. 'Hey, buddy,' it demanded, a note of irritation creeping into it now, 'you gonna talk to me or what?'

'Go away!' he muttered. 'Some of us are trying to sleep up here!'

When the voice called up at him for a third time, there was no mistaking its owner's exasperation. 'Hey! You *dead* up there or what?'

Henry opened his eyes, blinked tentatively and leaned sideways to peer over the edge of the stone block. Below him was an odd-looking little man standing with his feet planted firmly apart and his hands resting on his hips. He had a black eye and a split lip, and was mud-streaked, heavily tanned and wearing a grubby loincloth and what appeared to be a homemade grass skirt.

Henry pursed his lips and propped himself on an elbow. 'Er, sorry,' he said, 'but were you talking to me?'

The little man sighed and looked down at his feet. 'You see somebody else round here, buddy?' he asked, waving a hand at the nearby standing stones.

Henry gazed thoughtfully around the stone circle. 'Um, well,' he said, 'no, it's just that I thought . . . '

'How'd you get up there, anyhow? I mean I'm impressed. Really I am!'

Henry blew out his cheeks. 'Oh, well . . . I climbed up,' he said with a shrug, as if scaling stone monuments in bath towels was all in a day's work for him. 'Sort of,' he added with less conviction. 'I think.' He fell silent and gazed with unfocussed eyes at a nearby standing stone. 'I just wish,' he muttered, 'I knew how I got *here*!'

He took a very deep breath and looked down at the little man again. 'I mean,' he said, more to himself than the new arrival, 'I know what happened right up to the point where I passed out,' he frowned at the memory of Sam hitting him in the side of the head with the pool cue, 'I think . . .'

He touched his temple gingerly and was disappointed when his fingers failed to come away coated with blood. 'He hit me *really* hard, though,' he said, blinking several times at the lichen-covered stone block beneath him. 'But after that,' he added, looking up, 'it's all gone a bit hazy, really.'

'You was kidnapped, then. That's about the size of it, right?'

'Well,' said Henry, 'I wouldn't have put it that way myself. But now that you come to mention it . . . '

'Uh-huh, uh-huh,' nodded the little man with a distracted glance around the circle of standing stones. 'And you don't know where you are, right?'

'Oh yes,' said Henry, confidently, 'I know where I am all right.' He frowned. 'Except for all those trees . . . '

His voice tailed off into silence as he stared at nothing in particular. 'Only I thought there was a visitors' centre,' he added, pushing himself into a sitting position with his legs dangling over the edge of the stone lintel, 'over there,' he pointed, 'somewhere?' He looked around and then down. 'You know?'

'You comfortable up there, are you buddy?' asked the little man. The trilithon was almost three times his height and he was beginning to get a crick in the neck from looking up at Henry sitting on top of it. He turned his head slowly from side to side to ease the strain, raising and lowering his chin as he went and listening with ghoulish satisfaction as the bones in his neck clicked and cracked into place. He flexed his lower jaw in elaborate fashion and blinked at the base of the nearest standing stone. 'What in all the hells is a visitor's centre when it's at home?' he asked it, quietly.

Henry wasn't listening. 'I wouldn't say it was comfortable, as such,' he admitted. 'I mean, it feels sort of safe, if you know what I mean? It was hell getting up here, mind,' he added, sidling on his buttocks closer to the edge of the stone block, careful to keep the hem of the bath towel tucked coyly between his knees as he moved. He looked up and waved vaguely at the surrounding countryside. 'There were some pretty weird things happening down there last night, I can tell you.' He frowned at the newcomer. 'I thought wolves were extinct, though, aren't they? In England I mean?'

'England?' said the little man, absently. 'What's *England* when it's at home, buddy; if you don't mind me askin'?'

'Good question,' snorted Henry, 'after what I saw last night! Makes you wonder, doesn't it: people keeping things like that for pets and experimenting on them and stuff? I mean, it doesn't seem right, does it?'

He shook his head. 'I thought we were supposed to be a nation of animal lovers. You know, fair play, cricket, and all that?'

'Cricket?' muttered the little man, whose neck twisting seemed suddenly to have rendered him deaf in both ears. He stuck an exploratory index finger into his right ear and opened and closed his mouth like a beached carp. There was a soft click inside his skull and his hearing returned to normal.

'What's with the loincloth, and the, er,' Henry coughed diplomatically, 'grass skirt?' With nothing but a bath towel covering his own modesty, he felt he was in no position to be critical of the little man's eccentric attire. 'You been to a fancy dress party or something?'

'Don't ask,' he replied, flapping irritably at the hem of the skirt. 'Got bleedin' ambushed, didn't I? Should've seen it comin', mind? But they caught me off me guard havin' a shit. Bastards! Took everythin' I had, an' all.' He reached down to hitch up his loincloth. ''Cept me jockstrap and me strikes.' He flapped at the grass skirt again. 'Had to make this lot meself to look halfway decent.' He gazed up at Henry with rounded eyes. 'Reckon the bastards was gonna eat me if I hadn't got away.'

Suddenly, something about a motorway service station jogged Henry's memory. 'I had three Arsenal supporters after me the other day,' he blurted with a clarity of recollection that surprised him. 'Bastards chased me for miles, they did! I was scared stiff,' he added as the image in his mind's eye came into even sharper focus. He thought for a moment. 'Well,' he admitted as the image changed into something that he wasn't quite so sure of, 'I say Arsenal supporters, but they could have been . . . '

'That bad, then?' interrupted the little man, a stubby index finger exploring the depths of his left ear. 'Arsenal, like?'

Henry snorted. 'This lot was bloody terrifying! One of 'em was wandering around chewing his shirt.'

'I had to eat me shoes, once,' offered the little man, trying not to be outdone. 'And half me mate's chinstrap. Basic survival trainin' that is. To be fair,' he mused, 'it was better than most of the crap they used to give us.'

'I had a Vegetarian Chicken Supreme at a service station the other day,' muttered Henry, unwittingly upping the ante as even more memories came flooding back to him. 'You could've used that as a shoe. I don't know how they get away with it, do you, fast food?'

The little man lifted the front of his grass skirt with one hand and delved inside his tatty loincloth with the other.

'You hungry, then?' he asked, bringing out a stiff, furry bundle and holding it up. 'Got a rat,' he said, waggling it proudly. 'Wanna bite?'

Henry curled his lip. 'Er . . . no, I don't think . . . '

'Big bugger, mind?' enthused the little man, examining it closely. "Nough for both of us, I reckon?'

'No, really! Thanks for the offer, though, eh?'

'Up to you buddy. Just be more for me, that's all.'

'You're a Yank, then?' hazarded Henry. 'I was wondering: you not knowing anything about cricket and that.'

This time it was the little man who wasn't listening. He was wandering around picking up sticks and twigs and handfuls of dried grass. When he had collected as much as he thought he would need, he took a flint and tinder from his loincloth and sat down close to the base of Henry's trilithon.

'You gonna stay up there all bleedin' day, buddy?' he asked, twisting to glance awkwardly over his shoulder and up at the soles of Henry's bare feet. 'Only it's a real pain in the neck, y'know, keep havin' to look up.'

His name was Titus Andronicus Plebius, and he was a fine, upstanding citizen of the Glorious Roman Empire. Or at least, that's what he said when he thought the Romans might be listening. As survival strategies went it had been reasonably successful for him so far and a lot safer than telling the truth. On the other hand, he had found that it wasn't quite so effective if you tried it with the Visigoths, or the Vandals, or the Huns, or the Atrobates, or the Icenii, or the Durotriges, or any of the many independent tribes that lived within a few hundred miles of the Roman Empire, because they were inclined to rip your heart and lungs out with their bare hands if they had the slightest suspicion that you might be some sort of Roman, or, worse still, a Roman collaborator. Most of them hated the Romans so much that they could even get pretty violent if they thought you had ever considered, no matter how fleetingly, having a bathhouse built next to your mud hut. The tribes of northern Europe were sticklers for hygiene and avoided it like the plague whenever they could.

Titus thought he knew all there was to know about the Romans and their attitudes towards personal hygiene, but he had never seen a towel like the one Henry was wearing around his waist. True, it was purple, the colour of Roman nobility, and apart from the singed bits around the edges looked like just the sort of thing any highborn Roman might have been wearing. That didn't mean that Henry was either highborn or Roman, of course: he could just as easily have picked the towel up off the street after some rich patrician had discarded it because it was damaged. But Titus didn't think so. There was something about the way Henry talked that suggested that he was from a wealthy family and had only recently fallen on hard times. By his own admission, he didn't really know where he was, or how he had got there, and in Titus's book that could mean only one thing: magical abduction by witchcraft and a female person or persons unknown. Someone like the fearsome warrior queen Cartamandua of the Brigantes, for instance, who was rumoured to have magicked away her royal partner Venutius so that she could have her lustful way with his not so royal, but extremely well hung, stable boy, Vellocatus.

Titus knew that you had to be very careful who you talked to in this neck of the woods, because magical abductions happened all the time, and if you didn't take the proper precautions you could find yourself spirited away from your nearest and dearest for the personal gratification of some insatiable bit of royal totty who would use and abuse you until you were nothing more than a dried-up husk of your former self. He had thought long and hard about such appalling misuses of magical powers, and was furious that they only ever happened to virgin bumpkins from villages down the road, and never to really deserving cases like himself who would have known how to make the most of a bit of magical debauchery. It was a source of constant irritation to him that his own experience of abduction was not of the really interesting slippery, wet and groaning variety, but of the infinitely more painful blood, guts and massacring type where Roman soldiers hacked your friends and family to bits before dragging you off at the tender age of eleven to serve as a stable boy for the Roman army: and not, to his eternal regret, for Cartamandua's cavalry.

On his sixteenth birthday he had been forced to join an auxiliary regiment with the XX Valeria Victrix where he'd fought bravely alongside men with tribal origins similar to his own who he had come to regard not only as his friends but also his surrogate family. But all that had changed in the blinking of an eye on the day, three years later, when, at the Battle of Watling Street, he and his comrades had been ordered by their commander, Gaius Suetonius Paulinus, to slaughter every last man, woman, child and animal in the wagon train following along behind Boudicca's defeated army. Tens of thousands had been massacred that day: many of them women and babes-in-arms from his own tribe, the Durotriges. He had deserted later that night and been on the run ever since, living off the land as best he could and making life as difficult as possible for the now hated Roman invaders.

His real name was Corio Boc, and he was what Henry would have called 'an Ancient Briton' or 'a person of Celtic extraction'. Not that Titus would ever have thought of himself as either. For one thing, he was only twenty years old and had nothing obviously 'ancient' about him. And for another, the word 'Celtic' hadn't been invented in his time and could just as easily have been translated as meaning 'A Scottish football team based in the city of Glasgow' as 'Of or pertaining to any of a group of ancient peoples of Western Europe including the Britons and the Gauls', especially if the translation had been rendered by the occasionally erratic device that Henry was wearing unwittingly around his left wrist: a sophisticated piece of cybernetic circuitry that made it possible for him to converse more or less coherently with Titus without either of them suspecting that they weren't speaking the same language. It was a truly remarkable piece of micro-electronic engineering, not least because it removed the sort of lip-syncing problems you get in movies when one language is dubbed into another: with the result that Henry's and Titus's lips seemed to be moving in time with whatever it was that each of them thought the other was saying. More remarkable still was the fact that in spite of its occasionally idiosyncratic rendering of one or two of the lesser-known ancient European dialects (Latin with a strong Durotriges accent, for instance) its translations were provided as near instantaneously as made no difference. The practical upshot of which was that Titus had decided that Henry was some sort of sex slave of noble Roman extraction recently escaped from the clutches of a powerful witch queen like Cartamantua, while Henry had come to the conclusion that the little Ancient Briton was an eccentric ex-patriot American with a penchant for dressing in filthy rags and wandering around the countryside at weekends and on bank holidays in the company of other, like-minded inadequates pretending to be a Roman soldier.

2

TITUS ANDRONICUS PLEBIUS

Henry eventually plucked up enough courage to make his way down from the top of the huge trilithon to the short, spiky grass at its feet. After dangling for a while by his fingertips, with his toes scrabbling for an elusive purchase on the slippery rock making him feel vulnerable and the knowledge that the flapping bath towel offered an unimpeded view of his nakedness if the little man chanced to look up making him feel even worse, he finally let go and tumbled to the ground in a heap. After righting himself and adjusting the towel to preserve what little remained of his dignity, he looked up and saw that the little man had got a fire going.

As the flames took hold in the handfuls of dry leaves and grass that Titus had collected for the purpose, he tucked the flint and tinder back into his loincloth and started adding twigs and small branches to the growing blaze.

Henry padded around the fire on bare feet and squatted opposite the little man, grateful for a chance to get some warmth back into his aching body. 'I'm impressed,' he said, leaning forward into the wispy smoke and rubbing his hands together over the crackling flames. 'Where'd you learn to do that?'

'All part of the training,' said Titus, looking up. He grinned. 'You . . . er, wanna be careful, buddy,' he twiddled his fingers at his own face, 'you've singed yer,' and then at Henry's hair and eyebrows, 'and yer . . . wosnames.'

'Sorry?' said Henry, putting a hand up to his head. 'What do you . . .?'

But there was that odour of burnt hair again. He glanced at the fire and leaned hastily away from the flames.

'Here,' said Titus, holding up the rat and a sharp stick, 'you wanna do the grub?'

Henry shied away from the carcass with a mixture of disbelief and disgust. 'Er, no,' he said, smiling stiffly. 'You're the . . . er, the culinary expert, right?'

'Bagsie I gets the 'ead, then,' grinned the little man.

Henry looked away, and tried to think of something other than what it would be like to eat a rat's head. But curiosity got the better of him and he turned to watch through slitted eyes as Titus held the rat in one hand and rammed the stick into its mouth with the other.

Something in the action jogged Henry's memory. 'He was the boss's nephew,' he said, flinching at the sight of the dead rodent being skewered on the end of the stick. 'Adams? And I didn't get on with him very well.'

'What,' said Titus, twisting the stick, 'and the bastard shafted you, did he?'

'Not exactly,' replied Henry, wondering as he said it why he was confiding in this strange little man. 'I think it was his Auntie Kitty who did that. The trouble is I can't really remember.' He frowned. 'Must have been the bang on the head,' he added under his breath. 'Anyway,' he continued with a sigh, 'she thought the sun shone out of his . . . ' He winced as the point of the stick emerged from the rat's backside. 'You know?' he ended, lamely.

Titus pushed one end of the stick into the ground at an angle to the fire and sat back as the rat started to smoulder over the flames.

Henry leaned forward, extending a hand through the thin smoke and careful to avoid getting burned. 'I'm Henry, by the way. Henry Kite.'

'Titus,' said Corio Boc. 'Titus Andronicus Plebius.'

Henry nodded, knowingly. 'Liked Shakespeare, did they, your parents?'

Titus threw a couple of sticks onto the fire. 'Don't know what the old man liked,' he muttered. 'Never got a chance to ask the bastard, I didn't! Left home when I was eight years old. Ran off to fight the Picts, they said,' he added, looking up. He poked vigorously at the fire. 'She never saw 'im again after that, me old mum. Probably been shacked up with some pox-ridden tattooed Scottish tart ever since.'

Henry shrugged, glumly. 'Yeah, my dad left when I was only a couple of months old, too. Moved to Australia,' he added, nodding absently to himself as if that explained everything. 'I used to think it was my fault, you know? Like he took one look at me and decided he couldn't cope? Maybe he did, too, because my mother buggered off after him as soon as she got the chance.'

He sighed and gazed into the fire. 'Still, at least she waited 'til my sixteenth birthday. So I guess she deserves some sort of credit.' He looked up. 'She lives in the States now. Miami?' He took a deep breath. 'But I don't have much to do with either of them anymore.'

He shook his head, slowly. 'He used to send me lots of stuff for Christmas and birthdays when I was a kid, though, my dad? Probably just feeling guilty,' he added, morosely.

He brightened and waved an arm at the standing stones. 'It was mostly pretty good stuff, though: books about archaeology, ancient history, all that? I thought it was great. Lots of stories about Vikings and Romans and Celts and that sort of stuff. Perfect for a growing boy, you know?'

He smiled encouragingly at Titus, but the look went unnoticed. The little man was staring distractedly into the fire.

'You're one of those, what do you call 'em,' said Henry, tentatively, 're-enactors, aren't you? Doing battles and things? Like the Sealed Knot Society? I never realized you went into it in so much detail, though. You know, with personal histories and all that?'

Titus shrugged non-committally and poked at the fire with a stick, gazing into the flames and nodding sagely as if he had the faintest idea what Henry was talking about.

Henry had a sudden thought. 'So your lot built this place, then,' he ventured, 'to do your re-enacting and stuff in?'

Titus looked up with a sudden snort of derision. 'Yeah, right! Listen, my lot couldn't build a stone karsey if their backsides was on fire.' He looked down at the smoking carcass and waved vaguely at the stone circle. 'Some bunch called the Belgae built this lot, they say, before my lot was even born.'

Henry frowned and stared into the fire with a growing suspicion that he was missing something fundamental about his new companion. For want of something better to do, he glanced surreptitiously at his watch, only to find that it had gone missing along with the rest of his things.

'Bastard!' he thought bitterly as Sam's grinning face seemed to hover in the smoke above the fire, taunting him.

He frowned and did a quick double take, peering down at a band of letters and numbers that seemed to have been printed around his wrist in place of his watch. He licked a fingertip and rubbed at his skin, expecting the markings to come off, but they didn't even smudge. Something at the back of his mind told him that this was important, if only he could remember why.

'Got the time?' he asked, looking up.

Titus turned towards him. 'What for?'

Henry looked at the little man's wrist and saw that he wasn't wearing a watch either. 'Ah,' he nodded, knowingly. 'Got yours, too, did they?' He turned to glance over his shoulder at the rising sun. 'What time do you think it is, then; five, maybe six o'clock?'

Titus shook his head. 'Can't be more'n an hour after cockcrow,' he gazed up at the sky, 'if that.'

He picked up the stick with the rat on the end of it and thrust the smoking carcass under Henry's nose. 'Done yet, you reckon?' he asked.

Henry leaned away from the thing with a grimace of distaste. It smelled like charred guts and looked like bubonic plague.

'A bit longer, I think,' he said, hoping to put off indefinitely the moment when he would be forced to decide if he was brave enough to take a bite out of the vile thing.

Titus nodded and jammed the stick back into the ground. 'How'd you get here then?' he asked, glancing at the bath towel. 'I mean, you're not from round here, are you?'

Henry shrugged. 'I don't really know,' he admitted, screwing up his face in thought. 'But I think there was a woman . . . '

'I knew it!' crowed Titus, slapping his thigh in delight. 'I bloody knew it, didn't I? Soon as I saw you up there,' he waved at the trilithon, 'I said to meself "That poor bugger's been dumped by some tart! Poor schmuck!"'

Henry tucked the towel more tightly between his knees and looked self-consciously up at the sky. 'Well, not exactly dumped,' he said, his face reddening with embarrassment, 'more sort of . . . '

'You're one of them sex slaves, right?' said Titus with a broad grin. 'You can always tell.' He gazed intently at Henry for a moment. 'It's in the eyes, see,' He nodded, knowingly. 'Rich bitch, was she? Had her way with you and kicked you out? I know the sort. Happens all the time, buddy. You oughta be thankful she left you with your left and right intact.'

He gazed at Henry, again. 'She did though, didn't she, buddy,' he asked, nodding at Henry's groin, 'leave you with your goolies attached?'

Henry frowned. 'Um, yeah, but I don't think that's got anything . . . '

Titus nodded his understanding. 'One of those Brigantian witches, was she? Wouldn't mind a go at one o' them meself! Saw that Cartamandua in one o' them Genounian bathhouses once. Fittest bit o' totty I ever seen in me life, she was.' His eyes lit up with admiration. 'Smack me arse with her charioteer's whip any time she wants, that one could.'

'Um,' ventured Henry, 'you, er, you don't think you're taking this roleplaying thing a bit far, do you? I mean, with the Ancient Brit patois, and all that? I'm sure it's essential if you want your Boy Scouts' Badge for Historical Realism, or whatever it's called,' he gazed around with a shrug, 'but there's no one here to judge your performance, is there?' He had a sudden thought. 'Unless – look, *I'm* not some kind of judge, if that's what you're thinking?'

Titus stared at him in silence for a moment, his eyes suddenly hard and watchful. 'Judge?' he echoed with a tight-lipped smile. 'Not with you buddy,' he added, softly. 'Not suggestin' I'm some sort of,' his voice dropped to an ominous whisper, '*criminal*, or something, are you?'

Henry was taken aback by the sudden lack of warmth in the little man's eyes. The last thing he wanted was a physical confrontation with him. He wasn't dressed for it. And besides, there was something about his otherwise jovial demeanour that suggested that Titus would be capable of acts of unwelcome violence if the fancy ever took him. Worse still, an unnerving suspicion had just begun to worm its way into his confused mind.

'No, no,' he said, hastily, 'of course not! I mean it's just a bit of fun, isn't it? It's just that, well, I mean, you aren't a *real* Roman soldier, are you?' He tried a friendly smile for size, but saw instantly that Titus wasn't impressed by it.

The little man rose stiffly, silently, and stood facing him with his fists clenched and his feet planted firmly apart.

'Reckon I'm gonna need a bigger fire,' he said, coldly. 'Your scabby carcass ain't gonna cook proper over this piddlin' little thing, is it?'

'Ah!' said Henry, getting awkwardly to his feet and backing away a couple of steps in preparation for rapid flight. 'Yes, look, what I meant was . . . I mean, I didn't mean . . . ' He hesitated: Titus wasn't looking at him any more. His jaw had sagged open and he was staring wide-eyed past him at something over his left shoulder.

Henry turned to follow the little man's gaze and blinked in astonishment at what he saw heading towards them.

A young woman was approaching out of the red haze of the rising sun. She was tall, apparently naked, and striding across the short grass silhouetted against the glare like a catwalk model with her hips swaying provocatively and her long hair streaming behind her in the wind of her passage.

Henry felt rooted to the spot. This was partly because every inch of the young woman's body was outlined against the ruddy morning light, leaving almost nothing to the imagination: but mostly because the heavy metal object held in the fist of her right hand, and lying flat across her right shoulder pointing back the way she had come, was an enormous double-edged sword.

His mouth dropped open in comical imitation of the little Ancient Briton's, and time seemed to stand still as the apparition came swaying lithely towards them in what felt like slow motion.

He tried to swallow, but couldn't. His lips were suddenly bone dry, and his teeth felt as if they had been glued to the inside of his mouth. He tried to speak, but all that came out was the familiar high-pitched squeak, like the forlorn mewing of a lost kitten, that always seemed to afflict him at moments of heightened anxiety.

'Hells!' hissed Titus behind him in an awe-stricken whisper. 'Don't ever, *ever*! let 'em tell ya prayin' to chicken guts is a waste o' time, buddy. OK?'

'Do you know her then?' whispered Henry.

When Titus didn't reply, he took a couple of faltering half-steps back towards him with his eyes still fixed on the young woman. 'I said,' he insisted, leaning close to his ear, 'do you know who she is?'

Titus nodded, clasped his hands together and sank to his knees.

Henry looked down at him in astonishment. 'What the . . .?' he hissed, glancing quickly at the young woman and then back again. 'Who . . .?'

'Venus,' murmured Titus, blinking and licking his lips in appreciation. 'Kallipygos, Morpho, Ambologera . . .!'

Henry frowned. 'No, I mean,' he snapped, 'who is she *really*?'

'Surfeit of female pulchritude, lover,' said the young woman, striding up.

Henry flinched and turned to squint at her as she stepped out of the glare of the sun and into the shadow of one of the standing stones. He could see immediately that she was every bit as stunning as he had imagined her being, and that apart from a tight leather thong and a mass of jewellery that clinked as she moved, she was as near naked as made no difference. Swirling tattoos decorated her face, neck and breasts. Gold bands wound tightly around her wrists and upper arms. Chunky gold rings glistened from the fingers and thumbs of both hands, and a plain gold circlet sat snugly on her tattooed forehead. Thin discs of beaten gold dangled from her ears, and a magnificent torc of braided gold wire clung to her slim neck, its twin animal-headed terminals snarling a warning at anyone who might dare to approach their exotic mistress unbidden. Embossed leather straps crisscrossed invitingly between her tattooed breasts, and a studded leather belt, bearing a pair of silver-handled daggers in leather sheaths, sat low on her slim hips.

Henry had the feeling that he had met this magnificent young woman before, although for the life of him he couldn't remember when or where.

They looked at one another in silence for a moment. Then the young woman raised a mocking eyebrow and blew him a kiss.

Something in the gesture tugged hard at his memory and a name surfaced at the back of his mind. He leaned forward slightly with a tentative hand stretching towards her.

'Err, excuse me,' he said, aware how ridiculous his question might sound, 'but is your name . . . I mean, is it . . . are you, are you *Blossom*, by any chance?'

'Course I am, lover,' she grinned, with a flash of perfect teeth. 'Who'd you think I was, Aphro-bleedin'-dite?'

She thrust the point of the huge sword into the soft ground at her feet, and struck a pose with her hands resting on its silver pommel. 'Lots of similarities, mind,' she said, turning this way and that. 'But, see, she's had the tucks,' she took her hands from the sword pommel and pointed delicately at her naked breasts with the tips of her painted fingernails, 'here an' here,' she turned her back on Titus and thrust her buttocks towards him, 'and here. And as you can see,' she said proudly, spreading her legs and bending to look at him upside-down between her knees, 'I haven't.'

'Dead,' breathed Titus. 'Dead an' gone to Elysium.'

Blossom stood up and turned towards him. 'Hello,' she said, looking down with her hands on her hips. 'Is that a gladius under your grass skirt, lover, or are you just a horny little Roman?'

'*Woof*,' barked Titus, gruffly. '*Woof-woof!*'

'Your dog's got a boner, Henry,' said Blossom, breezily. 'You ought to keep him on a lead you know.'

Then, with her feet planted wide apart and her legs straight, she bent at the waist and gazed into Titus's saucer-like eyes. 'You're an enthusiastic little fellow, aren't you?' she said. 'Ooh, sorry,' she grinned, looking down, '*big* fellow, I mean.' She touched his cheek with the tip of a finger. 'And getting bigger all the time, too, I reckon. Tell you what,' she breathed, huskily, 'how would you like to come with me, lover, eh?'

Titus's body shuddered violently.

'Oh, dear,' she said, 'looks like you already have.'

She stood up and turned to Henry. 'I'll just have to take this one instead, then, won't I?' she said, reaching out and grabbing him by the wrist. 'Come along Henry. Time we was somewhere else.'

'What?' he said, tugging against her surprisingly powerful grip. 'No . . .!'

'Don't be silly,' she chided, sliding the fingers of her free hand under her studded leather belt. 'Look what I brought . . . ' She hesitated and felt around her waist in growing agitation, eventually letting go of his wrist and thrusting her hand all the way down the front of the leather thong.

Kneeling at her feet, Titus went glassy-eyed and started to drool.

'Bugger!' she said, withdrawing her hand and stamping her foot in frustration. 'Forgot the soddin' . . .!' She fell silent and gazed at the ground. 'Oh, well,' she said, looking up, 'just have to go back and get it, won't I?'

She pulled the huge sword from the ground and slid it expertly up over her shoulder and down into a scabbard strapped to her back.

'Don't go away,' she insisted, pointing at Henry's chest. 'I won't be long.' She gripped her left wrist with the fingers of her right hand, and started to tap.

The action tugged hard at Henry's memory, and he knew without understanding why that he must stop her before something terrible happened to them both. '*Don't!*' he cried, reaching for her arm. '*Wait!* There's something I really need to know.'

Blossom looked up at him with an expression of mild disinterest. 'What's that then, lover?' she asked, cocking her head to one side.

Henry coughed uncertainly, and shot a furtive glance at Titus before asking plaintively 'Where am I?'

Blossom's brow wrinkled in disbelief. She waved a hand at the circle of standing stones. 'You're kidding me, right?'

Henry followed her glance. 'I know that,' he said, miserably. 'I know *that*, don't I? What I mean is . . . ' he frowned, ' . . . what I mean *is* . . . ' he took a deep breath, ' . . . *when?*'

Blossom closed her eyes for a moment. 'Oh, er . . . 61, I think they said.'

She opened her eyes and nodded. 'Definitely!' Then she reached for her left wrist, again. 'OK?'

'*No!*' cried Henry. 'No, *wait!*'

Blossom sighed and raised an enquiring eyebrow. 'What?'

'Sorry,' he said, 'sorry, but 61 . . . *what?*'

Blossom tilted her head to one side. 'Comes after 60, lover,' she said with a shrug. 'You know, 60, 61 – like that?'

'Yes, yes, but it's not *just* 61, is it?'

Blossom pursed her lips.

'But it *can't* be! Can it? I mean, that would mean . . . It's got to be . . . ' his shoulders slumped, 'well, something . . . *else!* Hasn't it?' he ended, weakly.

Blossom shook her head. 'Just 61,' she said. 'Ammo Domino,' she added with an uncertain smile. She touched his upper arm, solicitously. 'Don't worry about it, though, eh?' She beamed. 'I won't be long. Oh,' she added with a smirk, 'I like the no-eyebrows look, by the way. Really suits you!'

Then, as Henry frowned his incomprehension, she tapped her left wrist with the fingers of her right hand, and vanished.

Titus was the first to move, wiping the drool from the corner of his mouth with the back of a hand and struggling to his feet.

'Where'd she go?' he asked, plaintively, turning his head this way and that. 'Bloody Brigantes witches,' he muttered, fiddling with his loincloth. 'Get you up for a bit of the old rumpy and then just bugger off. Happens every time!' He turned to tug at Henry's elbow. 'She the one, buddy?' he asked, pointing at the stone trilithon. 'She the one left you up there with your dick hanging out?'

When Henry didn't answer, he tugged harder. 'Come on, buddy, snap out of it, eh, and tell ol' Titus what the bloody hells is goin' on.'

Henry shook his head several times before taking a deep breath and saying without expression 'You're a Roman soldier, aren't you?' as if he was seeing him for the first time. 'A *real* Roman soldier, I mean?'

Titus regarded him, thoughtfully. 'You're not from round here, are you?'

Henry smiled wanly. 'Not recently Titus, no.'

'Meanin' what?'

Henry's smile faded. 'Meaning no, I'm not.'

'You're Roman, though, ain't ya?'

'No. No, I . . .'

Titus silenced him with a finger held to his lips. 'Workin' for 'em, then?'

Henry shook his head.

Titus watched him for several seconds. 'You sure?'

Henry nodded, emphatically. 'I only just got here, didn't I?'

'Yeah,' said Titus, as if he was trying to convince himself, 'course you did. Course you did. Look at you!' He sucked his teeth and looked Henry up and down. 'You seen what they do to deserters,' he asked, 'the Romans?'

'No,' said Henry in a small voice. 'No, I haven't.'

'No,' said Titus, flatly, 'but I 'ave, and it ain't pretty.'

He turned and gazed into the distance. 'I seen what they done to Boudicca's people at Watling Street. What *we* done to Boudicca's people. I was there. I was one of 'em and I were ashamed.'

A tear ran down his cheek. Suddenly, he looked very young.

'That's why I left 'em,' he said, pulling himself up to his full height and puffing out his chest. 'Durotriges, I am, and proud of it! Only joined that filthy Roman rabble 'cause they said they'd burn me village down if I didn't.' He shrugged. 'I joined 'em an' they burned the bugger down anyhow.'

'You were press-ganged?' asked Henry, softly.

'That what they calls it where you comes from?' said Titus. 'Client kingdoms, they calls it round 'ere.' He spat on the ground. '*Civitates*! All it means is . . . You do what you're told you miserable little turd, and tell every other bugger you likes it, or we burns down your village and rapes your whole bleedin' family.' He looked Henry in the eye, then turned and spat on the ground again. 'Civilizin' influence, that dickhead Cogi Numb Nuts said it was when they built that bloody great palace for him over Fishbourne way. Soddin' collaboration's what I calls it!' He took several deep breaths and grinned self-consciously. 'Now look what you done,' he joked, dragging grubby hands down his tear-stained face, 'got me feelin' all sorry for meself again, you bastard.'

'Sorry, I didn't realize. I thought when you got angry with me just . . . '

'What'd you expect?' cried Titus. 'Askin' stupid bloody questions! I don't know you from a skid mark on a Legate's toga, do I? For all I know you're a Roman spy sniffin' round to see if I'm loyal to the murderin' bastards!'

Henry held his arms out and looked down at himself. 'Seriously?'

Titus mirrored the gesture with a grin. 'Yeah, don't reckon I look much like any Roman soldier you ever seen, do I?'

Henry shrugged. 'Wouldn't know. The next one I see will be my first.'

Titus nodded. 'You're lost, ain't ya buddy? Serious lost, I mean? I am an' all, but this is my country, so it don't matter so much. But you . . . ' He pursed his lips and shook his head.

'Listen,' he added, with a hand on Henry's arm, 'you wanna tell me what's goin' on round 'ere? P'rhaps I could help. Who knows?'

'I don't think so,' sighed Henry. 'It's . . . complicated. Very complicated, I think. What's it to you anyway, you were gonna kill me just now.' He pointed at the fire. 'Not big enough for my miserable carcass, you said.'

Titus waved an airy hand. 'That was just a joke, wasn't it buddy? Pullin' your leg I was. No, look,' he wheedled with an arm around Henry's waist, 'what I'm sayin' is . . . you and me got to stick together, right?'

He glanced over his shoulder at the spot where Blossom had disappeared.

'Here,' he added, solicitously, tugging Henry back towards the fire, 'come an' 'ave a bite of me rat. Nice rat. Gotta keep your strength up, right?'

He glanced over his shoulder again. 'Gonna bleedin' need it when that one gets back!'

He bent to pick up the stick with the rat on the end of it. 'Tell you what,' he said brightly, holding it out, 'you can 'ave the 'ead.'

Henry sat on the ground by the fire while Titus tried to tempt him with delicacies like rat's-brain-on-a-stick and rat-off-the-bone; but he only turned green at the thought, and stared into the fire with a queasy shake of the head.

'Look,' said Titus, unable to contain his curiosity any longer, 'who is she buddy, eh, if you don't mind me askin'? At least you can tell me that, can't ya? It's only fair, innit? I give you me rat!' He glanced across the clearing and lowered his voice to a whisper. 'You reckon she'll come back, or what?'

'I don't know,' said Henry, with a sigh.

'Yeah, I reckon,' said Titus, hopefully. 'Don't you?' He nodded and gazed across the clearing again. 'How long you reckon it'll be, then,' he coaxed, ''til she, you know, gets back an' that?'

'I don't know. But I think it'll be a lot longer than it looks.'

'Yeah?' said Titus, gazing around, absently. 'Yeah, the thing is, who *is* she, buddy: that's what I wanna know.'

'Like I said,' sighed Henry, 'it's a long story. And the trouble is that I can't remember most of it. And even if I could, I don't think it would make much sense to you.'

'You're sayin' I'm thick, right?'

'No, no! Look, have you got any idea what a Filofax is?'

'Nope. But you 'ave, right?'

'Yes, but . . . '

'You can tell me, then, can't ya?' said Titus. He glanced across the clearing. 'What else you gonna do 'til she gets back?'

Henry gazed around at the standing stones. Then he looked at Titus. Then he gazed into the fire. Then he looked at Titus again. 'All right,' he sighed. 'But don't blame me if you don't understand a word of it. OK?'

Titus grinned, broadly. 'Great!' he said, rubbing his hands together. 'Great! Hang on,' he added, hurrying around to the far side of he fire to sit facing Henry, cross-legged. 'Let me get comfy first.' He took a deep breath, folded his hands in his lap and gazed intently into Henry's face.

Henry stared back at him for a long moment before looking into the fire for several seconds, nodding and looking up. 'It's like I said,' he began, 'when you were doing the . . . ' he nodded at the smoking rat. 'I think it started the morning Adams decided to make himself rich.'

'Sorry,' hissed a voice in a harsh whisper from just above their heads, 'but that isn't strictly true, is it?'

Henry and Titus looked up, and immediately scrambled to their feet in alarm. A tall, hooded figure, covered from head to foot in a long black robe, had appeared, apparently out of thin air, and was looming over them with its arms folded and its head bowed. It seemed to be watching them, but they couldn't be certain because all they could see was a shadowy void, and the hint of bright gold, under the huge cowl-like hood where its face should have been. They didn't wait to find out if it was human, or friendly, or if it had something else it wanted to say. They just turned in panic and stumbled around in opposite directions, colliding forehead to forehead on the far side of the fire in their desperation to get away.

'Holy shit!' hissed Titus, holding his nose and peering at Henry through watering eyes. 'How many more you got waitin' to jump out at us, eh?'

Then he reached around to grab Henry by the arm and pull him across in front of him as a shield. 'Tell you what,' he said with an unnaturally high-pitched laugh, 'I don't fancy your one at all.'

'Who are y-you?' quavered Henry at the figure, squinting against the pain in the bridge of his nose. 'And w-what do you w-want from us?'

'Do not be afraid, Henry,' hissed the figure in a voice like sliding gravel. 'I merely wish to put your mind at ease.'

'Yeah?' said Henry in a bitter, rising falsetto. 'Well you're not doing a very good job of it, are you?'

'Sit down,' rasped the figure. 'We really must talk.'

Henry and Titus looked questioningly at one another.

Titus shook his head.

Henry turned to the figure. 'N-no thanks,' he stammered. 'That's . . . I mean we're, we're fine. We've been sitting down quite a lot today already.'

'As you wish,' said the figure. 'Do you mind?'

Henry and Titus stared at the figure in tense anticipation.

The figure sighed and spread its arms to indicate the ground at its feet. 'Do you mind if I do?' it hissed, tiredly. 'Sit down?'

'Oh, no!' gasped Henry in sudden understanding. 'Not at all, no! Be our guest. Please, go ahead!'

'Yeah, really,' agreed Titus, nodding vigorously and pulling Henry after him as he backed away. 'Take the weight off, eh?'

'Thank you so much,' hissed the figure, lowering itself awkwardly to the ground with a dry, cackling laugh. 'My sense of balance isn't what it used to be, I'm afraid.'

Henry and Titus laughed too, a little louder than was strictly necessary, and took a few more surreptitious steps backwards, away from the fire.

'Where are you going?' asked the apparition sharply without looking up. 'You have an urgent appointment elsewhere, perhaps?'

'Well,' said Titus, letting go of Henry's arm and turning to run like hell, 'now that you come to mention it . . . '

Left to its own devices, Henry's fight or flight reflex took the only decision it could come up with at such short notice, and forced him to turn on his heel and flee after Titus as fast as his legs would carry him.

It didn't work. They had gone only a few paces when a dark and hooded figure appeared in their line of flight. 'Pity,' it hissed at them as they skidded to a halt. 'I was rather looking forward to a little . . . *chat*!'

Henry and Titus grinned uncertainly, licked their lips and took a couple of steps back the way they had come. Then, as one man, they looked over their shoulders at the patch of ground by the campfire. The shrouded figure was no longer there. But, when they turned back, it wasn't in front of them either.

'Confusing, is it not?' hissed a voice behind them.

They turned quickly to find the hooded figure sitting in its original position by the fire. 'I really do not like making dramatic gestures,' it said in a tired, and slightly irritable, voice. 'So please do not make me do that again.'

'That,' said Henry, jerking a thumb over his shoulder, 'was you?'

The apparition shrugged its bony shoulders. 'It's complicated,' it wheezed. 'Now, please, come and sit down. We really *must* talk.'

'If it's all the same to you, buddy,' said Titus, turning to flee, 'I reckon I'd better be gettin' back to . . . '

The figure was suddenly standing in front of him again.

'Where,' it hissed, looming over him and then switching instantaneously to his left side, 'do you,' then to his right side, 'think you are,' then behind him, 'going,' then in front of him again, 'Corio Boc?'

Titus stood perfectly still, his eyes flicking nervously from side to side. 'Ah,' he said, 'it's like that, then, is it?'

'Yes, *buddy*,' hissed the figure, 'it is!'

The figure vanished. And when Titus turned to look, it was sitting in its original position by the fire.

'I'll sit down, then, shall I?' said the little man, walking back across the clearing with his shoulders hunched in defeat. 'Yes, right,' he muttered as he sat cross-legged by the fire, 'I'll do that, then. *Fine*!' He pursed his lips and closed his eyes. 'Should've known, shouldn't I? Soon as she turned up I should've bleedin' known it wasn't gonna be my day. *Bugger*!'

The dark apparition raised a hand and motioned for Henry to join them.

'The libidinous one is never on time,' it hissed. 'Even so, she will be back a lot sooner than you might think.'

Henry walked over to the fire and sat down next to Titus. 'What do you want from us?' he asked, surprised to find that he was only moderately terrified now that there appeared to be no possible means of escape.

The apparition pointed at Titus. 'This is Corio Boc, Henry: part soldier, part thief, sometime mercenary, oft-times nasty little thorn in the side of the Romans. Tell us, Corio my lad, what you and your fellow prepubescent tribal commandos were doing on that spring evening, all those years ago, in the land of the Great Unwashed. No, no,' it added, holding up a commanding hand with a hasty, wheezing laugh as Titus opened his mouth to speak, 'not really. Not really: no! Leave it to me, boy, or Henry will never get to hear the truth.'

Henry and Titus waited in silent anticipation, glancing uncertainly at one another as the hooded figure sat, head bowed, rubbing scarred and bony hands together in front of the fire.

'You see, Henry,' it said, 'in order to explain your current predicament,' it spread its arms wide, 'we have to go back a very long way: a very long way indeed from your point of view. Ten years further back even than this – it really is AD 61, by the way, you know that now, don't you? – to the night when Pickfight the Acolyte left Nobrot and his friends . . . '

'Oh, come off it!' blurted Henry. 'Now you're taking the p . . .!'

He fell silent as the cowled head turned towards him with lightning speed. 'I assure you, *Mr. Kite*, that I have no reason *whatsoever* for telling you anything other than the absolute *truth*! Or at least, as much of it as I am privileged to have in my possession.'

'Well, yeah,' said Henry, glancing uneasily at Titus, 'but I mean, Pickfight? What kind of a name is Pickfight when it's at home? As for Nobrot . . . '

'Yes,' said the figure, pointing at Henry's wrist, 'well you can thank your wonderful universal translator for those little gems, can't you?'

Henry looked down at his hands. 'Sorry? What . . .?'

'Your left wrist?' said the figure, pointing again.

Henry turned his hand over to inspect the tattoos he had noticed there earlier. 'Yeah, but they're just . . . '

'No, they are *not*!' snarled the figure. 'On the contrary, they are not *just* anything! They are the visible manifestation of a complex . . .!'

There was a sudden pause as the figure fell silent and looked down at its gnarled hands, twisting in its lap. After a moment's hesitation, it took a very long and very deep breath. 'I am sorry,' it said softly, a note of regret creeping in to its husky voice, 'I allowed my emotions to get the better of me, and I should not have done so.'

It looked up at Henry. 'You are right, of course: the names are, by modern standards, ridiculous. But then, the device that is translating them instantaneously into English from their origins in the Dumnonii and Faeceantii tribal dialects is neither as universal nor as devoid of a sense of humour as its makers would have you believe.'

'Erm,' said Henry, completely out of his depth now, 'what do you . . .?'

The figure held up a hand. 'I am sorry Henry, but we have a great deal to get through, and only a limited amount of this linear timeframe in which to do it. So please believe me when I tell you that the marks on your wrist are, amongst other things, the keypad that controls the device that is currently making it possible for you and our friend Corio Boc to converse with one another in your native tongues. You are, of course, unaware of the fact, but he is speaking in an ancient dialect – ancient to you and me, that is – with its origins in a crude amalgam of Latin and the language of the Durotriges, the tribe of his birth, which, much to its eternal regret, was, and indeed, *is*, forced to live uncomfortably close to the Faeceantii tribe of which Pickfight and Nobrot were, and indeed, *are*, both members. Do you see?'

'I, er . . . no.'

'Hey . . . look,' said Titus, 'd'you reckon we could get back to . . .?'

The figure silenced him with a gesture. 'Be *quiet*!' it commanded.

It turned back to Henry. 'Please do not pursue the matter further at this juncture, Henry. All will become clear eventually. In the meantime, we have a great deal to get through before Miss Blossom returns with . . . that which she has gone back to fetch.'

Titus perked up. 'Yeah, now, see . . . that's what I'm talkin' . . . '

'*Silence*!' snarled the figure.

Henry and Titus looked at one another with the uncertain expressions of naughty toddlers who have, against all expectations, had the backs of their legs smacked by a normally placid maiden aunt.

The figure drew a long shuddering breath and shook its head wearily. 'Don't they think of anything other than sex?'

For a moment, Henry feared that Titus would make the mistake of answering truthfully. But to his relief, the little man contented himself with pursed lips, arched eyebrows and a speculative tilt of the head.

The hooded figure stared at him in silence for a while. Then 'Very well,' it said. 'And now, do you think I might continue my narrative?'

Henry and Titus nodded in silent unison.

'With no further interruptions, I trust?'

Henry and Titus nodded, again.

'Excellent,' said the figure in a tone that suggested that it didn't altogether believe them. 'Now,' it continued, gazing down at its hands, 'where was I? Ah, yes, the Faeceantii.' It took a deep breath. 'It was a warm night, Henry,' it looked up, 'was it not, Corio my lad?'

Titus wisely remained silent.

'A very warm night, and tempers were starting to fray.'

The hooded head turned towards Henry.

'You should understand, Henry, that Pickfight was the senior acolyte, and his status in the tribe depended very much upon everything going to plan for the duration of the celebrations. Indeed, you could say that his very life depended upon it.'

The figure looked from Henry to Titus, and then into the fire.

'It was the night of the Big Spring Festival,' it continued, 'and the arch druid was due at any moment.'

It looked up. 'But someone, some really *careless* someone, had gone and lost the virgin . . .'

* * *

3

PICKFIGHT THE ACOLYTE

'Look,' said Pickfight through clenched teeth, 'where's the bleedin' totty?'

Nobrot the horse frightener stood with his hands behind his back and tried to look innocent. 'Totty?' he said, wide-eyed. 'What totty's that then?'

Pickfight reached out and grabbed him by the throat. 'You're really pissin' me off! You know that, don't you?' he snarled. 'I leave you alone with her for five minutes – *five bleedin' minutes*! – and what do you do?'

Nobrot looked blank. 'What?'

'You let her bleedin' go, that's what!'

Nobrot's lower lip trembled. 'Didn't,' he pouted.

'Where is she, then?'

'Who?'

'The *tart*!' screeched Pickfight, clenching his fists and stamping his foot. 'Where's the bleedin' tart, you tosser?'

Nobrot flinched and blinked as a hail of spittle splattered his mud-streaked face. 'T'wodden my fault,' he wailed, his fingers fluttering defensively around his head. 'Only done it 'cause 'er said I wodden man enough.'

Pickfight felt the icy hand of doom wrap itself around his thumping heart. He swallowed uneasily and squinted at the grubby little man cringing in front of him. 'You didn't bleeding kill her, did you?' he asked through gritted teeth.

Nobrot shook his head, vigorously.

Pickfight breathed a sigh of relief. 'So,' he asked with exaggerated patience, 'where is she, then?'

Nobrot stuck a filthy index finger up his nose. '*Errrrr* . . .?' He screwed up his face and gazed at a faraway hill. '*Ummmmm* . . .?'

Pickfight looked away with a mournful shake of the head. 'Ye gods,' he sighed, 'it's like trying to get a Pict to lend you money. Listen,' he added, turning back, 'all I want to know is . . . ' he paused, and frowned: a very nasty thought had just struck him. 'Look,' he said, examining his fingernails casually, 'you didn't bleeding shag her, did you . . . at all?'

Nobrot bit his lower lip and looked at the ground.

'Well?' prompted Pickfight.

Nobrot flinched.

Pickfight put a paternal arm around his scrawny shoulders. 'It's all right, mate,' he said with a friendly squeeze, 'you can tell me. Did you or did you not shag the sodding virgin?'

Nobrot screwed up his face. 'Might 'ave,' he offered.

'Might have, what?'

Nobrot shrugged. 'Might 'ave.'

Pickfight waited for clarification, but none came. 'Yes,' he urged, 'but that means *what*, exactly?'

Nobrot shrugged. 'Might 'ave,' he frowned, 'only once?'

Pickfight swallowed, dryly. 'Only once?'

Nobrot nodded.

'You shagged the virgin?'

Nobrot nodded again.

'On the night of the Big Spring Festival?'

Nobrot nodded for a third time.

Pickfight folded his arms and looked at the ground. 'I see,' he sighed. 'Well, that's all right then, isn't it?'

Nobrot grinned back at him in relief. 'Yeah, that's alright then, innit?'

'Just so long as we know.'

'Jus' so long's we know,' agreed Nobrot. 'Yeah.'

Pickfight's face contorted with rage as he reached out and took the grubby little man by the throat with both hands. 'That was the last one you stupid *bugger*!' he shrieked. 'What're we gonna sacrifice now?'

He shoved the startled Nobrot up against one of the massive ceremonial standing-stones and hissed into his face. 'Listen mate, you do realize the arch druid's coming tonight, don't you? What's he gonna say when I tell him: It's alright, your worshipfulness, she's almost as good as new really, she's only been shagged once?'

'Er . . . twice?' suggested an apologetic voice behind him.

Pickfight let go of Nobrot and whirled around to find Grovel shifting uneasily from foot to foot. He stared at him, blankly, for a moment. Then 'What,' he asked with numbing certainty, 'not . . .?'

Gobshite stepped out from behind another of the standing stones, coughed politely, and held up an uncertain index finger. '*Umm*, sir . . .?'

Pickfight's shoulders sagged. 'Not . . .? What . . .? *Three*?'

'*Eight* actually,' said a self-satisfied female voice behind him.

'*Eight*!' squawked Pickfight, spinning around and clasping his head in his hands. 'What d'you mean, *eight*?'

'Well, *five*, really,' said the ex-virgin. She pointed at Grovel. 'Him twice, them three over there, once each, and him,' she added, nodding at Gobshite, 'three times. Mind you, that's only 'cause I didn't realize he'd started 'til after he'd finished. If you see what I mean?'

Pickfight crouched motionless for a moment like a trapped animal, his eyes narrowing in horrified suspicion as his world crumbled around him. 'You did it on purpose, didn't you,' he snarled with sudden bitterness, 'you dirty little slag? Just so's you could ruin my sodding life!'

'Who, me?' asked the ex-virgin, wide-eyed. 'What on earth would I want to do a thing like that for, lover, when I could have had my throat cut, my heart and lungs ripped out, and you lot dancing on my grave 'til Monday-week? Shame on you! How could you suggest such a thing?'

'Her were dyin' for it,' smirked Nobrot. 'I give it her, an' all!' He cleared his throat, loudly, to demonstrate his machismo, turned his head to one side, and spat over his shoulder. But a chance gust of wind caught the slowly revolving wad of slime and blew it back into his face, where it slapped into his left eye socket with a soggy *splat* and started to slither wetly down his cheek.

The ex-virgin curled her lip in disgust, and looked away. But Nobrot didn't seem to notice. Then, at the last moment, just as the slime was dribbling chunky and green towards his chin, he puckered his lips to one side and sucked the whole, lumpy mass back into his mouth with a loud *slurp*.

The other acolytes, long starved in preparation for the coming feast, looked on hungrily. Grovel, whose craving was greater than the rest, sidled up to his friend and started licking the damp trail from his face.

'Gods,' said the ex-virgin, 'I bet that's as close as they ever get to a bath!'

The acolytes frowned: bathing was not a concept with which they were familiar. Muck in all its forms was essential to their daily lives and they valued it highly. They bartered with it, they built with it, they wore it, they carved their crude artefacts out of it, and, when they were too knackered to get up off their skinny backsides to go out looking for food (which was most of the time) they ate it. They even slept in it, courtesy of their ponies, buried up to their straggling beards in its slowly steaming piles, with Pickfight in the middle, as befitted his station, and the rest radiating outwards in descending order of seniority: the whole flyblown bunch of them protected from the cold night air by the warmly fermenting clods.

They were not the most popular of tribes, the Faeceantii. No one traded with them, no one visited them (except by accident), and no one wanted to invade them. Indeed, when the wind was in the right direction, the borders of their squalid little plot in the middle of what we now know as Dartmoor grew significantly without so much as a single arrow having to be fired in anger. They were unwashed, unloved and unwanted, and in spite of the fact that it had been all hands to the pump in Ancient Britain since the arrival of the Roman invaders, the other tribes had never once invited them to a council of war. Everyone else had got to go: the Brigantes from the north with their proud and noble queen Cartamantua resplendent on horseback: the Icenii from the east with their warrior queen Boudicca astride her chariot: even old Caratacus, with his peripatetic court of eccentrics in tow, had been consulted: but never the Faeceantii, with their corrupt and cruel leader, the Arch Druid Stonking Rod, lurking in the rear.

The name meant He Who Carries His Genitals In A Small Wicker Basket, and it was well given, even though the genitals in question were not strictly speaking his own. In fact, they were the rightful property of the only other candidate for the office of arch druid at the last election, one Po-faced the Unprepared, to whom they had once been attached in the conventional manner, and from whom they had been unceremoniously removed by Stonking Rod with a dull knife while Pickfight and Ramskull held him down. They had hung around the arch druid's neck ever since, shrivelled and mouldering in their intricately woven container, as a warning to the rest of the tribe that this particular politician was not to be campaigned against lightly. Stonking Rod was not to be lied to lightly, either, and Pickfight knew it only too well.

'So that's it then, is it?' he said, bitterly. 'That's what you lot expect me to tell him, is it? Sorry your worshipfulness, the party's off, the sodding virgin's just been gang-banged!'

Most of the acolytes shifted from foot to foot uneasily. But Nobrot stood still, concentrating hard. His eyes lit up, suddenly, and he pointed at Grovel. 'What 'bout 'is daugh'er? Her's a virgin, inner?'

'Of course she's a sodding virgin, scrotum-brains,' snapped Pickfight, 'she's only two years old! Not even you would sacrifice . . . ' He paused and shook his head. 'Ye gods, what am I saying?'

'So,' said Grovel after a long and uncomfortable silence. 'He won't like it, then, you reckon, ol' Stonkin' Rod, like?'

'Like it?' hissed Pickfight. 'Bleeding *like it*! The Big Spring Festival ruined by a bunch of horny sods who can't be trusted to keep their loincloths on? Oh yes, he's gonna bleeding *love it*, isn't he? I just can't *wait* to tell him.'

'I'm not a vindictive person,' lied Stonking Rod when he heard the news, 'but can you give me one good reason why I shouldn't rip your dicks off and roast 'em over the fire on a sharp stick? I don't want to do it, believe me, although the gods know I could do with the protein, but if you haven't come up with a really good answer by the time I count to three I'll have no choice but to let Pickfight turn you into a bunch of girlies.'

Pickfight levered himself up from the sacrificial stone and strolled over to where the prisoners, Nobrot, Grovel, Gobshite, Drivel and Turdfancy, were hanging by their thumbs from a ring of hastily erected prompting posts.

'Look lads,' he said in comradely fashion, 'ask yourselves if it was really worth it. I mean, all this aggravation for a few brief moments of pleasure?'

'Brief is right,' muttered the ex-virgin, winking suggestively at Ramskull.

'Look,' said Pickfight, warming to his theme, 'how d'you expect us to sympathize with you randy little toe rags, when all you've done is risk bringing the wrath of the gods down on the lot of us? I mean, how do you think *we* feel? Why don't you try seeing it from *our* point of view for a change?'

It wasn't a fair question really, because, after hanging by their thumbs for half an hour, with rocks tied to their genitals to discourage them from running away, the accused were having difficulty seeing anything at all, never mind someone else's point of view.

Pickfight regarded them thoughtfully for a moment. 'Why don't you tell us about it, then?' he urged. 'Eh? We might understand. Who knows? I mean,' he added, gesturing at the other acolytes, 'we wouldn't mind hearing about it, would we lads: all the gory details?'

The tribe nodded eagerly and shuffled closer.

'That's right,' said the ex-virgin, 'tell the whole world, why don't you?'

'Come on,' said Pickfight, 'we can take it. We're all men here, after all.'

Nobrot glanced painfully sideways at Stonking Rod. 'Well he ain't,' he said through tightly gritted teeth, 'for a start!'

There was a collective in-sucking of incredulous breath. '*Uh-oh*,' muttered someone at the back of the bunch, 'that's torn it!'

Everyone knew that Stonking Rod was a woman. But they also knew that you didn't mention the fact unless you had no further use for your testicles.

'You fancy trying to prove the heresy you just uttered?' asked Stonking Rod, gripping the rock hanging from Nobrot's balls and tugging it fiercely.

'What I meant to say, your worshipfulness,' wheezed Nobrot through the agony of his slowly lengthening scrotum, 'was . . . was . . . '

'That you didn't think gang-banging virgins was a suitable subject for such refined company?' prompted Stonking Rod, slyly.

Nobrot nodded. 'Yeah, yeah! That, that! What you just said then!'

'Bollocks,' said Stonking Rod, letting go of the rock so that it bounced back up and thudded into the junior acolyte's unprotected groin. 'I like a bit of rape and pillage as much as the next bloke, actually. Specially rape, as it happens.' Her voice suddenly became ominously quiet. 'You're not suggesting I'm some sort of raving *poofter*, are you, by any chance?'

'No, no!' insisted Nobrot, breathlessly. 'Not that! Never! Never! No! No! Not ever! Never! Never! No, no!'

'Glad to hear it,' said Stonking Rod, with a voice like a treacle dagger, 'even if it is a barefaced lie. Right,' she added, sitting down on the judging stone. 'Guilty as charged! Chop their dicks off and roast 'em over the fire!'

'What about the ceremony?' whispered a frightened voice from the back of the crowd. 'What we gonna sacrifice, now?'

Stonking Rod pointed at the accused. 'That lot, of course! What did you think? And him,' she added, pointing at Nobrot with undisguised relish, 'you can do that little shit-for-brains first.'

The acolytes exchanged anxious glances, but no one moved.

'Well, what're you waiting for?' demanded Pickfight. 'You heard what her worshipfulness . . . ' He swallowed hard. 'I mean, *his* worshipfulness,' he corrected himself. 'His . . . *his* worshipfulness!' He simpered and bowed until his forehead almost touched the ground. 'You heard what *his* worshipfulness said.' His face hardened. 'So get on with it! *Now*!'

Still no one moved.

'Well?' demanded Pickfight with another sidelong, simpering glance at the arch druid. 'You lot suddenly gone deaf or what?'

'I think you'll find,' said the ex-virgin, winking at Ramskull again, 'that they're a bit worried that ol' Nobrot and his mates ain't your actual virgins no more. Not after what they just done to a certain beautiful young lady, they ain't. And I mean t' say, that kinda buggers up your little ceremony, don't it?'

Stonking Rod fixed the ex-virgin with a stare that would have roasted Nobrot's penis without the need of a fire.

'Who the hell are you?' she demanded.

'No one special,' admitted the ex-virgin, leaning close and stroking the palm of Ramskull's meaty paw with a finger. 'Not anymore. Just thought I'd mention it, that's all, about the gods getting angry and calling down a plague of something really nasty on the tribe, I mean?' She grinned at the wide-eyed acolytes huddling together nearby. 'Not that you have to take my word for it, do you? You can just go ahead and see what happens, can't you? I mean, they might not shrivel your knobs to dust, but then again they might. Who knows? The question is: have any of you got the balls to give it a try?'

'You don't believe in all that old bollocks, do you?' scoffed Stonking Rod at the vacant faces around her. 'I mean, for the gods' sake, who believes that load of old crap anymore?'

But it was clear from their anxious expressions, and the way they were muttering and hanging on to one another, that the acolytes did indeed believe it. The arch druid herself had told them to believe it often enough, after all, so why shouldn't they?

'All right,' she said, peevishly. 'We'll just have to find someone else, won't we? So,' she added, standing up and gazing around the crowd, 'who's a virgin, then, eh? Come on, we haven't got all sodding night!'

In fact, there was only one person who fitted the bill, and as soon as the ex-virgin pointed it out to them, the acolytes heaved a collective sigh of relief.

'You are, lover,' she said over her shoulder as she led the submissive Ramskull, beaming shyly, behind a massive granite boulder. 'Isn't that lucky: you being Protector of the Faith, an' all that?'

Stonking Rod tried to wave her to silence, but it was too late: the damage had already been done.

The acolytes looked speculatively at one another and started whispering. If there was one member of the tribe no one had ever wanted to shag, they decided, it was Stonking Rod. Not even Drivel had shown an interest, and he had been known to get amorous at the sight of a hole in the ground. No one had ever *seen* her being shagged, or *heard* her being shagged, or even heard *of* her being shagged. Which, given the tribe's rampant promiscuity and propensity for gossip, and the fact that they all lived packed tightly together in one huge mud hut, was pretty amazing now that they came to think about it. Could this be a sign from the gods, they asked themselves? Had the ex-virgin shown them the way to their own salvation? If they strapped the arch druid to the altar, and ripped out her heart and lungs, and drank her blood, and ate her flesh, and shrivelled her head in a big clay pot filled with boiling water, and ate and drank and shagged and buggered each other to a standstill over the coming week, would the bogweed bloom again in the spring? They rather thought it might. Besides, it was getting late and they hadn't eaten for a week, so it was certainly worth giving it a try.

Stonking Rod's eyes opened wide in disbelief as the crowd turned suddenly and surged towards her. She swallowed hard, and backed away.

'Now hang on a minute, lads,' she pleaded, gazing over their heads and signalling wildly. 'Look! No, wait! Stop! Over there! There's been a mistake! It's not what you think.' She pointed, despairingly. 'Look! Over . . .!'

* * *

'And there we must leave them, for the moment at least,' hissed the hooded figure, turning to face Titus. 'In spite of the fact that we have omitted to investigate the starring role that you and your young friends were hoping to play that night in the demise of Stonking Rod's tribe of degenerates.'

Titus pursed his lips and looked up at the sky.

The figure nodded. 'No matter,' it said, briskly, 'we will return to the subject in due course. Because this is not the story of what happened to Stonking Rod on that fateful day in AD 51, it is the story of what happened when the ripples of that event finally reached the twentieth century and entered the life of an unsuspecting young man in an office in a leafy part of Essex, England, on 27 April AD 1987. His name, of course, was Henry Kite, and something would happen that day to change his life forever: and in spite of appearances to the contrary, it had almost nothing to do with Adams.

'Ah, but wait a moment,' it wheezed, dryly. 'We are moving a little too fast for our young friend here, are we not, Henry? As you have rightly observed, he is not in a position to comprehend fully the nature of that most arcane of twentieth century artefacts, the Filofax. No indeed! And we would not wish to leave him behind in our little narrative, would we? So excuse us, if you would be so kind, while the lad and I take a short excursion. We will not, I assure you, be gone for more than a second or two at the most.'

The hooded head turned towards Titus. 'I think a little tutorial is in order,' hissed the gravelly voice, 'is it not, my lad? A brief visit to the twentieth century, and a lightning tour of the shops?'

Titus opened his mouth to speak, but whatever he was about to say was drowned in hissing static as he and the shrouded figure shimmered, faded and vanished into thin air.

But the figure was as good as its word, and they were gone for only the briefest of moments. When they reappeared, with an all-but inaudible hiss and a crackle of white noise, only a second or so after vanishing, Titus had undergone a remarkable transformation. The grubby loincloth and crude grass skirt had gone and been replaced by a snappy wide-shouldered two-piece suit of some shiny grey cloth that looked not unlike brushed aluminium. Beneath it he was wearing a white shirt with its cuffs turned back over the jacket's rolled-up sleeves. He had a pair of white woolly socks and a pair of mid-grey slip-on shoes with knotted tassels, a pair of red braces, and a thin red and black piano-key tie. His hair had been feather-cut and streaked with blonde highlights, and he was clean-shaven and reeked of an aftershave that Henry recognized instantly as Yves Saint Laurent's *Kouros*. He had a diamond stud in each ear and a silver brooch shaped like a bass guitar pinned to the lapel of his jacket. Most staggering of all, though, to Henry's way of thinking, was the makeup he was wearing: an alarming combination of blue eye shadow, black mascara, crimson rouge and a metallic purple lipstick that gave him an unnerving, chisel-cheeked, androgynous pout.

'Holy shit!' gasped Henry, getting up and backing away. 'What the . . .?'

'Calm yourself, Henry, calm yourself,' cackled the shrouded figure from its position on the ground by the fire. 'Do not be alarmed. I assure you that there is nothing more sinister in our young friend's appearance than an overly exuberant approach to retail therapy. Or to put it another way: I let him loose for two days in the West End of London. He spent much, but perhaps not all, of his time on Oxford Street, and in Covent Garden and Soho, learning about the culture of Britain in the 1980s.'

'Whaddaya think?' drawled Titus, chewing gum and holding the jacket open to reveal a pink iridescent lining that dazzled the eyes. He took a pair of Raybans from his top pocket, snapped them open with the flick of a wrist, slid them onto his face, and struck a pose. 'Pretty cool, eh?'

'*Eh-hem*!' coughed the hooded figure.

'What? Oh yeah, right,' said Titus, bending to pick up a brown paper bag. 'Here,' he said, handing it to Henry, 'this is for you.'

Inside the bag was a bathrobe. Henry took it out and held it up at arm's length. It had the logo of the Savoy Hotel embroidered on its breast pocket.

'You nicked it!' he said, glowering indignantly at Titus. 'You two-bit, cheapskate little . . .! You couldn't even be bothered . . . '

Titus' beaming smile wavered. 'We was busy,' he said, chewing with defensive vigour. 'And, look,' he held out a hand, 'if you don't want the bloody thing . . .'

'Sod off!' said Henry, clutching the robe to his chest with one hand and pushing Titus away with the other.

'Only tryin' to help,' muttered the little Celt, glancing with a sly grin at the shrouded figure. 'Some people . . .!'

'Sit down,' rasped the figure, 'we have a story to tell.'

'Right,' said Titus, eagerly. 'Oh,' he added, turning to pick up a pair of crumpled Marks & Spencer carrier bags, slightly charred around the edges. 'I, er, *we* got you some stuff,' he said, handing the bags to Henry. 'Keep us – *you*! – goin' for an hour or two, I reckon, yeah?'

Henry wrapped himself grudgingly in the robe and sat down.

Peering cautiously into the bags, he found two bottles of wine and a selection of sandwiches, yoghurts, cheesecake and fresh fruit. When he saw that Titus had also brought paper cups and plates, plastic cutlery and a corkscrew, he conceded, albeit reluctantly so, that the debt of the stolen bathrobe had been greatly reduced.

'Now then,' hissed the shrouded figure, as Henry uncorked a bottle of wine, 'if we are all sitting comfortably, we will return to AD 1987 and the day on which Nigel Adams decided that he knew how to make himself rich.'

4

NIGEL QUENTIN ADAMS

Nigel Adams had finally decided what he wanted most out of life and had just finished writing it in his personal organizer to make it come true. Two hundred and forty-nine times he had written it in the diary section: once for each day from 27 April right through to the end of the year. Each time he had written it he had used large, carefully rounded capital letters and bright red ink. And each time he had finished writing it he had underlined it with a ruler, twice. According to the digital timer in his other personal organizer, the pocket electronic one, the whole thing had taken him 2 hours, 24 minutes and 53 seconds, precisely. He decided to round it up to 2 days, 3 hours and 45 minutes exactly, and to put it down on the personal timesheet he had created for the purpose under the heading Staff Morale. Adams had no staff and their morale would have been of very little interest to him if he had. It was just that he liked things to be neat and tidy, just in case.

'In case of what?' Terry Smith asked Sam Johnson one day down the pub.

'In case he has to prove that he wasn't there when it all went wrong,' said Sam around a mouthful of mashed cheeseburger and chips, 'but you were.'

'Me?' said Terry in alarm. 'Why me?'

'Well,' said Sam, looking him over thoughtfully, 'you're older than he is,' he cocked his head to one side, 'and probably a good deal smarter.'

Terry shook his head at the unfairness of it all as he trudged off to buy another round. 'Why me?' he asked Ted the barman. 'What'd I ever do?'

'You forgot your nuts, for a start,' said Ted, handing him a bag. 'You wanna hang on to 'em tight round 'ere, mind,' he added, glancing over his shoulder before winking and touching the side of his nose. 'That bleedin' lot would steal your friggin' granny if her wasn't nailed down!'

Henry Kite had also decided what he wanted most out of life, but he didn't think that writing it in his personal organizer would make it come true. This was partly because he didn't have a personal organizer worthy of the name, but mostly because he didn't think that life would ever be *that* kind to him.

What Henry wanted most out of life was for Nigel Adams to drop down dead. This was not a new experience for him – not some spur-of-the-moment whim, or mere passing fancy – he had always wanted Adams to drop down dead: ever since he had first set eyes on him, in fact. And, now that he came to think about it, even before that. Adams had that sort of effect on people like Henry. And when you got right down to it, he had the same sort of effect on an awful lot of people, all of whom seemed to sense that they weren't going to like him as soon as they had heard his name. His effect on someone like Sam Johnson was even more dramatic. Adams was, Sam was inclined to tell anyone who would listen, just the sort of person he would like to see die a slow and horrible death. It wasn't strictly true, of course, because Sam had a weak stomach and a suspicion that death wasn't much of a spectator sport, even when it was happening to a truly deserving case like Adams. But it was a close-run thing and if something terminal were to strike Adams within the next ten years or so, Sam hoped that he would be around to see it: just so long as it wasn't too bloody.

The thought made him hungry, so he opened a drawer and took out the lunchbox his sister had packed for him that morning. The pink Tupperware didn't fit well with his self-image, so he hid it under the desk as he peeled off the lid and took out a sandwich. A moment later, he was munching contentedly and beginning to feel at peace with the world. Then Terry turned up with another note from Minnowfield and the sandwich lost most of its savour.

'Wha'?' he grunted around a half-chewed wad of tuna and cucumber.

'Note from Mr. Minnowfield,' said Terry, holding it out.

Sam regarded it with obvious distaste. 'By bussn't 'e wing?'

"Cause you don't bleedin' answer, that's why!'

A shower of damp crumbs sprayed from Sam's mouth. '*Po?*' he asked, indignantly. 'Po? Wad ovid?'

Terry jerked the note forward tentatively, half expecting Sam to snatch it away from him with his teeth.

Sam shook his head. 'Bo awah!'

'Please?'

Sam shook his head, again. 'Mo! Bo awah!'

'He said I gotta make sure you read it.'

Sam nodded at the desk. 'Pud id dare.'

Terry didn't move.

Sam shrugged and looked away. 'Pease y'selp.'

Minnowfield had started sending notes to Sam because Sam had stopped answering his telephone. He didn't have the time, he would explain when people asked. 'Soon as I pick it up, some idiot starts talking at me. How am I supposed to concentrate with that going on all the time?'

'Well,' Minnowfield had offered, 'we all have to make sacrifices, don't we?'

'I need peace and quiet, I do,' Sam had insisted. 'I can't go picking up the phone every five minutes to listen to some stuck-up bint rabbiting on about the expenses I shouldn't have claimed, or the holiday I haven't got left.'

Minnowfield had blushed with suppressed indignation on Charlotte Piece's behalf. 'I hardly think Charlotte, Miss Piece . . .'

'All those bloody idiots rabbiting on about their poxy products,' Sam had complained, staring into the distance. 'I haven't got time for . . .'

'*Clients*!' Minnowfield had asserted, timidly. 'Sir Richard is always very . . .'

'To *listen*,' Sam had countered, fixing Minnowfield with a withering stare, 'to a bunch of wankers eulogizing about their sodding tampons! That's not my job, is it? That's what you're there for, isn't it? You and that irritating little shit, Adams.'

Minnowfield had coughed, reproachfully. '*Eh-hem*, yes, well, Mr. Adams is still trying to learn how to . . .'

'Stab people in the back?' Sam had suggested with his head cocked to one side. 'Seems pretty good at it already, if you ask me! And why wouldn't he be:

he's got the perfect bloody role model for it, hasn't he?'

Minnowfield had blushed an even deeper shade of red. 'The fact that Mr. Adams is the chairman's nephew has got nothing to do . . . He was offered the job purely on merit, I assure you. And I feel certain that if you would just give him a chance you would see . . . '

'How old is he, anyway?' Sam had demanded. 'Twelve? Thirteen?'

'I . . . er, I believe that he has just turned . . . erm, actually, I'm . . . er, not entirely . . . And I admit that he seems rather young to be, er . . . yes. Nevertheless, I assure you that he is *perfectly* capable of . . . '

'Answering the telephone? That's settled then, isn't it?'

Minnowfield believed in maintaining eye contact with his staff at all times, but his own had begun to water so fiercely that he'd been forced to look away.

'I'll send you a note, then, shall I?' he'd asked, hopefully, looking obliquely out of the window. 'And you can read it when you have the time?'

Three weeks had passed since then and Sam still wasn't answering his telephone. He wasn't reading any of Minnowfield's notes, either. It was an experiment, he would say when people asked, to find out how effective alternative methods of communication really were. 'Because you don't really know, do you?' he would add, archly. 'You just take it for granted, don't you? Everyone keeps telling you it's the right thing to do, so you do it. But think of the man-hours you could be wasting. Think of the money you could have saved. You'll thank me for it one day,' he'd told Minnowfield with the wagging of an instructive index finger. 'By the way,' he'd shouted across the office as Minnowfield had hurried away in defeat. 'It'll take me about a year, I should think,' he'd shouted even more loudly at Minnowfield's retreating back, 'to decide? I'll let you know when I've finished, then, shall I?'

Minnowfield had disappeared into his office to nurse his anxiety about Sir Richard, and to try to decide what to do about Sam's insubordination. He couldn't let it go on indefinitely, he'd told himself, in case it spread to the rest of the staff. But he was always desperate to avoid any kind of confrontation with someone as unpredictable as Sam because it was bad for morale. Especially his own. So he'd decided he would continue to monitor the situation and await developments. Perhaps it would all turn out for the best in the end? But whatever else might happen, he'd told himself as he'd sniffed suspiciously at the armpit of his freshly laundered shirt, it would probably take him about a year to decide what to do next.

Terry thought the bickering was totally and completely and utterly pathetic. Why couldn't they behave like grown-ups, he wanted to know, instead of acting like a couple of big kids and wasting everybody else's time? There must be more important things they could be doing, surely, than arguing about who was going to answer the telephone and who wasn't? He had plenty of important things he could be doing, anyway, even if they didn't. Lots and lots of important things, as it happened. But they never listened to anything he said, so what was the point in him saying?

He pouted at the frustration of it all and wondered how long it would be before he could get back to the really important business of finding out what the new girl in Charlotte Piece's office was wearing under her tight little black skirt. He was almost certain that he had glimpsed the bump of a suspender clip there earlier, outlined against the inviting curve of her right thigh. But he wasn't sure, and the longer he had to stand in front of Sam's desk, waiting for him to take the note and read it, the longer it would be before he could get back up to the first floor and find out for sure.

Not that the precise nature of the girl's underwear mattered to Terry in the least. He was sixteen years old and so pumped full of testosterone that he had already seen and imagined more than enough to justify abusing himself furiously as soon as he got home, and indeed for many angst-ridden weeks and months after that. In the meantime, he was having to stand in front of Sam's desk, red-faced, half-hard and increasingly anxious that one of the randy bastard salesmen in Tony Orlando's office would get their filthy hands on the girl before he could get back up there and get his own filthy hands on her first. He sighed heavily at the injustice of it all, and favoured Sam with the most hangdog expression he could manage.

Sam took pity on him eventually. And although he wasn't prepared to interrupt his breakfast for something as insignificant as another note from Minnowfield, he decided that the least he could do was eat faster and put Terry out of his misery that little bit sooner. He started washing down half-chewed lumps of sandwich with gulps of warm tea, all the while staring fixedly at a spot about three feet in front of Henry's desk in an attempt to avoid the look of reproach in Terry's doe-like eyes. If Minnowfield and the marketing man with the gold-plated coffee beans didn't get him, Sam decided with a belch, a burst abdominal ulcer certainly would. And for a moment, a very brief moment, his future looked almost promising.

'At least it'd be a way out of this God-forsaken hole,' he told himself. 'The bastards are never gonna sack me at this rate.' He sighed. 'I'll just have to do something *really* nasty to that slimy little tosser,' he thought, eyeing Adams on the other side of the office. 'And hope Uncle Merv doesn't come over all sanctimonious and disinherit me for getting myself thrown out.'

He prodded his upper abdomen in the hope that he would discover there the first signs of a malignant growth so terrible that it would allow him to be invalided out of his job without having to forfeit his inheritance. He didn't find one. Worse still, when he looked up to share his frustration with the rest of the office, he found himself staring at something infinitely more unpleasant than a cancerous growth. It was Adams, shuffling across the office towards him with an open Filofax on the palm of his outstretched hand and a smug expression on his lividly pimpled, adolescent face.

A snarl, and a few damp crumbs, burst from Sam's mouth as he bent forward to scan his desk for the letter opener his demanding Uncle Merv had given him for his last birthday. If memory served him well, it would fit perfectly into Adams's chest, somewhere between his third and fourth ribs.

A moment later, as he glanced up again to see how much time he had left to arm himself, he realized with a wave of relief that Adams's lifeless, watering eyes were fixed not on him but on Henry behind the desk to his right. Grateful that he wouldn't be forced to commit murder in the middle of elevenses, he leaned back in his chair to grin around magnanimously at a suddenly benevolent world. There were worse things in life, he told himself, as he winked at Henry and inclined his head in Adams's direction, than dying in agony from a ruptured gut, and the one that was about to happen to his best friend was not, after all, about to happen to him.

Henry grimaced at Sam's over-stuffed smile and looked quickly away, only to find himself staring straight at the shambling Adams. He looked away from that too in the hope that the odious little creep would have veered off in someone else's direction or, better still, dropped down dead by the time he looked back. But it was no good: he was still coming, and the only thing he dropped was his Filofax, which he slid onto Henry's desk with a flourish.

'What do you think of that, then?' he asked. 'Pretty impressive, eh?'

He struck a pose with one hand on his hip and the other close to his face for a minute inspection of his fingernails.

Henry shook his head. 'Idiot can't even pose properly,' he muttered.

'What?' asked Adams, leaning forward over the desk and peering into Henry's face. 'What did you say?'

Henry ignored him, and hunched forward to scan the pages of the Filofax in slow irritation. Suddenly, he grinned, and glanced across at Sam.

Something in his expression made Sam stop slouching and come upright in his chair, his jaws working feverishly as he chewed his way to a higher level of concentration. Self-diagnostics were momentarily forgotten as his eyes narrowed in anticipation and he reached forward to pick up his mug and gulp down another mouthful of tea.

'I want a Porch,' read Henry in a loud voice from Adams's Filofax. He looked up and added 'Don't you think you ought to get a house first?'

Adams frowned. '*Porsche?*' he said, uncertainly, leaning forward over the desk. 'It says *Porsche*!'

'It says *Porch*,' said Henry, leafing quickly through the pages of the Filofax. 'About two hundred times, I should think.' He cleared his throat and bit his lower lip to stop himself laughing.

Sam wasn't so lucky. He gagged explosively and sprayed the contents of his mouth across his desk in a fine mist, most of it splattering his untidy heaps of papers and dripping brownly from the leaves of his dog-eared rubber plant. The rest shot through the air in a mushy lump and slapped into the crotch of Terry's trousers with a wet *thwack*!

Having rid himself of the greater part of the obstruction, Sam bent double in his chair and retched wildly at the floor. Small, unidentifiable projectiles burst from his gaping mouth and something clear and stringy dangled from his nose. The top half of his body seesawed violently up and down, and he gave vent to a raking, choking cough like the death-throes of an iron lung.

Standing motionless and horror-stricken in front of him, Terry found that his ardour for the girl in Charlotte Piece's office had been instantly and utterly quenched. He remained perfectly still for a moment, looking down in stunned disbelief at the wad of slime that had suddenly attached itself to the fly of his latest and proudest purchase from Man at C & A. It started to move as he watched, slithering and writhing its way down the front of what he liked to call his 'slacks' like a small, animated pizza. He stared at it open-mouthed until it detached itself, more or less en masse, and fell with a wet slap onto his shoes. The spell was suddenly broken and he looked up.

'Bloody hell!' he croaked at Sam's heaving back. 'What'd you do that for?'

When Sam didn't reply, he turned to Adams. 'Look what he did!'

'*Piss off!*' snarled Adams without turning his head. 'It says *Porsche*, you *bastard!* Can't you even read?'

Terry's mouth fell open. 'But . . .!' he began, holding out a self-pitying hand and looking down at himself.

Adams rounded on him, and thrust his head forward until their noses were almost touching. 'Go *away* you little *shit!*' he hissed.

Terry's jaw worked soundlessly for a moment as he decided to stand his ground. But Adams glared so fiercely at him that he thought better of it and looked away. Then, taking a pinch of trousers' crotch in either hand, he turned awkwardly and waddled stiff-legged towards the toilets. 'Bastard!' he muttered under his breath. 'Bloody-bastard-sodding-son-of-a-bitch!'

Henry wondered if he meant Sam for getting him into the mess or Adams for not helping him out of it.

Adams seemed to be no doubt, and turned angrily after Terry with a murderous look in his eyes.

'It says *Porch!*' said Henry, loudly, hoping to prevent Adams from rushing after Terry and braining him with some handy, blunt object. 'And might I say that your modest ambition does you credit? Even though a porch without a house to stand in front of . . . '

'*Porsche!*' roared Adams, turning to face him again. 'It says *Porsche*, you bloody *bastard!* What's the matter with you people anyway? Can't you take *anything* seriously? You're all . . . you're all . . . ' He subsided, suddenly, like a punctured balloon, and for a moment Henry felt almost sorry for him.

'Look,' he said tiredly, 'just leave it, will you? I don't give a toss . . . '

'*No!*' shrieked Adams. '*That's obvious, isn't it?* And you can't bloody well *spell*, can you? No wonder the country's in such a friggin' mess!'

Henry took a deep breath. 'Look . . . '

'I'm not talking to you,' snapped Adams, gesturing widely to include the whole office, 'you're sick! The whole lot of you are! *Sick*! And I *hate* you! I hate *all* of you!' He turned to leave, but thought better of it and rounded on Henry again. 'I'll get you for this!' he snarled, jabbing a finger at Henry's face. 'Just you wait and see if I don't!'

He turned away again, and glared around the office, daring someone, anyone, to speak. Faces turned towards him, and eyes watched him from all parts of the office, but no one moved a muscle, and no one spoke.

With a toss of the head, he snatched up his Filofax, turned on his heel and strode off to find a dictionary. If there was one thing he really wanted out of life, he decided as he hurried away, it was to put Henry and Sam and all the other bastards in their smug-bloody, smart-arsed-bloody, cold-bloody-blooded, stupid-bloody, grinning-bloody places!

'And I'm just the boy to do it, too,' he told himself through the tears of self-pity as he shambled along a corridor, 'me and Auntie Kitty'll see to that!'

'You know what he really wants?' said Sam, surfacing from beneath his desk and wiping his mouth with a crumpled page from Henry's *Guardian*.

'Who cares?' said Henry with a sigh.

'Exactly,' said Sam, sagely. 'Ex-act-ly!'

Five minutes later, Charlotte Piece found Adams in her brightly lit office on the first floor. In the wastebasket beside her desk, she found the tattered remains of her copy of the *Pocket Oxford English Dictionary* torn to bits, and beneath it, the mangled remains of Adams' Filofax. She bent at the waist and with the carefully manicured and painted finger and thumb of her right hand, lifted the dictionary clear of the wreckage and held it out in front of her at a lip-curling arm's length. She looked thoughtfully at the torn pages for a moment. Then she looked sideways at Adams. In her face was the familiar mix of loathing and insincere beneficence that Sam liked to call her 'Thatcher in the presence of poor people expression'.

'What is this?' she asked, coldly.

'Kite did it,' blurted Adams.

Charlotte frowned and looked at him over the horned rim of a pair of non-existent spectacles. 'Henry Kite,' she asked, 'did this? Are you sure?'

'He made me,' said Adams, defensively.

'I see. And why, *exactly*, did he make you do it, Nigel, do you think?'

'You know what he's like?' pouted Adams, waving a hand at a collage of chunky film stars crowding the wall.

'Yes,' said Charlotte without emotion. She knew what Henry was like, all right, and Adams had no business lumping him together with real men like Lundgren, Stallone and Schwarzenegger. 'I do know what he's like, *actually*!'

She also knew what Adams was like, and it was lucky for him that nepotism was alive and well and living in Essex.

'Never mind,' she said, suddenly. 'I wouldn't take any notice if I were you. *Hmmmmm*?' She smiled one of her best red-mouthed smiles, and bent to retrieve the torn Filofax from her wastebasket. 'And I know what you're like, too, Nigel my lad,' she added under her breath, '*actually*!'

Adams's eyes narrowed, uneasily. There it was again, people saying things under their breath whenever he was around. He glanced anxiously at Charlotte to see if he could detect any sign of censure in her expression, but she smiled brightly back at him and winked.

Charlotte really liked smiling and practiced it every day in front of the mirror on her bathroom wall. She practiced it in front of the mirror on her bedroom wall, too, and in front of the one that someone had stuck so conveniently to the windscreen of her car. She practiced it so often, in fact, that it was a wonder that she still hadn't managed to get it right, and even more amazing that she had run so few people over. Nevertheless, as smiles went, hers was impressively toothy and red-lipsticked and, for the average male observer at least, as close to an unqualified offer of vigorously damp sex as it was possible to get without parting her legs and saying, throatily 'Come and get it, big boy!' But to anyone not paralyzed with lust at the sight of her fluttering eyelashes, heaving bosom and daintily moistened lips, it resembled nothing so much as a dinner invitation from a great white shark.

Charlotte turned smoothly and smiled at Tracey Greene, sitting wide-eyed and open-mouthed at her tidy little desk by the window. She had been sitting in the same spot, wearing the same expression of startled confusion, ever since the diminutive Adams had burst snorting and whimpering into the office and begun tearing pages from Charlotte's dictionary. She had only started work with the company that morning and was desperate to get away from it already. This was her first stab at employment and she had no idea what she was expected to do with it. She had no idea who Adams was, either, but had begun to suspect that he had escaped recently from a room with heavily padded walls. Until a moment ago she had thought that she had a reasonably accurate idea of who and what Charlotte was, but she was beginning to have serious doubts about that, too. The older woman seemed to be leering at her menacingly, and she could feel herself starting to panic. She tried to speak, but no words would come out: all she could manage by way of explanation for her dumbness was a shake of the head and the mechanical opening and closing of her mouth. She wondered if she was going mad or, worse still, becoming senile like Granny Morris. She didn't really know what senile was, but she knew what Granny Morris was and the thought that she might be going the same way filled her with horror. Instinctively, she looked down at her lap to see if she had peed in her pants. It was the sort of thing that senile people were inclined to do, she knew. It was what Granny Morris did, at any rate. She was relieved to see that her tight little skirt was still dry. But she reached down tentatively with a hand under her bottom to make certain.

'Isn't this nice?' said Charlotte with another frightening smile.

Tracey retrieved her hand and slapped it guiltily to her mouth. 'He just came in,' she gasped, suddenly regaining the power of speech, 'and he,' she pointed, first at the wastebasket, 'and he,' then at the torn Filofax in Charlotte's hand. Finally, she pointed an accusing finger at Adams and gasped 'and he . . . he . . . he . . .!' She hoped with all her little heart that she, Charlotte, would understand about the Filofax and the dictionary, and that she, Tracey, wouldn't get blamed for what had happened to either of them.

'Yes, of course he did,' said Charlotte with that same ghastly smile. 'He is allowed to, *actually*! He is a probationary account manager, you know.' Her tone suggested that Tracey had missed something that ought to have been obvious to a half-wit.

She gestured from Adams to Tracey, and back again. 'This is Mr. Adams,' she said. 'Nigel, this is Tracey. She only started this morning, so don't go pulling her leg, will you?' Then with an equal lack of warmth, she turned and grinned at Tracey. 'Nigel's a budding account executive,' she said, knowing that this would mean nothing to the poor girl. But since it meant nothing to Adams either, she couldn't see that it mattered a great deal.

'I'm sure you'll be seeing a lot of him from now on,' she added, grinning maliciously. 'Won't that be nice?'

Tracey winced and wondered, not for the last time, if she should have taken the job at the chicken factory as Granny Morris had suggested; and whether being senile and ripping the guts out of chickens with your bare hands for the rest of your life would be such a bad thing to do.

Adams sniffed defensively and took the Filofax from Charlotte's hand.

'Well,' she said, briskly, 'I'm sure we've all got plenty to be getting on with, haven't we?' And she looked at him in a way that left Adams in no doubt that he had better have.

As he sidled out of the room, he told himself that what he really wanted out of life was a telephone. Auntie Kitty was going to hear about what these nasty people were doing to him, and then the whole lot of them would wish they had never been born.

Charlotte closed the door behind him and turned to Tracey. 'Make coffee,' she said. 'And don't talk to anyone until I get back. Do you hear?'

Without waiting for an answer, she picked up her torn dictionary and stalked towards a door marked Private. It was her personal entrance to Sir Richard's inner sanctum, and she had every intention of making good use of it. She had been insulted, her property had been vandalized, and someone was going to have to pay a high price, if not with his testicles, then certainly with his miserable job.

'Yes,' promised the terrified Tracey, rising uncertainly from behind her desk and gazing around the office. 'But where's the . . .?'

'And take it to the boardroom,' snapped Charlotte. 'I'll be back in five minutes. Do you hear?'

Tracey bit her trembling lower lip. 'Yes, Miss,' she quavered, looking desperately around the room, 'but where's the . . .?'

It was too late: Charlotte had already gone.

* * *

5

CLIVE MINNOWFIELD

'What a ball-breaker,' said Titus, tilting his head back and draining his glass. 'What she needs,' he added, archly, pausing to wipe his mouth on the back of a hand, 'is a damned good . . .!'

'*Yes*!' hissed the shrouded figure, holding up a peremptory hand that silenced the little man as if he had been struck dumb. 'Thank you for your generous offer of enlightenment, Corio my lad. But I fear that we must continue our narrative without the benefit of your insights into the inadequacies of the most intimate aspects of Miss Piece's personal life.'

Titus' brow furrowed as the cowled head turned slowly towards him like the turret of a battlefield tank homing in on its target. 'The fact that your prejudices are a good deal closer to the truth than your limited knowledge of womankind has any right to predict, does not make your misogyny any the more palatable, you unfortunate little male chauvinist Ancient Briton, you.'

Titus squinted. 'You what?'

'The fact that Charlotte Piece is selfish, hard-hearted and manipulative,' offered Henry, 'doesn't mean it's OK for you to say that all she needs to set her straight is a right good shagging.'

'Quite!' agreed the shrouded figure.

'Although, actually,' mused Henry with a mischievous glance at the figure, 'now that you come to mention it . . . '

'*Eh-hem*!' coughed the figure. 'Let us move on!'

Henry nodded. 'Yes. Yes, I sort of remember some of that stuff about Adams and the porch, and Terry's trousers. But,' he sighed and shook his head, 'it's like looking at a book that's got nothing but blank pages in it until you tell me something and the pages fill up. But then, after *that* bit, the pages are all blank again.' He frowned. 'If you see what I mean?'

The figure inclined its head. 'That is because temporal displacement has distorted your memory – left the most recent bits of it behind, you might say. The events we are recounting happened only three days ago in your linear timeframe, and are, therefore, only three days in the past from your point of view, regardless of the fact that you have since travelled almost two thousand years backwards in time. Do you see?'

Henry shrugged. 'What I really don't understand, though,' he said, 'is how come you seem to know so much about what people were doing and thinking. You weren't there, were you? I mean, unless you were invisible or something? So unless you're making it all up . . .'

'That will become clear in due course,' said the figure. 'For the time being, I will say only that I have been around for a very, very long time.'

Henry's eyes narrowed. 'You're not some sort of . . . god or something, are you? I mean . . . you know?'

The figure regarded him in silence.

'Just thought I'd ask, that's all.'

'What I wanna know,' said Titus, 'is what's a suspender clip?'

The cowled head swung towards him.

'I mean, I thought you might 'ave some pictures, or somethin'. Y'know?'

The figure didn't reply.

'Only, it seemed kinda important to that Terry bloke, didn't it?' said Titus, raising a questioning eyebrow. 'Yeah?'

The figure nodded, thoughtfully. 'So how *exactly* did you occupy your time when you were sneaking in and out of those grubby establishments in Soho?'

'That's a no then, is it?' said Titus, turning to refill his glass. He looked across at Henry. 'Come on then buddy . . . what happens next?'

'Quite right!' said the shrouded figure, swinging its head around to look at Henry. 'You might recall that your colleague, Mr. Samuel Johnson, was called to the company's boardroom that day for a meeting with a man who said that he was looking for an advertising agency to help him market his company's coffee-based products?'

'No,' said Henry with a shake of the head. 'Not really.'

'Such was the case, nonetheless.'

* * *

'Well,' asked Sam, 'who is this guy and what does he want?'

'I'm glad you asked me that,' lied Minnowfield, glancing anxiously around his tiny office and wishing that Sam hadn't come. He had asked him to, of course – had sent Terry Smith to get him, in fact – but only because Sir Richard had told him that he must. He wouldn't have done it if he'd had a choice. He hated being alone with Sam in such a confined space. He hated being alone with anyone, for that matter, whether they were in a confined space or not. Unless it was with Charlotte Piece. And he had a suspicion that she didn't like being alone with him. Which only made him feel worse. He'd always had the uncomfortable suspicion that he suffered from some sort of social disability, like perspiration odour, or bad breath, or possibly, though he had no evidence to suggest it, a particularly nasty case of something that might one day develop into trench foot. No one had ever told him so – not in so many words, at least, or by any deed, direct or indirect, that he could remember. His wife Mary had certainly never mentioned it. All she had ever said on the subject of his personal hygiene was that he ought to be more careful about the time he spent in the bath or he might wash himself away. As far as he could remember, his children had never mentioned it either. Nor had any of his other relatives, friends, classmates, colleagues, superiors, subordinates, or any of the myriads of passing acquaintances he had made during his fifty-two years of life. And that, he told himself morosely, was the root of the problem: his affliction was so mind-bogglingly awful that not a single one of them had ever had the courage to confront him with it face to face. That's why Sam Johnson was such a frightening prospect. He was the sort of person who might just say it, whatever *it* might turn out to be, without warning or provocation. There was just no way of knowing with someone like him. He might come right out with *it*, if he thought *it* needed to be said, and he might just do it in company if you were really unlucky. And if that happened to Minnowfield he didn't know if he would cope with the stress. He would be grateful – of course he would – for the honesty of which no one else had ever been capable. But what good would honesty be to him when he was shrivelling to a crisp with the shame?

He wished that something would happen to take Sam's mind off of any unpleasant odours he had noticed since entering the office. Perhaps a mouse would suddenly run across the carpet, or a bird dash itself against the windowpane, so that he would be able to cry 'My word! Did you see that?' or 'You know, that reminds me of the time . . .'

He glanced hopefully from the skirting board to the remote patch of blue sky just visible through the little barred window above Sam's head, but there were no speeding or plummeting bodies to be seen. He sighed, and started to leaf half-heartedly through the neat pile of papers Charlotte had given him ahead of the meeting. He was almost certain that he had seen the man's name in there somewhere, but for the life of him he couldn't remember where. He sighed again and shook his head, dolefully. Thinking of birds plummeting made him sad because he often thought of himself as a bird: a delicate, caged songbird, perhaps, or a brightly coloured bird of paradise, tethered to a perch, its wings clipped, unable to fly. For the umpteenth time since joining the company, he thought how trapped his fragile spirit had become by the job he had allowed himself to be bullied into by his old school chum, and the tiny office in which that same old chum had seen fit to imprison him with such premeditated malice. When he had agreed to join the company, he had done so in high spirits and the hope of becoming the proud figurehead at the prow of his old school chum's corporate ship. But he had ended up with an office the size of a toilet, and a reputation for being the back-end of Sir Richard's pantomime horse.

'I want you near me,' Sir Richard had told him on that first day. 'So we can act together, as one man, without a lot of dashing about trying to find each other. Do you see? This way you'll be right next door, within easy reach, and none of that nasty crashing into the furniture, eh?'

Minnowfield had nodded his agreement, aware of the insincerity in his employer's voice, but mistaking it for the early signs of strep throat.

Sir Richard had reached out and run his hand along Minnowfield's shoulders with all the speed and greasy familiarity of a nervous molester suddenly grown bold. His short, powerful fingers had fitted snugly over and around Minnowfield's bony shoulder and levered him into his sweaty armpit with alarming strength. More than a head taller, Minnowfield had been forced to bend uncomfortably at the knees. He'd tried to retract his head into his suit jacket at the same time, like a wary tortoise, but Sir Richard had sensed the move, and had gripped him more tightly than ever, bringing his free hand up towards Minnowfield's face, making him flinch in anticipation of an open-handed slap that had never come.

'What's the matter?' he'd asked. 'Don't you like it, my old . . . chum?'

'Oh, no,' Minnowfield had replied quickly, swallowing hard. 'It's great. Really it is! It's just that I'd always thought . . . ' His eyes had taken on a hunted look and his voice had fallen away into silent confusion.

'Ah, yes,' Sir Richard had nodded, expansively. 'Yes indeed! This is just the thing for *my* managing director, isn't it?' Then he'd jerked them around, to face down the corridor. 'And there's the door to *my* office,' he'd added with exaggerated patience, turning to gaze into the uneasy Minnowfield's watering eyes with their faces so close together that Minnowfield had decided that he was about to be kissed. He'd had mixed feelings about the prospect, and had wondered if it aught to thrill him as much as it did. But to his relief, his employer had rotated them back into their original position.

'And there's yours,' he'd said, pointing with a quick index finger at a door marked Cleaning. 'Right next to it: do you see?'

Minnowfield's response had been tentative. 'Um . . . yes,' he'd replied. 'But don't you think it might be a bit . . .?' He'd paused, and gestured hopelessly. 'Well, I mean . . . for an M.D?'

'What?' Sir Richard had wheedled. 'A bit . . . what?'

'Well,' Minnowfield had offered with a sudden rush of courage. 'You don't think it might be a bit . . . small . . . at all? Do you?' He'd looked away from the door to a point about six inches in front of his boss's head: as close as he'd felt able to get to looking him in the eye.

'Too small?' Sir Richard had asked with feigned surprise. 'Good lord man, what d'you want, a drill hall?'

Minnowfield's apology had been quick and effusive. 'Oh, no!' he'd gasped. 'Absolutely not! No! Not at all! *Hah-hah*!' he'd laughed, too loudly. '*Hah*! Drill hall! Very good! Must tell Mary . . . I, mmm, yes – er, yes, er . . . umm.' His voice had drifted away into silence again, and he'd tried unsuccessfully to swallow the acidic taste of shame that had risen in the back of his throat.

Sir Richard had let him suffer in uneasy silence as they'd stood, locked together, in front of the door. 'Mmmm?' he'd prompted, quietly.

'Well,' Minnowfield had replied, anxious to please, 'I'm sure I could . . . '

'*My God*!' Sir Richard had exclaimed, slapping himself in the forehead with the flat of his free hand. 'Why didn't I think of it before?'

'What?' Minnowfield had asked, shying away. 'Think of what?'

'That!' Sir Richard had told him, shuffling them three paces to the left.

It had occurred to Minnowfield that they might look from behind like Siamese twins, joined at the hip, and he'd wondered if it could indeed be the case, and if the prospect ought to thrill him as much as it did.

Sir Richard had pointed straight ahead with his chin. 'There!' he'd said expansively. 'What do you think?'

Minnowfield had found himself staring at a door marked Stationery.

'What?' he'd gasped, on the verge of hysterics. 'You want me to use *that* one, instead?' He'd been stunned. 'I mean,' he'd added, his voice breaking into a wavering screech, *'what's the difference? They're both . . .!'*

'Good lord man, no!' Sir Richard had promised him. 'As well as! As well as! We can knock 'em together. Don't you see?'

'Really?' Minnowfield had sighed. 'What . . . we could do that . . . for me?'

'Oh, I'm sure we could,' Sir Richard had assured him with a sideways glance at his suddenly beaming face. 'Just you leave it to me.'

And Minnowfield had left it to Sir Richard. And the plasterboard partition between the stationery cupboard and the broom cupboard had duly been torn down, and a brand new managing director's office created out of the wreckage. And Minnowfield had moved into it as soon as the paint had been dry. And at first he had liked it. At first he had been grateful for it. At first he had felt secure. But that had only been at first. As time passed, he had begun to loathe it. As more time passed, he had begun to fear it. And as even more time passed, he had begun to think of it as a cage.

Sir Richard thought it was ideal.

* * *

'He's a nasty piece of work, though, isn't he, that Sir Richard?' said Titus. 'Reminds me of a centurion I used to know. Wouldn't trust the bugger as far as I could throw 'im.'

'Indeed,' said the shrouded figure. 'And you would be correct not to do so, Corio, my lad. But I suspect that you would be somewhat out of your depth with that particular entrepreneurial fish. Unless of course, you felt inclined to "tickle a blade up under his ribs", as I believe you and your erstwhile comrades were wont to put it?'

Titus shrugged. 'Couldn't happen to a nicer bloke, you ask me. Anyhow,' he added, 'who's been tellin' stories outa school?'

'As I said earlier, I have been around for a very, very long time.'

'Yeah, well, sneaky, I call it.'

'Perhaps so. But, as we shall see, it really wasn't my fault.'

'Whose fault was it, then?'

'All will be revealed in due course. In the meantime, let us return to Clive Minnowfield's oppressive little office, and the meeting orchestrated so carefully by Charlotte Piece that was to have such far-reaching consequences for our friend Henry's career. No doubt we will return to the secret lives of your little band of adolescent malcontents in the fullness of time.'

* * *

'Well,' urged Sam in a bored voice as he and Minnowfield sat in the cramped and airless place, 'who is he and what does he want?'

'Umm,' murmured Minnowfield, leafing uncomfortably through the papers Charlotte had given him, 'it's here somewhere . . .'

He was spared further embarrassment when the phone rang.

'Your visitor is waiting in the boardroom,' said Charlotte, and hung up.

'Yes,' said Minnowfield, as the phone went dead. 'Thank you Char . . . er, Miss . . . er, yes, that's, thank you. Tell Mr. . . . er, Mr. . . . er, yes, we will be with him . . . er, shortly.'

They got up and traipsed down the corridor to the boardroom where the marketing man who said he needed help with a great idea he'd had for selling his company's coffee beans was waiting to meet them with his buttocks tightly clenched. His name was Richard Choat, and he didn't give a toss about his company's products. What he *really* cared about was getting inside Charlotte Piece's knickers as often as possible, and having a legitimate reason for being close to her at her place of work had seemed as good a way of achieving that aim as either of them had been able to come up with on the spur of a very sticky moment. At the very least it would give them an excuse for being seen together, they had decided, and if they managed to create an award-winning advertising campaign in the process, so much the better.

'Say you've got a new idea for selling it,' Charlotte had breathed hotly in his ear a week earlier as they'd fumbled with each other's clothing in the back of her white convertible. Choat would rather have been doing it in his car (he sat in it as often as he could, whether it was moving or not), but a Ford Probe (especially a priceless limited edition bought at considerable expense from the shadowy Mr. Beoric of B. T. & A. Autos of Norway, or was it Finland?) was even less accommodating than a Rover convertible with the top down when a well-built woman like Charlotte has developed a taste for carnal gymnastics.

'Minnowfield won't know the difference,' she'd hissed, arching her left leg over the back of the passenger seat. 'I'll take care of . . . *Oh, Richard, not yet!* I'll take care of Kite and Johnson, so all you have to do is . . . *No, Richard! Not yet!* All you have to do is . . . *Ooh, Rich-arrrrd, not again!*'

The plan had been laid immediately after they had, and with about as much consideration for detail and timing. So it was hardly surprising that it started to go wrong as soon as they tried to put it into practice.

'It won't work,' said Sam, who hated having to work with amateurs like Choat who re-packaged clichéd ideas and tried to present them as their own. The gold-plated coffee bean campaign, promising punters a charm bracelet and trinkets to hang on it in return for impossible quantities of jars purchased and labels saved, had been a dud the first time around. 'It didn't work then,' he insisted. 'And it won't work now.'

'Oh, I don't know,' said Minnowfield, who particularly liked the mock-up gold jewellery Choat had spread out in front of them on the boardroom table. 'Let's not be too hasty, eh? I'm sure Mr. . . . er . . . Mr. . . . er . . . ' He looked down at his notes, but Choat's name still managed to elude him.

Charlotte came to his rescue. 'Richard,' she gushed.

Sam frowned, and glanced towards her. What was she up to, he wondered, and why had she stayed in the boardroom after she and the terrified Tracey had finished serving that disgusting coffee? More to the point, why was she being so attentive and pretending to take notes? It wasn't like her to act the dutiful handmaiden when Sir Richard wasn't around.

She giggled again, almost shyly.

Sam's eyes widened. Something really odd, he decided, was going on here.

'Choat,' blurted Choat. 'Richard Choat,' he added, as he glanced quickly at Charlotte. 'I must have made quite an impression.'

'Me too', thought Sam as his thumbnail sank into something soft and yielding. He held the thing up to his nose and sniffed at it, appreciatively. 'This is shit,' he said, holding up a squashed gold coffee bean between the finger and thumb of his right hand.

Minnowfield was horrified. 'Steady on,' he said. 'I mean, it's not the most original idea, perhaps, but . . . '

Sam ignored him and held the bean towards Choat. 'Who made this?'

Choat was taken aback. 'Made it?' he murmured. 'I, well, I . . . '

'And does he keep rabbits, by any chance?'

Choat tried to remember the story he and Charlotte had concocted between them. 'The boys in the art department.' He frowned. 'Rabbits?'

'Friends of yours, are they?'

'Rabbits?'

'The boys in the art department.'

Choat blinked like a boxer who had taken one head punch too many. 'I don't see . . . ' he stammered, 'I mean . . . ' but a suspicion of dirty dealing had begun to force its way into his brain. His daughter kept rabbits, he remembered, and she disliked him – hated him, would be a more accurate way of putting it – and he wondered if she hated him enough to try to wreck his career. On the whole, he rather thought that she might.

The gold beans had not been made by the boys in any art department. Choat had no influence over such things. He was an accountant, and the art department in the company he worked for had never even heard of him. Not that he would have involved them in his little project if they had. It was strictly between him and Charlotte. The bracelet hadn't been made by the art department at the company, either: Choat had bought it from a branch of Ratners Jewellers as a birthday present for his wife two years earlier, and had taken it from her jewellery box that morning without so much as a by-your-leave. Jacqueline was a jealous woman, and one to be feared with a potato peeler in her hand, who would kill him, or something worse, if she ever found out what he was up to with Charlotte. And now that he came to think about that, he wished that he'd thought about it earlier.

He crossed his legs and tried to look relaxed, but it wasn't easy: the situation was in danger of getting out of control, and he was beginning to wish that he hadn't allowed Charlotte to talk him into it. He glanced in her direction, hoping for a sign that she thought things were going well, but she scowled back at him over the rim of her coffee cup, and then looked away with a heavy sigh and a far from encouraging scowl.

'Idiot!' she thought as she turned her back on the room. 'What's he let that stupid girl get up to now?'

The 'stupid girl' in question was Choat's daughter, Victoria, who was 16 years old and wanted to go to art school. Her art teacher said that she had a talent for it, too, but Choat wouldn't hear of it. He wasn't, he had insisted, having any sex mad, longhaired, lefty scroungers getting their legs over *his* daughter, thank you very much: not on the money *he* was expected to pay for her education, he wasn't! She would go to the local sixth form college and study accountancy as he had before her, and she would bloody well like it, too! In the meantime, she would toe the line at home and stay away from troublemakers like that Elizabeth Bates girl, whose disgusting family were no better than a bunch of socially inept criminals.

He couldn't imagine why he'd allowed Jacqueline to talk him into moving to Chigwell in the first place. He couldn't deny that the house had seemed perfect for them at the time: all classical mock Georgian, in its own designer-built gardens, with one or two tasteful sculptures in and around the shrubbery. The mortgage had been crippling, of course, but he had always managed to cover it with a bit of careful accounting and a few extra-curricular funds acquired from elsewhere. But the architectural extras had made it seem worth every penny, especially the competition-sized swimming pool, the triple garage with its integral games complex at the back, and his own personal favourite, the walk-through combined lounge, dining room, breakfast bar, audio-visual alcove and cocktail pit, all supported by that subtle mix of Greek columns that held up the ceiling, framed the windows and afforded such a wonderful view of the garden. But it was typical of Victoria's bolshie attitude that the best she could ever say about the place was that it was 'a load of tasteless wank.' Her endless criticism had started to wear him down, and had been undermining his confidence for months, making him wonder if he had done the right thing. The glass-topped wall, the gates and the Doberman Pincher kept the scroungers out, and there were more than enough Rolls Royces and Porsches in the neighbourhood to remind him that he had arrived amongst the real high achievers. Yet he had a nagging suspicion that one or two of them didn't have quite the level of sophistication he'd been hoping for: not what he would have found in Ongar or Brentwood, perhaps? Rumour had it that two-thirds of them were armed robbers, drug pushers, limp-wristed cabaret artistes, or all three rolled into one. Not that he minded any of that, just so long as they didn't get caught in the act and cause property values to crash.

What really bothered him was that so few of them seemed to have any *real* class. Most of their wives and girlfriends still wore imitation leopard skin instead of the real thing, with gold lamé sling-backs and half a pound of mixed gold bric-a-brac hanging from every limb. It had taken him years to convince Jacqueline that such things were not in their best interests if they were to improve their social standing. Now she was surrounded by it again and showed every sign of sliding back into her old ways. She had even gone back to spelling her name with a K and letting people – people she didn't even know! – call her Jackie in public. And it was obvious that the expensive education he'd provided for his only daughter had been completely wasted. There had been a time when she'd looked up to him, admired him even, and asked for his opinion on everything she'd said and done. But those days were long gone. All she ever did now was criticize every aspect of his life: his politics, his clothes, his car, the police, the school and the government he so admired. Nothing he did was good enough for the stupid little bitch. Worst of all, was this ridiculous notion that she was going to be an artist. Well, he'd had enough of her, and her slut of a mother. As soon as he got the chance he was off with Charlotte to start a new life, and the pair of them could go straight to Hell. He would sell the house out from under them, and see how they liked that. It had been dawning on him for some time that the sooner he got away from his bolshie daughter and his embarrassing slapper of a wife the better it would be for his career. The only problem was that he couldn't do it immediately because Charlotte had said that she wasn't convinced that he was serious about her, and needed proof that he really wanted them to spend the rest of their lives together.

'Get the brat to make you some . . . you know . . . thingies,' she'd breathed in his ear as he'd tried to prise her knees apart on the back seat of her car. '*Stop it, Richard*! You know . . . models and things? I'll show you what to do, and you can bring them to the office and . . . *Don't do that*! *Listen to me when I'm talking to you*! Bring them to the office, and then we'll see about us.'

He had told Victoria that he was working in secret on an important contract and wanted her to make some mock-up jewellery as a test of her commitment to this arty-farty stuff she kept saying she wanted to do: and that if she made a good job of it, he would pay for her to go to the art school of her choice. He had thought that he'd lulled her into a false sense of security with his little scheme. But it was beginning to look as if she had seen through it, and had come up with a nastier scheme of her own.

She had locked her bedroom door as usual that morning, and had left the house without saying goodbye. If she had only given him the stuff the night before, as he'd asked her to, he wouldn't have had to break into her room. But she hadn't, so the whole sordid business was clearly her fault!

He hadn't found what he'd been looking for immediately. But he'd rummaged through her cupboards and drawers, her underwear and makeup, until he'd come across an old biscuit tin stashed in the bottom of her wardrobe. It had rattled when he'd shaken it, so he'd forced it open and found inside the gold-plated coffee beans he'd asked her to make. They hadn't been as convincing as he would have liked them to be, but there had been no time to find replacements, so he'd had no choice but to take them with him. He'd also found in the box what he'd taken to be her idea of a charm bracelet. It had been far too big and too ugly by half, and he'd wondered how anyone capable of creating such a tasteless pile of junk could imagine that they had the talent to make a living as an artist. But he'd tipped it into his briefcase along with everything else, and left the tin on the bedroom floor with a Post-it note stuck to its lid on which he'd written in felt-tipped pen 'Thank you, darling. They're wonderful. Daddy. XXX.'

Jacqueline hadn't been in the house at the time, either, so he'd gone into the master bedroom and taken a gold bracelet from her over-stuffed jewellery box. It was bigger and heavier than he would have liked, but he'd figured that anything was better than the grotesque atrocity that Victoria had made. His problem was that the bracelet he'd chosen was his wife's favourite piece of jewellery, and the fact that she'd left it behind could only mean that she'd gone to one of her many aerobics classes at the health club. Leaving it at home always broke her heart, but that was better than having it break her wrist as soon she started jiggling up and down. He'd known that she would be devastated when she got home and found it missing, and he'd hoped that she wouldn't do anything too dramatic, like screaming the house down, or calling the police, before he got back. After a moment's thought, he'd scribbled another note and stuck it to the lid of the box. 'Gone to the jeweller for inscription', it read. 'Love you. Richie. XXX.'

It had seemed like a good idea at the time. Now he wasn't so sure.

Charlotte frowned at him across the boardroom table. She had decided that he was making such a mess of things that it was time for her to take charge.

'I don't think Sir Richard would be very pleased with that sort of comment, *actually*, do you?' she said, fixing Sam with one of her most penetrating looks of disapproval.

Sam shrugged his indifference. 'This,' he repeated, holding up the squashed bean for her inspection, 'is shit. Rabbit shit, to be precise.' He sniffed at it. 'I'd recognize it anywhere.'

'Really?' said Minnowfield, with childlike wonderment. 'But how?'

'I don't think we need to go into that, do we?' said Charlotte, tartly. 'What we ought to be doing is . . . '

'*Shoosh*!' hissed Minnowfield, waving her to silence.

Charlotte glared at him in disbelief. No one but Sir Richard was allowed to speak to her in that tone of voice!

'Recognize it?' prompted Minnowfield. 'How do you mean?'

'Used to keep 'em myself,' said Sam, 'rabbits. Used to carry this stuff around to throw at people, put down girls' dresses, that sort of stuff?'

Charlotte shuddered. 'This is disgusting,' she said, jiggling her cup and saucer as she glared from Minnowfield to Sam.

Minnowfield shrugged: if the coffee wasn't to her liking, he decided, she only had herself to blame. She and the trembling Tracey had made the ghastly stuff in the first place, after all.

'Carry it around?' he prompted.

'In my pocket,' nodded Sam. 'When I was a kid.'

'God!' grimaced Charlotte.

Minnowfield was stricken with envy. 'Really?' he whispered, wishing that he'd been allowed to carry rabbit shit around in his pockets when he was a kid. But it was just another in a long list of things that his mother would have banned him from doing if the subject had ever come up. 'What, all the time?'

Charlotte's eyes opened wide. 'Are you mad? I really *don't* think . . .'

'*Shoosh*!' hissed Minnowfield, with an uncharacteristically aggressive chopping motion of his hand.

'Depended how wet it was,' confided Sam. 'If it got stuck to your hand it was too wet. If you could roll 'em together like this,' he added, picking up some of the gold beans from the table, 'they'd be dry enough.'

Choat sat with his mouth open, fascinated in spite of himself.

Sam held the beans up for Charlotte to inspect. 'See what I saying?'

She curled her lip, and backed towards the door.

'If they were *really* dry,' continued Sam, 'you could spit 'em at people in your peashooter.'

Charlotte gagged. 'I've had enough of this!' she said, slamming her cup and saucer down on a side table. 'It's *filth*!'

'Ah, yes,' said Minnowfield, as she opened the door and stomped out of the room, 'good idea.' He beamed at the others. 'Fresh coffees all round?'

Choat was no longer certain he understood what was going on, and was beginning to wonder if the whole thing was some sort of elaborate set-up to make him look ridiculous: a malicious plot of Charlotte's devising, perhaps, to pay him back for some perceived slight against her. He concentrated hard, glancing from Minnowfield to Sam and back again, in an attempt to work out if they were all in it together. He was reasonably certain that Minnowfield was genuine because he seemed too conventional to be anything else. But he wasn't at all sure about Sam, who seemed too untidy and too disrespectful to be any kind of businessman he had ever heard of, never mind met. He looked more like an actor, or a poet, or some other type of overweight degenerate of the sort he wanted his daughter to stay well away from. He even had food stains down the front of his shirt, and something that looked suspiciously like a piece of cucumber stuck to his shoe.

Choat glanced nervously towards the door, wondering how long it would be before Charlotte came back into the room. She already seemed to have been gone for a long time, and he wondered if he ought to cut his losses and make a run for it. He looked at Sam, and then at Minnowfield. They stared back at him inscrutably, and he decided that he had no option but to stay where he was and brazen it out. His mouth was bone dry and he wished that Charlotte would come back soon with a fresh pot of coffee. It had been awful the first time around, but he felt that he would gladly drink gallons of the filthy stuff now, no matter how revolting it might taste.

'I'm sorry,' said Minnowfield with an apologetic cough, 'what did you say your name was again?'

'Choat,' he croaked, swallowing dryly. 'Richard Choat.'

Minnowfield smiled. 'Ah, yes, of course!' He gave a nervous dip of the head. 'More coffee, at all . . . er, Richard? I mean,' he added, simpering, 'I know it's not even remotely up to the very high standards of your company's excellent products, but needs must when the devil drives, and all that, eh?'

Choat smiled wanly back at him.

Minnowfield nodded and glanced down at his notes. 'Now, this idea of yours, er, Richard, perhaps you'd like to run it past us again? I don't think we quite got the full flavour of it the first time around, did we?' He turned to Sam for confirmation. 'Wouldn't you say so, Mr. Johnson?'

'How many rabbits have they got, exactly?' asked Sam.

Choat blinked. 'What?'

Sam pointed at the pile of golden beans on the table. 'Who made these? And do they really hate you that much?'

Choat smiled, tightly. 'Like I said, the boys in the art department.' And in an attempt to change the subject, he opened his briefcase to take out a sheaf of papers he'd prepared for the meeting. Mixed in amongst them was the chunky bracelet he'd taken from Victoria's biscuit tin. It skittered across the table as he pulled out the papers. 'I – I've got a bit of a storyboard here,' he stammered. 'I thought we could . . . '

Sam leaned across and scooped up the heavy beads as they skidded towards him. 'These are good,' he said, turning them over in his hands. 'Did the boys in the art department make these, too?'

'What?' said Choat, looking up. 'No, no . . . they're . . . that's just . . . I mean, it's just a piece of junk. I don't think . . . '

'Is it really?' said Sam, thoughtfully. 'Well, it looks like a very interesting piece of junk to me.'

Choat nodded distractedly as he sorted through his papers. 'It's only rough, really. But, look, this is what . . . '

'How old is the boy who made these?' asked Sam, examining the heavy beads closely. 'They're really very good, you know. Bit big for a bracelet, but we could always scale them down, couldn't we? A lot better than,' he waved a hand at the gold beans, 'that pile of crap!'

Choat licked his lips, and shook his head. He seemed suddenly to have lost the power of speech, and was rapidly loosing the will to live.

Minnowfield narrowed his eyes and looked from one to the other. He had the feeling that he was missing something here. He glanced down at his notes, but was almost certain that he could remember seeing nothing there about the ages of the people in Choat's art department. He wondered if Sam was on the right track. Then it struck him that perhaps it was something to do with target groups or consumer profiles or something like that: the sort of technical stuff that always seemed to confuse him. If it was that sort of thing, he couldn't be expected to understand it, he told himself, because that wasn't his area of expertise at all. He sat back and smiled benignly at Choat.

'Twelve?' prompted Sam.

Choat sighed, and glanced anxiously at Minnowfield.

Minnowfield beamed back at him, nodding his encouragement in spite of the fact that 12-year-olds seemed a bit young as a target group for coffee beans. 'Still,' he told himself, 'Johnson's very good at that sort of thing. I'm probably a bit out of touch.'

Choat's heart sank. 'I don't know about any of this,' he said, miserably.

'No,' said Minnowfield, kindly. 'But we do. We're the experts.'

'Thirteen?' asked Sam.

Choat looked down at the table.

'Fourteen?'

'Sixteen,' blurted Choat, with a weary shake of the head.

'Ah,' said Sam. 'And he keeps rabbits, does he?'

'She! My daughter, actually! And, yes, she does keep rabbits, if you must know! Are you happy now?' He put his hands on the table, and started to get up. 'I'll be going now,' he said, 'since you clearly don't want our business.'

'Oh, but we do!' insisted Minnowfield, wringing his hands at the thought of Sir Richard's reaction if they lost another valuable contract. '*Really* we do!'

'Well, you have a very odd way of showing it,' sneered Choat, determined to maintain the charade to the end. He gathered up his papers and began shovelling them into his briefcase. Now that he had made up his mind to leave, he wanted to get out of the building as quickly as possible.

Minnowfield was mortified. 'Don't go,' he pleaded. 'I'm sorry about the coffee. It was awful, I know, but . . . ' he glanced at the door. 'I can't imagine what's happened to Miss Piece, she's usually so *very* efficient . . .'

'It's got nothing to do with the sodding coffee!' snapped Choat. 'I have no doubt that you will be hearing from us in due course. But I wouldn't hold my breath if I were you.' He backed towards the door with his briefcase clutched tightly to his chest. 'I'm going now, *if* you don't mind?'

'That won't be necessary,' said a deep voice behind him. 'Although I'm not so sure about this pair of incompetent morons.'

The sound made Choat's hair stand on end.

He turned, reluctantly, to find the squat bulk of Sir Richard blocking his only means of escape. Behind him, her head and shoulders outlined against the light, was Charlotte, a smile of smug superiority splitting her face.

'*Shit*!' mouthed Choat, under his breath.

6

LADY KITTY

'You,' Sir Richard snapped at Sam from the boardroom door, 'stay! I'll deal with you later!' His demeanour changed in an instant as he turned smoothly and gestured for Choat to accompany him into the corridor. 'Won't you come with me, Mr. Choat? I'm sure we can give you exactly what you need. Miss Piece has told me all about it.'

He smiled coldly at Minnowfield as they passed in the doorway. 'This little misunderstanding won't hold us up at all,' he said, 'will it?'

'No, indeed,' simpered Minnowfield. 'Absolutely not!'

With his briefcase and papers clutched tightly to his chest as Sir Richard hustled him out of the room, Choat glanced over his shoulder at Sam.

Sam leaned back in his chair, twiddled his fingers in an unsympathetic farewell, and winked at the expression of terror on Choat's face.

Whatever else might happen, Sam told himself as he tipped the forgotten piece of jewellery from hand to hand beneath the table, he was not going to hang around in the boardroom waiting for it to became obvious that Sir Richard had no intention of coming back to 'deal' with him at any time in the near future. Once the others were out of sight, he was off, and the chunky bracelet, or necklace, or whatever it was, was going with him.

'Both of them?' cried Minnowfield in alarm ten minutes later in Sir Richard's office. '*Today*?' He glanced from Sir Richard to Charlotte, whose hard eyes were cold and uncompromising, and across at Adams, whose soft watery ones made him look sad as well as demented.

'Do it,' Adams urged. 'Do it! Do it!'

Charlotte shrugged. 'They're troublemakers, aren't they?'

'But you *can't!*' insisted Minnowfield in desperation.

Sir Richard eyed him, coldly. 'What did you say?'

Minnowfield licked his lips, and hoped that the floor would open up and swallow him whole.

Choat had only just left, bemused and wishing, not for the last time, that he hadn't allowed Charlotte to talk him into this hare-brained scheme. Sir Richard had apologized to him for the fiasco in the boardroom and had assured him that the company would throw its full weight behind his new coffee bean campaign and ensure its success. Choat had smiled in apparent gratitude. But beneath the fixed grin he had been terrified by the prospect of what might happen to him if he and Charlotte were to allow the charade to go on for much longer. He'd tried to tell her of his concerns as she'd ushered him out of the building, but to his horror she'd been awash with passion and seemingly oblivious to the dangers they faced.

'Wait for me in the car park,' she'd demanded, hotly, in his ear. 'And keep your motor running. I'll be out soon, for . . . *you-know-what*!'

She'd kissed him on the mouth then, and squeezed his inner thigh, before flitting wraith-like back into the building with a wave and a blown kiss.

By the time she'd made it back to Sir Richard's office, Adams had been in the process of trying to explain the demise of her dictionary, and the meaning of a brief and typically cryptic telephone call from Lady Kitty.

'What is the meaning of this, Dickie?' she had boomed out of the receiver. 'I'll not have the boy made a fool of! See to it! Do you hear?'

Adams stood now with his hands behind his back, for all the world like an infant reciting its lines at the school nativity, and he told a rambling version of his encounter with Henry and Sam, embellishing it so richly in the process that he wouldn't have recognized it if it had been read back to him. He explained the destruction of Charlotte's dictionary rather more simply with the repeated accusation that 'Kite did it!'

It was more than enough for Sir Richard. He wasn't about to do anything on Adams's behalf because he was a snivelling infant of an inconvenience and ought to be made to fight his own battles. But no one in his right mind ignored Lady Kitty when she was on the rampage. And besides, he had already decided that something nasty needed to be done to Johnson for trying to sabotage Choat's new account. Kite was Johnson's friend and that meant that they were probably in it together. He wasn't sure what it was that they were in together, but he knew that you couldn't be too careful when it came to subversives. Besides, they both worked for Minnowfield, and that was more than enough reason for throwing them out on their ears.

He looked Minnowfield in the eye. '*What* did you say?'

'There's Mercantile & Federated Insurance,' gabbled Minnowfield, like an auctioneer on amphetamine sulphate. 'Johnson has the . . . '

'*Can't?*' hissed Sir Richard. 'Did you say *can't* to me?'

' . . . account,' continued Minnowfield, doggedly. 'And Mitsutoshi . . . '

Sir Richard's voice doubled in volume. 'Nobody says *can't* to me!' he roared. 'Not unless he wants his todger ripped off and shoved up his *arse*!'

'Do it! Do it!' urged Adams, wide-eyed. 'Do it now!'

Sir Richard grinned. That was more like it. He could almost believe that they *were* related when he saw the little twerp getting carried away like that over business. It reminded him of himself in his younger days.

Minnowfield pressed on. 'That's £2.3 million over . . . '

Sir Richard stopped dead in mid-rant. 'What did you say?'

'Yeah!' sneered Adams. 'Cut his balls off, an' all!'

'It's £2.3 million over two years. With an option . . . '

'How much?'

'Cut his dick off,' sniggered Adams, 'and stick it up his . . .!'

Sir Richard turned towards him. 'Shut up!'

'I was only saying . . . '

'Shut up, when I tell you to shut up!'

This idiot boy couldn't be related to him after all, he decided, regardless of what his bitch of a wife kept telling him, because no true seed of his loins would ever show such scant respect for turnover. And if it wasn't for those damned pictures, he would tell the old witch what she could do with her bastard nephew!

'Didn't you hear what he said?'

'I thought . . . ' began Adams.

'No you sodding-well *didn't!*' yelled Sir Richard. 'You're not capable of it, you stupid little *turd!*'

He turned back to Minnowfield, his voice dropping to a whisper. 'Tell me again . . . how much?'

'It's £2.3 million over two years,' said Minnowfield, quickly. 'With an option on a further two years if they like . . . '

'Don't give me sodding details, man!' snapped Sir Richard. 'I don't want sodding details, do I? What good are sodding details to me?' His eyes narrowed to slits. 'Just give me the facts!'

Adams pouted. 'I'll tell Auntie Kitty if you don't . . .!'

Sir Richard rounded on him in fury. 'You'll . . . *what?*'

Charlotte stepped quickly between them, grabbing Sir Richard's wrists and pressing them gently down by his sides.

'It's £2.3 million over two years,' she said, inclining her head towards Minnowfield. 'And there's more.'

'More?' echoed Sir Richard, glassy-eyed.

Charlotte nodded and turned him back to face Minnowfield. Then she let go of his arms and turned to face Adams. She had no intention of allowing him to disrupt proceedings further. So with a friendly nod and an encouraging gesture, she motioned him towards her.

Adams stepped forward and inclined his head as she made as if to whisper in his ear. But she lowered her hand at the last moment and gasped him firmly by the balls.

Adams made a hissing sound as his lips pulled back from his tightly clenched teeth. His eyes opened wide and he snapped to attention, his lower lip quivering as he squeaked like a frightened guinea pig, almost as astonished by her actions as Charlotte was herself.

'Why don't we let them get on with it,' she whispered, '*mmm?*'

Adams swallowed hard.

'I'll take care of Kite for you, all right?'

Adams nodded.

Charlotte bared her teeth in one of her more terrifying smiles, and gave Adams's crotch a tweak. 'Goooood,' she breathed.

Behind her, Minnowfield was talking as fast as his dentures would let him. 'And a possible £3.5 million over two years . . .'

Sir Richard's eyes narrowed. 'Really?'

'Yes! Yes, indeed!' Minnowfield nodded. 'Over two years if . . .'

'Million?'

Minnowfield nodded again. 'Absolutely!'

'That's £5.8 million,' mused Sir Richard, 'over . . . ' He paused and took Minnowfield by the arm. 'It wouldn't do to be too hasty, now, would it?'

'No, indeed,' simpered Minnowfield. 'I think we ought . . . '

'One of them has got to go, though,' said Charlotte over her shoulder. 'At least one.' She kept her eyes fixed on Adams's face and her hand hooked firmly into his groin. 'It's only fair.'

'Is it?' said Sir Richard, without taking his eyes from Minnowfield's face.

'I'm upset,' said Charlotte, flatly. 'I've been insulted in front of a client.' She clicked her tongue. 'And there's Lady Kitty to think about, too.'

'Yes,' said Sir Richard, hurriedly, 'quite!' His eyes narrowed. 'That's it, then,' he told Minnowfield. 'See to it now!'

'But,' pleaded Minnowfield, 'Johnson has the accounts . . . '

'Get rid of the other one, then. I never liked him. What was his name?'

'Kite,' said Charlotte. She smiled coldly at Adams as, with a final squeeze, let go of his balls. 'He's the one who did it, isn't he?'

Adams nodded rapidly, but was careful to keep his mouth shut as he stepped backwards out of harm's way.

'Yes,' said Sir Richard, darkly, 'he was the one with the CDs, wasn't he? I don't like him. Get rid of the little bastard today.'

'But . . . ' began Minnowfield, wringing his hands.

'No *buts*!' insisted Sir Richard. 'Or we might have to look closer to home.'

* * *

'Sam tried to tell me about it,' said Henry, 'didn't he?' He frowned. 'I think. But I wouldn't listen, would I? I was trying to work and he kept rambling on about . . . about . . . *what?*'

'Good,' said the shrouded figure. 'Very good! Your memory is beginning to reconstruct itself.'

'Is it? Well, I'm glad you think so. All I can remember is Sam showing me something . . . Some kind of jewellery, but there's nothing there when I try to look closer. The pages have all gone blank.' He fell silent and stared into the fire with a furrowed brow.

'Quite so,' said the shrouded figure, leaning to one side to look into his face. 'But do not despair, Henry, your memory really will return completely once it has had sufficient time to catch up with your body. Believe me, I know from personal experience.'

Henry looked up. 'You do?'

The cowled head nodded. 'Indeed. But the important issue at this stage in our narrative is not the current, fragmented state of your memory, frustrating and confusing though that must be for you, but the question of what impact Richard Choat's actions were to have on your career.'

'It is?'

The figure nodded again.

'He's a wimp, though, isn't he,' said Titus, sliding a slice of cheesecake into his mouth, 'tha' 'Innowfiel' b'oke?'

'I don't know,' sighed Henry. 'I always felt sorry for him. I think he meant well, even if he was a bit . . . ineffectual at times.'

'*Bowwocks*!' snorted Titus, spraying cheesecake around. "Ee's a *whoosh*!'

Henry squinted at him. 'He's a what?'

Titus swallowed with difficulty. 'A wuss! He's a *wuss*! I said . . . '

The figure held up a hand and the little Ancient Briton fell silent with a confused look on his face.

'How do you do that?' asked Henry. 'The thing with your hand?'

'It's . . . too complicated to explain,' said the figure.

But Henry thought he detected a note of pride in the voice: a sense that the figure was pleased that the question had been asked.

'Try me,' he said.

'No, I really don't' think . . . '

'Go on! Please? Humour me? It's very impressive, you know.'

'Is it?'

'Very!'

'Well,' said the figure, glancing briefly at Titus, 'the subject doesn't notice, of course, but part of its linear timeframe is deleted from the awareness of those around it – sidestepped, you might say – as if it had never existed? Then we pick up from the moment immediately after he has had his say.'

'So, you don't stop him speaking, you just sort of save us the trouble of having to listen to it?'

'Precisely!'

Henry had the feeling that if the figure's face had been visible it would have been wearing a self-satisfied grin.

'Look,' said Titus, irritably, 'what are you . . .?'

The figure held up a hand.

The little man fell silent.

Henry smiled. 'Brilliant!'

'You think so?'

'Absolutely!'

'I am gratified that you approve of my little parlour trick.'

'You know, you could make a fortune out of that.'

'Really?'

'Damn right! You could . . . ' He stopped, and a broad smile spread across his face. 'You already have, haven't you?'

The figure bowed solemnly from the waist.

'Well I'm damned!'

'Not yet, Henry, but the day is still young. The point is that your former employer was determined to make an example of someone, and it was just your great good fortune that the someone he chose turned out to be you.'

'I don't seem to remember it feeling like that at the time.'

'Yes, well, getting drunk didn't help matters much, did it?'

'I wouldn't know, would I? I can't remember little details like that.'

* * *

Henry was slumped in an armchair in Sam's flat with a suspicion beginning to dawn on him that he had a problem. Most of it had come from a green bottle and several green and white cans, and was called alcohol. It hadn't been pure – there had been too much water and too many trace elements mixed into it for that – but it was something that he wasn't used to in such large quantities, and it had begun to play havoc with his central nervous system. The effect had been 'done to a turn', as Sam had put it, when they'd shared a joint of what he'd referred to proudly as 'a drop of the old home-grown'.

'Home-grown?' Henry had asked through the clouds of billowing smoke.

'Yeah,' Sam had replied. 'Well, you know . . . Nigeria?'

By the time they'd finished smoking it, Henry had been more than happy to agree that Nigeria was close enough to be called home. He had also made a fair job of forgetting that he no longer had a job to go to, and that he might not have a home to go to, either, if he didn't find a way of paying his mortgage soon. But at least he'd stopped sobbing and was almost beginning to feel optimistic about his future, even though he hadn't the faintest idea what that future would bring.

Everything had felt very different eight hours earlier as he'd sat at his desk trying to work at his computer, and trying even harder not to listen to Sam.

'He was a tosser,' Sam was saying, 'you know?'

'Un-huh,' Henry murmured, 'right . . .'

'He drove a car called a Probe, for god's sake. I saw him drive it away. How am I supposed to take a cretin like that seriously? I mean, you might as well call it a penis, and have done with it.'

'Call it a prick,' Ron Posset offered as he wandered by with a bulging bin bag trailing behind him. 'That way you got the car an' the driver both!'

'See,' Sam nodded, pointing at Ron.

'Yeah, pro-bab-ly,' Henry muttered, doing his best to concentrate on the screen in front of him. He looked up. 'Who're we talking about, now?'

'This guy,' Sam replied, tipping Victoria Choat's lumpy piece of jewellery onto the desk in front of him with such force that it slid across the surface and bumped against Henry's mug, spilling coffee over the rim.

'For Christ's sake!' complained Henry, jerking backwards in his chair to avoid imaginary drips. 'Look what you're doing, will you?'

'He didn't want it. Can you believe that? Said it was a load of old junk.'

'You messy sod!' said Henry, reaching for a tissue.

'You're not listening to me, are you?'

'Can't you be more careful?' Henry asked, lifting the mug and dabbing at the ring of coffee beneath it. 'You come barging in here . . .'

Sam leaned forward, and snatched Henry's notebook from the desk.

'Don't mess about!'

'Are you gonna listen to me, or not?'

'Come on . . .!' said Henry, holding out a hand.

'Not 'til you promise,' said Sam, clutching the book to his chest.

'Give it back!'

'Nope!' said Sam, pursing his lips, and cocking his head to one side.

Henry sighed: 'OK,' and held out a hand.

'Not 'til I've finished!' said Sam. 'See, this guy . . . '

'The one with the rabbit's shit?'

'Oh, so you *were* listening?'

'And . . .?'

'His daughter made it.'

'The rabbit's shit?'

'Yes. No! How could she make rabbit's shit, Henry? Tell me that.'

'Give them a really hard squeeze?' suggested Henry. He thought for a moment. 'Or just yell: Look out, there's a fox behind you!'

'Who's telling this story?'

Henry sighed, and leaned back in his chair.

'So this guy,' he said, when Sam had finished, 'what was his name?'

'I dunno, Weasel or Stoat, or something.'

'Weasel?'

'Or Stoat – I forget.'

'And he gave you this, did he?'

Sam shrugged, and looked out of the window.

'I see.'

'You think I stole it, don't you?'

'And you're saying you didn't?'

'He left it on the table. Said it was a load of old crap.'

'Fine.'

'I was only thinking of you.'

'Really?'

'I thought: That's just the sort of thing Henry would like. Of course, if I'd known you were gonna get all pious about it . . . '

'I'm very grateful. And . . .?'

'What?'

'About Stoat?'

'What about him?'

'I don't know. You're the one telling the story . . . remember?'

'That's it.'

'What is?'

'That!' Sam pointed at the jewellery. 'I thought you'd be pleased.'

'Oh, I am. Really I am!'

'You don't sound it.'

'You dump stolen property on me and expect me to be grateful?'

'Give it back, then,' said Sam, reaching forward.

Henry clutched the string of heavy beads to his chest with both hands and swayed out of the way. 'How old was she, then, this Stoat's daughter?'

'I dunno . . . sixteen, I think he said.'

'And she's got a blacksmith's workshop in her bedroom, has she? This is metal, Sam, she couldn't have made it without some sort of forge.'

'Busy, are we?' asked Adams, sneaking up suddenly behind Sam with a predatory grin. 'Got a lot on, have we?' he asked Henry. 'Work I mean?'

'Piss off!' said Sam.

'Oh, I'm not the one who's going to piss off, am I?' Adams smirked at Henry as he flapped an envelope in front of his face. 'But I know someone who is, don't I?' He looked down at the envelope, as if he had only just noticed it in his hand. 'Oh, I wonder who this is for?'

'Go away,' said Henry, tiredly.

'It's for someone called Kite,' said Adams, looking around the office with raised eyebrows. 'Is there anyone here with that name?'

Henry held out a hand.

'Not until you say please.'

'Keep it.'

'Oh no, I want you to have it,' said Adams, handing it over.

That was how Henry found out that he had been sacked. There were no kind words, no offers of regret, no golden handshake, no clock, no redundancy payment: just a terse note from Sir Richard saying that, due to his 'recent acts of gross negligence and dereliction of duty', his services were no longer required by the company. The letter went on to add that if he wasn't off the premises within the hour he would be thrown off.

Sam was all for going up to the first floor and beating the living daylights out of Minnowfield, or Sir Richard, or both of them together. Or just staying where they were and beating the living shit out of Adams.

Adams backed away. 'You can't touch me,' he said, licking his lips.

'Yeah?' said Sam, picking up a desk lamp in his meaty fist. 'Says who?'

'Leave him,' sighed Henry. 'It's not important.'

He had come to a decision, and the calmness in his voice surprised him.

He stood up. 'I'm going to the pub,' he said. 'Where I will have a large lunch: a ploughman's, I think, possibly two or three. I will also have eleven pints of lager, or thereabouts, after which I will probably come back here and throw-up all over our great leader's car. On the driver's seat, I think, if I can get the door open. If I'm really lucky, he'll be sitting in it at the time.'

'Good idea,' said Sam, getting to his feet. 'I'm coming, too.'

'You just try it, that's all. I'll tell Uncle Richard and he'll have your jobs.'

'Really?' said Henry, waving the envelope at him.

Adams pouted and looked at Sam. 'He'll have his job, then.'

Sam hefted the lamp in his fist. 'He can have it for all I care,' he said, taking a step forward. 'By the way, who pays your medical bills?'

Adams backed away. 'I'll tell the police . . .'

'Not with your jaw wired shut, you won't,' snarled Sam.

Adams swallowed, and backed away further. 'You wouldn't dare.'

'Really?' said Sam, raising the lamp over his head.

Adams blinked. 'You better not! 'Cause I'll tell . . .!'

Sam lunged at him, and bellowed '*Boo!*' into his face.

Adams turned on his heel, and scuttled out of the room.

A lot of hard drinking had been done since then, and Henry was definitely feeling the worse for wear. He was slumped in an old armchair in Sam's flat trying to focus his half-lidded eyes on the shape in the armchair in front of him. The shape suddenly rearranged itself into human form and spoke. To his amazement, he recognized its voice as belonging to Sam.

'How 'bout a de-cider?' he shouted above the music booming from the huge speakers against the far wall.

Henry squinted in thought for a moment. 'Cider?' he said, nodding into his empty beer glass. 'Yes pease, I – I thing I will.'

Sam got to his feet and picked up a small black, rectangular object from the coffee table. Henry watched through a fuzzy haze as he did something with it that stopped the music being deafening and made it merely very loud.

'C'mon then,' said Sam, walking towards the pool table. "Is your br-break.'

Henry was concerned. 'Issit?' he replied in alarm, jerking the glass into his line of sight and inspecting it minutely. After a pause, he shook his head.

'No, no, nod br-breaked,' he said, wobbling his head around to look over his shoulder, more or less in Sam's direction. 'Mus' be your one,' he hiccuped as he narrowed his eyes and stared across the room. Sam suddenly seemed to be a very, very long way away.

Sam's warehouse flat was large and spacious, with a polished wooden floor, grimed with occupation, and a double line of ornate steel pillars supporting the ceiling. There wasn't much furniture to speak of, apart from a tatty sofa bed and matching armchairs clustered around a metal coffee table on the threadbare rug where Henry was sitting. But there were cardboard boxes in a variety of sizes standing around the place filled to overflowing with books and other personal belongings that hadn't been unpacked since the day, two years earlier, when Sam had moved in. There were several six-inch nails, seemingly banged in at random around the walls, from which Sam's meagre supply of clothing hung limply: or at least, that part of his scant wardrobe that wasn't lying in and around the two battered laundry baskets filled to overflowing in the bathroom. There was a heavy pine dining table on which a computer jostled for space with untidy piles of papers and books. Over by the three large sash windows that opened onto the street below stood an impressive sound system with an extravagant array of speakers attached to it. Against the opposite wall stood a video camera on a tripod and a large TV on a metal rack. Below them was a line of neatly filled boxes containing records, music cassettes, videotapes and CDs. At the other end of the room, in an alcove, was a large and untidy double bed that seemed to Henry to be about half a mile from where he was sitting. Against the opposite wall, in the kitchen-dining area, a massive fridge and fridge-freezer stood with a forest of empty bottles crowding over and around them. Finally, in pride of place in the middle of the floor, stood a full-size pool table with Sam leaning heavily against it. He was a man of modest tastes, and as long as there was plenty to eat and drink, particularly the latter, and lots of music for him to listen to at excruciatingly high volumes while he practiced at the pool table, he was as content with life as it was possible for any higher primate to be.

Sam's head rocked unsteadily on his neck as he gazed into the middle distance. 'I thing you're righ',' he called, thickly. 'You di-dit las' time!'

'D'you?' called Henry, looking at his glass. 'Mine's enmity.' He frowned. 'Empity . . .' He concentrated hard. 'Haven't god any lef',' he ended, sadly.

He went to put the glass down, but it slipped from his grasp and dropped to the rug, rolling immediately out of sight under the coffee table. He gazed at the empty patch of carpet for a while, wondered why, remembered, frowned, swivelled his head in Sam's direction and saw that he was doing something on the pool table. He opened his mouth to speak, thought better of it, looked down at the carpet again, sighed heavily, decided that he had no option but to leave the glass where it was, thought better of that, too, and bent slowly forward to pick it up. As his head came down level with the coffee table his eyes focused on a pile of metal objects in an ashtray.

'Objects,' he thought. 'Metal,' he thought. 'Nice!' he said out loud as he wondered where he had seen them before. He continued to fish half-heartedly around under the coffee table before forgetting why and giving up. But he stayed where he was, bent double and gazing through the ranks of empty bottles and cans at the pretty pile of things in the ashtray.

Sam looked up from the pool table, and was surprised to see that Henry had vanished. He stood for a moment with the cue in his hand, frowning at the back of the armchair where his friend had been sitting only a moment ago. He looked around: the bathroom door was open and he could see that Henry wasn't in there. The door to the spare room was closed, but he was certain that he would have noticed if Henry had tried to go in there. He turned to stare at the back of the empty armchair, trying to remember the last time he had seen Henry sitting in it. He couldn't, so he turned back to the pool table and crouched down to play his next shot.

On the other side of the room, Henry reached carefully through the obstacle course of bottles and cans, and picked up the metal beads. He held them in front of his eyes for a moment, before swaying to his feet and turning to weave unsteadily across the floor towards the pool table to ask Sam where they had come from. He had a vague suspicion that he ought to know the answer, but since he thought that about most things in life, and had seldom been proved right, he decided that it meant nothing.

Sam had turned the music up again, and it was booming out of the speakers at its usual punishing volume as he did a passable impression of a drum majorette, twirling his cue erratically from hand to hand between shots.

Henry hesitated in the maelstrom of sound before tapping his baton-twirling friend on the shoulder and yelling 'Wha's theesse?'

Sam jerked around in alarm, and struck him a heavy, glancing blow behind the left ear with the thick end of the whirling pool cue.

Henry had just enough time to say 'Why?' in a pitiful voice, before sinking to his knees, and pitching forward onto his face.

Sam blinked down at him for a moment with pursed lips. Then he flexed the cue to make sure that it hadn't been broken by the impact. Satisfied that it was still in one piece, he sighted along it to make sure that it hadn't been bent out of shape. It seemed straight enough, but he turned to the table and potted several balls to check that its action hadn't been impaired. A couple of minutes after that, with only the eight ball to pot, he was forced to concede that he couldn't finish the game properly with Henry's body obstructing one entire end of the table. He put the cue down, switched off the sound system with the remote control, and went to fetch a glass of cold water from the kitchen. He splashed some of it onto his face, and drank the rest. When he realized that the glass was empty, he turned and went back to the sink for a refill. He was weaving his way carefully back across the flat, with the overflowing glass spilling water onto his fist, when he decided that the time had come for him to panic. Henry's continued immobility beneath the pool table wasn't natural, he told himself, and it wasn't fair, either, because pretending to be dead and frightening your best friend out of his wits wasn't funny at all! He was just about to stagger off in search of a phone to call for an ambulance, the police, and perhaps the fire brigade, too, when he heard someone banging hard on his front door.

* * *

'I remember that!' said Henry, touching the side of his head with a fingertip. 'He hit me really hard!' He stood up and stomped around, flexing his legs and stamping his feet. 'It was the first thing I thought of when I woke up here. I don't remember anything about this Choat bloke, though. I don't think I met him, did I? I remember Sam showing me the jewellery, but I still don't see how a 16-year-old could have made something like that without, I don't know, some sort of heavy metalworking equipment in her bedroom, or . . .'

'Perhaps that is because a 16-year-old did not make it,' said the hooded figure. 'In fact, it was constructed by someone with many years of experience of working with the design and manufacture of such objects. And he was not a jeweller, Henry, but a physicist.'

Henry stopped stamping, and turned around. 'Really?'

'Indeed. However, let us leave that fact aside for the moment, and concentrate instead on the plight of Richard Choat's 16-year-old daughter and the unsettling discovery that she and her best friend were to make on the morning of her father's ill-conceived visit to your former place of employment. Because it is with that discovery that our plot, if you will pardon the populist expression, really starts to thicken . . .'

* * *

7

VICKY AND BETH

'Shit!' said Vicky, as she stared into the empty biscuit tin. 'They're gone! They're really gone, aren't they?' She turned the tin upside down, and shook it. 'What the hell are we going to do now?'

'Tosser!' said Beth. 'Why'd Jackie marry him in the first place?'

Vicky curled her lip. 'What do you think?'

'What . . . you?'

'You don't think we had a choice, do you?'

'Eh?'

'Forget it,' said Vicky, dropping the biscuit tin onto the hated fluffy pink carpet her father had insisted on buying to cover her bedroom floor. She screwed up the note he'd left for her and threw it across the room. 'Anyway, it's not my dad we ought to be worrying about, is it, it's yours.'

'Yeah,' said Beth, without enthusiasm. 'We shouldn't have taken 'em, should we?' Their eyes met. 'I wish we'd never seen the bloody things!'

'Yeah,' agreed Vicky, as she plucked handfuls of fluff from the carpet and threw them at the biscuit tin, wishing it were her father's head she had in front of her. '*Tosser*!'

They lapsed into silence; Vicky sitting in the middle of the room with her head bowed and her legs crossed, as if she were meditating; Beth leaning back against the wall with her arms folded tightly across her chest and her legs splayed out in front of her like a collapsed rag doll.

Like millions of others, they had been watching the TV as the story of the audacious robbery at the British Museum unfolded. But unlike everyone else, it had been with a growing sense of horror as the enormity of what they had become involved in had begun to sink in. Every archaeologist, historian, politician and new age druid in the country seemed to have been wheeled out, paraded in front of the cameras and quoted and re-quoted ad nauseam. But regardless of their professional speciality, every last one of them had agreed that the collection of artefacts unearthed two years earlier from a previously unknown burial mound on Salisbury Plain had been the most valuable archaeological discovery of the century, and, perhaps, the most important archaeological find ever made in the British Isles. The cache of grave goods had been unprecedented in its richness, and had included previously unseen quantities of armour, weapons and religious relics – not least an eye-popping assemblage of phallic objects that, though anatomically accurate in every other respect, were felt by many male authorities to be overly optimistic in terms of length and girth. With them had been found a staggering array of earthenware jars overflowing with enough beads, coins, brooches and other decorative items to fill the display cases of the UKs most prestigious museums several times over. Everything had been in an unusually high level of preservation, and the world's experts had agreed that the collection was priceless. Yet for most people, everything else in the hoard had paled into insignificance when compared with what had been found at the centre of the mound clasped in the skeletal hand of the only human occupant. Seated on an ornate throne, and dressed in sumptuous gold-plated armour, the figure of a female warrior had been found clutching a beautifully crafted gold chalice. Everyone who saw it agreed that there was only one thing it could possibly be, and when it was stolen, along with everything else in the hoard, only a week after being put on exhibition at the British Museum, the entire country had gone into mourning.

'ARTHUR'S GRAIL OF TEARS', 'MUSEUM GALA-HAD NO FAIRY GRAIL ENDING' and 'CAMELOT's MISSING GUARD G-RAIL' quipped the pun-obsessed tabloids. 'BRING BACK THE ROPE!' demanded the opportunistic *Daily Mail*. 'FLOG THE BASTARDS!' insisted a surprisingly hysterical *Hello Magazine*, and 'GUINEVERE'S LOST ORGASMS?' suggested an obscure article in *Cosmopolitan*. But whatever their editorial perspective, they had all agreed that the theft was a national disaster and those responsible for it must be caught and subjected to a swift, public and brutally painful revenge.

'WORLD EXCLUSIVE!!' screamed the speculative red tops the day after: 'CRACK KRAUTS IN GRAIL HEIST', 'CHINKS IN ARMOUR ROBBERY' and so on. There hadn't been a scrap of evidence pointing to the identity, never mind the ethnicity, of the thieves, but that hadn't stopped ratings-conscious TV executives and circulation sensitive newspaper editors declaring open season on immigrants, refugees and foreign nationals of every colour and creed. The editor of the *Daily Mail* must have thought Christmas had come early when he'd demanded that anyone who couldn't prove that they bathed at least once a day in roast beef and Yorkshire pudding should be detained as a suspect. The xenophobes were suddenly having a field day, and the National Front's popularity soared to previously unimaginable heights.

The day after the robbery, Vicky and Beth had found some of the stolen artefacts in the shed at the bottom of Beth's garden. It had been half term and they had been bored with nowhere to go and nothing to do. So, after standing around on chairs in the kitchen pretending to be terrified of the sort of conversation-stopping mouse that Minnowfield would have welcomed into his office, and which Vicky had thought she had seen run under the washing machine, they had gone down to the shed in search of the mousetraps Beth thought her father stored there. They hadn't really wanted to kill the mouse, but searching through the boxes in the shed had promised some excitement on a dull April day, and at least it had gotten them out of the house.

'Shouldn't we ask him first?' Vicky had said, as she'd opened a box.

'The silly bugger's in bed,' Beth had replied with a total lack of familial concern. 'Got the flu, he reckons. Bloody hangover, more like!'

The cardboard boxes filled with pottery and jewellery from the robbery had been under a workbench. They had opened them and rummaged through what Beth had insisted was nothing more than junk that her father had been collecting from car boot sales for years. It certainly hadn't occurred to them that the infamous Grail Gang, as the press had dubbed the thieves, could have hidden part of their haul in a shed at the bottom of a suburban garden.

They hadn't found any mousetraps, but they'd had a lot of fun sifting through the piles of bric-a-brac until Vicky had found, wrapped in some old newspaper, a handful of chunky, wedge-shaped pieces of engraved metal with diamond-shaped holes cut through their centres. She'd taken a fancy to them immediately, holding them up to her face as earrings, pressing them against her chest as brooches, and stringing them together as a necklace on a leather bootlace she'd found hanging on a rusty nail by the door.

'Take 'em like that,' Beth had urged. 'They'll go with that long dress.'

'I can't,' Vicky had protested. 'What if he finds out?'

'Him?' Beth had snorted. 'You're kiddin' me, right? He hasn't got a clue what's in here. Take 'em. Silly bugger'll never know the difference.'

It had seemed like a joke to them at the time, but there was nothing funny about it now. They had seen the photographs in the papers and the reports on the TV, and had been left in no doubt that, no matter how ridiculous it might seem, what they had found in the shed at the bottom of Beth's garden was a small part of the stolen Grail Hoard. They had thought long and hard about what to do with their discovery, and had decided that they had no choice but to see that it was returned to the museum undamaged. They would hand it over to the police anonymously, they had decided, and hope that it wouldn't be traced back to Beth's dad. The only problem was how to go about it.

'That's it then,' said Beth. 'We've gotta do it, haven't we? We can't just let 'em melt it down, or cut it up, or something, like they said on the telly.'

'What about the police? What are we going say to them?'

'We found it under a hedge?'

Vicky looked doubtful. 'They wouldn't believe that, would they?'

'Just hide it somewhere, then, and tell 'em were we left it.'

'Yeah, but what about your dad and, I don't now, the gang? They'll know we took it, won't they?'

Beth shrugged. 'Dunno. Maybe not.' She thought for a moment. 'What if we smash the lock on the shed?' She hesitated. 'Or something, and . . . I dunno . . . sorta chuck stuff about an' make it look like some druggie's broke in an' nicked it?' She looked hopefully at Vicky. 'What d'you reckon?'

An hour had passed since then and Beth's dad, William 'Nobbler' Bates, had an even bigger problem than the one his daughter and her best friend had been facing. It went by the name of Bonce Mangle, and it had him by what are referred to idiomatically as 'the short and curlies'. Unfortunately for Nobbler, there was nothing idiomatic about what Bonce had his huge fist clamped around: they were real, and it was beginning to make Nobbler's eyes water.

'I'm not a vengeful person,' lied Dolly Killjoy, 'but if you don't tell me where the rest of it is, I'll let Bonce rip your dick off and turn you into a girlie.' She smiled coldly at Nobbler and blew a cloud of cigar smoke into his face.

There was nothing subtle or ladylike about Dolly, but very few people had ever been rash enough to tell her so to her face. Those who had, were now either integral to the foundations of one of several executive dwellings on a housing estate in Basildon, or singing soprano in Holloway Prison's male voice choir. Nobbler had no wish to join them, and was determined to tell her everything she wanted to know. His problem was that he didn't know how.

'I dunno Mrs. Killjoy, honest,' he protested. 'They was there Friday mornin' when I left 'em. Honest they was!'

'That's *Miss* Killjoy to you, William,' said Dolly, sharply. 'Or do I look old and decrepit to you?'

'No, no!' insisted Nobbler, shaking his head. 'Sorry, sorry! Mrs. – *Miss* Killjoy! I didn't mean nothin'.'

'That's all right, William. But if I have to tell you again you're dead.'

Nobbler nodded, vigorously, and swallowed hard.

Dolly smiled without warmth. 'And Saturday?' she asked. 'Where was the stuff on Saturday, William, if you don't mind me asking?'

Nobbler looked uncomfortable.

'And Sunday?'

Nobbler glanced at the door.

'Well?'

'I dunno,' he admitted. He looked from Dolly to Vinny Trashman and back again. 'You said we was s'posed to lie low.'

Dolly's eyes narrowed. 'And . . .?'

'I been in bed.'

She stared at him in silence.

'Since Friday, early! I got in soon as we come back from the job.'

Dolly looked at Vinny. 'He's been in bed, Vinny. Fancy us not realizing that.' She turned back to Nobbler. 'Who with?'

'No, no, no one, Mrs. – *Miss* Killjoy! Honest! *Honest*! I bin sleepin' jus' like what you said. Jus' sleepin', an' lyin' low.'

'He's been lyin' low, Vinny, and sleepin',' said Dolly.

Vinny levered himself away from the wall and stepped into Nobbler's line of sight. 'You'll be sleepin' permanent, you don't tell the nice lady what you done with our stuff, Billy Boy.'

Nobbler turned pleading eyes towards Dolly. 'Honest, Miss Killjoy! Honest! It were all there Friday mornin'! Honest it were!'

Dolly nodded at Bonce.

Bonce tightened his grip.

Nobbler hissed through clenched teeth and tried to stand on tiptoe to lift his genitals out of harm's way. He failed.

'Not good enough, Nobby, me old mate,' said Vinny.

'You've let us down, William,' said Dolly. 'Hasn't he Vinny?'

Vinny nodded. 'Yes, Miss Killjoy, he has.'

'Hasn't he Bonce?'

Bonce rotated his wrist as if he was turning a door handle.

Nobbler inhaled sharply, and wished that he had been born taller.

'You should've stuck to dopin' the gee-gees, Billy,' said Vinny. 'You ain't got the 'ang of this game yet, 'ave ya? It ain't every man for hisself, first past the post, all that ol' diddly. We gives you somethin' to look after, you gives it back when we asks. An' that means *all of it*, Billy Boy! It's called trust, see, an' you don't break it 'less you want me an' 'im to break you!'

He took a bone-handled knife from the pocket of his jacket and pressed a stud. A six-inch blade snapped open in front of Nobbler's staring eyes.

'We all does our bit, Billy, see?' said Vinny. 'It's called teamwork. Your bit's takin' care of the guard doggies. You takes care of them, we takes care o' you, right? Only, if you ain't got it when we comes lookin' for it, we takes it anyhow.' He brushed the flat of the blade down Nobbler's cheek. 'You see what I'm sayin', Billy, me ol' son?'

Nobbler's Adam's apple jumped as if he had swallowed a football. 'But they was in the box, Vinny,' he insisted, desperately. 'I put 'em there meself. An' I 'aven't touched 'em, honest! The rest's still there, innit?'

He was standing on tiptoe, wedged into the corner of the shed with his head jammed against the underside of a shelf. Bonce was standing in front of him, with Dolly on one side and Vinny on the other. There were several cardboard boxes on the workbench. Two were open with a collection of ancient objects and a scattering of packing materials piled around them.

Dolly nodded towards the bench with a sigh. 'They're not all there now, though, are they, William? Bit like you really, wouldn't you say?'

'And there'll be even less of 'im in a minute,' smiled Vinny, sliding the blade along Nobbler's cheek. 'If he don't start playin' the game.'

'Hold his head,' said Dolly.

Bonce gripped Nobbler's face in one of his huge hands.

Dolly put her brightly painted fingernails alongside Nobbler's cheek and the tip of her cigar close to the end of his nose.

'Now,' she said. 'I'm only gonna ask you once . . . '

Vinny stepped suddenly across behind Bonce and jogged Dolly's elbow.

The tip of the cigar met the tip of Nobbler's nose with a hiss.

Nobbler flinched and grunted in pain.

Dolly turned angrily to Vinny. 'What're you . . .?'

'*Shush*!' he hissed. 'Someone's comin'!'

In a layby on a deserted country road not far away, Richard Choat was having problems of his own. One of them was called premature ejaculation and it was driving Charlotte Piece to distraction. She kicked the back of the driver's seat and put her hands over her face. 'Oh, Rich-*arrrrd*,' she moaned, 'not *againnnn*!'

Choat was pleased with his performance, as usual, and took her cry as a round of applause. He eased himself up off his knees and onto the back seat beside her as if it was all his weakened body could manage. 'Sorry, gorgeous,' he sighed. 'Only once I get going, look out, eh?' He fell back against the seat in what he felt was a convincing state of post-coital collapse.

Charlotte wasn't sure what was missing from their relationship, apart from warmth, affection and genuine pleasure, but she had begun to wonder if it might have something to do with the lack of time they seemed to spend on what she suspected might be the finer points of lovemaking. She didn't know what else they ought to be doing, but she had the feeling that it couldn't be achieved in the two or three minutes that Choat always seemed to allow for it. She had read everything she had been able to find on the subject in *Woman's Own*, *My Weekly* and, when she had felt in need of a bit of lurid detail, *Cosmopolitan*. But she wasn't any the wiser because she was a bit weak on anatomy, and felt that experimentation of *that* sort, especially on herself, would be too grubby for someone with her social pretentions.

She glanced sideways at Choat as he lay against the back seat of her Rover convertible. In the wooded lay-by and the semidarkness of early evening, it was difficult to see his face clearly. Still, she decided, that might be an advantage, given what she was about to tell him, because at least he wouldn't be able to see her too clearly, either.

'You won't miss me too much when I'm away, Richard, will you?' she asked without preamble. 'I wouldn't want you to be *too* upset. I won't *actually* be having lots of fun, you know, while I'm gone?'

Choat stirred uneasily, and frowned into his untidy trousers' fly.

'Away?' he asked, absently. 'What do you mean, *away*?'

Charlotte turned briefly towards him as he folded his clothing back into place. 'I won't be gone for more than two actual *weeks*, you know. So there really *isn't* anything for you to worry about, is there?'

'Weeks?' said Choat, in sudden alarm. 'What d'you mean, *weeks*?'

'And I want you to know that I actually *won't* go out with *any* of the men down there, even if they *do* pester me all the time.'

'Men? What men? What are you . . .?'

'Well, they can be *very* persistent, sometimes, can't they, men? But I won't let them actually *seduce* me, just because they *might* take me out to dinner or something. If they do, I mean . . . ' She let her voice fade into silence.

'What are you talking about?' he asked, glancing out of the window as if he expected gangs of would-be seducers to start breaking into the car at any moment. 'Seduce you? Who's going to . . .?'

'Dickie said he *might* come down at the weekends to look after me,' she said, quickly. 'I thought that was *actually* very nice of him, don't you?'

Choat was bewildered. 'What are you talking about? I . . .'

'Oh, didn't I tell you?'

'Tell me what?'

'About the house?'

'House?'

'Well, *villa*, actually! In the West Country? Torquay? Dickie says it has a *wonderful* view of the sea, and . . . '

'Just a minute! Just a *minute*!' he insisted. 'I've never heard about any *villa*, or any *Dickie* in . . . in any . . . *Torquay*!'

'I must have told you. Didn't I tell you? I'm sure I must have told you.

Didn't I tell you? Are you sure?'

'Of course I'm sure! I think I'd have remembered something like that!'

'There's no need to shout, thank you very much. And *actually*,' said Charlotte with what she judged was just the right level of indignation, 'you don't *always* seem to listen to what I'm saying, Richard, if you don't mind me saying so. *Sometimes* I don't think you listen to me at all, if you *really* want to know.' She turned towards him with her head slightly bowed, her lower lip trembling just a touch, and her eyelashes fluttering under the weight of what might or might not be gathering tears. 'S-sometimes,' she faltered, 'I don't think you care about me *at all*. And you wouldn't *even* care if I actually *never* came back.' She sniffed and turned away with a self-righteous sob.

Choat was in trouble, and he knew it. Suddenly, and without warning, he was alone in a car with an emotionally unstable woman and no idea how he had managed it. That was the trouble with women, he told himself bitterly: they were *totally* unpredictable. One minute they were rolling around with you in unbridled passion: the next they were complaining about the colour of the curtains or saying they had nothing to wear. He sighed inwardly and sat very, very still. The only signs of life were in his eyes, darting nervously from side to side in anticipation of the need to make a dash for freedom.

'I was actually think-ing,' said Charlotte with a nicely judged catch in her voice, 'that I might *actually* never see you again, after tonight.'

Choat squinted his concentration at the back of the driver's seat. '*Tonight*,' he echoed uncertainly. 'What's happening . . . *tonight*?'

'I told Dickie that I couldn't go right away, but he insisted. He said I had done *such* a good job that I deserved a rest. Wasn't that nice?' She gave an experimental sob and was pleased to feel him stiffen on the seat beside her.

'Dickie?' he asked, guardedly. 'Who's *Dickie*, when he's at home?'

'Umm? Oh, sorry,' she said, innocently, 'didn't I say? I mean Sir Richard, actually. It's just that he said I should think of him that way, you know, instead of being so formal? He *actually* said I had a lot of potential if I was prepared to open myself up to some new ideas.'

Choat snorted. 'Yeah, I bet he did!'

Charlotte's response was icy. 'What are you inferring, Richard Choat?'

'Nothing,' he said, quickly. 'Nothing at all!'

'I should think not! And I don't believe you *actually* said such a horrid thing, either. You should be pleased he's taking an interest in my career. It's more than some people do, *actually*!'

Choat let the criticism pass. He wasn't listening anyway. He had other, much more important things on his mind. He didn't know much about Torquay, but he didn't like the sound of it at all. It was by the sea, for one thing – Charlotte had just admitted as much – and he knew *exactly* what that meant. It meant that Torquay was the sort of place where women in skimpy clothing went on holiday, and where that happened there were always cold-eyed randy bastards lying in wait to seduce them. His mind was already recoiling in horror from images of suave yachtsmen, muscle-bound lifeguards, and fast-talking beach photographers, each and every one of whom would be only too ready, willing, and perfectly equipped to bounce up and down on Charlotte's ample body as soon as it hove into view. And he knew that if they weren't, that randy old sod, Sir Richard, definitely would!

'But, what are you saying?' he asked, desperately. 'He's taking you to Torquay? For two weeks? Just you and him?'

Charlotte sniffed. 'Don't be ridiculous! I've already said he's *far* too busy for that. But he said he might manage the weekends . . . if I was on my own?'

Choat say a straw that he could clutch at. 'What . . . you mean you could take someone with you?'

She pouted. 'He said I could take a friend, yes.' She glanced sideways at him in the gloom. 'Not a man, if that's what you're thinking?'

'But he wouldn't know, would he? How would he know? Tell him you're taking your mother, or something.'

'Don't be ridiculous! I couldn't lie to him, could I? And anyway, he might come down and check.'

He snorted. 'No he bloody well wouldn't! Not if he thought your mother was gonna be there, too!'

'You don't even know mummy,' she replied, icily. 'Besides, that would be dishonest. I don't *actually* think I could be dishonest, Richard, do you?'

'Yes,' he hissed in her ear. 'But think what we could do together. *Hmmm?*'

'Well . . . maybe,' she murmured, with feigned coyness.

'I could get away next weekend. If . . . '

'I'm going tomorrow, *actually*! Dickie thought it was best, after all the hard work I did on the new contract. Recharge the batteries, he said.'

Choat frowned. 'Contract? What contract?'

'Yours of course! What did you think?'

'Mine?' he said in disbelief. 'You mean all that stuff we did today? The coffee and the beans and the . . .? But . . .!'

'He really was very pleased, *actually*. He said I had done more business in one day than Minnowfield and Johnson had done in six months.'

'But it's not *real*, for Christ's sake! It was a joke, so we could . . . get together and . . . you know? What's he going to say when he finds out?'

'He won't, *actually*, will he? Not after you tell him you've changed your mind,' she shrugged, 'or something.'

'Changed my mind?' he echoed, dully. 'Changed my mind? Oh, yes, sure! Yes. There'll be no problem with that, will there?'

'Just tell him you can't get on with Minnowfield, or Johnson,' she paused for a moment, 'or both of them. Say they insulted you, or something. They did, didn't they? I haven't *really* thought about it,' she lied. 'But I'm sure you can think of *something*,' she snuggled up close to him and kissed him on the point of the chin. 'Couldn't you? Just for little ol' me?'

'He wouldn't believe that.'

She pulled away. 'Why not? He doesn't actually *like* them, does he?'

Choat shook his head in disbelief. But the longer he thought about it, the more he could see the potential. The extraordinary scenes he had witnessed earlier in the day were still fresh in his mind, and he had to admit that it was difficult to imagine Sir Richard liking, or even believing, someone whose arms he had threatened, and so obviously wanted, to tear out of their sockets.

'Well, maybe,' he said, grudgingly.

Charlotte had no doubts at all. She was sure that it would work, and as soon as Sir Richard had taken his revenge on Johnson and Minnowfield she would be free to make her next move. She had always fancied herself as an account executive, and now that her boss had finally shown an interest in her career she felt that it was only be a matter of time before she was promoted to the management team. She was deluding herself, of course: Sir Richard had no intention of allowing a mere woman to move that far up the company's chain of command. But he was willing to go along with the game because she had one huge advantage over Minnowfield and Johnson: regardless of what he might want to do to them with the empties, he definitely did not want to squirt the contents of a couple of bottles of Moet et Chandon up their gymslips. Charlotte was an entirely different kettle of bottle green gym knickers. Even if she hadn't realized it yet!

'I might be able to do it,' said Choat with growing enthusiasm. 'But I'd have to buy Jackie some flowers, or take her out to dinner or . . . I'll have to think about it. But the company's a different matter. They . . . '

'I thought you were the financial director?' said Charlotte, sharply. 'I thought you told people what to do, not the other way around? Of course, if you don't really *want* to come with me . . .?'

'Well, I am! And I do! Of course I do! Want to come, I mean.' He nudged her in the ribs. 'Like I did just now, eh?' He glanced out of the window. 'Don't worry. I'll sort it out. Just wait and see if I don't.'

At the bottom of Nobbler's garden, things were starting to fall into place for Dolly, too. 'Well, well,' she said as Beth opened the door and peered into the shed. 'What've we got here?'

'Oh, sorry,' said Beth. 'I was just . . . '

'No! No!' cried Dolly. 'Come in little girl. Come in! Come in!'

Beth started to back away when she saw the open boxes on the workbench. 'No, that's OK. We . . . I mean . . . '

Dolly's eyes narrowed. 'Help the young lady in, Vinny. And her little friend!' she added, catching sight of Vicky behind her. 'Let's not be rude.'

Vinny grabbed Beth roughly by the wrist and yanked her into the shed.

Vicky tried to back away, but he was too quick for her, too, leaning out of the door and grabbing her by the forearm to pull her inside.

'Don't be shy,' said Dolly, giving the girls the once-over as they stood close together looking scared. 'We're all friends here. Aren't we boys?'

Vinny pushed them further into the shed, pulled the door closed and stood in front of it with his feet apart and his arms folded.

'Leave her alone!' blurted Beth. 'It's got nothin' to do with her!'

'Really,' said Dolly. 'What's that then, lovie? What's got nothing to do with your little friend?'

Beth's eyes flicked nervously around the shed. 'Hey,' she demanded, 'what's he doin' to me dad's balls?'

Everyone looked at Bonce, who blushed and glanced quickly at Dolly.

She shook her head, and nodded at Nobbler's crotch.

Bonce released his grip and lifted Nobbler away from the wall to dust him down and straighten his clothing as if he was a conscientious tailor helping a favoured customer decide which side he wanted to dress.

Nobbler's expression was pained, but he managed to wink in comradely fashion at Bonce and aim a playful punch at his midriff. He felt the big man had only been doing his job, and it wasn't his fault that he enjoyed it so much. Then he turned to glare at Beth through the tears of returning circulation. He wasn't pleased to see her at the best of times, and not at all in the shed from which she had been banned since the day she'd discovered his store of girlie magazines and women's clothing under one of the benches. She was nine years old at the time and had brought mixed reactions from the quests gathered in the house and garden to celebrate her parents' eighth wedding anniversary when she'd appeared in the middle of the festivities wearing a beatific smile and a variety of garish lingerie items over her best frock. That had been bad enough, but when she'd started handing out hard-core pornography to all and sundry Nobbler's patience had finally snapped. Eight years on, and the ridicule he'd suffered that day was still fresh in his mind.

''Lizbeth,' he grated, ''ow many times you gotta be told?'

'Now, now,' said Dolly, turning to look at Vicky. 'Who's your little friend, lovie? Eh, Elizabeth? Come to see your Auntie Dolly in your daddy's shed?'

One of Dolly's bony hands – its fingers seeming to twitch in anticipation of a good throttling – snaked towards her. Vicky shrank away from it as if she expected to be stung. There was something synthetic about it and its owner, that made her skin crawl. It was as if Dolly wasn't really a woman at all, but some sort of artificial creation that was not only not human, but not animal, either. Her body was angular and ungainly, sinewy and stringy, and didn't look capable of habouring enough oestrogen to justify its being characterized as hermaphrodite, never mind woman. She walked with her toes pointing outwards in a halting gait as if she was walking through shallow water and stepping precisely to avoid making a splash and wetting the uppers of her shoes. It was as if she was trying to move quickly, but felt the need to hold back before each step, like a suspicious chicken strutting anxiously across an electrified lawn. She was tall for a woman, and seemed to be canted forward from the hips, as if she might at any moment fall flat on her face. Vicky wondered if Dolly would be able of get up again if that happened, or would need lifting back onto her feet by someone muscular like Bonce. She wondered, too, if setting Dolly on her feet each morning was part of the big man's daily routine and, if so, whether he found it easy to face that much cold meat on an empty stomach that early in the day. From the look of him, she rather thought that he might.

Dolly's outfit was strictly mid-80s Basildon chic, with the top half rigidly wide-shouldered in lemon yellow leather with beige appliquéd suede curlicues, embedded glass beads, and over-sewn, sharp-edged lapels. The matching lower half was above the knee, skin-tight and pencil-thin, with black, seamed stockings and two-tone lemon and beige sling-back stilettoes. Her gold-studded, beige leather handbag was enormous and had chunky gold strap that could easily have anchored the *Titanic*. All in all, she looked like an undernourished linebacker for the Pittsburgh Steelers with a penchant for black hosiery, blonde perms and painfully tight-fitting shoes.

From the neck up, she looked even worse. There was a pancaked pastiness to her face that seemed on the verge of cracking open: not into crazed sections like a dried-up riverbed, but right down the middle like a violently hatching egg. Vicky felt a sudden chill as she wondered what grizzly apparition would emerge if that were ever to happen, and how many razor blades it would get through before breakfast – eating them, or shaving with them, she decided, would make no difference, it would be a hell of a lot, either way.

Dolly's deep-sunk eyes flicked from Beth to Vicky and back again, staring out of her powdered face like a hyena's, black and soulless, devoid of human intelligence, but glazed over and sparkling with an ice-cold animal cunning.

'Your daddy's been helping us solve a little mystery,' she said. 'Only I think we've been talking to the wrong Bates, Vinny, don't you?'

'Want me an' Bonce to ask 'em nicely for ya Doll?' said Vinny, leering at the girls and hitching at the crotch of his jeans.

'That won't be necessary will it girls?' said Dolly.

'Won't it?' asked Beth, defiantly.

Dolly stared back at her for a moment. 'I see,' she said. Then she turned to Nobbler with a raised eyebrow. 'Well?'

'What?' he asked, hoping that someone would tell him what the hell was going on. ''S'nothin' to do with me! I dunno what they bin up to, Miss Killjoy, honest. I bin lyin' low an' sleepin', like what you said.'

'She's your sprog,' smiled Dolly, tightly. 'So you ask her!'

Nobbler frowned. ''Lizbeth! Where's the stuff from the robb'ry?'

Dolly groaned. 'Whose idea was it to use this tosser?'

Vinny pursed his lips and looked up at the ceiling.

Bonce turned and frowned at the wall.

'What?' asked Nobbler, looking from face to face. 'What'd I do?'

'We haven't got time for all this,' said Dolly, stepping forward suddenly and punching Beth in the mouth.

Nobbler frowned as his daughter staggered back against the wall of the shed and dropped to her knees. 'What'd you do that for?' he whined.

'You got a problem with it?' asked Dolly.

He shrugged. 'I could o' done it, tha's all. Been wantin' t' do it for years! Always walkin' in where she ain't wanted!'

'Whose fault is that, I wonder?' asked Dolly.

Nobbler shrugged and tried to think of an answer.

Vicky started to move towards her friend, but Vinny grabbed her from behind and held her tightly about the waist with her arms pinned at her sides and her buttocks pulled firmly back against his crotch.

Dolly took a step towards Beth.

'Leave her alone!' shouted Vicky.

'*Shut it!*' snapped Dolly, rounding on her.

Vinny put a hand over Vicky's mouth, and pulled her even more tightly against his burgeoning manhood.

Beth touched her mouth with the back of a hand. It came away bloody. Her eyes were watering, but she was determined not to cry. '*Bitch!*' she muttered, as she got to her feet.

Dolly remained expressionless. 'Where is it?'

Beth looked at Nobbler. 'Why don't you ask him? He's got all sorts of stuff stashed around here.'

The second blow came from lower down, and it wasn't so much a punch as a slap – a haymaking right hook that struck Beth on the side of the head. Its effect was stunning. Dolly's hand was cupped, forcing air trapped in her palm into Beth's ear. The impact sounded like a cannon being fired next to her head. Pain lanced into her skull, and she dropped back to her knees.

Vicky tried to break free, but Vinny held her tight. She bit his hand, and he let go. 'Leave her alone!' she cried as Vinny grabbed her and wrapped his arms around her again. 'You *bastards*!'

'Ah,' said Dolly with a sudden glint in her eye. 'No, Vinny, don't hurt the little girlie. Not if she's got something to say while her friend's having a rest.'

The smile vanished in an instant. 'Well?' she snapped. 'Where is it?'

'Leave her alone,' said Beth, getting up from the floor.

'Well now,' said Dolly, 'what we have here Vinny is a mutual admiration society. Isn't that nice?' She looked from Vicky to Beth. 'So, which one of you two little girlies is gonna talk to your Auntie Dolly, then, *mmm*?'

* * *

'Reminds me of me old mum,' said Titus, appreciatively. 'That Dolly type does. Only more sorta friendly, like. She do a turn, you reckon?'

Henry and the hooded figure remained silent.

'What?'

'Tough in the Iron Age, then, is it,' asked Henry, 'the old mating game?'

'Gotta keep on ya toes, buddy, I can tell ya that much. Step outa line with a bit o' wild Brit totty and she'll be wearin' your bollocks for earrings before you can say bugger me old boots, I'm a eunuch!'

'Or a necklace,' said Henry, 'if she happens to be called Stonking Rod?'

'Oh yeah!'

'And you find that erotic, do you?'

'What can I say, buddy? I like a woman what takes control.' His face lit up.

'Hey, you seen that, what's her name . . . ol' Iron Drawers, back at your place?'

Henry looked blank.

'On that telly-box thing?'

'No idea what you're talking about.'

'There,' said Titus, pointing at the breast pocket of Henry's bathrobe. 'In that poncy guesthouse me an' 'im stayed at in that London.'

'You mean the Savoy Hotel?' Henry's face lit up suddenly with the idea that a hotel that considered itself one of the finest in the world was, from Titus's perspective, nothing more than an overblown flophouse.

'When me an' 'im went back to that London.'

'Forwards,' corrected the figure. 'We went *forwards* in time.'

'Whatever,' said Titus. 'Smack me with 'er handbag any time she wants, that one could. Spitting image of ol' Stonkin' Rod, an' all.'

'I believe,' said the figure, 'that he is referring to the prime minister of the time, Margaret Thatcher MP? The so-called . . . Iron Lady?'

'Is he on drugs?' asked Henry.

'Only the opiate of the masses,' said the figure, wearily.

'I should be so lucky,' complained Titus. ''Aven't 'ad a decent bit o' gear since that home-grown I got off that bloke over Silchester way las' month.'

'Do I take it that you mean the marijuana you stole from that unfortunate merchant while he was lying by the roadside unconscious?' asked the figure.

'Not my fault he couldn't take his drink, was it?'

'Meaning the amphora of wine with which you hit him over the head?'

'Slipped out o' me hands, buddy, didn't it, when he said he was workin' for the Romans,' protested Titus. 'It was the shock!'

'In much the same way as the shock made the pool cue slip out of Mr. Johnson's hands when he rendered Henry unconscious?'

'Right! So why ain't we talkin' 'bout that 'stead of pickin' on ol' Titus?'

'Are you saying that Sam knocked me unconscious deliberately?' asked Henry with a frown.

'Indeed not! That collision was undeniably accidental. I was merely attempting to formulate the kind of wordplay referred to correctly, I believe, as sarcasm? Unfortunately, humour was never one of my strong points.'

'You don't say?' said Titus.

The figure ignored him. 'Nonetheless, not everything in Mr. Johnson's behaviour was as it might have appeared at first sight.'

'Meaning what?' asked Henry.

The figure thought for a moment. 'What do you remember of the immediate aftermath of the unfortunate coming-together of your skull and the carelessly wielded pool cue?'

'There was an aftermath?'

'Oh, most definitely there was.'

* * *

8

AMY JOHNSON

Henry was lying on his back with a loud and distorted voice booming down at him from somewhere seemingly miles above his head. What the voice was saying wasn't clear, but it seemed to be something about whose word someone was taking for something, and whether or not someone could handle something or other. The phrase 'pissed as a fart' emerged briefly from the general hubbub as he felt himself being lifted into a more upright position.

Suddenly, he was aware that someone was kneeling at his side, propping him up. Blinding lights were beating down on him, making him blink and screw his eyes tightly shut. When he risked opening them again, the figure towering over him seemed to be holding a garden implement or a weapon of some sort; a spear, perhaps, or a sword: and for one sudden and wild moment he had the impression that he was looking up at a medieval knight in full battle armour. He swallowed in alarm, and shook his head to clear it, but the light shining from behind the figure's head was still so painfully bright that he had to look away and focus on something closer at hand.

'Oh, God!' he groaned in sudden recognition.

'I think he's hurt badly,' said a concerned female voice from just above his head. 'I think you've really done it this time, you drunken *idiot*. You can't be trusted for a minute, can you?'

Henry was amazed: suddenly he could understand every word being said.

There was a snort of derision, and a slurred male voice, which he thought he recognized as Sam's, said 'He's lookin' at your tits, you daf' bint. He prob'ly things he's died and gone to h-heaven.'

'Not everyone's as depraved as you are, Samuel Johnson,' said the female voice. 'Look at him. He doesn't even know where he is, poor thing.'

But it was true: he *was* looking at the woman's breasts, and very appealing he was finding them, too. He hadn't seen such a perfect cleavage since the last office party when he'd staggered back to Sam's flat and stumbled drunkenly into the bathroom, only to find Sam's younger sister, Amy, standing at the mirror doing her hair in her bra and panties. He'd grinned appreciatively at her and raised his eyebrows in drunken admiration, forgetting that in his haste to get to the toilet he'd already undone his flies and taken out his cock.

As first impressions went it was not auspicious, and things hadn't got any better when Sam had tried to defuse the situation by making introductions with a light-hearted 'Henry, this is my sister, Amy. Amy, this is Henry. He's not as mad as he looks.'

Amy's response had been curt, but not unfriendly, in spite of the fact that she had refused to shake Henry's outstretched hand.

'How do you do?' she'd said, smiling tightly.

Henry had meant to apologize, but he'd tried to be witty instead. His face had lit up with an imbecilic grin. 'Aim-maimy?' he'd slurred, wobbling slightly in his attempt to stay upright. 'Aim-aimy Jo'-jo'son. You're kiddin' me, r-ride?'

He had known that it was a mistake as soon as he'd said it, but he'd been unable to stop himself making things even worse. 'Aimy-y Johnson? *Hah-hah!* Is thad wad they called you? *Hah-hah-hah!* Aimy Joh'son an' S-Sam'el Jo'son! *Hah-hah!* Wad stoopid names t' give your fri-fri-friggin' kids!'

Then his smile had faded and his lower lip quivered with hurt as Amy had placed the flat of her hand on his chest, pushed him backwards out of the bathroom with surprising force, and slammed the door in his face.

He was grateful that they hadn't met since that night – doubly so after Sam had confirmed his suspicion that 'never again' would have been too soon for his sister. 'She thinks you're a prick,' he'd said, bluntly. 'Probably the biggest she's ever met. And I don't mean down *there*! By the way, if you *must* wave your dick at my sister in future, try to do it when the weather's a bit warmer, will you? That way she might not think you're quite so . . . insignificant.'

The embarrassment had stayed with Henry for a long time after that, and whenever he thought about it he broke into a cold sweat. For months he'd gone in fear of meeting Amy again, and would only go to Sam's flat if he'd made certain well in advance that she wouldn't be around to look down her nose at him again. Luckily, she was a student in London and only visited Sam during vacations. He usually remembered to ask – as casually as he could, and much to Sam's amusement – if she was going to be around. He'd forgotten to do so this time because he'd had other, more pressing things on his mind.

The memory of that first encounter came flooding back to him as he lay on the floor, remembering with a jolt where he'd heard the girl's voice before. He immediately pretended to lapse into a coma in the desperate hope that she wouldn't recognize him if he lay still. He wasn't wearing the lop-sided party hat this time, or the straggly bits of tinsel, and he didn't have his cheeks covered in Suzie Bunt's bright red lipstick kisses from their drunken grapple under the mistletoe. Best of all, he didn't have his penis in his hand, and he thought that if Sam would only be sensitive enough not to mention his name he might get away with not being recognized.

'Really?' Sam was saying, scornfully. 'Well, if he's nod lookin' ad your tits why's he dribblin' down the front of 'is shirt?'

'He can't help it, poor thing, he's hurt,' chided Amy, brushing the hair out of Henry's eyes with her fingertips. 'Not everyone's like you and that sex-crazed friend . . . ' She paused and frowned. '*Urgh!*' she said in sudden recognition. 'It's *him*, isn't it?' She glared up at her brother. 'You *bastard!*'

The hands cradling Henry's head were pulled away suddenly, and he fell backwards, cracking his skull against the heavy leg of the pool table.

Amy stood up, and backed away, wiping the palms of her hands down the front of her dress.

'He's all r-ride,' said Sam, wobbling unsteadily.

'Really?' she sneered. 'You look after him, then!'

'*Oooh*,' moaned Henry, 'my h-head hurts.'

'Serves you right!' snapped Amy.

'Feel sick,' murmured Henry.

'Good! I bet there's nothing wrong with you, anyway, you sad little pervert. You're even more pathetic than I thought you were if this is the only way you can get a girl to take notice.'

She rounded on Sam. 'What're *you* grinning at, you moon-faced idiot! *Ooh-ooh, Amy, come quick*!' she sang in mocking imitation of Sam's drunken panic as she'd arrived back at the flat to find Henry spark out on the floor and her idiot brother dithering over what to do next. '*I think I've killed him*!' She glared down at Henry. 'Fat chance!'

There was a brief silence, during which Amy looked at Sam, Sam looked at Henry, and Henry looked a fool.

'How old are you?' Amy demanded.

The question took Sam by surprise: and for a moment he gazed around the flat as if he expected to see the answer written on one of the walls.

'And when are you going to grow up?' added Amy, folding her arms and eyeing him coldly. 'Well?'

For want of something better to do, Sam held his arms wide, inviting her to examine the flat. He stood with a pool cue in one hand, half a glass of beer in the other, and a moronic, vaguely hopeful smile on his face.

'Look at you!' snapped his sister. 'Like a couple of overgrown kids! Call yourselves executives?' She leaned forward and looked down at Henry: who was doing his best not to look up at her. 'Well at least you've got your flies done up this time. I suppose we should be grateful for small mercies?'

''E's upset,' said Sam, draining his glass and wiping his mouth with the back of a hand. ''E's 'ad a bid o' bad n-news.'

Amy smiled, tightly. 'Nothing trivial I hope?'

'As a madder of fac',' said Sam, wobbling across to the coffee table in search of something to drink, ''e's bin s-sacked.' He examined a can of lager, before dribbling its dregs into his glass. 'I's a bid of a bugger, a-a-ac-tu-ally!'

'I don't believe you. You're just trying to make me feel sorry for the dirty little sod, that's all.'

'No, no, no, no,' said Sam, flopping into a chair. ''S'true! 'S'true! 'E's god the push, the el-bow, the big E, the ol' 'eave-ho! 'E's t-taken the drob, bin wash'dup, god the boo-oot . . .'

Amy held up a hand. 'Alright,' she said, tiredly. 'I'll buy it. Who's he been waving his willy at this time? Not your lovely Miss Piece, I hope?'

Henry felt his face flush hot with embarrassment. He knew that he had made a fool of himself, *again*, and that it was getting worse with every passing second. He wished that the floor would open up and swallow him because he couldn't help looking up at Amy as she stood above him. Her dress was perilously short and of some revealingly thin material: and with the pool table light shining brightly behind her, he could see the outline of her body in all its remembered glory as she stood over him, square-on with her legs parted, her hands on her hips, and the point at the meeting of her thighs drawing his attention like a magnet. He groaned in the agony of his impromptu arousal and rested his head on the floor, closing his eyes and trying desperately to think of England. If there was one thing guaranteed to take his mind off sex at a time like this it was the dire state of the national cricket team.

'Worse'n thad,' said Sam, darkly, as he started to tell her about Adams and his desire for a Porsche, and Choat and the gold-painted rabbit shit, and Charlotte Piece and her dismembered dictionary, and how Henry had been sacked through almost no fault of his own. He rambled on for quite some time, but if there was one thing he was good at it was telling a story, and to Henry's relief Amy went over to the sofa and sat down next to him to listen.

While they were occupied, he got unsteadily to his feet and sloped guiltily off to the kitchen. He had decided that he would establish some semblance of competence by making Sam and himself cups of black coffee. In the meantime, he thought it would be best if he made himself scarce.

A moment later, he gave the coffee table a wide birth as he suddenly felt the need to leave the kitchen and head for the bathroom. Once there, he barely had time to close the door before giving of his all into the toilet bowl. As he crouched forward, retching painfully, he wondered if he had really eaten the vast amount of tomato that seemed to be pouring out of him.

As soon as he finished being sick he felt much better. He washed his face, flattened his hair with a damp hand, and rushed back to the toilet bowl to throw-up again. He felt even better the second time, and went back to the sink, cleaned his teeth with Sam's new toothbrush, gargled with Sam's mouthwash, and then staggered exhausted back to the toilet bowl. Nothing came out the fourth time, other than a clear and stringy liquid of the sort that he remembered seeing hanging from Sam's nose that morning. The thought made him retch for a fifth time. Nothing at all came out the sixth time, or the seventh, or the eighth, or the ninth, except the sound, and he wished that that had stayed where it was. He felt more wretched than he had ever felt in his life, and told himself that there was absolutely no way he would take another drink for as long as he lived. The thought made him feel ill again, and he stopped splashing cold water onto his face and head, and staggered back across the room in the hope that he would soon die with his head stuck down the pan. Five minutes later, he was on his knees, feeling utterly defeated, with his arms wrapped around the bowl and his head hanging below the rim, when Amy walked in to see if he was still alive. In spite of the many indications to the contrary, she decided that he probably was.

'Drink this,' she said, handing him the sort of cup of strong black coffee that he had been meaning to make for himself. 'You'd better sober up. They tell me suitcases are a bugger to pack when you're pissed.'

* * *

'So,' said Titus, 'this bra and panties she was wearin' . . .?'

Henry turned to frown at him. 'What?'

Titus cast a wary eye at the hooded figure and leaned closer. 'This Amy bird,' he said, nudging Henry in the ribs. 'When you walked in on her in that wosname . . . that bathhouse place . . . an' that?'

'That was an accident! How many more . . .?'

'Yeah! Yeah! Right! Right!' said Titus, impatiently, 'course it was. Course it was, buddy. Only listen,' he glanced at the hooded figure again and reached inside his jacket to pull out a dog-eared *Ann Summers* catalogue, opening it at a much-thumbed page and holding it up for Henry to see, 'didn't look like this, by any chance, did they?'

Henry found himself staring at a centre spread of two scantily clad young women wearing unconvincing come-hither pouts and ill-fitting see-through black bras and knickers that looked as if they had been hurriedly cobbled together out of a couple of cut-price kiddies' fishing nets crudely embellished with scraps of tatty, but strategically placed, red fur. The first thing he noticed, apart from the picture's obvious surfeit of bad taste, was that it was upside down. He looked up at Titus's expectant face. 'It's um . . . ' He made a circular motion with his hand.

Titus glanced quickly at the catalogue, turned it the right way round, and thrust it back in front of Henry's face.

Henry swayed away from it, shocked to see that it was even less appealing the right way up. 'Have you ever thought,' he asked, 'of finding yourself a really *good* therapist?'

Titus's face fell. 'What,' he said, turning the catalogue to look at the picture, 'you don't like 'em?'

'Honestly?'

Titus glanced from Henry's face to the catalogue and back again. 'What?'

'Well, apart from the fact that they look about as happy as if someone's just done a dump in their handbags, and those things are cheap, nasty, don't fit properly and have the erotic appeal of a double hernia, what's not to like?'

Titus squinted at him, closed the catalogue with a snap and thrust it back inside his jacket. 'I bet you *wish* she was wearing 'em, though.'

'Sorry?'

'You fancy her something chronic, don't you?' He tapped the side of his nose. 'I can tell.'

'Who?' said Henry, determined not to understand the question.

Titus raised a disbelieving eyebrow.

'Look, she hates my guts, doesn't she? So . . . '

'What's that got to do with the price of garum?'

'I . . . What?'

'*Eh-hem*!' coughed the hooded figure. 'I hope you don't mind interrupting your little debate, gentlemen, riveting though it undoubtedly is, but I really think we ought to be moving on, don't you?' It pointed a bony finger up at the sky, where the sun was rising towards midday. 'Time, as they say – wrongly, as it happens, but never mind that – waits for no man.'

'Fine by me, buddy,' said Titus. 'This useless tosser wouldn't know a decent bit o' totty if it staked him out over an anthill and sat on his face!'

'You're a very sick man,' said Henry. 'You know that, don't you?' He looked up at the sky and gazed around the stone circle. 'Shouldn't we be getting under cover, or something, then?'

'Why?' asked the figure. 'Are you cold?'

'No, I'm fine,' said Henry. 'Although, now that you come to mention it, a decent pair of pants wouldn't go amiss: and maybe a shirt and a pair of jeans? Oh, and some shoes and socks would be really helpful, too?'

'I will see to it at once,' said the figure, turning away and holding up a hand. 'Colonel Payne . . . ?'

'Thanks,' said Henry. 'But that's not what I meant. I was thinking there was a pack of wolves here last night and, well, they might come back again, looking for something to eat?'

'Ah, yes, of course,' nodded the figure. 'You are naturally concerned for your safety. And I have failed in my duties as a host. Please forgive me, Henry. I should have explained.'

'No, it's fine. Really! It's just that I thought . . . '

'One moment, please,' said the figure, turning to gaze across the clearing.

Henry and Titus turned to watch in wide-eyed fascination as a tall, lean figure, clad in crisp camouflage fatigues, appeared from behind a standing stone on the far side of the monument and came trotting towards them.

'Good morning, sir,' said the soldier, coming to attention in front of the hooded figure and saluting smartly.

'Good morning, colonel,' replied the figure. 'May I introduce Mr. Henry Kite and Mr. Corio Boc?'

'Good morning, gentlemen,' said the colonel, smiling tightly and nodding crisply to each of them in turn.

Henry's answering nod and welcoming 'Hello' were accompanied by a bemused frown. The man looked familiar, but he couldn't quite work out if, or where, he had seen him before.

'This is Colonel Payne,' said the figure. 'He is here to look after us. Is that not so, colonel?'

'Indeed it is, sir, yes.'

'And all is well, I trust?'

'Absolutely,' replied the colonel. 'An inner defensive perimeter has been established at a radius of five hundred yards – that's approximately four hundred and fifty-seven metres in new money – and will remain secure against all-comers for the duration of your stay.'

'Excellent! And have you brought the provisions I requested?'

'Yes sir. Everything is, I believe, as per your instructions.'

'Please be good enough to proceed with the installation immediately, then.'

'Very good, sir,' said the colonel, saluting again.

'Oh, and colonel?'

'Sir?'

'Mr. Kite would appreciate a change of clothing. He's feeling a little chilly. See to it immediately, would you?'

'Of course sir,' said the colonel, bowing to Henry. 'I will have a selection of items brought down for him at once.' He saluted again and turned away.

'Five hundred yards?' muttered Henry, gazing beyond the stone circle. 'That's a hellova long way, isn't it? What's he got out there, some sort of private army, or something?'

'One moment, colonel!' called the figure.

The colonel stopped, turned smoothly and came to attention. 'Sir?'

'Mr. Kite is concerned for our safety, colonel,' said the figure. 'He had a very disturbing encounter with a pack of wolves during the night.'

'Is that so, sir?' said the colonel. 'Sorry to hear that, Mr. Kite,' he added, without, Henry thought, any discernable note of sympathy in his voice.

'In order to help alleviate his fears, colonel, might I prevail upon you to provide us with a demonstration of your group's defensive capabilities?'

The colonel bowed to the figure, and then to Henry. 'Certainly, sir! When might be a convenient time?'

'They say that there is no time like the present, colonel,' said the figure with a dry chuckle. 'Henry, what do you think?'

Henry shrugged. 'Er, yeah: fine by me.'

'Very good, sir,' said the colonel, saluting smartly. Then, in a gesture that Henry found spookily reminiscent of Captain Kirk on the surface of an alien planet, he looked straight ahead and said 'Ares to Calliope: come in please.'

'Calliope to Ares,' replied a vaguely seductive, disembodied female voice. 'Good morning, colonel. How are you today?'

'Good morning, lieutenant,' said the colonel. 'I'm very well thank you. How are things looking up there?'

'Visibility is currently at two thousand yards, sir,' replied the voice, as smoothly as melting butter, 'slightly hazy with an expected high of twenty-seven degrees and an overnight low of between fourteen and sixteen degrees. The *Meteoroi* report that we can expect more of the same, at least until the end of the week, and Commander Helius suggests that you should, and I quote: "Be sure to cover up well or start slapping on the Factor 35"!'

'Indeed?' said the colonel with the flicker of Jim Kirk's self-deprecating smile. 'Inform the commander that her recommendations have been noted.'

'Very good, sir! Is there anything else we can do for you at this time?'

'Yes lieutenant, there is. Give me your latest tactical report, if you please.'

'Certainly sir!'

There was a short pause before the silky voice continued. 'Scanners are currently tracking a total of eighty-seven potentially hostile contacts within a fifteen-mile radius of your position, with threat levels ranging in severity from Code One to Code Five.'

The colonel nodded and smiled at the hooded figure. 'Nothing for us to worry about, then?'

'Indeed not, sir, no! It's all very quiet down there at the moment.'

'Just the way I like it, lieutenant,' said the colonel, briskly. 'Let's see if we can keep it that way, shall we?'

'Absolutely, colonel,' breathed the lieutenant.

'Eighty-seven?' said Henry, uneasily, leaning towards the hooded figure. 'That sounds like a lot, don't you think?'

'Excuse me, colonel,' said the figure. 'Would you be good enough to ask the lieutenant to be more specific?'

'Of course, sir. Lieutenant?'

'It would be my pleasure, sir.'

'And lieutenant?'

'Sir?'

'Just the basics, if you would be so kind?'

'Of course, colonel. We have three solitary adult *Ursus arctus* – that's the brown bear, sir – two female and one male; two medium-sized sounders of *Sus scrofa* – that is family groups of the wild boar; and two hunting packs of mature *Canis lupus*, the common or grey wolf. They are all currently within the central core, but represent no immediate threat to your security at this time. We also have a single Roman cavalry patrol, and three indigenous tribal hunting parties, two on foot and one mounted, traversing the outer ring. They are, however, apparently unaware of one another's existence at this time, and none is currently on an interception course with your position.'

'Pleased to hear it,' said the colonel. 'Is that all?'

'At this time, sir, yes.'

'Very good. Keep me informed.'

'Of course, sir. Will there be anything else?'

'Yes, lieutenant,' said the colonel. 'You will run the low level threat response programme SD-89 for us immediately.'

'Certainly, sir,' lilted the lieutenant. 'The programme is locked in,' she added after a short pause, 'and ready when you are, colonel.'

'Very good. Initiate it . . . now!'

'Programme initiated, sir. The group will be with you shortly.'

There was a barely audible metallic hiss, like the sharpening of fine steel, as a quartet of shimmering, disc-shaped objects, each about two metres in diameter, approached at astonishing speed from the four points of the compass, and came to rest at eye level in front of the colonel.

'*Wow!*' said Henry, getting to his feet with the smile of a little boy who had just been led into Santa's Grotto for the first time.

The colonel turned to him and bowed. 'May I present your personal security team, sir?' he said, indicating each of the discs in turn: 'Combat drones *Alpha*, *Beta*, *Gamma* and *Delta*.' He smiled that same tight smile. 'Or as we like to call them: *War*, *Famine*, *Pestilence* and *Death*.'

'Oh,' said Henry, his smile fading to disapproval, '*nice!*'

The colonel was unperturbed. 'We like to think so, sir, yes.'

'Powerful offensive weapons though they undoubtedly are, they are not all *Sturm und Drang*, by any means, are they colonel?' said the figure. 'They do have a less . . . coercive side, do they not?'

'Indeed they do, sir!' said the colonel with a curt bow. He turned to Henry, but motioned to a spot behind him. 'Might I draw your attention to a convincing case in point, Mr. Kite?'

Henry turned to see Titus hiding behind one of the standing stones babbling something about never stealing another horse or lusting after another man's wife for as long as he lived.

'Oh,' said Henry, peering around the stone to look at him, 'is he hurt?'

'Hurt, sir?' said the colonel. 'No: at least not in the physical sense of the word. Mr. Boc is, however, displaying precisely the sort of responses to the appearance of the drones that our field research predicted would be normal in a person of his relative . . . er, naivety. Primitive superstition and futuristic military hardware do not, as is clearly evidenced by the level of your unworldly colleague's distress,' he gestured again at the terrified Ancient Briton, 'make for the most . . . relaxing of bedfellows.'

'What you mean,' said Henry, dryly, 'is that you've scared the living daylights out of him with something he doesn't understand.'

'Precisely so, sir,' said the colonel. 'As, indeed, is liable to be the case with every human being on the planet – psychopaths, sociopaths and fourteen-year-old boys with crushes on their female biology teachers excepted, of course.' He smiled indulgently. 'Would you care for a more *comprehensive* demonstration of our little group's combat capabilities, Mr. Kite?'

'I don't know,' said Henry to the hooded figure. 'Would I?'

'You would, I think, find it informative,' said the figure. 'Not to mention mildly entertaining.'

Henry looked doubtful.

The figure tilted its head to one side. 'Why don't you give it a try,' it said with uncharacteristic jauntiness.

Henry shrugged. 'All right, then. Only . . . don't let them kill anything on my account, will you?'

'Indeed not,' said the figure, turning to gesture at the colonel. 'In your own time, colonel, if you would be so kind?'

'Thank you, sir,' bowed the colonel.

He turned on his heel and strode a couple of paces to his left where Titus was rolling his eyes and muttering to himself behind the standing stone with his back pressed hard against it.

'If I might make a suggestion, sir?' said the colonel, gazing down at him. 'I believe your viewing experience would be greatly enhanced if you were to return to your position by the fire?' He gestured with a hand. 'Sir . . .?'

Titus didn't seem to hear him.

'I assure you, sir,' insisted the colonel, raising his voice, 'you will not be harmed in any way if you do.'

Titus seemed to look right through him as he peered quickly around the stone to check that the hovering discs weren't coming to get him. '*Piss off!*' he hissed. '*The buggers ain't seen me yet!*'

The colonel glanced at the discs: and then back at the terrified Celt. 'Actually, sir,' he said, evenly, 'I think you'll find that, given the nature of their sophisticated detection systems, that is a practical impossibility. However, have it your own way if it makes you feel better.' He nodded curtly and strode back towards the centre of the clearing.

'The drones have been programmed to display a hierarchy of escalating threats, sir,' he said, bowing to Henry. 'Each of which has been calculated to discourage aggressive responses from the range of protagonists they are likely to encounter in this theatre of operations, and to do so without, as you put it so eloquently, actually *killing* anything!' He turned back to the discs. 'You may proceed with the demonstration when you are ready, lieutenant.'

'Very good, sir,' came the disembodied reply.

There was a faint click and the discs began to fluoresce a brilliantly vivid green, as each projected from its underside eight needles of scintillating green light that jerked and stalked as the discs moved through the ancient monument like gigantic, spindly legged spiders.

Titus flattened himself even harder against the standing stone, closed his eyes and started to burble and shake.

The colonel smiled and nodded to himself.

There was another click.

The discs stopped glowing and the beams blinked out.

Three of the discs floated to one side. The fourth slid forward, humming softly as, with an eerie sucking and grinding, one of the trilithons began to rise out of the ground as if it was being uprooted by a invisible hand.

'*Whoa!*' gasped Henry, turning briefly to look at the colonel, and then back to stare in amazement at the three huge blocks of stone as they rose, still in their original formation, high into the air, 'that's . . . *WOW!*'

'Yes, sir,' said the colonel, smugly, 'isn't it though?'

Henry wrinkled his nose as a whimper and an unpleasant smell wafted from behind the standing stone where Titus was hiding.

'You're really going to like this bit, sir,' said the colonel. 'I always do.'

There was a click, and a dazzling beam of red light stabbed from the rim of the disc and began cutting the blocks of the hovering trilithon into horizontal slices, each about eight inches thick and separated by the width of the light beam from its nearest neighbours.

There was a gurgle and a thud as Titus passed out.

The colonel nodded and smiled.

Then, as Henry watched in fascination, one of the huge, freshly cut slabs of stone glided soundlessly from its position at the centre of the trilithon's massive lintel and came to rest hovering at eye level in front of him.

'Would you care for a slice of *Pi*, Mr. Kite?' asked the colonel with the smuggest of self-satisfied smirks.

* * *

9

BONCE MANGLE

Bonce Mangle was a giant of a man who stood six feet six inches tall in his stockinged feet, and weighed in at a little over three hundred pounds. Everyone who knew him agreed that he was the salt of the earth – which was another way of saying that he had all the warmth and sensitivity of a pile of crushed rock. He was honest, and loyal, and a glutton for punishment: which was perfect for Dolly who paid him well to dish out large doses of it to anyone foolish enough to disappoint her. But there was nothing gratuitous about the way he hurt people: he did it for the money and because he wasn't any good at anything else. He was a quiet, modest man who liked a quiet life and preferred hurting people who took their punishment in silence and had the good sense not to try to fight back. Above all, he liked people to stay where he put them (which was often into hospital) and to keep still while he pulled out their fingernails or squashed their testicles or punched them in the mouth. Those who couldn't, or wouldn't, control the urge to retaliate, or scream, or thrash about, or pray too loudly to their own private god, had to be discouraged from doing so: which usually meant tying them up and gagging them, or hitting them over the head with something heavy and nailing them down. That was where Vinny came in. He did the tying up, the gagging, the hitting over the head, and the nailing down: especially if girls were involved. He was holding Beth now while Dolly leered into her face and threatened her with his flick-knife.

Bonce watched them in melancholy silence as he took a rest from the strenuous half-hour he had spent squashing Nobbler's testicles, and wondered how anyone, even someone as clever as Dolly, could think that being nasty to girls, and making them cry, was a good thing to do.

Dolly had no such reservations. On the contrary, she got almost as much pleasure out of leering into the faces of defenceless young women, and threatening them with Vinny's flick-knife, as Vinny got from rubbing himself against them as they tried to back away. It gave Dolly a kick to see the terror in their tear-streaked faces. It gave Vinny a hard-on like a length of steel wire.

Vicky curled her lip as she watched him grope her friend from behind. It was hot in the shed, and she was sweating. She could see that the others were sweating, too, but she didn't think it explained Vinny's appearance. Even in the dim light from the shed's tiny window, his skin seemed to glisten. Whether it was sweat or some other greasy secretion, she wasn't sure, but something slick seemed to cover his whole body, giving him the look of a predatory reptile basted in oil. It was as if he had been dipped in a vat of Vaseline as a baby and had remained coated in a thin layer of the stuff ever since.

In contrast to the chunky and sluggish Bonce – who Vicky thought might be related to some sort of heavy earth-moving equipment – Vinny was slim and lithe, and could even be described, albeit reluctantly, as good looking. But he wasn't attractive – not even remotely so – and she hoped that she wouldn't have to get close to him again. She had felt physically sick when he'd touched her. A reaction that she shared with the majority of women who'd ever had the misfortune of coming into close contact with him. Even those who were in every other respect perfectly sane and healthy had been known to develop a compulsion to wash their hands repeatedly, and/ or to blow-torch their clothing after meeting him: even if he hadn't come within a barge pole's length of touching any part of their body.

Dolly eyed Beth coldly as Vinny pulled her back against his erection. What really annoyed her was that the stupid girl didn't appreciate how lucky she was. Dolly ached to have Vinny grind his cock against her buttocks, but he had never shown the slightest interest in doing so. She could have ordered him to, of course, but she was a proud woman. She had never begged for sex in her life, and she wasn't about to start doing so now. She wasn't about to start losing her virginity, either, and that's what really annoyed her.

She rounded on Beth with a snarl. 'You got five seconds before I rip your pretty little face off, lovie!' she hissed. 'And don't think Vinny's gonna save ya, coz he ain't!'

Beth shook her head defiantly, and tried to turn away with her eyes squinting shut and her lips set in a tight line.

It was too much for Vicky, who didn't doubt for a moment how vicious Dolly was prepared to be in order to get what she wanted, and in spite of Beth's insistence that they should say nothing about what had happened to the missing jewellery, she started to tell Dolly everything she wanted to know.

'Right,' said Dolly, when Vicky had finished. 'You two are coming with us. The sooner we get the stuff back the sooner Vinny'll stop rubbing his dick against your sweet little arses. Still, you can't have everything, can you?'

Still sticky from his latest encounter with Charlotte Piece, Richard Choat shifted uneasily in the driver's seat of the Ford Probe and told himself that he ought to be more careful in future. His discomfort was due less to the clamminess in his underpants than a fear of what his wife and daughter might do or say to him when he got home. Somewhere in the deeper recesses of his mind a voice was suggesting that perhaps he shouldn't have taken their possessions that morning without asking their permission first. But it was a very small voice, and since he was a great believer in the power of positive thinking, he didn't allow it to distract him for long. Whatever he had done, he told himself, he had done for his own good reasons. It was not for Jacqueline or Victoria to stand in judgement over him, and he wouldn't put up with it if they tried. He was the master of the household, the head of the family, the breadwinner, he who must be obeyed: and his authority should not be questioned. Would not be questioned, in fact! They might not see the logic of his behaviour immediately, but he was in no doubt that, in the fullness of time, his wife and daughter would come to appreciate the wisdom of his actions. After all, it was plain to anyone with a modicum of intelligence that he and Jacqueline weren't suited to one another, and that the only sane option left open to him was to establish an alternative arrangement as quickly as possible and with minimal disruption to his career. Jacqueline was only a woman, and a housewife at that, and had no business meddling in matters that were beyond her limited powers of comprehension. And in spite of the fact that when he looked at her now it was difficult for him to credit it, he imagined that someone would take her on eventually (albeit someone of a much lower social class than his own) and in due course she would adjust to the agony of losing him. She might even come to terms with the inevitable pangs of guilt she would feel at having driven him away, and realize that what he had done had been in everyone's best interests all along. In the meantime, she didn't have the problem, as he did, of trying to advance his career while burdened with a partner who was about as useful in the world of finance as a subscription to the *Socialist Worker*. He realized that she couldn't be expected to appreciate the seriousness of his situation because it was beyond her limited intelligence to do so. But the bottom line was that their marriage was a severe drain on his ability to motivate himself, and the sooner she got out of his way the better it would be for them both. In the meantime, he would have to cope as best he could with the inconvenience of having her dragging him down.

He had given careful thought to how Jacqueline and Victoria would react to him when he got home, and was confident that he would be able to handle whatever they threw at him, whether the throwing was done literally or not. If they *did* try to get physical with him, he was in no doubt that his natural athleticism, allied to the superb hand-eye coordination he had been honing to such perfection for so many years on the squash courts at his club, would enable him to dodge whatever flying crockery and objets d'art might come hurtling his way, or pluck them effortlessly and unflinchingly out of the air as they flew at his head. If they tried to use silence against him, he would be ready for that, too, and would refuse to be intimidated by it. Not only would he show not the slightest interest in talking to them, he would behave as if they didn't even exist. And if they tried to engage him in a slanging match, he would refuse to be drawn into that, too, remaining cool, calm and collected, and rising above the level of their petty bickering to dismiss their primitive arguments with the contempt they would undoubtedly deserve. All in all, he had not the slightest doubt that he would be capable of dealing effortlessly with all eventualities and ensure that his leadership of the family would go unchallenged and his authority within the household remain undimmed.

If he hadn't been so preoccupied with thoughts of the coming battle, he might have noticed the two large cars parked outside his house. And if he had done that, he might have guessed that a reception party of an altogether more formidable nature than the one he had been psyching himself up for was waiting for him inside. As he turned the Probe into Tebbit Close, he smiled a self-satisfied little smile, glanced up to check his appearance in the rear-view mirror, drew a driving-gloved hand over his carefully brushed hair, smoothed the edges of his close-cropped moustache, and ran his tongue around his teeth checking for confidence-sapping bits of crud. He didn't find any, because, as usual, everything was lean, mean and perfectly in place for the coming fight. As he turned through the gateway of number 79, Probe's Rest, and the tyres crunched on the gravel of the drive, he felt pumped up and ready for anything. It was typical of the way his day had been going that he was thrown completely off balance as soon as he opened the front door.

Jackie came zigzagging down the hall towards him with her arms held wide in greeting, and a huge, lopsided smile on her makeup be-trowelled face. As she homed in on him like a malfunctioning guided missile, she veered momentarily towards the hall table to drop an overflowing gin glass onto its polished surface, her fingers imparting a spin to it as she let go, causing it to slide across the top towards him like a wayward ice hockey puck.

Choat's eyes widened in alarm as he crouched and lunged instinctively to his right, holding out a hand ready to catch the glass as it slid off the end of the little table. But it skidded to a halt at the last moment and came to rest with a little less than half of its base hanging over the edge. He was still crouching, like an expectant slip fielder waiting to pouch the thinnest of edges, when Jackie changed direction and staggered towards him.

"Ello Rickie, *darlin*'!' she slurred. 'Come 'ere, an' give us a fuggin' kiss!'

Before he could get out of her way, she had grabbed him by the shoulders and planted her deep red, gin-soaked lips over his left eye. He flinched away from this unfamiliar show of affection, and wiped the side of his face with the palm of a hand. It came away red and sticky, and he thought for a moment that she had bitten off one of his eyebrows. Fearful for his health, he tried desperately to disentangle himself from her surprisingly powerful grasp, but she held onto him with all the determination of an amorous limpet, albeit less out of drink-induced passion than the fact that she would probably have fallen flat on her face if she hadn't.

'You mus' be fuggin' knackered, darlin',' she said, hiccuping quietly, and trying to locate his face with both hands. 'Le' . . . le' me ta'e your thin's.'

Choat had no idea what was happening. The only thing he knew for certain was that his wife was as pissed as a fart.

Jackie had been drinking for the better part of six hours: ever since she'd returned home from the health club and found that her favourite bracelet had gone missing. She'd been instantly distraught. She'd read the note that Choat had left for her, but it hadn't helped. What if he'd lost her most precious possession on the way to the jewellers? What if the jewellers had lost it, or sold it to somebody else? Worse still, what if he'd taken the bracelet and given it to the fancy piece she was almost certain he was shagging behind her back? After a moment's hesitation, she had picked up the phone and the Yellow Pages, taken out a bottle of gin and a packet of Superkings, and started dialling. Half an hour later, she had been tipsy and starting to get angry. Half an hour after that, she had been paralytic and furious. She had been two-thirds of the way through the Jeweller's section of the Yellow Pages, and halfway through the bottle of gin, and still no one had admitted to being in temporary custody of her beloved bracelet. She'd decided that there was a conspiracy going on. Her ratfink of a husband must have sold the bracelet to one of these snivelling bastards and told them to keep quiet about it. That's what they were doing, and no amount of reasoning, pleading or haranguing on her part had made them admit otherwise. On the contrary, and without exception, they had denied all knowledge of her husband's craven behaviour. An assistant at H. Samuel Ltd had shown great patience in defence of her own integrity, and had refused steadfastly to confirm that her colleagues were 'no better than a bunch of thieving bastards'! A member of staff at Earnest Jones & Co. Ltd had had no truck with the suggestion that he and his employers were either 'lying little toe rags' or 'cheap-skate rip-off artists'! And although an ex-employee of the Ratner Group had been willing to concede that her employer's former chief executive had once described part of their product range as 'crap' it was the closest Jackie had come to an admission of guilt.

Five minutes later, when she had been on the verge of calling the police to lay before them the extent of the fraud she believed she was in the process of uncovering, her friend, Charlene, had called to invite her to a male strip show at the Spotlight Rooms later that evening. The thought of a night out with the girls hadn't appealed to her at first. But when Charlene had pointed out that it would be the perfect way of getting back at her two-timing rat-bastard of a husband she had begun to warm to the idea.

From that moment on, with the cordless phone clamped to her ear, she had rummaged with increasing enthusiasm through her extensively vulgar wardrobe in search of the most provocative outfit she could find.

'If you're gonna go,' Charlene had urged her down the phone and around an extra-long, extra-slim, decidedly phallic cigarillo, 'you might as well go all the way, sweetie . . . if you know what I mean?'

An hour later, having given nature a truly gruelling run for its money, Jackie had given up trying to improve on what she had achieved and had stood regarding herself thoughtfully in the dressing room mirror. She hadn't been entirely convinced that she'd managed to transform herself into 'an exotic thing of feminine beauty', as Charlene had suggested she might. But she'd had a pretty shrewd suspicion that she looked like the average male driver's idea of the perfect Belisha beacon and would be capable of stopping the traffic at a thousand paces on any high street in the land, day or night.

It was a view shared instantly by Vicky, Beth, Dolly, Vinny and Bonce when they arrived at the house and stood opened-mouthed on the doorstep like a group of carol-singers who'd left their song sheets at home.

Jackie's skimpy mini dress was a lurid scarlet, dotted copiously with sequins and diamanté, and apparently two sizes smaller than her own skin. The indentations made in her thighs by the red, patterned stockings and suspender belt were clearly visible through it, as were the seams of her matching bra and pants. The muscles in her calves, thighs and buttocks were stretched almost to bursting point by the incline of her steeply canted, scarlet stilettos, and her sharply up-lifted breasts looked like a pair of flesh-coloured grapefruit squashed together in a dangerously elastic string bag. She was dripping with costume jewellery, smothered in perfume, and had 'killed the look stone dead', as Charlene had put it, by piling a metre or so of bright red hair extension as high as she could get it on top of her head. Under the combined effects of a can of firm-hold hairspray, a tube of ultra strong styling mousse, and a sachet of multi-coloured Angel Dust, the finished confection flashed in the hall lights like a particularly vulgar lump of fool's gold.

Vicky stood rooted to the spot at the sight of the garish apparition in front of her that bore only a passing resemblance to her mother, while the others, equally stunned and in danger of crashing into the furniture as they gawped, traipsed silently past her, with many a backward glance, before disappearing, amazed and bemused, along the hall and into the lounge.

'You don't thin' it's too t-tarty, sweedie, d'you?' asked Jackie, as she surveyed herself in the hall mirror. 'On'y I wouldn' wan' your frien's to thin' I got no classssssss!'

'Don't be daft,' hissed Vicky. 'That lot know as much about class . . . ' She hesitated and bit her lip. She had been about to say 'as you do, mother,' but had stopped herself just in time.

'Anyway,' she hissed, 'they're not my friends, they're . . . '

But it was too late: Jackie was already turning away. Having taken her daughter's response as a no, she clapped her hands in delight and blew a kiss at her own reflection. 'I thaw so, too,' she confided. 'Lesssss go-win.'

Vicky shook her head in grudging admiration as her mother swayed unsteadily down the hall. 'That's it, then,' she said quietly to herself. 'If Cruella de Vil ever comes to life and is given the job of seducing the entire male population, I know *exactly* what she will look like.'

Choat's reaction was a good deal less sympathetic. He narrowed his eyes against the glare from Jackie's headdress, and wondered if the loss of her beloved bracelet had finally sent her over the edge of reason into insanity. But if that were the case, why wasn't she trying to tear his eyes out with her bright red fingernails instead of groping amorously at his dick and nibbling his ear? On the other hand, perhaps she had lost her marbles entirely, and had retreated into some hideously pornographic world of her own devising in which seduction was a prelude to a viciously perverted revenge. He flinched as she tugged the briefcase from his lifeless fingers and hefted it onto the hall table, where it dislodged the perilously placed glass, causing it to drop like a stone to the parquet floor, bounce miraculously and spray its contents a foot or so up the wall. He winced, but Jackie seemed oblivious. Using his shoulders for support, she sidled around behind him and gripped his jacket firmly by the collar. He flinched again, his eyes narrowing and swivelling nervously from side to side as he tried to see what she was doing. He half expected her to pull the jacket down to his elbows, pinning his arms at his sides and rendering him vulnerable to a sadistic, eye-scratching attack. Instead, she dragged it roughly down his arms and over his clenched fists, scrunched it into a ball, and lobbed it in the direction of the hallstand. Choat winced as it hit the wall and slid down into the pool of spilt gin. He wanted to go and pick it up, and place it neatly on its accustomed hanger, but before he could move Jackie had squeezed his buttocks, prodded him in the small of the back, and pushed him towards the lounge door.

'Look who's 'ere, darlin',' she gushed as they entered the room. 'Wasn' it nice of 'emmm t-t' come?'

Choat surveyed the guests with a marked lack of enthusiasm.

Dolly was standing by the fireplace, next to Vicky.

'This-sss is Beth's Auntie Dorothy,' gushed Jackie in the singsong voice she always adopted when she thought she was in the presence of her betters.

'How do you do?' said Dolly, raising an empty sherry glass at Choat.

Jackie gasped. 'Oooh, sorry,' she said. 'Lemme fill id-up.'

She teetered across the floor, took the glass from Dolly's hand, and headed towards the drinks cabinet.

'An' this,' she added, turning to smile at Vinny, 'is Beth's zuncle *oooops*!' she giggled as she misjudged the steps, and stumbled into the cocktail pit.

'Vinny,' he said.

'Vincent!' said Dolly.

'Yeah, Vincent,' he agreed. 'I forget.'

Jackie winked as she tried to fill Dolly's glass. 'We d'own stan' on cer'mony 'ere,' she said, turning to grin at Choat. 'Do we Ricky, darlin'?'

'Whatever you say, *darling*,' he grated.

Jackie tapped the side of her nose. 'He says I gotta call meself Jack-*leeen*. Bud I tell 'im I'm jus' Jackie. Always was. Al-al-always w-will be.'

She giggled again as she teetered over to Dolly and handed her the glass. It was almost empty. Dolly raised an eyebrow at it, and put it down on the mantelpiece behind her.

'Where woz we?' asked Jackie, scanning the room, snake-eyed, like a drunken sniper searching for her next target. 'Oh, yessss,' she said, trying unsuccessfully to snap her fingers at Bonce. 'This is Beth's other un-nuncle.' She screwed her face up in thought. 'Is . . . is . . . '

'Mortimer,' said Dolly.

Jackie clapped her hands. '*Yessss*! Is Mort-mer!' She winked at Bonce, who grinned back at her. 'Is Beth's uncle Mort-mer.' She sniggered, and bent forward at the waist. 'By the way,' she added with mock seriousness, 'this is Beth!' She slapped herself on the thigh, and doubled-up with silent laughter. 'Who's ever-body-else's *niece*!' She staggered backwards with a fit of the giggles and leant against the wall to stop herself falling over. It was a long time since she'd had so much fun.

Choat coughed. 'Jacqueline, don't you think you've had enough?'

Jackie put a finger to her lips, and shushed him to silence. 'Wait! Wait!' she sniggered. 'Wait!' She held out both arms like an unstable conjurer's assistant preparing for the final revelation. 'An' thisssss,' she said, triumphantly, 'is your daughter, Vic-tor-ria! *Dah-dahhh!*'

There was an uncomfortable silence, broken only by uncertain clapping from Bonce, and an embarrassed groan from Vicky.

Jackie was disappointed with the reaction. The more so because there suddenly seemed to be at least twice as many people in the room as there had been a moment earlier. Bonce and an identical twin grinned at her and nodded their heads vigorously up and down. Two Dollys stared blankly back at her, while two Victorias looked witheringly at the carpet. Behind her, a single Vinny smiled and clutched at a single Beth's right knee in what he hoped would pass for an exchange of familial warmth.

The single Beth knew better, and elbowed him in the ribs.

Choat clenched his fists in irritation. He had forgotten how nauseating his wife could be when she was drunk. But even as his face reddened with embarrassment, he was trying to work out what his next move ought to be. On the one hand, he was grateful that it looked as if he wouldn't have to slug it out with his wife and daughter as he had been expecting. On the other, he knew that he needed to prepare for his departure for Torquay and Charlotte's welcoming embrace. If he allowed himself to be distracted by these strange people for too long he might never make it, and would forever regret the advantage he would be handing to that dirty old sod, Sir Richard. He decided to make his excuses as soon as possible and go to bed, hoping against hope that Jackie wouldn't be feeling randy and want to follow him up there.

'Hi,' he said with a tight smile, and something approximating a military salute. 'To what do we owe this . . . this . . .?'

'Sorry to barge in,' said Dolly, who was anything but. 'Only there's been a bit of a cock . . . er, a mix-up with some jewellery.'

Choat's response was guarded. 'Oh?' he said, glancing guiltily at his wife.

'Just some old bits and pieces. A necklace actually! I lent it to . . . '

'*Bethy!*' sang Jackie. '*Tah-raaah!*

'Yes,' said Dolly, tightly. 'And she gave it to . . . '

'*Vic-tor-riaaaah!*' sang Jackie. '*Hah-haaaah!*'

'*Yes*,' grated Dolly. 'And . . . '

'You took it!' chided Jackie, clapping her hands in delight. 'This mornin'! With me bra-bracelet, you nawdy boy.' She stepped forward and slapped him playfully on the cheek. 'Wish is the mos' precious thin' I e-ever had.' She slapped him again, harder this time, and smiled around the room. 'Isn't he a nawdy boy, ev-ever-body?'

Bonce nodded, and started to get up. It seemed to him suddenly that he might have to slap Choat about a bit for being such a naughty boy.

Dolly glanced quickly across at him, and shook her head.

Bonce sat down, disappointed.

Unaware of the by-play, Choat smiled tightly at his wife. 'It's in my briefcase, *darling*,' he said. 'If you'd like to go and get it?'

'Oooh, yes please!' squealed Jackie with a childlike clap of her hands. She teetered precariously out of the room, and came back almost immediately with the briefcase clutched to her chest. Before Choat could stop her, she had undone the catch and tipped the contents of the case onto the coffee table. With a metallic thump, the heavy gold bracelet glittered into view. Jackie scooped it up with a whoop of delight, and wrapped it around her wrist.

Choat smiled his insincerity at her as he tidied the pile of papers back into the briefcase. 'Happy now, darling?'

'Yes darlin',' she said. 'Kissy-kissy.' She held her arm up to display the bracelet for everyone to see. 'Who wan's another dring?'

'Where's the rest of it?' asked Dolly.

'What?' said Choat, distracted by Jackie, who had started singing tunelessly to herself as she tried ineffectually to fill a large glass with gin.

'The necklace?' said Dolly, raising her voice above Jackie's monotonous droning. 'I don't see it?'

'Ah, well,' said Choat, 'no, I haven't got it, because . . . '

'What?' snapped Dolly, turning to glare at Jackie, whose singing was becoming louder and more tuneless by the second.

'I haven't got it,' repeated Choat, raising his voice. 'I . . . Someone took it. I think.' He shot an angry look at his wife. 'Jacqueline! Do you mind?'

'Took it?' insisted Dolly, glancing at Bonce. 'Who took it . . . exactly?'

Choat looked nervously to his right as Bonce got slowly and massively to his feet, blocking out the light.

'Well?' prompted Dolly.

'I . . . Well, you see,' mumbled Choat, 'what happened was . . . '

There was a sudden crash, and the sound of breaking glass.

Everyone turned to watch as Jackie slid down the front of the drinks cabinet with what sounded like a sigh of relief. She came to rest with her back against the doors, her eyes closed, her mouth open and her legs splayed out in front of her. A shiver passed through her body, and she started to snore. An overturned bottle of gin rolled to a standstill and started to decant its contents onto her head. The bouffant hairdo began to collapse over one ear, while the caked make-up, mingling with the gin and the Angel Dust, formed a spangled paste that ran down her cheeks and dripped into her cleavage.

Everyone but Vinny looked away.

Choat looked at the carpet and sucked his teeth.

Beth looked at Victoria, who shook her head and looked up at the ceiling.

Bonce looked at Choat, expecting him to rush to his wife's assistance. When he didn't move, Bonce glanced at Dolly for guidance.

Dolly shook her head and motioned for him to stay where he was, rubbing her hands together and staring hard at Choat. 'That's better,' she said, taking a step towards him. 'You were saying . . . ?'

Vicky was indignant. 'You can't just leave her like that!' she cried, waving a hand at her mother, whose indelicate pose and dishevelled clothing made her look like the opening shot in a particularly tasteless set of reader's wives photos. 'Not with her skirt like that! And everyone *staring*!'

'Yeah,' said Vinny, standing up and taking off his jacket. 'I'll just . . . '

'Sit *down*!' snapped Dolly.

'Yeah,' pleaded Vinny, 'I was only gonna . . .'

'No you weren't!' insisted Dolly, her eyes narrowing.

Vinny sat down with a disappointed grunt.

'But you can't just . . . *ouch*!' cried Vicky as Dolly's nails dug into her wrist.

'No need to make a fuss,' said Dolly, out of the corner of her mouth. 'You want to see how she looks after Vinny's had a go at her, lovie?'

Vicky subsided.

Dolly turned back to Choat. 'You were saying, Mr. Choat?'

It took a while for her to get the full story out of him. Or at least, enough of it for her to make out what had happened to the missing jewellery. He kept glancing nervously at Vicky and waffling on about why he had gone to Sir Richard's advertising agency that morning in place of Tony Marston, the company's marketing director. 'I had to go, you see?' he insisted. 'He was taken ill at the last minute. Something . . . something *tropical*, I think?'

Dolly didn't give a damn about Marston's attack of malaria, real or imagined. 'Where's the piece?'

'Piece?' said Choat. 'I . . . Well . . . Who? I don't think I know . . .'

'You said you took it with you – the necklace?'

'Unh? Oh, I see!' sighed Choat. 'Yes. Yes, I thought you meant . . .? I mean, I thought it was a bracelet.'

'Bracelet, necklace,' snapped Dolly, 'who gives a . . .?' She paused and inhaled deeply. 'So . . . where is it?'

Choat looked anxiously around the room. His glance fell on Jackie, lying like an erotic rag doll in the cocktail pit. 'Don't you think we ought to do something about . . .? I mean . . . get her to bed, or . . .?'

'She's fine,' said Dolly.

Vinny's eyes lit up. 'I'll go.'

'Leave it, I said!'

Choat looked confused.

Dolly smiled. 'Vincent's a bit clumsy, Mr. Choat. Wouldn't want him drop her or anything, would you?'

'I'll take her,' said Choat, moving forward.

Dolly stepped in front of him and put the flat of her hand against his chest. 'No,' she said. 'Can't possibly let you do that, Mr. Choat, can we? Not after you've had such a hard day at the office, an' all.' She jerked a thumb at Bonce. 'You and the girl . . .' she checked herself. 'You and *Victoria* take her mummy upstairs and . . . whatever.'

Beth stood up. 'No! Me and Vicky'll do it!'

Dolly nodded at Bonce. 'Go with 'em.'

She got the rest of the story out of Choat while Bonce and the girls were out of the room. 'So this Johnson's got the stuff, right?'

Choat nodded uncertainly. 'I . . . I think so. I mean I'm not really sure. He was there, and . . . I thought it was a bit of old tat, you see? I mean . . .'

'Yeah, yeah, right,' said Dolly, impatiently. 'Only it was me old mum's, see?

All I've got left of her now. Wouldn't mind otherwise. Only worth a couple of quid, I expect. Still, it's the sentimental value, isn't it?'

Choat smiled, weakly. 'If I'd known, I wouldn't . . .'

'Not your fault,' said Vinny. 'This Johnson geezer's the one, right?'

'Yes, but I could have stopped him taking it.'

Vinny's eyes narrowed. 'Why didn't ya, then?'

'Well, when I say stopped . . .'

'He's only joking, Mr. Choat,' said Dolly. 'Aren't you, Vincent?'

Vinny's teeth flashed. 'Yeah,' he said, stepping close to Choat, and putting a hand on his shoulder. 'Only kiddin', Mr. Choat. Nothin' to worry about, eh?'

'That's right,' said Dolly. 'It wasn't your fault.'

'No,' nodded Choat. 'And it all happened so quickly.'

'Of course it did.'

'One minute I had it in my briefcase. The next . . .'

'Could have happened to anyone.'

'Still, if there's anything I can do to . . .?'

'Nah,' said Vinny with a wink. 'We'll take care of Johnson, don't you worry.' The thought of holding Sam down while Bonce squeezed his bollocks and Dolly asked him, ever so nicely, about the missing jewellery was definitely something to look forward to.

He was still smiling five minutes later when they left the house, but it didn't last. He was just getting into the back of the Mercedes next to Vicky when Dolly tapped him on the shoulder.

'She doesn't need an escort. She's not going anywhere, are you lovie?'

Vinny looked down at the pavement. 'OK by me,' he said, turning towards the car with Beth and Nobbler sitting in the back.

Dolly caught him by the arm. 'In the front, Vinny, though, eh?'

He was crestfallen. 'Ah, come on Doll . . .!'

'Soon as they step out of line they're all yours. 'Til then, leave 'em alone.'

'What if she tries to get away?'

'She won't.'

'Yeah, but . . .!'

'Come here,' said Dolly, turning away and walking over to the other car.

'You don't think much of him, do you Elizabeth?' she said, leaning in at the rear window and pointing at Nobbler.

Beth didn't answer.

'But you wouldn't want your mummy getting his balls sent home to her in a box, would you?'

Beth looked at the floor.

Nobbler frowned. "Lizbeth? Tell 'er!' He looked up at Dolly. 'She don't mean it Miss Killjoy, honest!'

Dolly grinned back at him. 'Just pulling your leg Billy. You see,' she added turning to Beth, 'that bloke over there?' She pointed towards a car on the other side of the road. 'Nice lad, is our Cyril. Bit like Vinny, really; likes the ladies, if you know what I mean? I gave him a bell, just now, from the bog in your little friend's house? Thought her mummy and daddy might need someone to take care of 'em, in case something happened to their little girlie. In case she tries to run away and gets picked up by the filth? That sort of thing?' She grinned. 'What with them thinking she's staying at *your* house, and your mummy thinking you're staying at *her* house, someone could get lost, couldn't they? Still, if they did, I could give Cyril a bell, couldn't I? Give him the bad news? And he could go in and sort of . . . pass on my best wishes, personal like, to your mummy and daddy? You hear what I'm saying, lovie?'

Beth swallowed.

'See Vinny?' said Dolly. 'She ain't going nowhere.'

She turned to Bonce. 'Follow us.' She reached out and caught him by the arm. 'And Bonce . . .'

'Yes, Miss Killjoy?'

'Don't get lost.'

* * *

'So this *Reader's Wives* thingy,' said Titus from one of the newly delivered couches, 'where'd I get one of them, then? I mean,' he added, 'jus' so's I can keep up with the story, an' that.'

'Ah,' said the cowled figure, turning towards him, 'I am pleased to see that you are back in the land of the living, my lad. How are you feeling?'

'Me?' he said, with a dismissive wave of a hand. 'I'm fine buddy. Fine! Thanks for askin'.' He eased himself onto an elbow and waved an arm around the clearing. 'This lot's pretty cool, though, eh?'

'I am pleased that our efforts to provide you with a few meagre home comforts meet with your approval,' said the figure.

'Oh, yeah,' said Titus, sitting up and swinging his legs over the edge of the couch, 'this is definitely me!' He bumped up and down on it, patting the richly patterned cloth with the palm of a hand. 'Nice. Very nice!'

The clearing had been transformed out of all recognition while Titus was unconscious, and Henry was impressed by how quickly the little man seemed to be adapting to the changes.

It had taken only a few seconds for the colonel's drones, working at what had felt to Henry like the speed of light, to deliver and arrange the furniture and fittings that now filled the centre of the ancient stone circle. There were couches and tables, benches and chairs, tents with decorative awnings, and an array of storage vessels and chests. Everything seemed to be of the highest quality and looked at first glance to be authentically Roman in every detail of design and construction. The little campfire was still burning brightly, but there were now four strategically placed patio heaters waiting to be switched on if the night air became too chilly for comfort. Like everything else, they had been designed with such precision and cunning that Henry had to remind himself that the only thing Roman about them was their appearance.

The drones had also installed a portable toilet tucked discreetly behind one of the trilithons, and a cooking range and an upright fridge-freezer beside one of the tents. They were all solar-powered, and of twenty-first century design and manufacture, but they looked as if they had come straight out of the pages of *Elle Decoration's Roman Edition*, circa AD 59.

'Hello,' said Henry. 'We thought you were out for the count.'

'Who me, buddy?' scoffed Titus. 'Nah! Just 'avin' a bit of a lie down, I was. Restin' the ol' eyes, an' listenin' to the professor over there,' he waved a hand at the hooded figure, 'rabbitin' on about what a dickhead you was with that Amy bird.' He slipped down from the couch and looked around, stretching his arms and legs and opening his mouth in a cavernous yawn. 'Old army trick, see,' he said. 'Never know when you're gonna get a decent bit o' kip, so you takes it whenever you can.'

'You didn't pass out, then?' said Henry, with a meaningful glance at the trilithon – now reassuringly whole and planted back in the ground.

Titus stared at him open-mouthed. 'You're kiddin' me, right?'

Henry raised an eyebrow.

'What that lot?' sneered the little man, glancing nervously over his shoulder at the gigantic stones. 'No chance, buddy! You gotta get up early in the mornin' to scare an experienced military man like ol' Titus!'

'Crapping in your underpants was a diversionary tactic, then, was it?'

Titus went pale and put a hand down to the seat of his trousers. He felt around, tentatively, frowning. He looked up. 'Hey,' he demanded, 'who's been messin' with me kecks?'

'Actually,' said the figure in an uncharacteristically hesitant voice, 'it was the colonel and his associates who emptied your . . . that is . . . who cleaned out your . . . er, washed your . . . rectified your . . . er, laundry malfunction.'

'And *they*,' said Henry, pointing at the sky, 'are all girls. Lucky for you they brought a washing machine along, wasn't it?'

Titus frowned. 'So . . . what . . . you're sayin' the colonel's a poof?'

'Don't be absurd!' hissed the figure. 'And even if it were so, his sexual orientation is none of your business.'

'That's easy for you to say,' complained Titus. 'It's not your pants he's been messin' about in, is it?'

'It isn't yours, either!' snapped the figure. 'It was the drones that . . . tidied you up. And I think you might show a little gratitude for their assistance!'

'Yeah, well, all I'm sayin' is . . . I was in the Roman army, I was. An' that was a real *man's* army, that was, not some bunch of fudge-packing bum boys like them limp-wristed Greek mob!'

A sound like escaping steam came from beneath the cowled hood as the shrouded figure lurched to its feet.

Henry glanced nervously up at it as it towered above him. 'I thought you hated the Romans?' he said, quickly.

'What? Well, course!' said Titus. 'Obviously I hate the bastards, don't I? But what I'm sayin' is at least they don't go nancyin' 'bout the place holdin' hands, pickin' flowers an' spoutin' poetry like a bunch o' Greek homos. I mean, that's not gonna get you a bleedin' empire any time soon, is it?'

'Has he never heard of Alexander the Great?' muttered the figure.

Titus took no notice. 'All I'm sayin' is, if you're gonna do a bit o' serious fightin' it's no good worryin' 'bout gettin' yer hair messed up, is it? I mean, you can't go sayin' to some bloke who's gonna stick his sword in yer guts '"Ang on a minute, buddy, me lipstick's all smudged", can ya?' He held his arms wide. 'I mean, your Greeks don't know nothin' 'bout fightin', do they? I bet for every Greek with balls enough to stand up for hisself when the snot starts flyin', there's thousands o' the buggers runnin' 'ome to their mummies.'

The hooded figure's right arm shot out towards the little Celt with the speed of a striking cobra. There was a muffled crump, like the distant thunder of a sonic boom, and Titus and the figure vanished from sight.

Henry swallowed hard and stood up, scanning the clearing in front of him, and glancing over his shoulder, in anticipation of their reappearance.

When he turned back, he was just in time to see Titus and the figure flick back into existence.

The little man was crouching with his eyes scrunched shut, his splay-fingered hands held out in front of his face in a gesture of rejection, and his mouth open wide in an agonized scream.

Henry took a step backwards. 'Jesus Christ!' he gasped. 'What the hell's the matter with him?'

'They called it Thermopylae,' replied the figure. 'And the Persians were always *most* impressive when they charged.'

Henry's nostrils twitched. 'Oh dear,' he said, 'I think there's been another laundry malfunction.'

'Indeed,' sighed the figure. 'And I suppose I had better get the little twerp to a competent therapist before he has another psychotic event.'

Titus opened an eye and peered around him.

When no one attacked him, he opened the other eye and lowered his arms to his sides. 'They're gone,' he breathed, turning to look behind him. 'Thank the Gods, they're . . .!' His face hardened. 'You *bastard*!' he snarled, pointing at the hooded figure. 'Scarin' the friggin' life . . .! I'll kill you for . . .!'

The figure raised a hand.

The air shimmered between them and they vanished.

Henry waited apprehensively, wondering what manic behaviour Titus would be engaged in when he returned. But to his amazement, when the little Celt flickered back into existence, he was sitting cross-legged by the fire, smiling serenely.

The hooded figure reappeared next to Henry, and for a moment they stood side by side looking down at the little Ancient Briton.

'What's he got to be so happy about?' asked Henry.

'I have a friend,' hissed the figure, 'a psychiatrist to be exact, with a liberal approach to the prescribing of mood enhancing narcotics.'

'What, like Valium, you mean?'

'Prozac, actually.'

'Never heard of it.'

'No, you wouldn't have. A bit after your time.'

'A high dosage, was it?'

'About average for someone with his . . . psychological problems.'

Henry nodded. 'So where did you take him?'

'San Francisco.'

'Lucky sod!'

'Yes, the weather was most agreeable for the time of year.'

'Which year would that be?'

'AD 1995, if I remember correctly.'

'And did you stay long?'

'Three days. It took a long time to stop him trying to kill me.'

'Seems to have done the trick, though, doesn't it?'

'You don't think we might have . . . overdone it?'

'He's stopped talking.'

'Good point!'

Titus chose that moment to recognize Henry. His eyes lit up and his smile spread into a toothy grin as he lurched to his feet with his arms held out in front of him like a forlorn toddler suddenly catching sight of a missing parent on the other side of the school playground. '*Dada!*' he mouthed in the gum-smacking voice of a late-developer. 'Titi want *dada!*'

Henry leaned backwards in lip-curling alarm as the newly regressed Titus, his arms outstretched and his legs pumping up and down, stomped through the little campfire towards him, blissfully unaware of flying sparks, like a joyous incarnation of the title character from *The Curse of the Mummy's Tomb*.

'*Shit!*' cried Henry, backing away too slowly as Titus crashed into him and engulfed him in a rib-crushing embrace.

'Titi love dada,' he gurgled as Henry's face started to turn purple.

'Geddim ov nee!' was all he could force through his crushed lips as the world around him faded to grey.

The hooded figure thrust out a hand, and with a sizzle and a hiss, Titus was suddenly standing on the other side of the fire, staring at the cringing Henry with mild disinterest. 'What's up with him?' he asked, lowering a copy of *Razzle Readers Wives Magazine*.

'Nothing at all,' said the figure. 'He is just eager to continue with the story.'

* * *

10

BOBBY AND LOUISE

Henry woke with a start and the terrifying realization that he was being strangled. Someone had him pinned to the bed and was trying to throttle the life out of him. Blood was pounding in his temples and his eyeballs felt as if they were about to burst out of his head. His mouth opened and closed soundlessly as he clawed desperately at a cord that had been drawn impossibly tight around his neck. He couldn't breathe and knew that he was about to pass out. A maniacal voice was taunting him, wailing louder and louder, challenging him to get up even as he struggled to break free. In a final attempt to save his life, he struck out wildly to his left, where the voice seemed to be coming from, but only succeeded in wrenching his shoulder as his fist missed its target and whistled harmlessly through thin air.

'He's behind me!' he thought, raising his arms and flailing above his head with both fists. Suddenly, he connected with something hard and bony. But it didn't help: the cord only drew tighter around his neck and the voice droned on and on. '*Went to bed! Bumped his head!*' it sang in a crazy monotone. '*Couldn't get up in the mor-ning!*'

His life started flashing in front of his eyes, and he felt oddly embarrassed by it, caught in the act like an unwitting voyeur, watching himself trying to fumble his way into Louise Trimble's voluminous party frock during their breathy encounter in the wardrobe at Bobby Martin's thirteenth birthday party, all those long years ago. Louise was willing, and he was desperate, but he couldn't solve the wrist-numbing riddle of her thick woolly tights. Then, just as Louise was coming to his rescue with an irritable 'Oh, for heaven's sake, I'll do it!' Bobby's mother wrenched open the wardrobe door and yanked him unceremoniously out into the daylight by his hair.

He never got another chance at Louise after that, but the memory of his grapple with her in the wardrobe had enlivened his 'O' Level revision sessions no end. And, in spite of his mother's insistence, he hadn't gone blind

'If only it had stopped there,' he thought, as he tried to fight off his attacker, 'with Louise's skirt up to her waist and her floral knickers hoving into view, none of this would be happening now!'

It was all Bobby's mother's fault, he decided, parading him in front of the tightly knotted group of his 'little friends' and boasting that they would 'never catch my Bobby doing such dirty, disgusting, filthy things with a girl!'

She was right, too: they never did. But if they had, Louise might not have had to go away for three days to 'stay with her Auntie Susan in London', and Bobby might not have been expelled from St George's a week later and sent to a boarding school in the north of England, as far away as possible from the gossiping neighbours.

'Bloody woman!' thought Henry, as he felt the last vestiges of life draining from his body. 'Wrecking people's lives!'

He turned angrily to take one last desperate swing at her as she stood behind him holding his ear and cuffing the back of his head. His fist struck something hard that gave under the force of the blow, and he was suddenly free. He wobbled in mid-air for a moment under the force of his own forward momentum, before pitching over the edge of the bed and crashing heavily to the floor on his head.

He lay there in a crumpled heap for several seconds, with nothing but a whirling constellation of brightly coloured lights and the pounding in his temples to tell him that he was still alive. In spite of the pain, he felt elated. There was silence. He was free. And his attacker had surely been vanquished.

Or had he? What if the bastard was just lying low somewhere, ready to pounce as soon as he showed the first signs of life?

His first instinct was to flee: to get out of the bedroom as fast as his legs would carry him. He forced himself onto his hands and knees and scrambled across the room on all fours. When he reached the far wall, he whirled around, stood up, crouching, and stared into the gloom, listening intently. His right hand hurt as if it had been slammed in a car door. He cradled it delicately against his chest and wished that he hadn't hit his attacker so hard. He wondered for a moment if he had killed him.

'He might be lying dead, down there,' he thought as he scanned the carpet. But nothing he saw in the gloom resembled a corpse.

'Under the bed!' he thought. 'The bastard's gone under the bed!'

What he needed was a weapon – something to protect himself with.

'Umbrella!' he thought, suddenly. He would have preferred something more practical, like an elephant gun or a bazooka. But since neither of those was immediately available to him, he decided that the golf umbrella would have to do. And a whack over the head with it would certainly give his attacker something to think about . . . wouldn't it?

Without taking his eyes from the shadow under the bed, he reached back and slid his hand along the wall until it met the umbrella standing in its familiar place in the corner of the room. He grabbed it, turned it around handle first, and hefted it in both hands.

'All right you bastard!' he cried. 'You can come out now! I know where you are!' He thought for a moment. 'And you can come out with your hands up, too! And d-don't try anything, o-or you'll . . . you'll be really sorry!'

'Damn it!' he cursed, inwardly. If only his voice hadn't faltered like that. This threatening people business wasn't as easy as it looked on the telly!

He waited for something to happen. But apart from a ringing in his head, and the rasp of his own breathing, there were no signs of life in the room. He swallowed hard and wished that he'd been born braver. He'd never been convinced that 'having a go' was a good idea, and now that his chance to give it a try had arrived, he was absolutely certain that it wasn't. He didn't even know if he was doing it right. He had the feeling that he ought to be perfectly balanced, poised and ready for action. He looked down at himself. 'If only I knew where the balls of my feet were,' he thought, 'this would probably be a hellova lot easier.'

He shook his head and sighed. What a mess! Here he was, unemployed, hung-over, half-naked with a homicidal maniac under his bed, and all he had for protection was an umbrella! The thought made him bubble with anger.

'All right, you *bastard*!' he shouted. 'Come on out! Or . . . or . . . I'm gonna come in and get you!'

As soon as he said it he felt foolish. There was no way he was going anywhere to get anyone, unless it was outside to get the police. But he wasn't going to do that, either, because it would mean that he would have to turn his back on the room, if only for a moment, and God only knew what would happen to him if he did that.

He crouched, motionless, waiting.

Still nothing happened.

'Maybe he's really unconscious?' he thought, with a sudden flood of compassion: only to snort derisively at his own gullibility a moment later. 'Playing at it, more like!'

He gripped the umbrella tightly, and clenched his teeth. There was nothing else for it, he decided, he would have to find out.

Holding the umbrella aloft, and keeping a watchful eye on the gap between the rug and the bed, he started to inch forward.

'As soon as he makes a move,' he told himself, 'I'll whack him. I'll smack him. I'll hit the bastard so hard . . .!'

There was a sudden yelp of pain, followed by the sound of the half-crazed voice screeching the nursery rhyme at him again. He leapt backwards and stood trembling with the umbrella held out in front of him like a two-handed sword. He was sweating profusely: the more so because he realized that the cry of pain had come from his own mouth. He had trodden on something, or something had bitten his foot. He raised the umbrella above his head, and stared wildly at the carpet where the voice now seemed to be coming from. There wasn't much light in the room, and he couldn't see the thing clearly, but he could tell that it wasn't a human being – not unless they were making them ten inches tall these days. He started to shuffle backwards, inch by inch, groping behind him with an outstretched hand for the light switch.

When he found it, the overhead light flicked on, and he saw the thing clearly at last! It was ugly and its large bug eyes stared up at him as it flopped about on its back like a wounded animal, all the while wheezing its insane taunt and swinging its stubby arms up and down. A shiver ran up his spine as he stared back at it. He knew exactly what it was. He had seen it many times before. He knew where it had come from and to whom it belonged. Worst of all, as the memory of the night before came flooding back to him he knew exactly what it was doing in his bedroom. All the fear, all the anger, and all of the pain of the last few minutes welled up inside him.

'Sam,' he yelled at the top of his voice, 'you *bastard*!'

It was at that moment that he caught sight of himself in the wardrobe mirror, crouching on the far side of the bed with his underpants tented by an inexplicable erection, his legs splayed apart, the golf umbrella clutched tightly in both hands, his hair on end, his eyes staring wildly, and his lips drawn back from his teeth in a snarl of aggression. Around his neck was a garish piece of jewellery: the necklace that Sam had taken from the marketing man the day before. He recognized it at once, and knew that he looked ridiculous in it. It was the final straw. He raised the umbrella high above his head, and with every ounce of strength he could muster, brought it crashing down on Sam's singing alarm clock.

There was a satisfying crunch. The mechanism croaked one last distorted '*mor-ning*' at him, and fell silent. He grunted in satisfaction and kicked it across the room. It hit the wall with a gratifying *clunk*! But any satisfaction that he might have felt was short-lived. Indeed, a split second before his big toe made contact with it, he knew that he was making a serious mistake. Excruciating pain lanced up through his foot. He clenched his teeth and sucked a long, hissing stream of air into his lungs. His eyes opened wider and wider as he dropped the umbrella like a hot coal and started to hop on one leg with his damaged toes gripped tightly in both hands. The pain got worse rather than better, so he tried standing still for a moment, not breathing, motionless and contorted, like a child who had just discovered that someone had replaced his football with the granite knob from the top of the gatepost. Then, just as his lungs were about to burst, his eyes and mouth snapped open and he howled a mixture of agony and self-loathing up at the ceiling.

'*Oooh! Ow! Shit! Shit! Bastard! Bastard! Sodding! Bloody! Ow! Shit! Ootch! Bastard! Bastard!*' And so on, and on, for what seemed like a lifetime.

The shouting and howling didn't help. So he lowered his foot gingerly to the floor and tried hobbling around in erratic circles, cursing, puffing and screwing up his face as he went. That didn't help much, either, but he kept at until the pain in his toe started to subside. When it finally reached manageable proportions, he limped over to the bed and flopped down onto it, exhausted.

He didn't stay motionless for long. His eyes popped open, and he turned onto his side to stare at the mirror on the wardrobe door. His reflection stared thoughtfully back at him. He pursed his lips at it and raised a hand to the string of large metallic beads around his neck. Then he glanced sideways at the headboard. Then back at his reflection. Then back at the headboard again. Finally, he shook his head in sad recognition and flopped onto his back with a sigh. He had just seen incontrovertible proof that he was a moron!

He couldn't remember much about getting undressed or getting into bed the night before, but judging by the position of the pillows, he must have been sitting upright with his back against the headboard when he fell asleep. The headboard was made from a tightly woven lattice of bamboo canes, one of which had broken months ago on the side of the bed where he had been sleeping. Now it was snapped clean in two. The necklace must have hooked over the broken end of the cane and been pulled gradually tighter around his neck as he'd slid down into the bed while he was sleeping. When Sam's alarm clock had gone off, and he had tried to sit up, the necklace must have been pulled even more tightly around his throat, making him think someone was trying to kill him. Under the weight of his desperate struggle to escape, the cane had eventually snapped and released him. He felt for the necklace and wondered what the cord was made of. It must be very strong, he decided, not to have broken under the strain. He touched it and felt a twinge of pain in his hand. He looked down and saw that the knuckles were red and swollen where he had punched the headboard. His other hand looked just as bad. He shook his head in recognition of his own stupidity, and collapsed back onto the bed. Every part of his body seemed to hurt. He rolled over to ease the pain, and fell onto the floor with a thud. He looked up at the ceiling and wondered if his day could possibly get any worse. He decided that it couldn't if he ignored it and went back to sleep. And, since he hadn't had much luck with gravity so far, he decided it would be safer to stay where he was.

He was just beginning to nod off when the phone rang. He opened his eyes and looked around. The phone was an arm's length away, under the bed. He stared at it for a moment, wondering how it had got there.

The ringing was beginning to irritate him when he remembered Sam's voice from the night before, and the ugly little alarm clock being waved in his face. 'If your one don't get you up, this little bugger'll do it, no pro-problem!' said Sam's grinning face.

He remembered the rest of the conversation, too. How Sam and Amy had decided that he ought to take a holiday, and that he could use their parents' cottage on Dartmoor for the purpose. He wouldn't need to book into a hotel, they'd told him, and it wouldn't cost him a penny. What's more, he could stay there for as long as he liked – within reason. But he ought to go soon, because he needed to sort his miserable life out before it descended into total chaos.

He had protested, of course, but they had insisted.

'Have you looked at yourself lately?' they had asked him. 'Really looked at yourself, I mean?' Because if he hadn't, they'd told him, he really ought to. He was a mess: an alcohol-sodden mess who couldn't make so much as a cup of coffee without throwing-up, never mind hold down a respectable job. He needed to pull himself together, they had assured him, and to do that he needed a holiday, and they were going to see to it that he got one.

'Or else!' Amy had added, darkly. And now that he came to think about it, it had been Amy who had done most of the talking.

He should have protested more strongly, he told himself. But he had been too drunk and too embarrassed by Amy's presence to offer anything more than a token resistance. He had allowed himself to be bundled into her car and driven home. He had protested there, too, about the suddenness of it all and the fact that it wouldn't be fair of him to go away and leave Spike on his own. 'An' who's gonna water the plants?' he'd asked, as Sam had been stripping him down to his underpants and propping him up in bed. 'Who's gonna cancel the milk? Who's gonna let the man in to read the meter? Eh? Who's gonna do all them things? Jus' you an-answer me that!'

He had smiled at his own ingenuity. But his victory had been short-lived.

Amy had stopped pretending to examine the wallpaper in order to avoid being confronted by his private parts, again, should his disrobing go amiss, and had turned to face him. She loved cats, she had assured him, and had always been on good terms with houseplants, milk delivery persons, and all manner of uniformed officials. She would housesit for him while he was away: not least because it would give her a chance to revise without Sam driving her to distraction all the time with his offensively loud music.

Sam had thought it was a great idea, too, because he wouldn't have to put up with her trying to organize him all the time, telling him to watch what he was eating and drinking and smoking; and telling him to 'Turn that bloody noise down and find something useful to do for a change!'

He had beamed at Henry, and patted him on the head to show that there were no hard feelings over him letting himself get knocked unconscious with the pool cue. And as a further proof of his goodwill, he had dipped a hand into his jacket pocket and brought out Richard Choat's necklace.

"Ere,' he'd said with a lopsided grin as he'd jammed it over Henry's head, 'bring you goo' luck, tha' bugger will!'

It had been a tight fit, and if Henry hadn't been so effectively anaesthetized by the dope and the alcohol, Sam would never have been able to force it over his ears without making him scream. As it was, he hadn't felt a thing.

Sam had stood back to admire the effect. 'Perfec'!' he'd said. 'Give you a bell at seven o'clock, then, eh?' he'd added, picking up the phone and dumping it under the bed. 'So's you gotta ged up to answer it, eh?'

With the ghost of Sam's grin seeming to hover just below the bedsprings beside him, Henry reached out, snatched the phone off the hook, and yelled into it: 'Piss off, you bastard, and get out of my soddin' life!'

Too late he remembered Amy's voice from the night before. 'You couldn't get up at seven o'clock if your arse was on fire, Sam Johnson. I'll call him. That OK with you, Henry? Sleep well.'

Henry groaned inwardly, and wondered why it was that he couldn't keep his stupid mouth shut or his flies closed whenever that bloody woman was around. He clamped his hand over the mouthpiece and swore.

'Shit!' he hissed. 'Shit! Shit! Shit! Shit! Shit!'

'Good morning to you, too, Henry,' said Amy on the other end of the line. 'No need to ask how you're feeling today, is there?'

He closed his eyes. 'Why me?' he wondered. 'What'd I do to deserve this?'

More to the point, what was he going to do to get out of it? Should he put on a strange voice and pretend it was a wrong number? Should he hang up and pretend it had never happened? Or should he come clean and tell this irritating woman the truth about what he had just done? But if he did that, what would she think of him then? She already thought he was a lecherous, drunken idiot. What was she going to think of him if he told her that he had just fought himself to a standstill against her brother's singing alarm clock, having first tried to hang himself from the headboard of his own bed? At first glance, her probable reaction didn't bear thinking about. It didn't look all that promising at second glance, either. But he realized that he couldn't just lie there, hoping she would go away. He had tried that last night, and look where it had got him. He decided that, on balance, his best option would be to pretend that he was waking from a bad dream and couldn't be held responsible for anything that he might have said or done. It was as good as anything else he could think of, and not so very far from the truth, at that.

He moaned experimentally, and fumbled with the phone. '*Whun-hun? No! No! Huh!* Who . . .? Where . . .? Where am I?'

Amy clicked her tongue. She hadn't grown up in the same house as the adolescent Sam without learning to recognize the old 'I was asleep, so it couldn't have been me pulling your pigtails,' routine when she heard it.

'Hen-ry . . .?' she sighed.

'Who . . . who's that?'

'It's me, Henry, Amy. Look . . . '

'Amy? Amy Johnson? Is that you?'

'Who did you think it was . . . the Wright Brothers? Amelia Earhart? Or just Baron von Richthofen, perhaps?'

He flinched. 'I was dreaming . . . '

'How do you know?'

'What?'

'How do you know you were dreaming, if you were asleep?'

He screwed up his face in search of a plausible answer. 'Well, I . . . People do, don't they? When you wake up you remember . . . '

'What was it about, then, this dream of yours?'

'Oh, er, well, I . . . ' he mumbled, trying to think more quickly than his brain would allow. 'It . . . it was horrible!'

'Was it, really?'

'Yes, yes! Horrible! Something . . . something huge and horrible and evil was coming after me, and I . . .'

'It didn't have its flies open by any chance, did it?'

'What? No, I . . . Look, that was an accident! I told Sam . . . '

'Did you, really?'

'And he said . . . '

'I do hope you're going to be ready in time!'

'Yes! Yes, of course, and . . . '

'So I'll see you at ten o'clock, then, shall I?'

'Look, I didn't mean . . . What? Ten o'clock? Ten o'clock . . . *today*?'

'To pick up the keys?'

'No! No! I mean . . . yes! Yes! Only, no! I . . . I was thinking I ought to leave early, didn't I? I mean, it's a long way, isn't it? So I ought to make an early start . . . don't you think?'

Amy agreed that it was a long way, and that he ought to make an early start, and if he would just leave his keys where she could find them – say, under the boot-scrapper at the front door? – she would take care of the house until he got back. 'Besides,' she added, before hanging up, 'that way you won't have to see me again, will you? Have a lovely time, Henry. Oh, and don't forget to write.'

'*Write?*' he muttered as he crabbed his way out from under the bed. 'Don't forget to *write?* Sodding letter bomb's all she'd gonna get!'

He stood up, and knew at once that it was a mistake. Everything above his neck started to throb, while everything between his ears tried to crush his brain. He clasped his head in both hands and sank to his knees.

He stayed like that for several minutes, holding his head tightly as if it was a precious piece of porcelain and he feared that if he let it go, it would fall to the floor and shatter into a million tiny pieces.

After what seemed like hours of suffering, the pain started to recede and he decided that it would be safe to move. But he didn't think that it would be a good idea to stand up for an hour or two, at least. So with his head pounding dully, and his body aching as if he had been dragged behind a galloping horse, he eased himself onto his hands and knees, and started to crawl towards the bathroom door.

11

RICHARD CHOAT

Charlotte Piece sighed with a delicious sense of anticipation as she lowered herself into a hot and steaming aromatherapeutic early-morning bath. The water swirled across her ample breasts and lapped at her chin as she lay back and closed her eyes luxuriously. It felt good as she ran her hands over the warm smoothness of her belly. It felt even better as her fingers probed down between her legs, and she wished, not for the first time, that Choat would touch her delicately like that instead of always thrusting his hand down her knickers as if he was pulling raffle tickets out of a sock. It would be even nicer, she decided, if he would show her the occasional moment of tenderness instead of groping at her without preamble and banging away for what usually amounted to little more than a couple of sweaty, grunting minutes.

The thought unsettled her and she decided to have nothing more to do with it. There would be plenty of time for that sort of thing once they were married. Although, if she was honest with herself, she wasn't convinced that marriage to Richard Choat would be such a good idea, after all. A lot had changed in her life recently, and she wondered if, by marrying him, she would be selling herself short. The other Richard, *Sir* Richard, had recognized her potential at last, and *her* Richard had just agreed to go with her for a fortnight's holiday in Torquay: and she was beginning to wonder if she had been underestimating her womanly powers for too long, and that, perhaps, men weren't *actually* as difficult to handle as she had thought.

She sighed, and closed her eyes. In spite of her misgivings about Richard Choat, she had decided that her world was almost perfect, and far better than her wildest dreams could have made it. She was a scarlet woman – she thrilled at the prospect! – off for a romantic affair with her lover at an exotic resort by the sea. It wasn't *exactly* the South of France, perhaps, but Sir Richard had called it 'the English Riviera', so it couldn't be *that* bad, could it? And to add to her excitement, she and her lover had arranged to meet clandestinely at a motorway service station on their way down to the West Country – her in the virgin white Rover convertible; him behind the wheel of his red hot Ford Probe. She had read about such assignations in her favourite romances, but had never believed that she would one day be doing something similar herself. She had wanted to, of course, and had daydreamed about it often enough. But she hadn't *really* believed that it could happen to her: not at her time of life: not after the way that she had been brought up to think about sex.

It wouldn't be perfect, she cautioned herself as she caressed her pubic mound absently with soapy fingers: not like it was in the *Mills & Boons* she had been reading for so many years. *Her* Richard wasn't really tall enough, or slim and muscular enough for that. And he didn't *really* have quite enough of the right sort of hair. But she wasn't worried because she had decided that life was what you imagined it to be, and for all his many short-comings he could be tall enough, lithe enough, handsome enough, Latin enough, and have a tanned-enough body with long-enough, muscular-enough limbs and a huge-enough, throbbing-enough, blue-veined-enough, purple enough . . .!

Her eyes snapped open and she sat bolt upright with her hands clasped to her mouth in alarm at the disgusting thoughts that had been rampaging their way through her mind. Water sloshed over the edge of the bath and splashed onto the floor as she chided herself. What had she been thinking? What had she been feeling? Worst of all: what had she been doing with the fingers of her right hand? She gagged as she realized that she now had those same fingers pressed to her mouth. She tore them away and plunged them into the bath to wash them clean of the filth with which they had become infected. Then she scooped up handfuls of water and splashed it at her face and into her mouth, spitting it out instantly as if it tasted of vinegar. She picked up the flannel and scrubbed vigorously at her fingertips before thrusting it down between her thighs to wash herself clean down there, too. It was the last conscious thing she did for several minutes.

The first touch sent a shiver of pleasure racing up through her body and into her head, where it burst inside her brain like the first rocket on Guy Fawkes Night. Her face lit up like a sparkler, her mouth dropped open like an oiled trapdoor, and her eyes bulged and stared at nothing in particular as every muscle in her body trembled with a lustful vibration. She was like a virgin tuning fork that had been plucked for the very first time. She was a big woman in a small bath, and as the vibrations grew more powerful, water splashed into the air and rained down across the floor. Her knees shook and her heels drummed against the bottom of the bath as she gritted her teeth and gave vent to a high-pitched, keening sound like the attack cry of a ninja field mouse. The sound grew gradually in intensity until it broke suddenly into a celebration of salvation and glory, and she sang at the top of her voice: '*A-amay-zi-ing grace, h-ow swee-eet the sound* . . . YES! *Tha-at say-aved a-ah* . . . YES! YES! . . . *a wre-etch li-ike-ah* . . . YES! . . . *meeeeeeee-ah! I-ah once-ah w-aas-ah lost* . . .!'

She was suddenly slapping at the water with her free hand, sending spray and foam flying into the air above her head, across the little room and against the frosted window. Soon the floor was awash, and the curtains drenched: and as she flailed about wildly, she dragged a towel into the water unwittingly and pounded it into the swirling foam with her fist. She was like a long-dormant volcano that had finally decided that it didn't give a damn what the rest of the world thought about it, it was going to erupt with every ounce of energy in its superheated body and to Hell with decorum!

As the waves of pleasure shot up her spinal column and into her brain, the vaguest of suspicions began to stir in a previously uncharted corner of her mind. By the time she had regained some semblance of control over her body it had formed itself into a certainty. It spoke to her softly, intimately, and she nodded her agreement slack-jawed, bright-eyed and seemingly reborn. There could be no doubt, she told herself through the soporific haze of her newly awakened libido, something very important had just happened to her, and this, finally, was the very first day of the rest of her life. The prim and proper Miss Charlotte Emily Piece had become a floozy, a trollop, a nymphomaniac, and from this moment forward the entire male population had better keep a tight hold on their dicks! The thought that they might be doing so, even as she lay supine and open for their dirty business, was one that she had never before allowed herself to dwell on. But she dwelt on it now as she slid slowly, luxuriously back into the gently swirling waters and dwelt on it again, and again, and again . . .

* * *

'Now that,' said Titus, 'is my kinda woman!'

'Is there any kind that isn't?' asked Henry.

Titus ignored him and reached inside his jacket to pull out the *Ann Summers* catalogue and lay it on the ground in front of him next to the copy of *Razzle Readers Wives Magazine*. 'What I was thinkin',' he said, pointing from one to the other, 'is she'd look really horny in one o' them.' He looked up eagerly. 'What d'you reckon?'

Henry and the hooded figure watched him in silence.

'No?' he said.

He turned a couple of pages and pointed again. 'What about them?'

'Remind me,' said Henry, 'what *exactly* is he doing here?'

'It's complicated,' sighed the figure.

'Yes,' said Henry, testily, 'but *he* isn't!'

Titus pursed his lips, turned another page, and pointed. 'Gotta be one of them, then, yeah?' he said, gesturing at a double-page spread featuring a quartet of long-legged, busty young women in an assortment of ill-fitting, transparent cat suits.

Henry shook his head. 'What he needs is a cold shower.'

The cowled head turned towards him. 'Do you really think so?'

'Either that or send him back to primary school.'

There was a brief but agitated sizzling as the hooded figure stood up, shimmered, faded, disappeared for a fraction of a second, and came back into focus with a steaming wooden bucket dangling from one of its bony hands.

Henry took one look at the bucket, got hurriedly to his feet, and backed as far away from Titus as he could get.

The little Romano-Briton was too busy thumbing his way through the Classified Section of *Razzle Readers Wives Magazine* to notice.

The hooded figure looked down at him for a moment before tipping the contents of the bucket over his head.

There was a ragged gasp from Titus, followed by a lot of spluttering and cursing, as water, slush, snow and a few chunks of ice splashed, clung, bounced and slithered over his head and shoulders.

'What the . . .?' he cried, looking down at himself with an expression of baffled indignation as steam rose around him and thick water and icy slush dripped from his nose, chin and eyebrows.

'Not *quite* what I had in mind,' said Henry, sucking his teeth.

'Really?' said the figure, turning towards him. 'It was the very best the alpine pastures could offer, I assure you.'

'I don't doubt it,' said Henry, looking down at the spluttering, cursing, cloud-enveloped little Ancient Briton. 'But I mean . . . *ice*? That's a bit strong, even for him.'

'It was snow when I scooped it into the bucket.'

'It isn't now, though, is it?'

The figure looked down at Titus. 'I keep forgetting that temporal displacement has a habit of altering the temperature of things if they aren't properly shielded. It's the friction, you see? Under normal circumstances one would expect the temperature to rise. However, in certain . . . '

'You *bastard*!' cried Titus, finally finding his voice and staggering to his feet. 'Why d'you keep doing this to me?'

'One moment, please,' said the figure.

It shimmered, faded, disappeared, and returned a moment later without the bucket. 'Temporal displacement brings with it certain obligations,' it explained, open-handed, 'of a moral and ethical nature?'

The others looked at it blankly.

'The owner of the bucket . . .?' said the figure.

'What about *me*?' demanded Titus, 'you faceless, brainless *arsehole*!'

'Indeed,' said the figure, with its head tilted to one side. 'Excuse us for a moment, Henry, will you?'

There was the now familiar fading and disappearing of Titus and the figure: followed by their almost instantaneous return.

Henry's eyebrows shot up his forehead as Titus re-materialized wearing sunglasses and the most garish combination of Hawaiian shirt and shorts he had ever seen. There was a floral garland around his neck, a straw hat on his head, and a pair of flip-flops on his feet. In one hand, he held a tall glass containing a purple liquid, ice cubes, assorted fruit and foliage, a purple bendy straw and a mini umbrella. In the other, he cradled a coconut with a yellow straw sticking out of it.

'*Aloha*,' he said with a grin.

'Are we warm enough now?' asked the hooded figure as Titus seated himself in a throne-like chair by the fire.

'Yes, we are, buddy,' said Titus, happily. 'Thanks for askin'.'

'Excellent,' said the figure. 'Excellent! You will have no further use for these pamphlets, then, will you?'

It picked up the *Readers Wives Magazine* and the *Ann Summers* catalogue and tossed them onto the fire.

'*Hey*!' cried Titus, surging to his feet. 'What the hells . . .?' But with the tall glass in one hand and the coconut in the other, he was powerless to intervene as the magazines burst into flames. He gazed mournfully at the curling pages for a moment before shrugging and sucking loudly on both straws at once.

'Now then, let me see,' said the figure, rubbing its scarred hands together dryly, 'where were we?'

* * *

Richard Choat tiptoed guiltily along the hall towards the front door. Halfway there, he paused to listen for the sound of following footsteps, but there were none, only the distant rumbling of his wife's snores. Satisfied that his departure had so far gone unnoticed, he lowered his suitcase carefully to the floor by the hall table, and bent to put on his shoes. It wasn't easy standing on one leg in the semidarkness while trying not to make a sound. Not that there was really any need for silence. A twenty-one-gun salute would normally have been hard pressed to wake Jackie on the morning after a heavy night before. And if no one got around to throwing a bucket of water over her, she would probably remain unconscious until lunchtime. Even so, Choat wasn't taking any chances that she would wake up and catch him trying to sneak out.

He hadn't dared to bathe or shower before leaving. He hadn't even risked having a shave for fear that the sound would wake her up. Instead, he had packed into his travelling case everything he thought he would need to do his ablutions at the first service station he reached on his way down to Devon. He wasn't due to meet Charlotte at South Mimms until 11.30, and there would be plenty of time between then and now to stop at a service station and smarten himself up. He would call his employers from there, too, with some excuse for his absence; a sudden illness perhaps, or the death of a family member in some distant part of the world; something that would sound dire enough to keep him away from the office for the two weeks that he and Charlotte were planning to spend together in Torquay. As for Jackie, he wasn't sure that he cared what she thought anymore.

He finished cramming his feet into his shoes, and picked up his suitcase. He took his car coat from its hanger, and smiled to himself as he padded softly along the hall. 'You're a cunning devil, Richie Choat,' he told himself as he opened the front door. 'Deadly with the birds, an' all. Poor sods!'

He had decided to travel light, and had packed only a few bare essentials, including just a few changes of clothes. He had a wallet filled with credit cards and would buy whatever he needed as he went along. It was exciting. By the time he got back, he might have a whole new life, not just a whole new wardrobe! His smile faded, and he glanced guiltily up at the ceiling.

'If *ever* come back,' he breathed. After all, he might set up home with Charlotte immediately, and never set foot in this house again.

In a car park ten miles away, Dolly Killjoy sat in the passenger seat of her yellow Mercedes convertible and smoked a cigar, while Vicky Choat half-sat, half-lay on the seat behind her, trying to ignore the smell.

Curly Hare dozed in the driver's seat next to Dolly with his head against the side window and his mouth open. They had been there for almost an hour, waiting for Sam Johnson to arrive at his office for work. It was still only half past seven, and he wasn't expected until nine, but Dolly wasn't the sort of person who liked leaving things to chance.

Parked next to them was a black Mercedes saloon, with Vinny, Bonce and Nobbler sleeping inside it. On the back seat next to her father, Beth had long since given up trying to sleep. Nobbler was curled into a foetal ball with his back towards her, snorting like a pig after truffles and impervious to her attempts to shut him up. She clicked her tongue in annoyance, and elbowed him in the ribs for the umpteenth time. His only response was to moan and shift position, his left hand rising slowly into the air like a hypnotized cobra to waft at an imagined body beside him.

'Not now, Maggie,' he whined, 'feelin' . . . knackered!'

Beth glared as she elbowed him even harder. Her mum's name was Patsy

He grunted and twitched, and his right leg shot forward as if it had been hit on the knee with a reflex hammer. His foot slammed into the back of the passenger seat where Vinny was dozing.

'Christ sake!' he hissed, bunching his fists and turning to glare at Nobbler on the seat behind him. 'Keep it down while you're havin' it off, will ya?'

Beth curled her lip. 'You *wish*!'

Vinny raised his fist and leaned towards her. 'Cheeky slag! I'll . . .!'

Bonce's huge hand snaked out and wrapped itself around Vinny's wrist. 'That bloke,' he said, impassively, 'is lookin' at us.'

'Bloke!' snarled Vinny, trying to break free. 'What *bloke*?'

Bonce nodded at Ron Posset, who was standing in front of the big car with a yard broom in one hand and a black bin-liner hanging from the other. 'He don't look 'appy t' me.'

'I don't give a shit what he looks like,' snapped Vinny, trying again to wrench his hand free from Bonce's iron grip. 'Get *off* me you bleedin' . . .!'

He was interrupted by a sharp tapping on the passenger window.

He turned to see Dolly glaring into the car.

'Sit down!' she hissed, as she opened the door. 'And smile Vinny, smile! Let's show the nice little man what friendly people we are.'

She turned and smiled stiffly at Ron as he sidled towards her. 'Kids!' she said. 'Who'd have 'em, eh?'

Ron sucked his teeth and looked pointedly at his watch. The company wouldn't be open for business for half an hour at least, and he wanted to know what these people were doing in his car park at this time of the day.

'I expect you've got 'em yourself,' offered Dolly, 'kids?'

Ron shook his head. 'Me and the missus prefers budgies,' he said. 'Course they shits on the floor, but contained like, on newspaper, an' that? None o' that gettin' dragged down the police station in the middle of the night.' He squinted at the occupants of the two cars, and decided that they didn't look like any family he'd ever seen, unless it was Ma Barker and her boys. 'Big then, is it,' he said, turning to look Dolly in the eye, 'this family o' yours?'

She nodded. 'You're probably wondering . . .'

'What're you doin' 'ere, then? This ain't a bleedin' caravan site, y'know!'

'We were hoping to find a Mr. Johnson?' said Dolly with a politeness that galled her. 'A Mr. Samuel Johnson?'

'Ain't nobody 'ere,' said Ron. 'Won't be neither for half-hour, at least. You better come back later. 'Bout nine-ish, I reckon. They'll all be 'ere then.' He looked at the ground. 'Them as is capable o' bein' anywhere, that is.'

'We thought we'd wait,' offered Dolly.

Ron sucked a hissing breath of disapproval. 'Oh no! Can't 'ave that! More than me job's worth, that is. 'T'ain't worth a tinker's bollock as 'tis.'

'There you are then,' smiled Dolly. 'Where's the harm?'

Ron shook his head, and turned towards the main entrance. 'Nope,' he insisted. 'Can't 'ave that. 'Ave to call the police.'

Dolly heard a familiar metallic click behind her, and turned to see a flash of steel in Vinny's fist. She was about to tell him to put it away when an imperious, but rather squeaky, voice trilled 'I don't think you're qualified to make that kind of decision, Posset, do you?'

'Bugger!' muttered Ron. 'Look what the cat jus' dragged in!'

'I'd watch my language, if I were you, Posset,' said Nigel Adams, emerging head first from the shrubbery next to the main doors. 'If you expect to be working for my uncle's company for much longer, that is.'

'My orders is . . . ' began Ron.

'To do what I tell you. Yes?'

'I was told . . . '

'Yes or no?'

Ron looked at the ground. Then 'Whatever you say, Mr. Adams,' he said, looking up and turning to leave. 'And where did you spring from, my lad, eh?' he added, under his breath. 'Sniffin' round people's offices, I shouldn't wonder. Lookin' for somethin' to use against 'em, p'rhaps?' He snorted softly to himself. 'Sniffin' round our Charlotte's swivel chair, more like!'

Adams smiled stiffly as Ron trudged towards the main doors. Then he turned with an ingratiating smile and bowed to Dolly. Anyone who drove a car like the big yellow Mercedes was his type of person, he was thinking, and he wanted to be certain that she appreciated the fact.

'Hired help!' he snorted. 'All the same, aren't they, the plebs?'

Dolly inclined her head. 'Dorothy Killjoy,' she said, holding out a limp hand. 'Miss,' she added with a coyness that would have made anyone who knew her tremble with fear. 'And you are . . . ?'

'Nigel Adams, account executive,' he said with a Teutonic bow as he took her hand. He stood up straight and wiped imaginary sweat from his brow. 'Been up all night,' he added. 'You know how it is when you've got important decisions to make? Course, they don't know what real work's about, do they?' he flicked a thumb at Ron. 'Don't even know they're born, most of 'em don't!'

'Some don't even know when they're dead,' replied Dolly, with a tight smile and a gesture to let Vinny know that his flick-knife wouldn't be needed.

Adams grinned, uncertainly. 'Yes, er . . . very good! Now then,' he added, 'what can I do for you, Miss Killjoy?'

'We're looking for a Mr. Johnson? A Mr. Samuel Johnson? He works here, I believe? We have a matter of some importance to discuss with him. You wouldn't happen to know when he's expected in his office, would you?'

Adams smiled obligingly and invited her into the building.

When Sam arrived a couple of hours later, hung-over and looking like death warmed up, he found Adams, Dolly and the girls waiting for him in the boardroom. Adams simpered over Vicky and Beth while Dolly told Sam the story she had told Choat about the necklace being a family heirloom.

Sam nodded dully through an excruciating headache. 'Thought it was too good to be true,' he mumbled. 'But I haven't got it anymore. I gave it to a friend.' He shrugged apologetically. 'Sorry.'

When Adams heard that the friend in question was Henry Kite, he dismissed Sam with an imperious wave of a hand, and rang the Personnel Department. Five minutes later, with Henry's address on a piece of paper in her handbag, Dolly thanked Adams for his help and suggested that if he was ever 'in town' he should look her up.

Adams grinned widely at the generosity of the offer, and waved after her as the yellow convertible and the black sedan sped away. It was almost three hours later that it dawned on him that he had no idea where she lived.

Eight miles away, in the main bedroom of his house, Henry glanced nervously at his watch as he crammed a last few hastily selected items into his holdall. He frowned uneasily, and looked closely at his watch. Surely, he told himself, it was after 9:30? He held the watch to his ear, and listened intently. There was silence. He shook his wrist and listened again. Still there was nothing. Or was that the faintest of ticks? He held the watch close to his face and stared at it without blinking. There could be no doubt about it, he decided, the second hand was definitely moving. So it probably was 9:30, after all. And if that was the case, there was no time to lose.

'Better get a move on,' he told himself, as he finished stuffing things into the holdall. Amy had said that she would be arriving at ten o'clock, and he wanted to be well away from the house before then.

He glanced around the room to make sure that he had packed not only everything he would need on his holiday, but also all the things that he didn't want Amy to find while he was away. She might not be the nosy type, but he wouldn't want to bet on it, and he was determined not to leave behind anything that might incriminate him. Which of his belongings she might decide to rummage through during the odd moment of boredom, or while she was looking for a spare light bulb or a 13amp fuse, was anyone's guess. So the very least he felt he could do was make sure that there was nothing too obviously damning left lying around for her to find and gloat over.

Some of his underpants and socks had rather more than the regulation number of holes and should have been consigned to the waste bin long ago. But if he put them in there now she would probably see them anyway. So he scooped them up and stuffed them into the bottom of the holdall. As luck would have it, there were more than enough of them to cover the porno mags and ancient, dog-eared packet of condoms he had remembered to take from the drawer in the bedside table. They in turn had reminded him of the knobbly monstrosities in the bread-bin which Sam had brought back from a holiday in Amsterdam, and which he occasionally took out as a conversational gambit when after-hours drinking sessions started to flag. Their popularity had been waning of late, and now seemed as good a time as any to be rid of them. He made a mental note to lose them, and the magazines, and the holey underwear, in a litterbin at the first service station he came to on his journey. In the meantime, he stuffed them into the bottom of the holdall.

It was then that he remembered the playing cards with naked women on them that he had bought as a spotty fourteen-year-old on a school trip to Brighton. After a frantic search, he found them under an old gym bag in the bottom of the wardrobe. He wrapped them in a pair of tatty socks, and hid them in the holdall under the magazines. Then he went quickly back through the house, checking that he hadn't left anything else of an incriminating nature for Amy to find. On his way through the sitting room, he stopped to say goodbye to Spike, who showed not the slightest sign of regret at his imminent departure. On the contrary, he lifted his tail in a gesture of disdain and strode haughtily over to his basket to lie down.

'Rather you than me, mate,' said Henry. 'Probably have you picking your hairs off the carpet by lunchtime.'

As he was passing through the kitchen, on his way to check that the backdoor was locked and bolted, his eyes widened in horror when he glanced at the sink and saw that it was piled high with washing-up, some of it dating back a couple of weeks. He realized that there wasn't time for him to clear it away completely, but he thought that he might reduce it to a less offensive level if he was quick. He picked up the dishcloth, turned on the hot tap, and remembered that he hadn't had any washing-up liquid for months. There weren't any alternatives left, either. He had used the last of the washing powder to remove the curry he and Sam had shared the Friday before last, and the bubble bath had gone the same way a week or two before that. He put down the dishcloth, turned off the hot tap, and looked at his watch. It was 9.39, and already too late to go to the corner shop to buy washing-up liquid, if he was going to be out of the house before Amy arrived.

He decided to leave her a note of apology in the hope that she would have forgiven him for his slovenliness by the time he got back. Not that he was optimistic: the kitchen was just the tip of the iceberg. The bedroom still bore the scars of his early morning battle with Sam's singing alarm clock, the shattered remains of which were lying in a corner by the wall. And the bed was neither made nor as sweet smelling as he would have liked. Add to that the fact that clothing was strewn about the floor or draped over the furniture, and the wardrobe door was open revealing a jumbled mess of belongings he had made worse during his search for the playing cards. The bedside table was littered with a variety of oddments, including a collection of fluff-encrusted cough sweets and a packet of rubbery biscuits. There was a coffee mug containing a growth that looked as if it might be in the process of developing antibiotic properties, and a litter of paperbacks, newspapers and magazines flowing over and around the wastebasket and under the bed. It wasn't just the bedroom that bore witness to his obvious lack of domesticity, either: the rest of the house was just as bad. He had been so busy making sure that he wasn't leaving anything of an incriminating nature for Amy to find, that he hadn't even noticed how dishevelled and unloved the place looked.

He checked his watch again. It was 9.45: just enough time, he told himself, to get out of the way before she arrived. Whatever he hadn't managed to tidy-up, or hide, or take with him would have to stay where it was and, in the fullness of time, bear witness against him.

He checked to make sure that he had his keys, his wallet, his glasses case, and the headache pills he knew he was going to need during the drive. Then he picked up the holdall, his camera case, and his overnight bag, and staggered as fast as his legs would carry him to the front door. There was no time to lose, because Amy was the sort of swot who would always be on time. Worse still, she was just as likely to be early!

He opened the door and looked around to make sure that he wasn't being watched as he slipped the keys under the boot-scraper. Then, satisfied that he had done all that was humanly possible to protect what was left of his good name, he closed the door, picked up his belongings and hurried down the path to the front gate.

Dolly and the others arrived at the end of the road just as he was putting the last of his luggage into the boot of his car.

'Wait!' said Dolly, taking hold of Curly's wrist in a grip of steel and forcing him to slow down. 'It's him! Pull in!' She pointed at the curb, and glanced over her shoulder to make sure that Bonce was doing the same. She turned back and peered across the road. 'Yeah, green Volvo. That's him!'

Curly stopped the car, and opened the door.

Dolly grabbed his arm. 'No!' she hissed. 'Not here!'

Curly frowned.

'Too risky,' she said. 'Stay put!' She opened the passenger door and scuttled, hunched forward, back along the pavement to the other car.

Vinny saw her coming and wound down the window. 'What's up?' he asked as she crouched by the door.

She ignored him and pointed at Beth on the back seat. 'You,' she hissed, jerking her thumb at the other car. 'In there! Now!'

Beth folded her arms and looked away.

Dolly clicked her tongue. 'OK,' she said to Vinny, 'she's all yours.'

'OK! OK!' said Beth, opening the door and starting to get out. 'I'm going! Don't get your knickers in a . . .!'

'Not *that* way!' snapped Dolly. 'He'll see you! *This* side! You stupid cow!'

Nobbler pressed himself back against the seat as Beth climbed over him, kneeing him in the groin as she went.

Dolly grabbed her by the hair and pulled her out on to the pavement, holding her head down. 'With Curly!' she hissed. 'If Kite sees you you're dead! You,' she added, looking at Vinny but pointing at Henry's Volvo, 'follow him! Get the gear off him soon as you can. No rough stuff, mind, unless you have to. We don't want a bleeding audience. Understand?'

Vinny bared his teeth in a wolfish grin.

'I mean it,' she hissed. 'I won't be happy if you bring the law down on us.' She glanced at Bonce. 'That means you an' all! OK?'

Bonce nodded, glumly.

'Right,' she said, 'if you get him somewhere quiet, do him.'

Vinny nodded.

Dolly looked across at Henry's Volvo. 'OK,' she said, 'he's leaving. Me and Curly'll stay and search the house. If we find the stuff, I'll give you a bell. If he starts coming back let me know.'

Vinny nodded again.

'And Vinny,' she added, coldly, 'don't piss about.'

She looked at Bonce. 'Make sure he behaves!'

As Henry's Volvo pulled away from the curb, Bonce slipped the clutch and pulled out to follow him at a safe distance.

Dolly stood up and walked back to the convertible, tapping on the window and motioning for Curly to get out. 'OK, let's do it,' she said. 'You two,' she added, jerking a thumb at Vicky and Beth, 'out! And don't even think about trying to get away. I ain't in the mood!'

At the end of the street, a man in a black silk shirt and black leather jeans watched from the driver's seat of a metallic black Range Rover as Dolly, Curly and the girls crossed the road and went in through Henry's front gate. As they walked up the path towards the front door, he spoke quietly into a remarkably small, remarkably slim mobile phone.

'He's just left,' he said, as he put the car into gear and released the handbrake. 'Hang on a minute,' he added, pulling slowly away from the curb as Curly forced open Henry's front door. 'She's here with her muscle and the girls,' he said. 'They're just going in, and I'm on my way.' He listened briefly. 'Yeah, catch you later.'

He tossed the little phone onto the passenger seat, reached forward and pressed the play button on the car stereo, grinning broadly as the muffled roar of the car's exhaust was joined by the spiky opening bars of Steppenwolf's *Born to be Wild*. As he turned at the end of the road, he took out a stick of chewing gum and folded it into his mouth.

'*Yeahhhh*,' he breathed, tapping his gloved fingers on the steering wheel and thrusting his head backwards and forwards in time to the music. '*Get yer mo-tor run-nin'! Earn-ah-earn-ah-uh-uh! Head out on the high-way! Nurn-ah-nurn-ah-nuh-nuh! Lookin' for ad-ven-turrrre . . . in whatever comes ourrrr wayyyyy!*'

12

VINNY TRASHMAN

The atmosphere in the big black Mercedes started to deteriorate almost as soon as they set off in pursuit of Henry's Volvo. The heating system jammed itself on, and in spite of Vinny's best efforts to club it into submission with the butt of his machine pistol, refused to do anything but blast them with a suffocating mix of hot air and diesel fumes. As if that wasn't bad enough, Nobbler developed a serious attack of the farts, and his foetid output, caused he said, by too much excitement and the Indian takeaway they had made him eat the night before, soon made the air in the car un-breathable. Bonce wound down a window to get some relief from the stench, but the wind-chill factor of the air whistling into the car as they sped along would have challenged a polar bear to keep warm. They were soon shivering like cats in a freezer.

Vinny was furious and all for pushing Nobbler out of the car. 'Pull in there!' he urged, tugging at Bonce's sleeve. 'Chuck the little shit-arse out!'

Bonce shrugged him off as the big car swerved and narrowly missed a group of startled pensioners gathered at the pavement's edge lamenting the perils of pedestrian life. As the Mercedes sped away into the distance, it was with mixed feelings that they shook their fists after it and cursed in morbid relief. On the one hand, they were pleased that the day was living up to their gloomy expectations of life as a senior citizen. On the other, they were disappointed that at least one of their number wasn't lying bloody and dying at the side of the road. They wouldn't be telling a harrowing tale on the *Six O'clock News*, after all, and the knowledge that two of them had pissed in their pants was scant consolation for missing out on their fifteen minutes of fame.

What little there was of Bonce's hair stood on end as the big car swerved off down the road with Vinny cursing and tugging at his sleeve. And things didn't get any easier when Vinny tried to clamber over the passenger seat to get at Nobbler cowering and farting in the back. With a knee in his ribs and the stench of diesel and undigested curry making his eyes water, Bonce was having a hard time of it keeping the Mercedes from mowing down a sizeable chunk of the population. He was worried about what would happen to the car if he hit someone, and terrified of what Dolly would say to him if he ran too many people over without her permission. Car chases weren't really his speciality and he had no idea if he was doing it right. For instance, how was he supposed to know if he was keeping the sort of distance behind Henry's Volvo that Dolly would approve of? It wasn't easy trying to work out what Dolly would approve of, and the trouble with trying was that if you got it wrong she was likely to turn up with someone several sock-sizes bigger than you were and have them squeeze your bollocks until you'd had enough of it. Or, more to the point, until Dolly had had enough of it: which wasn't usually the same thing at all. The only thing you could be certain of was that it would be as uncomfortable as Dolly thought it needed to be, and that, no matter how uncomfortable that might be, it would be more than uncomfortable enough for anyone who wasn't already dead. Bonce had seen the effects at close quarters and didn't like the thought of it happening to him. Doubly so because anyone several sock-sizes bigger than he was would be unlikely to know his own strength and inflict a good deal more discomfort than was really needed. He had done it himself often enough, making people's eyes water when all he had meant to do was make them grit their teeth. Dolly was always very tolerant on such occasions, and as long as her victims didn't start passing out before she had finished leering into their faces and threatening them with Vinny's flick-knife, she didn't seem to mind how much discomfort they felt: just so long as it was more than enough. But you had to be careful because she much preferred taking her pound of flesh from people who weren't too comatose or too dead to appreciate the subtleties of its removal. Appreciation was very important to Dolly, and anyone who didn't show her enough of it was inclined to end up embedded in reinforced concrete with something small and bullet-shaped lodged in their brain. Although not before she had taken the time to explain to them exactly what was coming, who was going to give it to them, which part of their anatomy was going to get it, and how much of a mess they were likely to make of their underpants in the meantime.

But it wasn't the physical violence that Bonce was afraid of – he could take as much of that as anyone cared to dish out – it was the psychological torture that terrified him. That and the tricky questions that Dolly always wanted to ask. People had been subjecting him to physical violence for as long as he could remember, and as far as he could tell it had never done him any harm. But tricky questions were a different matter, because, try as he might, he had never learned how to come up with the right answers.

'Hey, thick 'ead!' his third father in as many years had yelled at him one day when he was seven years old, 'why don't you get lost, ye little arsewipe?'

'Don't know how,' Bonce had admitted through the gathering tears and the bubbling snot. 'No-one learned me.'

His third father had grinned and whacked him around the head to learn him. It had helped. It had helped him to learn that telling the truth wasn't such a good idea if you were smaller than whoever was asking the questions.

The next time his third father had told him to get lost he had smiled and run away as fast as his sturdy little legs would carry him.

After the police had found him and taken him home the following day, his third father had asked him another tricky question. 'You tryin' to be funny or what?' he had demanded.

'Yes,' Bonce had replied, thinking to be ahead of the game.

'That supposed to be some kinda joke?' his third father had asked, whacking him around the head twice – once for trying to be funny and once for taking the piss. 'That'll learn ya,' he had promised, 'ya little dickwad!'

It had been a red-letter day for Bonce, because it had taught him that asking tricky questions was a lot more fun than trying to answer them. It had also taught him that the one who did the whacking usually felt a lot better about things than the one who got whacked. From that moment on, he had decided to dedicate the rest of his life to asking tricky questions and to whacking anyone who couldn't come up with the right answers.

'Hey, thick 'ead,' he'd asked his friend, Gizmo Real, the following day. 'Is that there your dog?'

'Yeah,' Gizmo had nodded. 'Tha's Buster, that is.'

Bonce had frowned. 'No,' he'd explained, 'you're s'posed to say he ain't.'

Gizmo had grinned, uncertainly. 'What,' he'd asked, 'is it some kinda joke?'

Bonce had shied away. 'You ain't gonna whack me, are ya?' he'd asked.

Gizmo had frowned in confusion. The idea of hitting Bonce, who was a head taller and at least a stone heavier, had never occurred to him. 'It's a joke, that, then, innit?' he'd asked.

'Bugger!' Bonce had muttered. 'I was s'posed to say that!'

Gizmo had giggled. 'You're takin' the piss, right?'

'Bugger!' Bonce had cursed. 'Bugger an' bloody buggerin' damn!'

'What?' Gizmo had asked in confusion – all he'd wanted was to be friends.

'You're s'posed to say no,' Bonce had insisted.

'No, what?'

'He ain't your dog.'

'Who ain't?'

'He ain't!'

'Him?'

'Yeah.'

'Tha's Buster, that is.'

'I know that, don't I?'

'What?'

'Say he ain't your dog.'

'He ain't my dog.'

'Yes, he bleedin' is!' Bonce had crowed, triumphant at last.

Gizmo had thought about it. 'Yeah,' he'd admitted, 'he is.'

Bonce had clenched his fists and stamped his foot. 'No he bleedin' *ain't!*'

'No,' Gizmo's dad had agreed, coming up behind him. "E's mine, ya little arsewipe! So you can piss off for a start!'

'No,' Bonce had insisted, earnestly. 'You're s'posed to say he ain't.'

Gizmo's dad had said 'bollocks' instead and whacked Bonce around the head for taking the piss.

Bonce had given up trying to ask tricky questions after that.

Then one day, about ten years later, he and Gizmo were standing together in the saloon bar of the Strugglers' Arms when Dolly Killjoy walked in and ordered a pint and a packet of crisps.

Gizmo took one look at her and snorted: 'Christ, what a dog! Ol' Buster would've fancied that one, I reckon, don't you?'

Dolly looked sideways at Bonce. 'Is he taking the piss? Your mate?'

Bonce flinched at the prospect of being whacked by a woman.

Gizmo grinned, and nudged him in the ribs. 'No, darlin'! *Woof, woof!*'

Dolly raised an eyebrow at Bonce. 'I think he is, don't you?'

Bonce shrugged uncomfortably and looked down at his hands.

'Needs a good smacking,' Dolly added, 'you ask me. No way to talk to a lady, that, is it? Trying to be funny and taking the piss?'

It took Bonce only a second to come up with the right answer. He grabbed the back of Gizmo's neck and smashed his face down on to the bar.

By the time Gizmo was allowed out of hospital, with his ear sown back on and his jaw wired shut, Bonce had been a member of Dolly's gang for almost a month. She told him when people were trying to be funny and when they were taking the piss. She told him when to whack them and when to squeeze their bollocks. He did as he was told because he didn't have to think about it, and because Dolly paid him pocketsful of money and let him ride around in her beautiful cars. But working for her had its drawbacks. There was an edge to her tongue sometimes that was a lot sharper and more deeply cutting than the blade of any flick-knife. When she wasn't around to tell him what to do, he had to decide for himself, and he still wasn't very good at that sort of thing. Trying to be good at it always made him anxious. And when he was anxious he worried even more about what Dolly would say to him when she found out about all the things he had done wrong.

He was anxious now as he tried to work out if he was close enough to Henry's car not to lose him, or so close that he would realize that he was being followed and try to get away. To add to his misery, Dolly had told him to keep an eye on Vinny and make sure that he didn't do anything stupid, like killing that Henry Kite bloke in public. The trouble was that keeping an eye on a psychopath like Vinny wasn't easy. Especially when you didn't know what a psychopath was.

'He's a malignant little sod, though, isn't he?' Dolly had said admiringly the first time she had seen him in action. 'Could use a nasty little shit like him in my lot,' she'd added, as she'd watched him grind his crepe-soled heel into the face of some unfortunate hippy. 'Got a nice little arse on him, too!'

Then there was Nobbler to be looked after. And Bonce definitely had mixed emotions about doing that. On the one hand, he felt a certain kinship with the shabby little man after having spent such an agreeable time in the garden shed squeezing his bollocks. On the other, he wished he would shut up and stop trying to be friends. Bonce never liked being friends with people whose bollocks Dolly had told him to crush – it wasn't professional. But Dolly had told him to look after the little sod, so what choice did he have?

He sighed inwardly at the weight of responsibility that Dolly had heaped on his shoulders, and hoped that he would be strong enough to bear it. He hoped even more that Vinny wouldn't cut Nobbler's throat before they got to wherever it was they were going. Dolly loved the big black saloon almost as much as she loved the yellow convertible, and he hated to think what she would say to him if he allowed Nobbler to bleed all over its expensive interior.

Vinny had no such reservations. One the contrary, he reckoned that bleeding was the only thing that Nobbler was any good for. The snot-nosed little bastard had been listening when Dolly had told Bonce to keep an eye on them both. Up until that moment, he had been enjoying having a new and impressionable gang member to show off in front of. But Dolly had put an end to that, and every time he looked at Nobbler's stupidly grinning face he was reminded of the fact. He was desperate to regain his place in the gang's hierarchy, and wiping the smile off of Nobbler's gormless face would be as good a way of doing it as any he could think of. The trouble was that every time he saw a perfectly good reason for chopping Nobbler into little chunks of dog meat, Bonce got all defensive about it and told him to stop.

'Who the hell's he think he is anyhow?' Vinny muttered to himself as he sat hunched up on the front seat. 'No way I'm takin' orders from that stupid sod!' The thought cheered him up, and he set to pondering the best way of filleting a live Nobbler, because filleting a dead one would be no fun at all.

If Nobbler had known what was going through Vinny's mind, he would have jumped out of the car without having to be pushed. Instead, he sat unhappily on the back seat, fidgeting, trying not to fart, and hoping that the others would eventually accept him into the gang and let him be friends. He had always wanted to be a part of somebody's gang, and this one looked like being a better bet than any of the others he'd wanted to join. For one thing, it had half the police forces in the country chasing after it. That was something for a bloke to be proud of, he reckoned, and just the sort of thing he could boast about to his friends. Not that he had many of those. For as long as he could remember he had wanted to belong somewhere and have someone let him join in with all the important and exciting things they were doing. Then again, at that moment, he would have been more than happy to settle for someone letting him get out of the car for a shit.

'Do it in your hands!' snapped Vinny, turning to point a finger at the little man's face. 'Just don't wipe it on the friggin' seats, that's all!'

Bonce glanced nervously at Vinny, horrified at the thought of what Dolly would say if someone wiped *that* on the upholstery of her beautiful car.

'It's not toilet paper, that, you know, birdbrain!' he could hear her saying. 'That's leather, that is! Or can't morons like you tell the difference?'

When Henry turned south onto the A12, Vinny decided that it was time for him to take control of the chase. 'Brentwood!' he said, suddenly.

Bonce frowned. 'Eh?'

Vinny turned in his seat and clicked his fingers at Nobbler. 'He's goin' to Brentwood,' he said. 'You'll see I'm right.' He turned back to Bonce and tapped the steering wheel. 'Watch him! He'll try an' lose us at the turnoff.'

Bonce was hurt. 'He don't know we're 'ere.'

Vinny grinned at Nobbler. 'Yeah?' he said. 'That's what he thinks, innit?'

Nobbler tried to grin through the pain of his tightly clamped arse. 'That's what you think,' he told Bonce, tapping him on the shoulder. 'Innit?' He smiled: this was just the kind of friendly banter he had always imagined himself getting involved in when he was part of a gang.

Bonce eyed him in the rear-view mirror. 'Is he takin' the piss?'

Vinny's mobile phone chose that moment to ring.

Nobbler flinched and squirted something hot and sticky into his Y-fronts.

'Bugger!' he moaned. 'Sod, an' buggerin' damn!'

'It's only me bleedin' mobile,' sneered Vinny, leaning over and snatching it from the back seat. 'Ain't you ever seen one before?'

He sat back in the passenger seat with the phone to his ear. He liked to flash around so that people would know what an important person he was. The fact that it was about as mobile as a house brick, and in most parts of the country, about as useful as a piece of string with a tin tied at each end, didn't seem to bother him at all. It was a status symbol, like his bone-handled flick-knife, his ruffle-fronted shirt and his bootlace tie, his drape jacket, his drainpipe trousers, and his crepe-soled, blue suede shoes. Although precisely what status along the evolutionary road towards Homo sapiens he thought they gave him wasn't always easy to fathom.

'It's not here,' said Dolly on the other end of the line, as she stood in Henry's bedroom with the contents of his chest of drawers scattered at her feet. 'Unless he's stashed it in the garden, or, I dunno, somewhere. Curly's outside checking the bushes and stuff. Where's Kite?'

'Goin' to Brentwood,' said Vinny, wrinkling his nose at a new and more pungent odour wafting through the car. 'I'll bell ya when he gets there, OK?'

Bonce frowned when Henry drove past the turning for Brentwood without so much as a glance at the slip road.

'No he ain't,' he said. 'Not goin' to Brentwood, he ain't.'

'Who said 'e was, eh?' sniggered Nobbler, who had taken off his sweater and his shirt and was fumbling with the fly of his jeans. 'Who said . . .?'

'Shut it!' snapped Vinny, turning and pointing a warning finger at his face.

'I was only sayin',' said Nobbler, pulling the sweater back over his head.

Vinny sniffed. 'Listen, if you've shit . . .'

Nobbler shook his head, vigorously. 'No! No! I was jus' . . .'

'What the bleedin' hell's that, then?' demanded Vinny, pointing at the bulge in the seat of the little man's jeans.

His phone rang again. He ignored it.

'I's yer phone, innit?' said Nobbler, grateful for any distraction.

'What of it?'

'Ringin', innit?' he said, squirming on the lump of the shirt stuffed down the back of his jeans.

'I'm warnin' you. If you've shit . . .?'

'She won't like it,' said Bonce. 'Dolly won't. You don't answer . . .'

She was standing at Henry's front door with Curly and the girls when Vinny picked up his phone. 'We're leaving,' she said. 'Where's Kite?'

'Goin' into town,' he said. 'I'll give you a bell when he gets there.'

'What happened to Brentwood?'

'Bonce screwed up,' said Vinny. 'Bell ya later.' He hung up.

Dolly stared at the phone for a moment, but decided to leave it at that. 'All right,' she said to Vicky and Beth, 'get moving.'

They were on their way out of the house when Curly noticed a young woman coming in at the front gate. 'Doll!' he hissed out of the corner of his mouth as they walked down the path towards her, 'What're we . . .?'

Dolly waved him to silence. 'Do as I tell ya,' she warned the girls in a hissing whisper, 'or I'll kill your mummies, your daddies, your dogs, your cats and your soddin' budgies! You got that?'

Amy was running late. She'd been stuck in traffic for more than an hour on her way to the house, and was feeling guilty about it.

'Hello,' she said, as she stood aside for Dolly, Curly and the girls on the path. 'I don't think anyone's in. Can I help you, at all?'

'Just got to get these two back home, lovie, that's all,' said Dolly. 'Their mummies have been worrying themselves sick.'

She turned to the girls. 'How many times have I told you to tell your mummy when you're going to stay out all night, Victoria, eh?'

Amy frowned: first at the girls and then at the house. 'Sorry?' she said, reaching for Dolly's arm. 'Are you saying they've been . . .?'

Curly stepped forward and pushed her hand away. 'Leave it out, darlin'!'

'Now, now Rowland, darling,' said Dolly in her best housewifely voice. 'There's no need to get carried away, is there? The young lady was only asking a simple question.' She turned to Amy. 'Weren't you, lovie?'

Curly's eyes widened in alarm at the thought that he was Dolly's 'darling'.

Dolly stared at him, stonily, waiting for him to say something helpful.

'Oh, yeah, right, er . . . Dorothy,' he said, suddenly aware that his continued good health was on the line. 'Yeah, right, sorry an' all that,' he blushed beetroot red, 'er, Doll . . . Dorothy . . . er, darlin'.'

Dolly smiled at Amy. 'Take no notice, lovie, he's just a bit tetchy, that's all. Been up all night chasing after these two again, see?' She shook her head at the girls. 'Your mummy's upset, too, Elizabeth. You should be ashamed!'

Amy was baffled. 'Sorry, but did you say . . . *again*?'

'You know what they're like at that age,' said Dolly. 'Once they get it into their heads to fancy a bloke there's no stopping 'em, is there?'

'No!' said Beth, suddenly. 'We've been kid . . .!'

Dolly dug her fingernails into her wrist. 'Now don't go telling fibs again, Elizabeth!' she warned. 'Remember your poor mummy and daddy, back home. You know how they worry about you, don't you? And Vinny? Don't forget about poor little Vinny, lovie. He's very upset, too.' She turned to Amy and smiled. 'Her little brother, Vincent,' she explained. 'Worries himself sick when she goes off without him.' She pushed Beth out into the street. 'And you, Victoria. Auntie Dolly's takin' you home now, too. So come along, both of you, and don't dawdle. We haven't got all day!'

Amy stood for a moment, looking from the house to the girls and back again. 'You mean,' she asked, uncertainly, 'they've been in there . . . *all night*?'

Dolly turned as she and Curly pushed the girls along the pavement towards the car. 'You know how it is?' she called as they crossed the road. 'They'll do anything at that age, won't they? And they never think about the dangers, do they? The clap, aids, rape: all that? All they think about is the money, lovie, isn't it? Makes you wonder about the men, though, doesn't it? I mean, look at 'em, for Christ's sake! No more than a couple of kids.'

Amy looked at the girls as Curly opened the car door and ushered them onto the back seat. 'Money?' she said, weakly. 'But . . .?'

'Not your problem though, is it, lovie?' said Dolly. 'Have a nice day,' she added as she got into the car and slammed the passenger door.

Amy stood perfectly still and watched in dumbfounded silence as the car drove away. Then her face stiffened into a scowl, and she turned and strode purposefully up the garden path towards the front door.

* * *

'You randy ol' bugger!' said Titus. 'It's always the quiet ones, innit?'

'Sorry?' said Henry. 'What are we talking about now?'

Titus gave him a knowing wink and leaned forward in his seat. 'You and the lov-el-ly E-liz-a-beth,' he said, rolling each syllable around his tongue like a lecherous gourmet, 'and the de-li-ci-ous Vic-tor-ria!' He leaned further forward and lowered his voice. 'Come on then, tell us, what were they like?'

'I don't know. I've never met them.'

'That's what they all say, buddy!'

'Yeah? Well, sorry to disappoint you, but in my case it's true.'

Titus pointed at the hooded figure. 'That's not what he said.'

'Yes, it is. You just weren't listening.'

'I heard enough,' said Titus, pointing at him with a pencil. 'Don't you worry 'bout that! Anyhow,' he added, looking down at the notebook in his lap, 'some of us 'ave got more important things t' do.'

'Really?' said Henry. 'Like what?'

'Wouldn't you like to know?'

'Probably not,' said Henry, turning to the hooded figure. 'Sorry, what were you were saying about . . .?'

'All right!' said Titus. 'I'll tell ya! Jus' don't keep goin' on about it, that's all!'

'I wasn't,' said Henry. He glanced at the hooded figure. 'Neither was he.'

'You wanted to, though, didn't ya? I could tell.'

'You've been sitting in the sun for too long,' said Henry. 'Your brain's starting to get frazzled.'

'Yeah, well, that's what 'appens to people . . . when they're in love.'

'In love! You?'

'What's so funny 'bout that?'

'Nothing! It's just that I never thought of you as romantic, that's all. Lots of other things, yes – sexist, racist, and maybe a bit psychopathic – but definitely *not* romantic! Still, we all live and learn, don't we? So,' he spread his arms wide, 'who's the lucky girl, then? Anyone we know?'

Titus tapped the side of his nose and held up the notebook. 'Bet you wanna know what this is, don't ya?'

'I doubt it,' said Henry. 'Knowing you, it'll be something disgusting.'

'OK, I'll tell ya. It's for her.'

'Is it really?'

'It's a wosname.'

'What . . . a begging letter, a ransom note, a final demand?'

Titus turned to the figure. 'What's he so bitter and twisted about?'

'You really *haven't* been listening, have you?'

'He needs a good slappin', you ask me.'

'Perhaps so,' hissed the figure. 'But I would be grateful if you would refrain from giving it to him until after we have finished his story.'

Titus stared hard at Henry. 'It's a ode, if you must know,' he said, tartly. His face fell as he looked down at the notebook. 'Only it ain't goin' so well.'

'You surprise me,' said Henry. 'I wouldn't have thought a silky-tongued ladies' man like you would've had too much difficulty coming up with something to whet the poor girl's appetite.'

'Leave it out! We've only just met!'

'Sorry? What're you . . .?'

'Muff-divin', buddy,' said Titus, with a click of the tongue. 'Try an' keep up!' He tucked the pencil behind his ear. 'I mean, I'm not gonna . . . y'know, am I, with some tart I've only just met? What kinda bloke d'you think I am?' His face lit up, suddenly. 'Mind you, after five minutes with ol' love-'em-an'-leave-'em Andronicus, they can't get enough, can they? So who knows?'

'Would I be correct in assuming,' asked Henry, 'that "muff diving", as you put it so quaintly, is what we grown-ups would call . . .?'

'*Eh-hem!*' coughed the figure.

Titus winked at Henry and leaned towards him. 'Do owls shit in the trees, buddy?' he asked. 'An' there's no need to get all hoity-toity about it with me, mate! Anyone can do it if he's got the right equipment, can't he?' He took the pencil from behind his ear and slurped at the end of it with his tongue.

'Oh, God!' groaned Henry, his body shuddering as his imagination tried desperately to rid itself of the unwelcome mental image that had suddenly been planted in the fertile compost of his brain. He closed his eyes, and his whole body shivered, as if an icicle had just slid down his spine.

Titus watched him for a moment before turning to the hooded figure. 'You sure he ain't some kinda poofter?'

Henry took a deep breath and opened his eyes. 'OK, look, can we get this over with, please? Just tell us who, *exactly*, you think you're in love with.'

Titus jerked the pencil up at the sky.

'What? You're in love with a cloud?'

Titus shook his head.

'The goddess of rainbows, thunder and lightning, April showers . . .?'

His sarcasm was wasted on the superstitious little Ancient Briton, who shook his head and jerked the pencil ever more vigorously up at the sky.

Henry sighed. 'I give up! If it isn't some sort of . . . ' He hesitated, and thought for a moment. 'You don't . . . you don't mean the lieutenant, by any chance . . . do you?'

A huge grin spread across Titus's face.

'You *do* mean the lieutenant!'

Titus puffed out his chest. 'The colonel introduced us.' He jerked a thumb over his shoulder. 'I was over the bog for a shit.'

'So much for romance!' muttered Henry. He thought for a moment. 'So you met her, then, did you?'

Titus nodded.

'Face to face?'

'On the . . . wosname?'

'The way to the bog?'

Titus shook his head.

'The way *back* from the bog?'

Titus shook his head, again.

'Bloody hell!' thought Henry. 'I'm playing Twenty Questions with Boudicca's idiot cousin at Stonehenge!'

'He means the communicator,' said the hooded figure.

Titus smiled, and nodded. 'What he jus' said, then!'

'OK,' said Henry. 'And . . . so . . . what did you say to her, exactly?'

'Asked for a date, didn't I?' smirked Titus.

'Excellent,' said Henry. 'A bit surreal,' he added under his breath, 'but so what? And, er,' he asked out loud, 'what did *she* say to *you*?'

'1815 is one of her favourites,' said Titus, uncertainly.

Henry thought about that for a second or two, trying hard not to laugh, nodding with his jaws clamped shut and his lips puckered against his teeth. 'Unh-huh!' he murmured, looking anywhere but at Titus' expectant face.

'So,' asked the little Celt, staring at him intently, 'whaddaya reckon?'

Henry cleared his throat. 'Well, I . . . *eh-hem*! I think that's . . . really,' he clenched his fists and hunched forward, 'really . . . *well done*!'

'Yeah,' said Titus, his face lighting up with a toothy grin. 'Yeah, right!' He stood up with his arms held above his head and his fists clenched. 'That Cartamandua can go shag herself now, can't she? Ol' Titus has pulled!'

'Absolutely,' blurted Henry. He took a deep breath. 'And er, . . . and what did you say to her? The . . . um, the lieutenant, I mean?'

'Let's go for it babes!' said Titus. 'Pretty cool, eh?'

Henry nodded with his teeth clenched and his arms gripping his chest.

'What?'

Henry shook his head.

'What?'

'Well, er . . . nothing! Nothing at all, really! Only . . . only it didn't occur to you that she might have been playing a bit hard to get?'

Titus frowned. 'I got a date.'

'Yes of course you have. But you don't actually know when it is, do you?'

Titus smiled and lowered his voice. 'I asked the colonel,' he said, tapping the side of his head.

'Good thinking! And he said . . .?'

'Seven hours an' fifteen minutes from now,' recited Titus. Then his face froze in the semblance of a smile and a hunted look came into his eyes. He drew back his left sleeve and looked down at a Rolex watch strapped to his wrist. 'Trouble is,' he said, tapping the watch face with a fingernail, 'this bleedin' thing don't work proper!'

Henry glanced at the hooded figure. 'Where did he get that?'

'Suite 218, 888 Brannan Street, San Francisco, CA,' replied Titus, without looking up. 'It says on the box.'

'You can read?' asked Henry.

Titus clicked his tongue. 'I was in the bleedin' Roman army, I was!'

'Yes, but . . . '

'And,' added Titus, rolling up his other sleeve to expose a band of symbols tattooed around his wrist, 'there's them.'

Henry gave the hooded figure another quizzical look.

'It will help to avoid confusion.'

'Really? So he can read, but he can't tell the time. Is that it? Sounds pretty confusing to me.'

'This bloody thing's broke,' said Titus, shaking his wrist and tapping the watch face with his fist.

'Come here,' commanded the figure.

Titus hesitated before getting up and walking reluctantly around the fire.

'Give me your hand.'

Titus glanced sideways at Henry.

'*Now!*' hissed the figure.

Titus flinched and thrust out his left arm.

'The other one . . . *idiot!*'

Titus thrust out his right arm.

The figure gripped it firmly and pulled it closer, pushing back the sleeves of the little man's shirt and jacket to reveal the tattoos on his wrist.

Titus closed his eyes and tried to lean backwards, curling his lip as if he thought he was about to be bitten.

'Now then,' murmured the figure, bending forward, 'what we need to do is that, that . . . that, that, and . . . *that!*' as it tapped the symbols in quick succession, turning Titus's wrist over and back again, before releasing it and leaning back in its chair. 'Look at it now!'

Titus opened his eyes and looked down at the watch.

When he looked up, he was wearing the widest grin Henry had ever seen.

'It's 11:34,' whispered Titus. 'I can tell time!'

He looked at the hooded figure. 'It's 11 . . .' he looked down. '*No!*' He hesitated, and corrected himself. 'It's . . . it's 11:35!'

He looked up at the sky. 'It's 11:35 . . . in the morning! 11:35am! 1135 hours, military time.' He grinned. 'An' I've got a date!'

He squinted into the distance, muttering. 'That's 1815 hours, military time.

That's . . . that's 6.15pm G.M.T.!' He thought for a moment. 'Tonight!'

'Yes,' said the figure, 'but you do realize that the lieutenant isn't . . . '

'English!' interrupted Henry.

The figure turned towards him. 'I was going to say human.'

'I'm not prejudiced,' said Titus. 'You can say what ya want!'

'But *she* is not really a *she*,' said the figure. 'At least, she is not a *human* she! *She* is a computer: an anthropomorphized machine: a digitally mapped computing device. *She* is a robot, an android, an automaton, a facsimile of humankind. *She* may *look* like a human female . . . '

This was too much for the translating device on Titus's wrist, which, having missed out on some of the most recent updates relating to gender stereotyping, advanced cybernetics and cutting edge marketing techniques, interpreted what the figure was saying as meaning 'Your new girlfriend is a cross-dressing, mixed-race, illegal immigrant, part accountant, part mathematician, part confidence trickster, who likes having sex with gorillas.'

'So what?' said Titus. 'If it's got two arms, two legs an' a wosname, I'll shag it!' He grinned and held up the Rolex. 'An' now I'll know when!'

'But . . . ' began the figure.

'Why not let him get on with it?' said Henry.

'Because the lieutenant is a robot.'

'He has an adventurous spirit, though, doesn't he?'

The cowled head swung slowly towards him. 'Your point being?'

'He has to find out sooner or later, doesn't he?'

The figure was silent for a moment. 'Find out what, exactly?'

'What his father could, and should, have told him if he had hung around long enough and hadn't been so busy beating up his mother and having sex with his sisters before he ran away to fight the Picts.'

'And you know those things to be facts, do you?'

'Come off it! You only have to look at him to see that!'

'You do?'

'Of course.'

'Really?'

Henry shrugged. 'OK, so he was talking to himself ten to the dozen when he thought the drones and the standing stones were coming to get him: praying to his gods to forgive him his sins and those of his family and friends. He went on and on about his father for God knows how long, and I thought,' he hesitated and pursed his lips, 'I thought . . . ' he took a deep breath, 'I thought it was really . . . *sad* . . . if you must know!' He cleared his throat. 'I'm surprised you didn't notice.'

'I didn't need to. I already knew. Indeed, there is very little that I do *not* know about our young friend's life. Or yours, for that matter.'

'Yes, well that's been obvious for a while, hasn't it? But what I really want to know is,' he pointed at Titus, 'why isn't he moving?'

'Ah,' said the figure, turning to look. 'That would be because he is temporarily outside of our time-stream. Displaced to one side, you might say.

I thought it best while we were discussing him. But he is quite safe and unharmed. In fact, he can't feel a thing. His metabolism has been slowed to such an extent that he is, well . . . *dead* is one way of putting it. *Not alive* is another. Either definition works well in this context, I find. Do you see?'

'No,' said Henry. 'How could I?'

'Quite. But the important thing to remember is that none of him can really be said to exist in this time or this place until I call him back to it.'

'Do you have to?'

'You think I shouldn't?'

'He looks happy enough.'

'That is because he has yet to discover that he is unlikely to make it to the Battle of Waterloo with the lieutenant!'

'He could if you let him.'

'Why would I want to do that?'

'Because, that way, everyone wins.'

'Including the lieutenant?'

Henry shrugged. 'She can look after herself, can't she?'

'Perhaps,' said the figure, thoughtfully, 'but it is essential that he should be present during the telling of your story.'

'All the time?'

'Time is relative.'

'You know what I mean.'

'Well,' said the figure, looking across at the little immobile Ancient Briton, 'he could catch up, I suppose, in his spare . . . while he is away. And he did seem to enjoy his stay in Tahiti, and only managed to get himself arrested twice for sexually harassing the locals . . .'

'Would they arrest him if he went back?'

'Oh, yes, definitely they would!'

'And could you get him out again if they did?'

'Of course,' said the figure, haughtily. It cocked its head to one side. 'Although, it might take me several hours to arrange it . . . don't you think?'

'In our timeframe, you mean?'

'In our timeframe, as you put it, yes.'

'And that would be good for his education, wouldn't it?'

The figure remained silent.

'That *is* the point of all these little trips he keeps making into the past and the future, isn't it?'

The figure inclined its head.

'And would he be back in time for his date with the lieutenant?'

'If that were thought to be desirable, yes! But don't you think that would be rather . . . unkind?'

'Would it?'

They looked at one another in silent contemplation for several seconds. Then the hooded figure raised its right hand. 'I have a better idea!'

'Hello, lover,' said a voice.

'Blossom?' said Henry, turning towards her.

Gone were the tattoos, the weapons and the tinkling gold jewellery. In their place were a pair of high-heeled purple ankle boots, a matching silk cat suit, brightly coloured plastic rings, bangles, hooped earrings and a necklace of chunky beads. Her hair had been cut expensively short and dyed a dusky shade of pink, and her makeup was characteristically excessive.

'Looking good,' she smiled, touching the collar of his shirt. 'Nice duds!'

Then to Henry's amazement, she bent at the knee in a gesture somewhere between a bow and a curtsey. 'Your choice, I assume, your grace?'

The figure inclined its head in acknowledgement. 'Blossom, my dear, thank you for coming at such short notice.'

'You look . . . different,' said Henry. 'But still very . . . er, nice.'

She grinned and dipped her head. 'Thanks,' she said. 'A lot of water under a lot of bridges, eh?' She frowned. 'Or maybe not, depending on where . . .?' Her eyes flicked across to the figure.

The figure shook its head, minutely.

Blossom nodded and turned back to Henry. 'Anyhow,' she smiled, 'you don't look too shabby yourself!'

'What was that all about?' asked Henry, suspiciously. 'That sly little look between you and . . .?'

He was interrupted by a thud and a rustling of papers as Titus stood up, knocked his chair over backwards, dropped the notebook and pencil on the ground and hurried forward. 'H-hello,' he stammered, stepping through the fire with a hand held out in greeting. 'I-I'm Titus. O-or Corio if . . .? We met over,' he pointed behind him. 'And you . . . We could . . . I'm . . .' He took a deep breath. 'You can call me anythin' you want!'

Blossom looked him over. 'I think I like Titus.'

He swallowed hard. 'Yeah! Yeah! Me too!'

'That's settled then,' said Henry.

'Not jealous, lover, are we?' Blossom chided. 'You know,' she added, leaning close and lowering her voice to a whisper, 'we could have had a wonderful time if they hadn't dragged me away.'

'I . . . We . . . Sorry?'

She turned to the hooded figure. 'Apologies, your grace. How can I help?'

'Our young friend here is about to take a short holiday, my dear,' hissed the figure. 'I am afraid that being with Henry and myself has quite worn the poor fellow out.'

'No,' said Titus, licking his lips and glancing from one to the other. 'I . . .!'

'And I was rather hoping that you would do me the courtesy of arranging it for him? And perhaps going along with him for the duration?'

Titus blinked as his mouth dropped open.

'No problem,' said Blossom. 'When would you like me to start?'

'It is said that there is no time like the present. As we both know, that is untrue, of course. But no matter: the poor lad is so exhausted that the sooner he gets away from our stifling influence the better, I think.'

The look in Titus's eyes became distant and glassy.

'Take him somewhere quiet,' added the figure, 'where he can spend some quality time on his own in contemplation away from . . . '

Titus frowned. 'No! Listen I don't . . .!'

'. . . the hustle and bustle of life to . . . '

'No? That's not . . .!'

'. . . catch up on some sleep, read a good book or two, find himself a new hobby. Preferably something educational and healthy, I think.'

'Yeah,' said Titus. 'Yeah, only . . . No! What I . . .'

'And don't let him overdo it, staying up late and eating and drinking too much. You know the sort of thing? Oh, and please make sure that he gets to bed early, and stays there. None of that sneaking off to the disco or the late night pictures when he thinks no one's looking. All right?'

'Yeah,' said Titus, turning pleading eyes on the figure, 'only I don't . . .!'

He was still trying to convince them that peace and quiet were not what he needed, when he and Blossom sizzled, shimmered, faded and vanished.

* * *

'You told a bad lie,' said Bonce. 'She won't like it, Dolly won't, she fines out.'

'Yeah?' sneered Vinny. 'Well who says she's gonna find out? Anyhow, she won't like it even more if *he* gets away, will she?' He pointed at Henry's Volvo. 'So I'd worry about *that*, if I was *you*!'

'He's alright,' said Bonce. 'I know where he is.'

'Yeah, well you bleedin' ought to! You're the bleedin' driver!' He leaned across until their faces were almost touching. 'So soddin'-well drive! I'll worry 'bout where he's goin'. I'm the bleedin', soddin' . . . wosname . . . I am!'

'Navigator,' said Nobbler, glancing up from his flies. 'Hey, can we . . .?'

'Shut it!' snapped Vinny. 'I know what it is!

Nobbler shrank away in alarm. The journey wasn't turning out to be the sort of friendly jaunt he had been hoping for. And the worst of it was that he had crapped in his pants, and although he had stuffed his shirt down the back of his jeans to soak it up, he had no idea what to do next.

'Who d'you think you're talkin' to, anyhow?' demanded Vinny. 'You're the bleedin' pain-in-the-arse, you are! The soddin' tart-in-the-tace! The shit-in-the-pants!' He raised his fist. 'So shut it, or else!

'Anyhow,' he added, turning to Bonce, 'I say where we go an' you do it!'

Bonce pointed at Henry's Volvo. 'What 'bout 'im then?'

'Funny,' said Vinny. 'Very bleedin' *funny*, I don't think!'

'Yeah,' said Bonce, after a pause, 'only he don't know we're 'ere.'

'Says who? He could 'ardly bleedin' miss us, could he? Stuck up his friggin' arse like a friggin' homo! Might as well stick up a bleedin' great sign!'

'Yeah,' sniggered Nobbler. 'Stick it up 'is bleedin' arse'ole an' . . .!'

'You're really gettin' on my tits, you are!' snapped Vinny. He pointed at Bonce. 'You're gettin' on *his* tits, an' all!'

'Dolly said watch 'im,' said Bonce.

'She didn't say give him a bleedin' push, though, did she?' sneered Vinny, turning and winking at Nobbler. 'Eh?'

'Yeah,' giggled Nobbler, feeling that perhaps they were all going to be friends, after all. 'She didn't say give 'im a push, did she? I didn't 'ear 'er . . . '

'For Christ's *sake*!' snarled Vinny, turning and glaring into the back of the car. 'Will you *shut* your soddin' cakehole for once?'

He turned away. 'Anyhow, he's goin' down town to flog it. You'll see.' He raised an eyebrow. 'Hatton Garden, I reckon.'

He changed his mind when Henry turned onto the M25. 'OK, so he's goin' south, down Dartford way, up the A2, through Cannin' Town an' . . . '

Henry turned north, not south, and Vinny changed his mind, again. They had been heading for the M11 all along, he told them. 'Roadworks on the A2, see? Heard it on the radio, las' night. He's goin' down the North Circular, right? Quicker that way, innit? Every other bugger'll be stuck 'ere, won't they?' He pointed at the queues of traffic on the opposite carriageway. 'See?' He nudged Bonce in the ribs, and turned to smile smugly at Nobbler.

It didn't last. 'The bastard's goin' north!' he said, when Henry ignored the turning for the M11. 'Up the A1!' His eyes narrowed. 'Or . . . or down Mill Hill. Down Edgeware Road. All them jewellers . . . '

'All them jewellers,' echoed Nobbler.

Bonce eyed him in the rear-view mirror. 'What's he know 'bout it?'

Vinny curled his lip. 'Naff all!'

When Henry left the M25 at Junction 23, Vinny nodded, knowingly. 'See? What'd I tell ya! Edgeware Road, innit?'

Nobbler tapped Bonce on the shoulder. 'All them jewellers, see?'

'Piss off!' said Bonce. 'Anyhow, he ain't.'

Vinny shrugged when Henry headed towards the service station slip road. 'So?' he said. 'South Mimms, innit?' Stoppin' for petrol an' a piss . . . '

'I wanna piss,' said Nobbler, who thought it best to understate his needs.

'Yeah?' said Vinny. 'You'll be lucky, mate! You'll 'ave a piss when I say you can 'ave a piss. An' you'll bleedin'-well like it, an' all!'

He picked up his phone. 'Gonna give Dolly a bell.'

Waiting in the service station car park, a man in a black Ford Cosworth took a sleek little mobile phone from a pocket and spoke into it as the gang's Mercedes drove past.

'Nils?' he said. 'Gary!'

He paused as the man in the black Range Rover cruised past, nodded in recognition and headed towards the exit.

Gary nodded in reply. 'Max is on his way home,' he said, as Bonce pulled the black saloon into a parking bay. 'Yeah. Yeah, right! OK, I'll take it from here. See you back at the ranch.'

13

SIR RICHARD

Sir Richard stood at the entrance to the company's offices shaking with suppressed fury and pointing at the car at the bottom of the steps. 'Posset!' he roared. 'What is the meaning of this?' When no answer came, he turned his head to one side, swivelled his eyes as far as they would go in the direction of the doors behind him and shouted 'Posset, you bastard! Get out here now!' Then, with the air of one accustomed to being obeyed, he turned his head back to its original position and waited, tapping his foot in time with his mounting frustration.

Ron Posset pushed through the double doors and ambled onto the paving at the top of the steps to stand with his hands thrust deep into his pockets, gazing at the back of his employer's head. 'What now,' he sighed, 'sir?'

Sir Richard's voice hissed in a venomous whisper. 'Is this supposed to be some kind of a joke, Posset?'

Ron shook his head. 'Does it look like I'm laughing?'

Sir Richard turned almost far enough to see his underling's face. 'What is that *thing*?' he demanded, pointing at the car.

Ron smiled to himself as he shuffled forward. 'Questions,' he sighed, 'always muckin' questions!' He stopped next to his boss, and for a moment they stood side-by-side looking down at the car at the bottom of the steps.

'Well,' he began, 'it's a . . . '

'No,' snapped Sir Richard, 'it's not *well*, Posset! Nothing is effing *well* about it! And if this isn't some kind of a *mucking* joke, you had better start looking for another *mucking* job!' He looked Ron in the eye. 'Do I make myself clear?'

'If it *is* a joke it's all right, though, is it?' asked Ron, without expression.

Sir Richard raised a warning finger. 'Don't push your luck!'

Ron pursed his lips. 'It's a car . . . '

'I said *don't*!'

Ron sighed. 'It's a Rover . . . '

Sir Richard's eyes narrowed. 'I know who made it, you moron!'

' . . . 2000 SE.'

'I don't give a monkey's left bollock what model it is! Just like I don't give a commie's tadger whether it's turbo-charged, fuel injected or wants to have your sodding babies! It's a Rover, mister, and I do not drive sodding *Rovers*!'

The morning was getting on, and he should have been on his way to Torquay by now in search of Charlotte Piece and what he hoped was going to be the dirtiest long weekend of his life. All he needed was for the surly pillock standing next to him to find a car appropriate to his stature as a knight of the realm and he would be on his way like the proverbial rat up a drainpipe. Charlotte had never shown the remotest interest in him before – not sexually, at least – but he had offered her two weeks holiday at his villa by the sea and she had jumped at the chance. He didn't know what had changed her mind, but he suspected that it had something to do with his masterful handling of the debacle with Minnowfield and Johnson the previous day. Or perhaps she was simply open to bribery. If so, it was a pity that he hadn't thought of using it on her earlier. But whatever the reason for her change of heart, she had apparently seen the error of her ways and was as desperate as he was to make up for lost time. He licked his lips at the prospect, and glanced anxiously at his watch. If he was going to get there ahead of her and prepare the ground for her arrival, he needed to get a move on. But he had no intention of arriving in anything less than the biggest, most impressive motor he could get his hands on, and the thing at the bottom of the steps wasn't that. His voice dropped to an ominous whisper again. 'Well,' he breathed, 'this had better be good!'

Ron sniffed. 'The Merc's knackered and won't be ready 'til tomorrow night, they said. The garage can't get the parts. Her Ladyship took the bum-wiper.' He nodded at the Rover. 'That's all they had left.'

Sir Richard's eyes widened. 'Knackered? Did you say . . . *knackered?*'

Ron nodded.

'And she's got the . . . *what?*'

'Bum-wiper.'

Sir Richard looked blank.

'B-M-W?' said Ron, carefully. 'Sorry, private joke!' He sniffed. 'Anyhow, her ladyship took it.' He smiled. 'She didn't happen to mention it, then?'

Sir Richard ignored the jibe and turned his attention back to the car at the foot of the steps. 'Can't get the . . .? It's the top of the sodding range, man! The single most expensive piece of automotive machinery the sodding Krauts have ever produced! Are you seriously trying to tell me that this . . . this *pile of crap* is the best you can come up with?'

'All be the same one day. Buy 'em out, the Germans will.'

Sir Richard turned disbelieving eyes towards him. 'Don't talk to me about corporate strategy, Posset. I don't give a tart's nipple about corporate strategy. Particularly a corporate strategy about which you know as much as that half-wit nephew of mine in there knows about the sodding clitoris! What I'm talking about here is quality. Have you any idea what would happen to it if I hit that *thing* along the wheel arches with a lump hammer? Well, *have* you?'

Ron shrugged and sucked his teeth.

Sir Richard held out his right hand, palm-up, and closed it into a tight fist. 'Crumple like tinfoil,' he sneered. 'Just like that!'

'Yeah,' agreed Ron, 'but if you hit a bum-wiper along the wheel arches it'd crumple, too, wouldn't it? Stands to reason . . .'

'Don't talk bloody daft man!'

'You hit it hard enough, even a Merc would . . .'

'Why?'

'What?'

'Who,' demanded Sir Richard with an index finger prodding at Ron's chest, 'in his right mind, would want to hit a Mercedes or a bum . . . ' he checked himself, 'a B-M-W along the wheel arches with anything! Eh?' He waved at the building behind him. 'Except one of those pathetic little envy-stripers Minnowfield mollycoddles in there!' He glared at Ron again. 'Well?'

Ron thought for a moment. 'I think . . . '

'Don't give me that! What I want is a decent sodding motor! And I do not now, and never did, give an angel's tit what *you* think!' He thrust his head forward until Ron could feel his breath on his face. 'Get me a decent set of wheels in fifteen minutes, buster, or you can kiss goodbye to your flat, your job and your sodding bollocks! Although not necessarily in that order! Do I make myself clear?'

Ron stared back at him, impassively. 'You do . . . *sir*!'

Sir Richard grunted. 'Fifteen minutes, or else!'

He pushed past Ron and strode into the building.

Ron allowed himself a half-smile as the doors banged shut behind him. 'Jolly good,' he said, quietly. 'So far, so jolly-well . . . lovely!'

At his flat on Chequers Road, Sam Johnson was doing his damnedest to keep out of trouble. Something violent was happening on the other side of the room, and he was trying hard to ignore it. He was still hung-over, and didn't feel that he had either the energy or the inclination for the sort of fight that seemed to be brewing around him. Besides, he'd already had a fight that morning, and felt that one-a-day was enough for any man.

'You stole that bracelet, didn't you?' Adams had sneered at him after Dolly and her gang had left the office. 'Telling them where Kite lives won't get you out of it, you know. Just wait 'til Uncle Richard hears about it, that's all!'

'Bracelet, necklace,' Sam had muttered, looking up from the magazine he'd been reading, 'who gives a toss? You know,' he'd added, putting the magazine down, 'you really ought to wash more often. That way there wouldn't be such a nasty smell about the place whenever you're around. Come to think of it, why don't you have a bath now?'

Minnowfield had been loitering near the reception desk, trying ineffectually to chat-up Suzie Bunt, when Sam had pushed his way through the doors to the main office with Adams slung over his shoulder in a sketchy fireman's lift and walked to the edge of the ornamental pool by the main entrance. He'd looked down into its gently lapping waters with Adams dangling over his back flailing his arms and legs about like a puppet with most of its strings cut.

'Ah! Umm . . . yes, umm . . . er, excuse me?' Minnowfield had called with a diffident impotence, holding out a limp hand in alarm. 'Excuse me, but don't you think . . .? Um, excuse me? Mr. Johnson? I really don't think this is the way to settle our differences, do you?'

Sam had turned and beamed at him. 'What do you reckon?' he'd asked. 'A triple somersault with full pike and tuck, or just chuck the little bugger in head first and let him get on with it?'

Without waiting for a reply, he'd nodded, said 'Yes, I thought so, too,' and heaved Adams, arms and legs jerking wildly, into the pool.

A lot of splashing, spluttering and waving of juvenile arms and legs had followed as Adams had tried desperately not to drown. He'd surfaced, slipped, done the splits and gone under again, before lurching to his feet to stand gasping for breath with his trousers around his ankles and a bit of plastic weed draped over one ear.

Sam had stepped back and rubbed his hands together in satisfaction. 'Well,' he'd smiled at Minnowfield, 'that's that then, isn't it? It was really nice knowing you, Clive old bean! And don't worry,' he'd added as he'd turned towards the main doors, 'I can find my own way out. Just stick the old P45 in the post for me, will you? Toodle-oo!'

He grinned at the memory, and tried to pretend that all hell wasn't breaking loose on the other side of his flat.

There was a loud thud and the sound of breaking glass, followed by another and another and another. He flinched, but kept his head down. There was another crash, followed by a stream of muttered invective. He realized that his sister's cursing was deliberately audible. But he was determined not to rise to the bait. The wisest thing he could do, he told himself, was stay quiet. The worst thing he could do was look up.

He looked up.

Amy was twenty feet away from him in the open plan kitchen with her body turned towards him and her head cocked to one side as she stared down at her feet like a hawk plotting the progress of a distant field mouse. The work surface beside her was cluttered with empty wine and beer bottles. Without looking at her brother, she turned and picked one up, raised it above her head and hurled it down at the floor.

Sam winced as he heard it smash. He couldn't see where it had landed because the kitchen units were in his way, but judging by the fact that broken glass hadn't scattered in all directions, he guessed that it was in the bottom of his flip-top bin.

The shattering of the bottle seemed to have a calming effect on his sister. She lowered her arms and let them hang limply at her sides for a moment. Then, after a few seconds, she straightened her shoulders, stuck out her chin and eyed the remaining bottles as if daring them to try to get away.

After another pause, she inhaled deeply through her nose and held her breath for a second or two before exhaling through her mouth and reaching for another bottle. She held it in the palm of her hand for a second or two, like a wine connoisseur examining the label. Then, apparently satisfied with what she saw, she cocked her head to one side, raised an enquiring eyebrow and pursed her lips tightly together. '*Un-grateful!*' she muttered, her face contorting into a snarl of aggression, '*bastards!*' she hissed, raising the bottle above her head and hurling it into the bin with a crash. '*Selfish!*' she hissed as she snatched up another bottle. 'They're all the frigging *same!*' She hurled the bottle into the bin with another crash. '*Men!*' she hissed, picking up another bottle and throwing it into the bin. 'Useless,' crash, '*bastards!*'

She was gathering speed now, snatching bottles from the work surface and hurling them into the bin. 'What bloody *good*,' crash, 'are they?' crash, 'That's,' crash, 'what *I'd*,' crash, crash, pause, crash, 'like to *know*! You offer to,' crash, '*help*,' crash, pause, crash, 'and what,' crash, 'do they,' crash, crash, '*do*?' pause, crash. '*Take*,' crash, '*ad-*,' crash, '*vant-*,' crash, '*age*!' crash. Pause. Crash, crash. '*That's*,' crash, '*what*!' crash, pause, crash, crash, crash!

Sam had to admit that her timing was very impressive. But he couldn't help wondering if she had given enough thought to the probable consequences of her actions. Had it occurred to her, he wondered, to consider what would happen to a plastic bin liner under such an assault? Was a flip-top bin filled with broken glass and the tattered remains of the bin liner really what she had set out to create? Had she thought about that aspect of it at all? Did she care? And in the unlikely event that the hapless bin liner managed to survive such a vicious onslaught intact, was she confident that it would be able to bear the weight of several dozen broken bottles without coming apart at the seams like damp tissue paper when some hapless someone tried to pull it out of the bin and carry it away?

It was while he was contemplating these and other technical problems, such as how he – for he it would certainly end up being – was going to get the dangerously sharp remains out of his bin, not to mention out of the flat, that he forgot to stop grinning to himself and look in some neutral direction. So it was that when Amy looked up, it was straight into his startled eyes.

'Well?' she snapped, with her fists bunched on her hips.

Sam's eyebrows shot up his forehead. 'What?'

'Haven't you got anything better to do?'

He couldn't remember if he had or not. So he gazed around the flat in the hope that some useful chore would present itself for his consideration.

It didn't.

Amy pointed at the crowd of empty bottles beside her. 'Well?' she demanded. 'What have you got to say for yourself?'

Sam shook his head dumbly, wondering why it was that he felt so guilty about a few empty bottles. Well, forty or so at the most, he told himself. After all, it was his flat, wasn't it, not hers? The trouble was that it had been like this ever since they were kids. It had never mattered that he was her older brother, she had always been the one who took charge.

'I was going to get a box,' he said, waving uncertainly in what he imagined was the direction of the company's offices where Rosie Posset was in the habit of saving cardboard boxes for him to cart his empties away in. 'I . . . '

'They're dis-*gusting*!' snapped Amy, fixing him with a hard stare. '*Well?*'

He smiled weakly and tried to explain.

He hadn't thought they looked too bad, he told her as he walked nervously across the room towards her: not until she'd started smashing them, he hadn't. Unsightly, he asked: surely not? They gave the place a sort of lived-in feel, didn't they, and a certain human warmth? And he had been meaning to get rid of them, really he had, as he did regularly, by the way – well, every four to ten weeks or so, if he remembered – but he hadn't managed to get around to it. And now, he explained, hanging his head in apparent disappointment, it looked as if he was going to have to miss out on his usual, and much needed, therapeutic trip to the bottle bank. Smashing bottles could be very good for the soul, he told her forlornly. Perhaps she should give it a try?

Amy sniffed and ran her tongue over her teeth. 'Really?' she said. 'And why would that be, do you think?'

He shrugged. 'No idea,' he said, standing next to her and peering into the bin. 'Did you, er, see Henry this morning, by any chance?'

Her head jerked around towards him. 'You can leave that ungrateful little sod out of it, too!' she snapped. She pointed at the bottles again. 'And you're no better than he is, are you?'

He nodded his understanding. 'Left the house in a bit of a mess, did he?'

She reached into the hip pocket of her jeans and snatched out the crumpled note that Henry had left for her on the kitchen table.

'Here!' she said, throwing it at him. 'See for yourself!'

He picked it up.

'Sorry about the mess,' it read, 'but I was in a bit of a hurry. Don't bother to tidy up. I'll do it when I get back. Thanks. Henry.'

Sam nodded. 'Still, I thought you'd have seen enough of his place last . . . '

Amy's eyes narrowed to slits. 'He didn't mention his little live-in guests, though, did he?'

Sam frowned. 'Yeah, but cats . . . '

'Cats?' she snorted. 'Cats? *Pussy* more like! Isn't that what you call us? Or should I say *pussies*? I'm not sure what the plural for whore is these days!' She glared at him. 'Are you?'

Sam was suddenly out of his depth. 'Sorry? Old Spike . . . '

'Old Spike?' hissed Amy. '*Old Spike*? What about young *Elizabeth*? And even younger *Victoria*? I suppose you just forgot about them, didn't you? Or does he have so many little girls hanging about the place that it's hard for you to keep track?'

Sam's eyes widened. 'Women?' He glanced across the room at nothing in particular, and then back at his sister. 'Henry?'

'Not *women*!' she snapped. '*Little girls*! And you needn't sound so bloody innocent, Samuel Johnson. I bet you thought it was really funny, didn't you, your dumb sister going round there to . . .?'

'Yes, but . . . *girls*? Are you sure?'

'Listen, I go round there in good faith, and what do I find?'

Sam looked blank.

'They were coming out of the front door, for Christ's sake! With their bloody auntie in tow. I mean, what kind of man is he, this friend of yours?'

She had gone to the house in good faith, she reminded him, and what had she found? Two little girls, that's what, with their clothes all rumpled and creased, looking tired and shagged out as if they had spent the night in God only knew what debauched sexual activities, being hustled down the path by some middle-aged harpy of a woman and a man the size of a small truck.

'Do you know how I felt?' she demanded.

'Two?' beamed Sam. 'What . . . *real* girls?'

'It's not funny!' snapped Amy. 'And it's probably not legal, either!'

Sam sat on the sofa and listened with undisguised admiration as his sister told him of Henry's hitherto unsuspected pulling power. 'Well,' he said, when she slowed down enough to take a breath, 'who'd have thought it, eh? I mean, if you'd told me . . .!' He fell silent when he saw the thunderous look on her face. 'What I mean is . . . '

'I know *exactly* what you mean!'

'Still, you've got to admit . . . '

'No . . . I . . . haven't! You can admit whatever you like. And you can go over there and clean up his house, if you're so bloody impressed by his disgusting behaviour. *And* you can look after his flea-bitten cat! *And* his virus-infested plants! *And* you can do his filthy washing! You can even *marry* the dirty little sod if you think he's so bloody wonderful. Just don't expect me to come to the wedding!' She fixed him with a hard stare. 'You'd better get a move-on, though, because I wouldn't put it past *Auntie Dorothy*, or whatever her name is, to turn up with a shotgun next time around!'

'Dorothy?' said Sam, sharply. 'Did you say . . . *Dorothy*?'

Amy clicked her tongue and looked at the ceiling.

'Tall? Skinny?' hazarded Sam. 'Leather two-piece? Bloody great handbag with a strap like the anchor chain of the *Titanic*?'

Amy gave him a withering look.

'And the bloke: big, balding, broken nose?'

'So you use the same pimp. How quaint!'

'They were at the office this morning,' said Sam, quickly, 'about nine o'clock. They were looking for Henry. She said he had something that belonged to her.'

'Yes,' snapped Amy, 'her *niece*!'

Sam shook his head. 'No, no! They were there, too! One of them was blonde, right? Long hair, short skirt, good legs?'

Amy raised her eyes to the ceiling again.

'The other one was shorter?' he added. 'Dark hair? Permed? Jeans and a T-shirt? Well,' he said, holding his hands wide, 'don't you see? If they were *there*, at the office, they couldn't have been at Henry's place all night, could they? I mean, I told them where he lives. They wanted that necklace-thing back. They must've gone straight round to get it.'

Amy stared at him in silent contempt.

He shrugged. 'What?'

'You're pathetic! You know that, don't you? Both of you are! I'm not surprised they sacked him. Why anybody would want to employ a couple of useless . . . ' she frowned. 'Hang on a minute! Why aren't you at work?'

He took a deep breath and told her.

'Idiots!' she said. 'My brother is an idiot, and his best friend is an idiot. And that probably makes me an idiot by association.' She went on for quite a while after that, making certain that he understood what an idiot she thought he was, and how unfair it was that their parents had forced her into being the younger sister of an idiot who had only idiots for friends. And if it hadn't been for the knock at the front door, she would probably have gone on about it for an awful lot longer than that.

Sam sighed with relief, and stood up.

'Stay where you are!' she snapped, pointing at the sofa. 'We don't want you attacking the Avon Lady, or anything, do we?'

'He made a nice splash, though,' offered Sam as she stomped towards the front door. 'Adams? About 5.8 for style, I should think?'

'Let's see if you're still laughing when the building society sends in the bailiffs, shall we?'

Sam sighed. 'I was wondering,' he called after her, 'if I ought to go down and see Henry? You know, stay with him for a while? Perhaps we could do something together?'

Amy turned with her lips pursed. 'Well,' she said, primly, 'you could get pissed together, couldn't you? You're both pretty good at that!'

'True,' said Sam, as she left the room. 'Only I don't think we could make much of a living out of it, somehow.'

'*Friends* of yours, I believe?' said Amy, coming stiffly back into the room a moment later with Vicky and Beth trailing behind her. She stomped past Sam, flounced into the spare bedroom and slammed the door behind her.

Sam smiled wanly at the girls. 'Sorry about that, it's just . . . '

'She your wife, then?' asked Beth.

'Sister,' said Sam. 'Got a vivid imagination, though. Sorry!'

'Yeah, we saw her this morning. She looked pretty pissed off then, too.'

Sam smiled, uneasily. 'Yes, well, she thinks . . . '

'We know,' said Vicky. 'Was that her boyfriend's house, then?'

Before Sam could answer, the bedroom door was flung open and Amy thrust her head into the room. 'You can stop talking about me, Sam Johnson, and get on with whatever disgusting things you and your little *friends* do when you're alone. And don't mind me. I've got some dusting to catch up on.' She withdrew her head and shut the door with a bang.

Vicky and Beth exchanged glances.

'Look,' said Vicky, 'where's your friend Henry? We need to talk to him urgently about something important.'

Before Sam could answer, the bedroom door was wrenched open and Amy thrust her head out again. 'Sounds like they don't think you're up to it, Sammy old son! Just as well really: I don't think I could cope with the grunting!' She withdrew her head and slammed the door again.

'Is she gonna keep doin' that?' asked Beth.

Sam shrugged. 'No idea.'

'Look,' said Vicky, 'about your friend . . .?'

The bedroom door opened and Amy came striding out.

'On second thoughts, I don't think I'll risk it,' she said. 'I'm going to the café on the corner. Let me know when you've finished, will you? If you've got any energy left that is!' She lifted her coat from a nail on the wall and strode towards the front door.

'Oy, tight-arse!' called Beth. 'Where d'you think *you're* goin'?'

Amy stopped and turned around, slowly. '*What* did you call me,' she demanded, frostily, 'you little *tart*? You come in here, flashing your tits . . .!'

'For Christ's sake!' cried Beth. 'We haven't got time to fanny about listenin' to you pontificatin', you stupid bitch! Your boyfriend, or whatever he is, is gonna be dead if we don't do somethin' about it quick!'

'Damned right!' snapped Amy. 'Just as soon as I get my hands on the lying little sod!' She smiled with sickly sweetness. 'Oh, and by the way, he isn't my boyfriend! He never *was* my boyfriend and he never *will be* my . . .!'

'It's not funny, you know?' interrupted Vicky, almost in tears.

'No,' said Amy, 'and you can tell him from me . . .!'

'*Jesus Christ*!' hissed Beth in exasperation. 'Will you shut your friggin' gob for a minute and *listen*! They're gonna *kill him*! Don't you understand? *Dead*! They're gonna kill him *stone-friggin'-dead* if we don't stop them!'

'If they haven't already,' said Vicky.

'It's not some silly bloody game, y'know?' insisted Beth. She looked at Amy and then at Sam as they stood in silence, too stunned by the ferocity of her outburst to move. She looked Amy in the eye. 'Look,' she said, evenly, 'that woman, that Dolly, is not my soddin' auntie, or our bleedin' pimp, whatever *you* think Little Miss Tight-arse!' She paused to draw breath and to shake her head with suppressed anger. 'We never even clapped eyes on her 'til yesterday morning. She's some sort of *gangster* or something! I don't . . . But,' she pointed at herself and then at Vicky, 'believe it or not, *we* are not *hookers*, or *tarts*, or *slags*, or whatever *you* wanna call us. She,' she nodded at Vicky, 'is a schoolgirl. *Just* a schoolgirl! And I'm an unemployed beautician. If you think that's some sort of crime – and some people do, believe me – OK! Only shut up for a minute and *listen*!'

She looked from Amy to Sam and back again. 'Well?'

Sam shrugged, and cleared his throat. '*Eh-hem*, yes, well . . .'

Amy folded her arms, and raised both eyebrows in mock anticipation.

'Right,' said Beth. 'Good! I think you'd better sit down.'

'I'll stand,' said Amy, 'if it's all the same to you?'

Sam raised both hands, as if to ward off any possible accusations of misconduct, and sat on the sofa.

Beth took a deep breath. 'Look . . . they nicked that Holy Grail thing,' she pointed across the room, 'on the telly? Her, that Dolly, my dad, that *thing* they call Bonce, and that slimy little bastard, Vinny! We nicked a bit of it back from my old man. Only we didn't know what it was. Right? Her dad,' she said, pointing at Vicky again, 'nicked it from us. Only he didn't know what it was, either. Then he,' she said, pointing at Sam, 'nicked it from him. Her dad? Yeah? And gave it to your friend, Henry.' She looked at Amy. 'You with me so far?'

Amy shrugged, non-committally, and sniffed. 'And . . .?'

'Now they – that Dolly and her lot – want it back. Only they don't know where it is. So they smashed his place up looking for it this morning, just before you got there, and followed him when he drove off . . . '

'Clever,' snapped Amy, 'being in two places at once!'

Beth looked her in the eye. 'Her,' she said, evenly, 'that Dolly and that Curly, took me and her with 'em to search the house. Right? That Bonce and that Vinny, and my dad, followed him when he left. Got it now?'

Amy shrugged and looked at the wall.

Beth looked at Sam. 'Then they let us go and told us to keep our mouths shut or else.' She sighed. 'Sod 'em, I said!' She pointed at Vicky. 'She used to go out with that Terry Smith at your place. So we called him and said we'd give him a blowjob if he told us where you lived. We reckoned you'd wanna help.' She looked at Amy. 'Maybe we shouldn't 'ave bothered.'

'And what proof do you have for any of this?' asked Amy, coldly.

'It's that necklace-thing,' said Vicky, reaching into a pocket and bringing out a wad of newspaper cuttings. 'Look,' she added, handing them to Sam. 'There,' she said, pointing, 'there and there?'

Sam shook his head. 'No, I don't see . . . '

'*Christ!*' said Beth, barging forward and pointing. '*There* and *there* and *there!* Talk about bleedin' *dense!*'

'I put them on the leather thong,' said Vicky. 'They weren't like that when we found them. It wasn't really a necklace. They were just sort of . . . loose.'

Sam glanced sideways at his sister. 'I think you'd better have a look at this,' he said, handing her the pictures.

It took the girls several minutes to convince Amy that she could stop wringing her hands and apologizing. 'Oh God,' she kept saying, rigid with embarrassment, 'I'm really sorry! Really I am! Only I thought . . . I mean when that Dolly woman said you were . . . '

'Forget it,' said Beth. 'If she'd told me I was a hooker I'd probably 'ave believed her.'

Amy smiled, weakly. 'Yes, but . . . '

'It doesn't matter,' said Vicky. 'Really it doesn't! The thing is . . . what are we going to do now?'

'I'll ring the cottage,' said Amy, 'and see if he's got there yet. No answer,' she said, a moment later. 'God, what if they've got him already?'

Sam looked at Vicky. 'What time did he leave?'

Vicky thought for a moment. 'About quarter to ten?'

Sam looked at his watch. 'He wouldn't have got there yet. He'll be another couple of hours, at least.'

'Shouldn't we call the police, then?' asked Amy. 'I mean, surely they could do something to stop them?'

Beth shook her head. 'No! Don't do that! She's got lots of friends, that Dolly has. She'd find out somehow and send someone round here to get us. You should've seen what that Bonce was doin' to my dad's balls.'

Sam crossed his legs uncomfortably and was glad that he hadn't.

Vicky nodded. 'You don't know what they're like.'

'But we can't just *sit* here!' said Amy, wringing her hands. 'Doing *nothing*! And let them,' she shrugged, hopelessly. 'I mean . . . can we?'

'If they haven't already,' said Beth.

'Don't keep saying that!' pleaded Amy. She looked hopefully at the girls. 'They wouldn't, though, would they? I mean . . . *really*?'

Vicky and Beth exchanged glances . 'Yes they would!' they said together.

Nothing happened for the next five minutes, except that the four of them sat staring into space, each with their own thoughts, most of which featured images of Henry lying at the side of the road with his head bashed in. Every so often one of them would look up and say: 'Maybe we could . . .? No, that wouldn't work, would it?' or 'How about if we . . .? No, that's no good, either!'

'Look,' said Amy in exasperation, 'we've got to do *something*! We can't just sit here and let him *die*!' She cocked her head to one side and listened. 'What was that?' she asked in a whisper. 'I thought I heard someone at the door.'

'I didn't hear anything,' said Sam, hopefully.

'There!' said Amy. 'You must have heard it that time?'

'What if it's them?' hissed Vicky.

'Don't answer it!' whispered Amy. 'Perhaps they'll go away?'

'We don't know it's them,' said Beth. 'It could be . . . '

'*Sssshhh!*' hissed the others.

On the other side of Sam's front door, Nils de Boer was starting to feel a bit peeved. He wasn't a patient man at the best of times, and he really hated it when people pretended they weren't in. He took something that looked like a high-tech hair dryer from a pocket of his leather trench coat, slid the nozzle of the thing over the handle on Sam's front door and pressed a switch. There was a high speed grinding noise, and a faint click. When he withdrew the device and pointed it at the floor, the doorknob and most of the lock mechanism fell out.

He put the device back into his pocket and kicked open the door.

Everyone inside the flat froze as it banged back against the wall.

Nils walked up to Sam, and pointed a large, shiny pistol at his head.

'Hello,' he said with an amiable grin. 'Time we all went for a little ride together, don't you think?'

14

NOBBLER BATES

Nobbler was having trouble walking. The damp wad of his shirt had wormed its way up into the crack of his arse and was forcing his bumcheeks apart. He waddled along with his knees bent and his feet splayed out, feeling cramped, dejected and smelling like a cesspit. From behind, he looked as if he had grown a painful third buttock. From in front, he looked as if he wished it was that simple. With his head down and his fists clenched against the pain in his spasming rectum, he made a shambling beeline for the Gents toilets. People stopped, turned and sniffed the air uneasily as he passed, wrinkling their noses and shaking their heads in distaste.

Vinny grinned wolfishly as he and Bonce watched the unhappy little man crab his way across the service station car park towards the main entrance. 'Tosser!' he said. 'Hope he falls down the bog an' drowns!'

'Don't like him,' said Bonce. 'He ain't funny!'

Vinny nodded. 'He ain't comin' with us, neither!'

Bonce frowned. 'Dolly said . . . '

'Dolly ain't 'ere, though, is she!' snapped Vinny. 'Anyhow,' he added, 'I jus' give her a bell and she said do what we want,' he bared his teeth, 'jus' so long as it's quiet.' He sniffed. 'She's gonna sort that Johnson geezer out, an' all.'

He gazed across the car park. 'Hey! Where's that bastard got to now?'

Bonce pointed at Nobbler.

'Not *that* bastard! That *Kite* bastard!'

After a brief and acrimonious search, during which Bonce sulked and Vinny blamed him for everything from the state of the roads to the contents of Nobbler's underpants, they found Henry sitting in the restaurant staring blankly out of the window with an untouched mug of black coffee and a dubious-looking plate of food on the table in front of him. Satisfied that he wouldn't be going anywhere for a while, Vinny decided to leave Bonce to keep an eye on him. 'Right,' he said, hitching at his jeans, 'I'm goin' for a piss. If 'e moves, smack him.'

Bonce's lower lip trembled. 'Yeah, only Dolly said . . . '

Vinny thrust his head into the big man's face. 'I told you: Dolly ain't 'ere, is she? How many more times? I'm givin' the orders! Got that?'

Bonce thought about smashing his fist into Vinny's nose, but decided that Dolly probably wouldn't like it if he did. 'Call that looking after him, dumbo?' he could imagine her saying.

He turned away, reluctantly, and looked for somewhere to sit.

Vinny grabbed him by the arm. 'An' for Christ's sake try an' look like a bleedin' tourist or somethin'! Don't jus' sit there! Eat somethin'!'

'Eat?' said Bonce, glancing at the self-service counters. 'Eat what?'

'Have a soddin' drink, then!' snapped Vinny, turning away with a shake of the head. 'Jesus Christ . . .!'

'Drink?' muttered Bonce.

After much careful deliberation, he bought a coke – the least challenging thing he could find – and started to sidle across the room towards Henry with the can balancing in the middle of a tray. Halfway there, he hesitated and stood still: should he sit close to Henry, he wondered, so as to be sure not to lose him if he moved, or should he sit as far away as possible so as not to draw attention to himself? As he dithered over what to do for the best, heads turned towards him. He shuffled first one way and then another, glancing repeatedly from Henry to a distant table and back again. More people turned to watch, following every glance back and forth, like the crowd at an impromptu game of tennis. When he finally settled for a table somewhere between the two extremes, sporadic applause broke out around him.

He blushed, and glanced anxiously at Henry, hoping that he hadn't noticed the commotion he'd caused. But he needn't have worried: if the restaurant had exploded in a shower of sparks and Dolly turned up to do the *Dance of the Seven Veils* in front of the flames, Henry would still have been too overcome by self-pity to notice.

He had tried unsuccessfully to revive himself with a mug of black coffee. It wasn't something he usually drank, hangover or no hangover, and even with six heaped teaspoons of sugar in it, wasn't something for which he felt he was ever likely to develop a taste. Sam and Amy had tried to make him drink what had seemed like gallons of the stuff the night before, and the memory of the retching and straining that had followed only increased his sense of revulsion. He left the coffee untouched and continued to gaze out of the window, trying to work out why the hell he was there. He got as far as Adams handing him the letter of dismissal, and decided that he didn't want to go any further. He had lost his job and needed to get used to the fact. It was a mixed blessing, he told himself, and he would just have to make the best of it: whatever *it* might turn out to be. On the one hand, he was glad that his four-year period of servitude with the company was over. On the other, he knew that being unemployed was a serious drawback when you had a mortgage to pay and a cat to look after, and a petrol tank to fill . . . He closed his eyes and swallowed hard. He wasn't going to think about any of that for a day or two yet, he decided, because he was going to be too busy having lots of fun.

He opened his eyes and felt in his shirt pocket for the scrap of paper with the address of Sam's parents' cottage written on it. He was going there because he didn't know what else to do, and because he didn't dare turn around and go home for fear of what Amy would say to him if he did. He shook his head in morose satisfaction at the thought that he had allowed himself to be bullied into his present predicament by a girl.

'Story of my life,' he told himself, bitterly. 'Women! Always telling me what I should do and what I shouldn't do, and . . .!'

He pushed the coffee mug away and stared out of the window some more.

The journey from his house to the service station had been uneventful. He'd driven slowly and carefully at first, completely unaware of the black

Mercedes behind him. He'd felt tired and fragile, and had decided that it would be a good idea to avoid doing anything that might stress him out. So when people had come barrelling up behind him, flashing their lights and waving their fists, he'd moved out of their way with nothing more animated than a curled lip. When they'd cut in front of him, or slammed on their brakes without warning, he'd sighed resignedly and shaken his head in pity at the time and effort they'd been wasting. And when he'd found himself caught up in heavy traffic, he hadn't lost his temper, changed lanes to gain a momentary advantage, thumped the steering wheel with the heels of his hands, or cast doubt on the parentage of a single one of his fellow drivers. The true measure of his fragility, however, had been evidenced by the fact that the word *knobhead* hadn't passed his lips even once during the whole journey. His hangover had been bad enough when he'd left the house, but as the slow miles had passed it had become even worse. By the time he'd reached the service station at South Mimms he'd decided that death would be a welcome alternative. His mouth had been dry, his bladder full to bursting, and his head throbbing like the speakers on Sam's pitiless stereo. He'd decided that if he was going to get himself back into the land of the living, he'd need a drink, a piss and a handful of headache pills. Although, not necessarily in that order.

As he'd parked the car, he'd wondered if Granada did blood transfusions as well as tanksful of petrol. He'd turned off the engine, slumped back against the driver's seat, and closed his eyes. After a while, he'd forced himself to get out and go in search of a glass of water. He was going to need one, he'd told himself, if he was going to make a serious dent in the bottle of Paracetamol he'd been clutching so tightly in his left fist.

Ten minutes later, he was sitting in the restaurant wondering if there were worse ways of starting a holiday than with a large dollop of animal protein substitute for lunch. The menu had said that the glutinous mass on the plate in front of him was Vegetarian Chicken Supreme, and that it had been 'Specially formulated to amuse the most discerning of palates'. He wondered if that could really be true, because, as far as he could remember, he hadn't so much as cracked a smile since the surly waitress at the service counter had dumped it on the tray in front of him and made it clear that, in her opinion at least, it was his duty to 'enjoy' it from the moment it left her protection.

He eyed it suspiciously, wondering if the only way to get some real amusement out of it would be to push it into someone else's face – the surly waitress would be a good place to start, he decided, as he gazed out of the window. Better still, the sociopathic marketing man (woman, child?) who had come up with the idea for the stuff in the first place. He looked sideways at it, squatting in the middle of his plate, glistening, beige-tinted and apparently held together by epoxy cement. The bulk of it – and bulk was the operative word – crouched menacingly on top of a perfect ring of congealed rice that looked so devoid of nutritional value that he wondered if it would be kinder if he allowed *it* to eat *him*, instead of the other way around. He eyed it uneasily as it sat there, looking like one of those malignant alien blobs, so familiar in science fiction B movies, that leapt huge distances through time and space to attach themselves to their victims' most vulnerable bodily parts. If it was truly vegetarian, he decided, it was probably only that way because it wasn't fast enough to catch anything that wasn't rooted in the ground. On the other hand, if the lumps sticking out of it were really bits of chicken, as he was beginning to suspect, then it was not only *not* vegetarian, but a good deal faster than it looked! As for it being in any way 'supreme', he doubted that he knew enough about alien invertebrates to make a meaningful judgement.

He prodded at it with a fork. The surface gave under the pressure, but the prongs didn't penetrate the skin. It seemed to have coalesced into an impenetrable lump: a smooth-surfaced agglomeration that could rival the most advanced modelling materials known to medical science and make beautifully accurate impressions of peoples' teeth. He was almost certain that if he turned the plate upside-down, the blob would detach itself, en masse, with a faint sucking sound, leaving behind nothing but a damp patch, like a giant thumb print, to show where it had been. It might not have any nutritional value, he decided as he pushed it away, but there was a better than even chance that it would one day make dishwashing obsolete.

When he pushed it away and turned to gaze out of the window, his attention was caught by a red sports car whose driver was trying to park next to a Volvo estate. He winced as the car's rear bumper nudged the Volvo's front wheel arch. The grinding of precision engineered cogs that followed could clearly be heard through the double glazing of the restaurant window as the driver tried to extricate himself from the tight spot into which he had just reversed. Henry blew out his cheeks and looked down at the thing on the plate. There was a depressing similarity between it and the driver, he decided.

'Taste has got nothing to do with it, has it?' he said. 'These days it's all about looks!'

Without thinking, he picked up the coffee and took a swig. It tasted vile. He held it in his mouth for a moment, before spitting it back into the mug. He put the mug down and pushed it away. 'Cretins!' he muttered, screwing up his face in disgust. 'Millions of 'em, wherever you look!'

His muttering didn't go unnoticed. A woman at a nearby table eyed him anxiously and wondered who she should call if he decided to go berserk.

He didn't go berserk. But he noticed her gawping at him and smiled reassuringly. He did it for no other reason than that he was supposed to be on holiday and smiling at people seemed like the right thing to do.

The woman didn't appreciate the gesture. She stood up, covered the heads of her two little girls with her coattails and headed for the exit, looking over her shoulder with many a fearful backward glance a she went.

Henry sighed and shook his head. The woman's behaviour proved his point. But how many cretins were you likely to meet in the average day, he wondered? Hundreds? Thousands? There were cretins like the one in the car park who drove red sports cars, and cretins like Adams who didn't but wished that they could. That was the trouble with cretins, he told himself, they all looked the same. He sighed, and stared out of the window some more.

The cretin in the sports car was still out there, inching this way and that, backwards and forwards, and getting nowhere in a hurry. Henry couldn't see the driver's face, but even if he had been able to he wouldn't have recognized Richard Choat because they had never met. But he did remember Sam's comment about him driving a Ford Probe, and Ron's joke about calling it and the driver a prick. But he didn't see the connection. He smiled at the memory and realized that he was going to miss Ron and some of the others at P.A.&D.

'There'll be no one to clean my car,' he thought, remembering Ron's weekly ritual. 'I'll just have to do it myself.' The thought reminded him of something. He frowned. 'My car,' he thought. 'What was it . . .?' As he gazed out of the window, the answer hit him like a kick in the teeth.

'Hey,' he cried, placing his hands on the table and levering himself upright, 'that's my car! That bastard's backing into . . .! Hey! That's . . .! Right!' He turned away from the table and barged past several startled customers on his way to the exit. 'We'll see about *that* won't we?'

Richard Choat had arranged to meet Charlotte Piece in the service station restaurant on the first stage of their journey to Sir Richard's villa in Torquay. He was a few minutes later than expected – mainly because it had taken him so long to park – and was walking briskly across the foyer when Henry came bustling out of the restaurant in the opposite direction. They passed within inches of one another without recognition.

Henry strode through the main doors and out into the car park, looking for someone to fight. Choat continued across the foyer towards the toilets, and was almost flattened by an anxious-faced Bonce who came lumbering out of the restaurant, looking for Henry.

Henry reached the Probe and stopped, disappointed to see that its driver had gone. He walked around to the side of the car and knelt next to the front wheel of his Volvo. He could definitely see what might be a scratch in the paintwork, and what he thought could possibly be a dent. He stood up and glared around the car park. 'Bastard!' he hissed. 'Look what he did!' he demanded of a passing motorist.

It was the woman from the restaurant with her two little girls trailing behind her. Her eyes opened wide in alarm. 'No,' she pleaded, gathering the girls in her arms and hurrying them away, 'don't hurt them! Please?'

Henry took no notice. He gestured from the Probe to the Volvo and waved his arms in the air. 'Can you believe it?' he cried. 'Can you bloody well believe it? I mean, what kind of idiot does something like that?'

All the anger and frustration that had been building up inside him over the past twenty-four hours came tumbling out of him suddenly, and he kicked one of the Probe's front tyres. The impact hurt the big toe he had bruised when he'd kicked Sam's singing alarm clock across his bedroom, and he hopped about, cursing and wondering if he was ever going to get it into his head that kicking things that weren't meant to be kicked was never a good thing to do.

The Probe's alarm started wailing mournfully in time to his erratic hopping and cursing, but no one took any notice of him or the car.

The pain in his foot subsided eventually. And when the alarm died with a final strangulated *whoo-ooh*! he felt suddenly calm.

'Right!' he said, folding his arms, and planting his feet apart. 'I'll wait!'

Vinny came out of the toilets just in time to see Bonce go blundering across the foyer towards the main entrance. He caught up with him as he was about to go charging out into the car park. 'Where d'you think you're goin'?' he demanded, grabbing his arm. 'I told you to watch 'im! Not go . . .!'

'He's run away!' wailed Bonce, taking Vinny by the collar and pushing him backwards. 'I watched 'im, Vinny, honest I did! I 'ad a coke! On'y a coke!'

'*Chrissake*!' croaked Vinny, back-peddling wildly and trying to dislodge the huge hands crushing his windpipe. 'Le' go o' me ya . . .!'

'Don't let 'er shout at me, Vinny,' pleaded Bonce. 'I'll squeeze any bollocks you want!'

Vinny grunted as his back slammed up against the tiled wall at the side of the foyer. And for a moment he hung there like a wet dishcloth in Bonce's huge hands, winded and gasping for breath.

Choat came out of the Gents toilets and was immediately grabbed from behind by Charlotte Piece. 'Quick!' she hissed in his ear. 'Or he'll see us!'

'What the . . .?' he croaked, as he was dragged backwards towards a group of potted palms near the rear entrance.

'He's after us!' insisted Charlotte. 'Quick! Hide! Before he comes back!'

'Hide?' gasped Choat. 'Charlotte, is that . . .? What the hell are . . .?'

'He's out there! Look at him! Don't you see?'

'Who . . .? Who's out . . .?'

'Look!' she urged, pressing his head back against the wall. 'No! Don't look! Get down! Out there! By the car! It's him!'

Choat tried to peer through the palm leaves, but she pulled him away.

'The green car! Next to yours! He's just standing there waiting!'

'*Who's* waiting?' pleaded Choat. 'For Christ's sake, what are you . . .?'

'I don't think he saw me. I parked over there . . . just in case.'

'In case of *what*?' begged Choat. 'What the *hell* are you . . .?'

Charlotte dragged him back into the potted palms to explain.

Out in the car park, Henry's resolve was starting to wilt. His bladder was full again and the April wind was bitingly cold: a combination that had brought many a strong man to his knees. He was soon shifting from foot to foot uneasily and wondering if waiting for the driver of the Probe to come back was really such a good idea. Even if he did come back, it might not be for another hour, especially if he had stopped for a hot meal.

Henry thought for a moment, shrugged and hurried back towards the toilets, just as Nobbler was squelching his way out of one of the cubicles.

Nobbler's first thought, when Vinny finally gave him permission to get out of the car, was to wash his shirt and pants in one of the hand basins in the Gents toilets. But faced with the prospect of doing it in front of an audience of other men, some of whom might think it a bit odd that he was wearing his shirt entirely inside his jeans, he decided to use one of the toilet bowls instead. He saw nothing strange about the idea: the porcelain looked a good deal cleaner, and the water a good deal clearer, than anything he was used to at home. So after locking the door behind him, he took off everything but his shoes and socks, and knelt in front of the bowl with his jeans and sweater in a pile on the floor beside him. Then he jammed the screwed up bundle of his soiled shirt and underpants into the crystal clear water and reached for the chain. A moment later, he was struggling manfully with a torrent of freezing cold water, punching, kneading and squeezing his dirty clothes for all he was worth. Soon, he was up to his armpits in darkening water and feeling pleased with himself. It was then that he noticed that it wasn't just his arms and hands that were feeling the effects of the cold water: his knees and shins were starting to go numb, too! He looked down and saw that the tiled floor was awash with water overflowing from the clogged bowl, and his jeans and sweater were turning several shades darker as they soaked it up. He flailed and flapped to his feet in alarm, and managed to yank his shirt free from the powerful undertow, but not before the water had drained away with a final vicious gurgle, taking his underpants with it! After a moment's slow deliberation, he decided that he might as well finish the job. His knickers had disappeared for good – there was nothing he could do about that – but at least his shirt was almost back to its original colour, and he couldn't get any wetter if he tried: so with a shrug and a muttered 'What the bugger?' he wiped his bum on the shirt, dropped it back into the bowl, and reached for the chain. Five minutes later, he was sloshing his way out of the cubicle fully clothed, but looking as if he'd spent an hour or two in his own personal monsoon.

On his way back into the Gents toilets, Henry passed an odd-looking little man coming out. He was short and wiry, and had a furtive look about him that Henry put down to the fact that he seemed to have had a shower fully clothed. The man shied away from him as they drew level, held a hand up to his face and veered into the nearby gift shop.

Henry raised an enquiring eyebrow at him, but carried on walking. 'See what I mean?' he muttered. 'Cretins! Millions of 'em! Everywhere you look!'

'It's him!' hissed Vinny on the other side of the foyer as Henry hurried back in to the Gents. 'I thought you said the bastard had gone?'

Bonce stopped banging his own head against the wall in anticipation of what Dolly would say to him when he told her that Henry had run away. He looked around. 'I'll get 'im, Vinny!' he promised. 'Don't worry 'bout . . .'

'No!' hissed Vinny. 'I'll watch him! Get back to the car!'

'It's him!' hissed Charlotte, as she pulled Choat out from behind the potted palms and hustled him away. 'Quick! Before he comes out! Follow me!'

'Where?' asked Choat, glancing over his shoulder for a sight of their mystery pursuer as Charlotte dragged him towards the main entrance.

'To Torquay, you *idiot!*' she snapped. 'Where d'you think?'

'No,' said Choat, craning his neck, 'I meant . . . *idiot?*'

'You missed him! Quick! Get back to the cars!'

Peering out from behind a postcard rack in the gift shop, Nobbler sighed with relief as Henry disappeared into the toilets. When he turned away, wondering what to do next, a display of red clothing on a nearby shelf caught his attention. He walked over to look at it with a smile spreading across his soggy face. He could see a way of getting into Vinny and Bonce's good books, if only he had enough money on him to buy what he would need. He reached into the sodden back pocket of his jeans and took out his wallet.

Inside the toilets, Henry was staring at himself in one of the mirrors. He looked pale and in need of a shave. There was a foul taste in his mouth, and his eyes were red-rimmed and puffy. He poked out his tongue, shook his head at its pallid appearance, and decided that it was time to get back on the road.

Water splashed up around him as he walked past the cubicles. 'That little guy must have fallen flat on his face in that lot,' he thought as he stepped gingerly through it, screwing up his face and wincing at the thought of the infectious diseases that must have leapt and slithered onto the little man's body as soon as he'd hit the floor. He shivered and headed for the way out.

By the time he got back to his car, the Probe and its driver had gone. He decided that it was probably just as well because he doubted that he would have been up to a slanging match; much less something that might have turned into a fistfight. He got into his car, checked the road map, and set off wearily on the next leg of his journey.

As he headed for the exit, the engine of the big Mercedes growled into life.

Bonce was about to pull out of the parking bay when Nobbler ran up wearing a huge smile, and with a bulky plastic bag in each hand. He wrenched open the rear door and clambered into the car.

The others turned to glare at him, disappointed that they hadn't managed to leave him behind.

'Right,' he said, grinning at their doom-laden faces, 'where we off to now?'

Bonce looked at Vinny. 'Is he tryin' to be funny?'.

Vinny looked at Nobbler, clad from head to toe in the bobble hat, scarf, sweatshirt, tracksuit bottoms and gloves of an Arsenal supporter.

'Does he look funny to you?'

Bonce shook his head. 'No he bloody don't! My team's West Ham!'

15

BOADICEA

Henry glanced at the dashboard clock and saw that it was a little after midday: and in a moment of wistful regret, he sighed and wondered what he would have been doing if he'd still had a job. Then an image of the man with the Whoopsie Glove flashed into his head, and the moment, and the regret, and a slowly surfacing suspicion that he was going to miss working for the company, disappeared in a wave of relief. He knew exactly what he would have been doing: the dross that no one else wanted: the sort of commissions where the company took obscene sums of money from clients for the development of marketing campaigns which no one, except perhaps the deluded clients, thought had the slightest chance of success. The sort of campaigns that were doomed to failure before they got started because no one in their right mind was going to want to buy whatever it was the client was trying to sell them. There had been no actual square wheels, glass hammers or left-handed screwdrivers for him to promote, but it had been a close-run thing, and the sheer banality of what had come his way after the debacle with the CDs had been grinding him down for weeks before he'd been sacked.

The terminal decline in his career at the company had begun on an otherwise innocuous day in February when Sir Richard had assembled the creative and marketing teams in the boardroom for an announcement.

'This,' he'd crowed on that chilly winter's morning with his nervous staff standing and sitting uneasily around him, 'is the future of advertising!' Then he'd held up a plastic box, and, with a flick of the wrist like a conjurer proving that the white rabbit really *had* disappeared, he'd snapped it open to reveal a row of shining compact discs. 'These little beauties,' he'd gloated, 'have got everything we're ever going to need to make ourselves . . . *rich*!

'Beds!' he'd cried, suddenly. 'Underwear! Pets! DIY! Underwear! Cars! Personal services! Underwear! Garden furniture! Tools! Underwear! And,' as his voice faded into nothingness and the room's occupants held their breath, 'it's all . . . *mine*!' He'd smiled tightly. 'That is to say, it's all . . . *ours*!'

He'd paused, then, waiting for the enormity of what he had just said to sink in. It hadn't. No one had had a clue what he was talking about. And although a few of the faces had suggested in their degree of contortion that their owners had either been trying hard to understand his meaning, or had needed desperately to empty their bowels, the rest had stared at him, blankly.

'All you have to do,' he'd continued, holding up a disc with a note of irritation creeping into his voice, 'is take a bit from here, and,' as he'd held up another one, 'a bit from here! And *wol-lar*! you have a completely new, totally original advertisement! None of our competitors will be able to touch us for speed.' He'd arched an eyebrow and lowered his voice. 'Or . . . *price*!'

As everyone had turned to look at everyone else, his voice had boomed out again. 'Think of it!' he'd cried, sending shockwaves of guilt through minds drawn tight by confusion. 'That vast, untapped market out there! And every last bit of it will be *ours*!' His voice had dropped twenty decibels and a couple of octaves. 'All of those newspapers,' he'd breathed, scanning the room from blank expression to fixed grin, like a lion deciding which zebra to kill, 'all of those magazines . . . all of those menus . . . all of those holiday brochures, just queuing up and begging us to make them look *glossy*!

'You!' he'd cried without warning, pointing an excited finger at Henry's face. 'What're *you* gonna do with the power of these little beauties?'

Then he'd sat down at the head of the table and leaned forward with a menacing stare. 'Think not what your company can do for you,' he'd intoned. 'Think what you, and these little beauties, can do for . . . *me*!'

His boss had never deigned to speak to him directly before that moment, and Henry had found the experience unnerving. 'Ah yes, well,' he'd begun, 'I think I would like to see,' he'd swallowed and gestured at the box of CDs, 'what's on the um, what's in the, er . . . how they . . . before making a . . . '

Sir Richard's eyes had narrowed a warning. 'We don't want any of that arty-farty crap, mind! It's got to be punchy! Punchy and brief! Punchy, brief and to the point! Like that little advert of mine for the perfect wife.'

He'd surged to his feet and struck a pose. 'All you have to do,' he'd declaimed, holding a jacket lapel in one hand and pointing at Suzie's Bunt's chest with the other, 'is screw it on the bed and it'll do all the housework!'

Then he'd sat down and smiled threateningly at the faces around him, daring them not to convulse with helpless laughter at the depth of his wit.

There had been some sporadic coughing from around the room; a ripple of applause from the foot of the table; and a muttered 'hear-hear' from Minnowfield, standing alone by the door.

Terry Smith had giggled.

Nigel Adams had smirked.

Tony Orlando had chuckled loudly, nudged Suzie in the left breast and raised a meaningful eyebrow at her cleavage.

Charlotte Piece, who still hadn't got the joke after eight years of trying, had clapped in delight and frowned at the dissenters, Henry and Sam.

Minnowfield had caught Sam's shake of the head and had looked away in confusion. The first time he'd heard the joke he'd hurried home to tell it to his wife, who'd slammed the bedroom door in his face and refused him conjugal rights for a month. 'Women!' he muttered. 'What's the point?'

Sir Richard had allowed his left hand to slid into his trousers' pocket beneath the table to reposition his erection against his thigh. Then he'd winked at no one in particular, given Minnowfield a hard stare and said: 'Right, that's enough frivolity for one day. Talk is cheap, whisky costs money!

'Time's up!' he'd added, getting to his feet and pushing back his chair. 'Tea break's over! Back on your heads in the shit!'

'Brilliant!' Minnowfield had enthused as he and Henry were wandering back towards their respective offices. 'He's self-made, you know? It really shows, too, don't you think?'

It was true; Sir Richard was a self-made man who never tired of boasting about the fact. 'You wanna know how I did it?' he would ask with a nudge and a reptilian grin. 'Give us a million quid and I'll tell ya! Eh? Eh? *Hah-hah!* Million quid! Eh? Eh? Get it? Make myself rich? Eh? Eh? *Hah-hah-hah!*'

'Thank Christ he keeps it to himself,' Ron had muttered as he'd shuffled along behind Henry and Minnowfield with his trademark bin-liner trailing in his wake. 'Wouldn't want another one of them greasy buggers about the place, knobbin' your wife, would ya? Get it? Eh? Eh? *Hah-hah-hah!*'

There had been a lot of screwing going on in the sort of adverts that Sir Richard had wanted Henry to work on after that, with a lot of dubious little devices that had apparently been intended to be screwed into clothing, or onto the furniture, or the wall, or the floor, or the dashboard of what Sir Richard had decreed should always be referred to as 'the family car'. There had been a lot of strapping-down and tying-up going on in them, too: most of it in doubtful pen and ink sketches of meaty men and women in girdles and trusses and frighteningly fortified 'smalls'. There had been elastic bandages for weak-kneed ramblers and sporty types with tennis elbows; penknives with attachments that could just as easily have been designed for getting boy scouts out of girl guides' tents as removing stones from the hooves of unfortunate horses. There had been sofa beds and futons, orthopaedic mattresses and vibrating armchairs, shoe racks, tie racks, bottle racks, toast racks, clothes racks, tool racks and a multitude of other racks and cunningly devised gadgets designed to be used in the gardens, kitchens, bedrooms, bathrooms, sitting rooms, garages, workshops and greenhouses of the many 'truly discerning home-owners' who had not previously realized that such items were essential prerequisites if they were going to keep up with the Joneses next door.

Sir Richard had dictated the copy at first, because, he had explained straight-faced to Henry, it was his 'calling' to do so. Henry hadn't been quite so easily convinced. Somehow the 'sexy, slinky underwear' that his boss had seemed to think had been designed for that 'special romantic occasion' had seemed to him more suited to the Witchfinder General's torture chamber than the honeymoon suite at the Ritz.

But Sir Richard's enthusiasm had been short-lived, and he had lost interest in the project after less than a week. That had been when Henry's problems had really got started. After working with the CDs for a couple of days on his own, he had come reluctantly to the conclusion that he had no choice but to tell the truth about what they contained. It was a decision that had marked the beginning of the end of his career at Pate Advertising & Design.

Minnowfield's feelings about Henry's predicament since that moment had been mixed. Part of him had been as embarrassed about it as he was about all the other things that had happened in the company over which he had had no control. But another part of him had felt that Henry ought to be grateful that he still had a job. His wife was the director of a charity for homeless people, and he'd seen at first hand, in the refuges and shelters where she worked, just what a disastrous effect being unemployed could have on a person's morale.

He'd known, of course, that Henry was being punished unfairly for having dared to question Sir Richard's judgement. But since he'd been subjected to similar indignities for years – and had seen no evidence that they had done him any harm – he had been inclined to think that Henry ought to stop moaning and make the best of what he was being given. Besides, he rather liked all of the eccentric people and products that they had been working with together since the demise of the CDs. They were all so quintessentially English, so refreshingly parochial, and not at all like the flashy Americanized frippery over which the advertising industry seemed habitually to drool.

The Super Dooper Whoopsie Scooper had looked like being a case in point, and he'd barely been able to contain his excitement at the prospect of getting his hands on the prototype of such an inventive device. The only downside to the initial meeting that he and Henry had been scheduled to have with its inventor had been the fact that the unpredictable Sam Johnson had been ordered by Sir Richard to 'sit in on it' with them.

'You can fold it away after use, and put it in your pocket,' the Whoopsie Glove's inventor had explained. 'That's the beauty of it. Do you see?'

'Yes,' Sam had asked, dryly, 'but why would you want to?'

The dapper little inventor had tapped the side of his nose, and winked. 'Well, you wouldn't want anyone to see you walking down the street with it in your hand, now, would you?'

'Having it in your pocket is OK, though, is it?' Henry had asked.

The inventor had opened his eyes wide and smiled a knowing smile at Minnowfield, who had smiled somewhat less knowingly back at him.

'And what about this?' Henry had asked, holding up a complicated piece of clear plastic that looked as if it was intended either as a caped condom for a man with multiple penises, or a surgical glove that could fly.

The inventor had tapped the side of his nose again, and taken a large char-grilled sausage out of his briefcase and placed it in the centre of the boardroom table. 'Imagine that's your whoopsie,' he'd encouraged.

Minnowfield had grinned like a child in the presence of his first conjurer. 'Yes, yes,' he'd enthused. 'It's very good, isn't it? Very convincing indeed!'

'You take your Whoopsie Glove,' the inventor had continued, 'like . . . so. Slide your hand into it like . . . so. Place your hand over the offending article like . . . so.' Then he'd held his hand over the sausage as Minnowfield had held his breath. 'And then, with the interstitial webbing preventing what we like to call "squeeze out", you lift and pick up cleanly . . . like so!' With a look of triumph on his well-scrubbed face, he'd held up the transparent package for them to inspect. 'And then,' he'd continued, 'to avoid any possible embarrassment, you wrap the wings around it . . . like so, and whip it into your pocket . . . thusly! I ask you, what could be simpler?'

Minnowfield had beamed around the table with a smile that had said that he was willing to pretend that he had no idea where the sausage had gone.

Sam had nodded, glumly. 'Old is it, that sausage?'

'Fresh this morning,' the man had assured him, a note of reproof creeping into his voice. 'Boadicea is very regular. I can always rely upon her to produce the goods when I have a demonstration.'

'Boadicea?' Minnowfield had frowned. Then his face had lit up with a knowing smile. 'Ah, yes, I see! I see! Ancient Britain, you mean? Traditional values and all that! Something you can really rely on? Yes! Yes! Excellent! I like it! Yes I do! We can definitely work with that, can't we chaps? Suits your product right down to the ground, if I might say so.'

Henry had eyed the little man, uneasily. 'You mean that thing is . . . *real*?'

'Oh, but of course, of course,' Minnowfield had nodded, breathlessly. 'Wonderful, wonderful! Tell me . . . where did it go?'

The man had frowned at Minnowfield, but spoken to Henry. 'Of course it's real,' he'd said, proudly. 'Some of our competitors use fakes, you know? But we believe in showing the customer *exactly* what he's going to get.'

'Quite right,' Minnowfield had nodded. 'So where is it, then, exactly?'

'Lots of them, are there?' Sam had asked. 'Competitors I mean?'

'Absolutely!' the inventor had replied. 'You wouldn't believe how cut-throat the doggy pooh market is getting these days.'

'Yes,' Henry had said, sourly, 'but you just put a real dog turd in the middle of the boardroom table.'

'Would you rather I had put it on the carpet?' the inventor had asked, turning and smiling apologetically at Minnowfield. 'More realistic, I know, having to bend down to pick it up, and all that. But our code of practice is very strict where demonstrations are concerned. I mean, we wouldn't want to lead anyone astray, now, would we?'

Henry and Sam had frowned at one another.

But Minnowfield had shaken his head to show that he, at least, didn't need to be told that dog pooh was usually to be found at ground level.

'And I thought you ought to get a bird's eye view of what we in the profession like to call the "swoop and scoop",' the inventor had added. 'Or "the clutch", to give it its more technical name, so that you would be better able to appreciate the ease of operation and the way the fingers curl under what we like to call "the quarry". Do you see?'

Henry had continued to stare uncomfortably at the telltale damp patch in the centre of the table, wondering how much longer he would be able to hold on to his breakfast.

'Of course,' the inventor had told Minnowfield, 'we don't always use live, er, *turds*, as your colleague put it so eloquently. However, on this occasion . . . '

'Live?' Henry had blurted. 'What do you mean, *live*?'

The inventor had laughed. 'Well, not actually *alive*, as such! Boadicea has a touch of worms, of course. You probably noticed some little white specks just now?' He'd pulled the thing out of his pocket and inspected it. 'Nothing moving, though,' he'd added, thrusting it under Henry's nose. 'See?'

As soon as Henry caught a whiff of the thing he'd started to retch. And by the time he'd finished throwing-up in the toilets, the inventor had gone.

Sam told him later that Minnowfield had wound up the meeting with unaccustomed aplomb, assuring the enthusiastic little man that the company would pull out all the stops to make sure that the Super Dooper Whoopsie Scooper campaign became an award-winner.

When Henry had gone back to the boardroom to pick up his notebook and pen, he'd found Adams standing by the window, looking smug.

'If you've come sneaking back to nick that sausage Johnson said you were saving for your dinner, you can forget it,' he'd crowed, holding up the soiled Whoopsie Glove and licking his lips. 'I've had it, matey! So there!'

Henry had wondered if he'd ever be able to face a sausage again after that. And he'd felt even worse when all his attempts to devise a campaign for the whoopsie glove had fallen on stony creative ground. Try as he might he hadn't been able to see the slightest merit in the thing and had found it impossible to believe that anyone in their right mind would want to buy it, much less place it 'fully loaded', as the inventor had put it, in their pocket, no matter how glossy the advertising campaign might be. There were some things that the average human being just would not do. And the more he'd thought about it, the more his mind had rebelled against the potential shortcomings in the thing's mode of operation. Never mind that it might leak its contents into your pocket. What would happen if the offending whoopsie wasn't as solid as Boadicea's had been? What if it was just a brownish-orange puddle with the broken lumps of the bung that had held it in the dog's arse sticking up in the middle of it like tiny, odious islands? As you bent forward to pick it up with your whoopsie glove in place, your natural impulse would be to scoop up what the inventor had called 'the quarry' with both hands. Without thinking, you would perform a pincer movement, only appreciating the enormity of your blunder when the warm, steaming, granular substance was already forcing its way under the fingernails of your unprotected hand. He would never be able to live with himself, he had decided, if he managed to come up with a campaign persuasive enough to tempt innocent people, people he had never even met, people he had no reason to hate, into clogging up their cuticles with *that*!

He shied away from the memory of the fruitless time he'd spent trying without conviction to produce a campaign for the whoopsie glove, and tried instead to concentrate on his driving. That was the trouble with working for Sir Richard's advertising agency, he reminded himself as he cruised along the M4, if you were honest about what was going on there, you were likely to end up working with shit!

Even so, he had to admit that his demise had been partly of his own making. If the CD technology hadn't looked so new and exciting, and if he hadn't allowed himself to be seduced by its apparently boundless potential, he might have seen its inherent dangers straight away, instead of messing around with it for days before eventually allowing the penny to drop. What's more, he might have had the good sense to keep his mouth shut about it and let some other poor sod take the blame. Someone like the shadowy 'legal people', for instance, that Minnowfield had kept rabbiting on about. In the event, it had been Ron who had planted the first seeds of doubt in his mind.

'Where'd he get that lot, then?' he'd asked one evening when they were both working late. 'Off the back of a lorry or what?'

'Eh?' Henry had grunted without looking up.

'That thing,' Ron had insisted, pointing at the ROM drive on Henry's desk. 'Bet he nicked it, didn't he? Like everything else the bugger owns.'

'I don't know,' Henry had admitted, 'Finland, I think. Some company called Beoric, Troth and something or other. There's a picture in his office with him looking smug and pompous in the snow on the banks of a fjord.'

'Is that thing legal, she's wearing?' Ron had asked, pointing at the drawing of a heavily corseted woman. 'Looks like summut outa the Chamber o' Horrors, you ask me!'

'It's for the woman with a fuller figure,' Henry had informed him, 'apparently.' Then he'd sighed and leaned back in his chair. 'He went over for a day trip, Sam said. They flew him in a helicopter. Gave him the VIP treatment. You can just imagine the self-important sod loving all that, can't you? He bought the bloody thing for, I don't know, Minnowfield reckons it cost a quarter of a million quid.'

'What . . . that piddlin' little thing?'

'No, not the ROM drive. Just the disks.'

'He's mad! I knew it all along.'

'He will be when he finds out. All that's on them is a bunch of crappy line drawings. Hundreds of the bloody things! Thousands! Just about every crappy small ad ever made, from the looks of it. We're supposed to make new ones by collaging bits of them together. It'll be cheaper and quicker, he says. Give us an edge over the competition.'

'Sounds dodgy, you ask me! Like them bloody wosname, thingies – them bootlace videos, an' that.'

'Shoestring, more like!'

Ron had nodded, and they'd stared at the ROM drive in silence together.

'You know,' Henry had added, with a heavy sigh, 'you can get a hell of a lot of crap for a quarter of a million quid.'

'I know, mate,' Ron had agreed. 'I've seen where the silly sod lives!'

You certainly did get a lot of crap for a quarter of a million pounds, and most of it had landed on Henry a week after he'd decided to tell Minnowfield the terrible truth.

'But you can't just use it like that,' he'd protested in Minnowfield's office after the reality of what he'd been asked to do had finally sunk in. 'There's copyright on this lot. There must be! You can't just go churning it out like there's no tomorrow. Someone'll find out and sue the pants off us!'

Minnowfield had been horrified. 'No, no, no!' he'd objected, shaking his head. 'Sir Richard was quite clear, we should . . . '

'But it's illegal, for Christ's sake!' Henry had insisted. 'If we start selling this stuff as our own, someone's going to come down on us like a ton of bricks. I mean, it might be a load of crap . . . ' He'd paused, and frowned. 'Actually, it *is* a load of crap! But the point is that it's somebody *else's* load of crap! *Everybody else's* load of crap, from the looks of it, and they are not going to be best pleased when they find out we've been palming it off as our own!'

Minnowfield had been deeply hurt by the implied criticism of the company's approach to creativity. 'I don't think there's any need for that sort of language, do you? Not everyone thinks he's Rembrandt you know!'

But Henry had persisted, and Minnowfield had finally agreed to ask 'the legal people' for their opinion on the copyright issues.

'Look,' he'd whispered, staring resolutely up at the ceiling, unable to look Henry in the eye, when they'd bumped into one another in a corridor a week later, 'it's a bit awkward, really. The legal people say we can't use them. The CDs, I mean. So I thought you'd better, you know . . . tell him about it? I'd do it myself, of course, only I don't really understand all the . . . er, issues.'

Henry had been incredulous. 'Not bloody likely!'

But he'd allowed himself to be talked into it on the understanding that everyone would realize that none of it was his fault.

'Phew!' Minnowfield had breathed with relief after Sir Richard's office door had closed behind Henry with a snap the following morning. 'That was lucky, wasn't it? I mean, it's a good job Kite told us about the copyright thing before we made fools of ourselves, don't you think?'

'I'll have his balls on a plate for this,' Sir Richard had snarled, 'the nasty little backstabbing bastard! I want him out! Do you hear?'

'Yes. Yes, of course,' Minnowfield had nodded, backing away in alarm. 'It's just that the legal people say that we really ought to be careful. I mean, you know, in case he goes to the press?'

'In case he does what?'

'With the story? To the newspapers? The legal people said it might look bad if we sacked him and he went to the newspapers about it? Do you see?'

'Bad? Sacking the little shit would look bad?'

'Yes, well, yes,' Minnowfield had ventured, wringing his hands, 'that, and the, um, the er, copyright . . . er, thingy?'

'What are you blathering on about, man?'

Minnowfield had swallowed hard and glanced at the door. 'Well, er, theft,' he'd added, uncomfortably. 'Copyright, er, theft on a . . . er, corporate, er, scale. The, um, er, legal . . . er, people er, . . . said.'

He'd swallowed even harder and tried not to look at his employer, who, he had noticed, had started to turn an unhealthy shade of green. 'If you see,' he'd added, nervously, 'what I . . .? That is, what *they*!' he'd corrected himself, 'what *they*! . . . *the legal people* . . . mean?'

Sir Richard hadn't expressed an opinion immediately. Instead, he'd sat rigidly upright in his chair and stared at the wall.

Recognizing the signs of an impending eruption, Minnowfield had taken the opportunity to tiptoe out of the room.

Sir Richard had continued to stare blankly at nothing in particular for several minutes, blind to everything but the fact that he'd been diddled out of millions of pounds worth of profits, and stabbed in the back, by a little weasel called Kite. A little weasel, moreover, whom he had unwittingly been nurturing in his bosom, and who was, even at that very moment, plotting corporate blackmail against him. It had been bad enough that his own wife was into him for anything that took her gold-digging fancy. Now his filthy employees were getting in on the act, too!

'Right you little bastard!' he'd hissed. 'We'll see about that won't we? The bloody discs go down the pan – no choice in the matter. But no case to answer then, either. And your day will come you little toe rag! Your day will come, all right! Make one mistake – just one *little* mistake – and your feet won't touch the ground all the way down the road to the sodding dole queue!'

A thought had occurred to him suddenly. 'Get me a number,' he'd told Charlotte, over the phone. 'Beoric, Troth and . . . what was his name? Lawby, was it? In Lapland, I think.'

'Norway,' Charlotte had informed him. 'I remember you going.'

'That's as maybe. Right now I want a quiet word with the buggers.'

'There's no record of a company, or an individual, of that name on file, sir,' Charlotte had told him, two minutes later. 'You must have handled it yourself. Shall I look in your book?'

Sir Richard's face had frozen into a tight smile as he'd remembered the clandestine nature of his dealings with Mr. Beoric . . . or was it Mr. Troth?

'No,' he'd replied, 'you won't find it there, either, I'm afraid, Miss Piece. In fact, I have a nasty suspicion that you won't find it any-bleeding-where.'

'Will that be all, then, sir?'

'No it won't. Get me Anderson in Accounts. I have a feeling we are about to discover the company's pension scheme is short of a quarter of a million pounds. Isn't that terrible? Just tell him I'd like a quiet word with him, will you? Then call him a cab. He won't be needing his company car after today.'

Henry had survived for all of six weeks after that. It doesn't sound like much, but it had been six weeks longer than Anderson had managed, and a good deal longer than he'd had any right to expect. Right up until Sam's fracas with Choat and the rabbit shit, in fact.

All in all, he told himself, he was pleased to be out of the place. And the more he thought about it, the better he felt. In fact, he was actually beginning to feel quite good about his life as he drove along the M4 on the way to his first holiday in years. His headache had almost gone, and his natural good humour was gradually beginning to reassert itself.

'That's right, *knobhead!*' he yelled, with his hands held palms-up above the steering wheel in mocking invitation as a car cut across in front of him without warning. 'You go right ahead mate! Don't you worry about me! I'll work it out! Got no bleeding choice with dickheads like you around, have I?'

He glanced in his rear-view mirror as yet another Mondeo came up behind him, flashing its lights only inches from his back bumper.

'Sod off!' he muttered. 'I'm not going anywhere, so you might as well get used to the fact!'

He glanced in his mirror again and saw that the Mondeo was changing lanes, slipping to his left, inside him, getting ready to undertake.

'Over my dead body!' he snarled. 'Don't think you're gonna get away with that one, matey!' he gloated, as he drew up as close as he could get to the car in front of him. 'Not on my watch, you ain't!'

And so it continued, for mile after reckless mile. As each new indignity swerved in front of him, or gesticulated at him from ahead or behind, his lips became more firmly set and his brow more deeply furrowed. His fingers gripped the steering wheel like the talons of some predatory bird, or balled into fists and punched at the air, or splayed out and slapped open-palmed at the leather in frustration. Sweat ran down his legs and pooled in his socks as he hunched forward and peered through the windscreen in search of new targets, his muscles tensing and twitching as the adrenaline surged through his veins. His speed became increasingly erratic as he braked, swerved, accelerated and changed lanes with the worst of them; signalling, yes, but only at the last moment, and only then because it gave him a perverse pleasure to show the rest of the bastards on the road how this driving business really *ought* to be done. He might be out of control, he told himself as he rocketed along, but he knew *exactly* what he was doing! He tailgated, flashed his lights, honked his horn and generally behaved like all the other basket cases on the road around him. It no longer mattered to him whether an advantage gained was real or imagined: the race was well and truly on, and he meant to beat all-comers to wherever it was they were all going. Even if that was straight down to Hell!

Bonce had been watching Henry's antics thoughtfully from a safe distance for almost an hour. The big Mercedes was still only three cars behind the Volvo estate, and he hadn't even had to try to keep up. In fact, he'd spent much of the time wondering in a ponderously philosophical sort of way why Henry was driving like a maniac when doing so was obviously such a waste of his time and effort. Eventually, he'd given up trying to figure it out. After all, he'd reasoned, how could anyone possibly understand a bloke who drove a Volvo estate out of choice?

He shivered. The heating system was still blasting out hot, diesel-laden air, but it was deathly cold in the big car with a window open. He thought he could have coped with the heat and the smell if he'd been on his own, but every time he'd tried to close the window Vinny and Nobbler had got angry and told him to stop. They were asleep now, wrapped tightly against the cold in the Arsenal supporters' gear Nobbler had bought at South Mimms.

Vinny was slumped in the passenger seat with a scarf wrapped around his face, and two bobble hats pulled down over his ears. His long legs were bent up to his chin and his head lolled down onto his chest as he dozed.

Nobbler was even more snugly cocooned. Curled into a foetal ball on the back seat, with a thumb in his mouth, he twitched occasionally, and made soft whimpering noises like a dog dreaming of rabbits.

Bonce craned his neck and eyed him enviously in the rear-view mirror. He would have wrapped up warmly himself, if the stuff Nobbler had bought for him had been for any club other than Arsenal.

"'Cept Spurs, o' course,' he muttered, nodding as he ticked off the names, 'Chelsea, Millwall, Wimbledon, Leyton Orient . . . '

Three cars in front of the Mercedes, Henry was feeling ill again, and had come to the conclusion that if he didn't stop swerving around soon, he would be forced to throw up. Behaving like a boy racer was all very well, and could even be described as fun in a *Space Invaders*, game-playing sort of way. But he had never been very good at that either, and was becoming increasingly aware that if the 'Game Over' sign flashed up in front of him while he was hurtling along the outside lane only inches from the car in front of him, there was a better than even chance that it wouldn't be followed by 'Congratulations: You've Just Won A Free Play'.

He was beginning to wonder how he could withdraw from the battle without appearing to chicken out (he was male enough and insecure enough to care about such things) when the road layout came to his rescue. As he turned off the M4 for the M5, one of those strange quirks of the motorway system that can happen, even at the height of the rush hour, overtook him and he found himself on a road that was almost deserted. Suddenly, there was nothing much in front of him or behind him. The nearest vehicle ahead of him was a lorry, ponderously slow and at least two hundred yards away. The only things behind him were a pair of black saloons, neither of which seemed in any hurry to catch up or overtake him. He took his foot off the gas and drifted into the inside lane. If anyone passed him now, he decided, it would be on *his* terms and at a time and a place of *his* choosing. He might be withdrawing from the fray, but at least he was doing so with his honour intact.

He settled back into the driver's seat with a sigh.

'Time for a piss and a sarnie, I reckon,' he said, glancing in the rear-view mirror. 'And the rest of you can go straight to Hell!'

As he turned off the motorway for the service station near Bristol, he saw that the cars coming up behind him were a Mercedes and a Ford.

'Too late,' he said, as they followed him on to the slip road. 'Gotta get up earlier than that to catch Henry Kite!'

16

CHARLOTTE PIECE

Vinny was dreaming when Bonce parked the car a short distance from the service station entrance and tried to wake him up. It was one of his favourite dreams, too, in which girls of every shape and size threw themselves at his feet, or, more precisely, at his cock, while he fended them off so that he could get on with the task of achieving world domination.

'Leave me alone, you dumb bitches!' he snapped, as he prised yet another fifteen-year-old nymphet's fingers from around his engorged member. 'Can't you stupid cows see I'm busy?'

'Vinny! Vinny!' she pleaded. 'Take me! Take me, please?'

'How can I rule the world with you lot hangin' off me dick all the time?'

'Yes, but take me, Vinny! Please? You can move into Buckin'ham Palace next week. Only take me to McDonald's, Vinny, please? Me and me thirteen bestest friends?'

'Get off me, you stupid bitch! I 'aven't got time for all this!'

When Bonce squeezed Vinny's thigh a second time, he woke with a start, a diminishing hard-on and a growing sense of betrayal.

'He's turned off,' said Bonce. He nodded at the service station entrance. 'An' he's went in.'

'Lucky bastard,' said Vinny, yawning and adjusting the crotch of his jeans. 'Where are we, anyhow?'

Bonce shrugged. 'Said Bristol back there.'

Vinny sat bolt upright. '*Bristol?* Whaddaya mean *Bristol?* What're we doin' in soddin' *Bristol*, for Christ's sake?'

Bonce thought it was obvious. 'Dolly said follow 'im . . . '

'Right,' said Vinny, reaching into his jacket pocket and taking out his flick-knife. 'The bastard's takin' the piss!'

Bonce grabbed Vinny's leg as he opened the door. 'Dolly said no!'

Vinny turned and held the knife in front of Bonce's eyes. 'You keep sayin' that I'm gonna cut your soddin' face off, moron! You hear?'

'Yeah,' said Bonce, unconcerned, 'only Dolly said . . . '

There was a metallic click, followed by a wet thud.

The first was the blade of Vinny's flick-knife slicing into view.

The second was Bonce's fist smashing into Vinny's nose.

'Hey!' said Nobbler, sitting up on the backseat and wiping specks of blood from his newly acquired Arsenal sweatshirt. 'Look what you done!'

Bonce turned and stared at him, balefully.

Nobbler swallowed hard. 'It'll wash off, I reckon, yeah?'

When Vinny regained consciousness, he found himself on his own in the Mercedes, slumped forward in the passenger seat with his head throbbing and his nose leaking blood. He touched it gingerly with the tips of his fingers and winced at the pain. '*Bastard!*' he said under his breath as he sat up and squinted through the windscreen. He could see Bonce and Nobbler not far away, peering through the glass at the entrance to the service station foyer.

'*Bastard!*' he hissed again. 'No bugger does that to me!'

He bent forward, picked up his flick-knife, and opened the door.

Not far away, Gary Harmsworth opened the driver's door of the Ford Cosworth and got out. Careful not to draw attention to himself, he walked briskly across the car park towards the telephone boxes near the main entrance on an interception course with Vinny. Halfway there, he reached inside his jacket and gripped the butt of the .57 laser-guided Magnum revolver nestling in the holster under his armpit. If there was going to be any violence done that afternoon, he decided as he released the safety catch, he was the one who was going to be doing it.

Inside the service station, Henry was wandering around the shop looking for something harmless to eat and drink. No more black coffee, he told himself, or Vegetarian Chicken Supremes: nothing that had the slightest chance of biting him back. He settled for an egg and cress sandwich and a bottle of mineral water, and walked over to the checkout to pay.

Bonce watched him through the plate glass while Nobbler stood muttering to himself, spitting saliva onto the club badge on his sweatshirt and sucking the fading blood spots into his mouth.

Vinny came up behind them and put the flick-knife to Bonce's throat. 'Time's up, bastard!' he hissed. 'And I ain't bein' funny, neither!'

Bonce frowned, and reached back with his right hand to grab Vinny by the balls. There were very few men who could have concentrated on the business at hand while Bonce had his fingers locked around their testicles, and Vinny wasn't one of them. His eyes bulged and he stood on tiptoe, trying to hoist his rapidly distorting gonads out of harm's way.

Bonce turned and took the knife from his paralyzed fingers.

Henry chose that moment to walk back to his car.

Bonce saw him coming and immediately let go of Vinny's crotch, hid the knife behind his back and peered up at the sky.

Vinny grunted and was about to punch Bonce in the head when he saw Henry approaching out of the corner of his eye. He changed his snarl of aggression into the rictus of a smile, halted his swinging fist in mid-air, reversed the motion and ran his fingers nonchalantly through his hair.

Nobbler was the last of the trio to see Henry coming. He immediately stood stock still, with his teeth clamped tightly on a mouthful of sweatshirt, and tried to pretend he was part of the shrubbery.

Henry eyed them uneasily as he walked past, and glanced nervously over his shoulder at them as he hurried back to his car. He had been intending to sit there and eat his sandwiches in peace, but he didn't think that it would be such a good idea now. The men seemed to be watching him, arguing and gesticulating, and he wondered if they could tell, just by looking at him, that he supported Manchester United.

'I's 'im! I's 'im!' squeaked Nobbler around a mouthful of bloodstained sweatshirt. 'Kick! Kick! E's 'ettin' array!'

'No he bleedin' ain't!' snapped Vinny, turning to Bonce and holding out a hand. 'Gimme the shiv!'

Bonce shook his head. 'Dolly said no!'

'Sod it, then! I'll do 'im with me bare 'ands!'

'Dolly said you gotta behave!' insisted Bonce, grabbing him by the arm.

Henry glanced across at the struggling men as he fumbled his keys into the steering column. The first two, the big one and the young one with blood on his face, were fighting their way towards him, while the short, wiry one was following along behind, chewing his shirt.

'Jesus Christ!' muttered Henry, as he tried desperately to start the car. 'If that's what supporting Arsenal does for you . . .!'

The engine roared into life as he pressed too heavily on the accelerator pedal. 'Why me?' he groaned, releasing the pressure slightly and engaging the clutch. 'What'd I ever do to deserve this?'

The car slipped suddenly into gear, lurched forward, and stalled. 'Shit!' he cursed. He looked up. The men were still coming towards him. 'Oh, god!' he muttered. 'They're gonna kill me for certain now!'

He turned the key again and pressed less heavily on accelerator as the engine coughed into life. He put it into gear and started to release the clutch.

'Get off me you moron!' snarled Vinny, as the Volvo jerked out of the parking bay and headed for the exit. 'The bastard's gettin' away!'

Gary Harmsworth eased the big handgun back into its holster, turned on his heel and walked calmly over to the Cosworth. He got in, started the engine, and waited until the gang had scrambled into the Mercedes and were driving away before following them back towards the motorway.

By the time they reached the M5, Henry's car had vanished.

'You've lost him, you arsehole!' accused Vinny. He poked a finger at Bonce's face. 'Dolly'll 'ave your bollocks for this! Wait an' see if she don't!'

For a while it looked as if he would be proved right on both counts. Then, just as they were giving up hope, Nobbler spotted the Volvo up ahead.

'There!' he said, pointing. 'Tha's 'im innit?'

Vinny's eyes narrowed. 'Yeah,' he said, 'yeah, maybe.' Then 'Yeah! Yeah, tha's 'im! Right run 'im off the road. I'll do 'im on the 'ard shoulder!'

Bonce glanced sideways at him.

'All right!' he snapped. 'All right! Just don't bloody say it, that's all! If he gets away it'll be your bollocks hangin' round Dolly's neck, not mine!'

A little way behind them, Gary was talking into his mobile phone. 'We're just leaving Bristol. The kid lost his rag, but I didn't have to whack him.' He smiled. 'Yeah, maybe next time. Yeah. Yeah! Catch ya later.'

Five cars ahead of him, Henry was still glancing nervously in his rear-view mirror, eyeing each car with suspicion and expecting at any moment to see a bloodstained, bobble-hatted head leering at him through an approaching windscreen. Ten minutes had passed since he'd left the service station and he was beginning to calm down. He had no idea what sort of vehicle the men were driving, but he figured that if they'd been chasing after him they would have shown themselves before now.

'Bastards!' he muttered. 'How dare they. . .? Scaring the living . . .! For two pins I'd go back there and . . . and . . .!' Well, no, he decided, he wouldn't go back anywhere to do anything. What point would there be in bothering with people – animals, sub-humans! – like them?

He glanced in the mirror again, and sighed with relief. They obviously weren't coming after him, and he wondered why he had ever thought that they would. Even hard-bitten football supporters weren't *that* crazy, were they? He smiled grimly at his own paranoia, and drifted into the inside lane.

''E's slowin' down,' said Bonce. 'He don't know we're 'ere.'

'Yeah, well he better not!' said Vinny. He picked up his phone.

'She's havin' a kip,' said Curly on the other end of the line. 'I ain't wakin' her. More than me bollocks is worth.'

'Yeah,' said Vinny, relieved not to have to tell Dolly that they were a hundred miles away, and had no idea where they were going. 'I'll bell 'er later, then, yeah?'

'Yeah,' said Curly, thumbing through a copy of *Penthouse* and picking his teeth with a match. 'So . . . what's up your end, then?'

Vinny shrugged. 'Jus' bidin' our time, like, y'know?'

'Right,' said Curly, tilting his head to one side. 'And . . . so what'll I tell her when she . . . you know, wakes up an' that?'

'Everythin's . . . y'know . . . no problem.'

'Right,' nodded Curly, turning the centrefold sideways, 'right. Yeah, look, catch ya later, then, eh?'

Vinny hung up and glared at the back of Henry's Volvo. 'Bastard's takin' the piss,' he muttered. 'Needs a bloody good smackin', you ask me.'

'Yeah,' agreed Nobbler, 'you an' me could give 'im a good . . . '

'*Shut it!*' snapped Vinny, turning around. 'Just friggin' *shut it*, that's all!'

They drove on for an hour, keeping a safe distance behind Henry's Volvo and bickering with one another as they went. By the time they reached the Sowton service station at Exeter, Vinny had convinced the others that Henry was trying to make them look stupid. They hated him for it. Hated him, in fact, almost as much as they hated each other. And despite the cold air streaming in through the open window, you could have cut the atmosphere in the big black car with the meat cleaver Bonce kept stashed in the boot.

Henry eventually left the M5 and drove onto the filling station forecourt at Sowton. He had been wondering if he ought to stop for a rest, but had decided that, with only about another thirty miles to go before he reached Sam's parent's cottage, he might as well press on and finish the journey.

He stood with the petrol pump in his hand and his head bowed, staring at his feet and thinking how wonderful it would be to get to the cottage and go to bed. The way he was feeling, he might easily sleep for a week.

Bonce had followed him into the service station, but had stopped short of the forecourt so that they could watch him from a safe distance.

Vinny was all for getting out of the car and shooting up the place. He had always fancied making a name for himself in some public act of senseless violence, and thoughts of glory and an anonymous appearance on the *News At Ten* were running through his mind as he caressed the snub-nosed machine pistol he'd taken from the glove compartment. He kept telling Bonce that, if he would only let him get out of the car, everything would be sorted in a matter of seconds, and they would be free to pack up and go home.

But Bonce wouldn't have it.

Not far away, Gary was speaking into his mobile phone again. 'Yeah, OK, they're all yours. I'm heading back as soon as they leave. Watch out for the kid. He's got a new toy.' He listened. 'No,' he said, shaking his head, 'just an Uzi.' He listened again. 'Yeah, sure! Yeah, see you back at the office. '

On the other side of the filling station, out of Gary's line of sight, a man in a black Range Rover switched off his mobile phone and slipped it into his jacket pocket. His name was Tom Hertz, and he was not only Gary's boss, he was also the head of a bespoke global security agency that specialized in surveillance, protection, and the neat, clean contract killing of anyone his clients didn't like. It was a modest operation that neither advertised its existence nor boasted about its achievements. It didn't need to do either: there were always plenty of people *in-the-know* with lots of money, wanting to have other people, who were not so *in-the-know* and who didn't have quite as much money, followed, threatened, maimed or rubbed out. But the agency was picky, and worked by recommendation only, with Tom and his associates selecting their clients, rather than the other way around. If Hertz Global Security Inc. thought you could be trusted, you would be contacted. If they didn't think you could be trusted, or if they didn't like the sound of what you wanted them to do, you could shout and wave your money about until you were blue in the face, all you would get for your trouble was a bad case of repetitive strain injury in your wrists and a very sore throat.

Tom's fees were high because with him on the case, the success of your project would be guaranteed. But if you commissioned him to do a job for you, you had better come up with the money once he had finished it, because if you didn't, it wouldn't matter how heavily you were armed and guarded, you would be guaranteed to come up dead.

There were always plenty of would-be clients waiting in line to make use of Tom's services. But only a few ever got the call. Just a handful of the less morally corrupt governments, a selection of the top global brands; and a few of the world's wealthiest people. The client on whose behalf he was following Henry Kite was one with whom he had worked many times before. His true identity was the stuff of legends, and an even more closely guarded secret than Tom's own. More to the point, he was the only person on the face of the planet of whom Tom would admit to being more than a little afraid.

He looked up and nodded, almost imperceptibly, as Gary drove past him on his way back to the motorway. Then he put the Range Rover into gear, and pulled smoothly and unobtrusively into the position Gary had just left.

Inside the filling station, Charlotte Piece was tapping her foot as she waited impatiently for the assistant to hand over her change. The day wasn't going as smoothly as she had hoped it would, and she still hadn't quite managed to put the close encounter with Henry Kite at South Mimms out of her mind. Worse still, she wasn't at all certain that Choat believed that it had really happened, and his lack of faith in her was playing on her mind.

In the burger bar at Membury Services, two hours earlier, she had tried to convince him that Kite was not only real, but following them in an attempt to gather information about their affair.

'He was following us. You know that, don't you?' she had insisted

'What?' he'd asked, absently, looking up from the menu.

'Don't listen to me then!' she'd snapped. 'And what are we doing in this place, might I ask? I don't like it; you know that, don't you? It's common, and I don't like it! Why can't we go to a restaurant like nice people do?'

Choat's only interest at that moment had been in ordering a burger with everything on it, and not at all in mysterious strangers who might, or might not, be following them. 'Us? What d'you mean *us*?'

'Oh, so you *were* listening to me, were you? Well, thank you very much, Richard! I'm *so* grateful! He was spying on us, you know that don't you? Trying to get me into trouble because I . . . Because he got himself sacked.'

'Who?' he'd asked, as he'd tried to decide if he ought to order a Knickerbocker Glory with hot fudge topping or a Double Choc Sundae with extra nuts. 'Who's following you . . . again?'

'*Us!*' she'd hissed as she snatched the menu away from him and jammed it back into the stand in the middle of the table. 'You're in it, too, you know! And,' she'd added with a victimized sniff, 'I think you could just take it all a bit more seriously, don't you?'

He had leaned back in his seat, as if to listen, but had continued to eye the menu, hungrily. 'Who,' he'd asked, 'is following us . . . exactly?'

'*Was!* *Was* following us, Richard! Not anymore, he isn't! No thanks to you, I might add! I should think he's halfway to Coventry by now.'

'Yes, but . . .? Coventry? What do you . . .?'

'Him, of course! Henry Kite! Back there! At that other place.'

'What . . . the service station, you mean?'

'I know what it's called! I'm not *stupid*, you know! And I saw him, don't forget, not you! If you'd just *listen* to me for once you might understand what's going on!' She'd clicked her tongue and reached forward to slap his hand away from the menu, again. 'For goodness sake! Listen to me, will you?'

He'd stopped stroking the menu and had stared down at his hands.

'He's trying to get into Sir Richard's good books, that's what! He's jealous of me, Richard, and it's just *awful!*'

'I see.'

'Is that all you can say? Someone's trying to ruin my life, and all you can say about it is . . . *I see?*'

'Well, it seems a bit far-fetched, don't you think?'

'You think I'm making it up, don't you?'
'No! No! I just thought . . . '
'What?'
'Nothing.'
'Nothing?'
'No.'
'Are you sure?'

He'd nodded, unhappily, as his eyes had flicked briefly up at her face and then back down at his hands.

After a meaningful silence, Charlotte had stopped glaring quite so fiercely.

'May I continue, then?' she'd asked, acidly, cocking her head to one side. 'I mean . . . do you mind if I finish what I was saying . . . at all?'

He'd nodded without looking up.

'Is that a *yes*, or a *no*?'

'It's a *yes*! I mean *no*! I mean . . . *yes*, you can go on with what you were saying. I mean . . . yes, *please* . . . go on with what you were saying.'

'Are you sure?'

He'd nodded again, but his eyes had strayed jealously back to the menu.

'Thank you! You're *so* kind! And for goodness sake stop sulking and sit up straight for a change!'

He'd gritted his teeth and sat up straight. It was like being back at school. All it had needed was for her to tell him that he couldn't have a pudding until after he'd finished his greens and the illusion would have been complete.

'Anyway,' she'd continued with a sniff, 'he thinks – and don't ask me how I know this, I just do! – he thinks that if he can prove it, Dickie will give . . . '

'Prove it? Prove what?'

'Us, of course! What do you think? Myself and yourself in an affair!'

'Really? And what's he gonna say: I saw them in a café having a burger together? That doesn't prove anything, does it? All it proves is . . . '

'And what about the pictures, might I ask?'

'Pictures? What pictures?'

'Pho-to-graphs, *actually*, Richard! You know what photographs are, don't you? With a camera? He could have seen anything, couldn't he? All of those times in the back of my car with . . . '

'So what?'

'And that's what you're going to say to your wife, then, is it . . . so what? Yes, Jacqueline, my darling, that is my bottom you can see through the window of that Rover convertible, but . . . *so what?*'

'He doesn't even know her!'

'Really? And what about Johnson? Johnson could have told him, couldn't he? You don't know him like I do. I can just imagine . . . '

'But why would he bother?'

'Because they're *jealous*, that's why! And because he wants to get his job back! They're always sniggering at people, those two! Grinning like idiots. They think they're so bloody superior! It makes you want to kick them in the sodding . . .!' She'd stopped when she'd seen the alarm in his eyes. 'Anyway, he took that bracelet thing, didn't he? Johnson? And that Dolly person knew it was yours, so she probably told him so he could get back at me.'

'I thought you said his name was Kite? And what has Elizabeth Bates' auntie got to do with . . .?'

'Oh, for heaven's sake! She told Johnson, didn't she? She must have! And Johnson told Kite! They're all in it together, don't you see? You do remember Johnson, don't you, Richard? In the boardroom? I really don't know why you're being so dense!'

'But you don't know that any of that is true, do you?' he'd ventured, eyeing the way out.

Her eyes had blazed with suppressed fury. 'You don't have to *keep* criticizing me, you know. You could just *listen* for a change. I wouldn't *mind* if you took me seriously for once!'

'Why me, though? What have I ever . . .?'

'You? *You?* It's always *you*, isn't it? What about *me?* *Your* job's not on the line here, is it? All *you've* got to worry about is that *thing* you call a wife! Why you married her in the first . . .! Listen, my career's at stake here Richard, and I really think you might just take it all a bit more seriously, don't you?'

Choat *had* taken it all a bit more seriously after that. So much so that he'd left a mountainous Monster Burger unfinished and a Double Choc Sundae with extra nuts almost untouched.

Charlotte had led the way back onto the M4, and at first their progress had been slow and ordered, as Choat had striven to demonstrate that he really *could* take things seriously when he tried. But as thoughts of Henry Kite had drifted to the backs of their minds their mood had started to change. Soon they had been cruising playfully along like a couple of love-stricken kids, drawing along-side one another now and then to smile and wave and blow kisses in a two-hour-long bout of foreplay that had lasted all the way to the outskirts of Exeter. By the time Choat had drawn alongside her to indicate that he needed to fill up with petrol, Charlotte had been feeling more than a little bit horny. She'd followed him onto the filling station forecourt like an obedient puppy and had waited in line until he'd finished fuelling his car. Then she'd taken his place at the pump as he'd blown her a kiss and driven around to the side of the building to wait until she was ready to drive on.

She was smiling to herself now as she stood at the counter thinking of all the things they would be doing to one another when they got to Sir Richard's villa in Torquay. Rude things! Disgusting things! Things that might even involve her being on top for a while! Her body twitched involuntarily as a tremor of anticipation rippled through her pelvis. Feeling embarrassed, she turned away and gazed out of the window.

She frowned: there was a man by one of the petrol pumps who bore a striking resemblance to Henry Kite. He was even driving a battered green car like Henry Kite's. Still, she decided, there must be thousands of green Volvos in the country. She squinted at the man again. His hair was the same colour as

Kite's, and he was about the same height. He had that same stoop-shouldered look about him, and the same dishevelled clothing. And as he lifted his head and gazed vacantly across the forecourt, she saw that he had the same face!

Charlotte clenched her fists and sucked a long racking breath through her nose. Where had he . . .? How had he . . .? She exhaled with a snort, and snatched her change from the hand of the startled assistant. Then she turned on her heel and marched angrily out of the building.

Henry sighed as the pump switched itself off. He pulled the nozzle from the filler pipe and returned it to the slot on the side of the pump. He was just replacing the filler cap when he was dowsed with wet sand. He looked up in shock and disbelief to see Charlotte standing alongside the bonnet of his car with an empty fire bucket in her hand.

'He won't take any notice of you, you know!' she told him. 'He's a good friend of mine, *actually*! So you can stop following us and go home. It doesn't matter what you say, anyway, because it's only your word against mine!'

She dumped the bucket on the bonnet of the Volvo with a bang.

'He hates your guts, anyway,' she added. 'You know that, don't you? We all do, *actually*. Oh, and by the way, if I see you following us again I'm calling the police. OK? So you'd better just go and . . . and . . . and *piss off!*'

With that, she flounced past him, got into her car and drove away.

Henry stood for a moment with his mouth open, looking down at himself. '*Us?*' he asked, weakly. 'Who the hell is *us?*"

Around at the side of the building, Choat frowned as Charlotte stopped her car next to his, got out and walked quickly towards him.

'What's up?' he asked, as she leaned in at the window. 'Hey, why're you all covered in sand?'

'It's Kite,' she said, pointing. 'He's still following us.'

'What?' he said, reaching for the ignition key. 'Where?'

'Back there! But it's all right,' she assured him, as the Probe's engine burst into life. 'What are you doing? Look, I told him I'd call the police if . . . '

'The police?' he gasped, putting the car into gear and revving the engine. 'No! No! No! Don't do that! I'll just . . .! Look, I'll see you there, shall I? Yes, that's what I'll do! No sense in us hanging about, is there?'

'Wait!' she called as he pulled away with a squeal of smoking tyres. 'You don't know how to,' she clenched her fists and stamped her foot in frustration, 'get there! *Moron!*' she finished, as the Probe swerved out of sight.

Tom Hertz smiled as he watched her get back into her car and roar off towards the exit in pursuit of her cowardly lover.

'Unbelievable,' he muttered as the Range Rover's engine purred into life.

Henry finished paying for his petrol and turned back to his car, aware that an audience of astonished drivers was watching his every move. They had witnessed his encounter with Charlotte with their mouths open, and had parted like the Red Sea a moment later as he'd trudged to the counter, shedding sand as he went. They'd parted again as he'd turned and headed back to his car. Now they were clustered at the window, waiting to see if anyone else was going to attack him. To their immense disappointment, no one did. Instead, he stood next to his car for a long time, unmoving, staring into space and wondering why the world had suddenly gone mad.

After a while, he looked down at himself and slapped at the sand still clinging to his clothes. Then he looked up at the sky, took a long shuddering breath, got back into his car and, under the expectant gaze of the little knot of gawping drivers, drove away in what instinct told him was the right direction to get back the motorway. Only when he had disappeared from view, and they had convinced themselves that the entertainment had finished for the day, did his audience break into an excited analysis of what they had just witnessed.

'Pathetic,' said Tom Hertz to himself, as he waited for the gang to pull out behind Henry, before following them back to the M5.

Choat didn't get far in his wild dash for freedom. Not long after leaving the filling station, he got caught in heavy traffic and wasn't much further on when Charlotte cut in front of him and forced him onto the hard shoulder.

'Where do you think you're going?' she demanded, leaning in at the driver's window. 'I don't think you know, *actually*, do you?'

He was evasive at first, but he eventually admitted that he had no idea.

'Well I *do*! So why don't *you* follow *me* for a change, and that way we *might* get where we're going in one piece! And for God's sake stop . . . *messing about*!'

He pulled out behind her as soon as there was a break in the traffic. But he wasn't really concentrating on where they were going, and kept glancing in his rear-view mirror on the lookout for marauding green Volvos. He was so busy watching the road behind him that he didn't notice when Charlotte signalled her intention to turn onto the A380 and head for Torquay.

By the time she realized that he wasn't behind her, it was almost too late. But with an admirable presence of mind, and a complete disregard for her fellow road-users, she swerved as the road divided, cut back across two lanes of traffic, bumped over the road markings and raised gradient at the intersection, swerved again to avoid a container lorry in the inside lane of the A38, and came to rest at a rakish angle at the bottom of the embankment.

The driver of the container lorry saw her coming just in time, braked savagely, yelled '*Stupid bitch*!' as she slewed left and then right in front of him, honked his horn aggressively, and ground to a halt in front of a woman in a Citroen 2CV.

The woman in the Citroen braked savagely, yelled '*Male chauvinist pig*!' through the windscreen, swerved to avoid a collision with the lorry, beeped her horn as aggressively as she could manage, and came to a wobbling stop in front of Richard Choat's Ford Probe.

Choat braked savagely, yelled '*Stupid tart*!' through the windscreen, leaned aggressively on his horn and skidded to a halt in front of Henry's Volvo.

Henry braked savagely, yelled '*That's all right, mate! Don't you worry about me!*' through the windscreen, leaned aggressively on his horn and slithered to a halt in front of Bonce Mangle's Mercedes saloon.

Bonce braked savagely, but not quite savagely enough, and slid into the back of Henry's Volvo with a bump.

Choat shook his fist at the woman in the 2CV, then glanced in his rear-view mirror and made a similar gesture at the driver of the car behind him. But his invitation to 'Get lost, knobhead!' came out as a strangulated gurgle when he realized that the vehicle was a green Volvo and the figure behind the wheel might, just might, be none other than the apparently relentless Henry Kite. His aggression evaporated in an instant, and he cringed down into the driver's seat, drawing his head into his shoulders, and praying that the woman in the 2CV would get out of his way before Kite managed to catch him.

Henry was too busy composing his features into an expression of self-righteous indignation to notice Choat's sudden change in demeanour. He smacked his lips in theatrical exasperation, applied the handbrake with an irritable click, and prepared to get out for an exchange of insurance details with the driver of the car that had just run into the back of him. But the expression of contemptuous superiority he was wearing as he opened the car door and looked behind him, changed instantly to one of wide-eyed horror when he recognized Vinny's angry, bobble-hatted face leering at him from the passenger seat of the Mercedes. Panic-stricken, he slumped back into the car, slammed the door and locked it, and fumbled with a trembling hand for the ignition keys. He started the engine, wrestled it into gear, gripped the handbrake, ready to release it, depressed the clutch and let his foot hover over the accelerator pedal. Then, with his eyes screwed almost shut and his lips clamped in a tight line, he prayed to any deity that would listen to him that the idiots in the cars in front of him would get the hell out of his way before the maniacs in the one behind him dragged him out onto the tarmac and tore his wretched body apart limb-from-limb.

His prayers were answered almost immediately when the Citroen inched forward past the container lorry and slipped into the inside lane.

Choat's Ford Probe followed it in an instant, snaking away with a squeal of tyres, overtaking the 2CV, and racing up the hill towards Plymouth.

Henry followed it as quickly as he could, desperately urging his aging car up the hill with the gang's Mercedes only inches from his back bumper.

Charlotte, red-faced and furious after an undignified period of gear-grinding to-ing and fro-ing, and some uncharacteristically bad language, managed to get her car back onto the carriageway to join the procession.

As she roared away up the hill in pursuit of the terrified Choat, Tom Hertz shook his head in mock admiration for the pantomime he had just witnessed, slipped the Range Rover back into gear, and pulled out from behind the container lorry to follow at what for him was a leisurely safe distance.

17

TOM HERTZ

Traffic on the westbound carriageway of A38 wasn't heavy that afternoon, but it wasn't easy to negotiate either. Some drivers dawdled in the mistaken belief that if there was such a thing as a Sunday driver they weren't it. Others, wishing that they were behind the wheel of something redder, sleeker and more penis-shaped were deliberately obstructive in retaliation for the company Vauxhalls and Fords with which they felt they had been lumbered by an uncaring world. The rest were either too busy urging heavy goods vehicles past others of their kind, or too pre-occupied with the pitifully inaccurate notion that the rest of humanity envied the supposed freedom afforded them by their wind-slalomed caravans, to care whose way they were blocking. Richard Choat, Henry Kite, Bonce Mangle, Charlotte Piece and Tom Hertz did their best to find a way through the confusion, but it was hard going.

Choat wasn't much of a driver at the best of times, anyway. Competent enough when travelling in straight lines and at constant velocities, he was inclined to go to pieces when called upon to perform complex manoeuvres like braking, accelerating, or changing gear at speed. Driving with his head down, his eyes scrunched half-closed, his tongue poking out between his thin lips and his gloved fingers locked onto the steering wheel as if they had been glued there, he tried in vain to pretend that there was nothing at all for him to worry about. Henry Kite didn't really exist, he kept telling himself, and even if he did he couldn't possibly be in cahoots with his wife Jackie as Charlotte had kept insisting. He tried to console himself with the thought that she had imagined the whole thing and the green Volvo they had been running away from belonged not to Kite but to someone completely different. Several completely different someones, most likely, he thought, since there must be millions of Volvos in the country, a high proportion of them green, and he was beginning to wonder if he might not have been running away from every single one of the damned things in turn. Nothing he had seen in Charlotte's character had suggested that she was capable of telling the difference between them, anyway. On the contrary, her knowledge of things automotive seemed to be of a typically female variety, and he would have minded betting that she only knew which one was the steering wheel because it was right in front of her when she sat in the car. On the other hand, he decided, swallowing hard, she might just be right about Jackie and Henry Kite, and if that were the case, then he was up the proverbial creek without so much as a boat, never mind a paddle. Jackie was a jealous woman, and try as he might he couldn't rid himself of the mental image of her standing over his mangled body with a potato peeler clenched in a bloodstained fist.

'I'll cut your ball bag off, darlin' and use it to put me knick-knacks in,' she'd promised him on their wedding night, 'if I ever catch you so much as *looking* at another tart!' Then she'd smiled winningly and slipped her hand down the front of his trousers. 'Oooh, diddums,' she'd added with a malicious pout, 'where's my lovely, one-eyed trouser-snakey got to, then, *mmm*?'

The memory chilled him to the bone. 'Neither rain, or snow, or threat of doom,' he misquoted as he raced along, 'shall pay these . . . something-somethings . . . from the swift depletion of their anointed hounds.'

He didn't really know why he was running away, other than through some vague hope that if no one managed to confront him with the uncomfortable question of what he was doing in Charlotte's company, he would always be able to deny that anything improper had been happening between them – a sort of ostrich-like 'If I don't have to admit that you exist and have caught me at it, I can always pretend that it's a figment of your imagination, and therefore completely untrue', head-in-the-sand sort of approach to the problem.

'Nor iron bars a prison make!' he intoned, glancing in his rear-view mirror and thumping the steering wheel in relief when he saw that Henry's Volvo had fallen out of sight behind him.

'Got you, you bastard!' he grinned. 'Thought you could catch old Richie Choat, did you, *Mr.* Kite? *Hah*! No chance, mate! Nooo sodding chance! This – *this*! – isn't your average motor. Oh, no! This is your actual *Ford Probe*, this is!' He broke suddenly into song. '*Ev-ery-thing we do-ooo is driven by you-ooo*! And this isn't your average accountant either, Mr. Kite! Oh, no! This is your . . . '

He frowned as a lorry pulled out in front of him without warning. He braked hard, and shook his fist at it. '*Oy*! *Outa the way tosser*!'

'This is *the* Richie Choat, this is,' he continued, tapping the steering wheel and baring his teeth at the back of the lorry. 'Not your average, every-day wimp of a . . .! *Oy*!' he yelled again at the uncaring driver, '*bollock-brains*! *Get outa the way*! This isn't your average motor, matey. Oh no! This is . . . Oh, *shit*!' he finished, as Henry's Volvo came up behind him again.

'Our Father, which art in Heaven,' Henry was chanting as he slowed down behind the Probe and shook his fist at it. 'Get outa the way, *idiot*! Oh, God,' he added, pleading with the dashboard, 'why is this happening to me? Don't let them catch me, God, please? Hallowed be thy name. Thy kingdom come. I'll never . . . I'll never . . .!'

But what would he 'never', he wondered? What could he possibly give up that would justify the saving of his miserable skin? Drink? No, that wasn't much of a sacrifice was it? He didn't even like the stuff that much. Women then? No, that wasn't any good either because he never had any to speak of. What about fantasizing about girls he saw in the office, or on the street, or in the pub? No, that wasn't realistic, either, because people had been telling him for most of his life that he would go blind if he didn't stop doing it, and it hadn't even slowed him down, much less made him give it up. Taking himself in hand was instinctive, he decided, and besides, eye tests were free on the National Health Service when you were unemployed . . . weren't they?

He glanced in his rear-view mirror for the umpteenth time and felt a shiver of fear run up his spine. 'Oh, God!' he moaned as the black Mercedes came up behind him again. 'Our Father which art . . . '

'This,' said Vinny, as he raised the machine pistol and pointed it at the back of Henry's Volvo, 'is a .44 Magnum, the most powerful handgun . . . '

'No,' said Nobbler from the back seat, 'i's a Uzi, innit?'

Vinny turned to glare at him. '*Shut it*!'

He turned back. 'The most powerful . . . '

'Yeah, but i's a Uzi, innit?' insisted Nobbler.

Vinny turned and thrust the barrel of the gun into the little man's face. 'An' it might jus' blow your friggin' 'ead clean off,' he grated. 'Are you feelin' lucky, punk?'

Nobbler decided that he wasn't, and ducked down behind the passenger seat to prove it. "T'isn't fair!' he muttered, as he cowered on the floor. 'No bugger ever lets me be friends!'

Vinny grinned and turned around to stare at the back of the Volvo.

Choat sighed with relief a moment later as the lorry slipped slowly into the inside lane. If there was one thing he was certain of it was that his Ford Probe could out-run Kite's elderly Volvo any day of the week. He put his foot on the gas, and was soon pulling away into the distance, leaving Henry with only the gang's Mercedes for company.

Vinny grinned and pressed the Uzi to his lips. 'Not long now,' he crooned, as he kissed and caressed the barrel. 'Not long now at all.'

Charlotte was still some distance behind them, but gaining fast. Choat was an idiot and a coward, she had decided, as well as a lousy lover, and what she had seen in him in the first place she really couldn't imagine. But she had no doubts about what she thought of him now, and as soon as she caught up with him he would be finding out in no uncertain terms.

'Call yourself a man?' she muttered, as she rocketed along the outside lane. 'Insect, more like!'

He'd left her – just like that! – gone off and left her to save his own cowardly skin. Well, she wasn't having it! And if he thought she was going to take it lying down he had another think coming. She'd tried that already, and look where it had got her. That morning she had given herself more pleasure in five minutes with a hot bath and her middle finger, than she had managed in six months with his whole, useless lump of a body! He wasn't an insect after all, she decided, he wasn't that highly evolved! He was a worm or a slug or some other slimy, crawling thing. Although not even *almost* as sexy!

Half a mile ahead of her, Choat saw himself as an entirely different member of the animal kingdom. He was cunning, he told himself, like a fox, or . . . or . . . a . . . a hyena! No, that didn't sound quite right, did it? He must have meant something else. He frowned. Perhaps he had meant . . . jackal? Yes that was it. He was a jackal! There was *The Day of The Jackal*, wasn't there? And that sounded much better, didn't it? Yes, he decided, he was a jackal, and he wasn't running away, whatever it might look like. Oh no, he was making a strategic withdrawal to leave the field of battle so that he could regroup and prepare for a counterattack. And when he was ready, the mysterious Mr. Henry Kite had better watch out, because he wouldn't be taking any prisoners.

There would be no quarter asked, and none given. When Richie Choat got mad at people, people got hurt – permanently! And the malicious Mr. Kite was next in line for a good thrashing!

But that would be then. This was now, and discretion, he told himself as he headed for an approaching slip road in a desperate attempt to get away, was definitely the better part of . . . of . . . well of something that he couldn't quite remember. But that didn't matter because he knew *exactly* what he meant and Henry Kite had just better watch out, that's all!

He checked his rear-view mirror one last time before heading onto the slip road. If he could just get out of sight before Henry Kite saw him, he would be safe. That is to say, he corrected himself, he would be safe to regroup, muster his forces, and prepare for a counterattack.

'Once more onto the beach, dear friends,' he intoned as he left the carriageway at what was, for him, breakneck speed, 'once more. To block off their deckchairs with our English beds!'

He needed time to think, he told himself, as he reached the end of the slip road and turned right towards the flyover that spanned the carriageway he had just left. There would be a bit of fast-talking to be done when he finally met up with Charlotte again. Not to mention when he got home and had to explain to his wife and daughter where he had been. But he meant to have his story clear long before any of that happened. Besides, they were only women, so there was nothing for him to worry about . . . was there?

'Now then,' he said, as he pulled into a layby at the far end of the flyover to gather his thoughts. 'It was like this Charlotte, Jacqueline, Victoria . . . '

A mile or so behind him, Henry managed to overtake a caravan just as it was about to pull out in front of him to pass a line of heavy lorries. As he squeezed past it, he glanced in his mirror and saw with relief that the thugs hadn't managed to follow him. He closed his eyes and took a long, tension-relieving deep breath. This was just the sort of lucky break he had been waiting for, and if he could only put a mile or two between him and his pursuers before they came after him again, he might get away.

'Come on! Come on!' he urged, rocking backwards and forwards in his seat in a vain attempt to make the ageing Volvo go faster. He made a vow, as he gradually picked up speed, that if he ever got out of this alive he would seriously consider buying something with a bit more oomph behind it. Something like a Golf GTi, perhaps, or even, heaven forbid, a Porsche! He immediately shook his head in disgust at the thought. No, he decided, he wasn't *that* desperate! He was scared all right, but he wasn't as terrified as Adams or Choat or Sir Richard – not yet, at any rate. Besides, he had just spotted a sign telling him that there was less than a mile to the next exit.

'He's gonna get *away-ay*,' warned Vinny in a sing-song voice as they laboured along behind the caravan. 'I told you *so-ooo*! Dolly'll have your bollocks for *th-issss*!'

'Can't,' said Bonce, miserably. 'Can't get past 'im!'

'If I was drivin' . . .!' sneered Vinny. 'But you wouldn't 'ave it, would you?

Noooo! Dolly said! Dolly said! Can't think for yourself can you, you moron? Got no friggin' brains! *Jesus!* If he gets away Dolly'll hack your bollocks off with a meat cleaver! You know that, don't ya?'

When the caravan finally managed to get past the line of heavy goods vehicles and pull into the inside lane, Henry was nowhere to be seen.

Charlotte Piece, on the other hand, was right behind them, flashing her lights and gesturing angrily for them to get out of her way.

'*Christ!*' said Vinny looking over his shoulder in disgust. 'Even the tarts round 'ere 're faster than you are!'

Nobbler turned to look out of the rear window. 'I'd give 'er a good wosname,' he offered. 'If 'er asked me nicely.'

'Might as well,' said Vinny. 'This tosser's lost the other bastard, anyhow. Get 'er to pull over. I'll give 'er a good twonkin' – you can hold 'er down.'

Nobbler's face lit up at the prospect.

'I bet he's turned off,' ventured Bonce, as they approached the slip road.

'No he ain't,' sneered Vinny. 'Where? No he bleedin' ain't!'

'Yeah,' said Nobbler, pointing, his sweaty head thrusting between the front seats. 'Tha's 'im there, innit?'

'Bollocks!' said Vinny. 'No it bleedin' ain't!'

But Nobbler was right. Not for nothing had he spent years staring into the distance, waiting for horses he had doped to keel over. The motorway was running downhill, with the slip road splitting off to the left and climbing up and around towards the flyover that spanned the carriageway they were on. Henry was at the end of the slip road, waiting to turn right.

Bonce nodded. 'Yeah, tha's 'im, there, innit?'

'Hey,' said Nobbler, prodding Vinny in the neck. 'What d'you reckon?'

Immediately behind them, Charlotte sat transfixed by the sudden appearance of his naked buttocks in the rear window of the Mercedes. So mesmerized by the sight of it was she that for a moment she forgot what she was doing and followed it and the Mercedes onto the slip road.

Ahead of them, Henry turned right at the junction, just as Choat, parked in the layby at the far end of the flyover, reached into the back of his car for a road map. As he stretched between the seats, he glanced up and saw to his horror that a green Volvo was heading straight at him.

'*Jesus Christ!*' he shrieked, turning hurriedly away and fumbling for the ignition keys. 'What did I ever do to him?'

Henry braked and skidded to a halt at the end of the flyover as the Probe snaked out of the layby in front of him and accelerated away.

'*Bastard!*' he yelled after it. 'What is it with these people? Don't they have *any* consideration for the rest of us poor sods?'

He glanced in the rear-view mirror to check that he wasn't blocking the road, and saw the gang's Mercedes coming up behind him again. 'Why,' he whined as he slammed the car back into gear, 'are they doing this to me?'

As soon as the Mercedes turned at the junction, Charlotte snapped out of the trance-like state she had fallen into.

'What are you doing, girl?' she muttered. 'They're just a bunch of . . . '

But a movement beyond the Mercedes caught her eye.

'*Worm*!' she hissed as she recognized Choat's Probe disappearing around a bend in the road. 'So *that's* where you've been hiding, is it, you *cockroach*? And you think you can get away from me, do you? Well, we'll see about that!'

It didn't take her long to catch up with the Mercedes. But having done so, she found herself in a quandary. She had already guessed that the car behind Choat's belonged to Henry Kite. Which meant that if she included the bunch of sexist bullyboys in the Mercedes immediately in front of her – and she had already decided that she might as well – all of the people she most loathed in the world at that moment were within fifty feet of her front bumper. The downside was that she couldn't get at any of them until they stopped running away. And even if she had been able to, and was given a choice, she wasn't at all certain which of them she would want to dismember first. It was a moot point anyway, she decided, because any chance she might have of visiting a righteous justice upon any of them would only present itself to her when Choat crashed into something immovable – sooner rather than later, she hoped – and the others ploughed into the back of him, leaving her free to mop up the lot of them at her leisure.

Thoughts of a leisurely approach to any aspect of his life were not even close to entering Henry's mind at that moment, as he drove frantically along roads that were becoming increasingly treacherous. On the contrary, the last thing he was thinking of doing was taking things easy. He didn't know where he was, or how far he'd come since he'd left the motorway, but if the desolate landscape and the winding roads were anything to go by, he reckoned he was probably somewhere on Dartmoor. Even so, he wouldn't have been surprised if the car radio had burst into life and a tinny voice in a thick Texan drawl had asked 'For the benefit of the folks back home, fella, how about tellin' us what it's like up there on the moon?'

The barren terrain seemed to stretch away in all directions, dotted here and there with granite boulders and stunted, wind-bent trees. The road was narrow and bumpy, and when it wasn't plunging down or climbing steeply up rolling hillsides it was winding its way between high hedges that obstructed his view of everything but the few yards of tarmac immediately in front of his car. From time to time, as he raced along, he would round a corner or pop over the brow of a hill and catch sight of a red sports car swerving along ahead him. Twice he had caught up with it, but no matter how hard he had tried, flashing his lights and sounding his horn, the driver had refused to get out of his way. And each time he'd been forced to slow down, he'd glanced anxiously in his rear-view mirror to see the black Mercedes coming up behind him, with Vinny's blood-smeared face snarling at him through the windscreen. It seemed only a matter of time before he lost control and veered off the road into a hedge or a ditch. And the thought of what would happen to him if that happened, filled him with horror.

Choat wasn't happy about the way things were going, either. He was only too aware of Henry's Volvo following close behind him, and took the light-flashings and horn-soundings as demands for him to stop. He careered along, scared half to death and wondering which he was most likely to suffer first: a heart attack or a fatal, head-on collision with some heavy piece of farm machinery coming in the opposite direction. Nothing in his life had prepared him for what was happening to him now and he was so terrified by it that he was in danger of becoming hysterical. It was one thing to frighten shaky octogenarians by steaming up behind them, superfluous spotlights blazing, in broad daylight and perfect weather conditions, and with the tailgater's unrealistic expectations of immortality spurring him on. It was something quite different to be running for his life along narrow, winding roads, the like of which he had never seen before in his life, behind the wheel of a car that he was only just beginning to realize he wasn't skilled enough to drive safely, and with the prospect of emasculation by potato peeler waiting for him if Henry Kite managed to catch up with him. Or to put it another way, what was happening to him was not what he'd always thought driving was really about.

His idea of motoring was a leisurely cruise along the nearest high street in his mirrored shades with one hand looped over the steering wheel and the other hanging nonchalantly out of the window. Cars were meant for posing in, not for driving. Ever since his days as a spotty seventeen-year-old prowling around the streets of Romford in his hand-painted, yellow Ford Escort with its perforated silencer and plethora of fake fog lights strapped to the front bumper, he had known that being able to handle a car wasn't important: what really mattered was looking macho and cool while you did it.

The driving test had been a major inconvenience to him, and one that he had only managed to master at the seventh attempt. Just in time, too, given that the only thing he had ever learned about the Highway Code was that it was a boring little book without a single bit of naked totty in it anywhere. Now, as he tried desperately to get away from Henry's Volvo, he wished that he'd learned a lot more about it. And that he really *had* taken the test at the seventh time of asking, instead of coughing up a hundred quid for his smart-arsed cousin Trevor to take it for him.

As he skidded around yet another blind corner at breakneck speed, he was on the verge of giving up – just stopping and letting Henry Kite catch up with him and do his worst – when an image of Jacqueline and her potato peeler loomed up in front of him and he thought better of it. Death in a head-on collision wasn't something he wanted to experience, that was certain. But at least it would be quick and relatively painless compared with bleeding to death after his malignant tart of a wife had hacked off his goolies with a razor-sharp kitchen utensil!

Not far behind him, Henry was being plagued by similar thoughts of disfigurement: although in his case, it wasn't only his testicles he was afraid of losing. He didn't normally take risks when he was driving, but he was beginning to think that if he didn't start doing so soon the result could be catastrophic. If Vinny's expression was anything to go by, the gang meant to run him off the road and start tearing off any bits of his body that came immediately to hand. And although gruesome dismemberment wasn't a pleasant prospect, he had begun to realize that as incentives to reckless driving went, it was the most effective he had ever encountered.

Suddenly, when he was on the verge of giving up, he crested a hill and saw that the road ahead of Choat's car ran for perhaps a quarter of a mile straight, level and empty of traffic. The hedges on either side had dropped away to nothing, and he realized in an instant that he might never get a better chance to escape. He sounded his horn as a final warning to the driver of the red sports car, and pulled out to overtake.

Choat flinched at the sound of the horn, and swerved involuntarily to his right, cutting off Henry's way forward and forcing him onto the grass verge.

As the Volvo ploughed across the rough ground, its tyres threw up clods of earth that slapped into the windscreen of the Mercedes, causing Bonce to flinch and slew the big car around to face back the way it had come.

Following so close behind him that she was forced to brake and swerve to avoid a collision, Charlotte skidded on the damp grass and disappeared down a shallow gully at the side of the road. A moment later there was a bang as her Rover crashed into an outcrop of granite.

She sat for a second or two, unmoving. Then, realizing that her part in the chase had come to an end, she slapped at the steering wheel in her anger and frustration, and screamed unintelligible curses up at the sky.

On the road above her, Choat had seen his chance to get away, and was racing across the moor with Henry now trailing a long way behind him.

Bonce meantime, had turned the Mercedes around, and was accelerating after them as fast as he could.

In the passenger seat beside him, Vinny had decided that the chase had been going on for too long. With a snarl, and a muttered curse, he hung himself and the Uzi out of the window in the hope that he would soon get close enough to the Volvo to shoot Henry Kite dead.

* * *

'Fun this, innit?' said Titus. 'Better than them Wacky Racers on the telly.'

'Fun?' said Henry. 'You think being chased by a bunch of bloodthirsty psychopaths armed to the teeth is *fun*?'

'Happens all the time, buddy.'

'Not to me, it doesn't!'

'That's coz you never met the Roman army, innit? Bloodthirsty, murdering wosnames don't come into it, do they? Women, children, babies, dogs, cats, horses, pigs, sheep, cockroaches . . . if it breathes they smashes its head in and eats it. If it's a girl, they rapes it, buggers it, smashes its head in, *then* eats it.' He grinned. 'Bit like your British Empire before you lost it, I reckon?' He tapped the side of his nose. 'I saw a wosname.'

'I believe our young friend is referring to a television documentary entitled

The Rise and Fall of the British Empire at which he threw peanuts while we were in our London hotel,' said the figure. 'As I recall, the only part of the programme in which he showed the least interest contained gratuitous and unnecessarily graphic portrayals of hanging, drawing and quartering.'

Titus nodded. 'The burning at the stake bits was pretty cool, an' all.'

'Really?' said Henry. 'Well, I guess it takes all sorts, doesn't it?' He eyed the little Ancient Briton for a second or two. 'Anyway, how long have you been earwigging? I didn't hear you come back.'

'Snuck round the back, didn't I?' he said, jerking a thumb in the direction of the portable toilet. 'With the missus when the professor was rabbitin' on about what a chicken you was runnin' away from them blokes.'

'Missus?' said Henry, glancing up at the sky. 'What, you mean . . .?'

'Do me a favour! I'm talkin' 'bout *real, livin'* totty, I am: not some tart that don't really exist!'

'I take it you mean Blossom, then?'

'In his dreams,' she said, stepping out of Titus' tent. 'An' after a week of babysitting that little sod, I can tell you that dreaming's all he's any good at!'

'She loves me t' bits really,' said Titus.

'Yeah,' said Blossom, 'and *bits* is what you'll be in if you *ever* try that on me again!' She turned to Henry. 'Have you seen what he keeps in that place?'

'It's all part o' me education, innit?' said Titus, glancing uncertainly at the others for support.

Henry shook his head, minutely.

The hooded figure showed no sign that it had heard.

'Looks like you're in a minority of one, *buddy*,' said Blossom.

She turned and bowed to the shrouded figure. 'Sorry to come back so early, your grace, but lookin' after this *infant* wasn't as much fun as I thought it was goin' to be! So if it's OK with you, I'll be getting' back to somethin' more relaxin' like havin' my whole body dowsed in Sulphuric acid.'

'Horniest body I ever seen, though,' smirked Titus, coming up behind her and slapping her hard on the arse.

What happened next happened so fast that Henry wasn't certain that it had happened at all. But according to the lieutenant, who described it to him later in detail, one moment Blossom was bowing to the hooded figure, with Titus grinning like a gargoyle and slapping her arse from behind, the next, she had turned full-circle and had struck him three times: once in the chest, which had held him rigid; once in the testicles, which, against the laws of physics, had straightened him up; and once on the chin, which had sent him flying through the air to land on the far side of the campfire unconscious.

When Henry dragged his eyes away from the little man, lying spark out on his back with an inexplicable smile on his face, Blossom was back in her original position, bowing to the figure, without so much as a hair out of place.

'My apologies, your grace,' she said, 'but he's been askin' for it for days.'

'I don't doubt it, my dear,' hissed the figure, inclining its head towards her. 'The level of restraint you must have had to exhibit in the face of such puerile provocation can only be guessed at. But it is greatly to your credit that you have taken the time to demonstrate fully the dangers inherent in stretching your good nature beyond its normally elastic constraints.'

The cowled head turned towards Titus. 'I only hope that he will eventually show an appropriate level of gratitude for the invaluable lesson with which he has just been presented.'

The hooded head swung back towards Blossom. 'In the meantime, my dear, do take care of yourself, and please be good enough to give my kindest regards to your son and his colleagues, if you should have the pleasure of their company before our next meeting?'

Blossom bowed. 'They will be pleased to know you're looking so well.'

She turned to Henry. 'See you soon, lover. And keep taking the garlic, eh?'

She turned away and started to tap the symbols on her left wrist with the fingers of her right hand.

'No, *wait*!' cried Henry.

She looked up.

'You said you had something for me?' He pointed across the clearing 'The first time you were here?'

Blossom thought for a moment. 'Oh, yeah, right!' She glanced quickly at the hooded figure, and them back again. 'Only now's not the right time. Don't worry, though, eh? It won't be long now.'

Before he could ask her what she meant by that, she had vanished.

When Titus regained consciousness, he thought that he had been transported into the episode of *Star Trek* that he had watched while under house arrest at his hotel in Tahiti. There were banks of brightly lit screens all around him with flashing lights, shifting patterns and what, had he possessed even a rudimentary understanding of aerial photography, he might have recognized as views of that part of England that we now know as Wiltshire.

'How are you feeling, sir?' asked a concerned female voice.

He turned his head and saw a young woman in military fatigues.

'I'm fine darlin',' he said, in spite of the pain in various parts of his body.

He tried to sit up, but found that he was pinned to a couch by straps across his chest, wrists and ankles.

'One moment, sir,' said the lieutenant, turning to look at a bank of instruments behind her. 'Please do not attempt to get up until I have ascertained whether it would be safe for you to do so.'

'Listen, buddy, you got no right to keep me prisoner in this . . . *thing*!'

'I assure you, sir,' replied the lieutenant, as she disappeared behind a screen, 'that you are not being held prisoner. On the contrary, you are an honoured guest aboard the surveillance satellite *Theta*, and your continued physical and psychological wellbeing are of primary importance to the success of its current mission. The restraints were applied to your person to ensure your safe transportation to this vessel from the planet below. They will be removed once the medical examination has been completed and we are satisfied that there exist no further threats to your health, mental or physical.'

'Yeah, well,' he said, with grudging acceptance, 'you wanna watch it, tha's all. Warriors like me don't take kindly t' bein' tied up.'

'Forgive me, sir,' said the lieutenant from behind the screen, 'I do not wish to contradict you, but according to our extensive profiling, being tied up is one of your favourite pastimes. Or are you informing us that we have somehow managed to misinterpret the data?'

He sniffed. 'Yeah, well, jus' don't go takin' liberties tha's all!' He turned his head to look at the lieutenant as she came out from behind the screen, and was struck dumb by the sudden change in her appearance.

'If that is the case, sir,' she said, walking towards him across the flight deck, 'we may have been mistaken in our assumption that this uniform would meet with your approval.'

'Hells bloody bells!' he whispered. 'You're friggin' gorgeous!'

'Thank you, sir,' she said with a perfect smile. 'I think this head and this body are probably my favourites.'

He frowned. 'Yeah, but how come you . . .?'

'The uniform, sir? Us girls have our little secrets, you know.' She struck a pose. 'Would you agree that it is an accurate facsimile of data acquired from your memory banks?' She turned on a heel like a model reaching the end of a catwalk runway. The miniscule skirt of a nurse's uniform that could only have been designed by Jean Paul Gaultier in one of his more frivolous moments, flicked up and flew out to reveal the lacy tops of her seamed stockings, matching eight-strap suspender belt and pair of ruffle-back panties.

There was a sudden beeping from the control panel behind her.

'I regret to inform you, sir,' she said, looking up from a battery of flashing lights, 'that our instruments suggest that you are suffering from the sudden onset of an abnormally pronounced, and probably rather painful, tumescence of the penis. Please excuse me while I attempt to ascertain from our clinical database the most appropriate course of action for me to take in order that you might be spared further discomfort.'

'Yeah, well,' muttered Titus as the translation device on his wrist went into overdrive, 'you could stop bendin' over them friggin' lights for a start!'

* * *

18

PERCE PRATT

Lance and Gavin Clatworthy were a lot smarter than most people thought. It wasn't difficult: most people thought they were as thick as two short planks.

'Don't talk bleedin' daft,' old Merv, their father, would say. 'They idden even *that* clever! Look at 'em for Christ's sake! Puggled, the pair of 'em is!'

He had a point: his sons looked as if they were caught in a time warp. A heavy metal born-in-the-middle-of-nowhere, raised-in-the-middle-of-nowhere, destined-to-stay-in-the-middle-of-nowhere-for-the-rest-of-their-yokel-lives sort of time warp that had encouraged them to think that it would be a good idea to grow their hair down to their waists and wear more denim than was good for the eyesight of everyone who had to look at them. Everything they owned seemed to be made out of denim: with most of it covered in metal studs and patches embroidered with heavy metal insignia and marijuana leaves, and embellished with mildly eccentric messages scrawled in shaky ballpoint pen. Things like 'Heavy Metal Anarchists Rule UK'; 'Iron Maiden Do It With Their Guitars'; and the particularly anti-climactic 'Black Sabbath Grand Funking World Tour 1977/ 78, Bovey Tracey Town Hall. I woz there!'

They had denim bracelets on their wrists, floppy denim hats on their heads, and skin-tight cut-off denim jeans for swimming trunks when they went off, pale and wan, to Fernworthy Reservoir to pose as surfers in front of non-existent gaggles of giggling, pubescent girlies. The most damning of all of their many sartorial idiosyncrasies, however, were the triangles of Paisley patterned curtain fabric sewn into the seams of their Levi 501s below the knee that flapped as they walked and might have given them the air of gauchos home from the pampas were it not for the occasional glimpse as they swaggered along of anaemic, sockless ankles and grubby plimsolls beneath. In short, they possessed all the fashion sense, but none of the glamour, of mannequins in a charity shop window done on the cheap.

The problem was that life in the wilds of Dartmoor was dull: deadly dull and gut-wrenchingly, brain-numbingly, energy-sappingly boring and bloody awful. And sitting on a windswept hillside in the middle of nowhere for eight hours out of every day, watching the diversion signs for Perce Pratt with nothing but the occasional carload of tourists to heckle and wave two fingers at from a distance, did nothing at all to lighten their mood. What they really wanted out of life was action; fast and furious action with blood and guts and good guys and bad guys and fist fights and fire fights and the deafening explosion of thousands of megatons of TNT all around. They wanted martial arts and swordplay, with the rescuing of damsels in distress, piracy on the high seas, bravery above and beyond the call of duty, and burning dive-bombers spiralling out of control into snow covered mountainsides. They wanted covert operations in a dinner jacket with miracle-working gadgetry and a licence to kill. They wanted anonymous telephone calls about albatrosses flying with sardines at midnight and lions lying down to have cryptic sex with lambs. They wanted daring moonlit raids behind enemy lines with secret codes and cyanide pills, and orders to divulge nothing but their name, rank, and serial number, no matter how many burning electrodes were attached to their scrotums. All they wanted in return were universal acclaim and an endless supply of nubile bodies writhing at their feet ready to indulge in every sexual perversion known to mankind – not to mention one or two they had dreamed up for themselves. They wanted all of those things, and they wanted them badly, especially the last. Their problem was that they couldn't be bothered to get up off of their lazy backsides to find them.

Gavin's home-grown grass was one of the reasons. The fact that they had bales of the toxic stuff stashed in the hayloft was another. One of the most potent hallucinogens on the planet, it was even more powerful than Perce Pratt's home-brewed scrumpy. And when the two were taken together, with a pinch of magic mushroom thrown in to taste, the effects on the average human psyche could be dramatic. Just enough and you started to see tiny pink elephants. Too much and you got the munchies and wanted to eat the little devils by the handful. The brothers had smoked and drunk and taken a pinch or two of more than enough, and had been eyeing a herd of rose-tinted miniature pachyderms hungrily ever since. So far the perfectly formed little hallucinations had managed to avoid being eaten. But, now that the ice cream had finally run out, it was beginning to look as if their luck had run out, too.

It was bitterly cold in the harsh April wind on the side of the hill overlooking the moorland road, as the boys slouched in rickety deckchairs surrounded by a litter of sweet papers, empty cider flagons, dog-ends and cigarette packets. Protected from the worst of the wind by bobble hats, woolly gloves and sleeping bags pulled up tight beneath their chins, they had binoculars in their army surplus duffel bags to see who was trying to creep up on them from behind, and walkie-talkies to call for help if they thought they were in danger of being overwhelmed by the forces of evil. They had been sitting in their current position since nine o'clock that morning, hoping against hope that something new and interesting would happen to them for a change. But, since nothing new or interesting had happened to them in more years than they cared to remember, they weren't optimistic. What they didn't know was that in less than five minutes, they would be having a dramatic effect on the lives of five people they had never met, and who weren't going to thank them for the experience. The latter wasn't so surprising, given that one of the five was about to have his car riddled with machinegun bullets, while the other four would be knocked senseless: one of them twice! If the boys had realized just how exciting their lives were about to become, they might have sat up straight for a change and concentrated on something other than destroying even more of their limited quota of brain cells.

Gavin paused in his vain attempt to scrape something tasty from the bottom of the ice cream carton he had been cradling against his chest for the past half an hour to gaze wistfully at a pair of tiny, salmon pink elephants in lime green tutus unicycling around his feet.

'Wish they little sods'd stan' still long enough to catch 'em,' he muttered, pausing to suck his dry fingers knuckle-deep into his mouth. 'Tidden fair the way they always buggers off soon as you tries to catch 'em.'

'What I wanna know,' said Lance, ignoring the elephants, but eyeing the carton jealously, 'is what're we doin' 'ere?'

Gavin looked across at him with a frown. ''Ere?' he asked, leaning precariously sideways in the creaking deckchair and prodding the ground with a finger. 'Or 'ere?' he added, flinging his arms wide to indicate the moor, the earth, the galaxy and the whole massively expanding universe beyond them. In his enthusiasm to probe the depths of existence, he accidentally threw the empty carton into the air, and watched with lip-trembling regret as it caught on the wind and went cartwheeling down the hill towards the road.

Lance watched it too for a while, torn between a powerful desire to chase after it and an equally potent urge to beat his brother to death for throwing it away. But the conflicting emotions soon cancelled one another out and he stayed where he was, nursing a deepening sense of betrayal.

'What're we doin' 'ere?' he said with one eye on the bouncing carton. 'That's what I'm sayin'. What're we doin' halfway up a bloody hill in the middle of bloody nowhere, freezin' our bloody taters off like a couple of bloody . . . ' he paused as the carton bounded into the air one last time and dropped out of sight over the hedge two hundred yards below them. 'That were the last one you stupid tosser!' he snapped. 'What we gonna eat now?'

Gavin shrugged, defensively. 'What?'

'*What?*' mimicked Lance. '*What?* You chucked our bloody grub away that's bloody *what?* you stupid wazzock!'

Gavin pouted. 'Didden!'
'Yes you bloody did!'
'No I bloody didden!'
'I saw you!'
'When?'
'Then!'
'What?'
'Jus' now!'
'No I bloody didden!'
'You're always bloody doin' it!'
'Bloody not!'
'You jus' bloody did!'
'Bloody didden!'
'Bloody did!'
'Didden!'

Lance frowned. 'You 'ear that?' he asked, as an echo of Charlotte Piece's Rover convertible smashing into the granite outcrop further down the valley reached them on the wind.

Gavin shrugged. 'What?'

'That.'
'That?'
'Yeah.'
'No!' Gavin shrugged. 'An' what if I did, anyhow?'
Lance thought for a moment. 'Yeah,' he said. 'Right. Who gives a bugger?'
He blew out his cheeks and looked down at the ground.
Gavin blew out his cheeks and looked up at the sky.

They turned and squinted at one-another, looked away, looked back, then down, then up, then off in opposite directions. There was silence as they sat with their faces screwed up, chewing their fingernails, trying to remember what it was they had been arguing about. It was a problem they had, this short-term memory loss: one of the many. And if Perce Pratt had been able to see them then, he might not have thought he was getting value for money.

Perce was the landlord of the Green Dragon Inn, an ancient public house that stood at the end of the even more ancient road that ran through the middle of the treacherous Sodmire Bog. Unless you fancied the trek across Sodmire – and no one in their right mind ever did – the track was the only way to get to the Dragon. It was narrow and deep-sunk, and at the height of the holiday season, drivers were forced to crawl along it, bumper-to-bumper, stopping at a passing place here to wave an oncoming vehicle forward: then moving up one place as they were waved forward themselves. When everything was working smoothly, vehicles moved from one passing place to the next in ordered lines, waiting, moving, then waiting again before moving on singly or in twos and threes, each one taking its turn in the queue. When things weren't working smoothly, which was most of the time, there was chaos.

Only a handful of the exhausted drivers who found themselves trapped on Sodmire Lane each day would have been there at all if Perce hadn't put up a sign at the junction with the main moorland road advertising an exciting range of attractions at his isolated public house that included a fun fair, a boating lake and a petting zoo. The eager tourists only found out when it was too late that these were all essentially figments of Perce's imagination, consisting as they did of a patched and leaning bouncy castle, a stagnant duck pond where Lance and Gavin liked to churn up the foul-smelling water with their battered radio-controlled speedboats; and a rabbit hutch housing a grumpy hedgehog named Chloe who had been rescued from under the wheels of the local dustcart by Perce's live-in waitress, Jo Cornwall.

Congestion on Sodmire Lane wasn't helped by the fact that many of the lost souls who found their way on to it each day hadn't had more than a passing acquaintance with their vehicles since their last holiday on the moor twelve months earlier. Or to put it another way: most of them had forgotten how to drive. They dawdled along, getting in each other's way from dawn 'til dusk in perfectly preserved Nissan Sunnys, Vauxhall Astra 1300Ss and Austin Maestros. According to a census taken on behalf of Devon County Council's Department of Tourism, there were to be found crammed into the few idyllic square miles around Sodmire each summer more cars belonging to their original careful owners than you could find in all of the car parks at all of the garden centres and DIY stores in the country on any given Easter Sunday, and only one in a hundred of the damned things had more than 3,000 miles on the clock. Expecting these eternal day-trippers to show consideration for their fellow road-users was fruitless. Most of them had only one speed, dead slow; and only one direction, straight ahead: and if they signalled, it was invariably accidental. Half of them were stone deaf, shortsighted, or both, and only used their rear-view mirrors to admire the antics of the pampered Jack Russells, Yorkshire Terriers, and Miniature Dachshunds that yapped incessantly from the glazed safety of their pristine parcels shelves. If they acknowledged you at all, it would be to boast that they had never taken a driving test in their lives and hadn't had an accident in sixty-odd years of driving, so it clearly couldn't be their fault that they had just crashed into you.

At the other end of the spectrum were the lantern-jawed, Brut-soaked, wetsuit-encased, unshaven, mop-headed, baggy-shorts-clad sporty types with mountain bikes, surfboards, windsurfers and canoes lashed to the roofs, or hitched up behind, their battered VW Beetles, campervans and mud-spattered Subarus. They were free spirits and knights of the road – whose foreheads were generally lower and hairier than their balls – who braked without warning and took pride in having learned how to park on hills, roundabouts, humpback bridges and blind corners. Of the rest, the majority were too preoccupied with screaming kids, steaming radiators and wing mirrors trapped in hedges to know or care how many cardiac arrests they were leaving slumped over steering wheels behind them. Mixed in amongst them was the occasional driver who really *did* know where he or she was going and why, and who wished fervently that they had remembered to strap a bazooka to the bonnet of their car before setting out. When road rage eventually got the better of these normally placid souls they were inclined to shake their fists and leap from their vehicles, slamming doors, throwing hats and sunglasses on the ground to be trampled under foot, and snapping off bits of canoe, windsurfer or mountain bike with their teeth. All in all, Sodmire Lane was a dangerous place to be between the months of June and September, especially for considerate drivers with dentures, and/ or a weak heart.

A year earlier, in the summer of 1986, the traffic jams on Sodmire Lane had reached such road- and artery-clogging proportions (with the ambulances and breakdown trucks ferrying the injured and clapped-out away from the scene only adding to the congestion) that the local highways committee had decided that something drastic needed to be done if they were to put an end to the annual carnage. The solution they had come up with was the removal of Perce's sign and the erection in its place of one of their own devising on which was to be written the legend 'Danger! Unsuitable For Motor Vehicles!'

Their decision had been met with scepticism, not to say derision, from the locals who'd felt that the sign hadn't got an ice cream's chance in Hell of making a difference. But to everyone's amazement, not least the members of the highways committee, the new sign had worked like a dream. The numbers of hyperventilating tourists and broken down vehicles had fallen away to almost nothing, and for the first time in living memory there had been peace on Sodmire Lane.

As the chairman of the local highways committee, and Perce's sworn enemy, Jack Strawbridge had been especially pleased with the outcome. Suddenly, only a few diehard locals had been going to the Green Dragon each day, and he had felt able to sit back in the comfort of the Blasted Pheasant with his cronies and toast the council's decision as a personal triumph.

Perce had been devastated by the sudden downturn in his business, and had taken to wandering through the all-but deserted building wearing the martyred expression of a bloodhound that had left one of its testicles hanging on a barbed wire fence.

'All that bloody money down the drain,' he had muttered. 'Might as well 'ave flushed me savings down the bleedin' bog!' His eyes had glazed over then, and he'd stare forlornly across the empty saloon bar at the brand new toilet facilities that he'd had installed that spring for the summer rush of visitors that had suddenly seemed destined never to come.

'Them's bloody fine bogs, an' all, mind,' he had insisted, with a mournful shake of the head. 'Cost a bleedin' fortune gettin' all they tiles grouted, an' all!'

'Gert 'eller they tiles is, Perce,' Hubert and Horace Naggs had assured him in dutiful unison (and the hope that their blatant toadying would win them a pint or two of scrumpy on the house). 'Tiles like they makes all the difference, mind, when you'm bustin' for an eye-waterin' shit!'

Perce had nodded and sniffed, and allowed his lower lip to protrude self-righteously. 'That there disabled bog wodden cheap mind, neither. 'Ad the bugger brought all the way 'cross yer from Plymouth, special, I did. No other bugger's got one o' they round yer, 'ave they?'

'Course they bleedin' 'aven't,' Jack had sniggered to his circle of devoted sycophants at the Blasted Pheasant. 'What good's a bloody bog when he's disabled? Eh? That's what I wants t' know!'

'Why don't I break both yer legs, lover?' Rooter Pengardon had growled as he'd stalked to the door. 'That way you'll find out, won't 'ee?'

Perce had been given a lot of moral support by friends like Rooter, and Hubert and Horace – and some of it might even have been genuine. But it hadn't really helped: his pub had still been empty most of the time, and there had been nothing for him to do but wander aimlessly from room to room stroking the gleaming brass drip trays lovingly and taking down the occasional spotless tankard to breath on and polish with a cloth.

'It's all that bastard Strawbridge's fault, mind,' he had insisted. "E's the one what's at the bottom o' this lot, don't you worry. Puttin' up signs without askin'. Wouldn't mind bettin' 'e were behind my Aggie goin' off, an' all.'

Whenever he thought of Agnes Morehead, Perce's eyes would mist over and he would stare slack-jawed at nothing in particular as most of the sharp-eared locals remembered that they had urgent business to attend to elsewhere.

'There 'er was one minute, an' there 'er wasn't the next,' he would add, to a rapidly diminishing audience, as he recalled his last night of passion with Aggie on the back seat of his ancient Vauxhall Viva. 'An' 'ere's me left with a bloody great you-know-what, an' no Aggie about t' help me shift 'im!'

The 'you-know-what' in question was an erection, and the reason for the hasty retreat of his customers. Not even the Naggs brothers, who were eager to sympathize with anyone if they thought there might be a free pint in it for them, wanted to hear about it again. More to the point, they didn't want to see it again, and Perce was inclined to get it out if anyone in the room showed the least signs of interest or appeared to doubt the truth of his story. Everyone who knew him had long-since learned that the safest course of action, if you didn't want to have an erect dick thrust at you for recognition, was to head for the hills as soon as his eyes went glassy and he reached for his flies.

No one had been able to get rid of it, he would explain to the few unfortunates who hadn't managed to get to safety quickly enough. Urologists had prodded it and squeezed it and peered at it through lenses. Neurologists had shown him faintly pornographic diagrams of erectile tissue, then squeezed it and X-rayed it and tapped it with little hammers. And an enthusiastic female physiotherapist from Tavistock had squeezed it and squeezed it again, and then again, and again, until – breathing rather heavily, Perce had thought at the time – she had pronounced herself satisfied that no course of exercises that she had heard of would ever make such a magnificent looking thing lie down. 'After all,' she'd added, bright-eyed and moist-lipped, 'why would you want it to, my lover? Now, if you'll just come and lie down over 'ere, on this lovely big couch o' mine, I'll strap 'ee in to it, an' climb on top, an' bounce up and down 'til you'm better!'

Perce had given up the treatment after six months because something had told him that she hadn't really had his best interests at heart. 'I don't reckon 'er knows what 'er 's on about,' he'd confided to the ancient Naggs brothers with their tongues hanging out. 'I mean, 'ow's all that ol' rubbin', an' grindin' an' smearin' o' cream s'posed to make 'im lie down? 'Ave's completely t'other effect, you ask me! Don't make no bloody sense, now, do it?'

Hubert and Horace nodded sympathetically each time he told them the story in graphic detail, and at their asking, and hoped that he wouldn't realize just what a brainless tosser they thought he was being.

'Tha's right, Perce,' Horace would nod, extending his tankard for a refill. 'Bloody shame 'bout that, innet? Where'd you say 'er lives, by the way?'

After years of exhaustive testing, the medical experts had been unanimous in their opinion that only a miserable whinger like Perce would have complained about having had such amazingly good fortune in the first place. They had gone on to add that if he didn't start showing some gratitude for it soon they would have no alternative but to chop it off and give it to someone who would. Even so, it had only been when the President of the British Medical Association, with a calculating glint in his eye and the flash of cold steel in his fist, had suggested that he would himself make the perfect recipient of a transplant, that Perce had finally begun to realize what a truly dangerous thing penis envy could be. He had been hiding in the depths of Sodmire Bog ever since.

But the threat of surgical reprisals hadn't stopped him wanting to discuss his predicament with anyone who could be persuaded to listen. He had studied his condition in great detail, he would explain, and had come to the conclusion that his problem was psychosomatic, and the consequence of his having been abandoned by the only woman he had ever loved just as he had been about, as he put it, 'to give vent'. The experience had been so traumatic, he would add, that his member had been in denial ever since, pretending that everything was fine and that Aggie hadn't really gone off and left him. Indeed, he would inform his cringing audience, he was convinced that his dick believed that Aggie was still very much around, ministering to his personal needs in the manner to which he, and it, had, for so long, been accustomed.

'See what I'm sayin'?' he would ask with a look of anxious enquiry. 'He won't accept it, will he, the old tadger? He reckons he stays like that – up, like? – Aggie mus' still be about. Else what's the ol' fella good for?'

But all the theorizing hadn't made any difference. He was still very much erect, and left to face the fact that not only had Agnes gone off without him, but it had probably been someone he knew well that had convinced her to go. Privately, he thought it had been Jack, or Rooter, or even old Merv. But none of them had ever been prepared to admit it. On the contrary, Rooter had said that it was Merv's fault. Merv had said that it was Rooter's. Jack had said that he didn't give a toss either way, just so long as Perce had a miserable life.

'Better off without the old tart, anyhow, you ask me,' he had sniggered to his mates in the Snare and Coney. 'At least the clap clinic's quieter than it was!'

Perce had heard about that and had decided that it wasn't a nice thing to say about a lady. So he had hidden in the bushes at the Stratton Hunt, and had shot Jack in the arse with his 22-rifle as he'd trotted past. Jack had been catapulted from the saddle by the impact and had landed in the middle of the pack, where he'd been savaged by confused hounds that had seemed to think he smelled more interesting than a terrified fox. The sight of him in tattered jodhpurs, and with a bullet hole and several sets of teeth marks in his skinny backside, had cheered Perce up no-end for a while. But enjoyable though the screaming and thrashing about had been while it had lasted, it had been scant consolation for the besmirching of Aggie's good name. Besides, it hadn't brought her back, and although Perce hated to admit it, Merv might just have been right when he'd said that she hadn't really loved him at all in the end.

'I know it's hard, Perce,' he had added. 'No pun intended, by the way. But think about it for a minute, will you? She couldn't really have loved you, could she? I mean, if she had she'd still be here now. And it's no good looking at me like that, is it? It wasn't my fault she went off and left you. Ask that randy little sod, Rooter, if you really want to know what happened that day.'

Perce no longer cared who was to blame for Aggie's sudden disappearance. All he wanted was to get her back: if for no other reason that it would give him something useful to do with his dick. People seemed to think that what he had to put up with was amusing, sniggering behind their hands or coughing their drinks across the bar every time some joker asked if he had a gun in his pocket or was just pleased to see them. And every time he tried to explain what it was really like, the bastards would snigger even louder and head for the hills! They never seemed to take his condition seriously, or stop to wonder what it was like to be so conspicuously aroused. Or perhaps they did and were just grateful that it hadn't happened to them? Perhaps they had some inkling of how it felt never to be able to wear swimming trunks in public without being arrested: or how dangerous it was to have an audience when you went to the loo? There could be ten of you standing in line at the urinal, except that you had to stand six feet further back to allow for the parabolic trajectory. Some men were easily offended by that sort of thing.

'Wha's up with you, then, mate?' they were inclined to snarl as a prelude to acts of gratuitous violence. 'Think you're better than the rest of us, do ya? You want a smack in the mouth, then, or what?'

No, it wasn't easy carrying a thing like that around in your underpants every day. Just once he wished he could piss on his shoes without having to wait for it to bounce off the ceiling first. Better still, he wished that Aggie would come back and put him out of his misery, and the highways committee would relent and take down their horrible sign.

But Jack and the committee had shown no such intention: not even after he had written them dozens of self-pitying letters explaining what a disastrous effect it was having on his income. On the contrary, they had written back telling him to shut up and stop wasting their time. Their decision, they'd added, was final, and what they did with their signs was none of his business.

Perce had eventually come to the conclusion that the council's uncaring attitude had left him with no alternative but to take the law into his own hands, and he had let it be known amongst his regulars that he would be happy to guarantee free scrumpy for life to anyone who could come up with a way of bringing the tourists back to the Dragon.

News of the offer had spread like wildfire amongst the locals, who, despite knowing only too well that unlimited access to the green stuff he brewed in his cellars would probably reduce what was left of their grey matter to something resembling liquidized porridge, had begun racking their brains for an answer.

19

ROOTS PENGARDON

To everyone's amazement, especially their own, it had been Lance and Gavin who had come up with a plan to solve Perce's problem. They had called it 'Our Plan', and had explained to Perce that it consisted of them taking it in turns to stand on a chair with their arms held out sideways in front of the council's sign to block it from the view of approaching tourists.

Perce had been sceptical of Our Plan's chances of success, but had decided not to discourage the boys from giving it a try. The theory had been that while one of them was standing on the chair in front of the sign, swigging from a flagon and looking innocent, the other would be on the grass verge at the junction, swigging from a flagon of his own, looking equally innocent, and directing traffic towards the Green Dragon. But as the first day of Our Plan's implementation had worn on, the boys had found it increasingly difficult to balance on the chair with so much scrumpy sloshing around in their bellies (not to mention their bladders) and had been forced to swap places frequently to avoid committing acts likely to offend public indecency.

This simple rotation system, which they had decided to call 'Our Other Plan', had worked well enough while they had both remained sober, but it had begun to break down by mid-afternoon when they had been so drunk that they had both been a) on the chair singing excerpts from *Iron Maiden's Greatest Hits*; b) in the middle of the road directing each other; or c) in the field behind the hedge flat on their back in a drunken stupor. Even so, their efforts had not gone entirely unrewarded: a trickle of tourists had arrived at the Dragon throughout the day, and it had seemed to Perce that his business would soon be back on its feet – even if Lance and Gavin probably would not.

Perplexed by their failure to stem the tide of mechanical breakdowns and human casualties littering Sodmire Lane, the highways committee had responded by putting up a succession of ever taller and wider signs at the junction, each warning of progressively more frightening dangers from Road Works to Flooding, Subsidence to Avalanche, and from Earthquake to Attack by Wild Animals. But as each new sign had been erected, so the brothers had simply found something taller and wider to stand on.

In a final act of desperation, the council had put up a truly enormous sign that had spanned the full width of the junction and borne a black skull and crossbones motif on a fluorescent yellow ground above the legend Beware! Devourment by Cannibals.

That had done it! The tourists had taken one look at the boys beaming drunkenly down at them from their makeshift scaffolding and had fled past the turning in droves. Perce's takings had fallen back to almost nothing, and the boys had been forced to go back to buying their own scrumpy.

But as luck would have it, only a couple of days after the erection of the council's monstrous new sign, the boys had been driving home across the moor in Lance's ancient Land Rover with a load of steaming horse manure hitched up behind it, when they had broken down on the outskirts of Princetown. Gavin had called Rooter from a phone booth in the village, and they had sat back and waited for him to come and tow them away with his tractor. It had been a swelteringly hot day, and hundreds of sweaty drivers in over-heated sweaty cars, filled with over-heated sweaty relatives, had been forced to make a slow detour around the Land Rover and its stinking cargo, passing uncomfortably close to the walls of Dartmoor prison in the process. Dozens of joyously steaming inmates had crowded at the windows of their steaming cells to jeer and make sexually explicit gestures at the scandalized tourists with a creative assortment of garishly painted papier mâché dildos.

'Never 'ad so many visitors in one day, that lot 'aven't,' Gavin had giggled with a pint in one hand, a spliff in the other and his feet up on the dashboard. 'Mus' thing their Christmases and birthdays 'ave all come at once! We oughta come down 'ere more often, and ged them buggers t' pay for the priv'lege. With all them grockles 'bout the place, you an' me could make us a f-fortune!'

It had taken a while for the penny to drop. But when it had, their faces had lit up like merchant bankers who had found a defenceless beggar to kick.

That night they had stolen a set of barriers and signs from roadworks near Okehampton and used them to set up their own diversion at the junction. Then they had cut the fixings on the council's massive sign and lifted it out of position with the winch on the back of Rooter's huge tractor. The following morning, they had settled back on the side of the hill to await developments.

A steady flow of punters had soon been following the signs onto Sodmire Lane, with the majority so close to garrotting their nearest and dearest by the time they arrived at the Dragon that they had been only too pleased to make the most of its amenities: not least the newly installed toilet facilities after the lugubrious Perce had informed them that the only way back to the nearest public conveniences was along the same high-hedged, traffic-clogged track down which they and their carload of straining and complaining relatives had just struggled for a bladder-bursting hour in the heat.

Guarding the signs had turned out to be the perfect way for Rooter and the boys to keep themselves busy. Or if not exactly busy, then out of everyone else's way. In return for their efforts, Perce gave them as much food from the pub's menu as they could eat and as much scrumpy from its cellars as they could drink. So far no one had questioned the legality of the signs, or tried to remove them. The locals knew when to leave well enough alone, and it never occurred to the tourists to go anywhere other than where they where sent.

From their vantage point halfway up Gallows Hill, the boys could see the road for a mile or so in both directions at once, and at the first signs of trouble they could call Rooter behind the hedge at the bottom of the hill and have him remove the makeshift barriers and hoist the council's huge sign back into place. By the time any inquisitive police officer or council official arrived at the junction, everything would be back to normal. Or at least, that was the theory. So far it hadn't been tested. Not a single police officer or council official had come within a mile of the place since the signs had been set up. So Perce was finally getting the customers he needed, while they were getting fed and watered – whether they had set out to do so or not.

It might be useful to note at this juncture that Perce's home-brewed cider was rather more than just an acquired taste. A green and vinegary vintage, known to the locals as Young Love's Dream or A Drop o' the Ol' Lovers', it not only made the drinker fancy anything that moved, including the curtains, it also contained the most effective spermicide known to medical science. The average human male had only to drink a pint of the stuff to be guaranteed sterility for up to twenty-four hours. Even so, only the desperate had ever been tempted to see it as a viable alternative to the more conventional forms of contraception, because it had long been rumoured that, when taken on a regular basis, it was inclined to cause the progressive shrinkage (not to say, the eventual disappearance) of a drinker's genitalia. Whether this was true or not, the boys weren't saying. But there were those who suggested, albeit carefully out of their earshot, that you needed to look no further for the cause of their many psychological problems than the fermentation vats in Perce's cellars.

Gavin shifted uneasily in the sagging deckchair and turned to gaze out across the moor. 'Anyhow,' he said, suddenly remembering their earlier argument, 'tidden nowhere, is it? Bloody Gallows Hill this is!'

'Yeah?' said Lance. 'An' what dif'rence does that make?'

'Well, tidden bloody nowhere then, is it?' insisted Gavin. He leaned sideways and patted the ground. 'This 'ere's Gallows Hill, innet?' He pointed across the valley. 'That over there idden.'

Lance squinted at the hill. 'Yeah,' he said, 'what of it?'

'That's Stratton Tor, that is.'

Lance's eyes narrowed. 'So . . . ?'

'Tidden Gallows Hill then, is it?' said Gavin. He pointed at a hill off to their left. 'Tha' idden Gallows Hill, neither.'

'I know that. I bloody know that, don't I?'

'Tha's Maidenhead Tor, that is.'

'Look . . . all I'm sayin' . . . '

'That idden Gallows Hill, neither,' said Gavin, pointing to the right.

Lance clenched his teeth. 'Listen . . . !'

'Tha's Dead Man's Dyke, that is.'

'Look,' said Lance, balling his fists in frustration, 'jus' bleedin' *listen* will ya?'

Gavin stood up, and pointed across the valley. 'An' that idden Gallows Hill, neither. Tha's . . . '

'Shut up!' snapped Lance, surging to his feet like a swimmer coming up for air. 'Or I'll bloody well . . . !'

' . . . Pratt's Knob,' ended Gavin, serenely.

' . . . brain ya!' snarled Lance, clamping his fist over his brother's mouth.

Gavin blinked owlishly.

Lance belched in the wake of a sudden attack of vertigo. 'Look,' he said, resisting the temptation to vomit, 'all I'm sayin' is . . . '

He hesitated and turned at the sound of distant gunfire. 'You 'ear that?' he asked, tilting his head to one side.

Behind the hedge at the bottom of the hill, Rooter was dozing in the spring sunshine with his faded check shirt open to the waist and his cut-off Levi's pulled tight against his crotch. His face was brown and weather-beaten, his hair close-cropped and greying at the temples. Lying back in the battered two-seater sofa that he'd strapped to the driving platform of the massive tractor for added comfort, he smiled contentedly up at the sky and closed his lids against the glare of the sun. He was blissfully unaware of the gunfire echoing down the valley. This was partly because the sound didn't carry into the hollow where he was sheltering from the wind, but mainly because he was so busy daydreaming about getting his hands inside some sexy holidaymaker's knickers that he wouldn't have noticed if a shotgun had been fired next to his head. The afternoon had turned out warm and sunny, and with three veggie pasties and a quart of Perce's scrumpy inside him, he was feeling at peace with the world. There were worse ways of warding off creeping senility, he told himself, than toasting your old bones in the spring sunshine. And better things than roasting to be done, too, if you could get some gorgeous bit of vacationing crumpet to give you a hand.

'Reckon I'll get meself over Chagford way tonight,' he mused as his stubby fingers moved down over the wiry hair of his chest and belly. 'Wouldn't mind betting there'll be . . . ' He paused and rotated a finger in his naval. 'Well, I'm buggered!' he said, sitting up. 'Will you look at that, Roots, me old son!'

He tweaked a wad of belly button fluff out of his navel with his little finger and held it up for a close inspection. Where did it come from, he wondered? How did it get there? And, most perplexing of all, why was it always blue?

He sighed and flopped back against the battered old sofa. Belly button fluff was one of life's great unsolved mysteries, and he pondered it often in his quieter moments: not because he expected to find an answer to the riddle of its existence, but because his therapist had told him that doing so would help him control his natural aggressions. It was better, she'd added, for his psychological wellbeing than thinking about all the things that made him feel angry. Unfortunate things happened to people when he felt angry. Lots of scary, violent, mind-altering things that left badger baiting sorts of people, fox hunting sorts of people, and any of the other habitually-cruel-to-animals sorts of people he so detested, writhing on the ground if they were lucky, and hanging naked and upside down in a tree if they weren't. But you couldn't just go around beating people to a pulp, the therapist had told him; even when they deserved it and it made almost everyone else, including the therapist, clap their hands in delight. Belly button fluff was a useful distraction, she'd told him, like stealing people's trousers and thinking about how to get himself laid.

'Blue,' he thought. 'Is that 'cause I wear blue jeans? But if it is, how come it gets through me shirt when the bugger's tucked in? And why's it always the same size? It don't keep on growing 'til it overflows an' hangs down me legs to me knees, does it? So who tells the bugger when to stop?' He belched, and squinted up at the sky. He would probably never know the answers, he decided, but he didn't care because his therapist had told him that philosophy was good for the soul, and a willingness to indulge in it was what separated sentient beings from religious fanatics, masters of the hunt and politicians.

'Never mind,' he muttered, 'be goin' home time soon. Then I'll get . . . '

There was a rattling sound nearby. He opened an eye and squinted at the empty ice cream carton that had just blown over the hedge. He nodded as it came to rest amongst others that had been arriving at intervals throughout the day. 'Yep,' he said, 'goin' home time soon! Always leaves raspberry 'til last, does our Gav.' He folded his arms across his midriff and settled back on the sofa to dream of sexy bits of totty wriggling as they sat on his face.

On the side of the hill above him, Lance was squinting in concentrate.

'D'you 'ear that?' he asked again, bending awkwardly sideways to reach for the binoculars tangled in the folds of the sleeping bag at his ankles.

'What?' said Gavin, gazing in the wrong direction.

'Not *there*!' said Lance, pulling the binoculars free and holding them up to his eyes. '*There*!' he pointed. 'Some buggers racin'!'

Gavin peered to his right. 'Ice cream men?' he asked, hopefully.

Lance lowered the binoculars. 'You're really, really stoned, man, you know that don't you?'

Gavin shrugged. 'It's a car. I can see the bugger from 'ere.'

'*Two* cars!' Lance corrected him. 'Goin' like the clappers. One of 'em's a *Volvo*! T'other one's a . . . a . . . *Ford*!'

'Grockles!' snorted Gavin. 'Grockles racin'! An' . . . an' shootin'! Tidden bloody right, that, is it? Fright'nin' the liddle bunnies an' . . . an' . . . !'

He flopped onto the deckchair and groped on the ground for a flagon.

When he found one with cider still in it, he raised it to his lips and tilted back his head until it was empty. Then he dropped it onto the grass, stood up, belched and wiped his mouth along a sleeve from elbow to wrist.

'Gonna call R-Rooder,' he muttered, reaching into a pocket of his denim jacket for a walkie-talkie. 'Tell 'im to block the buggers off. Teach 'em a lesson. Can't 'ave 'em chargin' 'bout the place fright'nin' the bunnies.'

'No, no, no, no, no!' insisted Lance, wagging his head unsteadily from side to side. 'Don't tell 'im wha' for, Gav! 'E won't do it, you tell 'im wha' for, will 'e? Shrink tol' the ol' bugger no more f-fightin'!'

Gavin thought for a moment as they stood side-by-side on their trampled sleeping bags swaying gently together in the breeze.

'Riiiiide,' he said, putting a finger to the side of his nose. 'N-no prob'em!'

He held the walkie-talkie upto his ear and slurred 'Roots? You . . . you there, y-ya bugger, or what?'

20

LANCE AND GAVIN

Rooter was dropping off to sleep with a pair of sexy young women whispering disgusting things in his ears, when the walkie-talkie in his breast pocket burst into life. 'Roots?' came Gavin's disembodied voice. 'You . . . you there, y-ya bugger or what? Is me, Gav, innet?' He belched. 'Listen R-Roots, ged Irene on the road an' . . . an' . . . an' make . . . make it *quick*!'

Rooter didn't answer.

'Roots?' came Gavin's voice again. 'You listenin' t' me ya ol' bugger?'

Rooter opened a jaundiced eye and regarded the walkie-talkie with distaste. Then he closed the eye and went back to dreaming about sex.

'Please yoursel',' slurred Gavin. 'Jus' thought you'd wanna know there's a ned-ball team comin' in . . . in a bus, is all. Bud if you're too busy . . .'

Rooter had the walkie-talkie clamped to his ear in a flash.

'Gav? Gav? That you, boy?'

'Ged 'er on the road quick, or you'll miss 'em! Mus' be a couple dozen ad leas'. Two of 'em's ridin' on the roof in them liddle skirts an' navy blue . . .!'

There was a click, and the walkie-talkie went dead.

Rooter held it at arm's length, shook it, stared at it, shook it again and clamped it back to his ear. 'What? Hello? Gav? You there? Navy blue *what?*'

There was no answer. He held the walkie-talkie at arm's length again and pursed his lips, uncertain whether to believe what he had just heard. Lance and Gavin were tricky little sods, and he was never quite sure when they were being serious and when they were taking the piss. This could be just another in a long line of their wind-ups. But if it wasn't, and he missed a netball team riding on the roof of a bus in short skirts and navy blue . . . whatever, it would be a seriously sad day for his libido.

He spoke into the walkie-talkie again. 'Gav? You there boy? Where . . .? Which way . . .? Gav? *Gav?* Which way're they comin'?'

Still there was no answer. He cursed under his breath, pushed the walkie-talkie down the side of the sofa, and reached for the tractor's ignition key.

When the huge vehicle burst instantly into life, he grinned proudly at the throaty rumble of the engine. 'Good boy, Robbie,' he muttered, as the massive thing started to roll up the short incline towards the road.

Two hundred yards above him, Gavin clenched his fist in triumph as the sound of the powerful engine drifted up the hill on the wind.

'Yes!' he grinned as he stuffed the walkie-talkie into his jacket pocket at the third attempt. 'Now then,' he said, searching through the litter at his feet for a flagon with cider still in it, 'jus' 'ave a liddle ol' drinky-pooh an' go for a bid of a chad with them noisy v-varmints . . . down . . . down . . .'

At the foot of the hill, Choat's Probe skidded around a bend in the road and flashed past the front of Rooter's tractor just as it was lumbering up through a gap in the hedge.

'*Bastard!*' yelled Rooter, waving his fist at the car as it swerved to avoid the diversion signs and disappeared down Sodmire Lane. 'Stupid, soddin' . . .!' He paused with his head on one side, listening intently. Suddenly, his eyes widened and he slid down onto the sofa with his arms wrapped over his head.

When Henry rounded the corner a moment later, he found the road blocked by the biggest lump of farm machinery he had ever seen in his life. He hauled the steering wheel to the right, skidded past the thing's massive rear wheel, and clipped a granite gatepost with the nearside front wing of the Volvo as it ricocheted through the gap in the hedge that Rooter had just left.

'*Bastard!*' yelled Rooter, sitting up to peer over the back of the sofa.

Henry was too busy trying to stay alive to notice as the car bounced out of control over the hard ground from one grassy tussock to the next as if it was in a giant pinball machine. Just when he was beginning to think that it would go on bouncing forever, it ploughed into a tangled clump of gorse bushes and came to a sudden halt.

'Bet that hurt,' muttered Rooter, winching from the safety of the old sofa. His face brightened. 'Serves the silly bugger right.'

Then it occurred to him that serious damage could be done to a frail human body when it was crushed against a steering wheel, and he decided that perhaps he ought to go and see if the driver of the car needed his help.

He jumped down from the tractor, cursing his sentimentality as he went, and started to run across the open ground towards the Volvo. The netball team would have to wait, he told himself, glancing over his shoulder as he ran. Although he doubted that they would be going anywhere fast with Irene blocking the road the way she was.

Henry shook his head in disbelief when he realized that he was still alive.

Then he remembered the gang and started to panic.

'Gotta make a run for it!' he told himself, as he fumbled with the safety belt. He pushed open the driver's door and started to get out.

'You all right, lover?' shouted Rooter, running up. 'You shouldn't go . . .!'

But he tripped on a tussock of grass and fell against the driver's door, crashing into it with both hands and slamming it back against Henry's head.

The last thing Henry saw before he blacked out was a shadowy figure hurtling through the air towards him, screaming like a banshee.

When Bonce rounded the bend a moment later, his reactions weren't as quick as Henry's had been, and although he braked as hard as he could, the Mercedes thudded into the rear wheel of Rooter's tractor and stopped dead.

Nobbler, who was peering between the front seats at the time, was thrown forward by the impact and cracked his forehead against Bonce's left temple.

The impact made a sound like a cricket ball being hit for six, and Nobbler passed out.

Bonce's skull was a good deal thicker, and his brain buried more deeply beneath it, so it was a bit longer before the blow took effect. He looked down at the unconscious Nobbler, lying in a heap across the handbrake, and said 'You tryin' to be . . .?' It was as far as he got. His mouth sagged open, his eyes glazed over and he drifted into unconsciousness with a grunt.

In the passenger seat beside him, Vinny pulled his head back through a hole in the windscreen, and peeled several layers of bobble hat and woolly scarf away from his face. '*Arsehole!*' he snarled. 'If I was drivin' . . .!'

He frowned, and prodded Bonce in the ribs. When he got no reaction, he grinned like a shark smelling blood in the water.

'Oh, dear, what a shame,' he smirked, turning away and looking through the gap in the hedge at the back of Henry's Volvo. He smiled and picked up the Uzi he'd dropped on the floor. 'Come in Mr. Kite,' he whispered as he raised it to his lips and kissed the barrel, 'your time is definitely up now!'

He reached for the door handle and was about to get out of the car when Lance staggered towards him with a cider flagon dangling from his fist.

'Hey man,' he said, peering into the Mercedes, 'you wanna dring?'

Vinny looked up a split second too late as the clumsily wielded earthenware jug arced in through the open window, bounced off his forehead with a soggy clunk and knocked him senseless.

Lance frowned down at him as he lay across Nobbler's unconscious body. 'Oh, hey, man,' he said. 'Sorry 'bout that, yeah?' Then his eyes lit up and he reached into the car to prize the Uzi from Vinny's lifeless fingers.

'Hey, look what I got, man!' he cried, holding it above his head and waving it at Gavin. 'Worth a bob or two, this one is, yeah?'

Gavin swerved towards him. ''Ere,' he said, pointing back along the road, 'what's this bugger want, then, you reckon?'

Lance turned to watch as Tom's Range Rover came to a halt a few yards behind the Mercedes. The driver's door opened, and Tom started to get out.

'Hello?' he called. 'Need a hand? Anyone hurt in there?'

Gavin pulled open the driver's door of the Mercedes and bent to examine the heap of unconscious bodies sitting in and lying across the front seats.

Lance turned away and walked unsteadily towards the Range Rover with the Uzi dangling from one hand and the cider flagon hanging from the other.

'No, no, no,' he said, slaloming in a different direction each time he wagged his head. 'Ev-everythin's fine an' . . . an' danny.'

'You sure?' asked Tom, glancing around for a sight of Henry's Volvo. 'They overtook me a couple of miles back. Chasing a guy in a Volvo, I think. Almost ran me off the road.' He looked around. 'What happened to him, by the way . . . the guy in the Volvo?'

Lance swayed to a stop. 'Look a' this liddle bugger,' he said, raising the Uzi and pointing it at Tom's chest. 'You seen one o' these liddle buggers be- before?' he hiccupped. 'How mush you reckon 'e's worth, then?'

Tom knew exactly what the gun was worth. He also knew how easy it would be to snatch it out of Lance's hand, smack him on the side of the head with it, and use it to blow his brains out. But there was no time for pleasure on this trip. He had a job to do for a client who was paying him and his operatives an indecently huge amount of money to keep an eye on Henry Kite. And that client would not be best pleased if Henry went missing. So no matter how enjoyable he might find the prospect, he didn't have time to waste on the extermination of irritating country bumpkins like Gavin and Lance. So he held up his hands in a gesture of surrender as the stubby barrel of the Uzi weaved a flat figure of eight in front of his face. 'Steady on,' he said, 'that thing's dangerous, you know.'

Lance wasn't convinced. '*Bollocks*!' he sneered. 'Pissy liddle thing, this is. I seen bigger p-peashooooders!'

Tom held out a hand. 'Look, why don't you give it to me, mate, eh? Before someone gets hurt?'

Lance pouted and hid the gun behind his back. 'Won't!' he said. 'Ge' your own one! I found 'im! 'E's mine!'

Tom pursed his lips. 'Yes, of course,' he said, tightly. 'Of course it is. I was just thinking, that's all: I could look after it for you 'til you sober up.'

Lance's eyes narrowed. 'You sayin' I'm pissed?'

'No, no, of course not! Only, look, about that guy in the Volvo . . .'

'Coz I'm friggin' nod, y'know,' insisted Lance. He held the gun out at arm's length. 'Steady as a s-soddin' r-rock, that is.'

Tom flinched again. 'Yeah, yeah, sure,' he said, bobbing and weaving as the gun homed in on his head. 'I'm impressed. Really I am! Only, would you mind pointing it at someone else for a bit?' He gave a hollow laugh. 'I mean, you wouldn't want my death on your conscience, now, would you?'

Lance thought for a moment. Then he shrugged, belched and pointed the gun at the Range Rover. 'I coul' shoo' the bollocks off . . . off a sparrow a' fif'y paces . . . me . . . no, no prob'em at . . . at all.'

'Yeah, sure you could. Look, about the guy in the . . .?'

'Hey!' cried Gavin, zigzagging towards them with Vinny's pistol held above his head. 'Look wha' I foun', man. Gert 'eller, this one, innet?' He crouched down with the gun held out in front of him and started miming potshots at imaginary enemies. '*Pee-yow*!' he mouthed to the left and '*Pee-yow*!' to the right, and then '*Pee-yow! Pee-yow! Pee-yow!*' at Lance, Tom and the Range Rover in turn.

Tom looked up at the sky. 'Jesus! This is all I sodding-well need!'

Being shot at was an occupational hazard in his line of work, but it had never occurred to him that he might end up getting his head blown off by a drunken hayseed doing impressions of Dirty Harry.

He took a deep breath and arranged his features into the semblance of a smile. 'Look lads,' he said, 'why don't you give the guns to me and we'll call it quits, eh? That way no one gets hurt.'

Lance wasn't listening. He had turned with a huge grin to watch over his shoulder as his brother pranced and posed with the automatic. As he swivelled around, the Uzi tracked from right to left and back again, coming to rest pointing at Tom's head.

Tom dropped instantly to his haunches. 'For Christ's sake!' he hissed. 'Stop pissing about with that thing!' He was running out of patience rapidly now, and while Lance wasn't looking he reached inside his jacket to release the stud on his shoulder holster. He was about to draw the huge Magnum revolver that nestled inside it when Lance turned towards him with a frown.

'Wha' you doin' down there, then?' he asked, wide-eyed, lowering the Uzi until it was in line with Tom's chest 'You lose somethin' or what?'

'Look,' said Tom, withdrawing his hand from inside his jacket and getting warily to his feet 'just put the guns down, will you? I haven't got time . . . '

'How-dee pardner,' said Gavin, standing up and blowing imaginary smoke from the barrel of the automatic. He pointed it at Tom, but looked at Lance. 'Hey, you gonna shood this 'ere no-good varmint or what?'

Lance's head wobbled on his neck as he regarded Tom in silence for a moment. 'Nah,' he said, smiling suddenly, and waving the Uzi vaguely in the direction of the moor. 'How 'bout you an' me mosey on down the ol' corral, Wyatt, an' shood us a couple o' mangy ol' ou'laws?'

Gavin didn't answer. He had started to feel queasy. All the jumping around had made him dizzy and he was beginning to think it was time to throw up.

'Dunno,' he said thickly. 'Gis a swig o' tha' ol' scrummy firs', eh?' He wafted the automatic at the flagon in Lance's hand. 'I'm fair parched an' plum tuckered out w-with all this ol' cowboy-type shit, pardner, y'know?'

Lance took no notice as he waggled the Uzi in Tom's face. 'You an ou'law, or wad?' he asked. 'Coz me an' ol' Wyatt's gonna . . . '

Gavin elbowed him in the ribs 'Hey! Give us a swig . . .!'

Lance flinched and pulled the trigger of the Uzi, sending a hail of bullets smashing through the windscreen of Tom's car.

Tom's reaction was instinctive. '*Jesus*!' he hissed, as he dropped to the ground and dragged himself under the Range Rover.

As he hit the road, the Magnum jarred out of his shoulder holster, skittered across the tarmac, and came to rest between Gavin's feet.

Gavin looked down at it, frowned, looked across at the Range Rover, frowned again, then smiled broadly and bent to pick up the gun.

Wedged beneath the car, Tom decided that enough was enough. He was going to have to kill someone after all. *Two* someones, in fact! And the more he thought about it, the more pleasurable the prospect became.

'*Stupid bastards*!' he snarled, reaching for the shoulder holster.

When he realized that the Magnum had gone, he cast around looking for it on the road, and was just in time to see Gavin's hand pick it up.

Lance, meantime, had turned the Uzi on himself, and was staring slack-jawed into the barrel. '*Eller*!' he breathed in wide-eyed admiration. 'You see *tha'* man? You see what it done to 'is wagon?'

Gavin grinned back at him like a small boy who had just been given a huge and unexpected present for Christmas. 'Look what I got!' he crowed, holding up the Magnum. 'They'm breedin' like bleedin' rabbits, man! Hey! Far out!'

Lance looked up from his inspection of the Uzi's barrel. 'Sorry 'bout your wagon, man,' he said at the place where Tom had been standing. He frowned and glanced across at his brother. 'Hey, where's that bugger got to now?'

'*Idiots*!' muttered Tom. 'I'm down here,' he called. 'Under the sodding . . .!' he checked himself. 'Under the car!'

Lance squinted at Gavin. 'You 'ear that?'

Gavin nodded. 'Where'd it come from, you reckon?'

'Unbelievable!' hissed Tom. He took a deep breath. 'I'm down here, you stupid . . .! I'm under the car! All right? Just put the guns down, and I'll come out. And for Christ's sake don't shoot!'

Lance and Gavin looked at one-another in mutual stupefaction, before getting down on their hands and knees to peer under the Range Rover.

'That you, man?' asked Gavin.

'Tight fit, that, innet lover?' mused Lance.

'Just put the guns *down*!' said Tom, snagging his jacket and smearing himself with mud and oil as he dragged himself forward. 'I'm coming out! And for Christ's sake don't shoot!'

The boys stood up and stepped back as he crabbed his way into the open.

'Sorry 'bout yer wagon, man,' said Lance, offering the Uzi for inspection. 'Don' understan' it. Bugger jus' wen' off in me 'and. An',' he waved the gun at the wide-open spaces around them as if to indicate that forces out there were acting beyond his control, 'dunno!'

Tom got warily to his feet and brushed himself down. 'Look, lads,' he said with a smile that was utterly devoid of warmth, 'why don't we all just calm down, eh? No need for anyone to . . . '

'Look what I got, man?' said Gavin, holding up the Magnum. 'Gert eller, this one is, inner?'

'Yeah,' said Tom, as he reached through the driver's window for his car keys. 'I'm very happy for you. Really I am! Look,' he added, edging cautiously towards the back of the car, 'I'm just . . . you know . . . gonna get the . . . er, the tool kit . . . outa the boot?' He smiled, tightly. 'OK?'

There was a pump-action shotgun in a case in the back of the Range Rover, and as soon as he got his hands on it he was going to blow this pair of drunken lumpkins to kingdom come. 'Just gonna . . .' he showed them the keys and waved vaguely at the smashed windscreen.

'*Oy!*' yelled a disgruntled voice. 'Wha's all the racket about, then? Some of us is tryin' to help injured people down 'ere!'

They all turned to watch as Rooter came striding through the gap in the hedge, his eyes wide, his fists clenched and an expression of extreme belligerence on his muddied face. 'Look at that!' he ranted, pointing at the Mercedes where it had crashed against the tractor's huge rear wheel. 'You see what that bugger's done to Irene?'

The driver's door opened as he strode towards it, and a dazed looking Vinny, flick-knife in hand, started to crawl out.

'Hey, you?' he blurted. 'Granddad! What the hell's . . .?'

Rooter turned and punched him in the side of the head. 'You can shut your gob for a start!' he snapped, without breaking stride.

Vinny's eyes turned up in his head as he thudded back against the doorframe and slid down to lay half in and half out of the car.

'See that?' demanded Rooter, pointing at the knife in Vinny's hand. 'Tha's all these young buggers understands these days, innet? Violence! Makes you wanna bleedin' weep, dunnet?'

Tom sucked his teeth as this new arrival came marching up the road towards them, waving his arms about and cursing. Two drunken yokels he could deal with without too much difficulty, he decided, but three might be a bit tough even for him. Besides, this one looked as if he wasn't quite as addled by drink as the other two obviously were. He glanced briefly at the Range Rover, but thought better of trying to get to the shotgun before Rooter reached him. He shook his head in irritation and shoved his hands deep into his trouser pockets. Retribution for his shattered windscreen was going to have to wait for a while.

Rooter stomped up to the Range Rover and stood for a moment with his hands on his hips, surveying the damage. Then he turned and wagged a disapproving finger at Gavin. 'I s'pose you thought that was funny?'

Gavin's eyebrows shot up his forehead. 'Me?' he pouted. 'That wodden me, man! What'd I . . .?'

'Netball team?' Rooter reminded him.

Gavin held up his hands in a gesture of denial. 'Oh, hey man, that . . .!'

'Look,' said Tom, 'do these two morons belong to you? Because if . . . '

Rooter cut him off with a gesture. 'That heap o' junk yours then, lover, is it?' he asked, with a nod at the Range Rover.

Tom frowned at the car. 'Junk . . .?'

'You better move 'im then, 'adn' ya?'

'Really?' said Tom. 'Well, in case you hadn't noticed, the Sundance Kid here's just blasted the windscreen full of bullet holes. I think it might be a bit difficult to drive it in that condition, don't you?'

Rooter ignored the question. 'Nope,' he muttered, shaking his head, 'can't 'ave that, can we? Makin' the place look untidy!'

He looked Tom over from head to toe. 'You're a bleedin' mess an' all. No one ever teach ya to look after yer clothes?'

Tom glanced down at the mud and oil stains on his knees, and the jacket pocket that had almost been torn off. 'Look, I haven't got time for all this. There was a bloke in a Vol . . . '

'Me neither,' said Rooter, snatching the Uzi from Lance and using it to knock out what was left of the Range Rover's windscreen.

Tom's eyes widened in disbelief. 'What the . . .? Look sunshine . . .!'

Rooter turned towards him with a finger held to his lips and the Uzi pointing at his belly. 'When I wants your opinion,' he said, 'I'll ask for it!' Then he walked around the car, smashing out the rest of its windows.

'There!' he said, standing back to admire his handiwork. 'You can piss off back wherever you come from, now, can't ya?' He took a deep breath. 'All the same, you lot are! Comin' down 'ere in your clapped out old bangers! Think you own the bloody place, don't ya? Parkin' all over . . .!' He shook his head in disgust. 'This idden a bloody scrapyard, y'know? Bloody national park, this is! An' look at you for Christ's sake! Covered all over with shite!' He sniffed his irritation. 'Some of us 'ave gotta live 'ere, y'know! We can't 'ave all this ol' crap litterin' up the place all the time!'

'Listen *mate*,' said Tom, coldly, 'that car was in perfect condition until Butch Cassidy's best mate decided to fill it full of bullet holes.'

Rooter clicked his tongue. 'That's right. Blame it on some dim bugger what don't know no better.'

Lance frowned. 'Dim . . .?'

'Shut up, you stupid wazzock!' snapped Rooter. He pointed the Uzi at Tom's chest. 'An' you got five seconds afore I turn you into a colander.' He raised an eyebrow. 'Well? You goin' or you goin', or what?'

'I don't think you understand what you're getting yourself into here,' said Tom. 'I strongly advise you to put the gun down and . . .'

Rooter raised the Uzi until it was levelled at Tom's head. '*One* . . .!'

'I'm warning you,' said Tom.

'Don't interrupt! *Two* . . .!'

Tom glanced at Gavin, who gave him a sympathetic shrug. 'Wouldn't push it, I was you, man,' he advised. 'Can't stop the ol' bugger when 'e gets a cob on like that there.'

'*Three* . . .!' said Rooter.

Tom looked at Lance.

Lance pursed his lips and inclined his head towards the Range Rover. 'Bes' be gettin' a move on,' he advised, 'I was you.'

'You're making a big mistake here,' warned Tom.

'An' you idden runnin' fast enough,' said Rooter. '*Four* . . .!'

Tom sighed and held up his hands in surrender. 'OK!' he said. 'OK! I'm going! I'm going! All right? Just don't shoot me, that's all.'

He wrenched open the driver's door, got into the car and inserted the ignition key. To his surprise, the engine started first time.

'That's right,' said Rooter, smiling amiably and nodding at the Mercedes, 'you jus' leave them other buggers to us, lover, you 'ear? We'll look after 'em, don't you worry.'

'Nice meetin' ya,' called Gavin, with a friendly wave as Tom put the Range Rover into reverse, and turned to leave. 'You-all come back an' see us agin sometime, pardner, y'hear?'

'Oh, I will,' muttered Tom. 'You can bet your sodding life on it, *pardner*!'

'Sorry 'bout yer wagon, man,' cried Lance, waving as the Range Rover roared back the way it had come.

'Right then,' said Rooter, as Tom disappeared around a bend in the road. 'Where were we?'

'Nice bloke,' said Lance, tip-toeing backwards. 'Could do with a sense o' humour, though, I reckon.'

'Yeah,' nodded Gavin, sidling along beside him. 'Bit skittish, an' all.'

Suddenly, they were both feeling sober. Very sober indeed!

'About time we had a little chat,' said Rooter, stalking after them as they backed away. 'Now, what was that you were saying about a netball team?'

Lance glanced nervously at the Uzi. 'That wasn't me, man,' he said, backtracking unsteadily.

Rooter nodded, and pointed the gun at Gavin.

Gavin held up his hands in instant surrender. 'Wow, hey, man! It was a joke, y'know?'

Rooter wasn't laughing. On the contrary, he told them, he was very disappointed that they had thought they could get away with such a childish deception. Did he, Gavin, think that he, Rooter, was soft in the head or something? Because if he did, he assured him, then he, Rooter, would have to put him, Gavin, straight on one or two things. Which, he confided with the barrel of the Uzi pointing menacingly at Gavin's groin, could well mean into the Intensive Care Unit at the Royal Infirmary.

'Thing is,' said Lance, tentatively, 'we was thinkin' . . . '

'Really? An' was that with both the brain cells, or jus' the one?'

'. . . 'bout the bloke in the Volvo?'

'Uh-huh?' nodded Rooter, stalking after them.

'I mean,' asked Lance, 'is he all right, or what?'

'What's it to you?'

'Only if . . . if he is – I mean, it's up to you, obviously – only . . . '

'Is it?'

'Yeah. I mean, if you was to take him over the Dragon? To see Jo?'

'Stand still!'

'No, hey, *listen* man! I mean, she was a nurse, right?'

'Don't you try making a run for it, mind?' warned Rooter. 'I don't wanna shoot you two sneaky buggers in the back.'

'OK by me,' said Lance, turning quickly.

Rooter grabbed him by the belt. 'Stand still, I said!'

Lance put his hands on his head, and turned around.

Gavin bent down and put Vinny's automatic and Tom's Magnum on the road as peace offerings. Then he stood up and put his hands on his head. 'Look,' he said, 'we was jus' thinkin', that's all . . . If she was a nurse . . .?'

Rooter squinted at him as an image of Jo in a nurse's uniform blossomed inside his head. 'Yeah,' he said, guardedly, 'what of it?'

'Well, I mean,' said Gavin, jerking his thumb in the direction of Henry's Volvo, 'you and him? Y'know? Bin in a bit of a smash-up?' He nodded and winked. 'I reckon you could do with a bid o' tender lovin' care an' that, right?'

Rooter's eyes narrowed. 'Are you suggesting I'd lie to the poor little maid?'

'Not exactly lyin', though, is it Roots?' said Lance. 'I mean, look wad them buggers done to Irene? You could've been killed!'

'Yeah,' added Gavin. 'Nasty lump you got there, innet?'

Rooter frowned. 'Lump?'

'On your hand?'

'Yeah,' said Lance. 'I mean, that bloke's head must o' bin hard!'

Rooter was beginning to see interesting possibilities opening up in front of him. 'Yeah, well,' he said, grimacing with a sudden imagined pain in the knuckles of his right hand, 'now that you come to mention it . . .'

'Here,' said Lance, reaching for the Uzi, 'better give me that, eh? Your hand's a bit tender, I spec, innet?'

Rooter bit his lip as he allowed the gun to be eased from his suddenly limp fingers. 'Yeah, well, I didn't have a choice, did I?'

'Course not,' soothed Gavin.

'Listen,' said Lance, taking Rooter solicitously by the arm, 'why don't you take matey there over the Dragon, and see Jo, eh? I mean, she'll know what to do with the bugger, won't she?'

'I don't know . . .'

'If you're not up to it, me and Gav could . . .'

'No, no! I'll go! Don't you worry 'bout me.'

Gavin moved in to support him on the other side. ''Ave a word with Jo then, eh?' He nodded at the Mercedes. 'An' we'll take care o' that lot.' He glanced across at his brother. 'Sodmire, you reckon?'

'Yeah, man,' grinned Lance. 'See the buggers get outa that lot, eh?'

It took them a couple of minutes to hitch the Mercedes to the back of Lance's Land Rover and tow it away from Irene's rear wheel. Then, with Vinny, Bonce and Nobbler still unconscious on the front seats, they drove away, singing at the tops of their voices, and zigzagging along the narrow road with the Mercedes swaying dangerously along behind them.

Rooter shook his head as they disappeared over Hangman's Hill. 'Happy as sandboys, mad as coots, and dimmer than a TOC-H lamp!'

He looked down at the road and began kicking broken glass into the hedge. He had just finished, and was about to go and tow Henry's Volvo back onto the road, when he heard a man shrieking at the top of his voice. His first thought was that Henry had regained consciousness to find that the blow from the driver's door had broken his neck and left him paralyzed from the head down.

'Bugger!' he cursed, kicking out at a final, non-existent shard of glass. 'Why's it always me has to pick up the pieces?'

* * *

21

TOBY BANNISTER

'Wha's a Uzi?' asked Titus.

'You're back then?' said Henry, turning towards him. 'You must be a hell of a thief, sneaking up on people like that. No wonder the Romans put a price on your head.'

'Takes years o' practice, that does, buddy,' said Titus. 'Course, I'm what you call naturally light on me feet.'

'I am pleased to see that you have recovered,' said the hooded figure. 'You had a rather nasty turn earlier, did you not?'

'Yeah,' said Titus, guardedly. 'Must o' bin somethin' I et.'

'That or the kick in the head,' offered Henry.

Titus was peeved by the suggestion. 'Hey, you don't wanna go listenin' t' none o' that ol' nonsense!' He sniffed. 'Lover's wosname . . . thingy, that was. She fancies the pants off me really.'

Henry pursed his lips. 'Of course she does. And what about the lieutenant? Kiss it better for you, did she?'

Titus's face split into an infantile grin. His eyes went glassy and he reached a claw-like hand absentmindedly down to his crotch.

'Hello?' said Henry. 'Anyone home?'

Titus turned towards him. 'What?'

'The lieutenant? How was she?'

The little man's face lit up with a beaming smile. 'Horny as hell!'

'For a robot, you mean?'

Titus' smile vanished. 'Listen,' he said, stabbing a finger at Henry's chest, 'I'd watch me mouth, if I was you! Or you'll get my fist in it! OK?'

Henry grinned. 'You got on well with her, then?'

'Just watch your mouth, that's all!' said Titus, turning away.

He turned back. 'An' show some respect!'

He turned away.

He turned back again. 'She's a person, too, y'know, not jus' the horniest piece of arse on the planet!'

Henry and the hooded figure exchanged glances.

'And before you ask,' added Titus, 'me and her's none o' your business, OK? So . . . ' he hesitated, 'so . . . so . . . *don't* ask . . . tha's all!'

He turned away.

He turned back again. 'You got that?'

'Our lips are sealed,' said Henry.

'Yeah, well, they better be!'

'It is an open-bolt, blowback-operated submachine gun capable of firing six hundred rounds per minute,' said the hooded figure.

Titus and Henry looked at one another.

'It was originally designed . . . '

'Is he takin' the piss?' asked Titus.

'On the contrary,' said the figure, 'given that the subject of the lieutenant is now, apparently, off limits, as I believe the saying goes, I was attempting to provide you with the information you requested earlier.'

Titus looked at Henry. 'He *is* takin' the piss!'

'The Uzi machine pistol?' said the figure. 'You asked for information about it? Or had you forgotten? I was merely attempting to provide you with . . . '

'Yeah, yeah, yeah!' said Titus. 'I know all that old bollocks, don't' I? I read the thingy in the wosname, didn't I?' He pointed up at the sky. 'What I wanna know is . . . where can I get one?'

The hooded figure hesitated for a moment. 'Why would you want to?'

'What?' said Titus, spreading his arms wide. 'You're kiddin' me, right? I'm a sportsman, buddy! I mean, *duh*!'

'Actually,' said the figure, 'you are a narcissistic, misogynistic proto-sociopath with a catalogue of moderately serious personality disorders to your name including, but by no means limited to, all of the insecure attachment patterns rolled into one. Or to put it another way: the slightest hint of genuine emotional commitment to any other living thing scares, as they say in the vernacular, "the living shit" out of you! To the best of my knowledge – and to all intents and purposes that is the best knowledge there is – you do not play football, rugby, hockey, baseball, basketball, netball, cricket, tennis, badminton, squash, snooker, pool, billiards or rounders: or indeed, any of a further eighty-five sports I could name, including archery, rifle, pistol and clay pigeon shooting. So please be good enough to enlighten me as to precisely how you believe you qualify as a sportsman? And more to the point, in what bizarre fantasy world of your maladjusted creation does anything defined correctly as 'sport' necessitate the use of a device that propels at six hundred rounds per minute lethal projectiles capable of destroying living tissue?'

'So that's a no, then, is it?'

'Yes it is!' said the figure. 'If for no other reason than the obvious eagerness with which you wish to acquire one. It has always seemed to me that those who desire most strongly to get their hands on such devices are precisely those who should be kept farthest away from them. And that includes one or two of the more dangerously psychotic individuals in our narrative. Speaking of which . . . '

* * *

Sir Richard was charging along the M5 in an attempt to make up for lost time. It had taken Ron Posset almost an hour to find a replacement for the unwanted Rover, and a further ten minutes to transfer his boss's personalized number plates on to it from the 'knackered' Mercedes.

'It's illegal,' he'd muttered, as Sir Richard had hovered over him tut-tutting and tapping his foot. 'Can't go changing' 'em round just like that, can you?'

'Stop wittering man, and get on with it!' Sir Richard had snapped. 'I'll be the judge of what is and what isn't legal around here.' Then he'd brushed his fingertips fondly over the bonnet of the Jaguar XJ6. 'Now *that's* what you call a motor, Posset. Beautiful piece of automotive machinery, isn't she?'

Ron hadn't ventured an opinion. But his silence had been of no interest to Sir Richard, who couldn't have cared less what his underling thought. He had no intention of arriving for his rendezvous with Charlotte Piece in anything as common as a Rover. But a Jaguar was a different matter. And what good were personalized number plates if you couldn't show them off when you needed that little bit of extra *oomph* for a special occasion? They had cost him a small fortune from the shady little man he'd bumped into at King's Cross on one of his visits to Madame Rawhide's House of Correction. And S1R RP was something to make his rivals (and everyone in the world was a rival) sit up and take notice. He could just imagine them squirming in their seats with envy as he cruised past. There was nothing subtle about it: nothing left to chance. Everyone who saw him knew they were dealing with a man of distinction; a man who went out and got what he wanted whenever he wanted it; a man who had been afforded the highest honour in the land for his contributions to the county's economy and the coffers of the Conservative Party. A pussy magnet, that's what the Jaguar was. A golden chariot perfectly suited to the man whom Charlotte Piece had finally discovered she couldn't resist.

'Get on with it man! I've got raving totty to catch!'

Ron had changed the plates almost as quickly as he would have done had he really wanted to help. And when he'd finished, Sir Richard had driven off in reckless pursuit of the woman he had been chasing for so many years that it hurt. He had been after her since her very first day at the company, and it was a measure of his determination that he had stuck at the task for so long. Other women who had refused his advances had fallen by the wayside, been sacked, passed over, or treated with such savagery that they had been forced to resign. But not the delectable Miss Charlotte Piece. He was desperate to get his hands on her, and to have her put her hands on him. The thought of the possibilities was driving him to distraction. The gymslips, the uniforms, the crotchless panties, the peephole bras and the whips! Especially the whips! And the oh-so high-heeled, sharp-toed, tight-fitting, black patent leather thigh boots, and the manacles, and the facemasks, and the big, black, shiny vibrating . . .!

He wiped his forehead with the back of a hand as he bombed along the outside lane of the motorway. If everything went to plan, he would never have to visit Madame Rawhide's again. Well, occasionally, perhaps, just to keep up with the latest trends in accessories.

In his eagerness to get at Charlotte, he had zoomed around the M25 and along the M4 as fast as the traffic had allowed. And by the time he'd reached the outskirts of Bristol he'd made up almost an hour on his quarry. Then he'd careered along the M5 at an average speed of just over a hundred miles an hour, and had only realized that he'd passed a police patrol car when it had come up behind him with its siren wailing and its lights flashing.

'Good afternoon, sir,' said the policeman who leaned in at the driver's window after they'd stopped on the hard shoulder. 'In a hurry, are we, today?'

'Ah, yes officer. I expect you're wondering why I'm, er, dashing along?'

'Would you mind getting out of your vehicle, sir?' asked the officer.

'Yes, of course,' said Sir Richard. 'But you see,' he dropped his voice to a whisper, 'I've got a lady waiting for me in Torquay.' He coughed conspiratorially and winked. 'If you know what I mean?'

'Very nice for you, sir,' said the officer. 'But she'll be waiting for a while longer if we don't get this little lot sorted out promptly, like, won't she?'

'Of course, of course,' said Sir Richard. 'Good man! And might I say,' he added, extending a hand, 'that I can see you're doing an excellent job?'

The officer looked at the hand without blinking. 'Got your apron in the boot, then, have you sir?'

'Good man! Good *man*!' said Sir Richard, his eyes sparkling. 'Glad to see we understand one another so well.'

'Yes, sir,' said the officer, without inflection. 'Me missus keeps tryin' to get me to wear one for the washing-up, like. Only I keep tellin' her it don't suit so well without boobs.'

'Really?' said Sir Richard, coldly. 'I dare say it suits your chief constable well enough, though, doesn't it?'

'Very likely, sir! Very likely! Only I don't see him around here at the moment, do you? Get out of the car, sir, if you would be so kind? I'm going to have to book you for speeding. One hundred and nineteen miles an hour, you was doing just now. Unless you think a handshake with my little black box back there in the car will make him change his mind?'

Sir Richard got out and followed the officer back to the patrol car. A quick check with the authorities later, and the officer's already peeved demeanour had changed to one of suspicion. 'Is that your car, sir?' he asked, pointing with his pen at the Jaguar.

'Of course it is!' snapped Sir Richard. 'What are you implying?'

'Only it says here it's registered to a Sir Richard Pate.'

'That is correct. I am he.'

'And it's a Mercedes,' said the officer, 'Metallic Silver, not a Jaguar XJ6. And what d'you reckon that is, then? Burnished Gold, would you say?'

'Ah, well, I can explain that, officer. You see it's perfectly simple . . . '

'Yes, sir. We'll have a nice little chat about it down at the station, shall we?'

Sir Richard complained all the way to the police station, threatening, cajoling and pleading by turns. But it did him no good. He was shown into a bleak little room with grey-green walls and a tiny, barred window, and told that the duty officer would be along to see him in due course.

'I demand to be allowed to call my solicitor,' he insisted as the door slammed shut in his face. 'Have you any idea who you're dealing with here? I'll have your badges for this!' He took off his jacket, and threw it onto the bare, stripped mattress on the battered metal-framed bed. Then he strode back to the door, and shouted through the grill. 'I'm going to be late for a meeting of national importance, you know? I've got people waiting for me out there, and they're not going to be best pleased when they hear about this!' He banged on the door with a fist. 'Are you listening to me? My secretary's going to be worried sick. If she doesn't hear from me in the next ten minutes she'll probably call The Palace! Do you hear?' He kicked at the door. 'All right then! On your own heads be it! Don't say I didn't warn you, that's all.'

At that precise moment, his secretary was twenty miles away as the crow flies, and not in the least bit interested in phoning anyone. There were three very good reasons for this; and all of which were bending over her slightly dented Rover convertible in lip-lickingly tight khaki shorts, while she sat on a granite boulder and regarded them with undisguised lust.

What she was admiring were buttocks. Three pairs of buttocks, to be precise, of a singularly taut-muscled variety that she had only ever witnessed in the sort of damply lurid erotic fantasies that she had always been especially careful not to let herself know about, never mind read. They belonged to a trio of the tallest, blondest, most disgustingly bonkable young men she had ever seen in her life, with legs that seemed to go on for ever, travelling upwards and downwards from the cutest of knees, tanned, taught-muscled, finely fair-haired and ending in thick, woolly socks and tough – oh so tough and manly! – walking boots.

She sighed, and tried not to choke on the lump in her throat.

'Well,' said a softly accented Scandinavian voice through the vibrant haze of her arousal. 'We think she is not so badly damage, ja? We push her back on dah road an' you are comings to help?'

Charlotte's blinked. 'Oh, yes,' she sighed. 'I think I probably am.'

Ole smiled. 'Gunna, and me, and Jon we push her up for you, ja?'

She nodded. 'Oh yes please! I think I would like that . . . a lot!'

'Good,' said Gunnar. 'Then we are walking to Torc-way, Ole and Jon and me? We have beds and breakfasts there, ja?' He turned, and gazed into the distance. 'It is a long, long way, I am thinking. But we are strong, ja? Very strong an' how you say . . . fit?'

Charlotte glanced at the bulge in Gunnar's shorts. 'Oh, yes,' she nodded, dewy-eyed, 'a very tight fit, I should think.' She frowned and looked up at his face. 'Where did you say you were going?'

'Torc-way?' ventured Ole. 'Torc-key?'

'Tor-*quay*!' she said, quickly. 'Yes, it's *Tor-quay*! That's what we call it! *Torquay*!' She giggled. 'Yes, yes, and,' she coughed, 'actually I'm going there myself . . . *actually*!' Her voice dropped by an octave. 'I don't suppose . . . I mean, I couldn't give you a lift there . . . at all . . . could I?'

Ole looked at Gunnar.

Gunnar looked at Jon.

Jon looked at Ole.

They all turned to look at Charlotte, who was busy trying not to look a gift horse in the mouth. 'If you want?' she offered, hopefully. 'To save you time? And I might be able to help you find somewhere to stay? If you like?'

'Ja?' smiled Ole. 'Places for all us boys to sleep?'

Charlotte nodded. 'Oh yes, I'm sure there will be enough room for all of you boys. If you don't mind ... squeezing in?'

'Ja,' said Ole, glancing at the others. 'That is sounding good to us boys.'

The boys nodded.

'Great!' said Charlotte standing up and straightening her clothes. 'What a wonderful day this is turning out to be.'

The mood was very different at Exeter Police Station, where her boss was anything but happy with the way his day was going.

'We've checked,' said the hard-faced detective on the other side of the table in the interview room, 'with the hire company you say you got it from, and with the DVLC, in Cardiff. The car registered in what you say is your name, licence plate number S1R RP, is still a Metallic Silver Mercedes. The car hired in what you say is your company's name from Town & Country Cars of Brentwood, Essex, is still a Burnished Gold Jaguar XJ6, licence plate number A1 SOB. How do you explain those inconsistencies, sir?'

'Posset,' said Sir Richard, simply. 'I told you: phone bloody Posset. He knows all about all of that!'

'We did,' said Detective Sergeant McGregor, looking down at his notes. 'A Mr. Ronald Posset, answering the telephone at the number you gave us, was pleased to confirm that the vehicle belonging to Sir Richard Pate is indeed the afore-mentioned Mercedes saloon, Metallic Silver. Not the aforementioned Jaguar XJ6, Burnished Gold.'

'What?' Ron had said in answer to the call from the Devon & Cornwall Constabulary. 'No, not a Jag. No, no it's a Mercedes, Metallic Silver. Yes, S1R RP. Yes, I know, pathetic isn't it? Still, definitely not a Jag. No, and not Burnished Gold, either. No, it's Metallic Silver. Yes. Yes ... like I said.'

He'd held the mouthpiece against his chest for a moment, and grinned at his reflection in the hall mirror.

'No, no,' he'd continued, with the receiver back to his ear, 'only too pleased to help! Yes! Yes! No, no, not at all. Not at all! Any time. Yeah, only too pleased to be of assistance. Yeah, you, too! See you later. Bye-bye!'

He'd hung up, and rubbed his hands together in delight, before walking into the sitting room and pouring himself a very large Scotch.

'I'm afraid,' said Toby Bannister of Craven, Craven, Toadmaster, Bannister & Welk, 'that we appear to be in some difficulty here. On the one hand we have a Mercedes saloon, Metallic Silver, registration number ... '

Sir Richard pointed an accusing finger at the solicitor's head. 'Whose bloody side are you on, anyway? You waltz in here like a refugee from bloody Rumpole of the Bailey and ... '

Toby smiled. 'My favourite programme, that is, actually.'

Sir Richard squinted. 'Really? I wonder why that doesn't surprise me.'

'Yes,' nodded Toby, eagerly. 'I particularly liked the episode about the wealthy business man who was suspected of murder when they caught him driving the dead man's car . . . '

'Look!' snapped Sir Richard, turning to DS McGregor. 'I don't want this *arsehole* anywhere near me. I want my own legal representation. Make a note.' He tapped the table with a finger. 'His name is . . . '

'Sir Jeremy Spence QC,' said the officer. 'Yes, you said. Unfortunately, Sir Jeremy has a prior engagement, according to a colleague of mine at the Met. At the Old Bailey, I believe? Along with Rumpole, no doubt. A little matter of a legal clerk's panties, I understand. His hands in them, against her will, so I am led to believe? He could be there for quite some time, I'm told. In the Old Bailey, I mean, not the legal secretary's panties.'

Toby shook his head, sadly. 'Not good, I'm afraid,' he admitted. 'But of course you needed representation so the duty officer very thoughtfully invited us along. Not really my sort of territory, though, you know? What our American colleagues call Grand Theft Auto, I believe? We do more sort of *conveyancing* really.' He giggled. 'Well I do, anyway. Still,' he added, with a sigh, 'we'll do the very best we can to help you out.'

He glanced at his notes. 'The confusion over the cars should be easy enough to sort out. But that still leaves the rather more serious matter of the cocaine.' He glanced at Sir Richard's frowning face. 'In your toiletries bag?'

Sir Richard's frown deepened. 'Don't talk nonsense, man! Never touched the stuff in my life!'

Toby cleared his throat. 'Yes of course. Absolutely! I suppose if you come clean about it, though, the police might be prepared to go easy on you?' He looked at the sergeant. 'Wouldn't you say?'

DS McGregor looked doubtful. 'Don't know about that,' he said. 'Cocaine's a Class A drug, and pushing's a serious offence.'

'Pushing?' said Sir Richard, in disbelief. 'Pushing? Are you mad? In case you hadn't noticed, I'm a Knight of the sodding Realm!'

'So is Bob Geldof,' said DS McGregor.

'Who?'

'Or . . . maybe not. Still,' said the detective sergeant with a smile, 'I think it's very amusing, sir, actually . . . come clean?' he suggested with a nod at Toby Bannister. 'Toiletries bag?'

Toby grinned. 'Oh, yes, I see. *Hah*! I hadn't thought of it like that. Pretty good, eh? *Hah-hah*! I must tell . . . ' He stopped when he caught sight of his client's withering stare. 'Um, yes, well, as I was saying: the cocaine . . . '

'Cocaine?' snapped Sir Richard. 'What d'you mean, man, *cocaine*? There's no *cocaine* in my toiletries bag! Have you gone *completely* out of your minds?'

'It's a very serious offence of course,' said Toby with an apologetic cough, 'and I recommend that you take the Fifth Amendment.' He frowned, and stared at the wall. 'Oh no, that's America, isn't it? Anyway, I think . . . '

Sir Richard ignored him and turned to the sergeant. 'Whose idea was it to lumber me with this wanker? Eh? It's some sort of joke, right? Cocaine? I mean you can't be sodding serious? And look at him, for Christ's sake!'

The sergeant smiled, and stood up. 'Yes, sir. As you say, it's just our little joke. Just one of the funny little ways we have in this part of the country.'

'Well I don't think it's very bloody amusing! And your superiors are going to hear about it. You can be certain of that!' He stood up. 'Now,' he said, haughtily, 'if you will be good enough to show me the way out . . .?'

'In a moment, sir,' said DS McGregor. 'We've just got the odd little formality or two to get through first, if you wouldn't mind?'

He cleared his throat. 'Richard John Pate, I am arresting you for being in possession of a Class A drug. You do not have to say anything . . . '

Sir Richard didn't hear the rest of the caution because he was too busy trying to cope with the shock.

High above the police station, a helicopter piloted by Nils de Boer banked and headed northwest. Vicky, Beth, Amy, and Sam looked down at the city spread out below them and wondered where they were being taken and why. All they had been told was that it wasn't safe for them to stay in Chelmsford because Dolly Killjoy was sending some very nasty people to kill them.

It hadn't taken long to persuade Vicky and Beth that they ought to leave, because they had already seen more than enough of what Dolly was capable of to last them a lifetime. Amy and Sam had been more difficult to convince, until Nils had pointed out that if they stayed where they were there was a better than even chance that they would be incinerated along with everything else in Sam's flat.

The journey to the rooftop helipad had taken ten minutes in a black sedan with tinted windows. Twenty minutes after that, they had been flying over London, heading west into the afternoon sun.

Sam swallowed uncomfortably, and nudged his sister in the ribs as the chopper banked to the right. 'If he does that again I'm going to throw up.'

'Where're you taking us?' shouted Beth, above the sound of the engine.

Max de Griese shook his head. 'Can't tell you that,' he said from his seat at the back of the aircraft. 'Sorry! But you'll find out soon enough.'

'How much further, then?' shouted Vicky.

Max looked at his watch. 'About ten minutes!' he shouted. 'Don't' worry about it, though! Just try and relax!'

22

JACK STRAWBRIDGE

Henry regained consciousness to find himself slumped across the front seats of the Volvo with an ache in his back where the gearstick was poking into his kidney, and a pain above the eyes where Rooter had slammed the car door against his head. He groaned as he tried to sit up; then whooped in alarm as someone grabbed him and dragged him out through the open driver's door by his ankles. The back of his head banged against the doorframe as he slid face-up over the edge of the driver's seat and landed on his back with a force that knocked the wind from his body. Before he could recover his senses, a frightening figure in tattered and smouldering clothing leapt onto his chest and grabbed him by the throat with both hands.

Henry's first thought, if you discount an obscure but heart-felt, 'Oh God, not again!' was that his attacker was one of the thugs from the Mercedes. The big car must have crashed and burst into flames, he decided, leaving this charred wretch as its only survivor.

His second thought, if you ignore a horrified 'Please God, don't let him drip any more of *that* on my face!' was one of astonishment that the man still wanted to fight after he'd suffered such terrible injuries. His clothes were smouldering and even as Henry watched, boggle-eyed and gasping for breath, the last few wisps of hair on the man's bright red, blistered head sizzled away into nothingness.

Henry squeezed his eyes shut in the hope that it was all a horrible dream, and he would wake soon to find himself slumped in the driver's seat of his car with nothing worse than a bruised forehead to contend with: or, better still, at home in bed with Spike laying on his chest, purring happily. But when he opened his eyes, the terrible apparition was still there, crushing his windpipe and mouthing obscenities into his face.

'Oh God!' thought Henry. 'I'm going deaf!'

It was true: his attacker was screaming with his teeth bared and his mouth working vigorously, but the sound of his voice seemed to be coming from a long way away, so that all Henry could make out was the odd word here and there. 'Thief' was one that penetrated his fading consciousness. That and a repeated cry of 'Mine! Mine! Mine!'

Henry realized something else, too: not only could he not hear what the man was saying, but he couldn't feel his fingers around his throat, either, or the weight of his body pressing down on his chest.

'This is it,' he thought, as he felt consciousness draining away. 'First your hearing goes. Then your other senses follow. Soon I'll be no more than a bag of putrefying water with a few assorted minerals scattered through it!'

He supposed his eyesight would be next to go, and felt a certain morbid satisfaction when the figure started to shimmer and fade. He watched in detached fascination as his attacker's scorched head and shoulders writhed with increasing violence in what appeared to be their own personal heat haze. There was a sudden and sizzling sound, like sausages frying in hot fat, and the tattered, singed creature shimmered even more violently, faded, shimmered again and then disappeared with a faint *whoosh*!

Henry closed his eyes and rested the back of his head on the ground. He couldn't decide whether he was alive or dead, and was too scared to move in case he found out it was the latter. For all he knew he was still slumped in a heap under Sam's pool table on a dope-alcohol-cue induced trip from which he would wake momentarily to find that he had imagined the whole thing. Or perhaps he was asleep at his desk and hadn't really been sacked from his job, or made a fool of himself in front of Amy Johnson, again, or been chased halfway across the country by Arsenal supporters with a bloodlust, or been doused in wet sand by Charlotte Piece at a motorway service station: and he most definitely had not just been attacked by an escapee from a painting by Hieronymus Bosch.

As he lay on the hard ground, trying to pretend that none of this was really happening to him, he decided that the best thing he could do was keep his eyes closed and wait for normality to reassert itself, hoping against hope that he would recognize it when it did.

Suddenly, a male voice spoke from nearby.

'You all right down there, lover?' it asked, in a quiet West Country drawl. 'You oughta get up, mind? You'll get they piles down there, you idden careful.'

When Henry didn't reply, the voice became thoughtful.

'You done it now, Pengardon, with yer fallollopin'. Poor bugger's dead, or dyin', I reckon. One or t'other, anyhow. Both, from the look o' the poor sod!'

There was the sound of heavy feet shuffling closer.

Henry decided to stay where he was, unmoving. Being dead, he decided, might not be such a bad idea for a while.

Rooter rubbed his jaw, and looked away from Henry to gaze thoughtfully at a faraway hill. 'Look after the bugger, they said. Take him to the Dragon, they said.' He looked down at Henry's inert body. 'Why is it always me who has to do the baby-sitting and that lot who get to have all the fun?'

Henry frowned inwardly at the change in the speaker's voice. The heavy West Country drawl had been replaced by something approaching Estuary English. Either there were two relatively normal people standing over him, he decided, or one, possibly very dangerous, schizophrenic!

A shadow moved across his eyelids, and he guessed that someone was bending over him for a closer look at his face.

'Hello,' said the voice, 'you in there, boy?'

Henry opened his eyes, and found Rooter's face about six inches from his own. He stared at it in silence for a fraction of a second, then opened his mouth and screamed for all he was worth.

Rooter screamed too, jerked away, rocked back on his haunches and fell over backwards to scuttle out of harm's way on the flats of his hands and feet. 'Now then, boy!' he said. 'Now then! No need for all that there screamin', is there? Nearly scared me bleedin' taters off, you did, carryin' on!'

'Don't touch me!' cried Henry, scrambling backwards on the flats of his own hands and feet. 'Don't you touch me! I know who you are! You and your murdering friends!'

'The boys?' said Rooter, mildly. 'They'm gone, lover.' He turned and pointed into the distance. 'Took them other lot over Sodmire way. Won't be back for a bit, I don't reckon, neither.'

Henry stood up, and looked around. 'You won't get away with it, you know? People saw you chasing me.'

Rooter held his hands up in a gesture of innocence. 'Not me lover. Them other lot, that were.'

'What other lot?' asked Henry, backing away.

'Them lot in that gert big Mercedes,' said Rooter, taking a step forward. 'With the 'ardware, an' that? The boys took 'em down Sodmire way for a bit.'

Henry shook his head, and backed further away. 'I'm warning you!' he quavered. 'Just you . . . you just . . . just stay where you are!'

'Warning you?' he thought. 'Warning who? About what? If you come any closer I'll run away? If you touch me I'll scream?'

He looked around. 'Where . . . where's your friend, then? Don't . . . don't you think you ought to get him to a hospital or something? I mean what . . .?'

'Look, lover,' said Rooter, 'you'm a bit puggled, tha's all. T'wodden . . . '

'He was on fire for Christ's sake!' cried Henry, gesturing wildly. 'I mean, what's the matter with you people? Jesus Christ . . .!'

'Fire?' said Rooter, suddenly alert. 'Who was on fire?'

Henry wasn't listening. 'What do you want from me, anyway? You chase me halfway across the country. I mean, who the hell do you think you are?'

Rooter shook his head in exasperation. 'Look after the bugger, they said. Where's the bloody straitjacket, then? That's what I wants t' know.'

He fixed Henry with what he hoped was a winning smile. 'They'm *gone*, lover! All right? The boys took 'em away. Over Sodmire? See the buggers get out o' that lot, eh? No place for a grockle, that idden.'

Henry frowned: the man was talking gibberish. *Puggled, Sodmire, grockle*; what kind of language was that? Like something out of a comedy sketch about village idiots. And look at him for God's sake! A great lump of a man, with hands like wicketkeeper's gloves and a face like parched leather, muddy old boots and a pair of tatty jeans cut off halfway up his thighs, a collarless, sleeveless shirt and a moth-eaten handkerchief knotted under his chin. If you gave him a straw hat, frayed around the brim, and a blade of grass to clamp between his out-sized teeth, the image of rural idiocy would be complete!

'You, er, you live around here, then?' he asked.

Rooter shook his head. 'No bugger lives 'round 'ere, boy, do they? I mean, there idden no bleedin' 'ouses round 'ere.'

'No. No, of course not. I just meant . . .! Look, I'm sorry about, you know, just now? I thought . . . I mean, I crashed my car, and someone slammed the door against my head and everything went black.'

Rooter cleared his throat. 'Yeah, well, what you doin' gallivantin' 'bout the place, anyhow? We don't hold with gallivantin' down 'ere!'

'Gallivanting?' said Henry, indignantly. '*Gallivanting*? They were chasing me, for Christ's sake! Three of 'em! In a bloody great Mercedes! I thought they were gonna kill me if I didn't get away!'

Rooter nodded, sagely. 'They was if we 'adn't come along an' stopped 'em. Cut your little dangley bits off, I reckon, if we 'adn't blocked 'em off. Not that your dangley bits, big or little, is any of my business, mind? I'm jus' sayin' you're lucky to still 'ave 'em, that's all.'

'That was you in the middle of the road? In that bloody great . . . *thing*!'

'Irene, that was, lover,' said Rooter, proudly. 'Gert 'eller 'er is, inner?'

'Gert . . .? You nearly killed me you stupid . . .! If I hadn't swerved . . .!'

Rooter held up a hand. 'No boy, it were *you* what nearly killed *you*, drivin' like a bloody maniac.' He clicked his tongue in disapproval. 'Can't 'ave that, can we? Makin' a racket an' fright'nin' the ponies!'

'Fine!' said Henry, turning away in an attempt to keep his indignation in check. 'All I know is . . . *JESUS – H – CHRIST*!' he shrieked, suddenly rooted to the spot as he stared open-mouthed at his battered car.

Rooter coughed. 'Not as bad as it looks, mind,' he offered. 'Soon get 'im straightened out, I reckon.' He sounded doubtful. 'P'rhaps?' He was silent for a moment. 'I towed 'im out o' they bushes. You was 'avin' a bit of a lie-down, inside, at the time. So I thought . . . '

'Look at it!'

'Could be worse, mind.'

'Could it?'

Rooter pursed his lips. 'Not really, no! Still the seats is all right, and the tyres. Get a few quid for scrap, maybe, if . . . '

'A few quid?'

'Bodywork's shot, see? 'Ave to rebuild the bugger from scratch.'

Henry stared dismally at the damage. 'It's a write-off, isn't it?'

'You could pro'bly drive the bugger if you knocked they wheel arches back out,' said Rooter. 'Maybe. Thing is, you shouldn't go messin' with blokes in Mercedes, boy. Never trust 'em, I say. They'm all the same: callous, 'ard-hearted buggers at best. Don't have nothin' to do with 'em, I was you.'

He gave Henry a quizzical look. 'What you been doin' t' piss 'em off like that, anyhow?'

'They don't think they liked the look of me. You know what football supporters are like?'

Rooter looked doubtful. 'There's Argyle supporters, down Plymouth way. Awkward buggers some o' them is. Course they don't go pointin' machineguns at folks. Not as far as I knows, they don't, anyhow.'

Henry frowned. 'Sorry?'

'Argyle never wins mind, so p'rhaps you could forgive 'em if they did, eh? Shoot the manager, like? Or the players? Still . . . '

'Excuse me?'

'. . . I don't hold with all that ironmongery meself. No sport in that, is there? I knows some blokes gets passionate 'bout football: tribal instinct, all that. Bit over the top, you ask me, though, shootin' folks jus' 'cause they supports t'other team. Whatever 'appened to wavin' your old rattle about, eh? What ever 'appened to fair play an'. . . .?'

'Hang on! Hang on!' said Henry. 'Just a minute! Sorry, but are you saying they had automatic weapons – machineguns! – in that car?' He glanced fearfully back along the road. 'The men in the Mercedes, I mean?'

'That's what Gav reckoned 'twas, yeah. Looked more like summut out of a kiddie's Action Man set, you ask me. Pissy little thing, it were. Give me a shotgun every time, mind, you wants to shoot a bloke dead.'

'Machineguns?' said Henry, weakly. 'They had machineguns?' He looked back along the road again. 'In the Mercedes?'

Rooter nodded. 'Bloke in the front seat 'ad one, all right. 'Ad a pistol, an' all. Big, silver bugger it were.' He started ticking things off on his fingers. 'Flick-knife,' he looked at Henry, 'bone handled; butcher's cleaver in the boot; couple o' baseball bats . . . '

Henry sat down with a bump, and put his head between his knees.

Rooter looked down at him with a thoughtful expression. 'You all right, lover? You'm lookin' a bit peaky to me.'

'I don't feel very good all of a sudden.'

'It's the air, see,' said Rooter, nodding sagely. 'Gets 'em like that down 'ere, that ozone, when they'm not used to it, like.'

'Really?' said Henry, with a feeble smile. 'And there's me thinking it was the shock of finding out I've just been chased halfway across the country by a bunch of homicidal maniacs armed to the teeth.'

Rooter pursed his lips. 'Dunno 'bout maniacs. They was mad, all right, but I reckon they was about as sane as you an' me.' He rubbed his chin. 'Anyhow, listen: I reckon we better get you over Perce's place, an' get a stiff drink or two down yer gullet. Yeah?'

'I don't know,' said Henry. 'I'm supposed to be somewhere by now.'

'We'm all s'posed to be *somewhere*, lover,' said Rooter. 'That's life, innet? But you can't go sittin' round 'ere all day, can 'ee?' He glanced at the Volvo. 'I mean, that thing idden gonna get you nowhere fast, now, is it?'

'Is there someone I could call, then? A garage, or . . .?'

'No need, boy,' said Rooter, holding out a hand and pulling him on to his feet. 'We'll tow 'im along behind Irene. Get 'im over Perce's place, an' worry 'bout fixin' 'im later. OK?'

Henry allowed himself to be led around to the front of the huge tractor and eased up into the soft safety of the sofa. He sat there in stunned silence while Rooter manoeuvred them into place, hitched the Volvo to the back of the tractor, and made ready to drive off. The big engine growled throatily, sounding more like a drag racer than an agricultural workhorse, as they rumbled along for a few yards before Rooter stopped again and jumped to the ground. 'You sit there quiet for a bit, eh?' he said. 'I got a bit o' clearin' up to do.' He frowned. 'Now then, who's been messin' with this lot,' he muttered as he picked up one of the barriers.

Henry watched as Rooter loaded a collection of signs and wooden barriers onto the back of the tractor, before jumping up beside him.

''Ave to leave the rest for later, I reckon,' he said, gazing at the hedge behind which the council's huge sign was hidden. 'Can't go movin' that big bugger now, can I?' He took a deep breath and looked around. 'Right then,' he said, brightly, 'time we was gettin' on. By the way, what's your name, boy? We ain't been introduced.'

'Henry,' he said, holding out a hand. 'Henry Kite.'

'Pleased to meet you, Henry,' said Rooter, grasping his hand and shaking it firmly. 'Leonard Pengardon. Only they mostly calls me Rooter round 'ere. Or jus' Roots, if you prefers?'

'Right,' said Henry. 'Thank you Rooter . . . er, Roots. And you work for the council,' he added, nodding at the signs, 'do you?'

'Not exactly, no. More sort o' . . . tourists, an' that.'

'Ah, yes: there must be lots of them down here. Tourists, I mean?'

Rooter shrugged without comment.

'Where are we, by the way?' asked Henry, gazing at the open countryside. 'I got a bit lost when those guys were chasing me across the moor.'

'That there's Stratton Widger,' said Rooter, pointing at nothing that Henry could recognize as a landmark. 'And we'm goin' down Perce's place, the Green Dragon Inn?' He pointed into the distance. 'Over Sodmire way?'

'Yes,' said Henry, doubtfully. 'But where are we, exactly? In relation to the rest of the country, I mean?''

Rooter frowned. 'You'm still a bit puggled, boy. That there bang on the 'ead's distangled yer brain. That there's Stratton Widger,' he repeated, slowly and more loudly. 'Down there, see? And we'm goin' down Perce's place: the Green Dragon Inn?' He pointed again. 'Over Sodmire way?'

'Yes, I see,' said Henry. 'Thanks. That's . . . that's much clearer. Um, and what happened to the men in the Mercedes?' He gazed around as if he expected to see them leap out from behind the hedge.

'Ah!' said Rooter. 'Now then: what 'appened to them lot was . . .!'

Henry listened while Rooter talked heatedly about the crash and his own heroic part in the ensuing pitched battle with the men in the Mercedes. 'Gave them big city gangster types a right good hidin', we did,' he said, proudly. 'Won't be seein' 'em round 'ere for a while, I don't reckon.'

'Sounds terrible,' said Henry, wide-eyed. 'Were you hurt?'

Rooter snorted. 'Me? No chance, boy! Take more'n a bunch o' pansies from up London-way t' trouble ol' Roots.'

'And your friends drove them away?'

Rooter nodded.

'To the police station?'

Rooter shook his head. 'No need for that, now, is there? We got our own ways o' dealin' with the likes o' them down 'ere, don't you worry.'

'How do you mean?'

'Sodmire,' said Rooter, rubbing his hands together. 'Leave the buggers in the middle o' that lot an' let 'em find their way out, ay?'

He leaned close. 'Never trust a man what drives a Mercedes, I say. Stupid, fat, selfish bastards the lot of 'em is. Only deceitful, connivin' men drives Mercedes, Henry, and don't you ever forget it.'

Henry nodded. He was thinking that Sir Richard drove a Mercedes. 'But where is it?' he asked. 'The car, I mean? I didn't see it back there. You didn't let them keep it, did you?' He looked around, anxiously.

Rooter shook his head. 'Bottom o' Sodmire by now, I reckon. There's parts that'd swallow a whole house.'

'You put it in a bog?'

Rooter nodded and made a sliding motion with his hand. 'The boys did, I reckon. Don't go messin' with the boys, Henry. Very bad news! Very, very bad news! They looks kinda stupid on the outside, mind. Sort o' placid an' dim? Bit like Sodmire, I reckon. Only very, *very* bad underneath! You watch out for 'em, mind?'

'Yes,' said Henry, solemnly, 'I will. But isn't that illegal? I mean, putting things in bogs? I thought this was a national park?'

'Shooting people's illegal, an' all,' said Rooter, gazing distractedly over the hedge. 'Thought you'd be pleased?'

'Well, yes, I suppose I am. But . . . '

'What?'

'Well, I was wondering. Why didn't the boys take *me* over to Sodmire, as well? I mean, how did they know I wasn't some sort of a gangster?'

'You ever 'ear of a gangster what drives one o' them?' said Rooter, flicking a thumb over his shoulder at the battered Volvo.

'Oh, I see,' said Henry, deflated. 'But . . . ' he paused when he realized that Rooter wasn't listening. 'Is something wrong?'

'You like horses, Henry?'

'Horses? I don't know. I've never had much . . . '

'I likes horses. Nice beasts. Don't like riders much, though, do you?'

'I don't like racing. Always seems a bit seedy to me. All those pinch-faced little men in cloth caps crammed into betting offices. Don't like show jumping, either. A lot of mean-faced, anal retentives feeling pleased with themselves for dominating dumb animals . . .'

'Nothing dumb about horses, Henry,' said Rooter, with mild reproof in his voice. 'Leastways, not none o' the ones I knows, there idden! Got a lot in common, they 'ave, mind, riders and men what drives Mercedes? Some of 'em does both! Hang on 'ere for a bit, will ya?' he added, stretching to look over the hedge. 'Got to 'ave a word with a friend o' mine for a bit. Keep your 'ead down,' he warned as he jumped from the tractor and headed back towards the gap in the hedge. 'Could be a bit o' snot flyin' in a minute or three.'

Henry stood on tiptoe and craned his neck to see what, or who, Rooter had been looking at on the other side of the hedge. He could just make out the head of a man in a riding hat, and he guessed from the sounds of heavy stamping and cursing, and the way the man was jerking about, that his horse was acting skittish. He wondered if it had been spooked by something at its feet: a dog or a rabbit or a snake, perhaps?

The man on the other side of the hedge was Jack Strawbridge, the leader and longest-serving member of Sodmire District Council. As such, he wielded considerable power in the local community, but he was not universally liked. 'Good Ol' Jack' or just 'Big Jack' he might be to all those who had been voting him into office for the past twenty-five years. But to all those, like Rooter, Perce and the Clatworthy boys, who had not, he was simply 'That long string o' gnat's piss from over Sodmire Farm way.' But regardless of what they thought of him, most people agreed that Jack took his role as a councillor very seriously. This dedication to public service was due partly to his strong sense of civic duty, but mostly because it had made him such huge amounts of money over the years. In his capacity as chair of the planning committee (he was also chair of the housing, highways, tourism, environment, education and finance committees), he could be relied upon to examine with due diligence any and all planning applications submitted to the council by his family and friends (and, indeed, by anyone else able to stump up his not inconsiderable fees) before coming down hard in their favour, in spite of the inconvenient demands of the relevant planning regulations, local, regional, national or European that might otherwise have got in their way. Over the years, he had shepherded many a rustic, double-glazed, two storey, centrally heated outside toilet or garage extension through the planning process and, in the fullness of time (say, the day after its completion), been proud to witness its transformation into luxury holiday accommodation to the short-term benefit of the local tourist industry, and the rather longer-term benefit of the Jack Strawbridge Retirement Fund hidden in a biscuit tin under the floorboards at Sodmire Farm Kennels. But while his influence in local politics had been increasing dramatically in recent years, his beginnings had been far from auspicious. He had been born the illegitimate and only child of one Celia May Strawbridge, a beautiful but slow-witted girl with the body of an underwear model and the intellectual capacity of an agony aunt. Not that her intellect, or lack of it, had mattered to the fertilizer salesman who had deflowered her in her father's hay loft on 1 April 1953. On the contrary, he would gladly have shagged his way through the entire membership of the Honourable Society of Pompous Meddlers and Fixers if, as he had been fond of putting it in after-dinner speeches ever since, 'they'd all had arses on 'em like that little maid!'

'Just you come in 'ere, darlin',' he'd wheedled, motioning the nubile Celia towards the shabby farm building with a hand fidgeting in his trouser pocket. 'And I'll show 'ee summut that'll make your eyes pop out on stalks.'

'No,' Celia had replied with a characteristic jutting of her lower jaw. 'Not 'til you gives me a present.'

'Oh, I'll give 'ee a present, all right. Just you wait and see if I don't.'

'Want a puppy,' she had replied, with a truculent shake of the head.

'If you lets me put my big thingy in your little thingy, I'll give 'ee a bleedin' puppy, all right,' the salesman had promised.

'Don't want a bleedin' puppy,' Celia had insisted. 'Want a Lassie-dog type puppy, that's what!'

'Fair enough. Lassie-dog type puppy it is, then. Now, how 'bout I gives 'ee a nice big bone to be gettin' on with?'

Nine months later, Celia had given birth to what she had fondly believed was a Rough Collie. She'd named him Jack after the salesman – who had lied: his real name was Roger – and had kept him in a cardboard box for the first twelve weeks of his life. She'd fed him on a diet of her mother's home-baked bread soaked in goat's milk and strips of her father's best pickled tripe. She hadn't bothered with nappies, or any of the other more familiar paraphernalia of human babyhood, limiting his grooming instead to an early morning dip in the horse trough and a twice-daily rubdown with wet hay. He'd done well on it, too: although not as well as Celia would have liked. No matter how hard she had tried to teach him, he had shown not the slightest aptitude for obedience training and had steadfastly refused to sit, stay, lie down, fetch a stick, or beg, even when prompted to do so with the careful application to his infant genitalia of one of her father's best battery-powered cattle prods.

Celia had been nonplussed by the infant Jack's total lack of canine characteristics, but had persevered with his training right up until the day when the local veterinary surgeon had arrived at the farm to give him his distemper injection and had discovered the terrible truth.

Until that day, Herbie Groins MRCVS had thought that he'd seen everything there was to see in veterinary practice. But what he'd found on that spring morning at Sodmire Farm Kennels had been the worst case of animal cruelty it had been his misfortune to witness during his forty-two years in the profession, and enough to make a strong man dilute his whisky with tears.

'Now look 'ere, Arnold,' he'd said to Celia's father after examining Jack's frail infant body. 'This 'ere idden right! They dogs is goin' soft wi' that there young whippersnapper stuck in among 'em like that there! The 'hole pack'll be ruined, mind, you don't take the little bugger out quick. I mean, how d'you expect 'em to catch ol' fox when they bin cuddlin' up to 'im all bleedin' night?'

Jack had been plucked unceremoniously from the bosom of his canine family and forced to live with his mother and her flea-bitten parents in the broken-down cottage attached to the kennels. But he'd never gotten over the shock of the separation – a trauma which he still blamed on the hounds – and had been exacting a terrible vengeance on the animal kingdom ever since.

For as long as anyone could remember, Jack had hunted and killed anything that moved on the Sodmire Estate – farm animals, farmhands and his grandparents excepted, of course (most of the time) – and had developed a particular fondness for terrorizing anything that couldn't protect itself and couldn't, or wouldn't, fight back. When killing things hadn't been an option, because some namby-pamby do-gooders had got in his way – the local hunt saboteurs, perhaps, or the RSPCA, or the village policeman (the last invariably by accident) he'd settled for maiming as a not wholly unrewarding alternative. He'd baited badgers, coursed hares and pitted dogs and cockerels against others of their kind. He'd blasted pheasant, grouse and partridge from the skies with a shotgun: and, when there had been none of those left for him to slaughter, he'd shot robins, thrushes, sparrows, blue tits and wrens: anything, in fact, that had wings. By the time he'd reached puberty, at the familial age of thirty-nine and a half years, there had been nothing larger than a grasshopper for him to kill within two thousand yards of the farm. Times had been hard for him then, and with playthings in such short supply, he'd been forced to find more creative ways of pursuing his hobby. Earthworms, he'd discovered, wriggled energetically when he cut them into halves, then quarters, then eighths, then sixteenths, and so on down until they were no longer divisible. Woodlice and beetles he'd dispatched with a hammer. Slugs and snails he'd squashed in a vice. He'd ripped the legs off spiders, the wings off butterflies, and, with aid of an industrial blowtorch, the skin from the backs of the guinea pigs, rabbits and hamsters he'd nailed to a fence. His doting grandparents, watching his development from a safe distance, had thanked God that he'd turned out so well. After all, as they'd never tired of reminding their friends at the hunt ball, nodding sagely, given the character of his unfortunate slut of a mother (who they had long since had banished to a sanatorium for her lewdness in conceiving their 'Little Jack' out of wedlock) he could easily have turned out a homosexual, or a communist, or even, horror of horrors, a coon!

Standing on the driving platform of the huge tractor, Henry could hear shouting, grunting and swearing coming from the other side of the hedge. Suddenly, there was a dull thud, followed by the sound of a man weeping. A moment later, Rooter re-appeared through the gap in the hedge, grim-faced, and with a garment draped over his forearm.

'You bloody bugger!' yelled a tearful Jack, shambling into view a safe distance behind him, minus his trousers, with his nose bleeding and a riding boot dangling from each hand. 'Come back 'ere, you *bastard*!' he snivelled. 'Come back an' fight like a man!'

Rooter walked up to the tractor and tossed Jack's jodhpurs at Henry. 'Hang on to them a minute, lover, will 'ee?' he said. 'Just gonna put that dirty little bugger to bed.'

'That's right!' yelled Jack, 'run away, you bas . . .!' He fell silent when Rooter turned to face him. 'Don't you touch me, you . . . you . . .!' he cried, glancing over his shoulder and backing away.

'You leave them animals alone, Strawbridge, you hear?' said Rooter, pointing an angry index finger as he strode forward. 'I catch you beatin' that mare again, it won't be just your bleedin' trousers that'll be comin' off. It'll be that fat, ugly head o' yours, an' all! You hear what I'm sayin'?'

'You can't talk to me like that! I'm an important man, I am!' whined Jack. 'An' I know all about you and them bloody Clatworthies messin' with my signs. You won't get away with it, y'know! I'll have the police on you!' He paused to wipe his nose on a sleeve. 'The *real* police, I'm talkin' about. Not that meddlin' bastard and his tart of a girlfriend!'

Rooter's body stiffened. 'You what?'

'Don't you touch me!' cried Jack, backing away even further. 'People round 'ere 'ave 'ad enough of the bullyin'!'

'Yeah, well you'd know all about that, wouldn't you?' said Rooter, walking towards him. 'Only thing you're any good at! You just remember what I told you, that's all! You leave them animals in peace, or I'll be comin' to get you, *snot nose*! I'll 'ave you Strawbridge, an' don't you forget it!'

He turned away, and climbed onto the tractor.

'Yeah?' shouted Jack, taking a hesitant step forward. 'Well, we'll see about that, won't we? You just try it, that's all!'

When Rooter didn't react, he took another step forward. 'You're not the only one who's got friends round 'ere, y'know? I've got friends, an' all. And they know where you live. And you!' he added, pointing at Henry.

'Me?' mouthed Henry, pointing at himself.

'Take no notice,' said Rooter. 'He's puggled.'

He turned the ignition key and the tractor's engine rumbled into life.

'That's right,' jeered Jack. 'Run off home to your boyfriends, why don't you? Bleeding poofter!'

If there was one thing he really wanted out of life, he decided as the big tractor disappeared down Sodmire Lane, it was to put Pengardon and his friends over at the Green Dragon Inn in their stupid-bloody, smug-bloody grinning-bloody places: and him and the lads down at The Lodge were just the ones who could do it, an' all! It was time for ordinary, decent country folk to put a stop to Pengardon's antics once and for all. The big shiny sign that his committee had put up to stop people going to the Green Dragon Inn still hadn't put that bastard Perce Pratt out of business, and Jack had heard that it was Pengardon's doing, helped by those drug-crazed Clatworthy boys. But Pengardon was the ringleader – Jack was certain of that – so they'd be sorting him out first. Him and that snivelling little sod, Perce Pratt. They'd get the little shit on Pengardon's tractor while they were at it, too. Trying to look innocent with that old 'Who, me?' bollocks wouldn't save him! In fact, nothing was going to save any of them now! As soon as he got home, Jack was raising a posse, like they did in the movies. Then him and an army of his best lads would be going after Pengardon and his commie friends. And when they found them, they would be stringing the bolshie sods up by their tadgers as a warning to all the other do-gooding, leftie shitehouses that you didn't go messing with decent, law-abiding Christian folk like Jack and his lads. Not if you knew what was good for you, you didn't! Not so long as God was in his sky with all the apostles and the baby Jesus sitting around his holy feet!

23

JO CORNWALL

Richard Choat was only seconds ahead of Henry when he rounded the bend, flashed past Rooter's tractor, and found Lance and Gavin's barriers blocking the road. With his eyes staring wildly and his mouth opening in a strangulated *'Gha-aaaahhhhg!'* he turned the steering wheel frantically to his right, scraped past the nearest barrier, and came to a skidding halt on the road to the Green Dragon Inn. He was about to drive off when it occurred to him that there might be a way of throwing the persistent Mr. Kite off his scent. With the engine still running, he jumped out of the Probe, crouched down, and hurried the few yards back to the junction where, with many an anxious glance over his shoulder, he hastily repositioned the barriers until they were blocking the road behind him. Then, glancing quickly back the way he had come, he ran back to the Probe, climbed in, and drove off as if his life depended on it: which, given what Jackie would do to him if she ever found out what he'd been up to with Charlotte Piece, it probably did.

With any luck, he told himself as he raced along Sodmire Lane, the irritating Mr. Kite would follow the signs past the turning and head off in completely the wrong direction. Better still, he would disappear down some unprotected, council-dug hole in the road, or go crashing into whatever lethal obstacle the barriers had been put there to protect.

'Cannons to the left of 'em!' he intoned, as he drove away with a screeching of tyres, swerving now and then to avoid anyone unlucky enough to be coming in the opposite direction. 'Cannons to the right of 'em. Cannons to the . . . cannons to the . . . Hah! Get out of that one, smart-arse Henry *Kite*!'

He breathed out heavily, and his shoulders sagged with relief as he felt himself moving further away from danger with every turn in the road.

'You shouldn't go messing with Richie Choat, my friend!' he crowed, as he drove on. 'Not if you know what's good for you, you shouldn't!'

When he arrived at the Green Dragon Inn, he was travelling so fast that he didn't realize immediately that he had run out of road. The old stone building loomed up at him suddenly as he raced over the brow of a hill and swerved into the car park. He skidded across the gravel, turning first one way and then the other in an attempt to find a way out. Finally, after a circuit through the parked vehicles, he realized that he was trapped.

He turned the Probe around and drove anxiously back towards the car park entrance, trying to work out what to do next. He could either stay where he was and await events, he decided, or he could go back the way he had come. But if he did that, there was a chance that he would run into Henry Kite coming in the opposite direction and find himself with no way forward, or back, and the one person in the whole wide world – apart from his wife, and, if he was honest about it, Charlotte and his daughter Victoria – that he least wanted to see blocking his way. He glanced at his watch and decided to stay where he was for the next ten minutes, and if Henry Kite hadn't appeared by then, he would decide what to do next. In the meantime, he thought it would be a good idea to get out of sight. He turned the Probe around and drove it to the back of the building. He turned off the engine and slumped back against the seat, wiping his forehead with the back of a gloved hand, and grinning with relief.

'Sharp driving, Richie me old son,' he told himself. 'Bastard thought he had you, though, didn't he? No chance! Just toying with him, you were. Take more than a wanker like Kite to catch old Richie Choat when he's feeling hot!'

It would make a good story, too, he decided: how he had been chased across a desolate wasteland by a homicidal maniac: how he had lulled that same maniac into a false sense of security by allowing him to keep pace for a while before burning him off and leaving him to eat dust in the wake of the powerful Probe: how he had cunningly switched the signs at the junction before pootling off to the nearest public house for a well-earned sarnie and a pint or two of something cool.

'All in a day's work when you've got a powerful machine like the Probe, of course', he could hear himself telling his enthralled audience in Accounts. 'But you've got to give these maniacs a bit of a chance, haven't you? I mean, if you don't keep 'em interested they go off and start murdering people with axes, don't they? Someone's got to take responsibility, see? And you don't think about the danger, do you, when you're in the middle of the action, like that?'

Yes, it would make a very good story. And the best part of it was that he still had a whole fortnight's holiday with Charlotte in which to embroider it.

But therein lay a significant problem. Charlotte had gone off and got herself lost. It was typical. Just like a woman. And of course, she would blame him, wouldn't she, because they always did, didn't they, women? They never saw the bigger picture. Everything was always so petty and so personal, and some other poor bugger's fault! He shook his head at the unfairness of it all, and wondered what he would say to her when, and if, he found her again.

A sound jolted him out of his reverie, and had him glancing anxiously towards the main gate. He looked over his shoulder towards it with his heart racing, but saw nothing there to cause him concern.

He slumped back in his seat, and sighed with relief.

When he heard the noise again, he turned quickly to his left, and saw a heavy metal door being pushed open at the side of the building. He watched with a rising sense of gratitude as Perce's live-in waitress, Jo Cornwall, in a mini-skirted, black and white uniform, backed out of the door with a bulging bin bag in her hands. She turned slowly and started to high-heel her way with careful precision down a flight of stone steps towards a line of wheelie bins close to the front of his car. When she reached the bottom of the steps, she stopped with her back towards him, dumped the bin bag on the ground between her feet and stretched up to lift the lid on one of the bins. She looked inside it, briefly, before closing it and moving on to the next. Each time she reached up to lift a lid, her tight little Lycra skirt rose further up her thighs until Choat found himself gazing in slack-jawed gratitude at the lace-trimmed tops of her stockings.

Apparently satisfied that there was enough space in the last of the bins, Jo bent forward, straight-legged, with the bag between her feet and started to tie a knot in the strings at the top.

Choat eyes widened as the little skirt gave up the fight against its own elasticity and snapped out of sight, like a recoiling roller blind, exposing Jo's buttocks and the string of a black thong that disappeared between them.

'Tease-errrrr!' he growled, wiping spittle from the corner of his mouth. 'You're doing that deliberately, you little tart. Just for ol' Richie's benefit!'

He glanced at his watch. Ten minutes had passed since he'd arrived in the car park. 'Right then,' he said, as he opened the car door and got out, 'come in number one, your time is *definitely* up now!' Henry Kite and Charlotte Piece could go to Hell, he decided, he had a far more interesting fish to fry now.

He closed the door and pressed the stud on the key ring, smiling and winking at the car as it beeped and flashed its lights.

'Down boy!' he hissed. 'Daddy's goin' huntin'. No need to wait up.'

He hitched up the waist of his trousers, checked his flies, ran his driving-gloved hands through his hair, smoothed down his moustache, pulled in his stomach, straightened his shoulders, and walked quickly across the crunching gravel with his eyes fixed firmly on Jo's buttocks.

'Hello darlin',' he grinned, stopping short to admire the view. 'You all right there, are ya? Or is there something I can do to help?'

'You could go and play with yourself somewhere else,' she suggested, without turning around. She stood up and hefted the bag into the wheelie bin, slammed the lid, and bent to pull her skirt back into place. 'The main runway at Heathrow Airport would do for starters, I reckon.'

'I might get lonely,' he pouted. 'How 'bout you come along for the ride?'

She turned around, and smiled tightly. 'Tempting, but no thanks!'

Choat jerked his thumb at the Probe. 'In my motor, I mean. How about I give you a ride, and you show me the way?' He pressed the key ring. The car beeped and flashed its lights. 'A ride for a ride, like, y'know?'

'You have lots of conversations like that, do you? You and your little car?'

'We're very close.'

'To what, the bottom of the evolutionary ladder? By the way,' she added, turning towards the steps, 'I wouldn't hang around here for too long, if I were you. The bin men'll be here soon to take away *all* of the rubbish.'

Choat grinned as she swayed up the steps and closed the door behind her. 'Gaggin' for it!' he smirked.

He turned, and walked briskly around to the front of the building.

Once inside the pub, he pushed his way through a crowd of people on his way to the bar, taking a ten-pound note from his wallet and waving it imperiously above his head as he went. 'A pint of your very best, my good man!' he called to the barman.

Perce turned a jaundiced eye towards him. 'Bes' what?' he asked. 'You want summut tastes good? Or summut makes you pissed as a fart?'

Choat wasn't listening: he had just spotted Jo making her way through the crowd and was trying to catch her eye. 'Don't mind,' he said over his shoulder to Perce. 'Just so long as it hits the back of the old throat hard, like, y'know?'

'And would you be wantin' the power o' speech after?' asked Perce, reaching for a tankard. 'Or ain't you bothered 'bout that, neither?'

Choat raised an eyebrow and grinned ingratiatingly at Jo as she pushed past him. 'Strong stuff then, is it, you reckon?'

'I'll take that as a no,' said Perce.

Choat nodded as Jo disappeared through a door at the side of the bar. 'Yeah, right,' he said, turning back to Perce. 'We've got some pretty strong stuff in Essex, y'know? One night me and a mate had eighteen pints . . . '

'Is that right?' said Perce. 'Pint of the Ol' Lovers' it is then.'

Choat smiled uncertainly at a tankard of cloudy green liquid that was placed on the bar in front of him. But he handed over the twenty-five pence he was asked for in return, and went to sit on an ancient wooden settle at a table next to an open log fire.

'How's 'er 'angin' then, me ol' lover?' asked a voice as he sat down.

He turned to see two elderly men grinning at him from a nearby table. They were Horace and Hubert Naggs, bachelors of the parish and cider drinkers extraordinaire.

Horace nodded and winked. 'Rot your kidneys that lot will, boy!'

'That?' said Choat, disdainfully. 'Dishwater to me, that is! You should see the stuff we got back home in Essex. I was just telling the barman . . . '

'You 'ad 'im afore, then, 'ave 'ee?' asked Hubert. 'The Ol' Lovers', like?'

Choat waved a casual hand. 'Always have a pint or two of the old scrumpy when I'm in this neck of the woods. Nine or ten, some nights . . .'

'Course you do,' smiled Horace. ''Course you do, lover. Us can tell.'

'What,' said Choat, 'you really think this stuff's strong? Like lemonade to me, this lot is.' He looked Horace in the eye, raised the tankard to his lips and drained half the contents in a single swallow.

He immediately wished that he was dead. Whatever the tankard contained tasted repulsive, like camel sick mixed with bat guano and cat's piss. His stomach muscles churned and clenched as he sat with his lips clamped on a final mouthful of the vile stuff in the certain knowledge that there were now only two options left open to him: neither of which appealed to him in the slightest. Either he could spit the disgusting stuff back into the tankard and suffer the inevitable loss of face that such a reaction would bring, or he could swallow it and risk looking an even bigger idiot when he vomited it back up.

He sat for a while, perfectly still, with his eyes fixed on the tankard. When he finally decided to accept that he had no real choice in the matter, he closed his eyes, took a deep breath through his nose, and swallowed hard.

After a moment, realizing that against all expectations to the contrary he was still alive, he opened his eyes and smiled unconvincingly at Horace and Hubert. Then, moving with great care and precision, he placed the tankard down on the table and tried not to think about what he had just done.

'Good stuff,' he said. He hiccuped. 'Jus' . . . just what I n-needed.'

Jo appeared beside him, collecting glasses. 'Watch yourself, tiger,' she said. 'Brewer's Droop's only temporary. What that stuff does lasts for years!'

Choat dismissed the idea with a curled lip. 'Hah! Stuff we drink in Essex makes this lot look like gnat's piss! I was tellin' the . . .'

'Really?' said Jo, wiping the top of a table with a cloth. 'Still, I bet you couldn't down the rest of it in one go, could you?' She grinned at the Naggs brothers. 'I mean, nobody could do that, could they boys?'

'Bugger I!' winked Hubert.

'Wodden chuckle!' agreed Horace.

'Yeah?' said Choat.

He looked down at the half-empty tankard; thought about it; thought better of it; thought about it again: then glanced up at Jo with what he hoped was an expression of casual disinterest. 'Actually, I was thinking . . . '

'Thought not,' she said, with a final swipe at the top of the table. 'All mouth and trouser, you grockles are!'

'Oh, yeah?' retorted Choat, as she turned to walk away.

'Yeah,' she said, turning back.

'Yeah?' said Choat, thrusting his chin forward.

Jo raised an eyebrow and stood with her hands on her hips.

'You don't think I can do it, do you?'

'Do you?'

'Course,' he said, with a marked lack of conviction. 'No problem.'

He eyed the tankard for a moment, placing a hand on either side of it and taking quick, shallow breaths through his nose. Then he reached out and raised it to his lips, closed his eyes, and tilted his head back.

When the tankard was empty, he put it carefully down on the table and stared dull-eyed into the distance. 'Great!' he said, through a series of involuntary abdominal spasms. He wiped his mouth slowly along a sleeve. 'Just what . . . what I fuggin well needed.' Then he belched with his mouth wide open and his tongue thrusting out over his teeth.

Horace thought he sounded like one of his pigs with the colic.

'Get you another?' asked Jo.

Choat's eyes opened wide in alarm. 'No! No!' he said. Then with studied nonchalance 'I mean . . . I'd love to, course I would, only . . . ' he waved a hand at the crowd standing between him and the bar.

Jo nodded. 'Yeah, busy today, isn't it?'

'Yeah,' said Choat, aware that his eyesight had gone hazy and there was a dull thudding in one of his ears. 'Think I'll wait 'til the rush dies down . . .'

'No problem, tiger!' winked Jo. 'Be my pleasure, won't it? Two pints this time, was it? Save you going back again later?'

He raised a hand to object, but she had already turned away and was disappearing through a knot of drinkers on her way to the bar.

'Gert 'eller, inner?' offered Hubert, with a lecherous grin that spoke of many long years of unrequited lust. He leaned forward, conspiratorially. 'You're in there, boy, I reckon. Fancies you somethin' chronic, 'er does!'

'Yeah?' said Choat, with an uncertain grin. 'You thing so?'

'Definitely! Likes a man what can 'andle 'is liquor, does our Jo.'

'Watch it, I woz you, though,' advised Hubert. 'Suck 'ee in and blow 'ee out in bubbles, you idden careful.'

'Bugger I!' said his brother. 'Wodden chuckle! Give 'ee a roight smiggin loike a good 'ne, you don't keep yer 'ands on yer winkle!'

Choat tried to grin through his incomprehension, but his facial muscles seemed to have seized up. His lips had gone numb, too, and his teeth felt as if they were multiplying inside his mouth. The sound in his ear had changed to a faint buzzing, and unless he was very much mistaken the walls of the pub had started breathing in time with the music from the jukebox. Something small and bright shot across in front of him and zoomed off towards the main entrance. He belched, and blinked after it like a startled owl.

'Good stuff, the Ol' Lovers', innet boy?' grinned Horace, as if he knew exactly what Choat had just seen. 'Put 'air on yer eyeballs that lot will!'

Choat levered his head into an upright position, and tried to locate the old man's face with both eyes at once. "Is nothin'! Should see some o' the stuff we got bag 'ome in Essex. One time, me an' a friend had eighteen . . .'

'There you go, lover,' said Jo, returning from the bar and placing two full tankards on the table in front of him. 'On the house – landlord's treat!'

Choat's head wobbled as he gazed down at the drinks. 'Yeah,' he said, looking up, 'how 'bout you joy-joinin' me for one? Know what I mean?'

'Later, lover, ay?' she said, patting him on the head like a pet dog. 'Get that lot down your neck first and we'll see.'

He grinned, and tried to touch the side of his nose with a finger. He missed several times and went cross-eyed with the effort. He gave up and licked his lips appreciatively as his eyes ran over her body from her stockinged legs up to her breasts and back down to the hem of her skirt. He grunted his approval and winked.

'Could do with somethin' hot t' get me teeth into, darlin',' he said. 'Know wad I'm sayin'?'

Jo winked back at him. 'Really tiger?' she said, leaning close and lowering her voice to a whisper. 'In that case,' she breathed, 'I think I've got just what you need.' She tapped him on the head again. 'Don't go away!'

When Henry and Rooter arrived, twenty minutes later, Choat was still chewing his way through the gammon steak with pineapple rings, chips and peas that Jo had slid onto the table in front of him with a request that he should 'Be a good boy and eat it all up for your Auntie Jo, eh?' His jaws were working mechanically, his head was listing to one side and his hooded eyes were barely managing to stay open. He paused momentarily to belch and take another swig from his third pint of scrumpy. Then he went back to his dutiful chewing, convinced that he was on a promise if only he could manage to eat every last scrap of food on his plate.

Rooter left Henry standing at the bar and wandered around looking for somewhere to sit. He glanced across at Horace and Hubert, who nodded when he pointed at their table. The brothers nodded at one another and drained their glasses as Rooter guided Henry towards them.

'Gotta be goin' now, my lover,' said Horace, getting to his feet and glancing at Choat. 'Got to muck out they pigs, see? You watch out for that Jo, mind? Don't want you gettin' laid to waste, as you might say.'

Choat squinted at the brothers as they made their way to the door. 'Don't you worry 'bout me, mate,' he called after them, wafting a hand. 'I got everythin' covered.' He gazed at the plate in front of him, empty at last. He belched his relief. 'Ev-ery-think!' he said, carefully. 'Ev'ry-thin' . . . *thing*! Every-*thing*! Every-thing's covered! I got everything . . . '

'You all right, boy?' asked Rooter.

Choat's head swayed into an upright position. He squinted at Rooter, and then at Henry. 'Every . . . thing's covered!' he said. 'Jus' a bid o' the ol' scrum'y is all. An' a hamung snake with ships and p-peeeas! Nothin' t' worry 'bout, though! Dring gallons o' the stuff on a reg'lar basiss . . . I do, me! You shoul' see the stuff we god bag 'ome . . . in-nin Essicks.' His arm suddenly described a wide arc across the table. 'One nigh' me an' a frien' 'ad eighteen . . . '

'That where you're from, then, lover, is it?' asked Rooter, absently as he turned away and motioned Henry towards him. 'Fancy a pint?'

'What?' said Henry, as he pushed his way through the crowd. 'Oh, yes. Yes, but I'll get them.'

Rooter shook his head. 'No you won't boy.' He pointed at the empty table. 'You take it easy. This one's on me.'

'I could do with something to eat,' said Henry. 'If they've got a menu?'

Rooter nodded. 'Watch out for ol' swivel-arse there, I was you. Looks like 'e's about to pass out.'

'He things I'm pissed,' confided Choat, as Rooter made his way to the bar. 'Dunnee? Bud I'm nod. Jus' a bid tired, is all. Had a h-h-hard day, me!'

'Yeah,' sighed Henry. 'Tell me about it.'

On the other side of the room, Rooter leaned across the bar and whispered something to Perce, who nodded and spoke softly to Jo.

Jo listened for a moment, glanced across the room at Henry, nodded, and took down a tankard. Rooter and Perce exchanged more whispered conversation and meaningful glances, before Perce put down his tea towel and stepped through a beaded curtain at the back of the bar.

Rooter smiled at Jo as she pushed two tankards of scrumpy towards him. 'Bon appetit,' she said. 'And try not to lose it this time, Roots, ay?'

'Very funny!'

'Never mind, tiger,' she smiled, patting his hand. 'Everything comes to him who waits. Even you!'

Rooter carried the tankards back to the table. 'There you go,' he said. 'Put lead in your pencil, that lot will! Back in a bit,' he added over his shoulder as he turned away. 'Gotta have a word with a friend.'

'Don't go getting into any more fights,' grinned Henry. He smiled at his own joke and took a heavy swig from the tankard. A moment later he was wondering what the hell he had done to deserve whatever it was that had just punched him in the throat and started to dissolve his back teeth.

'Bloody good stuff, that, innit?' said Choat, leaning towards him. 'Takes a while to ged use to it, mind. Bud, bloody good stuff when you do-oooo.'

'Christ!' said Henry, screwing up his face. 'It tastes like cat's piss!'

'Yeah, great, innit? 'Ave another taster. Geds bedder as you g-go along.'

Henry regarded the tankard with suspicion. He was beginning to feel light-headed already. Perhaps, he told himself, it was all the tension he had suffered in the last twenty-four hours? Or maybe he was still a bit drunk from the night before? Either way, he wasn't at all certain that drinking the rest of the vile-tasting stuff in the tankard would be a good idea. 'I dunno,' he said, looking sideways at it, as if he expected it to jump up and bite.

'Garn!' encouraged Choat. 'Get it down ya! Don't want these bum-bum-kins thinging we can't take it, d'you?' And as if to prove his point, he lifted his own tankard to his lips and drained it to the dregs.

'There's a good boy!' said Jo, appearing suddenly out of the crowd and patting him on the top of the head.

Choat grinned back at her like a two-year-old that had just done its first dump in a potty unaided.

Jo took a note pad and pencil from the pocket of her apron and turned to look down at Henry. 'Mr. Pengardon says you want something to eat?'

Henry nodded.

'What can I get you?'

Henry shrugged. 'I don't know. What have you got?'

'Bloody fantas'ic tits!' smirked Choat.

Henry looked uncomfortably at Jo.

'An' a bloody g-gorgeous assss!' added Choat, grinning as he leaned forward in his seat to slap her on the bottom.

Jo reached back, grasped his thumb and bent it back against the knuckle.

Choat's eyes opened wide in pain as she leaned towards him and spoke softly close to his ear. 'If you do that again, tiger, I'll break both your arms! You got that?' Then, without releasing her grip, she looked up at Henry. 'There's Steak an' Kidney, Gammon an' Pineapple, Cottage Pie, Lasagne, Plaice an' Chips, Cornish Pasty or a Ploughman's?'

'Well,' said Henry, with a wary eye on Choat, who was doubled forward in agony, 'I think I'll have a Ploughman's if . . . er, that's . . . yes . . . thanks.'

'Right,' smiled Jo, releasing Choat's hand. 'Won't be a mo.'

'Bloody 'ell!' whispered Choat, coming slowly up from below the level of the tabletop after she'd gone. There were tears in his eyes and his cheeks were puckered as if he was sucking an invisible pencil. 'God a bid o' the ol' cra-cramp,' he said, flexing his thumb, 'a-all of a sudden.'

Henry raised a knowing eyebrow, and glanced after Jo as she made her way back through the crowd. 'Yeah, I noticed.'

'Nah! Nah! Nah!' insisted Choat, with a shake of the head that almost rocked him out of his seat. 'Dyin' for it, that one is. Fancies me somethin' chronic.' He winked with out-sized precision. 'I can tell!' Then he lurched to his feet with his hand cradled under his armpit. 'Jus' gonna . . . you know?' He waved vaguely across the room. 'Run a bid o' cold water o-over 'im. Feelin' a bid, you know, sorta . . . wosname.'

It took him several minutes to find his way to the toilets, and several more to find his way out of them once he'd finished running cold water over his thumb. By the time he got back to his table, Henry had finished his second pint of scrumpy and was working his way through a gigantic ploughman's lunch. He was also looking and feeling a bit under the weather.

'There was this bloke,' he was saying to Rooter, as Choat plumped himself down on the settle by the fire. 'Polecat, I thing 'is name was.'

'Don't talk daft,' said Rooter. 'No bugger's called bloody Polecat, is he?'

Henry gave an exaggerated nod of the head. 'Honest!' he said, scrunching his face up in thought. 'Or . . . or it could 'ave been Weasel!'

'You reckon?'

'I's true! I's true!' insisted Henry, his voice sounding clipped and breathy, like an elderly Chinese with a hot gob stopper burning his tongue. He straightened his body with difficulty. 'Any-how, you'll never guess wad he was drivin'.' He grinned at Rooter. 'Go on! Go on! 'Ave . . . 'ave a guess!'

Rooter glanced across at Choat, who seemed to be staring through them.

'Moped?' offered Rooter.

Henry took a swig from his tankard and shook his head. 'No, no! Mudge worse 'an a moped.'

'Robin Reliant, then?' hazarded Rooter. 'You know, three-wheel jobby?'

'Wrong!' said Henry, triumphantly, with another shake of the head that almost shook him onto the floor. 'W-worse'n that!'

'Worse than a three-wheel jobby?'

'Definably!'

Rooter shrugged, and glanced at Choat.

Choat opened his eyes wide in sympathetic confusion.

'Can't be,' said Rooter, turning back to Henry. 'I mean, there's nothin' worse than a three-wheel jobby, is there?'

'Oh yes 'ere is!'

'What, then? A push bike?'

Henry giggled and shook his head. 'Nod a push bige! No, no, no, no!'

'I give up, then.'

'Thingy,' said Henry, thickly.

Rooter looked across at Choat and mouthed 'Thingy?'

Choat held his arms wide and mouthed 'Dunno!'

Rooter turned back to Henry. 'What's a *thingy*, then, when it's at home?'

Henry grinned, and smacked his lips. 'You know, *thingy*! Ford *thingy*! Ford Probe *thingy*!' He giggled, and slapped at his thigh.

Rooter looked at him, doubtfully. 'What they been feedin' you back home in that Essex, then, Henry, eh? Loco weed, was it?'

At the table by the fire, Choat stiffened at the use of Henry's name.

'Listen!' confided Henry, leaning sideways. 'Ron says . . . ' He paused and frowned. 'Ron works ad the o-office, by . . . by the way. He says: Mide as well call it a prick, an' 'ave . . . 'ave done with it!' He nudged Rooter in the ribs. 'Ay? Thad way you god the car, an' . . . an' the dri-driver both!' He grinned at his own joke. 'Ay? *Hah*! Ay? *Hah-hah*! *Hah-hah-hah-hah*!'

Rooter stared at him for a moment. 'Puggled, you are, boy,' he said. 'Must 'ave bin that bang on the 'ead.'

Henry had a sudden thought. 'What'd he wanna bother with the car for, ad all, is wad I wanna know? Mide as well walk roun' with 'is dick hang-hangin' out. Save a friggin' f-fortune in pedrol! *Hah-hah*!'

He collapsed sideways in gales of laughter with his head bumping against Rooter's shoulder.

Rooter remained impassive until the giggling subsided.

Henry straightened himself up with a jerk, and looked into his tankard. 'You . . . you 'ad to be there to appre-preciate the wosname . . . y'know?'

Rooter sighed and stood up. 'Sorry I missed it. Must 'ave been bleedin' hilarious.' He turned and craned his neck in the direction of the bar. 'Be back in a bit, boy, OK? Gotta drain the ol' spuds.'

At the table by the fire, Choat's face was set in a mask of silent fury. And he was feeling stone cold sober again. 'What about you, then, Mr. *Thingy*?' he asked. 'Didn't ca'ch your name, by the way. *Ploppy*, was it? Wad sort o' car d'you drive, then, Mr. *Ploppy*? Eh?'

'Ploppy?' echoed Henry, bewildered. 'Who . . . who's *Ploppy*? Hen-Henry is me! Hen-Henry Kite. Volvo!' he added, remembering. 'Bud is buggered, innit? Won't go,' he sighed. 'Nod proper!' His face sank, and he seemed on the verge of tears. 'Poor liddle thin' . . .'

'Is thad right?'

'Nod fas'. Nod straight. Have t' ged 'im mended some . . . somewhere.' He waved vaguely at one of the windows. 'Wasn' my fault, though, was it? There was these guys chasin' me for miles an' miles an' miles an' . . . The *buggerd*! All 'cross the . . . 'cross the,' he waved at the window again, ' . . . cross the thingy.'

Choat didn't believe a word of it. 'So,' he muttered to himself, 'Mr. Ploppy wants to play silly buggers, does he?' He looked speculatively at Henry. 'How 'bout another?' he asked, pointing at the tankard in front of him.

'Cross the friggin' . . . ' Henry frowned. 'Wad?'

"Nother pint?' asked Choat. 'For the road?'

Henry thought for a moment before shaking his head. 'Can't. Got to drive, see? God to ged to somewhere . . . somewhere . . .?' He squinted across the room, trying to remember where he was supposed to be going. He shook his head. 'Can' seem to remem'er . . . '

'Thawed you said your car was . . . was knackered?'

Henry's face lit up in sudden recollection. 'Tha's right! Tha's right!' he nodded. 'Main-ee-acks chasin' me cross the wosname . . . thingy.' He gazed distractedly at the window again. 'Out there . . . on the . . . thingy-wosname.'

'Is tha' right?'

'Now is buggered an' won't go.'

'Really?'

'Where's Ruder?' asked Henry, looking up and scanning the room. 'Was 'ere jus' now. Bedder go an' fine 'im,' he added, getting unsteadily to his feet and setting off through the crowd on his way to the bar.

Choat watched him go for a second or two before reaching across between the tables to pick up the keys to the Volvo. 'Right then,' he said, as he stood up and headed for the exit, 'let's see Mr. Henry Ploppy-Kite get outa this one!'

'Leaving us already, tiger?' asked Jo, as she bent over the table to clear away the empties. 'I thought you and me had a date?'

It was a measure of his preoccupation with thoughts of revenge, that he didn't even acknowledge her existence, much less answer her question.

* * *

'He needs a good smackin', you ask me,' said Titus's muffled voice, 'that Stoat bloke does! Takin' liberties with that waitress, an' that. And,' he added, with obvious indignation, 'where's he get off treatin' 'is wife an' daughter like he owns 'em? Eh? I mean, that can't be right, can it?'

Henry looked around for this newly reconstructed version of the little Ancient Briton. But he was nowhere to be seen.

'He's up there,' said the hooded figure, pointing at the sky with a bony finger. 'With the lieutenant?'

'Again?' said Henry, looking up. 'How long is that now?'

'In our time frame or theirs?'

'There's a difference?' asked Henry.

'Certainly there is a difference! Location has got nothing to do with it. In *our* timeframe he has been with the lieutenant for as long as you and I have been sitting here. But in *their* timeframe, several weeks have passed already.'

'Poor girl!'

'I heard that!' came Titus's disembodied voice. 'An' I'll have you know there's nothin' *poor* about her! Knock spots off any bit o' totty you're ever gonna get your 'ands on, buddy! An' that's for damn certain!'

There was the sound of a muffled slap.

'*Ow!*' cried Titus, his voice fading for a moment. '*All right! All right! I get it! I get it!*' he hissed. 'Women!' he added, out loud. 'An' for your information, buddy, her name's Calliope! *Lieutenant* Calliope, an' don't you forget it!'

'I'll try not to.'

'Yeah, well, I'm watchin' you, buddy, that's all! And I'm tellin' ya, you can see a hellova lot from up here!'

* * *

24

SIMON HAWKER

Sodmire looked to the untrained eye like just another ordinary expanse of green-brown moorland stretching away into the hazy distance and dotted here and there with granite boulders, scraggy bushes and the occasional wind-wracked tree. But appearances were deceptive, because there was nothing ordinary about Sodmire, and it wasn't a safe place for people like Vinny, Bonce and Nobbler to be wandering across without guidance. The fact that there were no signs of life – not a single animal or bird to be seen – should have warned them that the bright green, moss-choked surfaces around them weren't as harmless as they looked. But they were city folk and one patch of countryside looked to them like any other. So they trudged along with their heads bent into the chill wind, blissfully unaware that with every step they took they were only inches away from a nose- and mouth-clogging watery grave. To make matters worse, they had no idea where they were going, and even less of where they had been. The problem was that there were none of the familiar landmarks by which they normally took their bearings: no petrol stations, no pubs, no clubs, and no discotheques with queuing lines of mini-skirted crumpet for them to heckle and bait as they stumped past: no late night newsagents to rob: no hookers on street corners to lust after and verbally abuse: no prowling police cars to hide from: and, most dispiriting of all, no betting shops for them to duck into when they felt the need to fritter away some of their ill-gotten gains. In fact, there was nothing at all that spoke to them of civilization: just an endless supply of oppressive silence and a vast expanse of nothing remotely interesting for as far as their eyes could see.

If they had been more alert, they might have stopped to wonder why the furrowed tracks of Lance's ancient Land Rover, and those of the Mercedes hitched up behind it, had vanished without trace almost as soon as they had been made. But they hadn't. They might also have wondered why Lance had driven so fast and so precisely over such an impossibly winding route on his way to the place where he and Gavin had left them. But they hadn't done that either. And if they hadn't been so preoccupied with thoughts of revenge, they might have suspected that the gurgling hole into which their precious car had sunk so rapidly was not an isolated geological phenomenon. But even that glaringly obvious possibility had passed them by without so much as a frown. In fact, they had managed to deduce nothing at all about the open countryside into which they had been dumped so unceremoniously – other than that it wasn't a city street – until Nobbler stepped on a patch of what looked like solid ground, and sank into it up to his chest.

Vinny was all for leaving him there: just walking off and pretending that he'd never existed. Dolly wouldn't mind, he insisted, and besides, they had been wanting to get rid of the irritating little sod for days. But Bonce wouldn't hear of it, and, after getting Nobbler to throw him one end of his Arsenal scarf, managed to haul him out onto solid ground.

From that moment on, aware suddenly of the seriousness of their plight, they had been inching across the hostile landscape with the unhappy Nobbler leading, Bonce behind him and Vinny bringing up the rear, in what they hoped was the direction from which they had come.

After twenty minutes of heavy-legged trudging, feeling soggy and dirty, and looking as filthy as they smelled, they reached an outcrop of granite and sat down to rest. At least, Vinny and Bonce sat down to rest: Nobbler wandered off in a sulk. A moment later, he came hurrying back, pointing beyond the boulders and begging them to come and see what he had found.

'Danger,' he read from the Ministry of Defence sign. 'Un-ex-plod-ed or-ord-nance!' He looked up. 'What's one a them, then? Ord-nance?'

'Bollocks!' said Vinny, who wasn't going to be intimidated by signs in the middle of nowhere. 'Unexploded bollocks! That's what that is!'

Bonce's eyes opened wide in sudden alarm. He had always known that there were some pretty nasty weapons in the world, but that was nastier than anything he had even dared to imagine. He raised his right foot gingerly, and checked the ground beneath it. Then he raised his left foot and checked the ground beneath that, too. Nothing he saw under either foot looked to him like a bollock, unexploded or otherwise. 'No,' he thought, with a sigh of relief, 'none down there then, is there? Lucky for ol' Bonce, that is!'

Another thought struck him, and he turned to squint suspiciously at the surrounding landscape. What, he wondered, if these bollock-things were camouflaged, and just lying around in the open like funny-looking kiwi fruit? He liked kiwi fruit: liked putting them in his mouth whole and squishing them with his tongue until the flavour exploded onto his tongue with a zing. If he tried that with one of these new-fangled weapons he'd just learned about, he decided, it would probably *zing* his head clean off of his shoulders!

He eyed a sheep on a distance hill with suspicion, wondering if it could be some sort of suicide pilot – a *cami karsey*, or whatever they called them – just hanging about eating grass to lull him into a false sense of security so that it could sidle up to him, pretending to be friendly, and blow him off at the knees. He wouldn't stand a chance, would he? He watched the animal warily, and decided that if it took so much as a step towards him he was off. Vinny and Nobbler could hang around and get themselves blown to bits if they wanted, but he wasn't going to be caught so easy. As soon as the thing came anywhere near him he was getting the hell out of there fast!

'Like a bleedin' rocket!' he told himself, firmly. 'Sneaky liddle bugger ain't gonna get good ol' Bonce so easy!'

From now on he was going to treat every living thing with bollocks as a potential enemy, no matter how fluffy it might look. The trouble was that he didn't know enough about nature and stuff. Things like how you told boy-things from girl-things, and where *exactly* things other than people kept their balls. Living in the city was all very well, but it hadn't prepared him for anything like this. At least when a bloke came at you in a pub with a machete in his hand you knew to kick him in the balls quick and smash his head into the nearest wall. But here you had no chance! Kick so much as a fluffy bunny in the balls and it would probably blow your leg clean off at the hip! He shook his head in admiration for the mind that had thought up such a cunning device. 'Clever,' he muttered. 'Bloody clever thing, that is, an' all!'

Nobbler wasn't so easily fooled. 'No it ain't,' he said, glancing around, nervously. 'I been in the army, I 'ave, an' there ain't no such thing as that!'

'You?' said Vinny, scornfully. 'You ain't been in no soddin' army! You ain't man enough to be in the friggin' Girl Guides!'

But Vinny was wrong: Nobbler had been in the army; if only officially so for two days. Two days in the infantry proving that he wasn't fit to be cannon fodder, followed by six months in a top security research facility proving that he wasn't fit to be any other kind of soldier, either. He had signed up in a moment of unbounded enthusiasm at the thought of serving his country bravely (and because he couldn't get a job anywhere else) and of becoming a fighting British bulldog. But the army had seen his true potential immediately, and had turned him into a guinea pig for NATO instead.

His days at the research facility had been spent locked in a tiny windowless cell while an endless stream of white-coated doctors had fed him on every narcotic agent known to military science. Doses had been meted out precisely to within the nearest pound, and the effects plotted carefully on a board at the foot of his bed. They had fed him barbiturates and amphetamines washed down with heroin and morphine and opium and cocaine. They had pumped him full of LSD, STP, THC and even the odd aspirin or two when he'd been coherent enough to realize that he had a headache. They had given him blue uppers to make him high, red downers to make him low, and a patchwork quilt of hallucinogens on blotting paper to provide him with a multi-coloured roller-coaster ride in both directions at once. He had smoked Nepalese Black, Acapulco Gold, Lebanese Red, and a sprightly little home-grown grass that some enterprising old hippie from Cowes had nurtured lovingly in his greenhouse and christened AK47 Isle of Wight Skunk. By the time the army had finally seen fit to discharge him, he had overdosed on everything from Lemsip to CS Gas and been pronounced F4, F–, and the man least likely to say 'No thanks, man, I'm trying to give it up.' But he hadn't been so far gone that he'd neglected to take with him as a keepsake half of everything he'd found when he'd raided the medicine cupboards at the clinic on his way out: a not-so-little bit of *this* to give him a living as a dealer, and a damn great lump of *that* for his own personal use. Even so, his return to Civvy Street, and the post of Road Sweeper provided for him by a sympathetic Romford Council, hadn't gone as smoothly as he or the council would have liked, and he'd found himself hankering after what he'd come to think of as 'a proper job': something for him to get his teeth into; something in which he could be proud; something that might one day actually become a career. Being a part-time drug dealer had provided him with an income and a social status of sorts, but even for him it had been embarrassingly easy. Not exactly like taking candy from babies, perhaps (more like selling crack cocaine to primary school kids, in fact), but it had given him no real sense of achievement. Worse still, he hadn't been able to rid himself of a nagging suspicion that he had been letting his newly acquired knowledge of biochemistry, and the systematic torture of helpless and unrepresented life forms, go to waste.

Then one day, after his fifth line of speed in ten minutes, and while he was staring blankly at his sitting room ceiling trying to decide if he should scale the walls by his fingernails or just hang from the curtain rail by his teeth, a brilliant idea had hit him squarely in the creative centre of his brain where such things tend to hurt most.

His council flat had become a health hazard, with mouldering takeaways, festering coffee cups and overflowing ashtrays all around; and, in the middle of the sitting room floor, a dilapidated coffee table on which he had been cutting dessertspoonsful of speed with handfuls of talcum powder, lemon sherbet and three types of sugar. Flies had been attracted to this mountainous confection in their thousands, and it had occurred to him that in their eagerness to sample his wares without paying for the privilege they were effectively offering themselves up as subjects to be experimented on. So, in a spirit of creative adventure, he'd decided to start doing some research right away – that very afternoon, perhaps, or the next day, or the day after that; or even in a month or two's time. He'd eventually gotten around to it six months later in a modestly unadventurous sort of a way, with the clouds of bluebottles and houseflies as his willing, if unwitting, partners in science.

His initial experiments had not been successful. The insects, it had turned out, did not prosper on an exclusive diet of amphetamine sulphate, even if it had taken him several weeks of head-scratching to appreciate the fact. At first, he'd managed to convince himself that he'd invented a new way (?) of making living things invisible. Then he'd noticed the hundreds of tiny bodies squashed flat against the wall at the end of his makeshift workbench (the draining board in his landfill site of a kitchen) and been forced to accept the uncomfortable truth. It had been the speed, both literally and metaphorically, that had been causing the sudden disappearances: and what he had really discovered was a means by which the splattered windscreen effect could be reversed. Or to put it another way: the windscreens would no longer have to do any moving because his newly supercharged subjects would be doing all the moving they would ever need.

As soon as he'd realized that Britain's native invertebrates – or at least, those that he'd been able to corral – were too small for the sort of tests he'd been trying to conduct, he'd gone out looking for something more robust to experiment on. His next set of results hadn't shown the level of improvement he been hoping for (everything had still ended up dead). But at least he'd been able to follow the trajectory of a suddenly supersonic hamster, even if it hadn't been any easier to stop it battering itself to death at the end of its flight path.

It had occurred to him eventually, although not in so many words, that he had been getting the power-to-weight ratio seriously out of kilter – so far out, in fact, that by the time he'd gotten around to reducing the dosage to more suitable proportions, he'd all-but wiped out the stock at his local pet shop. The shop's owner, a fat and shabby little man known locally as Sleazy John 'The Beast' McCrittick, so far from being as sickened by this turn of events as one of his unfortunate parrots, had been over the moon at the improvement in his turnover that Nobbler's enthusiastic activity had brought about: and had suggested that they should go into business together, with him supplying the livestock for future experiments, just as fast as Nobbler could kill them off. It would be a double-whammy of a strategy, he had explained to the uncertain Nobbler, because it would allow him to continue making a decent profit while never having to open his shop to the public again.

Nobbler had still been mulling over the terms of the offer (including a clause requiring him to let McCrittick sleep with his wife and daughter on alternate Fridays), when his deliberations had been rendered academic by the detonation of several pounds of Semtex explosive in the sewers beneath McCrittick's shop. The Essex branch of the Animal Liberation Army had gotten wind of a dog fight planned for that very evening, and had taken the opportunity to blow McCrittick, two dozen sorry examples of Essex Man, and a pair of unfortunate pit bull terriers called Mitzy and Muffet, to kingdom come. The following day a representative of the ALA had written to the editor of the *Romford Beagle* claiming responsibility for the explosion and expressing her organization's sincerest regrets for the demise of any and all animals of a non-human variety caused by the blast.

With his supply line cut off so effectively, Nobbler had been forced to bring his research to a halt. But when an opportunity for a bit of impromptu experimentation had presented itself to him a few days later, he had found it impossible to resist. When the plumbing had gone wrong in the flat belonging to his visually impaired neighbour, Shamus O'Flynne (the proud owner of a large and powerful guide dog named Sabre), he had made the mistake of asking Nobbler for help. Nobbler had been only too pleased to oblige him, and had taken the opportunity to slip into Sabre's food bowl one of his homemade Mickey Finns. Half an hour later, the ecstatic Sabre (an impressive German Shepherd Dog with a pedigree as long as his tail) had overtaken a Porsche 911 on the ring road outside Romford: an achievement that would have been far less worthy of note (given that the flashy little car had been travelling at a modest 20mph in heavy traffic at the time) had not the portly, and occasionally airborne, Shamus been hanging on to the big dog's lead as he'd flashed past. The driver of the 911, a local bookmaker by the name of Don Gillies, a man not noted for his scruples, had seen in Sabre's joyous dash for freedom a chance to make for himself a very big and very fast buck. The rest, as they say, is history, and the legend of William 'Nobbler' Bates, the man who could make animals do anything, had been born.

'You ain't been in no soddin' army!' scoffed Vinny, again. 'They don't take snot-nosed little wankers like you! They only take *real* men like me!' He glanced at Bonce. 'An' real dumb buggers like him!'

'Why's that bloke wavin' at us?' asked Bonce, ignoring the insult. 'He found one a them bollock fings, you reckon, or what?'

'Bloke?' said Vinny. 'What *bloke*? There ain't no *blokes* . . .'

"E's comin' over,' said Bonce. ''E looks funny t' me.'

Vinny turned to follow Bonce's pointing finger, and saw a tall, thin man, dressed all in black, who did indeed look a bit odd, weaving his way rapidly across the boggy ground towards them.

'Right,' hissed Vinny, 'he gets close enough, we jump 'im.'

'Wha' for?' frowned Bonce. 'He ain't done nuffin t' us.'

'Just bleedin' do it, moron! Don't give the bastard a chance!'

'Hello,' called the new arrival. 'Do you need help to get back to the road?'

'Yeah,' said Vinny, sidling forwards. 'We was jus' . . . '

'Bleedin' lost,' said Nobbler.

'Hey,' asked Bonce, 'you seen any of them bollock fings round 'ere?'

'Right!' cried Vinny, striding forward. 'Get the . . .!' But he stepped onto a lush patch of greenery and sank into it up to his waist. '*Bugger*!'

'Ah, yes,' said the man in black, looking down, 'you want to be careful about that. It's very difficult to get out, once you're in.'

His name was Simon Hawker, but most local people just called him Shite.

Shite Hawker the Grockle Stalker they called him, because of his habit of wandering around the least accessible parts of the moor looking for lost and frightened tourists willing to pay him for guiding them back to their hostels, their tents or their cars. At least, that was how his career had got started. His expertise now lay in finding increasingly ingenious ways of exposing himself to shortsighted elderly ladies looking for cheap thrills. But he didn't so much prey on them as spice up their summer holidays a bit. He was good at it, too, and very popular: a far cry from how life had been when he was growing up.

No one had liked him as a child – least of the girls – because he'd been tall and gawky, with eczema-flecked skin that was pallid, flaky and covered with scabs. None of the other kids had wanted to play with him, or even talk to him. On the contrary, they had shunned him and excluded him from their gangs and their games. He'd been desperate to play pirates, and big game hunters, and cowboys and Indians with the other boys, but they had run away from him, and hidden, and mocked him, and refused to let him join in. Eventually, he had withdrawn from their presence in disgust at his own ugliness, and had taken to wandering the moor in his cowboy suit, with his father's old air pistol jammed into his plastic holster, pretending to be Butch Cassidy riding the range with his best friend, the Sundance Kid. He had felt painfully lonely and alone, but at least the air pistol had been more realistic than the shiny plastic cap guns the other boys had carried, and he'd had plenty of time to learn how to use it. So much time, in fact, that he had soon learned to shoot the seed head from a blade of grass at a dozen paces, nine times out of ten. But his prowess as a gunslinger had made no difference to the other boys, who had still mocked him and chased him away, leaving him to wander the moor alone and convinced that no one would ever want to be close to him, or touch him, or call him their friend. All that had changed on a day not long after his eighteenth birthday when a chance encounter with a myopic, but optimistic, elderly lady had given him a whole new outlook on life.

His mother had sent him to buy provisions in Buckfastleigh, and he'd stopped at the side of the road on his way home for a pee. A bulging string bag filled with groceries had been hanging down at his side with an errant German sausage, white-coated and tied with a knot at the end, poking through a hole and pointing at the sky when the elderly lady in question had appeared from behind a hedge in her all-weather gear. She had taken one look at the impressive sausage, swallowed hard and stopped dead in her tracks.

'My word,' she'd muttered with a slim hand pressed to her breasts, 'will you look at that, Doris old girl. Have you ever seen such a wonderful thing? A bit pasty, to be sure, but magnificent to behold all the same.'

Simon had turned his sad eyes towards her, grateful that someone had finally seen something in him worthy of note. Following the direction of her gaze, he had reached down and gripped the sausage with his free hand, raising it experimentally into a more vertical position and noting with interest how the change had broadened her smile. Then he'd waggled it up and down with increasing rapidity until her eyes had turned up in her head and she'd sunk slowly, but blissfully, to her knees in a matronly faint.

He'd pushed his penis back into his jeans, and the sausage back into the string bag, and gone over to help the slowly reviving Doris back to her feet.

'Oooh, young man,' she'd sighed, straightening her clothing and pressing her blue-rinsed hair back into place, 'you gave me *such* a turn! You don't do that sort of thing often, I hope?'

'Only every Tuesday and Thursday,' he'd replied, thinking quickly. 'Same time, same place, every week.'

'Really?' Doris had grinned with a trembling hand held up to her bosom. 'Just think of it, old girl,' she'd murmured. Then 'You know young man, I've got friends who'd pay good money for a fright like that. Here,' she'd added, taking a twenty-pound note from her purse and pressing it into his hand, 'a little something for you to be going on with. Bye-bye for now, lovely boy. See you soon!'

The following Tuesday, at precisely the same time and place, a car had arrived with Doris and four of her friends from the WI crammed inside it. The Thursday after that, a coach had turned up packed to the luggage racks with tightly permed hordes of ladies who lunched. The following Tuesday there had been two coaches and an ice cream van. And the week after that, five coaches, a hot dog stall and people selling postcards, toffee apples, candy floss, hotdogs, and extra strong smelling salts by the pound. By the end of the summer, Simon had established himself as the most popular tourist attraction in the South West of England.

Five years had passed since that day, and he had become a national institution, talked about at coffee mornings and bring-and-buy sales across the length and breadth of the land. He had supporters' clubs in all the major towns and cities, and even the odd one or two amongst the expatriate British in France, Portugal and Spain. Even so, he was not universally liked. There were those amongst the hoteliers, B & B and self-catering providers, campsite owners and amusement park entrepreneurs who took a very dim view of his business. They said that he lowered the tone, and gave Devon's holiday trade a bad name. Besides, they knew that he made more in a week from the franchises he let to the service sector than most of them made in a year.

The superstitious locals still shunned him, of course, talking about him behind his back, crossing the road when they saw him coming, and threatening their children with his imminent arrival if they wouldn't go to bed at the appointed hour or had refused to eat all of their greens. But none of that mattered to him anymore, because he had the adulation of his global army of fans to bolster his confidence during the summer months. And when the tourist season slackened off in the autumn, he simply went back to wandering the wide-open spaces in search of lost and disorientated souls to save from themselves. Only the hardiest of walkers ventured into the deeper recesses of the moor during the winter, so there wasn't usually much for him to do at that time of the year. But that suited him just fine because it gave him plenty of time to seek out new and more picturesque settings for his primary source of income, and to develop variations on the theme of salamis with which to keep his legions of admirers amused. Lately, he had been experimenting with a particularly promising range of fertility symbols that he'd picked up at a car boot sale in Bovey Tracey. He'd just decided to plump for the one with the six-inch nails hammered through it, when he'd caught sight of Vinny, Nobbler and Bonce making their way across Sodmire Bog.

'Need a bleedin' crane to get 'im out,' said Nobbler, looking down at the top of Vinny's head.

'You gonna stand there yakin' all friggin' day?' snapped Vinny. 'This ain't funny y'know? You wait any longer I'm gonna be drowned!'

Bonce and Nobbler looked at one-another. It wouldn't be their fault, they were thinking, if they couldn't get him out again, would it? And no one would blame them if he disappeared from sight altogether.

But for Simon it was just another day at the office, and Vinny just another grockle to be saved from himself.

'Grab hold of him like this,' he said to the others, pointing. 'You under there! You there! Me here! And . . . one, two, three . . . *heeeeeeave*!'

They all heaved together and Vinny came out of the mire with a pop.

'Like shit off a shovel,' thought Bonce.

'You stink,' said Nobbler, wrinkling his nose. 'That muck's all over . . . '

'Listen!' said Vinny, taking him by the throat. 'You wanna go back in there, you little shithouse?'

Nobbler shook his head.

'Shut yer friggin' gob then! OK?'

'Where's your car?' asked Simon.

'Down there,' said Bonce, pointing at the ground. 'Dolly's gonna kill us when she finds out.'

'She's gonna kill *you*!' sneered Vinny. 'Nothing to do with *me* mate, is it? You're the soddin' driver, ain't ya! How's it feel now then, eh? Not so bleedin' clever now, are we?'

Simon looked at the ground, and waited for them to stop bickering. They were a strange bunch of people, all right, dressed mostly in football supporters' gear and covered in mud. One of them had blood on his face, and the other two looked every bit as vacant as the wide-open spaces around them. But their personal problems were none of his business. All he wanted was to get them to safety. If they started killing each other along the way, that wasn't his problem. Just so long as whoever was left standing didn't forget to pay him when they got back.

'You'd better come with me, then,' he said, when Vinny and Bonce had stopped glaring at each other. 'There are some people over there in a campervan. I'm sure they would be happy to give you a lift if you asked them nicely.'

25

WPC GWEN EVERS

Henry Kite and Richard Choat were locked together on the ground like a couple of undernourished, trainee Sumo wrestlers who had missed out on the really essential lessons about gravity and human anatomy. It was true that they were facing one another, as is generally thought to be a minimum requirement in hand-to-hand combat. But they were not noticeably engaged in any of the other activities thought to characterize conflict. Not anymore they weren't! After a brief exchange of verbal insults, and an all-but ineffectual attempt at mutual battery, after Henry had caught Choat urinating into the petrol tank of his car, they had quickly subsided into a cursing, threatening inactivity. Now they were lying together in a desperate clinch in the dust of the car park at the Green Dragon Inn.

Henry's head was wedged tightly under Choat's right armpit and felt as if it was about to explode. He was sure that if Choat squeezed him around the waist one more time he would have no option but to throw up all over the back of his shirt. He had just decided to do it anyway, out of spite, when someone spoke from what sounded like miles above their heads.

'Now then, sirs,' said a quiet, and not unsympathetic, male voice. 'Can I help you two gentlemen at all?'

Squinting around Choat's elbow, Henry looked up to see a pair of uniformed police officers looking down at him. One was tall and unmistakably female, standing square on with her feet apart and her tightly clenched fists bunched at her hips. In addition to what looked like a painfully tight uniform, she wore two items worthy of note. One was a heavy calibre handgun in a finely tooled leather holster. The other was a look of distaste.

Henry got the impression that he and Choat might have been regarded with only slightly less enthusiasm had they been something soft and yielding the WPC had just stepped in. Choat was of the same opinion and, by mutual consent, like a couple of naughty schoolboys caught brawling behind the bike shed by their favourite games mistress, they let go of one another and got slowly to their feet to stand shuffling their shoes self-consciously in the dust.

The WPC looked them over, shook her head, and sighed. 'Pathetic,' she said as they hung their heads in shame. 'Pathetic, the pair of you are!'

The other officer, the one who had spoken first, was a sergeant in his mid-thirties. He was tall and broad with a handsome, smiling face. But in spite of his friendly demeanour, something told Henry that here was a man who was not to be taken lightly. It could have been the penetrating pale-blue eyes that did it, or the powerful, hairy forearms folded across his barrel of a chest. More likely, though, it was the finely tooled hardwood baseball bat dangling from his belt at the end of a stainless steel chain.

'Now gentlemen,' said the sergeant, in a soft West Country drawl, 'what's going on here, then, eh?'

'Ah, officer,' said Henry. 'I'm glad you've come.' He gestured at Choat, and spoke with halting precision. 'This . . . *person* jus' pissed in . . .!'

'Pissed?' said Choat, coming suddenly to life and pushing Henry out of the way. 'He's the one who's *pissed*! All I been doin' . . .'

'*Oy!*' said Henry, pushing back. '*I'm* talkin'! So you can jus' . . . *piss off!*'

'Yeah?' said Choat. 'Who's gonna make me?'

'I am!'

'Yeah? You and whose army?'

The sergeant sighed, and stepped between them. 'Now then, now then, calm down gentlemen, if you would be so kind.'

'There's no problem here, cons'able,' said Choat. 'What 'appened was . . .'

'Shut up!' said Henry, reaching over the sergeant's shoulder to slap Choat in the head. '*I'm* tellin' him!'

'No you're not!' retorted Choat, slapping back. 'I am! You can jus' . . .!'

'That's enough!' said the sergeant, pushing them firmly apart. 'Let's have a bit of decorum, gentlemen, shall we?'

Henry and Choat stood glaring at one another, breathing heavily.

They were at the side of the pub, next to Henry's dented Volvo. Choat's Probe was parked nearby, and a small crowd had formed in the hope of seeing one or other of the would-be combatants get seriously injured.

The sergeant turned and waved them away. 'That's all right, ladies and gentlemen. Nothing to see here! On your way, if you would be so kind?'

'That's better,' he said when the last of them had shuffled away. 'Now then, one at a time, if you please?' He nodded at Henry. 'You were saying . . .?'

'No good talkin' to him,' sneered Choat. 'He doesn't even know . . .'

'Yes, thank you, sir,' said the sergeant, 'but I think I'll be the judge of that, if it's all the same to you?'

'Please yourself.'

'Thank you, sir. That's very kind,' said the sergeant. He turned to Henry. 'You were saying, sir . . .?'

'Ah, yes!' said Henry. 'Thang you. I . . . er,' but now that his chance had come, he wasn't sure what to do with it. To gain time he extended a hand.

The sergeant ignored it.

'Er . . . Kite,' said Henry, smiling wanly and withdrawing his hand. 'Henry Kite? From Essex? Well . . . Writtle, really. You know? Jus' sorta left . . . Well, west, really, of . . . of Chelmsford?' He indicated with both hands, as if he had a map hanging in front of him. He tried to smile winningly through the effects of Perce's scrumpy, but it wasn't convincing.

The sergeant looked at him, impassively.

The WPC pursed her lips, and gazed at the ground.

Choat shook his head, and looked at the sky.

'Um, yes,' murmured Henry, unsure what to do next. 'An', er – this!' he gestured elaborately at Choat. 'This . . . this . . . *person* jus' *pissed* . . .'

'No I didden!' insisted Choat, who was also feeling the effects of the scrumpy and wishing that he'd made sure that the coast was clear before he'd started pissing into Henry's petrol tank. 'He's the one who's pissed! I jus' stopped for a . . . a pint an' . . . an' . . .'

Henry put his hand over Choat's mouth, and pouted at the sergeant. 'I was talkin',' he whined, 'wasn't I? Tell 'im I was talkin' an' . . . an' i's nod fair!'

'That's all right, sir,' said the sergeant, prizing Henry's hand away from Choat's face.

'Look . . .!' began Choat, before the sergeant silenced him by clamping his own hand over his mouth.

'You have a nice rest,' said the sergeant to Henry. 'Pace yourself, like.'

'Now then, sir,' he added, turning to Choat and taking his hand away from his mouth, 'why don't you have a go while this other gentleman's having a think?' He put a finger to his lips. 'Nicely, if you would be so kind?'

'Thank you, cons'able,' simpered Choat. 'As I was sayin' . . . I jus' stopped for a bite o' lunch and a chance to drain the ol' spuds.' He smiled suddenly at the sergeant in a man-to-man, man-of-the-world, matey sort of a way.

The sergeant gazed back at him without expression.

'Then this bloody id-idiot,' continued Choat, 'comes 'long, starts cadgin' drinks off me, geds pissed, an' . . . an' won't leave me 'lone! You know wad they're like when they ged like that? Then he follows me out 'ere an'-an' *attacks* me! Prob'ly tryin' to rob me, I shouldn't won'er . . .'

'I's lies!' insisted Henry, who had just decided that it was time to punch Choat in the head. He turned towards him and drew back his fist.

'Now then, sir,' soothed the sergeant, casually enveloping Henry's hand in his own massive fist. 'You just take it easy. We'll soon have this little lot sorted out, don't you worry.'

The sergeant's grip was unbelievably tight, and Henry began to crumple at the knees as his eyes and mouth opened wide in silent agony. The sergeant's expression of mild benevolence didn't change for a moment, and he gave no indication that he was aware of the excruciating pain he was inflicting.

Henry's mouth opened even wider in a voiceless scream as he sank slowly to the ground. Just as the mists of unconsciousness seemed about to engulf him for the third time in twenty-four hours, the sergeant let go.

He remained on his knees, gently cradling his injured hand against his chest and blinking back tears of self-pity. He looked up at the WPC for sympathy, but she clicked her tongue, and looked away in disgust.

'Look, c-cons'able,' said Choat, moving close to whisper in the big man's ear. 'I don' wan' any trouble. I mean, look at 'im, eh? An'-an' look at 'is car.'

They both turned to gaze at the battered Volvo.

'I ask you?' said Choat. 'I bet he 'asn't got two brass farthin's to rub t'gether. An-an', we've all done it, 'aven't we? Had one or two too-ooo many, I mean? I'd jus' as soon for-ged the 'hole thing. Live an' le' live, I always say.'

'Well, that's very generous of you, sir,' said the sergeant, as they turned and looked at Henry, who seemed to be grovelling on the ground, either praying to his own private god, or lost in the throes of delirium tremens.

'*Nah*!' said Choat. 'We've all done it, 'aven't we? Jus' led 'im sleep it-off.

He'll be ride as rain in the m-mornin'.' He put his arm across the sergeant's shoulders as they turned and walked towards the Ford Probe.

Choat took hold of the door handle and spoke softly as if he and the sergeant were discussing a favoured but wayward child. 'Look, why don' I jus' slip off now, and we'll say no more 'bout it, eh? I mean, you can 'andle 'im, can't you? Man of your ex-experience an' . . . an' that?'

'Well, if you think that's for the best then, sir?' said the sergeant, with a glance over his shoulder at Henry, who was shuffling forlornly towards them. The WPC had hooked a hand under his armpit and hoisted him to his feet. Now she was behind him, prodding him in the back with her truncheon.

'Yeah,' said Choat. 'No 'arm done, eh? I'll be gettin' 'long, then, shall I?'

'Excuse me!' said Henry with a jerk as the WPC poked him in the left kidney. He stood on tiptoe behind the sergeant and pointed at Choat like a nosy neighbour peering over a fence. 'Wha's he doin' then? If you don't mine me askin'?'

'You be a goo' boy, Mr. Ploppy,' mocked Choat. 'An' don't go givin' the nice off-off'cers any more . . . more trouble.'

Henry jerked as the WPC prodded him with the truncheon, again. 'You're not gonna let 'im ged away with it, are you?'

'What's that then, sir,' asked the sergeant, leaning against the driver's door of the Probe, 'get away with what, exactly?'

Henry wobbled out of the way as the WPC's truncheon stabbed at him again. 'All right!' he said, testily. 'All right! All right! I'm goin' for Christ's sake!' He turned to the sergeant. 'He pissed in my petrol tang, tha's what! How far am I s'posed to get on that? It's not bloody f-four star, y'know!'

The WPC smiled and winked, before turning away and strolling around to the other side of Choat's car.

Henry thought he heard her utter a high-pitched whistle. Then he frowned in confusion when he also thought that he saw something large and brown glide out of a clump of bushes near the front of the car.

'No,' said the sergeant, with a judicious nod and a quick glance at the WPC, 'I don't suppose it is, sir, now that you come to mention it.' He looked at Choat, who was tugging ineffectually at the door handle. 'Just a minute sir, if you would be so kind?'

'I'm in a bid of a hurry, act-ually,' said Choat, trying to open the door against the weight of the sergeant's body. 'Gotta get to the 'otel, y'know?'

'Yes, sir,' said the sergeant, mildly. 'Of course you have. It's just that this gentleman here, Mr. Kite wasn't it, sir?'

Henry nodded, dumbly. He was starting to feel sick again, and had decided that talking would not be a good idea.

'Well,' said the sergeant. 'Mr. Kite is making a very serious accusation against you, sir. By the way, I don't think I caught your name, did I?'

'It's Choat, cons'able,' said Choat, pulling at the door handle again. 'Richard . . . Richard Choat. Now, if you wouldn' mind . . .?'

'Yes, and that's *sergeant* if *you* wouldn't mind, Mr. Scrote. It's a small thing,' he added, apologetically. 'But I do like to get these things right.'

'Yes,' said Choat. 'So do I, *sergeant*! And it's *Choat*, if *you* don' mine! Not Scrote! Choat! C-H-O-A-T. Choat!' he glared at Henry. 'Not Stoat! Not W-Weasel! Not Polecat! Jus' . . . *Choat*!' He turned back to the sergeant. 'An' I really thing this has gone on long enough, don' you?'

'Oh, undoubtedly, sir,' said the sergeant. 'Make a note of this gentleman's name, Gwen, will you, just in case? This is WPC Evers, by the way,' he said, gesturing proudly towards his partner on the far side of the Probe as she copied Choat's name into her notebook. 'And I'm Sergeant Arthur, of the Devon & Cornwall Constabulary. That's both of us, by the way: we're a team.'

'Are you really?' said Choat.

'Yes, sir,' said the sergeant, brightly. 'Both of us! Anyhow, I'd be grateful if you could clear up the little matter of Mr. Kite's car. If you would be so kind?'

'I tol' you, sergeant, it's nonsense! An' I'm in a hurry. So if you don' mine, I'd like to be goin'.' He tried to get into the car, but the sergeant took hold of his upper arm and gripped it, tightly.

'Yes sir,' he said. 'All in good time.'

'You're h-hurtin' me!' whined Choat.

'Yes, sir, life's a bugger sometimes, isn't it? Now, if you would just . . .'

'This is p'lice bru-brutality,' said Choat, through clenched teeth.

'Yes sir, very likely,' agreed the sergeant. 'Now about Mr. Kite's car? He says you, er, drained your spuds, I believe your expression was, wasn't it, into his petrol tank?' He turned to Henry. 'That is right, isn't it, sir? That is the gist of your accusation against this gentleman, is it not?'

Henry nodded.

'I mos' certainly did not!' said Choat. 'All I did was . . .'

'He stole my keys!' blurted Henry, against his better judgement. 'In the pub! I was jus' gonna . . . ' He got no further, but turned with a throaty belch, and vomited over the back of Choat's car.

Choat's eyes opened wide in horror. 'What the . . .?' He turned to the sergeant. 'D'you see that?' He turned to the WPC. 'D'you see what he did?'

'Oh,' said the sergeant, sharply, 'so it's taking the keys as well now, is it?'

'Look what he . . .!' spluttered Choat. He frowned. 'What? No! No! Course it isn't! Do I look like the sord o' person who'd do a thing like that? I might 'ave picked 'em up by accident – by mistake.' He shrugged. 'In a crowded pub with people pushin' and shovin'.' He turned back to the Probe. 'Look what he . . .!'

'And after a drink, or two, sir?' prompted the sergeant.

'Yes. No! I mean . . . what are you suggestin'? I'm drivin' . . . '

'Yes, sir,' said the sergeant. 'Just what I was thinking.'

'He's lyin',' said Henry, who was feeling much better after ridding himself of what had been fermenting in his stomach. 'He 'ad two pints while I was there.' He wiped his mouth on a sleeve. 'An' he 'ad one before we got 'ere. Me and tha' man,' he added, looking around for Rooter. 'Well,' he said, when he couldn't find him, 'he was 'ere jus' now . . . '

'See?' said Choat. 'See? The man's ravin'! I might 'ave picked up his keys by mistake. Maybe I did. I don't deny it. But where's the 'arm in that? Anyone could o' done it, couldn't he? As for piss . . . urin-nating in 'is petrol tang . . . I ask you,' he gestured from the Probe to the Volvo, 'why would I do a thing like that?'

'That's what I was wondering,' said the sergeant.

'There y'are, then,' said Choat, tugging at the door handle. 'Now, if you wouldn't mine . . .?'

'Wasn't I Gwen?' continued the sergeant, unperturbed 'Just now when we was sitting over there behind the hedge in our little car? Having a bit of lunch? I said to WPC Evers – didn't I Gwen? – I said: What's that flashy looking bugger doing pissing in that petrol tank? I'll bet it's not his car.' He looked Choat squarely in the eye. 'Isn't that right, Gwen?'

Choat stopped tugging at the door handle, and stood perfectly still.

'Oh yes, sergeant,' agreed WPC Evers. 'You *did* say that. And I'd say we had him bang-to-rights, with the evidence in his hand, so to speak.'

Henry frowned. 'You saw . . . saw him do it?'

'Yes sir! We saw him all right,' said the sergeant. 'Didn't we Mr. Choat?'

'Not that there was much *to* see,' smiled WPC Evers. 'Not from where I was sitting, anyway! Still, what he hasn't got he won't miss, will he? Chop it off, I say. That way he won't do it again.'

'Oh, yes?' said Choat, his tone suddenly scathing. 'And you thing anyone's gonna care 'bout that pile o' junk, do you?' He waved at the Volvo. 'Or that nasty liddle bugger?' he added, pointing at Henry. 'He's bin af'er me all bloody day, y'know? Chasin' me all 'cross – all – every-bloody-where!' He wrenched his arm free of the sergeant's grasp and pulled open the car door. 'Well I've 'ad enough of it! So ged your filthy 'ands off of me! I'm leavin'!'

The sergeant bent down with Choat as he plumped into the driver's seat.

'I wouldn't do that, sir, if I was you,' he said, quietly.

'Is tha' right?' said Choat, who had a pretty good idea that if he could get the Probe started he would have no difficulty at all in out-running what the sergeant had referred to earlier as their 'little car'. He thrust his keys into the steering column. 'And why is that, mide I ask?' he added, playing for time

'Because Boadicea wouldn't like it, sir,' said the sergeant, nodding towards the passenger seat of the Probe.

An impossibly deep growl sounded in Choat's left ear.

'I should move very carefully, sir, if I was you,' said the sergeant. 'Or she might remove bits of your anatomy that you would be wanting to keep.'

'She is a bit peckish,' said WPC Evers through the passenger window.

Choat glanced to his left, and wished that he hadn't. For a moment he had found himself staring into the enormous drooling jowls and red-black eyes of the thing that the sergeant had called Boadicea. Then he'd turned quickly away, and decided that it would be best never to look back. From his brief glimpse, he thought the monstrous animal was probably some sort of dog, but he was too close to it to be certain, and it might easily have been a bear, or even a lion. Two things *were* certain, however: he had never been so frightened in his life, and he was in danger of ruining a perfectly good pair of trousers.

'Now, just you take it easy, Mr. Scrote, sir,' said the sergeant, pleasantly. 'As I said, she won't kill you if you do exactly what you're told. All right?'

'Kill?' hissed Choat.

'Well, not so much kill as maim,' confided the sergeant. 'I don't think Boadicea has ever killed any actual human beings, has she Gwen?'

WPC Evers shook her head, sadly.

'No, I thought not,' said the sergeant. 'Still, she can be a bit boisterous when she has a mind.' He suddenly cheered up. 'You haven't got a bit of liver about you, have you, Mr. Stoat? Other than your own, I mean?'

Choat's eyes swivelled slowly towards the sergeant in disbelief.

'No? Well, never mind. It was just a thought. She'll do anything for a bit of liver, will our Boadicea.'

'What is it?' asked Henry, peering into the car over the sergeant's shoulder. 'I mean I know it's a dog.' He frowned. 'It *is* a dog, isn't it?'

'Oh yes, it's a dog all right,' agreed the sergeant. 'That's Boadicea, that is. She's Gwen's little friend.'

'Little?' breathed Choat.

'In a manner of speaking,' said the sergeant. 'She don't get out much, see?'

'But, um,' continued Henry, 'I mide be wrong, but isn't that . . .? I mean I don't know mush about dogs, but hasn't it got . . .? Isn't that . . .?'

'It's a penis, sir, yes,' beamed the sergeant. 'Bless you! Fair size too, Mr. Smote, wouldn't you say?'

Choat bared his teeth.

'Well, then,' said Henry, 'doesn' that mean *she* is r-really a *he*?'

'It's not her fault, mind,' confided the sergeant. 'Boadicea's a dog all right: as opposed to a bitch, like. And it makes her a bit humpitty, all the name-calling. But it's not her fault: she was an only child.'

'Humpitty?' mouthed Choat.

'On account of how she'd rather be a he than a she,' said the sergeant. 'If you take my meaning, Mr. Stoat?'

'Only child?' asked Henry. 'I don' thing . . .?'

'It's a bit difficult,' agreed the sergeant. 'But how do you think she feels?'

For a moment they all contemplated Boadicea's personality disorder in respectful silence. All except Choat, that is, who was busy developing a fairly serious personality disorder of his own.

'Still,' said the sergeant, with a sigh, 'I reckon Mr. Sproat had better come out of there while he still can. Don't you?'

Choat swallowed. 'Is it safe?'

'Oh yes,' said the sergeant, happily. 'But . . . easy does it: one buttock at a time, like, and no sudden moves.'

'Don't you frighten her,' warned WPC Evers. 'She's very sensitive. I won't be answerable mind, Arthur, if he upsets her?'

'Arthur?' said Henry. 'Is that your name? Sergeant Arthur Arthur?'

'That's right, Mr. Kite,' he smiled. 'It's in the family, you might say.' He looked across at WPC Evers. 'That's all right Gwen. He won't harm her, will you Mr. Spote?'

Choat didn't answer. Instead, he turned and glared at the sergeant with an expression that said that he believed that he was in the presence, and at the mercy, of several seriously deranged minds.

'Great!' beamed Henry. 'Whadda fantas'ic name!'

'I'm glad you like it,' said the sergeant. 'It's not to everyone's taste, mind?'

'D'you think you could get me out o' here?' hissed Choat, in spite of his terror. "Stead of chit-chit-chattin' 'bout your bloody family tree?'

'I should worry 'bout your own family tree,' smirked Henry. 'Or what'll be left of it if Boadicea decides to give you a bid of an im-impromptu v-vasectomy.' He grinned at WPC Evers.

'She wouldn't bother,' said the WPC. 'She only eats Big Bite Mixer!'

Henry and Sergeant Arthur turned towards one another with self-pitying expressions that said that, against their better judgement, they were about to laugh uproariously at someone else's misfortune. They fought valiantly against the temptation for a second or two, but were eventually unable to quell it.

Their sudden and synchronized burst of laughter startled Boadicea, who threw back his head and let out a single eardrum-battering roar.

In the confined space of the Probe's cockpit, the sound had a spectacular effect on Choat, who shot from the car like a rocket.

Henry never could understand how he managed it without going straight through the sergeant. But one moment Choat was in front of them, sitting gingerly in the driver's seat of the Probe. The next, he was behind them, six feet away, standing bolt upright, with his hair on end, and a look of abject terror on his ashen face.

Henry felt that the day was suddenly starting to look up.

Then he realized that Choat had elbowed him in the side of the head on his way out of the car, and with a sigh of resignation and a muttered 'Oh no, not again?' he sank slowly to his knees.

The last thing he saw, as he lay on the ground wondering why the world around him was disappearing into a rapidly deepening heat haze, was Jo Cornwall kneeling beside him in her revealingly short skirt and button-straining blouse, with an unexpected, but gratifying, look of concern in her eyes.

* * *

26

NELL AND THE DRAGON

'You all right, boy?' asked Rooter. 'You wanna stay away from that there lamp, mind,' he wafted a hand at the little oil burner in the middle of the table, 'yer eyebrows is lookin' a bit . . . frazzled.'

'What?' said Henry, putting a hand up to his face as he gazed at the odd array of people around him. 'It's a bit dirty in here, don't you think?'

Rooter cast a cursory glance around the saloon bar of the Green Dragon Inn. 'Looks all right to me, lover,' he said. 'What I mean to say is: it's the whip, innet? If horses likes the bugger so much how come they runs away from him all the time?' He sucked his teeth. 'I mean, that's what they keep tellin' ya, innet? Bloody horse *likes* racin'? Well, if he *likes* racin' so much what's the point of whippin' the bugger? What's the point of a jockey in the first place? Just turn the horse loose, an' let him get on with it, if he *likes* it so much! It don't make sense, does it? Horse runs faster when you hits him with a whip, right? So why's he do that?'

Henry frowned. 'Those *are* spittoons over there, aren't they?' He pointed across the room. 'By the bar? Are they supposed to overflow like that?'

Rooter clicked his tongue. "Cause it hurts his bleedin' arse! He don't think "Oh, bloody good oh, that little bugger on me back's hittin' me arse, so must be time to win the soddin' race". No! He thinks: "Bugger me! Some soddin' dung fly's just bit me bum: better get the hell outa here before the little bugger does it again"! Only he don't stop, does he, the jockey? So the bleedin' horse keeps on runnin'.' He sniffed his irritation. 'That's what it's all about, innet? Bleedin' horse gets to the end of the race, an' he thinks: "Got away from that little bugger at last, didden I?"'

He picked up a mug of cider from the table and took a hefty swig.

'They say the bleedin' horse likes it when he wins. Course he bleedin' *likes* it! He got away from the bleedin' dung fly, didden he? That's what the bugger's happy about. Not 'cause he won the race an' some dozy fat bint in a silly hat comes up to him an' pretends she gives a flyin' doodah if he lives or dies. He's just thinkin': "This fat tart hangin' round me neck must a bin bit by the same bleedin' dung fly. Otherwise what's she so bleedin' happy about?" If he knew it was the jockey slappin' him on the arse he'd squash the little bugger flat, wouldn't he? Rear up on his hind legs and kick him in the groolies.' He sat back and stared glassy-eyed across the room. 'Like to see that, lover, I would. All they horses kickin' all them struttin' little buggers in the grownads. Fair warm me heart, that would!'

'Yes,' said Henry, 'but how come there's all that *stuff* on the floor? It's not very hygienic, is it?'

Rooter wasn't listening. 'Horses is good beasts, mind? A bit dim when you compares 'em to yer average nuclear scientist, p'rhaps. But I reckon most of 'em's more well-meanin'. Them fat buggers who buys 'em an' sells 'em for dog food when they gets tired of 'em, they're the nasty pieces o' work! T'weren't always so, mind.' he added, waving a hand around the room. 'People used to respect their horses, didn't they? Used to look after 'em proper, like.' He thought for a moment. 'Well, most of 'em did. Had to, see? Life or death in them days. Only way to get about the place, see?'

Henry followed the arc of Rooter's wafting hand, and came to the conclusion that the only explanation for what he was seeing around him was that he was dreaming. The Green Dragon Inn wasn't the most lavishly furnished public house he had ever set foot in, but surely it had never looked as disgusting as it did now? There were growths on the walls, the floor and the ceiling: and on the dogs, pigs and chickens rolling, snuffling and scratching in the sawdust of the floor. There was unpleasant-looking stuff encrusting most of the customers, too – those that he could make out through the gloom – their pox-ridden, scabby and altogether unwashed hides looking every bit as rancid as the mouldering splash of sick he could see under a nearby table. They were a filthy and bizarre looking bunch, apparently clothed in tatty garments left over from a second-rate production of *Les Misérables*: with Perce the landlord the most sartorially challenged of the lot, enveloped in some shapeless sack-like creation with sagging, coarse-woven tights clinging to his spindly legs and a codpiece like a rhino horn rising threateningly out of his groin. Henry swallowed hard at the sight of it. Then he realized with a shock that all of the men in the place were similarly attired. All except him, he noted, as he glanced down at his lap.

Then there was the barmaid, leaning over the table in front of him with her bosoms thrusting pertly, dangerously, pinkly rounded and a surprisingly long way up and almost out of her tightly corseted, lacily cleavaged dress. With a sight like that to greet them every time they looked up from their mugs of cider, he decided, it wasn't surprising that the male contingent had come equipped to cope with feats of spontaneous arousal.

There was a grunt from a customer at a nearby table. Henry turned and looked across at the man's imbecilic expression of lumpen bliss, just as a young woman backed out from under the table on her hands and knees. She stood up, wiped her mouth along her bare arm and held out a hand.

Her 'client' grinned back at her and shook his head.

She smiled, took a short wooden club from the folds of her scruffy dress and whacked him with it above the ear. As he slid unconscious from his chair to join two others already lying on the floor at her feet, she reached quickly forward and lifted a pouch from his belt. She extracted a coin deftly between her finger and thumb, and dropped the pouch onto his limp body as it slid to the floor. With a gap-toothed grin, she turned away, caught Henry's bemused expression and grinned even more widely as she swayed towards him.

'He likes his bit o' battery,' she said, flicking a thumb at the unconscious former client. 'Pays extra for a clip round the lugholes, does our Smegley.'

She raised an eyebrow at Henry, and the hem of her skirt to just above the tops of her stockings. 'An' what's *your* pleasure, my precious? What can young

Nell do for 'ee, eh? Nice fiddle under the table? Or a bunk-up 'cross the top?'

Henry shook his head, and held up his hands to ward her off. 'No, no! I'm fine!' he protested. 'Really I am! Thanks all the same.'

'Here,' said Rooter, tossing her a coin. 'Only make it quick: we got some serious debatin' goin' on here!'

Nell caught the coin deftly, put it between her teeth and bit it, before slipping it into the folds of her dress and bending to crawl under the table.

'No!' pleaded Henry, trying ineffectually to scrape his chair backwards and out of her way. 'I really don't think . . .!'

'You jus' lie back an' think of England, boy,' encouraged Rooter. 'Anyhow, hangin' offence it was to steal 'em, back in them days.' He sniffed and gazed into the distance. 'I remember one time at Waterloo . . . '

Henry flinched as Nell's fingers tugged at his zip under the table. 'The railway-*whoooo*,' he hissed, 'ra-railway station, or . . . or the battle?'

Rooter frowned. 'Railway station . . .?'

Henry's eyes bugged out, 'Whoa!' he exclaimed, as Nell's fingers delved into his clothing. 'I . . .! Look . . .! No! No! Just . . . That's not . . .!'

'There us was,' said Rooter, unconcerned, 'me, an' the boys on holiday, like, when up comes this little bugger in some kinda dress. Sorta kilt-thing, it was, only made outa grass an' that? Anyhow, he's got his fists all clenched an' his face all screwed up, lookin' to punch me lights out. "Listen, buddy", he says, all kinda threat'nin' like, "you ain't wanted round here!"'

He lifted his mug and took another swig. 'Well, I wasn't havin' any o' that, was I? So I smacks him in the gob an' knocks the cocky little bugger on his arse. Spark out he went like a telly bein' unplugged!'

He whipped his mouth along a sleeve. 'That weren't the end of it, mind.' He took a deep breath. 'I looks round an' up comes this flashy bugger on a gert big horse with his spurs rippin' the poor bugger's sides all t' pieces! "Oy, you!" I shouts. "You treat that bloody horse proper, mind! Or I'll have yer smelly guts for garters!" He looks at me an' "Piss off, you little shitehouse!" he says. "Piss off?" I says, "Who you tellin' to piss off, you festerin' cesspit?"'

Henry's eyes were almost popping out of his head. 'No, no!' he pleaded, trying without real conviction to push his chair backwards as Nell's cool hands groped through the tangle of his underpants. 'I – *no! No! Please . . . don't!*'

'What's up, my precious?' she grinned. 'You idden complainin', is you?'

'No, no! No! It's just that – Oh *God!* – what the hell's happening to me?'

'Reckon it's your lucky day, boy,' said Rooter, with a knowing wink. He reached for his mug and took another swallow. 'Anyhow,' he continued, 'he looks at me like I'm summut the bloody cat's just dragged in. "You bleedin' little shitehouse!" he says again. Then he comes at me with 'is gert big sabre up here, over his head. "Bugger this for a game o' soldiers!" I says. "Not very bleedin' hospitable, these army types ain't!"'

He looked at Henry. 'You listenin' to me, lover, or what?' When Henry didn't reply, he shrugged, and continued with his story. 'Anyhow, there's me standin' there like a lummocks with me mouth open waitin' for 'im to chop me head off. "This is it Roots!", I tells meself. "No more shaggin' for you!"'

He picked up his mug, and took another swig.

'He's about ten-foot away, see, when his head just sorta smashes t' bits! "Well I'm buggered," I thought, "there he goes again, interferin!"'

Henry was breathing heavily. 'Sorry?' he said. 'I-I'm a bit . . . a bit lost. You-you were on holiday, a-and a – oh my *God*! – a soldier charged at-at you with his s-sword out, and . . . and . . .'

'Lance shot the bugger through the gob with one o' they wosnames? They smart darts?' He sniffed. 'Silly bugger's charter, you ask me. Don't take no skill to kill a bloke with a gun with bullets what aims themselves, do it? Anyhow, blew the bugger's brains all over the shop! Made a hellova mess, an' all!'

Henry was panting. 'I w-wouldn't ha – *hah*! – have thought . . . ' His eyes and mouth suddenly opened wide, and he took a huge sucking breath. He gripped the arms of the chair as if his life depended on it, levering himself forward until his upper body was arching over the table. He shuddered once, twice, three times: then jerked part of the way back into the chair, shuddered forwards again, jerked back once, twice, three times, and then slumped against the chair with a long, drawn-out sigh. When he realized that Rooter was staring at him, he cleared his throat and tried not to look as guilty as he felt.

'So what . . . what happened?' he asked, blinking like a bush baby thrust suddenly into the harsh light of day. 'What did the police . . .? I mean . . . was it . . . was it self-defence, or . . . or . . .?'

Rooter frowned. 'You wanna go easy on that ol' scrumpy, boy.' He leaned forward. 'The bugger were on our side, see? Well, on our side as much as we was on any bugger's side – us being on holiday, an' that.'

Henry jerked again as he felt his clothes being tucked back into place. 'So what you're saying is you-*ooo* . . . you knew-*ooo* him, did you?'

'Didn't get the chance, boy. Wouldn't o' minded a word with the bugger about his horse. Smack him about a bit for treatin' it badly. Nice beast.' He shrugged. 'But they smart darts is a sod when they gets goin'. Blew the bugger's brains all over the shop. That's the trouble, with 'em, see: they're good, all right, but messy with it. Pointin' one o' them at a bloke's a bit of a double-edged sword. I mean it gets the bugger's attention, all right. But he's useless for conversation, after.'

Henry shuddered as he felt his zip being pulled back up. 'Sorry,' he said, squinting in concentration, 'but . . . what was a double-edged sword?'

'This is!' said a voice behind him.

He turned to look over his shoulder and saw that the stained glass window behind him had come suddenly to life. A medieval knight was snarling down at him with a huge sword raised over its head.

Henry's eyes widened as the massive weapon came swinging down towards his neck. He leaned to one side to get out of the way, and lurched out of his chair onto the hard stone flags of the floor.

* * *

'You like knocking yourself about, do you?' asked an amused female voice.

Henry opened his eyes to see a young woman sitting in front of him in an old wooden carver. She looked familiar, but he couldn't quite place her. It was one of those moments when he saw someone he thought he might know, but couldn't decide if he did or he didn't: and couldn't pluck up enough courage to talk to them in case they had no idea who he was.

'If you really want to kill yourself, there's easier ways than jumping on your head, you know,' said the young woman, with a nod at the settle behind him.

He looked around. He was in the Dragon again, and relieved to see that its decor had returned to something more familiar than the way it had looked in his dream. He was particularly relieved to see that the stained glass window had reverted to its inanimate self. He groaned, and pushed himself into a sitting position. Then he realized that his clothes were on fire.

There were charred patches on his jeans, and his jumper was smouldering in several places. He must have been lying on the settle by the fire and fallen off in his sleep to roll into the ash and glowing embers around the hearth. He slapped at himself in alarm, and rolled away from the fire, while Jo looked on with the hint of a smile. When the last of the embers had been put out, he closed his eyes and leaned back against the wall. He felt awful. His tongue seemed to have grown to several times its normal size and become Velcroed to the roof of his mouth. He smacked his lips together, wishing that the taste of natural yoghurt would go away, and that whoever had clamped his head in a vice would come back soon and release it. Better still, he wished he could remember if he knew the attractive young woman sitting in front of him.

'Still with us, then?' she asked.

'Could be,' he replied, with an uncertain smile and a hand reaching up to check that his head was still on his shoulders. 'Actually, I'm not really sure.'

He tried to focus on her face, hoping to remember her name, or at least, where he had seen her before. But he only managed to get as far as her legs, which were long, slim and encased in black nylon. He groaned: from his position on the floor he could see right up her skirt to the inviting black triangle of her panties.

He dragged his eyes away and looked down at the floor, trying to think of something other than what had just happened in his dream. He was acutely aware that he had an erection. He tried desperately to concentrate on the disturbing taste in his mouth as a means of steering his mind away from thoughts of sex. He had always felt uneasy about eating natural yoghurt. It was a deep-seated, primordial fear, perhaps, based on a mistrust of putting into his mouth anything that might be described, no matter how loosely, as 'living'! He didn't have the same problem with fruit and vegetables because, despite the fact that they were arguably still alive, there wasn't the remotest possibility that they would look up at him with large, puppy-like eyes as he prepared to pop them into his mouth and make him wonder guiltily if there wasn't a more humane solution to his hunger than crunching some living thing to death. He knew, of course, that the tiny microbes, or whatever it was that live yoghurt contained, weren't going to do that, either. But he couldn't get away from the thought that they might do something even more terrifying if ever they got around to realizing that they were amongst the fall guys in the perennial drama of life. What if they were to decide one day that being eaten alive wasn't such a great idea, and that what they really wanted out of life was to raise families and have careers and own homes of their own? And what if they discovered suddenly that they had organizational capabilities and could act as a collective, ganging up on other life forms as ants and bees and termites had been doing for millions of years? What if they wanted the microbial equivalent of holidays in Skegness, Majorca or Las Vegas, and the freedom to marry, buy their own homes, and keep pets? After all, ants kept aphids, didn't they? So why shouldn't bacteria keep viruses, or other microbes less advanced than themselves? The implications for humanity if dairy products ever decided to rebel against their lot in life were potentially horrific. There you would be at breakfast with a mouthful of live yogurt and muesli, just getting ready for that satisfying taste sensation as the mixture slid over your tongue and down your throat into your stomach. When suddenly, the bacterial equivalent of Genghis Khan would step forward from the masses and whip his billions of minuscule followers into a frenzy of microbial rebellion. Before you knew what was happening, they would have clumped together and stuck in your throat, choking you to a terrible death. He had seen enough episodes of *The Twilight Zone* to know that it would not be a pretty sight as the murderous little bastards frothed and foamed their way out of his ears and eyes and mouth and nostrils, and, quite possibly, his other bodily orifices, as well. And the whole gruesome business would be accompanied by a high-pitched keening and twittering as they communicated to one another their utter, vengeful delight at suffocating yet another disgusting and so-called 'higher life form' to death.

The thought made him shiver as if someone had walked over his grave. But he supposed that there were people for whom the prospect would be exciting. People like those bizarre individuals who went on the stage to demonstrate the art of live goldfish swallowing. The sort of oddball novelty acts that were inclined to appear during summer seasons at the end of the pier, or in down-market talent shows on TV: and his problem with whom wasn't that they were capable of such acts of cruelty, but that they had ever felt motivated to perform them in the first place. How had that happened? Had they once swallowed an insect inadvertently while riding their bicycle open-mouthed through the countryside at dusk on a midsummer's evening? Had an unfortunate maybug ricocheted off their back teeth, cannoned into that dangly thing at the back of their throat and disappeared down their gullet into their stomach? Had they dismounted and performed the Heimlich Manoeuvre on themself, regurgitating the maybug in pristine condition onto the palm of a lovingly upturned hand? Had they then waited patiently for its confidence to return before waving it a fond farewell as it flew off into the lowering sky only to be crushed infinitesimally flat seconds later against the windscreen of an on-rushing car? Was that how those things always got started? Or had the people who performed them been born with a sadistic streak, and seen the move from tearing the wings off butterflies to the swallowing of live goldfish as a natural progression? Had the fact that others had taken a ghoulish delight in watching them do it, been just an added bonus at first? Had they started with minnows at school, and moved quickly on from the role of playground eccentric to that of local celebrity on the strength of the miracle that, unlike the hapless butterflies, the goldfish got to come back again and again to the delight of a growing band of grizzly voyeurs? Had the increasingly adoring audiences at birthday parties, weddings and bar mitzvahs been more than willing to overlook the fact that taking part in the entertainment was probably not nearly as much fun for the hapless goldfish as it was for its celebrity-seeking bug swallower and his or her audience? Had it occurred to them that being lifted out of its natural environment, and held up for inspection as it drowned, was unlikely to be a pleasurable experience for the victimized fish? Or that being sucked into the belly of some gigantic entity and forced to swim around in a liquid designed by evolution to digest it, probably wasn't much of 'a laugh' for it, either? And, finally, that being coughed back up into the same hostile, drowning world from which it had been forced to depart a few seconds earlier, and held gasping for breath before being dropped back into its natural environment, would do nothing to convince it that the entities responsible for its near-death experience had anything other than contempt for all life forms, including, and perhaps most particularly, their own! It was like those little knots of posturing inadequates who gathered together in manicured fields with shotguns, flat caps, waxed jackets, green wellies and piles of ammo to blast pheasant, grouse and partridge out of the skies. Aided by posses of bearers, beaters and dogs, they demonstrated their courage and selfless sacrifice by standing their ground as dead and dying birds rained down from the heavens all around them with their little beaks gasping for a final breath as they thudded to earth. Did the shooters feel proud as they clubbed the mortally wounded to death with the butts of their guns or stomped the life out of the helplessly flopping bodies with the heels of their boots? And was it really only upon such acts of doubtful heroism that empires could be built, or a man's, or indeed a woman's, masculinity gauged? And what would happen if those same 'hunters' were invited to take part in a bit of role reversal, and were to find themselves naked, alone and unarmed in a metal cage with nothing for company but a dozen or so really pissed-off ostrich with steel-clad beaks, razor-sharp talons and a desire to rip human flesh and sinew from bone? Just how eager would even the psychopaths amongst them be to 'kick arse' then?

Henry shook his head and gazed up at the ceiling. He was beginning to sound like Rooter, rabbiting on about cruelty to animals and man's inhumanity to . . . well, just about all forms of life. He sighed and glanced self-consciously at the young woman.

She gazed back at him without blinking. 'Where've you been, then, tiger?' she asked. 'Somewhere nice, I hope, was it?'

'This keeps happening to me,' he said, remembering his fight with Choat.

'What, falling on your head? You ought to be better at it than that, then, didn't you?'

He dragged a hand over his face. 'Practice makes perfect they say.' He squinted at her for a moment. 'It's . . . Jo, isn't it?' he ventured. 'Only I . . .'

'Josephine,' she nodded. 'But Jo will do just fine. Welcome back.'

He looked around. 'This is the Dragon, right? How long have I been . . .?'

'Out cold?' She glanced at her watch. 'A couple of hours.'

He was indignant. 'What, and you just left me lying here unconscious? I might have been seriously hurt!'

She stood up. 'Doctor said not. Fancy a drink?'

He grimaced and got carefully to his feet. 'No thank you.' His whole body seemed to hurt as he moved. 'Anyway, which doctor?'

'Might have been,' she said, as she walked to the bar. 'But I reckon he was a grockle gynaecologist. Anyhow, he said you'd be fine. Have one of Perce's specials,' she added, over her shoulder. 'Be a bit of a pick-me-up. Well, pick-*you*-up, anyway. Here,' she said, holding out a glass, 'drink this.'

He shook his head. 'No thanks.'

'Drink it, I said!'

He looked at her for a while before taking the glass. 'What is it?'

'You don't want to know. Just knock it back.'

'Looks a bit . . . cloudy to me.'

'Are you going to drink it, or do I have to sit on your chest and pour it down your throat?'

'Well, if you're offering . . .?'

'Drink it!'

'Right!' He raised the glass to his lips. 'Just . . .?'

'In one go! And whatever you do, *don't* stop to taste it!'

'Is it really that bad?'

'Worse!'

'I see.' He took a deep breath, and raised the glass to his lips. 'Look,' he said, lowering it again, 'perhaps I should just   ?'

'Do it! You'll thank me for it later.'

'Will I?'

'No. But drink it anyway.'

'Oh, well,' he shrugged, 'what the hell!' He drained the glass, looked at it, and handed it back to her. 'Not bad: sort of sweet, with an after-taste of,' his eyes bugged open, '*sul-phu-ric acid*! Christ, what was that?'

'Sulphuric acid. Just to taste! Live by the sword, die by the sword, eh?'

'Don't talk to me about swords! I've had enough of them for one day!'

'Drink this,' she said, handing him another glass.

He backed away, shaking his head. 'Oh, no!'

She clicked her tongue. 'It's water. Take away the sting.'

He took the glass and sniffed at it.

'God, what a bunch of pansies, you grockles are!'

'Water?'

'Water!'

'Are you sure?'

She turned away. 'Gwen was right: you're pathetic!'

He took a sip. It was water. It was cool. He sipped a bit more of it. It tasted good. He took a mouthful, and swallowed it. It tasted even better. He drank half the glass, and put it back on the counter.

'Better?'

'Yes. Thank you.'

'Right then: off you go!'

'Off?' He looked around. 'Off where?'

'I've been hanging around for ages waiting for you to come back to life. Now, if you don't mind, I've got things I need to be getting on with.'

His face fell. 'I see. Yes, yes, well, thank you. Thank you very . . . ' He tapped at his pockets. 'I don't suppose you've seen my car keys, have you?' Then he remembered what had happened to his car. 'Damn, I can't . . .!' He looked up. 'You don't happen to know where Rooter is, do you?'

'He left after they carried you in here. Said I was to get you over to the Clatworthy's place.'

He brightened. 'You're going to give me a lift?'

She shook her head. 'Can't drive. Drew you a map, though.'

She took a paper napkin from the pocket of her apron. It had a few lines scrawled on it in black ink. 'It's a bit screwed up I'm afraid.'

She came around behind him, and peered over his shoulder. 'Any good?'

He thought the map was useless, like something created by a spider that had fallen into a pot of ink before tottering across the paper and popping its clogs. But he wasn't about to say so in case she stopped standing behind him. For years he had harboured a secret lust for the sort of waitress uniform she was wearing. Ever since his so-called Auntie Mandy – a waitress whose extra curricular activity had seemed to include the serving, or 'servicing', of every able-bodied man in the village – had cornered him in the bathroom during his sixteenth birthday party and introduced him to the joys of rough sex. As Jo brushed against him, she smelled the same way with that horny combination of strong perfume and stale beer – precisely the aroma that had wafted through his favourite fantasies together with mental images of the deliciously provocative Mandy up against a wall, on the back seat of a car, or down an alley with the echoes of 'time gentleman please!' ringing in his adolescent ears. Only this time he was sober, more or less, and he definitely did not intend to hate himself in the morning. Not unless he was very, *very* unlucky!

'You all right?' asked Jo. 'Not going to throw up again, are you?'

'No, no,' he assured her, 'I'm . . . it's just that . . . no, no, I'm fine!'

'You've gone a bit red.'

'Yes, look, I . . . How far is this place?'

'Two or three miles – maybe five?'

'Why don't I get a cab, then?'

She walked around to the other said of the table. 'Cab?'

He nodded.

'A taxi?'

'Yes.'

'Out here?'

He nodded again.

'Taxis don't come out here. Not any more. Especially not after dark.'

He looked at the windows. 'It isn't dark yet,' he said, turning back. 'What do you mean,' he asked, uneasily, 'not any more?'

'Sodmire. Easy to miss the road in the dark, and lots have. Never been seen again, some of 'em haven't.'

He glanced at the windows again. 'Really? Can't I phone a garage or something, then, and get them to come and pick me up?'

'No garages.'

'What about these people?' He pointed at the map.

'Clatworthies?' She shook her head. 'Don't have a phone.'

'Good God! What kind of primitive place is this?'

'Not so much primitive as practical.'

He frowned.

'They cut down the telegraph poles,' she explained, 'last winter. To keep their central heating going?'

'Isn't that illegal?'

'Is it?'

'Didn't the police do anything about it?'

'Police don't go out to the Clatworthy's place if they can help it. Not these days, anyway. Not without an escort, they don't.'

Henry was feeling more uncomfortable about his proposed journey by the second. 'Isn't there somewhere else I could go? I mean, could I stay here for the night? I'm feeling a bit tired actually. I could just doss down on the . . . '

She shook her head. 'Sorry.'

'But I can't drive, can I? My car's knackered and I can't just go traipsing across the moor in the dark.'

She delved into the pocket of her apron and brought out something that clinked. 'Gwen said to give you these.'

'Gwen?'

'WPC Evers. Remember?'

'What is it?'

She jiggled the things in his face. 'Rattlesnake's teeth!'

For a moment he believed her, and shied away.

'Car keys,' she said, with a pitying shake of the head. 'Your friend in the Ford Probe left them for you.'

'He's no friend of mine!'

'He left them for you, anyway. Here!'

'Yes,' he said, 'but I can't do that, can I? How can I do that? I don't know how to drive the damned thing, do I?'

'You'll learn. Besides, you don't have a choice.'

Then she told him what had happened after he'd passed out and been carried into the pub. How Choat had tried to bribe Sergeant Arthur and WPC Evers by offering to put fifty pounds in the Police Benevolent Fund if they let him go. How the sergeant had been inclined to accept, but WPC Evers had not. How she had told Choat that they were going to take him in and book him for affray and causing criminal damage. How he had protested his innocence. How they had taken no notice. How he had pleaded, and they had taken even less notice. How he had grovelled and pleaded, and they had relented with the suggestion that they might be persuaded to go easier on him if he were to make an act of contrition. How he had offered to put one hundred pounds in the Benevolent Fund. How WPC Evers had told him that that was not what she had had in mind. How Sergeant Arthur had not been so sure. How Choat had suggested one hundred and fifty pounds; then two hundred pounds; then five hundred: and, finally, how he had offered the keys to his beloved car, and WPC Evers had said 'That'll do nicely. Let's go!'

Henry was incredulous. 'But I can't drive that thing!' he protested. 'Even if I could, I wouldn't be seen dead in it!'

She rested her fists on her hips. 'Listen, either you drive that car to the Clatworthy's place, or you sleep in it. And believe me, I wouldn't want to be out there after dark. Not unless I had the engine running, I wouldn't.'

He swallowed and glanced at the windows. 'Why? What's . . .?'

'Because it's bloody cold, that's why!'

'Oh, well, I think I could cope with a bit of . . .'

'And then there's The Beast, of course,' she added, as she turned away.

'The what?' he asked, trailing after her. 'What did you . . .?'

'Probably just old wives' tales. But something's killing those sheep, isn't it?'

His Adam's apple jumped. 'Sheep?'

'They say it doesn't eat people, though. Just defenceless animals.'

'Oh, good! That makes me feel a hell of a lot better!'

'As long as they stay indoors.'

He tried to convince her to let him stay, but she wouldn't have it.'

'Right,' he said, with a hangdog expression. 'Right!' He took a deep breath. 'How far did you say it was to this . . . this Clotwarthy place?'

'Clatworthy! You can't miss it. Big house called The Stone Dancers. Follow the map and you'll be fine. Oh, and whatever you do, don't stop after dark. You never know what might be out there lurking in the bushes.'

She leaned forward and kissed him unexpectedly on the cheek.

'You might want to clean yourself up a bit first,' she added, looking him over. 'What with getting into punch-ups and setting yourself on fire, you're looking a bit frayed round the edges.'

27

MORRIS AND NORA

The couple in the campervan were Nora and Morris Oldroyd, and they had come all the way from Doncaster hoping not merely for a glimpse of Simon Hawker's mythical member, but also a chance to capture it on film with at least one of their Olympus *Sure Shot* cameras, preserving it for posterity and the slideshow they were planning to give to their friends when they got home. With their thermos flasks, bacon sarnies and binoculars at the ready – Morris in his flak jacket, camouflage trousers, flat cap and horn-rims; Nora in her best purple boob tube, rah-rah skirt and glittery tights – they sat patiently on candy-striped metal folding chairs at a remote spot on the moor scanning the horizon for their first sight of the fabled Devonshire Dong.

Nora was fifty-six years old, and stood five feet four inches tall in her stockinged feet. She was five feet eight inches tall in her white stilettos; and six feet two and a half inches tall with her bleached blonde hair backcombed on top of her head. A mother at fourteen, a grandmother at twenty-seven and a great grandmother at forty-one, she was the joyfully irresponsible matriarch of a northern tribe whose numbers had topped the two hundred and fifty mark with the turning of the year. Abused and fumbled at by her father and his friends as a little girl, she had grown up in the knowledge that the only thing that the men of South Yorkshire wanted from their womenfolk was that they should open and close their legs and their mouths only when they were told to. Which, in the case of the former, was every Saturday night after the master of the house had downed ten pints of Tetley's at the Miners' Welfare Club, and, in the case of the latter, never!

At the tender age of thirteen, heavily pregnant with Reginald her eldest, Nora had passed through the gates of Slaggs End Secondary Modern School for the last time, promising herself as she waddled away that she wouldn't get caught like that again – at least, not by the games master or the geography teacher, if she could help it – and certainly never by that horny little sod in 3D with the endless supply of her favourite bubblegum. Tutti-frutti had been her Achilles heel all along, and it would probably have led her to an irredeemable fall from grace had not the awkward Morris Oldroyd arrived in the nick of time to save her. Not Reginald's natural father (one of the few who could have said as much without laughing) he had taken willingly to the role of father and provider, and had stuck by Nora and her growing tribe of mewling sprogs ever since.

Morris had never wanted to be a father, or a husband, and had stepped into the breech only because his fellow miners had begun to ask too many awkward questions about his sexual proclivities. Things like why he was always the last one out of the showers at the pit baths, and why he was always so eager to continue scrubbing backs and buttocks when the need to get them clean had long gone. Most damning of all, though, had been the most obvious sign of his enthusiasm for the task, pointing as it had tent-pole-like at the ceiling as he'd lathered, kneaded and stroked. Nora's condition had offered him the perfect escape route, and he had run all the way to meet it at little Reginald's christening, arriving red-faced and out of breath only seconds ahead of the Slaggs End Colliery lynch mob. Nine months later, with Nora pregnant again courtesy of the paperboy or the milkman or any one of the dozen or so shopkeepers on the Slaggs End council estate happy to accept payment in kind, she and Morris had been married. The ceremony had taken place at Pope Pius RC Church, Slaggs End, with all the trimmings and Nora bulging brazenly in virgin white. There had followed the ultimate marriage of convenience, and, to everyone's amazement, more than forty years of something not unlike wedded bliss. Morris had remained uncomplaining, in spite of the fact that Nora had continued to drop other men's offspring with a regularity that had bordered on the careless. For her part, Nora had never asked what he got up to at night in the garden shed with the door locked and one of his extensive collection of dog-eared *Health And Fitness* magazines propped up on an old music stand under a shaded lamp.

All had been well in the Oldroyd household until the arrival of the menopause and a sudden slump in Nora's previously raging libido. While everyone in the village had been aware of the sudden change in her demeanour, it had been Morris who had been forced to bear the brunt. No longer guaranteed hours of uninterrupted pleasure astride his sit-upon lawnmower, in wellington boots and with Marigold gloves coated in Swarfega, he had found for the first time in their life together that Nora actually wanted to talk to him! Worse still, she had begun to demand that he take her to garden centres in search of petunias, DIY stores looking for shelves, and, horror of all horrors, to shops that sold spare parts for their ancient Ford Cortina. Most unsettling of all, though, had been the way in which she had suddenly begun forcing him to listen to gossip about their neighbours who, coincidentally, had finally stopped talking about her.

Morris had fretted for a year as he'd searched in vain for a solution to this new, and most unsettling, of problems. Then one day, he'd found wedged inside his copy of *Muscle Magazine*, a stray copy of *The Lancet*, in which, next to a beautifully illustrated article on penis enlargement, he'd found a brief editorial about Hormone Replacement Therapy. He'd read and reread it with a growing sense of excitement, before taking out a pen and paper and making a note of an address in the West End of London. The following morning, he'd rung Directory Enquiries to confirm the address and phone number, before calling the consulting room to arrange an appointment, followed by the local station to book a return ticket on the early morning train to King's Cross. By lunchtime the following day he'd been skipping along Harley Street with his bank account lighter by two hundred pounds, and a prescription in his pocket which the Norwegian gynaecologist, a Mr. V.E.R. Y'Oligin-Kvacksalvare, had assured him would return his life with Nora to something that he would recognize as normal.

Nora's response to the HR therapy had been immediate. In less than a week, she had burned her capacious bloomers, her elasticated tights, her ankle-length rose-printed dresses, and the recently acquired collectors' editions of *Knitter's Monthly*, *Crocheting For Beginners*, and *Gardening Which?* Then off she had gone on a weeklong retail therapy binge to *French Connection*, *Miss Selfridge*, *Top Shop* and the lingerie and rubber fetishists' sections at her local *Private Shop*. Soon, she had been ladling on the make-up again, swaying provocatively along the street, whistling lasciviously at building workers, and generally doing her best to seduce any male over the age of consent with a pulse. The change in her demeanour had been miraculous, and news of Morris's discovery had spread like wild fire through the local community. Nora had handed out information about her therapy willingly and without charge, and had quickly been joined in her metamorphosis by a growing posse of rejuvenated sex pots who, determined to make the most of their newly rediscovered libidos, had started terrorizing Slaggs End's male population in gangs. Out had gone the sewing patterns, the recipes for sponge cake, the flower arranging workshops and the instructions for making teasel hedgehogs; and in had come the contact magazines, the one-to-one chat lines and the long party evenings experimenting with peephole lingerie and big, rubber, handheld or strap-on machines. The next such gathering was to take place on the day after Nora and Morris got back from their trip to Dartmoor, with a select band of enthusiastic grannies invited along to push the boat out, and a variety of carefully contoured and lubricated rubber thingummies *in*, while Morris, in waistcoat, jock strap and bow tie, passed around the passion cake and occasionally showed them his dick. The high point of the evening was to be the showing of whatever footage of Simon's famous manhood they had managed to obtain on their travels.

Vinny, Nobbler, Bonce and Simon knew nothing of Nora and Morris's plans as they watched them from behind a granite outcrop.

'Don't let 'em know we're comin',' hissed Vinny. 'Single file an' no talkin'!' He grinned. 'You take the bloke,' he told Bonce out of the corner of his mouth. 'An' remember, we ain't takin' no for an answer. You,' he hissed at Nobbler, 'jus' . . . stay outa the way!'

Simon was confused. 'What is it: surprise party or something?'

Vinny grinned. 'Yeah, right! They're gonna die laughin' when they see us comin', ain't they? You stay close, an' all. I don't wanna send 'im,' he hooked a thumb at Bonce, 'out to get ya. You hear what I'm sayin', Uncle Fester?'

Simon nodded, unhappily. He had never liked surprise parties, because no one had ever wanted to talk to him at surprise parties: not even when they had been arranged in his honour. But he got to his feet with a sigh and a shake of the head, and fell in behind the others as they moved off at a crouching run in the direction of Nora and Morris's campsite.

They were within ten feet of Nora's chair, creeping up behind it stealthily, when Nobbler let his enthusiasm get the better of him. He stood up and sprinted past Bonce, only to slip on the wet grass and stumble forwards, grabbing Vinny's jeans and tracksuit bottoms as he fell and dragging them down to his ankles.

Morris and Nora stood up in alarm at the cursing and grunting that followed, and turned to find Vinny lying facedown with Nobbler's head wedged between his naked thighs.

Morris raised his eyebrows, enthusiastically. Then he looked away as Bonce came lumbering towards him. 'Hello,' he said, holding out a hand and smiling, coyly. 'How do you . . .?'

Bonce walked straight past his outstretched hand and grabbed him by the crotch. 'Borrow your motor,' he said, with a nod at Vinny. 'He said.'

Morris's eyes sparkled in sudden gratitude. It wasn't quite the way he had imagined being greeted by his first lover – the big man's grip was just a little too firm for comfort – but he had always wanted to be with a man who got straight to the point. He grinned sheepishly, and glanced across at his wife.

'Look,' he hissed at Bonce, 'this is a bit sudden, don't you think? Maybe we should wait while the others get acquainted?'

'It's you, though, innit?' cried Nora, with her eyes fixed on Simon's face. 'You from the brochure! I'd know you anywhere, duckie; even without your willy pokin' out!'

Simon smiled modestly, and looked at the ground.

'The girls at the club'll be *so* jealous,' cooed Nora, turning to her blushing husband. 'It's him, Mor, innit? Look! Him with the stonker?' She paused and winked at Bonce. 'Ooh, you're always so forward, aren't you, you boys!'

Morris grinned. 'Look,' he whispered to Bonce, 'why don't we go behind them bushes and . . .?'

'Let's get down there before the rush starts, I said,' babbled Nora to Simon with a delighted clap of her hands. 'Didn't I Mor?'

Morris rested his head on Bonce's chest. 'No need to – you know,' he said, 'make a song an' dance about it, eh? Let's you an' me just slip off to . . .!'

'Look at the pair of 'em!' cried Nora. 'Silly buggers, ain't they? Don't it warm your heart, though, eh, to see 'em at it like that?'

She looked down at Vinny and Nobbler, still wrestling together on the ground. 'Not like that one exposing hisself to the whole world!'

She nodded at Morris. 'He don't say much,' she confided. 'Least ways, not when he's – you know? – 'avin a bit of a thingy. But I know he's pleased as punch to see you. Aren't you Mor?' she shouted. 'Pleased as punch to see him, I said you was?'

Morris nodded as he nuzzled against Bonce's shirtfront. 'Be gentle,' he whispered. 'Or not, you know . . . whatever.'

'Used his redundancy money to buy her, he did,' added Nora, pointing at the campervan. 'Corn Nitch, that is! Innit Mor? Top o' the range, an' all!'

'Corniche,' said Morris, absently. He loved the smell of big, sweaty men.

'We'll go down there and 'ave a right good look, I said', beamed Nora, 'first chance we get! Didn't I, Mor?'

Morris sighed.

'Look,' snapped Vinny, finally disentangling Nobbler's head from his jeans and tracksuit bottoms and pulling them up. He got to his feet and turned to kick Nobbler in the arse as he grovelled on the ground. 'Shut it!' he told Nora. 'We're takin' over. Understand? No more friggin' about! From now on . . . '

Nora beamed. 'Oh, yes!' she enthused, clapping her hands. 'Yes! Yes! Yes! Be our pleasure, wouldn't it Mor? We'd love to have 'em, wouldn't we? All of 'em? Only, just one thing, duckie,' she added, tapping Vinny's chest, 'if you wouldn't mind? Let me get me *Sure Shot* out, eh?' She turned to her husband again. 'Eh, Mor? You wanna get your one out an' all?'

Morris didn't answer. He just stared into the distance with a faraway look in his eyes. A moment ago he had been sitting in the middle of this barren wilderness wondering how he had allowed himself to be talked into taking part in such a ridiculous adventure. Now he was in the next best thing to paradise with the hunk of his dreams hanging on to his private parts and showing every sign of wanting to bugger him roughly to death. He shook his head in amazement. 'Lovely place, this,' he sighed, 'innit, this Devon?'

Twenty-five miles away, in a whitewashed detached house overlooking the harbour at Torquay, Charlotte Piece would have agreed with the sentiment. But she would have added that it was even better when you had three strapping young Norwegians to help you enjoy it. The carpet was soft, and the Norwegians were hard, and she slapped at their backsides with a pork chop as they took it in turns to career from room to room with her on their backs.

'Geddy-up, horsey!' she yelled, as Gunnar whinnied and lumbered into the master bedroom on all fours. 'Off to the corral,' she shrieked, 'to give little ol' Lottie a right good seeing to, you naughty, naughty stallions, you!'

Ole and Jon looked up as the pair came into the room at a canter.

Ole smiled. 'You want we should move over, Lottie? You want to come back to beds, ja?'

'Whoa, horsey!' she cried, as Gunnar collapsed beneath her.

'You want we should do it again?' asked Jon.

Charlotte stood up, and rested the spike of a stiletto heel on the back of Gunnar's neck. 'Get down here,' she demanded, with a wave of the pork chop. 'I want all of you down there now, licking my feet. And you,' she added, pointing at Jon. 'I shall expect you to put that gorgeous thing to good use in a minute or two, so don't let its mind start to wander. Now then,' she added, looking them over, 'who's gonna take Lottie's panties off with his teeth?'

Yes, Charlotte would definitely have agreed that Devon by the sea was a wonderful place to be if you were an attractive woman at the height of your sexual powers with three imaginative and tireless young men to help make up for the time you had wasted on selfish idiots like Richard Choat. The villa was warm and private, and she had discovered that the silk sheets on the giant waterbed were perfect for wrapping around her body, fresh from the Jacuzzi, when she did her impression of Cleopatra being unrolled at the feet of Julius

Caesar. Jon and Ole had carried her above their heads, trumpeting and barrumpetty-tumpetting from room to room. When they'd reached the lounge, where Gunnar had been sitting wrapped in the tablecloth with a potato masher in one hand and a fish slice in the other, they'd lowered her to the floor and rolled her out for his close and very intimate inspection. It was a very good game, they had decided. So good, in fact, that the boys had taken it in turns to be Caesar, and, for the first time in her life, Charlotte had begun to appreciate just what a versatile combination hunky young Norwegians and kitchen utensils could be.

Twenty-three miles to the north of Tor Bay, Sir Richard was having rather less of a good time in the holding cell at Exeter Police Station.

'You like a bit o' rumpy?' asked his massive cellmate, Bumpy Oates, with shaved head, tattooed biceps and scars running down his left cheek.

'Don't be ridiculous!' said Sir Richard, haughtily. 'My personal life is none of your damned business!'

'Coz you're gonna get down on your knees, 'an' start kissing the beast!'

'Listen, you nasty piece of work!' snapped Sir Richard. 'I don't damned well take orders from . . . *ker-wurkle*!!' he croaked, as Bumpy grabbed him by throat and shoved him back against the wall.

'Wrap yer laughin' gear round this, granddad,' he said, 'or I'll split yer 'ead open like a grapefruit, an' eat yer brains out with a spoon. We all gotta do our bit in 'ere, sunshine. An' right now my bit is you!'

On the edge of Sodmire and, if he had but known it, only a ten-minute walk from the Green Dragon Inn, Richard Choat was standing in the middle of the narrow and deserted moorland road wondering what the hell had just gone wrong with his life. He had lost his car, his mistress and his bearings, and if something didn't happen soon to make sense of it all he was probably going to lose his sanity, too. He turned his head away from the empty stretch of moorland road down which Sergeant Arthur and WPC Evers had disappeared after dumping him and his belongings out of their 'little car' and into the cold.

He blinked in confusion and looked down at his bare feet. 'Why,' he asked them, miserably, 'does everything happen to me? What have I ever done to deserve this? It's not fair, is it? It really isn't fair! Nobody else has all this shit happen to them all the time, do they? Why's it always gotta be me?'

Sergeant Arthur had stopped the patrol car without warning and turned to look at him on the back seat. 'Right, out you get, Mr. Stoat! Give us your shoes, your socks, your tie and your belt!'

Choat had looked at him, blankly. 'What? Are you mad?'

'Standard procedure,' WPC Evers had informed him. 'Belt, socks, tie and shoelaces! Can't have you hanging yourself in the nick, now, can we? Come on! Chop, chop! Before it gets dark would be nice!'

'Hang myself? For pissing in a petrol tank?'

'Prison does funny things to people, Mr. Scrote. Can't be too careful with someone like you, can we?'

'But . . . they're slip-ons for Christ's sake!'

'Potential offensive weapons,' the WPC assured him, darkly. 'Hand 'em over! And your wallet! All your personal effects, come to that!'

Choat had shrugged and glanced out of the window. 'Yes, but can't it wait 'til we get to the police station? What's so special about here?'

'Better check this lot, too,' Sergeant Arthur had suggested, getting out of the car and opening the boot. 'Make sure there's nothing concealed.'

'Concealed?' Choat had echoed in astonishment, as he'd walked around on tender feet to stand at the back of the car. 'What do you mean, concealed? What do you think I've got in there, a bomb or something? You've got no right to go through my personal possessions.'

'Open them yourself, then,' the sergeant had offered as he'd dumped the cases on the short grass at the side of the road.

'What do you think I am, a terrorist or something?'

'No, sir,' the sergeant had assured him, 'we know *exactly* what you are. So if you would be so kind . . .?' He motioned at Choat. 'Get 'em off!'

'All right,' Choat had agreed, glumly. 'OK. If that's what you want.'

By the time he'd realized that the officers had got back into the car and started the engine, it had been too late for him to do anything about it.

Five minutes had passed since then and he was still standing where they had left him, feeling miserable and freezing from the feet up.

Suddenly, he heard an engine. He glanced up eagerly and saw a vehicle coming towards him. But it was clearly bigger than the little police car, and his face fell when he realized that it wasn't the officers coming back to get him.

The vehicle was an elderly Range Rover belonging to, and being driven by, Jack Strawbridge. Behind him, jammed together in a stinking horsebox, were a bunch of his best 'lads' and one very tough 'maid'. All of them were drunk and armed to the teeth with shotguns, rifles, axes, knives, swords and a variety of illegally held small arms. They had been drinking in the Blasted Pheasant for hours and had taken a vote on what needed to be done about certain people they didn't like. Now they were on their way to the Green Dragon Inn looking for Rooter, Perce, Henry and any of the Clatworthy clan they could get their hands on. Worse still, from Choat's perspective, one or two of them were feeling uncommonly horny.

He stood at the side of the road and waved his arms above his head as they approached. He wasn't to know it, but stopping them and asking for a lift was going to turn out to be the daftest thing he had ever done in his life.

Across the moor, and a little way to the east, in a luxuriously panelled underground gymnasium, Amy, Vicky and Beth were relaxing after a late lunch. Sam was leaning against a vaulting horse and watching what was happening around him with an expression of calculated superiority. They were still getting used to their surroundings, but on the whole they were pleased with what they had found. The girls certainly felt that they were being entertained royally as they sat together on a wooden bench wondering if they had ever seen a finer hunk of male musculature in their lives than the one that was flexing itself on the floor at their feet.

'Hi,' said Nils, looking up as he pumped himself up and down on one arm. 'How was your lunch? Two hundred and forty-nine, two hundred and fifty!' He stood up and reached for a towel. 'You girls want to work out while you're waiting? It'll be at least another couple of hours before he gets here, I reckon.'

Amy exhaled, sharply. 'Don't know if I could cope with that, really,' she said, her eyes shining with promise.

'I could!' said Vicky, jumping to her feet.

'Yeah!' said Beth. 'Me too!'

'Only you'll have to show me,' added Vicky, nudging Beth out of the way.

'Yeah!' said Beth, pushing back. 'Me, too!'

Sam shook his head and walked over to his sister. 'Shameless, aren't they?' he said. 'Like bitches in heat! I thought that Vicky was the quiet type. Still, you never know do . . .?'

Amy ignored him and turned towards a huge man on the other side of the room. 'Don't forget me?' she called, getting quickly to her feet. 'How does that thing with all those metal-thingummies work?'

'The weights, you mean?' asked Max de Griese.

'Yeah, those metally-weighty-thingumajigs,' pouted Amy. 'I liked the look of those when you were doing them just now. Could you show me how you're supposed to sort of *pump* them up and down?'

'Yes, of course. If you'd like to come and sit down here in front of me?'

Amy skipped across the room and sat down.

'Yeah,' said Max, 'sort of like that. Only you're supposed to face the other way. No, really! Really! Yes, like that. And, er, not quite so close?'

Sam shook his head as his sister cuddled up to her would-be instructor.

'Pathetic, isn't it?' said a female voice behind him.

He snorted. 'Damn right!' He started to turn: 'Just look at . . .'

'Hello, Sam,' said a young woman in the tightest of leotards.

Sam swallowed. 'Hello, it's . . . You're Kate, aren't you? Haven't seen you for . . . I dunno, must be . . . Anyway, how's . . . how's things?'

'Things are just fine, Sam: thanks for asking. And I've been hearing all about you. They tell me you've been doing a great job for the firm.' She nodded at the others. 'Do you fancy a workout?'

'I dunno about that. Not as fit as I'd like to be, y'know?' he said, thinking that a workout for him was a leisurely stroll to the pub followed by the intermittent ferrying of a bottle of lager up to his mouth. 'Always meaning to get started, but never seem to get round to it . . . you know?'

'No problem. I'm sure we can do something about that, can't we?' She looked him over. 'Better get you into something more comfortable first, though, don't you think?'

'Maybe,' said Sam, who had a feeling that he wouldn't look altogether inviting in Lycra. 'As long as you promise not to be too hard on me. I mean, I'm a bit out of practice with,' he waved a hand, 'this sort of thing.'

'I promise I won't spank you if you get it wrong.' She grinned. 'Not unless you're a really, *really* good boy!'

In a windowless room not far from the gymnasium, two men were sitting in front of a battery of monitor screens. One of them shook his head as he watched Kate lead Sam into a changing room with wood-panelled walls.

'I don't know,' he said, with a sigh, 'if he doesn't get here soon we're going to have an orgy on our hands.'

'Yeah,' said the other man, shifting in his seat, 'and with any luck I'll be right in the middle of it.'

The older man regarded him, thoughtfully. 'I don't understand it. All I can think is that he's used it somehow.' He shook his head and adjusted the crotch of his trousers. 'It's all getting a bit too familiar, don't you think?'

He pressed a switch. Various interior and exterior views appeared on the screens. 'By the way,' he asked, as a camera panned across the car park at the Green Dragon Inn, 'you haven't seen Jo, have you? I thought I might . . . '

'Yeah,' said the other man, 'so did I!'

'I'm being serious,' said the first man. He turned and pointed at a screen that showed an isolated parking place out on the moor.

'I don't like the look of that little shit,' he said, as they watched Vinny Trashman push Morris Oldroyd onto the driver's seat of the campervan. 'We might have to have him put down.'

He turned away from the screens. 'Get hold of Mr. Hertz for me, will you? If he's recovered from his meeting with the wild men of Gallows Hill, that is?'

He turned back and pointed at one of the screens. 'Tell him to get over there immediately, just in case. In the meantime, I'll try to raise Jo on the horn.' He sighed. 'Always assuming she's remembered to switch the bloody thing on!'

28

DOCTOR SPIEGEL

Morris Oldroyd drove the campervan across the moor with a renewed sense of purpose and a new zest for life. Bonce wasn't as hunky, or as well oiled, as the languid tarts he drooled over in his favourite magazines, but he was definitely masculine, with a masculine smell and a masculine feel: and as far as Morris was concerned he could grope and squeeze his private parts as hard, and as often, as he wanted to. In fact, he was mildly disappointed that Bonce hadn't seen fit to squeeze his genitals for a while now. But he hadn't given up hope that further indignities would be done to his person in the near future, and he smiled to himself as he imagined what it would be like when he and Bonce finally had a chance to be alone together. In his mind's eye he could see those strong arms like steel hawsers crushing their bodies together; those whipcord thighs wrapping themselves around his head; and those firm, pert buttocks, so vividly imagined, clenching and unclenching as they drove Bonce's massively engorged . . .!

Morris shivered and grinned out of focus as the van veered to the left, mounted the grass verge, and jiggled suggestively across the close-cropped turf at the side of the road.

On the bench seat beside him, Vinny leaned across and slapped him on the thigh. 'Oy, tosser, you tryin' to kill us, or what?'

'Sorry,' said Morris, reaching over and touching Vinny's knee to reassure him. 'I don't know what came over me. I felt sort of floppy all of a sudden.'

Vinny curled his lip. 'Floppy? Soddin' floppy? I'll make you feel soddin' floppy you don't watch where you're goin'!'

Morris thought about all the things Vinny might make him feel, but floppy definitely wasn't one of them. Still, he managed to keep the van on the road, more or less, for the rest of the journey, and to follow Simon's directions to the Green Dragon Inn, while the ecstatic Nora sat crammed tightly together in the back of the van with everyone else, talking non-stop about how pleased she was to have finally met Simon 'in the actual flesh' as she put it, and how delighted she was to have met all of his 'lovely friends', too! All of *her* friends, she assured him, would be as 'jealous as buggery' when she got home and told them about it. And 'Mor', she informed everyone, was also 'as pleased as buggery at meeting them', even if he didn't know how to show it.

Her endless chatter was getting on Vinny's nerves.

'Don't she ever stop yakin'?' he asked. 'Wonder she ain't starved to death, keep rabbitin' on!' He leaned across to Morris and hissed in his ear: 'You wanna smack her in the gob every now an' then, mate! Show the stupid cow who's boss. Wouldn't stand for it, if it was me!'

'Your, er, tracky bottoms are a bit . . . you know?' ventured Morris. 'With all that, er,' he swallowed hard, 'all that nasty *mud* on them like that?'

'You what?'

'I was only thinking, that's all,' said Morris, quickly, 'I could wash them out for you, if you wanted me to? You know? If,' he swallowed even harder, 'if you wanted to take them off?'

Vinny turned to see if anyone in the back of the van was listening. But they were all too busy listening to Nora.

He turned back to Morris and leaned menacingly towards him. 'If I didn't know you was married, mate, I might think you was some kind o' woofter! An' I *hate* bleedin' woofters! You hear what I'm sayin'?'

'Who me?' snorted Morris, his voice becoming suddenly gruff. 'I was a bleedin' miner, I was!'

'Yeah! Morris bleedin' miner!' giggled Vinny. 'Geddit? Ay? Like the car?' He turned and shouted at the others in the back. 'You hear that one? Morris bleedin' miner! Him? Geddit? Like the car?'

Bonce looked up with a frown. He couldn't be bothered with any more of Vinny's feeble jokes – not at that moment, at any rate – he was having far too much fun in the back of the van listening to Nora: the more so because he had finally managed to get away from her weirdo of a husband and didn't want reminding of their earlier encounter. There was something about Morris that made him feel uneasy. Something in the way he seemed to like being knocked about that didn't seem quite right. It worried Bonce, and he didn't like being worried because when he was worried he felt anxious, and feeling anxious upset him. He had been trying not to feel worried or anxious or upset ever since he'd been forced to stand by and watch the big Mercedes slip beneath the surface of Sodmire. What Dolly would say to him when she found out what had happened to her precious car didn't bear thinking about. So he hadn't been thinking about it. He had been trying to concentrate on nice things instead. Things like Nora, who fascinated him. She was like perpetual motion on legs, powdered and smelling of strongly exotic perfumes, and just the sort of female relative he wished he could have had when he was a boy. The sort of person who would have cradled his head against her sweet-smelling bosom when he'd felt lonely; licked her hanky and dabbed away his tears when he'd cried; kissed him sloppily on the lips whenever she'd visited him; and fed him lemonade and sticky buns whenever he'd visited her. Someone who would have noticed how much he had grown and not been terrified by it, and who would have been as nice to him as she was being to Hawker. Bonce envied him, and figured that he must be a really nice bloke for someone as sweet smelling and colourful as Nora to like him as much as she obviously did. Maybe living in the country wasn't such a bad thing, after all, he decided, if it made nice people like Nora be as nice to you as all that?

Simon was feeling much happier about things, too. He liked being the centre of attention, and having women like Nora fuss over him the way that she was. He liked how she touched his hands and his arms and his face and his thighs without cringing; and the way she kissed him and cuddled up to him and made disgusting suggestions about what she would be powerless to stop him doing to her if ever he decided to drag her off into the bushes by the hair and have his wicked way with her frail old woman's body.

As the journey across the moor continued, even Vinny began to feel better about life. He had decided that his big chance to take over the gang had finally arrived, and with Dolly on the other side of the country, and Bonce and Nobbler unable to understand what was happening around them, there was no one to get in his way. Suddenly, he was free to prove what a great leader he could be, and show how brilliant he was at making decisions. Most satisfying of all, though, he was free to demonstrate what a truly vicious, violent, and vengeful little shit he could be when he tried. The fact that they had lost Henry Kite, *and* the jewellery from the robbery, *and* Dolly's expensive Mercedes, *and* all their weapons, *and* his mobile phone, was a bit of a drawback, he had to admit. But he wasn't worried about any of that because he knew how easy it was going to be to lay the blame on Bonce's and Nobbler's shoulders, and turn their lives into his own personal vision of Hell. In the meantime, he needed to get to a phone quickly to call Dolly and tell her where they were, what they were doing, and why none of it was his fault.

He smirked as he rehearsed in his mind's ear what he would say to her when he got the chance. 'Bonce an' that little shit-arse screwed up, Doll. Why don't I jus' whack 'em, eh? Take 'em out? Kiss 'em goodbye? Get rid of the useless tossers once an' for all? Then it'd be just you an' me . . .'

Yes, he decided, the day was definitely starting to look up.

The only person in the van who was feeling thoroughly miserable with life was Nobbler. He sat on the floor in the back, forgotten, scrunched up and wondering if Bonce and Vinny and Simon and Nora and Morris, or anyone else in the whole wide world, was ever going to be nice to him ever again. His clothes were wet and cold and caked in mud, and he was lost in an alien world of grass and sky and potentially lethal, exploding wildlife, where people talked about him and at him, but never *to* him, unless it was to yell and sneer and point out what a useless dildo they thought he was being. He was lonely, confused and dejected. Worse still, he hadn't had any decent drugs for what felt like a lifetime. Being sober and straight at the same time was something he hadn't experienced for so long that he couldn't remember how it was supposed to feel. All he knew was that his nerves were as frayed in the middle as they were around the edges and at both ends, and he was beginning to wonder how much more sobriety he could take without cracking up.

After bumping along the narrow moorland roads for ten minutes, Morris pulled the campervan into the car park at the Green Dragon just as Henry was guiding the Ford Probe out from behind the building where Choat had left it.

They passed one another a moment later without recognition.

Vinny turned to Simon as Morris switched off the engine. 'They got a phone in this place, right?'

Simon nodded.

Vinny pointed at Nora. 'You an' her, stay here. You,' he added, pointing at Bonce, 'watch 'em! OK?'

'What about me?' asked Nobbler.

'You can get lost for all I care!' snapped Vinny. 'Only I don't reckon we're gonna be *that* lucky. You're comin' with me,' he told Morris. 'Try anythin' and the old scrubber gets it.' He turned to Bonce. 'You got that?'

'She ain't done nuffin',' pouted Bonce.

'That's right, duckie,' said Nora, with a hand squeezing his thigh, 'you look after little ol' Nora, eh? Lovely, strappin' boy like you!'

After Vinny and Morris had gone, Nobbler got out of the van in a sulk and wandered around to the side of the building looking for somewhere to take a leak. He stopped beside the back bumper of a battered green Volvo, and fumbled through the folds of his clothing in search of his dick. Thirty seconds later, he had finished drawing squiggly wet patterns all over the boot of the car and was lowering his trajectory onto its number plate, when something about it struck him as familiar. He squinted at it, frowned, squinted at it again, and then, with his eyes widening in recognition, pissed all over his shoes.

At the front of the building, there was no immediate answer to Vinny's peevish pounding on the main doors. But he kept at it, and eventually there was movement behind the glass panels.

Jo Cornwall threw the security bolt, opened the door, and peered out.

'Hello, darlin'' said Vinny, looking her over. 'Wha's a horny piece of arse like you doing in a dump like this?'

'Go away,' she said. 'We're closed.'

'Don't be like that gorgeous,' he said, grabbing the edge of the door as she tried to shut it. 'We only wanna use your phone, don't we?' He turned to Morris. 'We're lost, ain't we, Mor?'

Morris grunted as Vinny's elbow struck him in the ribs. His mind had been wandering, trying to make sense of his feelings. On the one hand he was excited by the prospect of a whirlwind love affair with Bonce – or even Vinny, if push came to shove. While on the other, their aggressive behaviour horrified him, and he was finding the contradiction in his feelings confusing.

'Unh?' he grunted. 'What?'

'I said we're lost,' grated Vinny, elbowing him again, 'ain't we?'

Morris shivered like a tree that had just been struck by an axe. 'Oh, yes,' he said. 'No hope of salvation, is there? On the road to ruin for sure!'

Jo raised a quizzical eyebrow. 'What's up with him?'

'Take no notice.'

'Forget his medication, did he?'

Vinny smiled tightly at Morris. 'Only messin' about, ain't ya Mor? It's me Auntie Dolly, see? She's expectin' us at 'er place, an' we're runnin' a bit late. Gotta give 'er a bell and put her mind to rest, yeah?'

Jo glanced at the campervan. 'Who's that lot, then?'

Vinny turned to look. 'Tha's me granny,' he said, pointing at Nora. 'Her with the hair? Them other two's me cousins.'

Jo narrowed her eyes when she saw Simon Hawker peering at her through a side window. 'He bring you here, did he?'

'Yeah. We was lost an' that, like. Look, the old dear's on her last legs.' He waved at the van. 'We don't get her to Auntie Dolly's soon she ain't gonna make it!'

'Looks healthy enough to me. With her tongue stuck in his ear.'

'Yeah. Grannies, eh? Always lookin' to see you washed proper, ain't they? You gonna let us use your phone, or what?'

She thought for a moment. Then she nodded, and opened the door.

'Wipe your feet,' she said, glancing at Morris. 'An' tell laughing boy here to behave himself, OK?' she added, as she walked across the saloon bar.

'Vinny!' wheezed Nobbler, running up. 'It's 'im, innit?' He waved towards the back of the building. ''I's 'is car, innit? Back there in the wosname!'

'Shut it!' hissed Vinny.

'Yeah, but it's 'is, innit? 'Enry wosname's wosname!'

'Bollocks!'

'Honest! I seen the number plate-thing an' . . . !'

Vinny clamped his hand over the little man's mouth. 'You sure?'

He nodded, wide-eyed.

'Right, shtum!' said Vinny, turning to smile disarmingly at Jo. 'Collects number plates, like, y'know? Pass the time on the road?' He tapped the side of his head with a finger. 'Just a bit . . . Wouldn't 'urt a fly, though, honest!'

Jo turned away. 'Runs in the family, does it? In here,' she added, nodding at a door next to the bar. 'The phone?'

Vinny jerked his head for Nobbler to follow him into the building. 'You got rooms, then?' he asked. 'People stayin', an' that? Only a mate said he was gonna stop for a couple o' days.'

'No rooms,' said Jo. 'I'll be in the bar if you want me.'

'Best offer I've 'ad all day.'

'Yeah,' smirked Nobbler, 'I wouldn't mind . . . '

'*Shut it!*' hissed Vinny. 'Only he drives a Volvo, like,' he said aloud to Jo. 'Nice picture, that, by the way.'

Jo looked at him for a moment. Then she turned to look at the framed photograph on the wall. It was a picture of the pub that Perce had taken a long time ago. She sniffed. 'Fifty quid to you.'

'On what they pay me?' he snorted. 'You 'aven't seen him, then, our mate?' He pretended to examine the photograph, closely. 'Who's the geezer on the 'orse, then? Lord of the bleedin' manor, or what?'

Jo shrugged. 'You could say that.'

'Still 'ave all that old diddly down 'ere, then, do ya? Serfs an' stuff? 'E's about so big, our mate, by the way. You'd know 'im if you saw 'im. Henry, his name is. Henry Kite?'

'He left five minutes ago.'

'Couldn't 'ave!'

'OK. He didn't.'

'No! I mean . . . I believe ya. Only . . . what, he was walkin' like, was he?'

Jo turned to look at him. 'What?'

'Our mate! We'd 'ave seen him, wouldn't we? If he was drivin'?'

'He borrowed someone's car. Look are you gonna use the phone or not?'

'Yeah! Yeah! Only he didn't say where he was goin', did 'e, our mate?'

'He went to the Clatworthy's place,' she folded her arms. 'Look, this isn't a tourist information centre, you know!'

'Yeah, right! Only, how far's that, then, this . . . wosname, this Clotwothy's place? If you don't mind me askin'?'

'Look . . .'

'No problem. No problem. Just thought I'd ask, like, tha's all.'

He turned away.

He turned back again. 'I was jus' wonderin' . . .'

'Why don't you ask Hawker?'

'Yeah, right. Only what was the name, again? Where our mate's gone?'

'Clatworthy. The phone's in there. Are you gonna use it or not?'

'Yeah, yeah. Right. Thanks.'

'You stupid *sod*!' snarled Dolly, when he told her what had happened. 'What'd I tell you? Keep an eye on him, I said. And what d'you do?'

'No, Doll,' he protested, 'it ain't like that, honest! Bonce an' Nobby screwed up. I couldn't do nothin' . . .'

'Don't give me all that old bollocks!'

'But we *know* where the bugger's at, Doll. We got 'is car an' . . .'

'And you've searched it, right?'

He swore silently as he held the receiver to his chest. 'Not as such,' he admitted. 'I was jus' gonna . . . '

'Why not?'

'We . . . '

'Idiot!'

'But he can't 'ave gone far, Doll! Soon as we get our 'ands on 'im. . .'

'Right. I'm coming down. Sort this mess out once an' for all. Well?'

'Well what?'

'Where are you, you moron?'

He had to admit that he didn't know.

'Bloody-well find out, then, and call me back!'

He smacked the receiver against the wall when he heard the line go dead. 'Bugger!' he muttered. 'How're we s'posed to . . .?' He frowned. Then he grinned and sneaked back to peer through the door into the saloon bar.

Jo was on the far side of the room, talking to Morris and Nora.

Vinny nodded, and stole quietly back along the hallway to the kitchen. He rifled through the drawers and found a meat cleaver and a steak knife with a six-inch blade. He slid the meat cleaver into a pocket inside his drape jacket, and slipped the steak knife into his sock. Then he straightened his clothing, and walked back down the hall to ask Jo for directions.

'Where from?'

'Town.'

'What . . . Exeter or Plymouth?'

'London.'

'That'd take hours.'

'Not the way Curly drives.'

'Yeah, well, you'll have to wait outside. I've got work to do in here.'

'Look,' he said, walking towards her, 'we don't want no trouble. All we,' He stopped and bent forward in agony. 'Bugger! Bleedin' ankle's been . . .'

Jo frowned and took a step towards him. But he straightened with the steak knife in his hand, and held it to her throat.

'Listen, *darlin'*,' he snarled, 'I decide who stays an' who goes round 'ere! You got that? So be a good little girlie and do as you're told.'

* * *

'Come an' get it!' called Titus, as he walked across the clearing with a tray held out in front of him. 'Get 'em while they're hot!'

He stopped next to Henry's chair and proffered the tray. 'He's a bit of a macho arsehole though, isn't he, that Vinny?'

Henry looked at him askance. '*You* think *Vinny's* an arsehole?'

Titus nodded. 'Can't go treatin' birds like that, can ya? Callin' 'em names an' knockin' 'em about. I mean, they're people, too, ain't they?'

'Very profound,' said Henry, looking down at the tray. 'What's this?'

'Muffins,' said Titus, proudly. 'Baked 'em meself!'

'That is incorrect, Corio Boc,' said a female voice behind him.

'Ooops!' whispered the little Celt. 'Ol' Titus is in trouble now!'

Henry turned to see a young woman walking towards them wearing an apron and a pair of impossibly high-heeled shoes. Her hair and makeup were impeccably done, if a little heavy for his liking, and she was carrying a tray with a teapot and assorted cutlery and crockery balancing on it.

'*Who* baked them?' she asked, as she stopped next to Titus.

'I read the recipe, though, didn't I?'

'And you set the timer,' she said. 'Aren't you a clever little boy?'

Titus grinned. 'Gorgeous, eh?' he said, nodding at the lieutenant. 'A lot cleverer than you an' me, an' all, buddy, don't you worry!'

'Please forgive the intrusion, sir,' said the lieutenant, bowing to the hooded figure. 'Good afternoon, Mr. Kite!' she added, bowing again. 'But the Sex Machine thought you might be in need of some light refreshment?'

'The *what*?' snorted Henry. He looked at Titus. 'Did she just say . . .?'

'*No!*' said Titus, hurriedly. '*No, no!* I keep tellin' 'er I'm jus' good ol' Titus, but you know what girls are like when they get a bit . . .?'

'On the contrary, Corio Boc,' interrupted the lieutenant, smoothly, 'you instructed me to refer to you . . .'

'*On our own, I said!*' he hissed. 'Not *now*! Not in front of . . .!'

'As you wish, your horniness. Would I be correct, then, in assuming that you no longer wish me to be known as your Little Love Bunny?'

Henry grinned. 'Your horniness . . .?'

'*No!*' said Titus, sharply. '*No!* I mean, not *now*! Not *now*, with,' he waved a hand at Henry and the hooded figure, 'that lot . . . all sort of . . .'

'Very good,' said the lieutenant. 'In which case, what manner of . . .?'

'I mean, *yes*!' hissed Titus, glancing at the giggling Henry. 'Look . . .' He took the lieutenant by the elbow and hustled her out of earshot.

Henry watched as they stopped some distance away and stood close together: the lieutenant still holding her tray, standing straight and erect, watching Titus intently and matching his every movement and gesture with minute adjustments of her head: the little Ancient Briton hunched forward and agitated, half-turned away from Henry and the hooded figure, glancing nervously over his shoulder at them from time to time, with one hand on the lieutenant's bottom and the other making sharp chopping and slicing movements to emphasize whatever message he was trying desperately, and apparently in vain, to get across.

'She doesn't look very,' said Henry, hesitating and glancing across at the hooded figure, 'very, well, er . . . *military*, does she?'

He had a point: beneath the apron, with its printed image of a matching black lacy bra, frilly panties, suspender belt and stockings, the lieutenant was wearing a matching black lacy bra, frilly panties, suspender belt and stockings.

'I mean, she would probably stop most armies in their tracks on sight, but somehow I can't see that being much good for discipline. Can you?'

'On the contrary, I believe our young friend there is perfectly happy to submit to the lieutenant's disciplinary regime. Not least, because it is based exclusively on her unparalleled knowledge of his sexual proclivities.'

'Not quite what I meant, though, was it?'

'Of course not. But it is just possible, Henry, that you are looking at their relationship through the wrong end of the telescope.'

'Me? You were the one who kept telling him she was a robot.'

'That is correct. But it was never my intention to force him to go against his instincts. Rather, I was hoping to spare him the potential embarrassment of learning the truth. The possibility of which, I might remind you, you seemed to find so very amusing.'

'Meaning what?'

The figure held up its right hand.

Henry turned to look at Titus, expecting to see him shimmer, fade and disappear. But he remained resolutely solid and engaged in an animated discussion with the lieutenant.

'Let me put it this way,' suggested a female voice. 'Do you find the lieutenant sexually appealing?'

Henry turned to see a mild-looking middle-aged woman sitting upright in an armchair, almost within touching distance, with her legs and feet together and her hands clasped loosely in her lap. She was watching him with an expression of friendly enquiry.

Taken aback by her sudden and unheralded arrival, Henry glanced at the hooded figure and back again. 'Sorry?' he said, 'But . . . who are you, exactly?'

'My name is Eve Spiegel, Henry. Doctor Eve Spiegel, to be precise. I am a psychotherapist, and I like to think,' she gestured towards the hooded figure, 'one of his grace's oldest and dearest friends.'

'And he brought you here, did he?'

'He asked me to come here, yes.'

Henry swallowed. 'Why?'

'I was rather hoping that you would answer my question.'

'Which question would that be?'

'The one about whether or not you find the lieutenant sexually appealing.'

'Why? What's that got to do with anything?'

'I don't know. I was rather hoping that you would tell me that, too.'

'You're rather hoping for rather a lot, then, aren't you?'

'Indeed,' said the doctor, with the trace of a smile. 'It is a personal thing, of course, and by no means all of my colleagues would agree with me, but I find that it is in the nature of my profession to be optimistic.'

'Meaning . . .?'

'Well, you know, I like to think that most of us have better ways of living our lives, if only we can find them. And it is my hope – my conceit, if you will? – that I will be able to make some positive contributions, however small, to the way in which people feel about themselves and the world around them.'

'Nothing Messianic about that, then?'

'Touché! Are you a religious man, Henry?'

'Good God, no! Haven't been near a church since I was a kid. I mean, except for marriages and christenings and, you know, that sort of thing.'

'So how would you describe your philosophy of life?'

'What: Life, the Universe and Everything?'

'If you like, yes.'

'It's forty-two, isn't it, according to Douglas Adams?'

'You're a fan of *The Hitchhiker's Guide to the Galaxy*, then?'

'It's OK. A bit like the curate's egg, really.'

'Good in places, you mean?'

'There are some really funny bits, yes – Don't Panic, Ford Prefect, the Vogons – and some bits that aren't quite so good. A bit like life, really.'

'And the robots?' asked the doctor. 'With their *Sirius Cybernetics Corporation's Genuine People Personalities* technology?'

'Is that what she is?' asked Henry, glancing across at the lieutenant.

'I have not had the pleasure of meeting her,' said the doctor. 'But from what his grace has told me about her, I would say that she is very far from being Marvin the Paranoid Android.'

'Certainly doesn't look like him, does she?'

'Indeed.'

Henry turned to stare at the doctor for a moment. Then he glanced back at Titus and the lieutenant. He nodded to himself and took a deep breath. 'I don't know. What do you mean by sexually appealing, exactly?'

'Do you think she's an attractive woman?'

'She's a robot!'

'Quite so.'

'What?'

'As you say, she is a robot'.

'So what do you want me to say?'

'As unlikely as it might seem, and as hard as it might be for you to put into words, the truth would probably be helpful.'

'She's a robot!' he insisted, gesturing towards the lieutenant. He lowered his voice. 'I mean, she's not a *real* woman, is she?'

The doctor nodded, impassively.

'She's not even human.'

'That would appear to be the case, certainly. But I think that, perhaps, the question is still an interesting one. Don't you?'

Henry shrugged and looked into the fire. 'Is it?'

The doctor watched him in comradely silence.

He looked up. 'Why are you asking *me*, anyway? I'm not the one who's,' he gestured at Titus, 'drooling over her, am I?'

'Do you think he is wrong to be "drooling over her" as you put it?'

'I don't know! What kind of question is that? I mean, it takes all sorts to make a world, doesn't it?'

'It would certainly seem so, yes.'

'And people do some pretty strange things, don't they?'

'Perhaps. But isn't *strange* a relative term? I mean, what may seem strange to you or me might be perfectly normal to someone else. And what exactly does it mean to be normal, anyway?'

Henry stared at her for several seconds. 'I don't know,' he said, turning away and gazing out beyond the standing stones. He thought for a moment. 'Maybe it's got something to do with having a living, breathing, blood-pumping intelligence. And some sort of self-awareness, perhaps?'

The doctor nodded. 'Do you masturbate, Henry?'

'Do I . . .? What the hell's that got to do with it?'

'Does the thought of masturbation upset you?'

'Yes! No! I mean, I don't know. I suppose it depends on who's doing it, doesn't it?' He turned to the hooded figure. 'Is this really happening to me?'

'I am afraid so,' said the figure.

'Why?'

The figure shrugged. 'Titus is an important part of your future. Or he will be in the fullness of what many of us prefer to call time.'

'He is?' Henry frowned. 'I mean . . . he will be?'

The figure inclined its head.

'Bloody Hell!'

'There was a survey done by a group of female researchers, Henry,' said the doctor, 'that looked to establish the prevalence of masturbation amongst the male population in North America. Their conclusions stated that of the men who were willing to answer the question "Do You Masturbate Regularly", 97% said they did. Of the remaining 3%, the researchers concluded that 2% were physically incapable – of masturbating, that is – while the remaining 1% were lying.'

'I'm sorry, but I don't see . . . '

'Well, it begs the question, does it not, why words like tosser and wanker are employed so widely as terms of abuse? After all, if the researcher's findings were even close to being accurate, all the name-caller is doing, when he or she refers to someone as a wanker, is telling them that they are just like everyone else. And that kind of defeats the purpose, don't you think?'

'So you're saying we've all been programmed to think masturbation is bad in spite of the fact that we all do it? And that, what . . .? You're saying it's all down to religion, or something?'

'Not religion as such, perhaps.'

'What then?'

'Well, perhaps it's more to do with those who seek to use religion, or some other form of superstition – economics or politics, say? – to justify their own prejudices and keep the rest of us in line. To control us?'

'What's that got to do with them?' He pointed at Titus and the lieutenant.

'My question still stands. Do you find the lieutenant sexually appealing? Notwithstanding that she is, as you rightly say, a robot.'

'Notwithstanding that,' said Henry, 'I suppose the answer is yes.'

He looked around the clearing, made a deprecatory gesture with his hands and said 'So what does that prove?'

'I would say that it proves that you are perfectly normal. Rather like all the rest of us who masturbate but don't like to talk about it.'

'Well good! I feel much better now that's sorted out!'

'Do you?'

'Absolutely! Definitely! No doubt about it! Never been so convinced of anything in my life.'

He took a deep breath, and thought for a moment.

He looked across at Titus and the lieutenant, who, much to his surprise, were standing side by side watching him in silent immobility.

He pursed his lips and shrugged. 'Well, I suppose,' he said after a pause, 'I suppose . . . now that you come to mention it . . . when you put it like that and I stop to think about it . . . all things considered, and all that . . . yes, I do! At least, I think I do. Feel good about it, I mean.'

'And would you say the lieutenant is fit?'

'Fit?'

'Yes.'

'What do you mean . . . *fit*?'

'An excellent question, Henry. What indeed?'

'I don't know. I mean, do robots do exercise?'

The doctor inclined her head.

'Do they eat? Or do the equivalent of eating? I mean, they must need some sort of energy, mustn't they? Fuel of some sort to keep going,' he hesitated, 'and a balanced diet?'

'You would think so, wouldn't you?'

'The right sort of fuel,' he mused. 'Or do you mean fit for purpose, like a machine, or a theory, or an ideology?'

'What if I said to you that I think Arnold Schwarzenegger is really fit?'

'What, you mean healthy?'

'That is part of it, yes.'

'So . . . what, you mean, you fancy him, then?'

'I think he looks horny, yes.'

'Horny?' Henry blinked. 'Really? Arnold Schwarzenegger? You think Arnold Schwarzenegger is sexy?'

'Yes.'

'But he's as thick as two short planks!'

'Actually,' said the doctor, evenly, 'I know Arnie quite well, and while I would have to say that he isn't the most knowledgeable, cultured or academically gifted person I have ever met, I don't think it would be fair to call him thick. On the other hand, I'm not convinced that it is fair to call anyone else *thick*, either. Intellectually or educationally challenged, perhaps. But not . . . *thick*!'

'So it's a purely physical thing, then? You and Arnie, I mean?'

The doctor nodded. 'As long as he doesn't move or speak.'

'So you wouldn't want to have a relationship with him?'

'I didn't say that.'

'So you *would* want to have a relationship with him?'

'I don't think I said that either. I like skiing, Henry. So I like to take the occasional holiday at Aspen in Colorado. But I don't like cold weather, so I wouldn't want to live there. I much prefer San Francisco where it's warmer.'

'So you're talking about a fling then, an affair, with Arnie? Not a permanent, live-in sort of relationship?'

'Something like that, yes.'

'And have you? Had an affair with him, I mean? If you don't mind me asking?'

'I haven't had an affair with him. And no, I don't mind you asking.'

'Why not? I mean, why haven't you had an affair with him? Just now you said you wanted to.'

'I think what I said was that I wasn't going to discount the possibility of having a relationship with him. But I didn't say what *kind* of relationship. Neither did you. But perhaps there was in our discussion an unspoken assumption that we were talking about an intimate, physical and predominantly sexual relationship.'

Henry was confused. He sat for a moment, blinking and gazing at the ground with unseeing eyes. The only thing he was certain about at that moment was that his brain was starting to hurt.

The doctor continued to watch him, unmoving.

He looked up. 'So,' he asked, measuring his words carefully, 'are you talking about some sort of *imaginary* relationship?'

'That might be one way of putting it, yes.'

He nodded to himself and looked down at his hands.

He was silent for a long time.

His brain hurt some more.

There were things that he wanted to say, wanted to ask. But something told him that the questions running through his mind were too personal for him to put into words. But whether he was afraid of embarrassing the doctor or of embarrassing himself, he wasn't so sure.

'What are you thinking?' asked the doctor.

He looked at her, pursed his lips, shrugged and looked down at the ground. He shook his head several times.

'So,' he said, aware that he didn't want to look the doctor in the eye, 'are you saying,' he swallowed, uneasily, but forced himself to go on, 'that you might *fantasize* about him? And have . . . *that* sort of relationship with him?'

The image that flashed into his head at that moment was just too unsettling for words. The prospect of Arnie Schwarzenegger as a languid, oiled centrefold with women drooling over him, and . . . well, perhaps doing a lot more than just drooling, too, did not compute.

A disconcerting shiver ran up his spine.

'What was that?' asked the doctor.

He shook his head and raised his hands, palms facing the doctor, as if he wanted to push her away. 'Don't ask!'

'How are you feeling?'

'A bit queasy, as a matter of fact.'

'You look as if you've just seen a ghost.'

He smiled. 'Do I?' He chuckled to himself. 'Well, not a ghost, perhaps, more sort of . . . Arnie in his underpants!'

'Mmmm,' murmured the doctor. 'Lucky you!'

'Not really.'

'No. No, I suppose not.'

'Do you mind if I ask you something?'

'No, go ahead.'

'Well, umm, are you married?'

'No, I'm not.'

'So you live on your own, then?'

'No, I live with my partner.'

'What, your business partner, or . . . or the other kind?'

'My domestic partner – my lover – yes.'

'And does he . . . or she! . . . know you fancy Arnie?'

'I don't believe we have ever discussed that possibility, as such. But it wouldn't surprise me to learn that he had worked it out for himself.'

'And what would he say if you did? Discuss it I mean?'

'I don't know, Henry. But I like to think that he would not be offended or challenged by it, if we did.'

'He wouldn't?'

'I like to think that he wouldn't. Because I also like to think that we understand reasonably well the depth of the commitment we have made to one another. And the difference between fantasy and reality.'

'What's he like? If you don't mind me asking?'

'How do you mean?'

'I don't know, really. Just,' he hesitated, 'I mean, how would you describe him to someone, if they asked you?'

'I think that would depend on who was doing the asking.'

'What if it was me?'

'Well, then I think I would say that he is loving, caring, thoughtful, capable, strong and creative: an intelligent man who is every bit as sexy as I need him to be. We talk a lot about how we think and feel about ourselves and about each other. And I like to think we are honest about those things. Or at least, as honest with one another as it is possible, and advisable, for two human beings to be.'

'Lucky you,' said Henry. 'Most girls think I'm a twat!'

'Really? Why do you say that?'

He shook his head. He wanted to say 'Because walking in on someone with your dick hanging out isn't the best way of introducing yourself to a girl, is it?' Instead, he said 'He sounds like a nice person, your guy.'

'Thank you, Henry,' said the doctor. 'Yes, I think so, too. And ours is, I think, a very rewarding relationship.'

He smiled. 'In spite of the fact that you fancy Arnie's pants off!'

The doctor smiled back at him. 'In spite of that, yes.'

Henry looked across at Titus and the lieutenant, who were deep in conversation, again. 'So is that what you're talking about, then? Titus and the lieutenant each has what the other one needs, or wants, or whatever, and that who and what they are isn't really important?'

'On the contrary, Henry, I think it is crucially important. But perhaps what matters most is knowing that they are both happy with the situation, and provided they are not harming anyone else, including each other, why should they not be allowed to get on with it? Indeed, why should they not be congratulated for having found something that so many of us seem to be searching for so desperately but are unable to find.'

'But, I mean, isn't the lieutenant being exploited? She doesn't have freewill, does she, if someone has programmed her to pander to a man's every whim? And if she can't feel emotions?'

'As I understand it, your grace,' said the doctor, 'the lieutenant is quite incapable of being exploited. Is that not so?'

'To all intents and purposes,' said the figure, 'yes. She has an IQ that is far in excess of any human capability. And she has been programmed with information from every available source of knowledge, historical, mythical, political, religious, scientific, economic, cultural and so on: all of it set within a strict, if relatively simple, moral framework. Which is to say that she will always act in what she calculates to be the best possible interests of everyone concerned, including her own.'

'So you're saying she likes dressing like that?'

'Certainly,' said the doctor. 'How many people do you know, Henry, who do not like being told they look fabulous?'

'I don't think *fabulous* is in Titus's vocabulary, is it?'

'And fit: do you think *fit* is in his vocabulary, Henry?'

'God knows!'

There was a faint sizzling sound as Dr. Spiegel disappeared.

When Henry stopped to think about it, he had to admit that in spite of, or perhaps because of, the fact that she didn't have a single human organ anywhere in her body, the lieutenant was, as robots went, a horny looking woman and apparently as fit as it was possible for any human or android to be. She certainly looked like a real woman, and he guessed that she felt like a real woman, too. The hooded figure told him that she had been modelled to resemble a human adult female in every aspect except one: she wasn't actually alive. Or at least, she wasn't alive by most people's definition of that word. On the other hand, since she had no human organs anywhere in her body, she was very probably a good deal healthier, and fitter, in every sense of those words, than any human being, female or male, was ever likely to be in his lifetime. Her skin was realistic, the hooded figure had told him, warm, flexible and pleasant to the touch, and she had even been given a complete set of carefully designed and constructed bodily orifices capable of replicating in every way human responses to intimate sexual activity.

Henry swallowed uncomfortably at the thought.

'I understand,' continued the figure, 'that she responds realistically to foreplay, and is capable of experiencing orgasm in a manner very close to that experienced by any healthy human female fortunate enough to have been gifted with an attentive lover.'

'Too much information!' said Henry. 'I really don't think I needed to know that, do you?'

His body shivered, briefly, and he shook his head in an attempt to rid his imagination of the unwelcome images flashing through it.

'Anyway,' he said, turning away and getting to his feet, 'that's enough of *that*, I think, don't you?'

He stomped around in a circle for a bit, flexing his arms and shoulders, and making gruff, manly noises, before turning back to the hooded figure and taking a very long and very deep breath.

'Right then,' he said, rubbing his hands together, 'what was that you were saying just now about the Green Dragon Inn?'

* * *

29

JACKIE CHOAT

Every evening at six o'clock sharp, Perce Pratt closed, locked and bolted the doors of the Green Dragon Inn and trudged wearily up to his bedroom for a ten-minute nap. And every evening he woke two hours later feeling refreshed and ready for another rigorous night's serving behind the bar. But this evening was different. This time he wasn't allowed to wake of his own accord. This time someone woke him earlier than usual with a knife against his throat and a whispered warning that if he made any sudden moves his head would part company with his body.

'There,' breathed Vinny, with his fist clamped over Perce's mouth, 'that's a good boy. Now you jus' get up nice and slow old man and show Vinny where you keep the artillery. Be nice, mind,' he warned, squeezing Perce's jaw in his fist, 'or Vinny'll cut your soddin' face off!'

Perce eased himself warily onto his elbows. 'What d'you want?'

'Where's the guns?'

Perce shook his head. 'It's a pub. We don't . . . '

'Don't piss me off!' snarled Vinny, holding the kitchen knife in front of Perce's face. 'Or I'll dig yer friggin' eyeballs out!' He stared hard at Perce. 'This is bumpkin country, this is, an' all you bumpkins got shooters. 'Sides, the tart downstairs says you 'ave!'

Perce tried to sit up. 'Jo? What've you done . . .?'

'I told you!' warned Vinny, forcing him back onto the pillows. 'You really don't wanna piss me off ol' man!'

'OK!' said Perce. 'OK! There's a cabinet . . . in the cellar.'

'And?'

'What?'

'The keys?'

Perce inclined his head at the bedside table. 'In the drawer.'

Vinny grinned. 'That's better. Now you jus' turn over granddad, an' put your hands behind yer back, an' Vinny won't 'ave to cut yer dick off.'

Downstairs in the room behind the public bar, Nora and Morris were sitting back-to-back on the floor with their mouths taped shut and their wrists tied together. They were frightened and trying not to think about what would happen to them if Vinny decided to get really nasty. He had sent Bonce and Simon Hawker out to fetch what he had called Simon's 'wheels' from his mother's house so that they could drive to a place called Buckfastleigh to meet someone called Dolly and guide her and her gang back to the pub. After they'd gone, Vinny had started taunting Nora, calling her an old slapper and a tart and a pox-ridden old whore.

Morris had tried to stick up for her and had been smacked in the face for his troubles. Then Vinny had kicked him, and called him a wimp and an iron and a woolly-woofter as he'd lain dazed and bleeding on the floor. Their holiday, which, until an hour ago, had looked like turning out precisely the way Nora had hoped and imagined it would, was suddenly going disastrously wrong. Nora's pride had been dented. Morris's face was bleeding and his ribs hurt. And neither of them thought they were going to get out of the pub alive.

Nora hoped that Vinny would get it over with quickly, if he decided that he couldn't afford to have them around any longer. On balance, she told herself, she and Morris had had a good life together. There had been hard times, yes, but she wouldn't have changed any of it for the world. All of those naughty little flings she'd had on the backseats of cars, and up against walls, in fields and bedrooms and barns and on kitchen tables and halfway up stairs; even on a pool table, or two, once or twice: the knee tremblers, whenever and wherever she could get them, that had been part and parcel of their life together for so many years. And Morris had always been waiting quietly in the background, looking after her, supporting the kids, bringing home the bacon and flogging himself half to death every night in the garden shed for the love of swarthy young men who didn't even know he existed. She loved him, even for that: especially for that, perhaps, and for always being there when she needed him and staying away when she didn't: and for never scolding, or moralizing, or leaving her and her sprogs in the lurch.

It had been a good life, all things considered, she reminded herself. Morris was a good man. And she wasn't such a bad woman, was she? Just a bit headstrong and wayward at times, perhaps: and, maybe, a bit hornier than most? She hoped now that they would go together when the time came, and that Bonce would make sure that Vinny got things over with quickly and without too much pain.

Morris reached back and gripped one of her hands. He squeezed it, and squeezed it again, hoping that she would feel better knowing that he still cared. He had always loved her, the little tart, even though he had never found her remotely interesting sexually. And he had always been pleased for her when some hairy-arsed miner, window cleaner, butcher, baker, candlestick maker, policeman, traffic warden, gardener, social worker or boy scout had given her a right good rogering and put a smile back on her face. He'd never begrudged her the affairs, and she'd never criticized the time he'd spent with the lawnmower. Their marriage had never been consummated. But now that it looked like coming to an untimely and violent end, his fondest wish was that she would get the chance to lay him down, rip off his trousers and pants, tear off her knickers, and ride him with all the lust in her libidinous body. If they had to go, he wanted them to go together, humping each other's brains out to the end!

Around the corner, in the saloon bar, Jo was sitting on the old wooden settle beneath the stained glass window with her wrists taped behind her back, watching Nobbler through half-closed lids as he ogled her. She parted her legs, and watched as his eyes opened wide in response. She smiled to herself and drew her knees together. Nobbler took a hefty swig from a bottle of lager, and frowned. When she opened her legs again, he raised both eyebrows in approval. When she opened her legs even wider, he licked his lips. It was like watching one of Pavlov's experiments with dogs. Only in Nobbler's case, the stimulus bypassed his taste buds and went straight to his dick.

'*Pack it in, Jo!*' hissed a voice in her ear.

She glanced at a wall light where she knew there was a concealed camera. 'Shouldn't be watching me, then, should you?' she whispered.

Nobbler looked up, guiltily. 'What?'

'What's a nice bloke like you doing in a gang like this?' she asked.

'Who?' he replied, turning to look over his shoulder.

'You of course. What other nice bloke is there?'

'Ay?'

'You don't belong with this lot, do you? I mean . . . '

'Bloody do! Well 'ard, me!' He took another swig from the bottle.

'Yes, but they're just thugs, aren't they? You're . . . '

'I'm a bleedin' thug, an all!' he insisted, emptying the bottle. 'Don't you worry 'bout that!' He belched. '*Bitch*!'

She opened her legs, wider this time, and smiled as his eyes were drawn irresistibly to the hem of her skirt. 'You couldn't untie my ankles, could you?' she asked, beating her eyelashes like hummingbird wings.

'*Jo . . .!*' warned the voice in her ear.

'Only the tape is ever so, *ever so* tight!'

Nobbler shook his head, but slid onto his knees and started fumbling with the ties at her ankles. 'Vinny said . . . '

'Vinny's not here, though, is he?'

'I wouldn't wanna bet on it, *girlie*!' said Vinny, from the doorway. He strolled into the room with a swagger, looking down his nose at Nobbler and pointing a twelve-bore shotgun at his groin.

'You useless little prick! Another friggin' minute, she'd 'ave 'ad you lettin' her go! Wanker!' He held out the shotgun. 'See that? Blow your horny little bollocks off that will you don't stop playin' with yourself. 'Sides, she's savin' herself for me. Ain't ya darlin'?'

'Of course,' said Jo. 'What else? Big, tough bloke like you.'

'*Jo! For Christ's sake!*' warned the voice in her ear.

Vinny stared at her for a moment. Then he put the barrel of the gun against her cheek. 'You better not be takin' the piss out of Vinny, girlie. He can shag you just as easy with half your face blown off, y'know! Don't make no difference to Vinny, girlie. He *likes* tarts what don't *ever* talk back!'

He looked down at her legs and moved the barrel of the shotgun onto her knees, before sliding it slowly up her thighs until it snagged against the hem of her skirt. He paused for a moment and looked into her defiant eyes.

'That big enough for ya, darlin', is it?'

When she continued to stare back at him impassively, he lifted the hem of her skirt on the barrel of the gun and pushed it up until he could see her knickers. He licked his lips, and slid the gun down between her thighs and against her crotch. 'Like that, do you, darlin', eh? Nice 'an hard for ya, is it?'

When she still didn't reply, he turned to Nobbler. 'Put her in the back.' He reached down and cupped his genitals in a claw-like fist. 'I'm gonna give the bitch what she's been askin' for since we got 'ere!'

'Not . . . not now, Vinny, ay?' stammered Nobbler. 'Later, eh? Listen . . .'

Vinny pushed him away. 'Piss off!'

'No, but it's them, innit?' insisted Nobbler. 'Bonce an' wosname come back?' He pointed at the window. 'Out there?'

Vinny listened. 'No it ain't!'

'Yeah, i's them, innit?' Nobbler nodded and stood up.

'Eyes like a hawk,' sneered Vinny. 'Lug'oles like a bat. An' a face like a monkey's arsehole.'

He poked Nobbler in the back with the shotgun. 'What you waitin' for, then? Go let 'em in!'

He turned back to Jo and hoisted her skirt with the barrel of the shotgun to get a better look at her knickers. 'Sorry, darlin',' he said, pulling the gun away, 'Vinny's got things to do. Not your day, is it? Still plenty o' time for that later, eh? Just you an' me?'

'Got it,' said Simon, as he and Bonce walked into the saloon bar. He frowned at Jo. 'Hey, what are you doing to her?'

Vinny pointed the shotgun at him. 'What's it to you?'

'Nothing. I mean, it's just that . . . well, I wouldn't do that, if I were you.'

'Yeah? Who's gonna stop me?'

'Well, there are a lot of people who . . .'

'You haven't got it yet, 'ave ya?'

'Sorry?'

'This ain't one of your little trips 'cross the wosname,' said Vinny, waving the gun at a window. 'Some hoity-toity stroll with a bunch o' wanky tourists out there! We ain't payin' ya, y'know? So you can forget all that ol' diddly. You do what you're told – we don't blow your head off. You got that?'

Simon nodded. 'Yes of course! It's just that . . .'

'You *got that*, I said?'

'Yes. I've got it. You're in charge.'

'An' you better get used to it! So, where's this bleedin' motor o' yours?'

'In the van.'

'In? What d'you mean . . . *in?*'

'My bike. We came back as quickly as . . .'

'*Bike?* What *bike? Wheels*, you said. Get your soddin' *wheels*! Wheels means a motor, not some friggin' push-bike!'

'Sorry, but *you* said wheels,' said Simon, apologetically, 'not me. I thought you knew. And anyway, it's a scooter, not a bicycle. It belongs to my mother, really, but it's got an engine and everything.'

'Has it really?'

Simon nodded.

Vinny pointed the shotgun at his face. 'You takin' the piss?'

'What? No! No, of course not! No!'

''Cause if you are . . .'

Simon held his hands above his head. 'No, really!' He looked at Bonce. Then back at Vinny. 'I don't understand. I thought you wanted me to get it?'

Vinny kicked a chair across the room. 'Arsehole! Bleedin' stupid . . .!' He took a deep breath. 'OK, so let's 'ave a look at it! Not you!' he added, waving the shotgun at Nobbler. 'You stay an' watch that!' He pointed at Jo. 'An' take this. He fumbled inside his jacket for the meat cleaver. 'An' try not to chop your soddin' dick off with it. Head yes. Dick no. An' don't go getting' your ears stuck in her sussies, neither!'

When they got to the campervan, Bonce opened the back doors and lifted Simon's mother's scooter to the ground.

Vinny stared at it in disbelief. 'What good's that piddlin' little thing, you tosser?' He pointed at Bonce. ''Ave you seen the size of that daft sod? That thing ain't gonna get you 'cross the bleedin' car park, never mind all the way to soddin' . . . wosname!'

'Buckfastleigh,' said Simon.

'I know what it's called!' He turned away. 'All right . . . get back inside!'

'I could take the other one,' offered Simon, as they traipsed back into the bar. 'He probably doesn't weigh much. It would carry both of us, I think.'

'Knobhead?' said Vinny. 'You ain't taking Knobhead nowhere. Useless little twat! Get somethin' else! This place has gotta have somethin',' he waved an arm, 'out in the middle o' friggin' nowhere!'

Simon shook his head. 'No, I'm sorry. It's like I said before: Mr. Pratt doesn't own a car. And Miss Cornwall only has a bicycle.'

'Yeah?' said Vinny. 'How come you know so much?'

'Everyone knows. Mr. Pratt never goes out. He has a fear of being kidnapped, I think. And Miss Cornwall never learned to drive. If she needs to go anywhere, someone always gives her a lift.'

'I bet they do. That right, *Miss* Cornwall? You the local bike, are ya?'

'I manage.'

'A ride for a ride, is it? That how it works?'

'Perhaps.'

'Meanin' . . .?'

'*Take it easy,*' said the voice in Jo's ear. '*No need to antagonize the nasty little sod!*' Jo shrugged, and looked away.

'What about the van?' asked Bonce. 'Me an' 'im could take . . .'

Vinny shook his head. 'I said no! Why d'you think . . .?' He clicked his tongue. 'Look, Kite comes back an' takes 'is motor, I ain't chasin' after 'im on string bean's soddin' moped, am I? You'll 'ave to take it, that's all.'

'What about 'is motor?' asked Nobbler. 'Henry wosname's?'

Vinny shook his head again. 'Tha's bait, that is, knobhead! He ain't gonna hang about long if it ain't 'ere, is he?'

'I could go on my own?' suggested Simon. 'It would be a lot quicker. If you tell me where you want me to meet your friends?'

'You're takin' him, I said! He don't know the way, does he? So you gotta make sure 'e gets there. You ain't goin' on your own 'cause you might decide you ain't comin' back. Or maybe you just comes back with the filth?'

'We'll 'ave t' walk,' observed Bonce, 'up the 'ills.'

'You better get goin', then,' said Vinny. 'Dolly'll be 'ere in a couple hours, an' you know what happens t' them as keeps 'er waitin'.'

Dolly was going to be there a lot sooner than Vinny realized, if Curly and the other drivers did as they had been told.

'You two first,' she nodded at Sid and Spider. 'Curly takes me and Boxer in the Merc. You take that lot in the wagons. And don't hang about! If we don't get there on time, you two don't come back. Got it?'

The two customized ambulances, fuel injected, turbo-charged and packed to the roof with weapons and the nastiest bunch of thugs Dolly's underworld connections could muster, set off with her lemon yellow Mercedes following along behind. It took them less than twenty minutes to reach the M25: and an hour after that they were almost a hundred miles closer to their destination. It wasn't really surprising, because traffic lights, roundabouts and hard shoulders were no obstacle when Joe and Joanna Public slowed down and pulled in at the side of the road to let them pass. It was the same tactic they had used on the night of the robbery at the British Museum when they had stolen the most valuable archaeological discovery the country had ever seen.

As the miles whipped quickly past, Dolly sat back in the soft luxury of the yellow leather interior, and smiled at the prospect of tortures to come.

'Yeah?' she said in answer to the shrill ringing of the car phone. 'Tell me something I want to hear!'

'All done, Miss Killjoy,' said a diffident voice on the other end of the line. 'Three turkeys roasted for dinner, as ordered.'

'And the giblets?'

'Can't help you there, Miss Killjoy, I'm afraid. Sorry,' said the voice. 'All the other birds had flown the nest by the time we arrived.'

'Pity,' said Dolly. 'And the trinkets I asked for?'

'Sorry again, Miss Killjoy. All sold out before we got there.'

Dolly clicked her tongue in annoyance. 'And the pictures of the barbecues? I take it you didn't forget them?'

'No, no, Miss Killjoy! Being developed as we speak. Be in the post for you first thing in the morning. I'll see to it personally.'

'OK, Bunny, see Matlock. You know where. He'll give you the balance.'

'Thank you, Miss Killjoy. A pleasure doing business with you, as always.'

'Yeah, right,' said Dolly, as she hung up.

'All done, boss?' asked Curly, over his shoulder.

She shook her head. 'Three drums taken care of, but no bodies. And Bunny didn't find the stuff.'

'We keep goin', then?'

Dolly didn't answer. She sat back against the soft leather and pursed her lips. So Bunny had torched the houses, but hadn't come up with the missing jewellery. Somehow she hadn't thought that he would. It was a shame, but the lack of bodies was even more disappointing. She had been looking forward to having another little chat with the likes of Sam Johnson, and Richard and Vicky Choat: not to mention Nobbler's mouthy slut of a daughter. She had a feeling that they hadn't been entirely honest with her the first time around. But Bunny and his boys hadn't managed to find them, so retribution would have to wait for a while.

'Funny that,' she mused, as she took out a bottle. 'Almost looks like they're all in it together. Couldn't be though, could they?' she told herself, as she filled a glass with two fingers of whisky. 'And they'll turn up sooner or later, won't they? So there'll be something to look forward to after I've finished with Kite.'

As the convoy sped west along the M4, Bunny 'Bunsen' McGinley's talent for fire lighting was causing havoc with the Essex Fire Brigade. Henry's house was the first to go up in flames after Bunny and his boys had searched it, doused it with petrol, and set a five-minute fuse. Then they'd walked casually down the garden path and climbed into a transit van with the Anglian Water Authority's logo painted on its sides. Bunny liked his little joke.

Ten minutes later, as Henry's front door was being blown off its hinges, Bunny and his boys arrived at Sam's flat. They cut the padlock and chain that Nils had installed, searched the place thoroughly, doused it with petrol, set the fuse, and sauntered back to their van.

Twenty minutes after that, they arrived at number 79 Tebbit Close, where their routine was the same as before. An hour later, yet another fire engine was rushing to the scene of a domestic blaze. All in all, it had been an excellent night for Bunny and his crew. Dolly was a regular customer who could be very spiteful if you didn't do things the way she wanted them done. But she was a prompt payer if you did a good job, and £15,000 was a satisfying return for a little over four hours work.

It was lucky for Jackie Choat that her body had a way of stirring male hormones into confusion and forgetfulness, or she would have been going up in flames with her house. As it was, Cyril Midgeley had been hooked from the moment he'd seen her come swaying down the path towards his Sierra. He squinted at her, frowned, wound down his window and stuck out his head.

'Jackie?' he called. 'Jackie Pleats? Is that you?'

She glanced at him, looked away, and would have walked haughtily on by had not something in his voice brought back sweet memories of sweaty nights in her uncle's lock-up garage in Chelmsford.

She stopped, turned, and broke into a smile. 'It isn't?' she grinned.

'It bloody is!' he grinned back.

'Sizzle! You dirty little bugger!'

'Not so little,' he winked.

As reunions went, it was brief and decisive. Jackie felt more than a little damp at the memory of the times they had shared together, while Cyril felt distinctly hard at the thought that those times might be about to be rekindled.

For a moment, he forgot about his guard duties and asked her where her 'gorgeous little fanny' was going.

She pouted. 'Town as it happens, Sizz. Why, you wanna come?'

He was out of the car in a flash. 'You know me,' he grinned. 'Jus' point me in the right direction, an' I'm off!'

They embraced, briefly.

He stood back and looked her over from head to toe.

She struck a pose and raised a knowing eyebrow.

He nodded his approval, and touched her arse with a firm hand as he opened the door and ushered her on to the passenger seat of his car.

She crossed and uncrossed her legs several times as they drove along, her short skirt riding a little higher each time.

He glanced sideways to show that he had noticed and was grateful.

'You look really great, Jacks,' he told her for the umpteenth time as they left his Sierra and headed for the centre of town. 'Really great, y'know?'

'You always was a sweet-talker, Sizz,' she grinned. 'Never could say no to you, could I? All them nights in that smelly old lockup!'

'On them cardboard boxes!'

'With me skirt up round me neck!'

'Me jeans round me ankles!'

'Me pants in your pocket!'

'On me bleedin' 'ead, more like!'

'Yeah. Dirty bugger!'

'Great, wannit?'

'Yeah,' Jackie replied, with a sigh. 'Yeah, it was, Sizz.' She pursed her lips. 'Sorry 'bout what happened after . . . y'know?'

'One day we was . . . you know? Next thing I hear you're gettin' hitched!'

'Yeah, you know how it was?'

'Mate o' mine said you was up the wosname.'

'I needed security, Sizz. Someone to look after the kiddie.'

Cyril took her by the arm and pulled her gently towards him. 'It was mine, though, Jacks, yeah: the kiddie?'

She looked down at the pavement. 'I don't know. We . . . '

'Go on,' he insisted, 'say it weren't?'

She sighed. 'Yeah,' she said, sadly. 'Yeah, it was.'

And yes, she admitted, she had felt bad about finishing with him. She still felt bad about it, in fact. But she had married Richard Choat because he'd had a steady job and could offer her and the baby a secure future. But she'd never loved him, and had never even liked him that much. He was cowardly, selfish and about as much use in bed as a concrete duvet. But he'd given her and her baby daughter a good home. Well, a clean and dry place to live in, if not exactly one filled with love and affection. And the baby had been given a good education and decent clothes and regular holidays, and . . .

'But she was *mine*, right?' Cyril insisted.

Jackie nodded, unhappily.

'You didn't trust me, then . . . that it?'

'What d'you expect with the probation and the GBH and the . . .? What was I s'posed to do? Would *you* 'ave married you, if you was me?'

Cyril nodded to himself as they walked along in silence for a while. 'So where we goin' then?'

'Bank,' she told him. 'Unlike you, Sizz, I'm gonna make a withdrawal before it's too late.'

He patted her arse as they turned into the bank on the High Street.

The amount she wrote on the check was £187,000, exactly.

'Can I ask you, Mrs. Choat,' the manager enquired, politely, 'whether you and Mr. Choat will be closing the account? There will be very little left in it after such a substantial withdrawal, you know.'

'He'll be round to get it sorted tomorrow,' Jackie lied. 'When he gets back from his business trip up north?'

The manager smiled, uncertainly. 'You don't mean . . .?' He hesitated. 'Mr. Choat *is* aware of this transaction, I take it? The account *is* in your name of course, in accordance with your husband's wishes, and it does require only a single signature, but is he fully aware of your intentions?'

'My intentions are always very proper,' she promised, batting her eyelashes and leaning close enough to make sure that he got a really good battering from her perfume and an unimpeded view down the front of her blouse.

'Only jokin', Mr. Livingstone,' she breathed, with a hand resting lightly on his arm. ''P'raps you'd like to spank me for being a naughty girl later?'

Mr. Livingstone swallowed hard, licked his lips and giggled. 'Well, if you think you really deserve it, Mrs. er . . . Mrs. er . . .?'

Jackie moved closer. 'How 'bout I come an' see you next week?' she asked, with her lips next to his ear. 'Just you and me, like? In your office?' She leaned heavily against him. 'And you can show me what you'd like to do to me if you could get your hands on my . . . *assets*!' She blew lightly in his ear. 'Or whatever you boys call 'em these days?'

Mr. Livingstone was still mulling over the possibilities as Jackie swayed out of the building and linked arms with Cyril on the way back to his car.

He had led a blameless life by modern standards, had Mr. Reginald P. Livingstone, and it really annoyed him. He wanted desperately to make up for lost time, and wondered if he had the courage for illicit meetings, the renting of a love nest close to his office, or for leaving his wife to live in disgusting sin with the deliciously provocative Mrs. Choat. The palms of his hands itched as he pondered his options.

'So,' Cyril asked, as they walked back to his car, 'where you livin' these days, then, Jacks?'

'You're kiddin' me, right?'

'What,' he frowned, 'not . . .? I thought you was visitin' or sellin' somethin' or . . . or cleanin' or . . .? I mean, you . . . in a place like that?'

'Cheek!' she cried, in mock indignation, digging him in the ribs with her fist. 'I'll 'ave you know, Cyril Midge . . .!' Her smile froze. 'What?'

'Not 79 though Jacks, ay?'
'Yeah. Why? What . . .?'
'Bugger!'
'What? Bugger what?'
'Look, don't go back there. It ain't safe!'
'What you on about, Sizz?'

When he told her, she stared at him in silence for a moment. 'You been watchin' me, Sizz? That what you're sayin', you bastard?'

He nodded, unhappily.

'What for?'

'Make sure you didn't do nothin' stupid.'

'Like what?'

'Jus' sorta stay in the house and leave the filth out o' it . . . y'know?'

'Filth? Outa what?'

'Best you don't know, Jacks,' he said, bowing his head.

She took a couple of steps away from him. 'So what's this then?' she demanded. 'You keepin' an eye on me now?'

'I dunno Jacks, honest! I didn't think. Soon as I saw you I thought . . .'

'Yeah, well you can forget about *that*, for a start!'

She turned and started to walk briskly away. 'So long, Sizz!' she said, over her shoulder. 'See you in another sixteen years, p'rhaps, eh?'

'Don't go back, Jacks!' he pleaded, following along behind her. 'Please? They're gonna torch the place tonight!'

She ignored him, and carried on walking.

He hurried past her, turned, and grabbed both of her arms in his fists. 'I mean it, Jacks!' he said, earnestly. 'This ain't some kinda joke!'

'Yes it bleedin' is,' she replied, smiling broadly. 'You know what I got in here, Sizz?' she asked, lifting her shoulder bag. 'A lot of bleedin' money, that's what! A *hellova* lot o' bleedin' money! And you know what I'm gonna do with it? I'm gonna take a bleedin' holiday. A *long* bleedin' holiday! A *permanent* bleedin' holiday!' She looked him squarely in the eyes. 'I'm leavin' him, Sizz. I'm leavin' the two-timin' little rat-faced bastard for good. An' I'm takin' all his money – *our* money! – an' all. See what the little tosser thinks about that! I had a phone call this mornin', Sizz, from a bloke callin' himself Max. "Max who?" I says. "Maximum Information Services", he says. "Your old man's shaggin' some tart called Charlotte", he tells me. Jus' like that! Charlotte Piece, he said her name was. Been bangin' her for months, he reckoned. "Gone away with her", he said. "Bollocks!" I said. "'Ave a word with your daughter, then", he says. "Hello, mum", she says. "Vicky?" I says. "Yeah", she says. "Listen mum, you gotta get out" . . .!'

'*Vicky*? You called her *Victoria*?'

'I couldn't hardly call the poor cow Cyril, could I, you daf' twallock?'

'That's me mum's name . . .'

'Well ain't that a bleedin' coincidence? I'd never 'ave guessed!'

'What, you mean . . .?'

'Shut up an' listen, Sizz, will ya?'

He shut up and listened.

'"So Vicky", I says, "what the 'ell's goin' on? I'm all right, mum", she says. "I'm with Beth. Where?" I asks. "Never mind", she says. "We're OK. Listen to what Max's tellin' ya. Sorry, but it's the truth. Get away from the house", she says. "Get out now, an' stay out. Wha's goin' on?" I says. "Jus' do it mum!" she says.

She shrugged. 'There was some other stuff about how her and her friend was all right, an' that. But you get the gist?'

'I dunno no one called Max, Jacks. I was told by . . . '

'You any good at packin', Sizz?'

He looked blank. 'Eh?'

'Got a few things I wanna take. You fancy a holiday? A long holiday? Jus' you an' me? No strings? Unless you still like that sorta stuff?'

'Still got the handcuffs, Jacks, if you're interested?'

She grinned. 'He never liked any of that, did our Tricky Dickie. Never had time for a bit of friendly spankin'. Wham-bam, thank you mam was all he was any good at. Half a minute, if you was lucky. Selfish git! Somebody'll teach the bugger a lesson one o' these days. Just a pity I won't be around to see it.'

She was right on both counts. Someone was going to teach her husband a lesson, and she wasn't going to be around to see it. But it was going to happen a whole lot sooner than she could ever have imagined. About an hour after she and Cyril boarded the ferry for Calais, in fact, on their way to what they intended would be a very long, very dirty weekend or two or possibly three, in Paris, and then on to who knew where? Jackie certainly didn't, and Cyril couldn't have cared less.

While they were toasting one another in the cocktail lounge of the *Herald of Free Enterprise*, Choat was being mercilessly threatened with buggery by a gang of willy-waving, gun-toting, scrumpy-sodden farm labourers in the back of Jack Strawbridge's horsebox as it bumped across Dartmoor. He was their little bit of light entertainment on their way to settle a few old scores with Rooter and his friends at the Green Dragon Inn. They draped a tatty bit of sheep's wool over his back, and forced him to make bleating noises to help them feel more at home. He would never understand how he'd managed to avoid being shafted by the whole lot of them in turn, but he had, and that was a blessing. A blessing that he had decided might even make him turn to religion one of these days. Even so, it would be years before he would be able to bring himself to look at a sheepskin coat without feeling queasy: and much, much longer than that before he could face a lamb chop without throwing up!

30

LA DEMOISELLE SAUVAGE

Henry was too busy trying to cope with the sense of trepidation he felt at having to venture out on to the moor alone after dark to give anything more than a cursory glance at the Oldroyds' campervan as he passed it on his way out of the car park at the Green Dragon. He gritted his teeth and pointed the Probe uncertainly towards the exit in preparation for what he hoped would be a short and uneventful drive to the Clatworthy's farmhouse.

He had mixed feelings about the making the journey, and about driving Choat's car. On the one hand, he was grateful that he wouldn't have to walk the three or four or five miles, whichever it turned out to be, that Jo had estimated so vaguely was the distance from the pub to the people she'd said would be able to repair his battered Volvo. On the other, he hoped that no one he knew (especially Ron and Sam) would see, or hear about, him driving the Probe: because if they did, he had a feeling that it was something that he would find it impossible to live down.

After edging hesitantly across the car park, skidding occasionally on the loose gravel as he pressed too hard on the accelerator or the brakes, he drove jerkily back to the place where he and Rooter had met after he'd crashed his car. He turned right at the junction, as Jo had instructed, and headed into the gathering gloom of the moor. With her crudely drawn map on the passenger seat beside him, and her instructions fresh in his mind, he felt confident that he knew exactly where he was going. He didn't, of course, and it wasn't long before his optimism began to disappear into the lowering sky. Nothing he saw as he drove along bore the slightest resemblance to anything Jo had described to him beforehand. No landmarks presented themselves, and everything looked the same, no matter which way he turned. The narrow road went endlessly up, down and around between high hedges, and it wasn't long before he began to suspect that everything *looked* the same because it *was* the same, and he had, for some time, been going around in circles.

It was the ancient standing-stone in the middle of the deeply sunk crossroads that finally convinced him that he was lost. He realized, as he gazed at it with the engine idling, that he had seen it at least twice before, albeit from a different direction each time. To make matters worse, the sky was growing darker and the fleeting landscape less distinct by the second, as the night, and the weather, closed in around him. Eventually, he was forced to admit that he had no idea where he was, where he was going, or where he had been. To complete his discomfort, it started to rain and the road ahead began to shimmer in front of his tired eyes as water flooded down the windscreen in sheets. He had just decided to stop, and try to work out how to turn on the headlights, when a set of temporary traffic lights took the decision out of his hands. He stopped the car, and sat waiting for them to change back to green.

Nothing happened for several minutes, except that the rain got heavier and the night darker, while he examined the dashboard for the switch that would turn on the headlights. He found something that looked hopeful, clicked it, and was pleased when the road ahead sprang into sharper relief. He pulled several times at what he thought was the dip switch and nodded in satisfaction as the beam dimmed or shone out brightly in response. He was about to congratulate himself on his cleverness when he noticed that the traffic lights had changed to green. He put the car into gear, released the handbrake and was about to pull away when they changed quickly back through amber to red.

'Bugger!' he muttered, as he put the car back into neutral and pulled hard on the handbrake.

He sighed, and fumbled for the overhead light to continue his inspection of the dashboard. He still hadn't mastered the heating system, and with the windows closed against the rain it had become uncomfortably hot inside the car. He flicked the controls and held his hands over the vents, but nothing he did seemed to stop a constant stream of hot air blasting into his face.

He leaned back in the seat and ran a hand across his forehead. Then he reached down and undid the top two buttons of his shirt. He had been keeping them done up so that no one would see the necklace Sam had jammed over his head the night before. He didn't go in for jewellery at the best of times, and this particularly gaudy item wasn't something he wanted to be seen wearing. He would have taken it off earlier, but it was such a tight fit that it hadn't been possible to get it back over his head without slicing off at least one of his ears. The leather thong had been too tough for him to break with his bare hands, and in his fragile condition that morning he hadn't dared to cut it with a knife or a pair of scissors for fear that he might sever a major artery in the process. As he stared disconsolately through the windscreen at the unchanging column of lights, he eased the lumpy metal beads away from his Adam's apple, and rubbed at the indentations they had made in his skin.

He yawned and stretched, and turned to glance through the side window, realizing with a shock that it had become so dark that he could barely see the hedge a few feet from the car. He shuddered at the thought that what Jo had called the Beast of Sodmire might be lurking out there somewhere, beyond the reach of the headlights, waiting for a chance to attack.

'Friends,' he muttered, remembering how Sam and Amy had bullied him into coming to this God-forsaken place for a holiday. If it hadn't been for them he would probably have been curled up in front of the telly at that moment, warm and safe with Spike purring contentedly in his lap.

'Never there when you need them, are they, friends?' he said, bitterly. 'I don't want much,' he told the windscreen, 'just someone to look after me and protect me and love me and cherish me, and obey my every whim.' He stared down at his hands. 'Actually, just someone to talk to would be nice.'

He glanced distractedly at the windscreen again, and sat up with a jerk. While he had been feeling sorry for himself, the lights had changed back to green. He put the car into gear, and was just about to pull away when they flicked from green to amber, and back again to red.

'Bugger!' he hissed. 'Bloody, sodding . . .!' He slapped at the steering wheel, flopped back against the seat and glared at the lights. It really wasn't fair! Not a single car had come his way while he had been sitting there. Not one single solitary car! He pursed his lips and narrowed his eyes in an attitude of aggrieved persecution. Then he put the car into gear, released the handbrake and the clutch, and accelerated past the lights. Almost immediately, he was forced to brake and swerve as a little red sports car shot across the front of the Probe at the crossroads beyond the lights and careered off into the night like a flock of teenage girls in pursuit of their favourite boy band.

The Probe bounced off the hedge before skidding to a halt straddling the crossroads. He put it into neutral and applied the handbrake with rather more force than was needed. Then he reached a trembling hand for the ignition key and turned off the engine.

In the silence that followed, he leaned forward to rest his forehead on the steering wheel. Then he closed his eyes, put a hand up to his throat and took a series of very deep breaths. 'Holy shit!' he muttered, in a hissing whisper.

After a while, he looked up, muttering in self-loathing. 'You stupid . . .! Jesus Christ!' he cried, slapping the steering wheel again. He leaned back. 'What the hell d'you think traffic lights are for . . . decoration?'

He was about to slap the steering wheel again when he noticed that someone was walking towards him down the middle of the road on the other side of the crossroads. He narrowed his eyes in concentration, turned on the ignition and flicked the switch on the steering column. As the windscreen wipers swished across in front of him, he realized that he was looking at a young woman whose long white dress, made virtually transparent by the rain, was pressed against her slim body, revealing white underwear beneath. Her long blonde hair was soaked against her head, and black mascara was running down her pale cheeks. But in spite of her bedraggled appearance, she walked proudly towards him, her smiling eyes apparently fixed on his face. He swallowed hard at the sudden appearance of this vulnerable apparition, and reached a trembling hand for the dipswitch to avoid dazzling her with the car headlights. When he looked up, she had almost reached the bonnet of the car. By the time he had wound down the window, she was beside him, with a hand on the doorframe, blinking her long lashes against the weight of the rain.

'Hello?' she said, brightly, her pale pink lips only a few inches from his face. 'How are you tonight?'

He tried unsuccessfully to swallow. 'Hi,' he croaked. 'I . . . '

'Going somewhere nice?'

'I, well,' he said, hesitantly. 'I . . . I'm going to the Clatworthy's place, actually. Do . . . do you know it, by any chance?'

She nodded, and pointed to the right. 'Down there? About half a mile?'

'Yes,' he said, grateful not to have to show his ignorance. 'Can I,' he hesitated, 'can I give you a lift somewhere . . . at all?'

'Oh, how lovely,' she said, with a beaming smile. 'I'll get in, then, shall I?'

He couldn't get the passenger door open fast enough.

'Of course, of course!' he assured her, leaning sideways and groping for the handle. 'Yes, do! You must be soaked!'

She walked quickly around the front of the car and climbed into the passenger seat, sitting down with a sigh and closing the door.

'You must be soaked,' he said again, glancing down at her body. 'What on earth are you . . .?' He hesitated and stared open-mouthed. An unsettling number of the buttons down the front of her long white dress had come undone, and the skirt had fallen open to reveal the tops of her tan stockings.

'How are you?' she asked, with a hand on his thigh. 'You look *ever* so hot!'

He looked up into her concerned, mascara-streaked face. 'Good God!' he thought, with a thrill of excitement, 'it's Auntie Mandy all over again!'

The memory of how he had fantasized over his so-called 'Auntie Mandy' through one entire summer – getting through so many boxes of tissues in the process that the chemist on the corner must have thought he was the sickliest kid in the village – was still achingly fresh in his mind. As a spotty eleven-year-old with a burgeoning libido he had spent many a guilt-ridden day in eager anticipation of Mandy's return home each afternoon from secondary school. From his perch in the branches of a tree at the bottom of his parents' garden, he had been able to see right in at her bedroom window. She had been five years older than him, and a world of creamy-white femininity away from his innocently pre-pubescent circle of friends. And at the mercy of his raging hormones, he had coveted her body jealously, even though he'd initially had no understanding of why. All he'd known was that his vestigial penis (hairless and cigarillo-thin) stood to attention whenever he thought of her bending over on the hockey field in her pleated skirt and bottle green panties.

She had always left the bedroom curtains open when she'd changed out of her school uniform, and even though he'd been unaware of the fact, her slow disrobing had been choreographed for his secret delight. His favourite branch had been at roughly the height of her bedroom window, and although he hadn't realized it at the time, he had been just as visible to her as she had to him. So pleased had he been with his cleverness in finding such an effective way of spying on her that it hadn't occurred to him that her provocative behaviour had been designed specifically to get him aroused. For weeks she had been using his reactions to help her develop the seductive techniques that she would use in later life to get what she wanted from all the men who were so easily swayed by the sight of a creamy white thigh or the hint of a pair of tight little white panties. Henry had merely been the first, and possibly the happiest, in a long line of testosterone-fuelled males who, she was to discover later in life, had more seminal fluid in their gonads than brains in their heads.

Fourteen years on, he could still remember in the minutest of detail exactly what she had been wearing as he'd watched from his perch on that fateful afternoon in July. First, she had removed – so very, *very* slowly! – her school tie, her white cotton blouse and her tiny, grey, pleated skirt. Then she had turned to sit on the end of her bed, facing the window in her regulation white bra and panties, with her legs parted carelessly and her knees drawn up as she bent forward to take off her little white socks. Henry had been watching intently for ten minutes, with a hand fiddling unconsciously in the pocket of his crumpled short trousers, when suddenly he'd felt an irresistible pulse in his penis and the warm, wet sensation of something liquid squirting with hair-raising strength down his leg. The sensation had lasted for the briefest of moments, but his whole body had jerked so violently that he had almost been thrown him out of the tree.

Unknown to him, Mandy had been watching closely from beneath hooded brows, and as soon as he'd started vibrating, she had lain back, with her legs thrown even wider apart, and reached down to the taut gusset of her knickers.

When he'd glanced up from his boggle-eyed examination of the sticky stuff dribbling down his leg, the sight of her lying so provocatively supine had made him come again with such muscle-twanging force that his body had catapulted him backwards off the branch and out into space.

The broken leg and sprained wrist he had sustained when he'd landed on Edgar Dare's dad's chicken hutch on the other side of the garden fence, smashing it to smithereens in the process, had been a minor inconvenience given Mandy's subsequent thoughtfulness during his long convalescence. She'd visited him every day after school while his leg had been in plaster, sitting at the end of his bed, sucking a lollipop or stick of rock, with her short skirt riding up her tanned thighs and her gleaming white knickers displayed for his shamefaced, hand-twitching pleasure. It had been a toss-up, both literally and metaphorically, which of the three had been the stiffer throughout that long, hot summer: his cigarillo-thin penis, the plaster cast on his leg, or the unwashed, semen-soaked football shirt he'd kept hidden under his bed.

Two months after his recovery, his frustrations had finally gotten the better of him, and he'd plucked up courage enough to creep into Mandy's back garden under the cover of darkness to fondle her coveted underwear where it hung on her mother's washing line. He hadn't meant to steal anything. All he'd wanted was to touch something the memory of which he'd hoped would lift his sexual fantasies to new and more pleasurable heights. Just a frisson of Mandy's femininity, perhaps, in the hope that it would give a little extra lift to the lonely hours of what the book his embarrassed mother had given him in place of a more informed education about sex had referred to, inexplicably he'd always thought, as 'self-abuse'.

He'd stood transfixed in the moonlit garden, with his eyes bugged out on stalks and his penis the girth and rigidity of a Biro. He'd been reaching up on tiptoe, with a pair of panties pulled down to his nose, breathing in imagined traces of Mandy's femininity, while he'd pumped his enthusiastic little dick for all it was worth. Paradise had been rapidly opening Mandy's soft thighs to his greedy imagination as he'd stood with his right elbow vibrating rapidly and his eyes glazing over with the look of a hypnotized trout. Then, just as he'd been about to ejaculate into the flowerbed, the backdoor of Mandy's house had opened to reveal her pyjama-clad father silhouetted against the kitchen light.

Turning towards him in horror, Henry had been too late to suppress the vigorous churning in his loins. And as his short life had flashed in front of his panic-stricken eyes, his unabashed penis had begun squirting into the delphiniums what had felt like gallons of spunk.

Mandy's dad, unaware of the sprinkler activity happening amongst his perennials, had thrust a hairy paw down the front of his pyjama trousers to scratch thoughtfully at his low-hung, middle-aged balls.

Henry meanwhile, had been trying desperately to force his spitting erection back through the zip fly of his trousers in preparation for running like hell. In his anxiety to bring both hands to bear on the problem, his fingers had become tangled in Mandy's panties, pulling them down until they'd snapped free of the clothes peg holding them in place. The washing line, and its cargo of freshly laundered smalls, had immediately rebounded into the air like a length of spring-loaded bunting at a wind-tossed village fete. To Mandy's drunken father, standing under the back porch with his dirty fingernails locked into the matted hair of his scrotum, this sudden semaphore message in his wife's and daughter's most intimate items of clothing had been like the proverbial red rag to a bad-tempered bull. As the bouncing line had continued to wave its frilly burden with indecent provocation at his neighbour's brightly lit kitchen windows, he had grasped its significance at once, let out a blood-curdling roar of disgust, and, with murder in his beery-eyed face, lurched down the back steps towards the garden path bent on revenge.

Luckily for Henry – bug-eyed and open-mouthed with his erection caught in his hastily part-zippered fly – Mandy's father had drunk his customary eight pints of stout that evening, and had failed to get his bearings in the dark. Staggering into the garden, he'd stubbed his slipper-clad toe on a concrete gatepost, hopped sideways off balance in his drunken agony, knocked over the dustbin with a clatter, and toppled facedown into its contents. Under cover of the resulting confusion, with his arse sticking out and his fingers tugging at his zipper-trapped dick, Henry had made good his escape.

Aware that a cloud of suspicion had been hanging over him, he had stayed well away from Mandy and her furious father for months after that. But any guilt that he might have been feeling had been more than adequately compensated for by the pair of trophy panties that had remained wrapped around his wrist as he'd fled into the night. It had been five years later, at his sixteenth birthday party, that one of his fantasies about Mandy had finally come true. She had trapped him in the bathroom and pointed out – cruelly he had thought at the time – as she'd pinned him against the sink and slipped her hand down the front of his jeans, that the pair of purloined knickers that he had been guarding so jealousy had actually belonged to her mother.

'Well, yes,' said Henry, coming back to the present. 'I . . . it's the heating, you see? And I can't find the . . . ' But his throat seemed to slam shut as his voice tailed off into silent embarrassment.

'Never mind,' said the girl, patting his leg. 'I'm sure we'll be fine.'

'Where . . . *eh-hem*!' He swallowed, and started again. 'Where did you say you were going?'

'With you,' she said, pointing ahead. 'You do want to take me, don't you?'

'Oh, yes!' he nodded. 'Oh, that's . . . that would be . . .!'

'It's so *cold* out there. And so *dark*, isn't it?' she said, shivering and hugging herself. 'And I get so *frightened* on my own at night, don't you?' Her breasts jiggled provocatively as she shivered, and her split dress rode even higher up her stocking-clad thighs.

'Well, er . . . *hah-hah*!' he laughed, 'I don't know about that!'

She turned to flutter her eyelashes at him. 'But it's so *warm*, and so *cosy*, and so *private* in here, isn't it?' she sighed. 'And we can look after each other, can't we? You don't *mind* taking me, do you?'

'Do I . . .? You must be . . .? No! No! I mean, yes . . . that would be . . .'

She nodded towards the windscreen. 'It won't take us long, will it?'

'Won't it?' he said, dazedly. Then 'Oh, no! No, no, I see!' as he caught her meaning. 'Yes of course! To get to . . .!' He pointed at the road ahead. 'Yes, and you must be . . .? I bet you can't wait to get out . . .?'

He turned away and fumbled for the ignition keys to cover his confusion.

The engine roared into life as he pressed too hard on the accelerator pedal.

'Sorry,' he said, cringing against the whine of tortured metal. 'Sorry! It's not my car you . . . I mean, I borrowed it. I didn't steal . . .'

'Will they have room for us to stay the night, do you think?' asked the girl as the Probe lurched off down the road.

'For the night? You and . . .? Don't you think we ought . . .?' He swallowed hard. 'I mean, I . . . I'm Henry, by the way. And . . . and you . . . you are . . .?'

'Magdaline,' said the girl. 'But most people just call me Mandy.'

He nodded, dumbly. 'Really? Mandy? That's . . . I used to have an aunt called . . . ' He cleared his throat. 'Yes, but that's not . . . I mean, do you . . . do you live around here, er, Mandy? And . . . what were you doing out there in the . . .? You must be wet . . .?' He glanced down at her body in the dim light from the instrument panel as the words of a Meatloaf song flashed into his head. 'Though it was cold and lonely in the deep, dark night,' it ran, 'I could see paradise by the dashboard light!'

He glanced quickly at her face, and smiled an apology for the lustful thoughts running chaotically through his mind. 'I'm sorry, I . . . '

'*Look out!*' she cried.

The car thumped over something and bounced along the grass verge.

He braked hard, and skidded the Probe to a halt.

'What?' he asked. 'What was it?"

'Oh, dear,' sobbed the girl.

'What? What did I hit?'

She didn't answer, but sat with her hands to her face, sobbing, softly.

'It's alright,' he said, leaning across to touch her shoulder. 'Don't worry about it, I'll . . . Was it an animal?' he asked, tearing his eyes away from her legs to gaze over his shoulder at the back window.

'It's not your fault,' he said as she sobbed, 'I should have been watching where I was . . . ' He glanced over his shoulder again. 'Was it a dog? A fox? What? Never mind,' he said, patting her wrist. 'I'll . . . I'll go and have a look, shall I? Yes. That's what I'll do. You just . . . I'll go . . . You just . . .'

He reached across to the glove compartment, and took out the torch he had seen there earlier. 'It's all right,' he said again, as he opened the driver's door. 'It's not your fault. Really it isn't! I'll just go back and have a look. You stay here and . . . I won't be long.'

He got out of the car, grateful that the rain had almost stopped, and walked back along the road, shining the torch across the tarmac and into the hedges as he went. Nothing he saw resembled an animal, living or dead.

He had just turned to glance back along the road at the Probe, when he tripped over something and fell sprawling across the grass verge.

Feeling foolish, he got quickly to his feet and rubbed his hands down the front of his jeans. Then he turned and shone the torch at the ground.

There was something in the grass just ahead of him.

He took a step towards it, wondering what horribly mangled corpse he was about to find.

He played the torch over it, and peered at it.

Then he knelt for a closer look.

He didn't recognize the thing at first. But when he pushed the grass aside with the end of the torch, he realized with a wave of relief that what he was looking at was the stump of a telegraph pole that had been sawn off about six inches above the ground. He smiled at it, and stood up.

So, he thought, Jo had been telling the truth about these Clatworthy people after all. But why had Mandy been so upset? What had she seen, or thought she had seen? He turned and played the torch over the road, and the hedges, and the grass verge. But he saw nothing that resembled a body.

'Funny,' he muttered, as he walked back to the car, 'why would she get so upset about a stump? Still, she'll be pleased to know that nothing's been hurt.'

There was sudden crack of thunder. He flinched and hurried back to the car. But when he got there, Mandy had gone.

He shone the torch along the road in both directions, and called her name.

There was no answer.

He shone the torch inside of the car.

It was empty.

He called her name, again.

Still there was no answer.

Suddenly, he felt very uncomfortable. Suddenly, he had to face the fact that he was alone in the middle of nowhere; and a very dark, very wet, very inhospitable, and very, very weird nowhere it was, too!

The girl's disappearance was just the latest in a long line of strange things that had been happening to him all day. Things like the homicidal football supporters who had chased him halfway across the country for no apparent reason, and the strange burning man who had tried to throttle him after he'd crashed his car. Then there were the heavily armed police officers with their massive dog-bitch-thing, Boadicea, sitting in Choat's passenger seat, and Choat's odd behaviour pissing in his petrol tank and rambling on about being chased. There was Charlotte Piece at the filling station throwing a bucket of sand over him and babbling on about a lot of people who hated his guts. Now he had met, or had imagined that he had met, an exotic and oddly familiar young woman who had appeared out of nowhere, metamorphosed into someone from his past life and his most erotic fantasies, and then vanished into thin air as if she had never been. To top it all, he had been knocked senseless no less than three times in the past twenty-four hours! He looked around and wondered if perhaps the blows to his head were beginning to take their toll on his sanity. Or perhaps, even worse, that he had gone out of his mind some time ago and was only now beginning to appreciate the fact.

'Perhaps,' he muttered, 'I'd better get the hell out of here!'

He shivered as a sudden prickling sensation between his shoulder blades made him whirl around and shine the torch at the hedge.

He could see something there, only a few yards away, at about head-height, half-hidden by the swaying branches of a tree. Despite his unease, he took a couple of halting steps towards it, shining the torch at the thing and squinting against the glare reflecting from the wet leaves.

As he drew closer, he realized that what he was looking at was a brass sign fixed to a granite pillar. 'The Stone Dancers', it read. Set back from the road were two wide stone columns. He was looking at a gateway with wrought iron gates standing open and a roughly metalled driveway leading down into the darkness under a dense cluster of trees. He remembered what Jo had told him about the entrance to the Clatworthy's farm.

'You can't miss it,' she'd said. 'Stone gateposts; big iron gates; and a sign saying The Stone Dancers. Go down there, and they'll take care of you. But stay in the car 'til you get there. You never know what might be lurking in the bushes at night. And don't go talking to any strangers. You get some very odd people wandering around the moor after dark.'

He shivered and hurried back to the car.

He got in, slammed the door and locked it.

He started the engine, and reversed back towards the gates.

He waited: telling himself that he had no choice but to go in.

He didn't like the look of it one little bit. But staying out on the moor on his own in the dark was even less appealing.

He took a deep breath. 'Oh well,' he said, with an unconvincing attempt at levity, 'what the hell!'

He turned the car through the gateway and disappeared into the darkness under the trees.

Almost as soon as the Probe's rear lights had vanished into the gloom, there was a flash of light on the road near the gateway, and a burning figure materialized out of the air. It slapped at the flames licking its body, turned quickly through 360 degrees, glanced at its smoking wristwatch, looked up at the sky, and screamed: 'Stampeasy, you bastard! Why're you doing this to me?'

* * *

'That's him, isn't it?' said Henry, excitedly. 'The one who dragged me out of my car?'

The hooded figure nodded. 'That is correct.'

'What does he want? And where does he come from?'

'Those and other questions will be answered in due course, Henry, as I have told you several times already. Please be patient. It is better that your story should unfold in its proper chronological order.'

Henry wasn't listening. 'And who's this . . . Stampeasy, was it?'

'That too is . . . '

'He's a time traveller, right?'

'No, Stampeasy is . . . '

'I meant the burning man. He's a time traveller, right?'

'He is also a time traveller. However . . . '

'And he's still after me, isn't he?'

'Yes he is. However . . . '

'So that's why the colonel and the lieutenant and the drones are here? To protect me from him?'

'Not exactly, no. Neither the burning figure nor Professor Stampeasy can harm you here. The colonel and his squad are . . . '

'How do you know that for certain?'

The figure sighed. 'I realize that this is difficult for you, Henry, but . . . '

'You said "professor" just now.'

'Yes, but that is irrelevant. It would not help you to regain your memory more quickly, or indeed, with any greater degree of accuracy, if we were to start shifting backwards and forwards willy-nilly through your recent past in search of answers to questions of that nature. On the contrary, I believe that to do so would almost certainly cause you more problems than it could possibly solve.'

'Yes,' sighed Henry, irritably, 'but what *exactly* does that mean?'

'I do appreciate something of the difficulties you are experiencing. But you must try to understand that your memory has been corrupted by an accidental journey through time. And not just any old journey through time, either, but an unscheduled shift of almost two thousand years. That is a jump of significant proportions for anyone. And its effects will have been much more disorientating for you because you weren't prepared for it in advance.'

'Yes, and why was that?'

'Excuse me, Mr. Kite,' said the lieutenant, appearing suddenly next to Henry's chair, 'but would you care for a cup of tea?'

'What?' said Henry, turning towards her.

'I think it would help you to relax.'

'Er, umm, no,' he said, absently, waving her away. 'I mean,' he added, turning back, 'no thank you!'

He turned to the hooded figure. 'I don't see . . . '

'It is one of Miss Cornwall's favourite recipes,' said the lieutenant, proffering a cup. 'She makes it herself from ingredients she grows in her herb garden at the Green Dragon Inn.'

'No, really!' said Henry, shaking his head. 'I don't really drink . . . ' He hesitated and turned towards her. 'What did you say?'

'I think it might help you to relax.'

'Not that bit! The bit . . .! Did you say . . . Miss Cornwall?'

'You better believe it, buddy!' said Titus, stepping out from behind the lieutenant with a plate of biscuits in his hand. 'And listen, you never told me she looked like *that*! You lucky old bugger!'

'You've met her?'

'Do owls shit in the trees, buddy? Listen . . . '

'Not now!' hissed the hooded figure, waving him to silence.

'Why does he keep saying that?' asked Henry. 'And what about him anyway? He hasn't lost his memory, has he? One or two of his marbles, perhaps, but that must have happened years ago.'

The hooded figure held up a hand just as the little Ancient Briton was about to reply. 'Our young friend's situation is different from yours, Henry. It is true that he has travelled relatively widely in time, yes. And that he has spent a considerable amount of that time in what, from your perspective, is both the past and the future. But he has not been in control of that activity. I have, or Blossom or the lieutenant have. And we use a technology that is more sophisticated than the one that brought you here. So that he has been given more protection from the potential ravages of the process than you were given when you made your unscheduled journey into the past. And it would do you no good at all if we were to attempt to unravel the tangled confusion that is your memory by picking up its thread in the middle of the story, as it were, rather than at what we might call "a loose end". We really *must* follow it through in its original sequence to its chronological conclusion, rather than go breaking into it halfway along its length and have to return to tie it back together again later. Your memory would become even more fragmented than it already is. Do you see?'

Henry sighed. 'If you say so.'

He turned and gestured at the cup in the lieutenant's hand. 'Jo made this, you said? There'd be no harm in giving it a try, then, would there?'

'No, indeed,' smiled the lieutenant. 'An excellent choice!'

* * *

31

ROBBIE THE MECHANIC

There were times when Henry wanted to commit acts of mindless vandalism, like putting his fist through a television set or tearing up a book and incinerating its pages with a blowtorch: or just standing up in the middle of a cinema, ripping up a seat or two and yelling 'I do not believe it! I do not bloody well believe it! No one in their right mind goes into that place, on their own, at night, unarmed and with incontrovertible proof all around them that all they're going to get out of it is a very nasty case of evisceration. Not unless they've had their brains replaced by cucumber sandwiches, they don't! This film is not realistic!'

It was infuriating how all of those dumb characters, in all of those dumb horror movies, never, but *never*, had the good sense to stay away from empty houses, ancient castles, fog-shrouded back alleyways, deserted churchyards and prehistoric burial mounds. It didn't seem to matter how dark it was, or how many headless corpses and severed limbs there were strewn about the place; nothing stopped the stupid sods from going in. It never seemed to matter how loudly the thunder crashed and the lightning flashed and the wolves howled and the wind blew, or how often the distorted shadows of axe-wielding, homicidal maniacs drifted across the wall behind them: they always, but *always*, did the one thing that no one in their right mind would even contemplate, never mind actually do: they opened the door and went in! It made him want to take them by the throat and yell 'What's the matter with you, mate, can't you see they're having you on? Can't you see all they want is to get you dead? And what kind of role is this for a serious actor? It's not the Royal Shakespeare Company, you know, with noble friends gathered around your deathbed praising your valour. No women weeping and gnashing their teeth – well, one or two in the wardrobe department who've got to get all that fake blood out of your costume ready for the next scene, perhaps. No children sobbing; no fanfare of trumpets, no posthumous laurel wreaths; no sun sinking slowly in the west to the sombre tones of the Last-sodding-Post! All you're going to get out of this lot, mate, is your arms pulled out of their sockets, your skull caved in, and your useless brains sucked out through your nostrils. You're just another second-rate wannabe, doing what second-rate wannabes do best: *dying*! No one's gonna mourn you – except, perhaps, your doting mother – you know that, don't you? And it's no good listening to that geezer with the camera lens hanging round his scrawny neck, because he's just a bleedin' throwback with a vested interest. He doesn't give a toss about your motivation. All he cares about is bums on seats. It's no good sitting in a corner trying to work out why your character is behaving like such an all-round dickhead. Old baldy doesn't give a monkey's gonad about any of that. He certainly isn't going to give a flying doodah when the critics pan you for being such a useless tosser and taking a role that required zero acting ability and still left you looking like an incompetent twat. It doesn't matter to him if you never get another job. So just tell him to stuff his sodding picture, and maybe then the rest of us can go home and get a decent night's sleep. At least we won't have any more of that stupid looking-under-the-bed rubbish, and leaving the light on, and pretending we really *wanted* to stay up all night in case we missed a total eclipse of the moon, or the dawn chorus, or the sun rising in glorious Technicolor over the gasometer at four in the sodding morning. I mean, what is it with you? Don't you care that people all over the world will be going without sleep for days and nights on end, arguing over precisely how they would like to see you meet your maker for being such an incompetent wally? Not only couldn't you see that pile of bloodless cadavers you had to wade through to get to that oh-so-bloody-convenient telephone box in the middle of sodding nowhere, it was blindingly obvious to the rest of us that you couldn't act your way out of a wet paper bag, either, even if you'd had a script decent enough to let you give it a try.'

Why couldn't they see that they were going to die whatever they did? If the thing with the eight-inch fingernails didn't stab the brainless sods in the back when they weren't looking, some critic with a poisoned pen definitely would.

He sighed: perhaps that was the answer to it all, really: they didn't have a choice. They were damned whatever they did: just as he was now. He could stay where he was, in a car in a dark, damp, scary forest, alone at night in a thunderstorm, or he could turn around and go back out onto the moor, also in a car in a dark, damp, scary thunderstorm, and with the possibility that the Beast of Sodmire was lurking out there somewhere ready to tear him apart, limb from limb, the moment he showed his face. Then again, he could keep going until he got to the Clatworthy's farmhouse: probably equally dark, damp and scary in a thunderstorm, and with no guarantee that the Beast of Sodmire wasn't waiting to kill him there instead. Of course, there was always a chance that the Clatworthies would turn out to be a perfectly ordinary, warm-hearted family of decent country folk with nothing more irksome about them than that horribly annoying West Country whine that everyone in these parts seemed to have perfected to a blackboard-scraping nicety. And even if they *were* strange, misshapen throwbacks from some savage, disease-ridden, dark, damp, medieval period of history when people with warts were burned at the stake and live virgins were even thinner on the ground than they were in Billericay, they would still be real, live, warm-blooded human beings, wouldn't they? And if there was one thing he really wanted out of life at that moment, it was someone to talk to; someone to take the scariness away; someone to tell him that everything was going to be all right. And he would be happy to hear it, even if it was uttered in the sort of accent that made him want to smack the speaker in the back of the head with a mallet.

He sighed again and tried not to feel too terrified as he drove the Probe down the narrow, rough-hewn track between high, moss-covered stone walls towards what he hoped, and feared, would turn out to be the Clatworthy's farmhouse. There was a sudden flash of lightning behind him, followed immediately by a crackling roll of thunder, and the densely packed trunks and swaying branches of the trees on either side of the track were cast instantly into stark relief against the utter blackness of the forest beyond.

'This is not a lot of fu-un!' he warbled to himself in a singsong voice as he crouched terrified over the steering wheel. 'Not a lot of fu-un at aw-alll!'

The trees seemed to crowd in on him from all sides in what he felt was an altogether unnecessarily threatening manner, bending low with their gnarled, lichen-hung limbs swaying down in the wind and rain like so many fossilized spider's legs clutching at him, slapping against the windscreen and scraping across the roof of the car as he passed. It was all a bit too much like a scene from one of those second-rate horror movies he so detested, and the typically clichéd prelude to the gruesome dismemberment of a hapless traveller. He only hoped that he wasn't about to star in the sequel to *The Night of the Bloodsucking Zombies*, or even the prequel to *Alien 28*.

What would he find when he reached the end of the driveway, he wondered; a collection of ramshackle farm buildings clustered around a wattle and daub hovel with rusting lumps of agricultural machinery and emaciated livestock glued to the front yard in a shin-deep slurry of bovine faeces and mud? A bunch of congenitally barefooted, slow-witted, dungaree-wearing, axe-wielding, rustic cannibals, freshly reincarnated from the set of John Carpenter's *Children of the Corn*, lurking in the undergrowth and desperate to whet their whistles on the blood of a freshly slaughtered tourist? He shivered at the thought of how their vacant faces would look staring down at him as he lay on the ground spurting blood from sundry severed arteries. Dead-eyed, they would be, beneath jutting, low-slung foreheads, with fist-like cheekbones, hair-sprouting pug noses, gap-toothed mouths, long arms, lump-knuckled hands, lump-knuckled feet, ragged, ill-fitting clothing, and that oh-so-bent-shouldered, stiffly shambling, knife-toting, scythe-wielding, body-dragging, offal-munching excuse for upright bipedal perambulation! The one thing he knew for certain was that they wouldn't be normal: not even remotely so, if the approach to the place was anything to go by.

The house, when he finally saw it, did nothing to bolster his confidence. It was large and dark and in an architectural style that could only have been described as Hammer House of Horror Transylvanian. It loomed up at him out of a rising mist as he approached, its high walls like battlements towering wet and black and massive-blocked above his head, curving forward from the left and the right to meet him, then rising into an imposing stone archway with iron-studded, wooden gates standing open and pointing the way to a starkly-lit courtyard beyond. It was definitely not the humble country cottage he had been expecting.

He brought the car to a halt and sat for a moment unmoving, wondering whether he ought to go in, or do the sensible thing and run for his life. It wasn't that he believed in the Beast of Sodmire, he told himself, not really, not as such: because that was just an old wives' tale, wasn't it? He had heard of the Beast of Bodmin, and had even seen pictures of it: photographs and video recordings. It was a big black cat, wasn't it? A puma, or a jaguar, or a leopard, or some other type of feline that he wouldn't know from a hole in the ground if it popped up in front of him and ripped out his liver. But then, there was the question of scale. How could he be sure that all of those pictures weren't fakes? Just snapshots of someone's ordinary moggy let loose in the wild and filmed from a distance with a deliberately shaky camera, like those supposed pictures of bigfoot that were just someone's mate in a gorilla suit, stumbling around in the shrubbery at the end of a suburban garden.

But what if the Beast of Sodmire wasn't a fake? What if it was real and could take human form? Surely then this was just the sort of place he would expect to find it, crawling headfirst down the wall from a high window or emerging with a bloodlust from a dirt-filled box in the dungeon. He had no way of knowing if the building had a dungeon, but he reckoned that if looks were anything to go by it must be riddled with the damned things.

As he drove around a corner at the end of the drive he passed a stone sculpture in the middle of an unkempt circle of lawn. The headlights threw it into harsh relief as he stopped the car and tried to steel himself to go on. He had no option, he kept telling himself, he couldn't just sit there waiting for someone, or some *thing*, to come out and ask what he thought he was doing.

He took a deep breath and inched the car forward under the brooding mass of the archway. The sculpted figures seemed suddenly to come to life and dance in the headlights as he drove past.

He smiled, tightly. 'The Stone Dancers!' he muttered. 'At least something around here makes some kind of sense.' Some sort of Bacchanalian orgy-type sense, he decided, as the granite figure of a woman, her granite skirts held high above her granite waist in alarm, stood on a rough-hewn granite plinth surrounded by a crowd of naked, granite men prancing along with their granite extremities pointing rigidly up at the sky. He turned past it with a shiver, and headed towards an arched entrance that seemed to lead to an inner courtyard. The bright light he had seen earlier was pouring through this opening. He drove towards it, passed slowly under the arch, and rolled the Probe to a halt. The rain had stopped completely, and he could see that the light was coming from four floodlights on tripods under an awning, like huge standard lamps without shades. Arranged in a square, they bathed the centre of the yard with something like daylight. Between them, racked up on an inspection platform, was an odd-looking vehicle, a bit like a Range Rover, a bit like a bulldozer, and a lot like a giant Swiss Army Knife on wheels.

After a moment's hesitation, he switched off the engine, got out of the car and walked towards the vehicle, conscious all the while of the sound of metallic taping coming from somewhere out of his line of sight. As he got closer, he saw a man in dirty overalls bending forward under the bonnet of the vehicle. He must have heard Henry's footsteps, but he didn't look up.

Henry coughed to attract his attention. '*Eh-hem*! Hello? Excuse me . . .?'

There was no response.

'Excuse me?' he said, more loudly. '*Eh-hem*? Hello?"

'Yeah?' said the figure, continuing to work under the bonnet.

'I'm looking for a Mr. Clatworthy? A Mr. Mervyn Clatworthy? I was told he would be able to repair my car?'

The mechanic carried on working. 'We don't do Probes,'

'It's not a Probe. It's a Volvo. I . . . '

'You a mechanic then, are you?'

'I . . .er, no, I'm . . .'

'Just as well.'

'Sorry?'

'If you can't tell a Volvo from a Ford, you'd never pass your City & Guild's,' said the man. He glanced over his shoulder. 'Oh, I don't know though. Anyhow, you drive a thing like that you don't need help from me.'

'I don't?'

'What you need is a psychiatrist.' He turned around. 'Or a plastic surgeon.' He seemed to be in his mid-twenties, but his face was smeared with so much dirt and grease that it was hard to tell. 'The one to help you overcome your understandable sense of sexual inadequacy: the other to add a couple of inches to your dick if that doesn't work.' He nodded, and looked down at the engine.

'Yes,' said Henry, moving closer. 'But it's not my car. I wouldn't drive one of those things if you paid me.' He frowned, and glanced over his shoulder at the Probe. 'Well, I would, if I had to. I mean, I did, didn't I? There it is. I drove it. Of course I did. But I didn't have a choice because . . . '

'Let me guess,' said the man, turning towards him. 'You only drive it 'cause the extra power lets you get out of trouble quickly if you have to. Right?'

'Sorry?'

'And you would have bought a BMW, only you're single and you thought it would be more environmentally friendly to buy a car that uses less fuel?'

Henry was beginning to get the drift. He smiled. 'Actually, no, I . . .'

'So you *are* married, and you *do* have a bum-wiper, because you need something big to get the whole family into, even though all you've got is a Yorkshire Terrier with a pretty pink bow between its ears, and a wife with nothing at all between hers?'

Henry grinned. 'Not exactly.'

'So the Probe's in *her* name, but *you* drive it because she uses the bum-wiper to take the kids to school. The wife, that is, not the Yorkshire Terrier. Or she would if you had any kids, but you don't because she keeps getting headaches whenever she's not off screwing some bum-wiper salesman in a layby on the M25. The wife that is, not the Yorkshire Terrier. Although, from what I've heard about Essex girls . . .'

'How do you know I'm from Essex?'

The man waved a torque wrench at the Probe. 'Registration?'

Henry nodded. 'Yes, I see. But . . .?'

'So you're twonkin' anything that hasn't actually got "I am HIV positive" stamped on its forehead. But only because you think tattoos are just too gauche for words: not because you're afraid of catching the disease. And you drive the Probe because it saves space in the driveway, and she drives the bum-wiper because she never knows when she might have to go off to the shopping mall with a coven of her shiniest best friends. She would rather drive a little red – sorry, *green*! – environmentally friendly hatchback if it wasn't for the fact that she wouldn't be seen dead in anything that isn't True Blue. She does vote Tory, of course? And besides, she knows men don't respect women in small cars, or men with small dicks, especially if they happen to be their own, and since she is determined to be treated as an equal in a male dominated world, and already earns more than most of the men in it after studying for one whole night a week, for two whole consecutive weeks, to qualify as a colour co-ordination consultant serving all those power-dressing androgynes in the City of London, she figures that she has the right!' He frowned. 'How did I do?'

'Pretty good, I imagine,' smiled Henry. 'But that really *isn't* my car so it's hard to tell. Mine really *is* a Volvo. But it got a bit smashed up, and someone pissed in the petrol tank.' He shrugged. 'The same person who lent me the Probe, as it happens. Funny old world, isn't it? Anyway, people kept telling me that Mervyn Clatworthy was the only person within a twenty-mile radius of wherever I was who could fix it, so here I am. Sorry it's late: I got a bit lost.'

'Most people do. Anyhow, you've been lied to my friend.'

'I have?'

'Yep! Merv Clatworthy couldn't fix a pair of roller skates, much less something with an engine, gearbox and transmission.'

Henry was crestfallen. 'Really?'

'Not so much as a Dinky Toy, I'm afraid.'

'I see.' Henry gazed disconsolately at the ground. 'In that case . . . '

'I can, though. Just so long as it isn't nuclear powered.'

Henry started to laugh, but stopped short when he realized that the young man wasn't joking. 'Er, well, no, it . . . '

'We haven't got the inspection chambers anymore, you see? Can't get the lead, or the suits. And I was never very keen on having my goolies fried in the name of automotive engineering.'

'No, I can see how you wouldn't be.'

The young man wiped his hands on an oily rag, and trust one of them forward for Henry to shake. 'Robbie Clatworthy,' he said. 'Son of Magic Merv.' He gazed at the Probe. 'So where's this Volvo of yours?'

'Henry Kite. Pleased to meet you. It's in the car park at the Green Dragon Inn. Someone called Rooter towed it there for me with his tractor. I don't suppose you know him, by any chance, do you? Rooter, I mean?'

Robbie nodded as he continued to wipe his hands on the rag. 'You better come in. You can leave that where it is: no one's gonna nick it. By the way,' he added, in a conspiratorial whisper as he opened a door at the side of the building, 'I ought to warn you, the natives can get a bit restless round here sometimes – the family? Don't let it bother you, though: they're harmless enough most of the time. Except Lance, of course. And Gavin. And I wouldn't trust Gareth or Kate as far as I could throw 'em. They're not too homicidal at the moment.' He stared off into the distance. 'Just don't like strangers, that's all.' He turned, and grinned brightly at Henry. 'I wouldn't turn my back on any of them more than you have to, though. OK?'

'Really?' said Henry, with an uncertain grin. 'Thanks, that's very . . . I'll try to remember that. By the way,' he added, in an attempt to lighten the mood, 'why do you call them bum-wipers? BMWs, I mean? I've got a friend who does it, but I never thought to ask him why.'

Robbie shrugged. 'Gotta be insecure to buy one o' them, haven't you? Trying to convince yourself you're a big boy now? Car means you don't have to look after yourself. Car does the looking after for you, doesn't it? And who looks after you best? Your mum does, right? And what does your mum do from the moment you're born?'

'Yes, I see. Fair comment.'

Robbie closed the door and leaned towards him. 'The trouble is,' he whispered, 'I'm the only sane one here. The rest of 'em's crazy as coots.'

Henry smiled nervously as they entered a large, high-ceilinged, sparsely furnished room lit by a single, naked bulb dangling from the centre of the ceiling at the end of a cobwebbed flex. The walls looked damp and mouldy, and there was no carpet, or mat, or covering of any kind on the dusty, redbrick floor. In one corner there was a pile of straw and a cardboard box where a cat eyed him suspiciously from amongst her litter of kittens, mewling feebly and clambering over each other. In the opposite corner, was a huge and ancient sofa with the stuffing pushing out of the cushions and the ends of the arms. Lying on it, watching Henry's every move with dark, baleful eyes, was an enormous dog that could easily have been the twin to WPC Evers' Boadicea. It was jet black, with a thick coat and slobbering jaws. Its teeth were yellowing and its tongue looked like a lump of diseased liver. It filled the sofa completely with its tail hanging down to the floor at one end and its chunky, leonine head thrusting over the battered, greasy arm at the other. There was an enormous bone, like the thigh of an ox, with mouldering flesh and gristle still attached, lying on the floor in front of the beast's massive head.

As Henry and Robbie started across the room towards a door in the opposite wall, the animal glanced down at its unfinished dinner, then up at Henry, and let out a deep, rumbling growl. The springs in the dilapidated sofa vibrated like distant thunder, and Henry got the distinct impression that he had just been compared favourably for tenderness and crunchability with the mouldering femur.

Robbie seemed to think so, too. He wagged a censoring finger at the giant beast. '*Unh-uh!*' he admonished. 'Eat what you got . . . greedy bugger!'

Henry grinned uneasily at Robbie. Then, as he turned back to make sure that the massive animal wasn't about to attack him, he almost collided with a shabby, wizened old man who seemed to have materialized out of the air.

'This here's Granddad,' said Robbie. 'Harmless old sod most of the time.'

Granddad shuffled forwards in a frayed dressing gown and tatty slippers, munching on his false teeth and peering into Henry's face as he came.

'Hello,' said Henry, pleasantly and in spite of the strong smell of unwashed flesh. 'Pleased to meet you.'

'Watch 'em!' hissed the old man, cocking his head to one side. 'They'm mad! All of 'em is, 'cept me!'

He peered around the room with a hunted expression, and then up into Henry's face. 'Only sensible bugger in the whole bloody place, me. Whole bloody country, come to that.'

'Yes,' said Henry, trying to avoid physical contact. 'Of course you are. Of course . . . yes, that's . . . that's . . . thank you, it's . . . '

'Here,' insisted Granddad, pressing a bladeless pocketknife into the palm of his shrinking hand. 'Take hold o' this. An' don't let the buggers get behind ya. Slit yer gizzard, soon as look at ya, most of 'em would.'

'No, I won't,' said Henry, with a fixed grin. 'That's . . . Thank you. Thank you very much.'

'Give us that,' said Robbie, taking the useless knife from his unresisting hand and dropping it into the pocket of Granddad's dressing gown as the old man shambled away. 'Told you,' he added, over his shoulder as they left the room. 'Mad as coots the lot of 'em are.'

'Is he all right, though?' whispered Henry. 'I mean, you know . . .?'

'What . . . some kinda psychopathic lunatic, you mean?'

'No, no!' said Henry, quickly. 'No! Well, no,' he added, thoughtfully. 'I mean, he isn't though, is he?'

'Nothing to worry about mind. Silly sod hasn't killed anyone for years. Forgotten how to, you ask me.'

'In the war, you mean?'

'War?'

'Yes, I thought . . .?'

'And this here's Uncle Bert,' said Robbie, as they walked towards another decrepit old man drooling down his chin in a bath chair by a window. 'Well, great uncle, really. Granddad's big brother?'

Henry smiled at the old man and nodded a greeting.

There was no response.

He was just about to turn away when a frail voice said 'And God spake unto Jedediah and said "Go smite ye the Samsonite." And Jedediah knew that it was good.'

Henry looked at Robbie.

Robbie shrugged. 'He hates luggage.'

'Ah!' said Henry. He turned to smile condescendingly at Great Uncle Bert just as the old man's bony arm whipped up from the bath chair, grabbed the beads around his neck and used them to pull his head forwards and down.

When Henry's face was level with Great Uncle Bert's mouth the old man hissed into his ear 'He hates tourists,' he said, cocking a thumb towards the door in the far wall. 'Beware!'

Henry grinned uneasily and tried to shrink away from the spittle-flecked lips and the yellowing teeth. But Great Uncle Bert was surprisingly strong and held him fast. Suddenly, as Henry grimaced and strained, the old man farted, and let go of the necklace. Henry jerked free and staggered backwards, away from the overpowering stench of bad eggs.

'Don't worry about him,' said Robbie. 'The old sod hasn't got enough energy to piss, never mind cut your throat.'

'A lot of violence in your family, then, is there?' grinned Henry as they left the room and entered a long, dark, wood-panelled corridor. 'You hear stories, don't you, about inbreeding, and that? Not here, of course! I wasn't suggesting that . . . It's just one of those things you hear about . . .'

'Inbreeding?' snorted Robbie. 'Fat chance. Impotent, the lot of 'em are. And just about as crazy as they can get without being locked up.' He lowered his voice and leaned closer. 'Only me and dad can still get it up.'

He looked quickly in both directions and leaned closer still. 'Mind you,' he whispered, 'I reckon the old sod's lying about that, too.'

Henry tried to grin, but found that his facial muscles had seized up.

'Where'd you get the necklace?' asked Robbie. 'Is it ugly or what?'

'This?' said Henry, pulling his shirt collar closed. 'It's not mine, actually. It belongs to a friend. I was just sort of looking after it for him.'

'You got anything belongs to you? Or you just go round borrowing things from people as and when? What about the jeans? They yours, or you just looking after 'em for some bugger you met in the street?'

'No, the jeans are mine: and the shirt, and the shoes . . .'

'And very stylish they look, too,' said a voice.

Henry turned to see a short man, possibly in his late fifties, standing in the doorway at the end of the corridor. He was unshaven and dishevelled. His greasy hair was flattened against his head and brushed clumsily to one side. He was dressed in a threadbare cardigan, a pair of scruffy carpet slippers and a shirt of indeterminate colour that looked in urgent need of a new collar and cuffs. His crumpled ensemble was completed by a pair of sagging trousers that had almost been denuded of what had once been brown corduroy.

'Who's this, then?' he asked, with his head tilted to one side and his eyes fixed gimlet-like on Henry's face.

'Wants his car fixed,' said Robbie. 'Some bloke pissed in his petrol tank, he reckons. Rooter's towed his car to the Dragon.'

'What about the multi? You repaired that bugger yet?'

Robbie nodded and jerked his thumb at Henry. 'Just finishing off when he turned up. His name's Henry by the way. Henry, this is Magic Merv; the bloke who can fix anything. He'll fix your car for you.' He winked at Henry, turned away, and started to saunter back the way they had come, whistling tunelessly.

'But,' said Henry, reaching out a hand towards him, 'I thought you . . .?'

'Take no notice,' said Mervyn, leaning close as they watched Robbie amble away into the gloom. 'Mad as a coot in a sack, that one is. Don't know why the bugger hasn't been locked up long before now. Right then,' he added, rubbing his hands together. 'I'll show you to your room.'

Henry's eyebrows shot up his forehead. 'Room?' he said. 'No, there must be some kind of mistake. All I wanted was to get my car fixed.'

Mervyn turned away. 'Can't go back to the Dragon, can you?' he said, as he strode off through the house. 'Couldn't find your way back, could you? And they wouldn't take you in even if you could.'

He stopped and turned to look Henry in the eye. 'And you wouldn't want to sleep in your car, would you, not with what's out there in the dark waiting to rip your throat out soon as you close your eyes?' He grinned knowingly. 'So, you'd best be staying here with us, hadn't you? Safer that way.' He grinned again. 'Don't you think?'

He turned away. 'Come on then!' he called, as he strode off down yet another dark corridor. 'And for Christ's sake try to keep up!'

32

MAGIC MERV

The massive house was old and dark, and smelled of mildewed leather. There was a layer of dust and fallen plaster over everything that crunched underfoot and skittered across the floor as they walked. The atmosphere was dank and oppressive, and there were powdery moulds and fungal growths sprouting from the walls and ceilings. Every now and then Henry's hand would brush against something wet and clammy and he would recoil in horror wishing that he hadn't watched that documentary about what a dose of amoebic dysentery could do to your bowels. He decided that if he ever got out of this place alive he would have his clothes incinerated and every last scrap of body hair removed by surgeons with sterilized scalpels. And after that he would have a shower in industrial strength disinfectant and go to sleep for a month. The place made his skin crawl. All he wanted was for one of these strange people to repair his car so that he could be on his way and out of their lives forever. He didn't care which one of them did it, just so long as it allowed him to leave this place in one piece and free from contagion. The trouble was that he didn't know how to break it to them gently.

'Look,' he imagined himself saying, 'I know it's getting late. And I realize that it's dark outside and you're probably about to sit down to your supper. But would you mind, please, just nipping across to the Green Dragon and towing my car back here to repair it first? You don't have to do much really, just straighten out the front wings and stop them rubbing on the tyres so I can drive it away. I haven't got far to go, so if you could flush the piss out of the petrol tank, it only has to hold up for about ten miles. And it wouldn't take you more than half an hour, would it? Well, maybe a couple of hours at the most. So if it isn't too much trouble, I'd be really grateful if you would just fix it now: and at least then I'd be out of your hair and you wouldn't have to go to the trouble of putting me up for the night. I wouldn't ask, only I'm in a bit of a hurry. I've got an important meeting to get to this evening. It's a family gathering, as a matter of fact. And you know how sensitive they can be, don't you? I realize that you don't know me from a hole in the ground, and there's no reason why you should go to all that trouble for a stranger. But how do you think my family must be feeling, wondering where I've got to at this time of night? Think how relieved my mother will be when her only son comes home safe and sound. I know I've just turned up on your doorstep without warning, driving someone else's car and with an unlikely story about how that same someone pissed in the tank of my car. But so what? Stranger things have happened, haven't they? I mean: some pretty weird things must have happened around here with you lot about! And where the hell do you get off being so bloody judgmental about it, anyway? I mean: look at you, for Christ's sake! It can't be long since you stopped using turnips for money. And what happened to the nit lady round here? Die of overwork, did she? Or just get snowed under by the weight of infestation? Good God man, you and your flea-bitten relatives are nothing less than a breeding ground for every bacterium, virus and parasite the human race has ever encountered, and a suppurating sore on the universe's syphilitic gonads to boot. In fact, your whole family's nothing more than a pus-ridden bunch of scabrous haemorrhoids dangling out of the arsehole of evolution, and probably a festering dung pile of congenitally maladjusted murdering bastards, as well. And if you think I'm going to spend the night in this revolting cesspit of a mausoleum you must be even nuttier than you look. Although, how anyone could ever be *that* crazy I can't even begin to imagine!'

Somehow he didn't think that such an approach would be helpful.

He frowned as he followed the old man through the humid darkness, hoping against hope that he would be able to get out sooner rather than later with the greater part of his health and sanity intact. And surely even this bunch of in-bred mutants would realize that his admiration for them was less than wholehearted, and would want to be rid of him as quickly as possible?

What little light there was came from the occasional naked bulb dangling from a crumbling ceiling at the end of an ancient, braided flex. There weren't nearly as many of these as he would have liked, and he hurried from one pale patch of sickly yellow light to the next for fear that something really nasty would happen to him if he didn't. The possibility that something just as nasty would happen to him even if he did was one that he was trying hard not to think about too deeply.

Ahead of him, Mervyn picked his way through the decaying interior with a speed and agility surprising in someone of his advancing years, and it was all that Henry could do to keep up. He always seemed to be lagging that little bit too far behind for comfort, and kept glancing over his shoulder, wall-eyed, to check that the flesh-eating demon he saw in his mind's eye wasn't just about to catch him and rip out his throat with its pitiless talons.

The further they went into the building the more apprehensive he felt. The place seemed infinite: a vast, dark labyrinth of stairways, musty corridors and half-seen rooms crammed with every sort of junk he could imagine. It felt like a bring-and-buy sale at a kleptomaniac's house. Everywhere he looked, furniture was stacked in untidy piles. There were crates of crockery and cutlery and china ornaments, and trestle tables heaped high with old clothes and hats and spectacles and jewellery. There were thousands of books and files and ledgers jammed onto dusty shelves or heaped vertically from floor to ceiling in precarious columns. As he hurried along behind the old man, trying desperately to keep up, he saw a room filled with walking sticks, umbrellas, crochet mallets and cricket bats; and then another containing only boots and shoes. In others, he saw collections of watches, and toys, and luggage, and false teeth, and stuffed animals. He even saw one containing nothing but dolls and teddy bears in what looked like every size and shape ever made. After a while, he began to wonder if perhaps he wasn't in a domestic house at all, but the vaults of some ancient lost property office where the possessions of untold generations of careless travellers had been sorted and filed and left to turn slowly to dust. Or maybe it was a vast, decaying Victorian institution where nameless unhappy souls had passed away in anonymous isolation leaving only their forgotten belongings as proof that they had ever existed? Or perhaps it had once been a military hospital, or a prison for the criminally insane? And if it turned out to have been either, he didn't doubt that, in Robbie's false-teeth-munching Granddad and the scary-eyed Great Uncle Bert (not to mention the alarmingly nimble Magic Merv), he had just met three of its original inmates. With a sudden chill, he wondered if the house had once been – was still? – a place into which luckless travellers like himself disappeared with a dreadful regularity, and from which not even their most insignificant possessions ever again saw the light of day. On the positive side, it was a bargain hunter's paradise: a place where you could find everything from a jam jar filled with assorted rusty nails and screws to a second-hand armoured personnel carrier. On the more negative side, it gave him the screaming willies!

It was while he was mulling over one or two uncomfortable questions, such as whether or not the various parts of his dismembered body would ever be found, that Mervyn led him into a room that stopped him dead in his tracks. It was like medieval banqueting hall: long, high and wood-panelled with a vaulted ceiling, an impressive granite fireplace and an incongruously welcoming log fire crackling in a huge iron grate. High above his head, the dimly seen arching beams were smoke-blackened and joined at the top of each vault by richly carved and gilded wooden bosses. Eerie shadows danced in the corners of the room and around the ancient furniture. The dark wooden floor had strips of threadbare carpet running down the middle of it and criss-crossing between ranks of grimy, glass-topped counters and display cases.

Henry blinked in the unaccustomed brightness of the roaring fire reflecting from the brightly burnished surfaces of countless weapons and gear of war hanging on the walls, standing on the floor, or lying in the cabinets. There were elaborate arrays of knives and daggers sparkling in the gloom; swords and axes, spears, maces, lances and shields, helmets, headdresses, breastplates and entire suits of armour standing singly or in groups. There were crossbows, longbows, blunderbusses, matchlocks, machine pistols, sniper's rifles, bazookas, rocket and grenade launchers, single barrelled, double barrelled and pump-action shotguns, heavy calibre machineguns, and several fan-shaped displays of handguns from flintlocks to stainless steel automatics.

Mervyn's eyes seemed to glitter dangerously as he turned with a half-smile.

'The boys got a thing about this sort of stuff,' he said, lugubriously. 'Can't get enough of it, they can't.' He bared his crooked teeth in a mirthless grin. 'I reckon they needs help.' He raised a questioning eyebrow. 'What d'you think?'

'I didn't know there were so many ways to kill people.'

Mervyn nodded. 'And the boys knows 'em all.' He pursed his lips. 'Scares the bleeding taters out o' me!'

'Remind me not to upset them.'

'Oh, you won't need reminding. Soon as you meets 'em you'll know.'

'It's not Robbie, then?'

'Robbie's got a sense of humour. This lot look funny to you?'

The collection certainly didn't look funny to Henry. And he decided that he didn't want anything to do with the people who owned it: not least because anyone who frightened this scary old man as much as the mysterious 'boys' seemed to, weren't people he wanted to meet. He turned away from the fire and came face to face with a particularly sinister suit of what he took to be Japanese armour. It was about his height, draped in dusty cobwebs, and had a snarling black mask instead of a face. He wasn't sure why, but he didn't want to turn his back on it. He tried to sidle past, took several steps backwards and stumbled against something that pricked him sharply in the ear. He flinched and swung around to find himself staring up at the gaping jaws of a massive brown bear with an iron-studded collar on its neck and razor-sharp, steel-tipped claws groping towards him. 'Damn!' he said, touching a hand to his ear and taking a step backwards. 'It cut me!'

'Always was a bit heavy-handed,' said Mervyn. 'Here, let's have a look.' He pushed Henry's hand away. 'Just a scratch. You'll live. I'll get the girl to look at it later. Can't have you dying of septic lugholes, now can we?'

Henry pouted. 'It's a bit dangerous, don't you think?'

'Not half as dangerous as he was when he were alive! In his prime he'd of ripped your head off and swallowed it before the rest of you hit the ground.'

He gazed lovingly at the massive creature. 'Course he wouldn't do you no harm now, would he? Not with that lot stuck in his gullet.' He touched the shaft of a spear sticking out of the animal's huge barrel of a chest. 'Old Lou Cornish saw to that, didn't he?'

'You mean,' said Henry, wide-eyed, 'he killed it? With a spear?' Suddenly, the wound in his ear seemed inconsequential.

'Killed it?' snorted Mervyn. 'Lou? With a piddling little thing like that? Don't talk daft, boy! Old Lou were mad, he weren't suicidal! That were an accident. Bruno were already dead, and old Lou after something a lot smaller than bears.' He lowered his voice to a whisper. 'A lot trickier, an' all!'

Henry was intrigued. 'Really?' He looked around, as if he thought the walls might be listening. 'What do you mean?'

'You met our Rooter, Robbie said?'

'He helped me with the car,' nodded Henry. 'By the way, why do they call him that? Rooter, I mean? Is it something to do with farming or . . .?'

Mervyn's eyes narrowed with obvious distaste. 'Always *rootin'* round in women's underwear, I reckon. Other people's women's underwear, come to that. Ain't a pretty picture, is it? A very naughty boy is our Leonard. Or was. Calmed down a lot since. Always had an eye for a pretty face. And one or two what weren't so pretty. Wasn't the faces he were interested in, see, was it?'

'Yes, when we were in the pub there was a waitress. Jo, I think her name was. Rooter kept trying to chat her up. I thought . . . ' He stopped, aware that the old man was frowning at him with his mouth compressed into a tight line.

'Sorry, I didn't mean . . . Please, go on with the . . . um . . . with the story.'

Mervyn sniffed. 'Yeah, well . . . he'd been having a bit of a thing with old Lou's wife, Irene, seemingly, Rooter had? Only Lou found out, didn't he?' He grinned. 'They always did, mind, the husbands? That's how come Rooter's a bit handy in a scrap. Not that he wouldn't avoid it if he could, mind – afraid of losing his looks, if you can believe it. He had plenty of practice, all the same. Most of the buggers caught up with him sooner or later. Law of averages, I reckon, when you're spreading it about as much as he did.' He pursed his lips. 'Still does, come to that.' His eyes lost their focus for a while.

Henry waited in respectful silence.

'He was up here one morning,' Mervyn continued, 'recovering from a hard night's you-know-what with Irene, when old Lou comes charging in with a shotgun and an invite to his funeral. Rooter's that is: not Lou's. Seems he'd had a set-to with Irene, and she'd told him she'd had it up to here with his boring ways, and was off with Rooter to a new life.' His eyes glinted in the firelight. 'It were news to Rooter, I can tell ya! Always was, mind: silly bugger never learned.' He grinned, and grabbed Henry's forearm in a surprisingly firm grip. 'Anyhow,' he said, turning Henry towards the door, 'me youngest's over there when old Lou comes charging in. Only a kid he was then, but he takes that bloody great gun off the old bugger as cool as you like. Only eight years old he was, and did it so neat the silly sod didn't know it'd happened.' He grunted, and laughed. 'Pissed as a fart, he was, and thought he'd dropped it. Looked all round the floor. Even stuck a hand in his pocket. Like Laurel and Hardy, it was. By the time he worked it out, the boy's chucked the gun to his brother. He's taken the cartridges out and handed the bugger to me.'

There was another long pause as Mervyn remembered the scene. 'Anyhow, old Lou was madder than a stoat in a sack, and grabs the boy by the throat ready to throttle him.' He shook his head with suppressed anger. 'I wasn't having that, was I? Not with *my* kid, in *my* house, I wasn't! I told him to let the nipper go or I'd rip his heart out with me bare hands.' He turned and looked Henry in the eye. 'He could tell I wasn't kidding. "Go on, Merv", he says, "give us it back!", meaning the gun. "I'm only gonna shoot the bugger. He deserves it, an' all. Everyone knows that".' Mervyn nodded. 'He was right. But I wasn't having it in my house. "You wanna kill him, you can do it outside", I told him. "And you can do it without this".' He shook his head. 'He didn't like that, did he? But I wasn't having shooting in my house: not 'less me or mine was the ones doing it. Course, Rooter was begging me to protect him, wasn't he? Telling me to chuck Lou out, call the police, all that old nonsense. But I told him to sort it out for himself.'

He looked Henry in the eye again. 'You do some other bugger's woman - in his own bed, mind? – I reckon you got it coming.'

Henry wasn't so sure. 'I suppose so. But you can't just go around shooting people, can you? I mean, that's murder . . .'

The old man's nostrils flared. 'That ain't bleedin' murder, is it? Bleeding pest control, that is!' He glared at Henry with a sudden, round-eyed craziness.

'You telling me you reckon the bugger weren't asking for it?'

'Well, I suppose . . . I mean he shouldn't have done it, perhaps, should he? Still you can't just go . . . '

'There's no bleeding *still* or *p'rhaps* about it!' snapped Mervyn, with a look that said the discussion was over. He took a deep breath, and fixed Henry with a menacing stare. 'I told the buggers to get outside and settle it. You could see he weren't keen on the idea, mind, Rooter? A bit too bloody knackered after shagging Irene all night, I reckon.'

He gave Henry another hard stare.

Henry tried to smile, but could only manage an expression that suggested that he was straining to empty his bowels.

'Bit too bloody pissed an' all,' continued Mervyn, 'after all day in the Dragon with his mates boasting about it. Anyhow, he made up his mind he wasn't having any, and took off through the house as fast as his spindly old legs would carry him. Lou took off after him, and the rest of us followed on behind as best we could.' He shook his head. 'What a bloody palaver that was. The boys was all right, but I was proper shagged out by the time we caught up with 'em back here. Went full-circle, right through the house and back again. Daft sods!' He paused, as if to get his breath back. 'Lou cornered the randy bugger over there, by them spears.' He pointed at a fan-shaped array on the far wall, where a spear was missing from the middle of the pattern.

Henry nodded at it, wide-eyed. 'Where there's a gap?'

'Right,' said Mervyn, turning to pat the shaft of the spear sticking out of Bruno's chest. 'This one.' He pointed across the room. 'See the one with the binding round the handle?'

Henry nodded.

'Rooter took that. So they had one each. I got here just as old Lou was taking a swipe at Rooter's head. Cut the bugger's spear clean in half, it did. Nearly took his nose off, an' all. Sort of *focused* his mind, I reckon, that did. Don't think he thought old Lou were serious 'til then.'

Henry was incredulous. 'But he had a shotgun!'

Mervyn shrugged. 'Wasn't the first time, was it? Most of 'em round here's had a pot shot at the silly bugger at least once. Still, I reckon it was the spear that did it, almost smacking him in the physog like that. Never was a good idea to hit Rooter in the face, mind. Still isn't, come to that. Too bloody vain by half, the bugger is. Gets a right cob on, anyone tries it.' He paused for a moment. 'Anyhow he backs off and grabs a big old sword off the wall.' He pointed across the room. 'See?'

Henry nodded at another empty space in an array.

'Then they really got down to it,' said Mervyn, with ghoulish delight. His eyes sparkled, and he rubbed his hands together at the memory. 'Chased all round the place hacking and jabbing and swearing and cursing and trampling the furniture. We had a hell of a job just keeping out their way, never mind stopping the buggers. Old Lou's spear's got this collar running down from the point, see?' He tapped the weapon in Bruno's chest. 'So Rooter can't cut it with his sword, can he? But he keeps hacking at it and old Lou keeps fending him off and dodging out the way. Had a longer reach, see? Jabbing and poking, and drawing blood every time he nicks Rooter's arms or his chest.' He grimaced. 'Got a bit messy round here after that.'

'It sounds horrible.'

'Damn right! There's a lot o' valuable stuff in here, and you can't have blood and guts splashed all over it, can you? Lowers the price.' He took a deep breath. 'Anyhow, it all comes to a head when Rooter gets fed up with the chasing about, and Lou catches him on the cheek with his spear.' He pointed to his own face. 'Bad it was. You probably seen the scar?'

Henry nodded.

'Course, Rooter goes berserk then, yelling and snarling – that vanity-thing again, see? And old Lou panics. I mean you couldn't blame the poor sod. He throws his spear as hard as he can and hopes for the best. But Rooter ducks and it whistles over his head and catches poor old Bruno in the gizzard. Been there ever since. Twenty-odd years, I reckon it is now.' He thought for a moment. 'Didn't stop Rooter, though, did it? He ups and charges at Lou with this bloody great sword held over his head in both hands like a dagger. Old Lou just stands there, transfixed, and pisses in his pants. I thought he was a goner for sure. So did he from the look on his face.'

'God,' said Henry, in a hushed voice, 'it must have been terrifying.'

Mervyn smiled. 'Rooter's just about to skewer the bugger, right?'

Henry nodded. 'Yes!'

'Got this damn great sword held over his head in both hands, pointing it right down ol' Lou's throat.'

'Yes! Yes!'

'Only Lou dodges out the way at the last second and takes off like a frightened rabbit. Charged right out the house and hasn't been seen since. Mind you, he only just made it. Rooter couldn't stop, could he? Bloody sword comes down like a bolt o' lightning. Missed ol' Lou by a gnat's foreskin and went straight through that armourer's block like a pickaxe through fresh liver.'

Henry turned to look.

'There,' said Mervyn, pointing. 'And that's seasoned oak, that is: a foot thick if it's an inch. Been like that ever since. Just like the spear.'

There was a long silence as Henry stared at the sword embedded in the oak slab. The visible part of the blade was in perfect condition, double-edged, unstained, and engraved with an elaborate pattern. It was about three inches wide, and half an inch thick where it disappeared into the wood. Twelve inches above the block, it was a little wider where it met what was left of the handle. A burnished knuckle guard stood out at right angles on both sides of the shaft, but the grip and pommel had been removed, leaving the handle little more than a dull metal bar ending in a roughened thread. Henry moved to touch the blade with the back of his hand, and was amazed to see his fingers reflected in it, as if in a mirror.

'How does it stay so clean?' he asked, in an awed whisper.

Mervyn shrugged. 'Beats me.'

'It's like Excalibur, isn't it? The sword in the stone, and all that?'

'Who?'

Henry felt deflated. 'Well, I just thought . . . ' he shrugged, and pointed at the sword. 'What happened to the handle? It looks kind of . . . sad like that.'

'Been that way since Rooter stuck it in.'

In spite of its ruined handle, the sword was an impressive weapon.

Henry reached out to touch it. 'Do you mind?'

'Mind what?'

'Well, I thought I might . . .? If you don't mind?'

'What?'

'I thought I could, sort of . . . try and, you know, pull it out?'

Mervyn stared at him. He frowned. 'What the hell for?'

'I don't know. It's something I've always wanted to do, I suppose. Silly, isn't it? I mean, I know it's not . . . It couldn't be, could it? It's just . . . ' He looked away and then back at the old man. 'Do you mind?'

'Get on with it, then, if you must. We haven't got all bleeding night! And mind you don't rupture yourself in the process. We ain't insured.'

'Great,' said Henry, with a beaming smile. 'Thank you! Thank you!'

He licked his lips and reached for the sword.

He grasped the handle gently at first, testing the feel of the cold metal.

Then he tightened his grip, and started to pull.

The sword didn't even seem to move by so much as a millimetre.

Mervyn shook his head, as if he believed he was harbouring an idiot.

Henry let go of the sword and wiped his hands down the front of his jeans. Then he took the sword in both hands again, tightened his grip, braced his legs against the base of the heavy oak table, and pulled with all his strength.

Still nothing happened: except that the veins on his forehead stood out in stark relief, and he had the uneasy feeling that he might have displaced a rib.

He let go of the sword and took a step back.

'Fun, was it?' asked Mervyn. 'All that yanking?'

Henry grinned and nodded with childlike satisfaction. 'I've been wanting to do something like that ever since I was a kid.'

'Really? And what d'you reckon you learned?'

'It won't move.'

'I meant the story.'

'Well, it's hard to believe that anyone could have done such a thing.'

'Even more amazing, if it was true.'

'What?' called Henry, as the old man turned and walked out of the room. 'What do you mean? Do you . . .? Are you saying . . .?'

'Get a move on!' came Mervyn's voice through the doorway. 'Or you'll be late for dinner! And our Blossom wouldn't be happy about that, would she?'

33

HUBERT AND HORACE

Hubert and Horace Naggs had never learned to ride the bicycles they pushed all the way to the Green Dragon Inn each evening at opening time. But they pushed them there anyway because it gave them something to lean on when they were staggering home at the end of the night with eight pints of Perce's cider sloshing around in their tight little bellies. While Henry was still driving in circles out on the moor, wondering why his life had to be *so* disappointing, the brothers were leaning their bikes against the wall at the side of the pub, just as they had been doing for the past fifty-odd years. When they found the front door locked and bolted against them they panicked and knocked on it with the flats of their hands, and drummed on it with their fists, and kicked at it with their muddy, steel toe-capped boots. When they got no answer, they went around to each of the windows in turn, peering in, shouting, and tapping at the glass in a desperate attempt to attract someone's attention. It was already well past opening time, they pointed out at the tops of their creaking voices, and if they didn't get an infusion of alcohol soon, Perce would have their untimely deaths from an excess of sobriety on his conscience.

'You better let them in,' Jo warned Vinny in the saloon bar. 'They'll call the police or the fire brigade or something if you don't.'

'Yeah?' said Vinny, suspiciously. 'What's it to you if they do?'

'You think I want to be in here when the police turn up, and you and the Brain of Britain over there,' she flicked her chin in Nobbler's direction, 'are trying to decide whether to shoot your way out, or just shoot us instead?' She looked him in the eye. 'Believe or not, that isn't my idea of a good time.'

Vinny was pleased that he had scared her, but told her to shut her mouth and keep quiet until the brothers got fed up and went away.

The brothers didn't get fed up, or go away: instead they re-doubled their efforts, wailing, stamping their feet, praying aloud to the god of cider drinkers, beating their chests, and threatening to set fire to the wheelie bins at the back of the building if someone didn't open the door and let them in for a pint of Perce's best. It was their life-blood, they pointed out: and the only thing that stood between them and reality, and therefore, more valuable than life itself.

Vinny got tired of listening to them eventually and untied Jo's wrists and ankles and pushed her towards the door at gunpoint with a warning to get rid of them quickly, and to do nothing stupid – like asking for help – or he would have no option but to blow her brains all over the walls of the pub.

Jo opened the front door and told the brothers that Perce wasn't feeling well and that she wouldn't be opening for business on her own so they might as well push their bicycles back home and have an early night. The suggestion had no effect on the brothers, who nodded and winked and smiled apologetically for disturbing her and asked whether she had time for a quick knee-trembler behind the bar while Perce was out of the way.

Horace grinned widely, tapped the side of his nose, and patted Jo's buttock as he and his brother pushed past her into the bar. She shouldn't let Perce's illness force her to keep the pub closed when they were around to help her out, he told her. And if she wouldn't mind just showing them where she kept the scrumpy they'd be getting on with some serious drinking while she worked out just how she could make best use of their latent talents as barmen.

Vinny didn't see the joke. He stepped out from behind the door with a scowl of disapproval, and pushed the shotgun against Jo's midriff. What did she think she was doing letting them in, he wanted to know; and where did they think they were going without his permission?

Horace and Hubert looked at him in round-eyed astonishment, turned and looked at one-another, swallowed hard in unison, and raised their trembling, blue-veined hands above their scrawny heads.

Vinny smirked his contempt. 'Not so bleedin' cocky now, are we boys?'

'I wouldn't do that, I was you,' offered Horace, with a mournful shake of the head. 'Some bugger'll get 'urt, you go pointin' guns at folks.'

Hubert nodded his agreement. 'Very nasty,' he muttered. 'Very, very nasty, guns is. Very nasty indeed.'

Vinny told them to shut their mouths and to get over by the bar before he blew their brains all over the walls of the pub.

'*Oy!*' he yelled, as they shuffled obediently backwards, 'Knobhead! Get out 'ere an' make yourself useful!'

'I'm all right,' quavered Nobbler, peering tentatively from behind the counter where he had been hiding since the brothers had begun their commotion. 'I'll just stay 'ere, then, yeah?'

'I said get out 'ere, and help me with this lot,' snarled Vinny. '*Now!*'

Nobbler shook his head, and ducked out of sight.

Vinny's eyes blazed. 'You *what?*'

'No,' came Nobbler's tremulous voice from behind the bar, 'can't!'

Vinny strode across the room towards him. '*Can't?*' he roared. 'Did you say soddin' *can't* to me, you *tosser*! You'll do what I tell ya or I'll . . .!'

'Do what?' asked Tom Hertz, rising from behind the bar and pointing the barrel of a huge stainless steel handgun at the centre of Vinny's forehead.

Vinny stopped dead, and stood perfectly still.

'Well,' said Tom, 'isn't this cosy? Tell me, are you going to put that thing down, or am I going to relieve you of ten pounds of useless fat by blowing your brains all over the walls of the pub?'

Vinny hesitated as he weighed up his options.

'Don't even think about it,' said a voice.

Vinny turned to see Gary Harmsworth standing in the office doorway, leaning against the jam and holding a pistol just as big and shiny as Tom's.

Vinny gritted his teeth. But he laid Perce's shotgun carefully on the bar without a word, raised his hands above his head and took a step backwards.

Tom motioned him into the middle of the room. Then he turned to Horace and Hubert, and nodded his thanks for their diversionary tactics.

'Played to perfection, gentlemen,' he said, 'if I might say so? I think that deserves a pint and a packet of crisps, don't you?'

Hubert and Horace nodded, and grinned, and headed for the bar, rubbing their hands together enthusiastically as they went.

'Hang on a minute, boys,' said Jo, holding up a hand.

The 'boys' stopped in their tracks, looking crestfallen.

Jo looked at Tom. 'Mind if I have a word with this one first?' she asked, nodding at Vinny.

'Don't you want to know who we are?'

'What makes you think I don't already?'

Tom pursed his lips, and nodded. 'Be my guest then,' he said, after a moment's thought. 'Only be careful: they tell me he's a nasty little shit.'

Vinny turned towards Jo with a welcoming smile. 'What's up gorgeous?' he smirked. 'Got somethin' nice for ol' Vinny, 'ave ya?'

Jo smiled. 'This,' she said, as she took the hem of her skirt in both hands and shimmied it up to the tops of her stockings.

Vinny sniggered and grinned across at Gary and Tom. 'Some of us got it,' he said, 'the rest of you can watch an' learn.'

'And *this*!' added Jo, now that she could move freely.

Her right leg whipped forward and slammed the point of her stiletto heel into Vinny's kneecap.

'*That's* for *Nora*!' she said through clenched teeth as his eyes bugged open in agonized amazement. The pain in his knee was so mind-bendingly hideous that it kept his leg locked rigidly in place just long enough for Jo to draw back her foot, take aim, and kick him in the bollocks.

'*That's* for *Morris*!' she said, as he doubled over like a folding chair snapping shut. 'And *this*,' she added, taking the shotgun from the bar and ramming the butt of it into the top of his head as he crouched in front of her, 'is from *me*!'

He pitched forward onto his face, unconscious.

Hubert and Horace clapped and cheered.

Tom inclined his head in appreciation. 'And would you like a word with this one as well?' he asked, hoisting Nobbler from behind the bar by an ear.

Nobbler flapped his hands around his head as if he was warding off a swarm of bees. 'No! No!' he pleaded. 'No, no! Please? *Please*? He made me! I didn't want to do it, honest? I didn't mean . . .!'

'Get out here,' said Jo, pointing at the carpet next to Vinny's inert body.

'No, no! Please, not me!' pleaded Nobbler.

Tom grabbed the waistband of the little man's tracksuit bottoms and half-dragged, half-threw him over the counter. He landed on his head, scrambled upright, and cowered back against the bar in a foetal crouch.

'No, no!' he babbled. 'Not me! Not me! Please? Please? *Pleeeease*?'

Jo shook her head in disgust and told him to go and untie Nora and Morris in the back room, and to be quick about it before she ripped his dick off and fed it to Horace and Hubert's prize pigs.

'Oh, arrh,' chuckled Horace. 'Loves raw willy, them pigs does.'

'Bugger I,' agreed Hubert. He grinned at Nobbler. 'Fresh testicules goes down a treat. You got any o' them on 'ee, 'ave 'ee, my lover?'

Nobbler fled from the room at a gallop.

'And then get your bony arse upstairs and untie Mr. Pratt,' Jo called after him, 'or I'll feed your balls to his goats!'

Hubert and Horace thought the whole thing was hilarious, capering about, giving each other hugs and high-fives like a couple of goal-scoring schoolboys. They would probably have celebrated all the way down to the cellars if Tom hadn't held up a hand and called for silence. He unclipped a remarkably small mobile phone from his belt, and held it to his ear.

'We've got company,' he said. 'Be here in a couple of minutes. Too many for us to take on alone, so everybody outside, quick. We'll have to leave the van for later. Sorry,' he said, as Nora and Morris came into the room. 'Gary will take you to the Jeep at the back of the orchard. I'll finish up in here.'

* * *

'More tea, Mr. Kite?' asked the lieutenant.

Henry turned towards her. 'Umm, yes,' he said, holding out his cup. 'This is really good stuff, isn't it?'

'Indeed it is, sir,' agreed the lieutenant in her liltingly, silken voice. 'Close analysis reveals that it possesses many natural healing qualities which modern medical science is only now beginning to rediscover.'

'Really?' said Henry, stealing a glance at Titus who was giving him a shut-up-now-and-talk-about-something-else signal from behind the lieutenant's back with an index finger slashing vigorously across his throat.

'So, lieutenant,' said Henry, suppressing a grin, 'what sort of things do you mean, exactly?'

'Well sir, the Ol' Sex Machine has been good enough to regale me with fascinating accounts of just how much of that wonderful ancient lore was possessed, and indeed *is* possessed in this period of history, by his ancestors, and, indeed, by the extant members of his immediate tribal group.'

'Has he really?' said Henry, glancing at the little Ancient Briton, who was standing on tiptoe, shaking both his head and a warning index finger while vigorously mouthing '*Sssh-shooosh*! *No, no, no*!' for all he was worth.

'Fascinating! That was very kind of the good Ol' Sex Machine, wasn't it?'

'Indeed, it was, sir, yes,' said the lieutenant, wide-eyed. 'Although, I feel I must confess to being surprised to learn that the shaman, soothsayer, druid, witchdoctor, magician or tribal elder of the ethnic grouping known as the Durotriges, to which, of course, the Ol' Sex Machine belongs, seemed to think that eating a bull's testicles or a wolf's penis or a bear's bladder stuffed with fresh goat's semen would be useful in restoring a flagging libido.'

'Did he really?'

'How about another biccy?' asked Titus, desperately proffering a plate.

Henry waved him away.

'Actually,' said the lieutenant, 'the shaman, soothsayer, druid, witchdoctor, magician or tribal elder was a woman, sir.'

'I made 'em meself?' offered Titus.

Henry ignored him. 'And was she laughing when she said it?'

'Well, sir, now that you come to mention it . . . '

'Hey,' cried Titus, pushing forward, 'she's a bit feisty, though, isn't she, that Jo Cornwall?'

'He has trouble getting it up, then, does he, the Ol' Sex Machine?'

'Up sir?' said the lieutenant. 'Would I be correct in assuming that you are querying Corio Boc's ability to achieve a tumescence of the penis?'

'*Whoa*!' cried Titus. 'That's . . . that's a bit bloody personal, don't ya . . .?'

'Yes, lieutenant, you would.'

'Actually, sir,' said the lieutenant, placidly, 'it would appear that when I wear something like this,' she stepped forward and did a twirl in a miniscule maid's uniform that seemed to consist of very little that wasn't either white, tight and frilly, or black, short and lacy – and reminded Henry of his Auntie Mandy in one of her tartier get-ups – 'the question is not so much can he get it up, sir, as will it ever go down?'

Titus's face lit up like a Christmas tree. 'See?' he said, stepping in front of Henry and striking a pose. 'That's what I'm talkin' 'bout, buddy!' He turned and strutted across the clearing. 'That Jack bloke's bunch o' bleedin' pansies better watch out when the Ol' Sex Machine rides in t' town!'

* * *

By the time Jack and his posse of angry 'lads' (and the one even angrier 'maid') arrived at the Green Dragon Inn, an eerie silence had descended on the place. Jack skidded his Range Rover to a halt on the gravel in front of the main entrance, and the gang staggered out of the horsebox in a rebellious rabble, pushing the terrified Richard Choat ahead of them, casually squeezing his biceps and fondling his buttocks as they went.

Jack told them to 'stop pissing about and let him go', because they had bigger fish to fry now. They agreed reluctantly and shoved Choat out into the cool evening air with a warning that if he didn't make himself scarce they would tie him to the bull bar on the front of the Range Rover, and bugger him senseless. Or as one of them put it so cheerily ''Til the spunk pumps out your cakehole, my precious!'

Choat vomited over his shirtfront, and fled shoeless into the night with his beltless trousers clutched tightly about his waist with both hands. The madmen in the horsebox hadn't actually buggered him during the journey. But they had bent him over and fondled his bum and his genitals with their filthy, callused hands, and whispered into his cringing ears full-blooded descriptions of what they would do to him if they ever got the chance. The thought of it made him throw up again as he stumbled into the gathering gloom at the back of the pub, where he fell over a stone wall in his haste to get away and landed on top of Horace Naggs, crouching in the shadows beyond. Hubert, Tom, Gary, Nora, Morris, Jo and Perce were there with him, waiting for a chance to make good their escape. Choat screamed in terror as Horace grabbed him and tried to hold him down. A moment later it was Horace who was doing the screaming when he realized that Choat's clothes were covered in sick. All hell broke loose then with Choat yelling incoherent threats and slapping limply at Horace's face and shoulders, while the old man gurgled his revulsion and tried ineffectually to keep him at arm's length. Jo came inadvertently to their rescue when the light from Tom's pencil torch picked out her stocking tops as she bent to help pull them apart. Both men stopped instantly and crouched on the ground, staring, open-mouthed.

'Christ,' whispered Choat, hoarsely. 'It's a woman. Thank God!' Then he burst into tears, and leaned forward to kiss her feet.

Jack's lads (and the solitary maid) had no idea what was going on at the back of the building because they were making so much noise at the front. There was a lot of shouting, stomping of feet and milling about as they waved their weapons above their heads and gestured defiantly towards the brightly lit windows in an attempt to psyche themselves up for the coming assault. So excited were they that Jack could barely make himself heard. He eventually managed to quiet them down, and get them lined up in some sort of order, so that he could tell them how proud he was to be leading them into battle. They were a fine body of men, he assured them (especially the woman), and when they attacked the building he would be guarding their backs in case Pengardon and his underhanded friends tried to creep up on them from behind. They had been persecuted, he reminded them, just because they liked wholesome country sports. And they had all suffered the indignity of the verbal abuse and the degrading theft of their most personal items of clothing. They had all been made to look stupid in front of their families and friends, and forced to sneak home with their arses hanging out of their underpants.

'You know what it's about, lads,' he told them in a voice modelled on Churchill at his most inspirational. 'We've all had to put up with it, haven't we? Scurrilous attacks on our way of life. Violations of our persons. The thieving of our most sacred personal garments, and the slanderous abuse of our good names. And for what, lads, eh: for *what?* Because they're jealous, that's for what! Avaricious of our shining way of life. Well don't you worry, lads,' he promised them, 'they'll pay for their transgressions tonight. The worm's gonna turn and bite the smug sods in their self-righteous backsides.'

Fox hunting and badger baiting were their birthright, he told them, and the birthright of all right-thinking, clean-living, Christian folk across the length and breadth of the country. And if they wanted to torture animals for the fun of it, it was nobody's business but theirs.

The lads (and the solitary maid) grunted, and belched and farted in agreement. Wads of steaming mucus were spat from curled lips, or snorted through pinched nostrils, and slicked and slimed the ground at their feet. Soon the air was thick with a stench like rotting liver in a rancid curry sauce, and the ground awash with gobbets of spittle and snot. Every time Jack exhorted them to vengeance, he was met with a snorting, spitting, farting volley of approval. Dimmer Bright got so caught up in the excitement that he crapped in his pants. But the fundamentalist fervour that Jack had whipped-up around him was so fierce that no one, not even Dimmer, noticed the difference.

When Jack had his lads (and the glowering maid) ready to visit a holy pogrom on Rooter and Perce and Henry and the Clatworthy Clan, he stood to one side and gave them the signal to attack. They roared past him up the steps, through the main doors, and into the saloon bar with guns blazing. By the time they realized that Vinny and Nobbler (gagged and bound under one of the tables) were the only people left in the building, it was too late for most of the decor. The mirror behind the bar shattered along with the optics, and at least half of Perce's beer mugs and assorted glassware were blasted to bits before Jack managed to call a halt to the carnage.

At the back of the building, Tom crammed everyone into the Jeep and drove away under cover of the brief but furious fusillade.

It was a lot quieter on the deserted stretch of moorland road where Bonce and Simon were approaching Buckfastleigh for their meeting with Dolly and her boys. Simon's mother's scooter had been of no real use to them, and they had abandoned it not long after setting out. Their combined weight had been too much for the poor thing, not least because with Bonce's huge bulk pressing down on the pillion, the front wheel had kept lifting into the air, making it impossible for Simon to steer. Five times they had veered off the road and into a ditch before deciding that it would be quicker to walk. The evening air was clear, but getting colder, and they marched along briskly to keep warm. Simon knew the way and there was plenty of time for them to talk.

Bonce had been impressed with Simon from the outset. More to the point, he had been impressed by the way Nora obviously admired him. Bonce liked Nora more than anyone he had ever met. So much so that he was willing to put his trust in this strange man without question: and would do anything he asked of him, follow him anywhere and risk everything to keep him safe. He was aware that this created a conflict of loyalties for him. But he didn't want to hurt someone on Vinny's say-so when that someone was so obviously admired by someone as obviously admirable as Nora. He wasn't nearly as enthusiastic about Morris, in spite of the fact that he was Nora's husband. But he couldn't see any good reason for insulting him and pushing him around the way Vinny had done. And the more he thought about it, the more he began to wonder if there was any real difference between the way Vinny treated people like Nobbler and Morris and Nora and the way he treated him. And if there wasn't a difference, he wondered why he kept putting up with it. As far as he could make out, Vinny was nothing more than a loud-mouthed bully who probably had a tiny little dick. This line of thinking was a new departure for Bonce, and about as close to a philosophical treatise on human nature as he was ever likely to get. More to the point, it gave him a warm feeling inside.

'I hope you don't mind me asking,' said Simon, as they strode along with the silence broken only by the sound of their breathing and the slap of their feet on the tarmac, 'but do you like what you do for a living?'

'All I got,' said Bonce. 'Dolly says I ain't no good at nuffin else.'

Simon nodded. 'Yes, but what do *you* think?' He stopped walking and turned to face the big man. 'I'm sorry, but I don't even know your real name. I mean, it's not really Bonce, is it?'

Bonce bowed his head. 'You don't wanna know.'

'Yes I do,' Simon assured him. 'I can't keep calling you Bonce, can I? It's not . . . It doesn't really suit you. You're more sort of a John, like John Wayne: or a Clint, like Clint Eastwood, or . . . '

'Me mum used t' call me Rocky,' mumbled Bonce.

Simon smiled. 'Yeah? What, like Rock Hudson, you mean?'

Bonce looked at his feet. 'Like that boxer in them films. Stupid that, innit?'

Simon stepped forward and punched him playfully on the bicep. 'It suits you! That's what I call onomatopoeia at its most perceptive.'

Bonce looked at him sideways. 'You takin' the piss?'

'No, of course not. All it means is Rocky suits you down to the ground. Rocky. Like in the films? And what do you think?'

'Yeah, if you want.'

He turned away and they walked on in comradely silence.

'She must be a nice person, your mum,' ventured Simon.

'Yeah, p'rhaps,' said Bonce. 'I don't remember so well. They put me away 'til I were adopted. Didn't see 'er, like, after that.'

'What about your adoptive parents?'

'Didn't stay long wiv most of 'em, did I? Didn't want me, did they? Said I made 'em scared.'

'It must have been tough?'

'Tha's life, though, innit?'

'I suppose so. I didn't have much fun when I was a child, either. I don't think my parents liked me at all. I was always ill, you see? I had eczema and things like that? I wasn't exactly what you would call a pretty child. I always had scabs on my skin. None of the other parents wanted me to play with their kids. They thought I'd give them a terrible disease or something. And I think my parents blamed me because they never had any friends, either.'

Bonce nodded. 'They was all scared o' me.' He held out his huge hands. 'Coz o' them. Said I hurt people deliberate.' He pouted. ''Twasn't fair! I didn't mean no 'arm, did I? Jus' couldn't 'elp it is all!'

They walked on through the darkening night.

'So Rocky,' said Simon, suddenly, 'what *would* you do, if you had a choice?'

Bonce smiled at the name. He thought for a moment. 'Dolly wouldn't let me,' he said, sadly. 'So it don't matter, do it?'

'Yes, but what if Dolly wasn't around? What would you do then? Imagine you could do anything in the world.'

'Big place, the world, though, innit?'

'Yes,' said Simon. 'Yes, I suppose it is. You know what I'm going to do, Rocky? When I've finished with all this? Next year?'

Bonce shook his head.

'I'm going to build a butterfly farm. Built it already, in fact,' he pointed, 'over there, on the site of an old quarry. I've got enough in the bank so I don't have to work for a couple of years. And I should have it all up and running by this time next year. What do you think?'

'Butterflies? What . . . like on flowers, an' stuff?'

Simon nodded. 'Big ones, and rare ones – there are lots of species that have started to die out, all around here. All over the rest of the country, too. All over the world, come to that. I'm going to put some of them back.'

Bonce thought that sounded like a good thing to do. 'I'd wanna do that,' he sighed, 'if I wodden so dumb.'

'You could help, if you wanted to? Feed them and stuff like that until you learned more about it? But only if you wanted to, of course: I wouldn't want to make you do anything you didn't want to.'

'They bin doin' that since I were a kid,' said Bonce. 'Nobody never asked what I wanted. Anyhow . . . too bloody stupid, I am.'

'You don't know until you try, do you?' Simon pursed his lips. 'Look, let's get this lot sorted out first, you and me, and make sure the others get out of it safely: you know, Nora and Morris, and Miss Cornwall and Mr. Pratt, and the others? Then when this Dolly and her friends have gone back to London, you can come and have a look at my place. See what you think?'

'Dunno,' said Bonce, for whom the idea of getting 'this lot sorted out' as Simon had put it, didn't seem very likely with Dolly on her way down from London to sort it out the way *she* wanted. 'Don't reckon she'd like that so much. Sometimes she ain't so nice.' He glanced sideways as they walked along in the moonlight. 'Still,' he added, guardedly, 'wouldn't do no harm t' look, would it? Lookin' ain't so bad, is it?'

'Absolutely not! I was thinking, what you could do if you wanted . . . '

They walked on through the cool evening air together. And as Bonce listened to Simon talking about his plans for the future, a whole new world of exciting possibilities started to open up in front of him.

Back at the Green Dragon Inn, a whole new world of possibilities was beginning to open up for Vinny and Nobbler, as well. After a brief exchange of threatening pleasantries, they found that they fitted in easily with Jack and his lads (and the aggressive maid). There was a natural affinity between them that transcended tribal differences. And by the time Simon and Bonce got back from Buckfastleigh with Dolly and her boys they were all drinking happily together, and discussing the finer points of knifing, clubbing and garrotting their enemies to death.

Dolly took one look at the chummy scene and ordered Stan and Boxer to drag Vinny into Perce's new toilet facility and jam his head down the pan. 'And make it quick,' she added. 'I wanna know what the tosser's been up to.'

'Where d'you thing you're goin'?' demanded Jack, as he and his drunken cronies moved to stand unsteadily shoulder to shoulder, blocking the way. 'Vinny's our mate, in' 'e? So leave 'im alone . . . or . . . or else!'

Vinny blinked his bleary-eyed gratitude, then turned and grinned at Dolly like a recently-rogered cherub. He was drunk, and prematurely hung-over, with a lump on his knee and a lump on his head and an ache in his balls where Jo had exacted a painful retribution for his mistreatment of her and the others.

'See,' he slurred, 'you can't tudge me! Jag's me frien', in 'e?'

Dolly wasn't impressed, and motioned Stan and Boxer to dump him in a chair to answer her questions. 'You got five seconds to tell me what's been going on,' she told him. 'And if I don't like what I hear, we're gonna blow you and your little bumpkin buddies away!'

Gummer Muttocks decided that he wasn't having that. He took a couple of drunken steps towards Dolly, unzipped his fly and took out his enormous penis. ''Ave a blow on tha' then, ya stuck-up cow,' he sniggered. 'Yer soddin' mouth's big enough for the bugger, innet?'

Jack's bunch roared their approval, banging on the tables with their fists and stamping their feet on the floor. But the laughter died on their lips in an instant when Spider whipped out his machete and brought it down in a hissing arc to rest menacingly across the root of Gummer's dick.

An awed silence descended on the room, and no one moved.

Eyes darted from side to side as the gangs weighed each other up.

Then, as if to a signal, everyone pulled out a weapon with a sound like the Honour Guard coming sloppily to attention at the Trooping of the Colour.

Silence fell again.

Again, no one moved.

Dolly waited for a while before taking the cigar from her mouth and stepping forward to blow a cloud of smoke over Gummer's dick. 'No thanks,' she said, 'I've just eaten. How about I have Spider chop it off and put it in the fridge for later? Make a nice little snack with me cocoa. What do you think?'

Gummer frowned, and glanced across the room at Jack.

Jack turned away, and looked at Dolly.

Dolly cocked her head to one side, and shrugged.

Jack smiled tentatively: then grinned: then chuckled: then threw back his head and roared with laughter up at the ceiling.

A moment later, Dolly's boys and Jack's lads (and the swaggering maid) were slapping each other on the back, sheathing machetes and axes, sliding handguns back into holsters, and pointing shotguns and machine pistols at the floor. It wasn't long before they were all laughing and drinking together like long-lost buddies, and deciding that, in spite of their differences, they really had a lot in common. And although sheep shagging wasn't one of them initially, it wasn't long before a pint or two of the Ol' Lovers' convinced a few of Dolly's boys that they wouldn't mind giving it a try.

Dolly left them to it, and had Boxer drag Vinny into the kitchen.

Stan sat him on a chair with his hands tied behind his back, as much to stop him falling off the chair as to keep him from running away. Then they force-fed him with black coffee and salt water until he was so sick of being sick that there was nothing left for him to do but sober-up.

It took longer than Dolly would have liked, but after half an hour of unbridled retching he finally managed to tell her what she wanted to know: or at least, as much of it as his scrumpy-sodden brain could remember and his dented pride would let him admit.

A gang of really big blokes had attacked him, he told her: three or four of them at least – possibly even five or six – with fancy guns and cowardly tactics, sneaking up on him from behind and beating the shit out of him while that snide little creep, Nobbler, ran off and hid. But he had given as good as he got, he assured her, taking at least two of them down with him before he was overpowered by the sheer weight of numbers.

Dolly didn't like the sound of it at all. She particularly didn't like the way he kept glancing sideways at her to see if she was buying his bullshit story: as big a load of crap, she reckoned, as any she was ever likely to hear in a party political broadcast. And her suspicions were confirmed soon after, when the terrified Nobbler came in to give his halting side of the story.

There had been a tart in a short skirt and stockings, he told her, goggle-eyed, who had kicked Vinny in the bollocks and hit him over the head with the landlord's shotgun. 'It was really, really short,' he repeated, 'an' she 'ad legs an' knickers, an' stock . . . '

'Yeah, yeah, right!' said Dolly, waving him to silence. 'We get the picture. What about the geezers with the fancy shooters?'

Nobbler shook his head. 'No, no,' he said, licking his lips and glancing furtively at Vinny. 'Dunno nothin' 'bout that.'

Tom's words, whispered menacingly in his ear as they'd crouched behind the bar together waiting for Jo to open the front door and let Hubert and Horace into the pub, were still too fresh in his mind.

'We're not really here, are we, me and my mate?' Tom had hissed, nodding at Gary with a finger to his lips and the barrel of the big shiny Magnum pressing between Nobbler's saucer-like eyes. 'You give us away and you're dead, Nobbler my son. Oh, yes,' he'd added, smiling at the little man's startled expression, 'we know who you are, Mr. William Bates of 16 Bradfield Road, Romford, Essex. We've been watching you for a very long time, haven't we? So be a good little boy, William, and forget all about us. OK? That way we won't have to come round and kill you, will we? You got that?'

Nobbler had got it all right, and he was still getting it as he tried desperately not to look Dolly in the eye.

'He's lyin'!' insisted Vinny. 'There was three or four . . .'

'Shut it!' snapped Dolly. 'I wasn't talking to you!'

'Yeah, but Doll. The little bastard's lyin'. I'm tellin' ya there was . . . '

Dolly nodded at Boxer, who turned and punched Vinny under the ribs.

Vinny grunted and slid forward on the chair, gasping for breath, his hands tied behind his back the only thing stopping him from sliding to the floor.

Dolly turned back to Nobbler. 'And . . .?'

'What?' he asked, staring in horror at the choking Vinny.

'Who,' said Dolly, with slow precision, 'was the tart in the skirt?'

'You . . . you mean that . . . that waitress bird?' stammered Nobbler, glancing quickly from Dolly to Boxer to Vinny and back again.

Dolly frowned. 'Waitress? What waitress?'

''Er . . . 'er name woz Jo,' stammered Nobbler. He licked his lips and glanced anxiously at Vinny, again. ''E said she was gonna do sex wiv 'im,' he blurted, his facial muscles alternating violently between a smile and a frown as he tried to decide whether he ought to be laughing or crying, or doing both at the same time. 'Only she kicked 'im in the wosnames.' He swallowed hard, his eyes darting about. 'For what 'e done to that Nora an' that Morris an' them.'

'What's he on about?' muttered Boxer, clenching his fists and taking a step towards the terrified little man.

Nobbler flinched away, his hands fluttering up in front of his face like dancing butterflies. 'That . . . that ol' poofter,' he said, cringing and pointing a trembling hand at the window, 'an' that tatty ol' scrubber in that . . . that wosname . . . that van-thing out there.'

'Well?' said Dolly, turning to Vinny.

He struggled to pull himself upright on the chair. 'Honest Doll, there was a bunch o' geezers with shooters an' . . .'

'How many?'

'What?'

'How many *geezers* was there . . . *exactly*?'

'Four or five . . . I dunno. It happened so fast . . . I didn't see . . .'

Dolly walked over to Boxer, pulled the revolver from his shoulder holster and turned to fire it at Vinny.

The first shot smashed a wine bottle on a table beside him.

Vinny flinched and cried out as glass whizzed past his face.

Nobbler shrieked and fell to his knees.

The second and third shots smashed a mixing bowl and a pasta jar behind Vinny's head.

Vinny cried out again, and Nobbler started to pray.

The fourth shot clipped the bobble from Vinny's woolly hat and pinged it up into the air. The fifth shot smashed the bobble to smithereens.

A cloud of pulverized red wool drifted slowly down onto Vinny's head as he and Nobbler pissed in their pants.

Dolly cocked the pistol and pointed it at Vinny's chest. 'How many?'

'*Two*!' he screamed. '*Two! Two! Chris'sake don't shoot!*'

'That all?'

'*Yes, yes! Them an' the old geezers on bikes!*'

Dolly's eyes narrowed to slits. 'Old geezers? What . . . *old geezers* on bikes?'

'Two of 'em! They banged on the door! I . . . I got confused.'

'And?'

'She let 'em in. That waitress let 'em in. The others must o' come in the back when I . . . I wasn't lookin'.'

Dolly turned to Boxer. 'They must have come in the back when he wasn't lookin',' she echoed.

Boxer took a knuckleduster from his jacket pocket and slid it onto his fist in anticipation of an intimate meeting between it and Vinny's face.

Dolly turned to Nobbler. 'Get up!'

He got shakily to his feet, with one hand clasped to his mouth and the other clamped over the damp crotch of his tracksuit bottoms. 'Please,' he pleaded. 'I didn't do nothin', Miss Killjoy, honest. Honest, I didn't!'

'Old geezers?' she asked.

'Yeah! Yeah! On bikes. Old an' wrinkly they was,' he said, gazing wall-eyed at Boxer. 'Must o' bin a hundred year old . . . an' . . . an' . . .'

'Really? As old as that, were they?'

Nobbler nodded, eager to please. 'An' . . . an' wrinkly . . . an' an' mad.'

'And . . .?'

Nobbler looked around. 'What?'

'Anything else you want to tell me?'

'No, no! Nothin'! Honest! Honest! Please don't . . . don't shoot me!'

'You sure?'

Nobbler shook his head, emphatically, then nodded, then shook his head again, his face a mask of confusion and fear.

'You lie to me . . . I kill you. Understand?'

'Yes! Yes, yes!' He bowed. 'Thank you! Thank you!'

'Right,' she jerked her head at the door, 'piss off!'

Nobbler bobbed and bowed and touched his forelock, thanking her for not killing him, as he backed out of the room.

Dolly sent Stan to fetch Jack.

'Never 'eard of 'em,' he said, after listening to Vinny's description of Gary and Tom. 'They ain't from round 'ere, tha's for certain!'

'Yeah? What about this waitress-type in the short skirt?'

Jack shrugged. 'That Cornwall tart, probably.' He belched and scratched his arse. 'Frigid lesbo bitch, you ask me!' he added, remembering a painful attempt to put his hand up her skirt.

'Just your ordinary, everyday waitress, then?' said Dolly. 'Not some kind of karate expert, or nothing?'

Jack snorted. 'Jus' yer ordin'ry, ravin' nympho scrubber, more like!'

Dolly regarded him, impassively. 'So you're saying she's a frigid, sex mad, lesbian, nymphomaniac, slapper, right?'

Jack narrowed his eyes.

'Forget it. And the old geezers on bikes?'

'The Naggs brothers,' said Jack, with a shrug, 'prob'ly. Feeble as farts in a windstorm. No need to worry 'bout them. '

Dolly turned to look down at Vinny. 'So you got done by a butch tart in a skimpy little dress and a couple of old geezers with their cocks in a splint. Why doesn't that surprise me?'

'No, Doll, honest,' pleaded Vinny. 'There was . . .'

Dolly gave a minute nod of the head.

Boxer turned quickly and hit Vinny in the face with a backhanded slap that sent him and the chair crashing over backwards. At a signal from Dolly, he grabbed the chair and the man, and hauled them both upright.

Dolly eyed him, coldly. 'And the motor?'

'Motor?' said Vinny, blood dripping from his nose and running from the corner of his mouth. 'What . . .?'

'Kite's motor, you *tosser*! You searched it, like I said, right?'

Vinny nodded. 'Knobhead did. The stuff ain't in it.'

'Check it,' said Dolly to Boxer. 'Now!'

She looked at Stan. 'Go get Bonce and that long string o' gnat's piss. No, wait!' She turned to Vinny. 'What's his name: Bonce's new mate?'

'Hawker,' said Vinny, spitting blood on the floor.

Dolly nodded at Stan.

Bonce shuffled into the room and stood with his head bowed, wringing his huge hands and glancing uneasily from Dolly to Vinny and back again. He and Simon had made the journey from Buckfastleigh in the front of the lead ambulance in Dolly's convoy so that Simon could guide them back to the Green Dragon. Bonce had agonized every inch of the way, terrified of what Dolly was going to say to him about the loss of her precious car, and their weapons, and Vinny's phone, and, most important of all, Henry Kite.

Dolly stared at him for a while in silence. Then 'Where's the Merc?' she asked. She already knew the answer, but she loved watching him squirm.

Bonce shied away. 'In that bog place,' he said, glancing quickly at Simon.

Simon didn't notice. He was too busy staring in horror at Vinny, slumped sideways on the chair, dripping vomit and blood.

'And you put it there, did you?'

Bonce shook his head, and looked down at his hands. 'No, it . . .'

'Forget it!' she snapped. 'So who's your wanky new friend, then, moron?'

Bonce smiled, uncertainly. 'He . . . he's Simon. His name's . . .'

'Is it really? Hello Simon,' she said, turning towards him. 'What've you and this idiot of mine done with my nice new motor, then, ay?'

'Answer the lady,' said Boxer, shoving Simon in the chest with a fist.

Simon looked up with a jerk. 'Sorry?'

'Over here,' said Dolly.

He turned towards her with rounded eyes. 'What . . . what happened to him?' he asked, looking down at Vinny.

'Tripped over his tongue, didn't he? Always happens to them as lies to me. You gonna be next?'

Simon's eyes opened even wider. 'Me? No! No, why would I?'

'Very sensible of you . . . Simon. So where's my soddin' motor, then, eh?'

He told her that, as far as he knew, it was at the bottom of Sodmire Bog, and that Lance and Gavin Clatworthy were the ones who had put it there.

Dolly turned to Jack. 'You know 'em?'

'Bunch o' hippy bum bandits!'

She turned back to Simon. 'Well?'

'I . . . I don't know them very well, really. But I don't think . . .'

Jack belched. 'Bunch o' soddin' pansies, you ask me.'

'And Henry Kite?' asked Dolly. 'He in Sodmire, too?'

'I don't know who you mean,' said Simon. 'I've never met him. But one of Mr. Strawbridge's friends said he'd gone over to The Stone Dancers.'

'And what's that when it's at home?'

'The Clatworthy's farm? About three miles away,' he pointed, 'over there?'

'And you know how to get there, I'm guessing?'

'Yes, but I don't think . . . '

'No,' interrupted Dolly, 'but I do. And that's all you need to know. So you'll be taking us there in the morning. OK?'

Simon looked at Jack. 'Well, if that's what you want. But it might not . . . '

'No buts,' said Dolly. She turned back to Bonce. 'He stays here tonight and you watch him. Got that?'

Bonce nodded, unhappily.

'And no more screw-ups, or you'll be staying in this shithole for the rest of your life. You understand what I'm saying, dumbo?'

Bonce nodded again and looked down at his shoes.

'You better. Now piss off!' She jerked a thumb over her shoulder. 'Both of you! Get outa my sight before I get *really* annoyed!'

She turned to Jack with the fixed grin of a predatory reptile.

'Looks like it's up to you and me to sort this lot out then, doesn't it, Jack my old son?'

34

BRUNO THE BEAR

There was nothing welcoming, nothing homely, and absolutely nothing 'Come and spend a relaxing weekend in one of our family-friendly Travelodges' about the room Henry had been given for the night. There were no paisley patterned curtains with matching bedspreads, no pale pink velour headboards, no wavy-edged candy-striped pillowcases, and no bedside lamps with shiny pink sateen shades and matching tassels that always made him wish he'd remembered to pack a flamethrower in his holdall. There was no remote control TV with a porn channel to embarrass him in the morning when the smarmy sod at Reception asked if the director's cut of *Naked Pussy Vixens* had 'kept him up all night'. There was no Gideon Bible, no trouser press, no telephone, and no Do Not Disturb sign for him to hang outside the door when he was pretending to be doing something more business-like than wanking. There was no clean cup and saucer, no spoon, no electric kettle plugged in and filled with water ready to boil, no complimentary sachets of hermetically sealed tea, coffee, sugar, Coffee Creamer and Long Life Milk, and no Rombouts biscuits to con him into thinking that he was staying somewhere more expensive than was actually the case. There weren't even any non-absorbent towels in three patronizing sizes folded over a frighteningly hot chrome-plated towel rail in a brightly-tiled, antiseptically clean en suite bathroom with minuscule bars of individually wrapped soap and sachets of shower gel ready for him to steal when he checked out. Under normal circumstances this lack of cloying sentimentality would have suited him just fine, because there were few things that the tourist in him hated more than smug hotels that required him to feel at home in rooms that were not remotely like any part of any home he had ever visited, never mind lived in. But his circumstances were far from normal, and a bit of self-satisfied Laura Ashley would have given him some welcome relief from the wood-panelled, neo-Elizabethan sensory deprivation chamber in which he was stranded.

The room was chilly and dark, and felt as if its walls were closing in around him, compressing the air and making it hard for him to breathe. He hoped that this was only a symptom of the panic attack that he was almost certain that he had suffered when Mandy had disappeared without warning out on the moor. But he wasn't certain, so he sat on the edge of the bed and fretted about it. There was plenty of room for him to fret in, too, because the bed was enormous: a huge, tapestry-hung four-poster that filled half the room and creaked every time he trembled with fear. He kept glancing around uneasily, convinced that at any moment a section of the oak panelling would swing open to reveal a would-be assassin lurking in a secret passageway and equipped with poisoned darts, garrotting wire and a deadly, razor-sharp dagger. He had read about secret passageways in old houses when he was a child, and he knew that if you wanted to find one all you had to do was look for the nearest life-size family portrait. The secret passageway would be behind it, and the eyes of the lifelike ancestor staring down at you would really be the eyes of the assassin waiting for the right moment to come out and strike. As theories went he had always found it very convincing, but it didn't help him in his current predicament because there were no fewer than six elaborately framed portraits of Clatworthy forefathers hanging on the walls around him. There was a Victorian Clatworthy, a Georgian Clatworthy, an Elizabethan Clatworthy, and three other Clatworthies from periods of history that he couldn't quite place. Their resemblance to Mervyn Clatworthy was uncanny, and a more disreputable looking bunch of conniving cutthroats it would have been hard to imagine. He stole a peep at each of them in turn from under hooded brows as he sat hunched-up on the creaking bed, half-hoping, half-fearing to catch a pair of eyes gazing back at him. He saw nothing of the sort, but the conviction that he was being watched wouldn't go away.

The more he thought about it the more he became convinced that his life was in danger and that there were only two possible courses of action he could take. Either he could stay where he was until the secret door burst open and some demented family member rushed in and battered him to death with a hideous medieval implement of torture, or he could go back into the dusty corridor and get battered to death by some equally demented family member, with an equally hideous medieval implement of torture, out there instead. He had no doubt that he would to be battered to death eventually, or that his only contribution to the whole sordid business would be in deciding where it happened. On balance, he felt that he would prefer to die in the bedroom. Dark and sombre it might be, but at least there he could meet his maker in some sort of comfort, breathing his last stretched out across the enormous four-poster. Far better that than dying in a filthy corridor where there would be no chance of making a (relatively) comfortable and dignified end.

While these and other morbid thoughts continued to eat away at his self-confidence, he became aware that eating was something he desperately needed to do. He hadn't had anything since the ploughman's lunch at the Green Dragon Inn earlier in the day, and since he had vomited most of that over the boot of Choat's car, he reckoned that he had lost whatever limited nutritional value it might have contained. Now he could feel that old, familiar emptiness gnawing away at the pit of his stomach, along with a growing conviction that his colon had developed an echo. Mervyn had told him to join the family for dinner, and although the idea hadn't appealed to him in the least at the time, he was beginning to find it an increasingly attractive proposition.

Mervyn had also told him how to get to the dining room. The trouble was that he had never been very good at listening to directions and had forgotten everything the old man had said to him after the bit about going out of the door and turning right. This would not normally have prevented him from venturing forth with complete confidence because, like most men, he had an unswerving belief in his ability to get from any point A to any point B with unerring accuracy, day or night, regardless of distance, mode of transport, or the prevailing weather conditions. The fact that this had never been borne out by experience (the weight of evidence suggested that he couldn't find his way out of a wet paper bag with a bulldozer) was something that he had always preferred to gloss over. But given what he had already seen of the Clatworthy clan, it wasn't the possibility of getting lost that concerned him; what he was really terrified of was being found.

All he could recall of Mervyn's directions was that the dining room was next to the room with the weapons in it. And that was a daunting prospect because it had taken him and Mervyn several minutes to walk from there to where he was now: and regardless of what he thought of his own abilities as a navigator, he didn't fancy his chances of making it back there without getting himself murdered along the way. In fact, he wasn't feeling positive about any aspect of his future. He was tired and hungry and beginning to suspect that the Clatworthies weren't being entirely honest with him. To the best of his recollection Mervyn had said nothing to Robbie, or to anyone else for that matter, about him being given a room for the night. Yet his bags had been waiting for him in the bedroom when he'd got there. Not only must Robbie, or a person or persons unknown, have taken it as his or their duty to carry the bags all the way to the room from the Probe in the distant courtyard: but he, or they, had managed it without passing Henry and Mervyn along the way. He realized that, given the size and sprawling nature of the house, this wasn't such an improbable achievement. But what wasn't so easy to explain was how they had known in which of the dozens of rooms he would be staying. Besides, if anyone had asked him, he would have said that his bags were still in the boot of his Volvo in the car park at the Green Dragon, because he certainly hadn't moved them from there. Why would he have done, when he hadn't been expecting to stay overnight? But it wasn't so much the how of the thing that bothered him as the why. On the whole he didn't think that the Clatworthies were the sort of people who went out of their way to help someone like him unless there was something in it for them above and beyond any warm feeling they might have got from playing at being Good Samaritans. So why, and by whom, had his bags been brought to the house? After a moment's thought, he decided there were only four possible answers.

The first was that the Clatworthies were opportunist cannibals who kept a room ready at all times for the arrival of chance visitors who they would invite into the house, lull into a false sense of security, and then chop into tiny pieces of shivering kebab to feed to the malformed relatives they kept chained in the cellars.

The second was that they had been given advanced warning of his arrival by a person or persons unknown and had prepared the room so that they could invite him into the house, lull him into a false sense of security, and then chop him into little pieces to feed to the relatives chained in the cellars.

The third possibility was that the room had been prepared for a victim who had yet to arrive, and the opportunist Clatworthies had seen him as a convenient hors d'oeuvre, to be enjoyed ahead of the overdue main course, who they could invite into the house, lull into a false sense of security, and then chop into tiny pieces . . . etcetera, etcetera.

The fourth, and by far the scariest, possibility was that the Clatworthies were just an ordinary farming family who liked nothing better than to help lost and weary travellers by offering them free board and lodging for the night and it was he, Henry, who was the dangerously paranoid psychotic.

He was so engrossed in trying to figure out which of these options he ought to worry about first that he didn't register the sound of footsteps in the corridor outside the room until it was almost too late.

He looked up, apprehensively, expecting the door to burst off its hinges and some manic family member to come rushing into the room to club him to death with a hammer. When that didn't happen, he felt oddly deflated. Then it occurred to him that perhaps he shouldn't allow someone who might know his or her way around the building to go by unchallenged.

Without pausing to consider the possible consequences of his actions, he jumped up, rushed to the door, pulled it open and peered out just in time to see a trousered leg disappear around the corner at the end of the corridor. He set off immediately in pursuit of the leg's owner, and a dozen strides later, turned the corner into an identical corridor just as a door halfway along it closed with a click. He hesitated, and looked anxiously in both directions, before walking up to the door and knocking with a hesitant fist.

Nothing happened for several seconds. Then the door opened a crack and a man of about his own age looked out. It was Gary Harmsworth, and he gazed at Henry for a second or two. Then 'What?' he asked, flatly.

'Hi,' said Henry, hoping he sounded braver than he felt. 'Sorry to bother you, only I'm a bit lost, and I was wondering if you could show me the . . .?'

'Wait,' said Gary, shutting the door with another ominous click.

Henry's confidence started to drain away as soon as the door closed in his face. Who was this man, he wondered, and what had he gone back into the room to fetch: a gun, a knife, a venomous snake that would bite him on the breast like Cleopatra and make his death look like an accident? Or was there some hideous, humanoid *thing* in the room that would spring out, grapple him to the floor, knock him senseless, suck his intestines out through his anus, and then rip out his backbone for use as a walking stick? He could just imagine how vile the thing would look with its wedge-shaped face mutated to fit neatly into bum-cracks, and its stubby arms and massive thumbs adapted for forcing its victims' buttocks apart. It would have bad breath – very, *very* bad breath! – and a very bad back from all the stooping. Which, of course, was why it would need a constant supply of new walking sticks.

All of these gruesome thoughts flashed through his brain in an instant. But before he could summon up enough courage to flee in terror, the door opened and a smiling Tom Hertz stepped out into the corridor to greet him.

'Good evening Mr. Kite,' he said, closing the door behind him with a doom-laden snap. 'I'm Tom Hertz.' He proffered a hand. 'And I'm pleased to see that you made it safely. Dangerous place at night, the moor, isn't it?'

Henry was encouraged by the use of his name. 'Yes,' he said, with an uncertain grin, 'You wouldn't want to be out there on your own, would you?' He frowned. 'Excuse me, but how did you know my . . .?'

'This way,' said Tom, turning to stride back along the corridor. 'It's easy to get lost in here, too, isn't it?' he added, over his shoulder. 'Such a big place!'

'Yes,' said Henry, hurrying to keep up. 'But how did you . . .?'

'There,' said Tom, stopping by a door in the next corridor.

Henry looked at it in confusion. 'What?'

'Your room,' said Tom. He turned to leave.

'But,' said Henry, 'I've just come from here. I was looking for the dining room, actually.' He frowned, and shook his head as if to clear it. 'I'm sorry, but have we met? Only, I was wondering how . . .'

Tom didn't wait for him to finish the sentence. 'Right,' he said, turning briskly away from the door and striding off along the corridor. When he reached the door at the far end, he opened it and motioned Henry into the room beyond. 'There,' he said. 'Door at the far end. Bon appetit.'

Henry looked through the door expecting to see the first in a series of rooms and corridors stretching away into the distance. What he saw instead was the weapons room. He was stunned. 'But,' he said, taking hold of Tom's arm as he turned to leave, 'how can . . .? I mean, I thought . . .'

Tom turned to gaze meaningfully at the hand on his wrist.

Henry swallowed and let go. 'Sorry,' he said, smoothing the sleeve with his fingers, 'I didn't mean . . . It's just that it took us ages to walk all the way . . .'

Tom pointed into the room. 'Through there. Door at the far end. Okay? Dining room's on the other side.' He stared hard at Henry. 'Got it now?'

'Yes, thank . . .'

'Better hurry, then,' said Tom, turning him by the shoulders and putting a hand in his back to push him into the room. 'It's bad manners to be late,'

'Right,' said Henry, as he stumbled forward. 'Thank . . .'

But the door had already closed in his face.

*　*　*

'I knew it!' cried Henry, getting to his feet. 'I knew I'd seen him somewhere before! Where's the colonel?'

'I don't know,' admitted the figure. 'Colonel Payne?'

'I'm sorry sir,' came the lieutenant's disembodied voice, 'but I am afraid the colonel is not available at this moment in time.'

'Really?' said the figure. 'And why is that lieutenant?'

'He felt that a developing situation would benefit from being given his personal attention, sir.'

'And what situation would that be?'

'A Roman mounted patrol was closing rapidly with your position, sir. And the colonel felt that they needed to be persuaded to reconsider their options.'

'I bet he went on his own, though, didn't he?' said Henry.

'Indeed he did, sir,' agreed the lieutenant. 'Although, having made contact with the patrol, he requested the assistance of combat drones *Alpha* and *Beta*.'

'Where is this Roman patrol now?' asked the figure.

'Scanners indicate that they are heading away from your position, sir,' said the lieutenant, 'at a surprising rapid velocity.'

'It would appear, then, that the colonel has been successful in convincing them to rethink their strategy, would it not?'

'Indeed it would, sir, yes.'

'And where is the colonel now?'

'He is aware of your desire to speak with him, sir, and will be joining you in approximately three, two, one . . . '

'Good afternoon, sir,' said the colonel. 'Good afternoon, Mr. Kite.'

'I knew it!' said Henry, pointing and accusing finger. 'I knew I recognized you! You're Tom Hertz, aren't you?'

'Well done, sir,' said the colonel. 'I am very pleased to see that your memory is returning to normal.'

'You are?' Henry felt deflated. 'Really?'

'Certainly! That is, as I understand it, the point of this exercise, after all.' He turned to the hooded figure. 'Is that not so, sir?'

'Indeed it is.'

The colonel turned back and smiled stiffly at Henry.

'Oh,' he said. 'Umm, well, in that case . . . thank you.' He sat down. 'By the way, the . . . er, the Payne-Hertz, name thing? Very clever! Onomatopoeia with a military bent.'

'I prefer to think of it as personal security services, sir,' said the colonel. 'The rank-thing is really just for show. A conceit, if you will? But be that as it may, I am pleased that my little subterfuge meets with your approval.'

He turned to the figure. 'If you will excuse me, sir, a matter of some urgency requires my attention.'

'Yes of course. Don't let us keep you. And thank you for responding to Mr. Kite's request so promptly. However, before you go, might I ask the nature of this new emergency?'

'Certainly, sir. Mr. Boc and Lieutenant Calliope urgently require my assistance in finalizing the details of the menu for your evening meal.'

'In which case,' said the figure, 'we really mustn't detain you, must we?'

'Thank you, sir,' said the colonel, saluting crisply. 'Mr. Kite,' he added, saluting again, 'good luck with your journey. Bon voyage, so to speak.'

* * *

Henry shook his head sadly as he surveyed the weapons room.

'See what I mean?' he asked of a suit of armour. 'What's it all about, eh? I mean, what the hell's going on in this place?'

He turned with another shake of the head and started to walk dejectedly through the flickering shadows, past the arrays of weapons, towards the door at the end of the room.

'I'm beginning to think I'm a pawn in all this, y'know?' he said, stopping to gaze at the fearsome suit of Japanese armour. 'All *what* do I hear you ask? All *what* indeed!' he said, when the armour didn't reply. 'Madness, that's all *what*! They're all mad and I'm rapidly going that way.'

He thought for a moment. 'Actually, I bet I'm the only sane person in the whole house. Whole country, for that matter. Probably the whole *world*, if it comes to that.' He regarded the suit of armour solemnly. 'What do you think?'

The armour didn't answer. But it looked so fierce that he stepped to one side to avoid getting too close to it as he sidled past on his way to the door.

'Of course,' he said, apologetically as he backed away, 'you probably don't speak much English, do you? Probably Shogun or Shinto, or something that sounds like an elderly asthmatic eating hot potatoes with his mouth open. Sorry,' he added. 'I didn't mean to be disrespectful. It's just that Kurasawa isn't that easy for us Europeans to follow without the subtitles.'

He glanced anxiously to one side, wanting to move on, but feeling reluctant to turn his back on the warlike thing. Then he frowned as he caught sight of something shiny out of the corner of his eye. He edged towards it, glancing nervously over his shoulder to satisfy himself that his insults hadn't awakened the suit of armour to murderous intent.

At the side of the room he stopped to gaze at the sword embedded in the oak tabletop. He was too intimidated by the magnificence of the thing to touch it again. But he bent forward slightly at the waist for a closer look. The delicate tracery on the blade was vaguely familiar, and the longer he looked at it the more he was convinced that he had seen something like it somewhere before. He looked up and frowned at the wall in concentration, trying to remember where he had seen it. There was definitely something at the back of his mind that he couldn't quite put his finger on. Something about . . .

'What you doin' 'ere, then?' asked a deep voice behind him.

He gasped, almost screamed with shock, and spun around expecting to be decapitated by an irate Samurai swordsman. What he saw instead was a great lump of a man standing uncomfortably close and gazing intently into his face with questioning, childlike eyes.

Henry staggered backwards and immediately yelped in alarm as something sharp prodded him in the back of the head.

He spun around, and held up his arms in surrender, only to find himself staring into the glazed eyes of Bruno the stuffed bear.

He swallowed hard in relief, took an instinctive step backwards, and trod on the foot of the child-man behind him.

'Sorry!' he gasped, whirling around to face him. 'Sorry! I didn't mean . . . It's just . . . You know, the bear . . . ? I . . .'

'Didden 'urt,' said the child-man, earnestly.

'Good,' said Henry. 'That's . . . '

'Gaga idden no cissy!' He thumped himself in the chest with a fist.

Henry frowned uncomprehendingly for a moment. 'Oh, isn't he?' he said with relief as the penny suddenly dropped. 'No, no, of course he isn't! Of course! That's . . . that's good, isn't it? That's . . . Well, I mean, *well done!*'

'Brubru,' said the overgrown infant, pointing first at the stuffed bear and then at himself, 'Gaga frien'.'

Henry's head nodded rapidly up and down to demonstrate that he understood. 'Yes, yes,' he said. 'Good, *good*! That's . . . that's *excellent*, isn't it? *Excellent*! Yes, yes! *Well done again!*'

This, surely, he told himself as he glanced around the room in search of somewhere to hide, was one of the inbred relatives the Clatworthies kept chained in the cellars. Gaga might look harmless – like an outsized toddler without an ounce of malice anywhere in his hulking body – but Henry had a feeling that his huge hands would be capable of splintering a human skull like a sledgehammer smashing an egg if he ever got riled.

The child-man held out one of those formidable hands for him to shake. 'Gaga be you frien', too?' he asked, with an uncertain smile.

Henry flinched at the sight of the spade-like paw. But he took it in a gesture of goodwill, and immediately wished that he had put it under the front wheel of a double-decker bus instead. His face dissolved in agony as if it was melting, and he stood on tiptoe like a ballet dancer suddenly stricken with rickets. His tongue worked frantically in a silent attempt to force the phrase 'Please kill me now' past his paralyzed lips. Then, just as a comforting blackness started to engulf him, a voice echoed, irritably, across the room.

'Leave him alone, you stupid bugger! How many times you gotta be told?'

Henry turned his head to watch as Mervyn Clatworthy strode across the room towards him through a pale fog. At first he couldn't work out why the old man looked so tall. Then he realized that it was because he had sunk to his knees while Gaga had been crushing his hand.

'You do *not* go near sharp things without permission,' snapped Mervyn, 'do you hear? How many more times you gotta be told?'

The big man let go of Henry and stood with his massive hands wrapping and unwrapping in front of his chest. He looked beseechingly at Henry and stuck out his lower lip. 'Gaga didden mean nothin',' he said, bending at the knees to wrap an arm around Henry's shoulders. When he straightened up, he lifted him clean off the ground. 'Gaga got new frien',' he said, with a rib-crushing squeeze. 'New frien' be Brubru frien', too!'

Suddenly, Henry thought he knew what it would be like to be hugged by an amorous gorilla. 'Wee-eeee!' he wheezed, as Gaga tightened his grip, 'w-were just t-talking about Bru-Bruno. Gaga was . . . '

Mervyn shook his head, irritably. 'Your name's *Gareth* for Christ's sake! *Gareth*! Not *Gaga*! What are you, some kind of *moron*?'

He looked at Henry. 'Let him go or you'll crush the poor bugger to death.'

It was at that moment that Henry realized that he was still kneeling, even though his knees were now three feet off the floor. '*No*!' he gasped, as the big man loosened his grip. '*Don't* . . .!'

But it was too late. Gareth let him go and he dropped to the threadbare carpet like a stone, landing on his knees with a dull crack, and remaining there bent forward with his eyes open wide as a barely audible whine, like a hound with its balls in a gin trap, forced its way through his clenched teeth.

Mervyn looked down at him with narrowing eyes. 'Well,' he snapped, 'you comin' to dinner or not?'

Five minutes later, Blossom Clatworthy minced provocatively across the dining room on dangerously high heels to help the limping Henry to a place at the table. Her face was plastered with makeup that looked as if it had been applied as she'd ridden a moped over a cliff. Her spiky orange hair looked terrified, too, standing out at right angles to her head as if it had realized long before its owner that they were plummeting to a horrible death. Her dress was minuscule, and an uncomfortable shade of lilac. It was fluffy and woollen, and Henry wondered if it had once been an ankle-length evening gown that some careless someone – probably Blossom herself – had left in a hot tumble drier for six weeks. Whatever it might once have looked like it was now tiny as well as topless and backless, and managed to cover her knickers, the tops of her fishnet stockings and her painfully tight uplift bra only if she stood upright and didn't move. In spite of the agony in his knees, Henry was embarrassed to feel his manhood rise in appreciation as this vision of sluttish perfection reached forward and helped him to his seat. His head swam as she lowered him with a hand around his waist and another at his elbow, the warmth of her left breast pressing momentarily against his cheek. Everything went grey for a second or two as he sank onto the chair, the pain in his knees combining briefly with the suffocating pungency of her perfume to lend him all the flexibility of an elderly rheumatic. His predicament wasn't helped by a growing fear that if he bent forward too quickly he would either fracture his painfully erect penis like a dry twig, or punch a hole with it right through the fly of his jeans. It occurred to him, as he allowed himself to be lowered into his place at the table, that if his dick got any harder he would soon be able to use it to pole-vault out of this hellhole to freedom.

He smiled wanly and nodded his light-headed gratitude as Blossom let go of his arm and allowed him to sit down. She winked and patted his inner thigh with her left hand as she took her place on the chair beside him. Then she brought a huge glass filled to the brim with red wine up to his lips. He reached a shaking hand to steady it, drank deeply, and nodded his thanks. Then he reached hastily for it again and drained it to the dregs.

The wine seemed to course through his veins like a shot of the best cocaine. 'Thank you,' he said. 'That was . . . that was . . . thanks.'

Then he looked for the first time at the faces watching him from around the table, and decided that those amongst them who weren't already unconscious had not been impressed by the manner of his halting arrival.

35

GRANDDAD AND GREAT UNCLE BERT

The dining room was dimly lit and sombre, and looked to Henry like a throwback to some indeterminate part of The Middle Ages. The floor was laid in dark granite slabs, foot-worn and bare. The walls were of a similar material, but rough-hewn and hung with ancient tapestries. The windows were narrow and high-arched with diamond leaded glass set in stone mullions and framed by black velvet drapes. The table and chairs were of some close-grained dark wood, rounded and grime-polished with age. What light there was came from a log fire, and a dozen or so guttering candles in brass sconces on the walls and a trio of wax-dribbled candlesticks in the centre of the table. Above a heavy granite fireplace hung an oil painting of a group of stiff-backed, moustachioed men dressed as knights, each holding a plumed helmet in the crook of an arm. Henry thought at first glance that they must be members of a Victorian football team in fancy dress. Then he recognized Rooter and Mervyn, and Hubert and Horace Naggs. Others in the picture also looked familiar, but he couldn't quite place them. Someone cleared their throat, and he dragged his eyes back to the table and the diners seated around it.

Lance was opposite him, hunched over a bowl of some sort of stew into which strands of his long hair hung lank and greasy. He had a wooden spoon in his right fist, and was using it to shovel the lumpy mixture into his mouth by the shortest possible route.

Gavin was on Lance's left, leaning forward over another unappetizing bowl of stew as he dunked into it a thick slab of the crusty white loaf that sat sliced into doorsteps on a wooden platter in the middle of the table. He slurped as he ate, and a brown drool dripped from the stubble of his chin.

Next to him was his sister, introduced by Mervyn as Kate, who gazed at Henry with a thoughtful expression as she stirred her stew half-heartedly with a large wooden spoon.

Mervyn was on Kate's left, at the head of the table, leaning forward with his fingers steepled together. His eyes were heavily lidded, and he seemed to be watching the others with his lips set in the semblance of a paternal smile.

Next to Mervyn, on Henry's side of the table, was Great Uncle Bert, slumped back in his chair with his eyes closed and his mouth open as he snored up at the ceiling. A bowl of stew, overlain with a skin of congealed grease, sat on the table in front of him untouched.

On Uncle Bert's left was Blossom. Then came Henry, and next to him Robbie, who greeted him curtly and continued eating with a haste suggesting that he expected the stew to be taken from him if he didn't finish it soon.

At the far end of the table was Granddad Clatworthy, his false teeth lying next to his plate and his pale lips puckered as he sucked stew through a thick plastic straw with a sound like a drain being unclogged.

On the other side of the table, opposite Robbie and next to Lance, was the childlike Gareth with a food-splattered, plastic bib around his neck and a spoon the size of a soup ladle clamped in a huge fist. He was obviously concentrating hard, and doing his best to get at least some of the stew from the bowl to his mouth without spilling it. But the lumpen trails down the front of the bib were mute testimony to just how far he was from getting it right.

Henry surveyed his fellow diners only fleetingly, but what he saw was enough to put him off eating in general, and stew in particular, for life. He looked down at the bowl steaming greasily in front of him, and wondered with a shiver if the lumps floating in it were the remains of the last guest the Clatworthies had invited to dinner: and, more to the point, whether at some time in the near future he was destined to become the main ingredient in a similar dish. He was just reaching for one of the slabs of bread on the platter in the centre of the table as the safest culinary option available to him, when Lance wiped his mouth with the back of a hand and looked up.

'What d'you do down that London way, then?'

Henry withdrew his hand. 'Ah, well,' he said. 'I work for an advertising agency. That is, I used . . . I mean . . . it's in Essex, not London. But we do have clients in London. You know?' he added, more in hope than expectation.

Lance grunted, and went back to ladling stew into his mouth with his eyes fixed firmly on Henry's face.

Henry wondered if he should leave it at that. But a quick glance at the stew convinced him that talking would be a safer option than eating. It was the sort of mistake that anyone could have made. 'I, er . . . that is . . . *we* create advertisements, mostly for newspapers and magazines and billboards?'

'Oh, how clever!' breathed Blossom, leaning towards him with one hand on his thigh and the fingers of the other running up and down the stem of her glass. 'How 'bout another drink?' she asked in a husky voice. 'All that drawin' an' writin' an' stuff must make you *ever so* thirsty!'

Henry nodded, absently. 'Yes, thank you. That's . . .'

'What,' said Lance, fixing him with a mocking grin, 'an' you go round tellin' people 'bout it? People you don't even know?'

Henry was thrown momentarily off balance: not so much by Lance's apparent antagonism towards the advertising industry as the sensation of Blossom's fingertips fluttering over the crotch of his jeans. He looked down at her hand just as she pulled it away and touched it to her mouth.

He looked up at her face, and grinned, self-consciously.

She grinned back at him with raised eyebrows and a series of sharp hissing sounds '*Tish! Tish! Tish! Tish!*' between her clenched teeth as she touched each fingertip to her lips in turn.

Henry glanced across the table at her brother, wondering if being seduced by someone's horny sister was a hanging offence in this neck of the woods.

He cleared his throat. '*Eh-hem*! Well, yes,' he began, in an attempt to lighten the mood, 'but the money's not bad and if we . . . '

Lance's eyes flashed. 'You write a load o' *crap* 'bout washin' powder and dog food and stuff to stick in women's knickers and all you can say is . . . the money idden bad?'

Henry had encountered this sort of attitude before – albeit expressed in a less aggressive fashion – and he felt that he was on familiar ground. It was another simple mistake that anyone could have made.

'*Hah*! Well, yes,' he said, a little too loudly. 'Not always the most moral of professions, is it? But some of us like to think that we adhere to a proper code of practice. And as I was about to say, if *we* didn't do it, someone . . . '

Lance stood up with such force that his chair crashed to the floor behind him. He leaned across the table with his spoon pointing at Henry's head. 'Don't *say it*! Just don't bloody well *say it*, tha's all! What d'you think we are, half-wits? You think we want all that crap you keep tryin' to flog us?'

'Well, I . . . ' began Henry, pausing and flinching as he felt Blossom's left hand rest on his crotch and give it a squeeze.

He looked quickly to his right and found her leaning towards him with her chin on the heel of her right hand and her little finger sliding in and out of her puckered lips. 'You idden hungry then, lover?' she breathed, removing the finger. 'Made special for you that were, an' all.'

His Adam's apple bobbed uncomfortably, as he picked up the wineglass and drained it in a single swallow.

'Well I . . . ' he said, pausing to wipe the back of a hand across his mouth.

'I'm talking to you!' snapped Lance. 'You always ignore people down London way when they'm talkin' to 'ee?'

He shook his head. 'No, no,' he said to confirm that he didn't ignore people when they were talking to him and didn't think that the Clatworthies were a bunch of half-wits, either.

'Tidden his fault, mind?' said Mervyn, nodding at Lance. 'He gets a bit tetchy when he's hung over.' He waved a hand at Blossom. 'Give the bugger a drink before he does him a damage.'

Blossom offered the bottle to her brother.

Lance ignored it and turned to pick up his chair. He sat down and glared at Henry. 'So,' he said, 'you knows 'bout writin' and stuff, then, yeah?'

Henry looked uncertain. 'Well, I . . . '

'You'll know 'bout poems an' that, then, right?'

'Well, I . . . '

'Show him one of yours,' Lance said to Gareth. 'Let's see how good 'e is at judgin'!' He turned to Henry. 'You don't mind havin' a look, would ya?'

Henry swallowed. 'Well, I . . . '

'Is that all you can bloody-well say? *Well I*? Don't it get on your bloody wick saying *well I* all the soddin' time?'

Henry blinked several times and opened his eyes wide the better to focus on Lance's face. But everything was starting to look hazy, as if he was seeing the world through a deepening fog. 'Poetry's not really my sp-speciality, I'm afraid,' he said. 'I mean I don't know mush about it, really.'

'You'll look at 'is, though, yeah?' insisted Lance. 'As a favour to us, like: for your supper, an' that? 'Cause we wouldn't wanna make 'ee sing for it, would us? It not being your *sp-speciality* an' all.'

He nodded at Gareth, who got up and lumbered out of the room.

Henry glanced anxiously at Mervyn for guidance.

'We makes our own entertainment down here, see,' he said. 'Nothin' much else to do, is there, living in the wilds, an' all that?'

Gareth came back almost immediately clutching a tatty piece of paper to his chest. He shuffled over to Henry and laid it on the table beside him.

'Bes' one I got,' he said. 'Couldn't fine t'other ones, any'ow.'

'Tha's fine,' said Henry. 'Really! An' . . . an' thank you. Well done!'

He picked up the paper and flattened it out on the table next to his plate.

Blossom leaned towards him with her left hand resting on his thigh.

'Well,' prompted Lance, 'any good, is it?'

'Give him time,' said Mervyn. 'Can't rush this literary appreciation business, can you, Henry?'

Silence fell around the table as everyone, except the unconscious Great Uncle Bert, turned to watch the wheels of literary appreciation in motion.

Henry wished that he was somewhere else. Anywhere else, he decided, would have been nice. He hoped that Gareth would turn out to be an undiscovered literary genius, and that he would be able to recognize the fact. But as he gazed down at the crumpled sheet of paper, his heart sank. It was a page torn from a spiral bound exercise book with a red margin line running down the left-hand side. Gareth's poem had been impressed heavily in thick pencil in the middle of the page, and Henry's heart sank even further as he noted its brevity and the unnerving simplicity of the sentiment it contained. It read:

<u>owed 2 the 1 wot i luvs</u>
<u>by gaga clattwarthee</u>

i hopes 4 e
i mopes 4 e
i recon i b a dope 4 e

i sings 4 e
i mings 4 e
1 day i all swing 4 e

i trys 4 e
i lys 4 e
1 day i all dy 4 e

this ears me pome
this ears me song
if u says u dunt luv i
i nose you b rong

A deep gloom descended on Henry as he read it again in the hope that he had missed something insightful the first time around. He dared not look up for fear that it would be taken by Lance as a sign that he was ready to make his pronouncement. He read the poem again, conscious all the while of Blossom's breath on his neck, and her fingers inching up his thigh towards his crotch. He was aware, too, of Gareth's huge bulk behind him peering over his shoulder, mouthing the words over and over again in an earnest whisper.

He knew that he couldn't stay silent for much longer.

He reached for the wineglass and emptied it in a gulp.

'*Ah-hem*, er . . . I er, I don't quite un-understand . . .?' He glanced over his shoulder at Gareth and pointed at the second verse. 'Here? Er . . . *ming*?'

'Yeah,' said Gareth, 'ming, innet?'

'Ah!' nodded Henry. 'Yes! Yes, I see. And, er . . .?' He tapped the page with a finger. 'It, er . . .? It, er . . .?'

'Wha'?'

'Well . . . er, what *exactly* does it . . . er, . . . mean?'

'Pot!'

'Pot?'

'Pretty pot,' nodded Gareth, wide-eyed. ''E come from long, long away!'

'Oh, *Ming*!' said Henry, understanding suddenly. 'As in *vase*, y-you mean?'

'Potty-vase, yeah,' nodded Gareth, eagerly. ''E cost lots. You knock 'im down, he breaks!' he added, with concerned wonder.

'Yes, of course!' said Henry, sweating profusely. 'Of course! Of course!' He reached for the wineglass and raised it to his lips. It was empty.

'I see,' he said, putting the glass down on the table with a heavy hand, like a condemned man denied a final libation. 'It's fr-fragile, you mean? Your love for the ob-objec' of the poem is fragile, like a prizeless ar-ardifac'?'

Gareth smiled uncertainly: apparently on the verge of tears. ''E's a potty-vase, in 'e?' he said, with a note of panic creeping into his voice.

'Here,' whispered Blossom in Henry's ear as she filled his glass to the brim. 'Let me . . . top you . . . *up*!'

Henry picked up the glass, and drank half the contents. 'Yesss,' he said, over his shoulder at Gareth. 'It's a m-medaphor, you mean?'

Gareth's lower lip trembled. 'No . . . 'e's a potty-vase, in 'e!'

'Of course,' said Henry, doggedly. 'Of course! But i's also . . .' He sighed and thought better of it. 'Yes, i's a potty v-vase, in 'e?'

Blossom leaned close to refill his glass.

'Well?' snapped Lance.

Henry sighed. 'I's brief,' he hazarded. 'A-an' to the p-point.'

'That good, is it?'

'Leave him be,' chided Mervyn.

'Well,' said Henry, as Blossom's fingers toyed with his zip. 'I don't know mush . . . I mean, look, po'try isn't my . . .'

'You know about words, you said,' insisted Lance

'Yes. Well, I mean, no . . . nod really. I jus' draw the pitchers, mainly. An' that,' he hiccuped, 'that sorta stuff.'

'I bet they're really *sexy* pictures, too,' breathed Blossom in his ear.

'He's tryin' to get out of it!' snorted Lance

'No, no I'm nod,' insisted Henry. 'I's jus' thad I'm nod an authotity . . .' He tried again. 'An authority . . . authrotity . . . I . . . I'm nod an experd, is all.'

'Yeah? Well, I'm not an expert on seducin' helpless women, am I? But I knows when some bugger's tryin' to get his leg over me sister.'

Henry twitched as Blossom poked her tongue in his ear.

'Leave the bugger alone!' hissed Mervyn.

Lance glared at his father.

'Not you!' snapped Mervyn, pointing at Blossom. 'That silly cow!'

Blossom leaned back in her chair and toyed half-heartedly with her dinner.

Henry smiled lopsidedly at the old man. 'Well,' he slurred, turning back to Lance, 'I 'ave a-an op-in-ion, bud I'm nod sure . . . '

'Come on then, let's hear it.'

'Well,' he said, keeping his head bowed, 'I thing,' he licked his lips and stared resolutely down at the page, 'I thing i's a bid prim'tive. Y'know, in the true sense o' the word? Like Berriryl Cook is a prim'tive pa-painter?'

Lance stood up. 'He's takin' the piss!'

'Sit down!' snapped Mervyn.

Lance scowled, but sat down. 'Well . . . that the best you can do?'

Henry looked over his shoulder at Gareth, whose face looked in danger of collapsing in on itself with a heart-rending wail of infantile hurt.

'I don' mean i's bad,' said Henry, raising a comforting hand towards him. 'Jus' sord of . . . ver' simple an' . . . no, no childlike . . . an' No! I mean . . . it h-has a childlike in-innocence tha' gis id a sorta strength an' . . . '

'Bullshit!' said Lance, standing up with his fists clenched.

'Sit *down*!' insisted Mervyn.

Henry swallowed hard, and got unsteadily to his feet. 'Look,' he said, trying to meet Lance's eyes but feeling he was seeing him through a frosted window. 'Wad d'you spec' me t'say? Eh? I mean, I thing in the grade scheme of thin's is not ver' good. Bud . . . *bud*! . . . given who-ooo rode it, I thing is ver' sweet. An' . . . an' sen'imen'al! An' . . . an' . . . an' . . . So, are . . . are you happy now?'

He sat down with a bump, and glanced towards Mervyn, not wanting to look at Lance, and not daring to look over his shoulder at Gareth.

There was a deadening silence around the table. No one moved. No one seemed even to breathe. Henry looked down at the page expecting to be stuck a heavy and fatal blow from behind. When nothing happened, he looked up. Everyone was staring at him. Everyone was smiling at him. Even Lance was smiling as he tossed a five-pound note to his father.

'All right,' he said, 'you win.'

Henry frowned. 'Wha' . . . wha' d'you . . . ?'

'Took him thirty seconds to write that,' said Lance. 'And all you can say is: I thing i's a bid prim'tive!' It's a load of crap, that's what it is! Anyone with half a brain can see that. I haven't even read it and I know it's a load of crap!'

'I am deeply, deeply hurt,' said Gareth. 'In fact I would go so far as to say that I am emotionally cut to the quick.'

Lance pointed at Mervyn. 'I bet him you'd try to talk your way out of it. He said you had more guts. He was right. Congratulations.' He dropped his spoon into the soup bowl, and strode out of the room.

Henry turned and squinted at Mervyn. 'Y-you plan dit?' he said, dully. He felt very weak and the fog in the room had become all but impenetrable.

'Spur of the moment,' said Gareth behind him. All trace of his drooling, juvenile persona had vanished.

'Y-you can talk,' muttered Henry. 'An' . . . bud I . . . You're nod . . .?' He gave a lopsided grin. 'You was testin' me, wasn' you? See if I wos a liar!'

'You thought about it, didn't you?' said Mervyn.

'Wad if I did?' slurred Henry, as the fog seemed to envelope him completely. 'Bud . . . bud . . . bud . . . *why*?

'This is our house, and we like to know who's in it. Besides, we had to do something to pass the time until the drugs took effect, didn't we?'

'Drugzzz?' said Henry. 'Wad . . . wad drugzzz?' He turned and frowned up at Gareth. 'An', bud . . . h-how comes you can talk prop . . .?'

It was as far as he got. His eyelids fluttered and drooped, his chin dropped onto his chest, and his body twisted and slumped forward until his forehead came to rest with a soggy clunk in his dinner.

'Right,' said Gareth, briskly, 'so much for the entertainment. Get him out of there and down to the lab before he drowns. We need that thing downloaded before the anaesthetic wears off. And,' he added, smiling at Blossom, 'time for another shot, I think, don't you?'

* * *

'Would this be an appropriate juncture at which to set the table for dinner sir?' asked the colonel, appearing suddenly behind Henry. 'Given the point you have reached in the narrative?'

'*Jesus*!' gasped Henry, groping at his chest. 'Would you please stop doing that? You're gonna give me a heart attack one of these days!'

'Doing what, Mr. Kite?'

'Just sort of . . . turning up! Couldn't you cough or something to warn us?'

'I'm sure we could manage that, sir. Make a note, lieutenant, would you?'

'Certainly colonel.'

'And dinner, your grace?' asked the colonel, turning to the hooded figure. 'In the main tent, if now would be a good time?'

'Are you hungry, Henry?' asked the figure.

'Actually, I'm starving, now that you come to mention it.'

'Yes, thank you, then, colonel. Proceed as soon as you and the lieutenant are ready.'

* * *

36

NURSE BLOSSOM

It was 7 o'clock the following morning when Blossom crept into the room where Henry had spent the night. She closed the door behind her and tiptoed over to the bed to look down at him as he lay on his back, his mouth open, snoring softly. It was a pity he wasn't awake because she was wearing precisely the sort of nurse's uniform he had been fantasizing about for so many years, with a perilously short skirt, a tight button-popping blouse, a pair of wickedly high stiletto-heeled shoes, fishnet stockings, and a tiny paper hat pinned high on her back-combed hair. The only part of her outfit never to have featured in his fantasies was the stainless steel kidney dish in her right hand containing a hypodermic syringe, a pair of forceps and a wad of cotton wool.

She stopped at the side of the bed and gazed down at his sleeping face. After a moment's thought, she nodded to herself and lifted the duvet to inspect his early morning erection. Apparently satisfied with what she saw, she sighed and let the cover fall back into place. She put the kidney dish down gently on the bedside table and turned to look at him again. As far as she could tell he was unconscious rather than merely asleep. But she wanted to be certain, so she reached down and pinched his cheek. When he didn't react, she opened her hand and tapped him on the side of the head with the tips of her fingers. When he didn't react to that either, she drew back her hand and slapped him in the face, once, twice, and then backhanded for a third time.

'Henry?' she called, softly. Then 'Henry! *Henry!*' more loudly.

She grabbed his shoulders and shook him.

His only response was a snuffled '*Munuh-huh-nuh-muh?*' through his nose

For a moment, as she stood over him, she was filled with doubt and self-recrimination. She knew that what she was about to do was wrong; or at least, that the rest of the family would say that it was wrong, and if they caught her at it they would force her to take yet another of Mervyn's potions to calm her down. But the urge was so strong in her that she couldn't resist the temptation of his unguarded manhood. And the fact that its owner was out cold was the icing on the cake.

Blossom had long been of the opinion that most men were at the height of their sexual powers when they were unconscious. If they happened to wake up in the middle of one of her performances it could make arranging their bits for maximum advantage that little bit easier. But on the whole, she had found that any improvement was marginal and the downside was that they invariably wanted to express an opinion about how things ought to be done. She had long-since come to the conclusion that discussions of that sort were a waste of her time and energy: and that it was far better to have sex with the average man when he wasn't looking. At least then you didn't have to tell him that the Earth had moved for you, too, or that, no, thirty seconds really wasn't *too* quick! In Blossom's book, a comatose man was close to the perfect sexual partner. Not as rewarding as a woman, of course (most men simply didn't have the same depth of appreciation for the subtleties of genital anatomy and physical performance), but a hell of a lot better than one who was fully awake.

She glanced at the bedroom door, tiptoed over to it, and jerked it open to check that no one was lurking outside in the corridor. She looked both ways, closed the door quietly, took a large wad of chewing gum from her mouth and stuck pieces of it onto two of the picture frames where she knew there were hidden cameras. She took the hem of her skirt in both hands and tucked it into the broad leather belt around her pinched waist. Then, with a predatory gleam in her heavily painted eyes, she walked quickly across the room and leaned forward with her left knee on the edge of the bed. She placed her left hand beside Henry's head and lifted her right leg over him as if she was mounting a horse. She eased herself into position on his chest before inching forward until her knees were on either side of his head.

'Now,' she said through clenched teeth, as she grabbed his ears and lowered herself onto his face, 'take me, you big horny bastard!'

Of all the masturbatory fantasies that Henry's imagination had ever conjured up, this one would have been right up there alongside his most productive. Over the years he had imagined a seemingly endless stream of sexual encounters, including the odd one or two in medical institutions where an insatiable nurse, or nurses, used and abused him to within inches of his ailing life. But in all of his lurid imaginings, he had always been wide-awake when the squelchy bits had got started. So it was his great misfortune that he was still fast asleep when Blossom jerked her way to an eardrum-searing orgasm with her crotch pressed against his face and her fingertips pinching her nipples with delicate vigour. Her head was thrown back and her eyes tightly closed on a fantasy of her own in which Henry was altogether more muscular, stubble-faced and animal than he was in real life. Her mouth opened in a final gasp of regret as she shouted '*Il massivo*! *Il bastardo*! God damn it, you monster! *Sì! Sì! Sì!*'

When her abdominal muscles finally ceased their rhythmic clenching, she took several deep breaths, inched her way backwards onto his belly, and slumped forward with her naked breasts pressing against his face. Henry meantime, slept on, oblivious of what had just happened to him, and dreaming of sucking lime jelly and caviar through a muslin sieve.

* * *

Henry sat unmoving at the dining table in the tent, staring distractedly at the plate in front of him. His face was painfully red.

'Are you not enjoying your meal, Mr. Kite?' asked the lieutenant, leaning over the table towards him. 'Is the Vegetarian Chicken Supreme not to your liking, sir? Corio Boc and I prepared it especially for you in light of the preference you displayed for that particular dish during your comfort break at the motorway service station at South Mimms.'

Henry didn't reply.

'Are you feeling unwell, Mr. Kite?'

He shook his head. 'So *that's* what she meant,' he whispered.

'Mr. Kite?'

He looked up. 'Sorry . . .?'

'The Vegetarian Chicken Supreme, sir: is it not to your liking? The original recipe called for chicken as the main ingredient, of course, but our research suggested that Tofu marinated in a delicate morel and kai-chi sauce would be indistinguishable from the real thing.'

'No,' he said. He looked down at his plate. 'No, no, it's fine.'

'But you are not eating it sir.'

He blinked, and looked up. 'No, I . . . I don't seem to have much of an appetite at the moment, that's all.'

'On account of he's jus' been told he's a human dildo,' said Titus, around a mouthful of food.

'Thanks for reminding me.'

'Didn't look like you needed much remindin' to me, buddy,' said Titus, putting his knife in his mouth and sucking it clean.

'Actually, Corio Boc,' said the lieutenant, 'a dildo is a device that is most commonly inserted into the female genitalia. Whereas what Miss Blossom was doing to Mr. Kite . . . ❥

'*Yes*! *Quite*!' interrupted Henry. 'Thank you, lieutenant! But do you think we could leave the anatomy lesson for another day?'

'Certainly, sir! When would be a convenient . . .?'

'Lieutenant?' hissed the figure.

'Sir?'

'I believe that what Mr. Kite is trying to say is that he would rather not discuss the subject at all. Not today, not tomorrow, not ever. Do you see?'

'My apologies, sir,' said the lieutenant, turning to bow to Henry. 'And if the Vegetarian Chicken Supreme is not appetizing enough, perhaps Corio Boc and I could prepare something more to your liking?'

'Go on, get it down ya!' encouraged Titus, pointing at Henry's plate with his knife. 'Nothin' like a decent veggie dinner to put lead in yer pencil.'

'That's rich,' said Henry, 'coming from someone whose idea of haute cuisine is charred rat's brain on a stick!'

'Not anymore it ain't, buddy,' He puffed out his chest. 'I'm a vegan.'

'You're a *what*?'

Titus pointed his knife at the lieutenant. 'I been converted. Not easy findin' decent recipes, mind. Them hoity-toity buggers over at that *Michelin* wosname don't like veggie grub much, do they? Stupid buggers!'

He stuffed a forkful of food into his mouth and waved the fork in the air. 'I mean, fancy thinkin' eatin' meat with all that salt an' fat an' gristle an' cholesterol an' stuff's gonna keep 'em healthy.'

'I don't know how you do it,' said Henry to the lieutenant, 'but you're a miracle worker.'

'Actually, sir,' said the lieutenant, 'miracles are cultural devices employed in the mythologies of superstitious cultures to explain the existence . . . '

'Yes, thank you, lieutenant,' hissed the figure. 'Very interesting, I'm sure. But could we just concentrate on finishing our meal?'

'Of course, sir. And would you care for a dessert, Mr. Kite? Or coffee? Tea? A liqueur? Or would you rather I brought you the cheese board?'

'How about a double brandy?' said Henry. 'Actually . . . make that two.'

'Certainly, sir. And would there be a particular manufacturer whose products you find most suited to your palette?'

Henry shook his head. 'I'll leave that up to you.'

'Very good. And have you finished with the dish from your main course?'

Henry waved a hand. 'Take it.' He looked up. 'Sorry, by the way: I'm sure it was very nice, but I'm just not feeling hungry at the moment.' He turned to the hooded figure. 'Come on then: get on with it! Let's see what indignities you're going to embarrass me with next.'

* * *

Blossom pushed herself into a sitting position and looked down at Henry with an oddly maternal expression in her eyes. She took a handkerchief from the sleeve of her blouse, wet it with saliva, and dabbed at his nose and mouth. '*Il buono!*' she pouted as she patted at his lips and chin. '*Il cattivo! Il brutto!*'

When she was satisfied that he looked respectable, she climbed off the bed, straightened her clothes, and bent forward to kiss him on the lips. Then she took the syringe from the kidney dish, held it upright, pressed the plunger and smiled as a jet of clear liquid arced across the bed. She pinched his cheek to satisfying herself that he was still unconscious, and bent to rub the muscle of his upper arm with the cotton wool swab.

After she had injected him with its contents, she dropped the syringe into the kidney dish, and lifted the duvet from above his groin, pursing her lips and murmuring 'Adequate. Definitely adequate, that.'

While she waited for the antidote to take effect, she took a tube of KY Jelly from her apron pocket, cracked it open with her teeth, and squeezed a generous dollop onto his groin, before lobbing the tube over her shoulder and kneeling at the side of the bed. She pushed the duvet aside and took his manhood in her fist. She knew that he would wake soon, and wanted to be certain that he would be too aroused by then to refuse her offer of help.

Suddenly, the door flew open and Mervyn thrust his head into the room. 'I thought I told you to leave him alone?' he hissed.

'Go away!' she snapped. 'Can't you see I'm busy?'

Mervyn shook his head. 'Look . . . '

'Go away! Just this once? Please? I won't be long. Honest! All I want . . . '

'I know what you *want*,' said Mervyn, soothingly. 'Everyone in the whole world knows what you *want*, Blossom, my dear. But we can't always *have* what we want, can we?' He picked up the syringe and examined it closely.

He nodded, and motioned Tom Hertz into the room.

'Get her out of here before he wakes up,' said Mervyn. 'Give her another shot, and make sure she stays out of the way until it takes effect.'

'No!' pleaded Blossom, with her hands slipping from Henry's manhood as Tom pulled her away. 'I'm not such a bad girl really, am I?'

'Take that tube of gunk away, too, and get a cloth,' added Mervyn. 'If he wakes up with that lot plastered all over his dick he'll think he's been sucked off by a giant slug. And I don't think he could handle the stress.' He glanced quickly around the room. 'And get that muck off of those lenses.'

When the antidote took effect, Henry woke with a crushing headache, a vaguely familiar and not unpleasant musky taste in his mouth, and a conviction that it would be a bad idea to open his eyes. He didn't know where he was, but he could feel what he thought was sunlight streaming through what he assumed was a window at the foot of what seemed to be a bed, and for the moment he thought he would be safer not to move. At least, he hoped he was in a bed with sunlight streaming through a window, because if he wasn't, there was a chance that he was out in the open air. And if that were the case, he wasn't sure what it would mean for his wellbeing. But regardless of where the sunlight was coming from, he could tell that it was very strong and knew that if he wasn't careful it would blast its way through his fragile eyeballs and weld his retinas to his brain. He decided to keep his eyes closed until he had worked out where he was and what he was doing there.

One thing he knew for certain was that he wasn't at home. In spite of the familiar hint of muskiness that he still couldn't quite place, the air around him smelled different from his own bedroom. There was none of that familiar, foetid staleness, characteristic of bed linen that has absorbed so many assorted bodily fluids that it has taken on a life of its own and is about to crawl into a corner to reproduce. His own bedclothes had a distinctive matt sheen and a lank, limp, moist clamminess that often made him feel that he was sleeping in a flannelette pizza garnished with flakes of desiccated seminal fluid, mucus and sweat; which, though he hated to admit it, wasn't so far from the truth.

After a while, his curiosity got the better of him and he decided to find out where the sunlight was coming from. He raised his head slowly, and opened his eyes just a crack. The result was a blast of light that forced his head back onto the pillow as if he had been punched in the face by a giant fist. He grunted, and wondered if he had been struck by lightning. He put a trembling hand up to his face to check that his eyeballs hadn't been fused into their sockets, and was comforted to see the shadow of his fingers moving behind his closed lids. He swallowed with relief, and decided that it would be a good idea to keep his eyes shut for a while longer.

So he wasn't at home, and he wasn't at Sam's place, either. He knew that he wasn't at Sam's because the characteristic smell wasn't there: that combination of flat beer, stale tobacco smoke and washing that hadn't been properly aired. Whenever he stayed at Sam's flat, he ended-up sleeping on the sofa bed, vying for space on it with the flotsam and jetsam that had been lost down the backs and sides of the cushions over the years. Some of the things he had found there – usually only after he had slept with them for several hours – had made his skin crawl with disgust. There were the usual bits of food, cooked and uncooked, rock hard or soft and squidgy according to vintage, with most of it coated in a fungal growth that looked just as likely to start an epidemic as cure one. There were bits of stale toast with hairy marmalade squashed into them; decaying banana skins and apple cores; lumps of fruitcake; bits of biscuit; and a mishmash of boiled sweets, cigarette ends and tea bags mixed together in a mouldering potpourri. Worse still was the scary menagerie of insects, too diverse to catalogue and too numerous to count, that were to be found scavenging over it all when the lights were turned off. Yes, sleeping on the sofa bed at Sam's place could be a frightening experience, and was not to be recommended to anyone who hadn't taken the precaution of drinking themselves into a comatose state beforehand.

His worst experience had come one morning when he'd woken to find a used condom stuck to the side of his head. Aware of a vague discomfort, he'd rolled onto his back and put a palsied hand up to his left cheek to peel the rubbery thing away like an Elastoplast that had lost most of its stick. Then, blinking owlishly in the early morning gloom, he'd lifted it in front of his red-rimmed eyes and gazed at it with mild disinterest, before lowering his hand down by his side and turning over to go back to sleep. His eyes had snapped open in anguish a moment later and he'd surged into an upright position with his mouth opening wide in a blood-curdling scream. His head had clicked forward like an automaton's, and he'd watched in skin-crawling horror as his hand had tried to flick the clinging thing away, flapping at it madly, but powerless to make it let go. When he'd been unable to cope with the tension any longer, he'd forced himself to pull it off with the finger and thumb of his left hand. He'd tried to throw it away from him then, too; but again it had been stuck fast. He'd flicked at it, and plucked at it in increasing desperation. But all he'd managed to do was transfer it back to his right hand. Backwards and forwards it had gone after that, from one hand to the other as he'd flapped at it and flicked at it, and grimaced and shrieked his disgust. Finally, when he'd been able to bear the torment no longer, he'd thrown himself sideways onto the floor and crabbed his way towards the bathroom on his elbows and knees. When he'd got there, he'd torn off a ragged length of toilet paper with the heels of his hands and used it to pluck the repulsive thing from his skin. Then, with a yelp of triumphant hatred, he'd hurled it into the toilet bowl like a vanquished rattlesnake, and lunged forward instantly with a foot on the handle to flush it away.

After washing and scrubbing his hands and face several times, he'd gone back to the sink and done it again; and again; and again; and again, and again; before storming into Sam's bedroom to demand an apology. What he'd got instead was a yawn of irritable indifference, and an invitation to 'bugger off!'

'D'you know what the time is?' Sam had wanted to know.

'Ten seconds before the arrival of the grim-bleeding-reaper,' Henry had snarled, 'if you don't get up and grovel at my feet, you mucky bastard!'

'Condom?' Sam had frowned, as Henry had stood over him, fists bunched, challenging him to a fight. 'Haven't got any, mate: used the last one Saturday night, if you must know.'

'I bloody well know that, don't I, you moron!' Henry had shrieked. 'I just shared a bed with the sodding thing, didn't I?'

'Wash it out then, if you want,' Sam had suggested, before rolling over to go back to sleep. 'Chemist's on the corner, though,' he'd added, as an afterthought. 'Be a bit more hygienic, don't you think?'

It had taken Henry a long time to eradicate the groin-tightening, anus-flinching memory of that morning, and an even longer time to forgive Sam his holier-than-thou indifference to the mental anguish it had caused. Almost as long, in fact, as it had taken him to satisfy himself that all the washing and scrubbing with every cleansing agent he had been able to find in Tesco's Household Cleaning Department had made him wholesome again. When he'd eventually gotten around to speaking to Sam without snarling, they'd patted one-another on the back, agreed to let bygones be bygones, and gone out on a pub-crawl to celebrate the rekindling of their friendship. When they had staggered back to Sam's flat, five hours later, Henry had been too drunk to drive, too tight-fisted to pay for a taxi, and too lazy to walk the mile and a half to his house. He'd swayed gently in the middle of the room and shaken his head as Sam had tried to get the sofa bed ready for him to sleep on.

'*Unh-nuh*!' Henry had insisted. 'Nod geddin' me on that bloody thin' again, mate. No soddin' chance!' He would sleep in the spare room, he had told Sam curtly: the spare room, he had insisted, would suit him just fine.

Sam had been equally insistent that the spare room was for use only by his sister: and there would be hell to pay if Henry sullied it while she was away.

'Sullied?' Henry had exclaimed, indignantly. 'Bloody *sullied*? You are lecturin' me 'bout bloody *sullied*, you mucky bastard? Where'd you ged off preachin' 'bout hygiene? All I wanna do is crash out!'

'Yeah,' Sam had nodded as they'd stood toe-to-toe prodding one another in the chest, 'but it's nod tha' bloody simple, is it? I mean,' he'd added, waving an arm in an arc around the flat to prove to Henry that he could have had the freedom of the place if Sam's had been the only opinion that counted, 'if it was up t' me, mate? Bud is outa my 'ands, innit? She leaves stuff in there when she's gone. An' I can't 'ave you sniffin' through it, can I? Her knickers and stuff?' He'd lowered his voice to a whisper. 'They know if you 'ave, don't they, women? Don' ask me how . . . they jus' do!'

'Why,' Henry had asked, with slow deliberation, 'would I wanna go *sniffin'* in your sis'er's panties? Wad kine o' pervert d'you thing I am?'

'You don' like my sis'er's panties? Was wrong with 'em, then?'

'Nothin'! Nothin' ad all! Far's I know they're perfec'ly good pan'ies . . .'

'Perfec'ly good . . .'

'. . . I . . . I ex-spec'.'

'. . . good pan'ies. An' . . . an' you won't fine any . . . any bedder.'

'I know! I know! I bloody-well know tha', don't I?'

'Yeah? What . . . you been sniffin' round in 'em then, or . . . or wad?'

'Me? What kinda pervert you thing I am?'

'Nothin' t' do w-with pervert, is it?' Sam had insisted. 'Wear 'em on your 'ead, all I care. Nothin' perverted 'bout that.' He'd leaned closer, and spoken in a whisper. 'Do it meself if it was somebody else's sis'er. All I'm sayin' is she'd bloody-well know, wooden she?' He'd gazed around the flat as if he expected to see Amy step out of a cupboard and confront them with their disgusting voyeuristic behaviour. 'Eh?' Then he'd leaned back to focus on Henry's face. 'An' . . . an' I'm the one who'd ged id i-in the neck . . . right?'

'I unnerstan all that. I unnerstan! I do, I do, I do! Bud . . . the thing is . . .'

The argument had gone on long into the night, and so had the drinking.

Henry had passed out at around three o'clock in the morning, and been left by Sam in an untidy heap on the sofa bed to sleep it off. When he'd woken bleary-eyed, ten hours later, he'd been clutching a used tampon to his chest with both hands.

No, it definitely wasn't easy to forget what it was like sleeping at Sam's flat. And wherever he was now, it wasn't there. But if he wasn't at home, and he wasn't at Sam's flat, where the hell was he? And why did his head hurt so much? Whatever he was suffering, it wasn't a hangover. At least, it wasn't one of the common or garden variety to which he had been subjecting himself for too many years. And if it wasn't a hangover, the only thing that could explain his discomfort was . . . foul play!

The pain in his head felt as if it had been caused by some sort of heavy cutting equipment – a chainsaw or an angle grinder, perhaps? – and a process that had involved the removal, and subsequent replacement, of the top of his skull. He couldn't say for what purpose he had been treated in such a disgraceful fashion by a person or persons unknown, but he was satisfied that the apparent lack of a motive didn't mean that the possibility should be ruled out entirely. It was while he was pondering this and other factors that might help to explain his discomfort, that the events of the past forty-eight hours started to come back to him.

The first thing he remembered was his encounter with Robbie, Granddad and the penknife-toting Great Uncle Bert. Then he remembered meeting Mervyn and listening to his story about Rooter and Lou Cornish in the weapons room, and suddenly everything began falling back into place. He remembered that he was in a house that belonged to a bunch of strange and probably congenitally maladjusted (not to say potentially homicidal) evolutionary throwbacks who doubtless would stop at nothing to achieve whatever their pathologically evil ends might be. He had no doubt that their ends would be both pathological and evil, because what other sort of ends could congenitally maladjusted evolutionary throwbacks have? And now that he came to think about it, it was a miracle that he had managed to get to sleep, never mind survive the night un-murdered, with people like *that* roaming the house. He must have been a lot braver than he gave himself credit for, he decided, or a lot drunker. And the Clatworthies must have been a lot slower in their dismembering of unsuspecting visitors than his experiences the previous evening had suggested would be the case. He frowned when he realized that he didn't remember much about the previous evening; or at least, nothing beyond the embarrassment of Gareth's poem.

Suddenly, he sat upright, with his eyes not just open but staring wildly. He inhaled deeply through his nose, and flopped back onto the pillows, wishing that they would swallow him up and make the embarrassment of what he had said and done at dinner go away. He gazed unblinkingly up at the ceiling for several seconds, like a rabbit trapped in the headlights of an onrushing car. The sunlight streaming through the window at the foot of the bed burned his eyes, but not as much as the memory of what had happened at dinner burned his pride. He turned onto his stomach and buried his face in the pillows as a savage mental image of the grinning Clatworthies surfaced to mock him.

It was while his was lying on his belly, feeling sorry for himself, that he realized that he had an erection, and that it had probably been that way since he'd woken up on the floor by the fire at the Green Dragon Inn.

He frowned into the pillows. 'That's almost . . . that must be . . . '

He levered himself onto his elbows, squinted at his watch and did a quick calculation. Assuming that it was now morning, and he had slept through only one night, it must be . . . 'sixteen hours!' he gasped.

His first emotion was one of joy at the thought that he could keep it up for that long without continuous stimulation. Then he frowned, turned over thoughtfully and raised himself into a sitting position. Satisfying it might be, he decided, but natural it most certainly was not! What if there had been some sort of malfunction? What if his erectile tissue had seized up? How would he know? What the hell was erectile tissue, anyway, and would masturbation make its effects go away? Would his dick be grateful for the exercise and lie down? It had worked in the past when he'd been feeling uncomfortably horny. And he wondered if it would be worth giving it a try now. Intentionally or otherwise, he had certainly been subjected to more than his fair share of sexual provocation in the past thirty-six hours, with Amy standing over him with the light behind her at Sam's flat; Jo sitting on the chair in front of him as he'd lain on the floor at the pub; Mandy with her stocking tops on display in the passenger seat of the Probe; and, most unsettling of all, Blossom's sluttish performance at dinner. Even so, he told himself, now definitely was not the right time to be thinking about taking himself in hand.

He glanced quickly at the door. Or was it?

He turned to look through slitted eyes at the brightly lit window. Closing the curtains might be a good idea, he decided, if he was going to get personal. He didn't want to go blind for real. And besides, with the curtains drawn anyone looking into the room would find it difficult to see what he was up to.

He got out of bed and advanced cautiously across the floor towards the window, with one hand shielding his eyes against the glare and the other feeling his way along the wall as he went.

In a basement room not far away, several people watched him on a pair of monitor screens, his erection swaying in front of him as he inched forwards. It wasn't too large, or too threatening: just average in length and thickness, with an apparent smile on its pinkly bulbous head that seemed to say 'Good morning. I'm really pleased to meet you: bouncy, bouncy.'

Halfway across the room, he stubbed his toe on the leg of a chair.

He cried out in agony and started hopping on one leg, while his undaunted penis bobbed up and down. '*Not again!*' he hissed through clenched teeth.

The people the basement room watched in fascination, their eyebrows rising and falling, and their heads nodding up and down in time with the rise and fall of his cock, like spectators at a game of vertical tennis.

When the pain in his toe reached bearable proportions, he stopped hopping and limped on towards the window, groping forwards with his head bowed until he found the edge of a curtain. He pulled it across, and reached over to do the same to the one on the other side of the window. When the room had been reduced to a manageable level of darkness, he leaned back against the wall with a sigh, and opened his eyes.

He was struck by an overwhelming sense of déjà vu. A tall mirror on a stand at the side of the room was tilted towards him, and he could see in it a dimly dishevelled reflection of himself. It reminded him of how he had looked in the wardrobe mirror the previous morning after his life and death struggle with Sam's singing alarm clock. Only this time he was totally naked. His hair and penis were both standing on end as if they, too, were shocked by his primitive appearance. Around his neck was the gaudy necklace that Sam had jammed over his head after he and Amy had put him to bed. He wondered who had put him to bed this time, if he hadn't been in a fit state to do it himself. He couldn't remember either way, and thought it best not to ponder the possibilities too deeply. But the image of himself in the mirror was a different matter. It had a sobering effect, pushing all thoughts of masturbation out of his head. He wandered, trance-like, across to the mirror, with his fingers tracing the contours of the beads around his neck. He stopped to stare at himself, feeling uncomfortable and intimidated by the sight of his blatant arousal. After a while, he turned away and walked thoughtfully back to the bed. He got in, lay down, and pulled the duvet up to his chin.

Memories of the previous day's events started to run chaotically through his mind as he stared up at the ceiling. Suddenly, he came to a decision. He threw off the duvet, got out of bed and walked over to his holdall on a chair by the wall. He reached inside it and fumbled around until he found the pair of nail scissors he kept in his toiletries bag. He'd been wearing the stupid necklace for too long, he told himself, and now was the time to be rid of it once and for all. He went back to the mirror and snipped the thong holding the beads together, taking great care not to cut his throat in the process.

There was a rattling crash and a skittering sound as the heavy metal beads fell to the floor and rolled at his feet. He bent slowly and picked them up one at a time, holding them protectively like water in the palms of his hands. He walked back to the bed and sat down to examine them closely. He switched on the bedside lamp and leaned back against the headboard with a frown. He hadn't taken much notice of the beads since he'd first seen them, and was astonished to see how intricate they were. Each one was elliptical in cross-section and had a diamond-shaped hole cut through its centre. When he looked at them from the side he saw that they were roughly triangular, like wedges cut from a slightly flattened sausage of metal. The curved outer surfaces were decorated with an elaborate tracery inlaid with silver and gold wire in a pattern that looked vaguely familiar. One side of each piece had been milled flat with a complex design etched into its smooth surface. The other side of each piece looked identical, except that the designs weren't etched into the surface but raised above it. He turned them over in his hands.

The people in the basement room watched him intently.

'Fifty quid says he'll get it in five minutes,' said one.

'You're on,' said another.

Henry frowned and examined the beads even more closely. A sudden thought struck him, and he held two of them together so that the etched surfaces touched. He shook his head minutely, and turned one of the pieces over until its raised surface was in contact with the etched surface of the other piece. When he twisted them against one another, there was a gratifying click as they slotted together.

'Told you,' said a voice in the basement.

'Hasn't got there yet, though, has he?' warned the other.

'He'll make it. He isn't as daft as he looks.'

Henry let go of one of the beads and pouted dejectedly as it unlocked itself and dropped into his lap. He picked it up and slotted it back into place, holding the two pieces together with the tips of his fingers. Then he laid the pair carefully on the duvet and sorted through those that remained until he found what he was looking for.

The third piece fitted into place on the end of the other two with a click, and the rest of the puzzle was easily solved. It wasn't long before he had all eight pieces of the necklace lying in his lap. When he fitted the final piece into place, it was as if they all suddenly became magnetized and locked together to form a rigid, ornate and slightly squashed metal cylinder about nine inches in length and a little over an inch in diameter. He looked down at it for a moment with a deepening frown. Then his eyes opened wide in astonishment and he leapt from the bed with a yelp.

'Told you!' said Jo, triumphantly, turning to Robbie and holding out a hand. 'That'll be fifty quid, please.'

'Come on,' said Mervyn with a heavy sigh, 'let's go and find him before he does something stupid.'

37

DOLLY KILLJOY

Snot and urine were thick on the ground outside the Green Dragon Inn, as Jack and his lads (and the lethargic maid) tried to rouse their stale bodies for the coming attack on the Clatworthy's farmhouse. They looked terrible and smelled worse, as they gathered at the front of the building like ambulant corpses risen from the grave to steam in the first light of Judgement Day. With dried vomit encrusting their clothing and clotted in their hair, they hunkered down in corners and shied away from the light. They felt queasy and fragile, and not nearly as confident as they had the night before when, after some hard bargaining and some even harder drinking, Jack and Dolly had come to an agreement over what would be done with Henry's body after he had been killed. Negotiations had been tough and Jack had given ground slowly, but he had eventually agreed that, if he got to Henry first, he would allow Dolly to search the corpse and burn whatever Gummer and Tickle Muttocks hadn't eaten, before scattering the ashes over her granddad's allotment in Peckham Rye.

Jack and his lads (and the cynical maid) had felt that this last demand smacked of a certain girlie sentimentality until Spider had pointed out that there were more bodies dug in around Grandpa Killjoy's potatoes than there were hairs sprouting from Tickle Muttock's bollocks. Most of the lads had been impressed by that suggestion, because Tickle was as hairy as a gibbon and they had figured that anyone nasty enough to rub out *that* many people wasn't someone they wanted to mess with. But Gummer and Dinger Bell hadn't been so easily convinced, and had decided to work out for themselves just how much of a murdering bitch Dolly was claiming to be. So, after foiling Tickle's frantic attempts to get away, Dinger and Alfie Driver had held him down while Gummer had started pulling out his pubic hair with his best set of electrical pliers. For a while, everyone except Tickle had been having a great time, taking bets and counting in unison. But when he'd bitten through the rubber boot that his brother had wedged between his teeth to stop him screaming, and had begun pleading with them to let him go, most of the lads (and the sniggering maid) had drifted away in search of someone less fragile to maim. Even so, Gummer, Dinger and Alfie had stuck doggedly to their tasks, and had eventually declared that the hair count had reached two thousand and ninety-eight by the time there had been nothing left around Tickle's groin to uproot. All bets had been off, however, after Dimmer Bright had pointed out that, since most of what had been harvested from Tickle's crotch had been torn away in bunches and no one, especially Gummer and Dinger, was any good at counting, the true number could be anywhere between Bert Newton's conservative thirty-seven and a half, and Spud Pady's optimistic twenty-two million and eight: and that, therefore, the only thing that everyone could agree on was that Tickle's crotch smelled worse than a dead badger's bum-hole.

Dolly had watched them with a growing sense of irritation, fearing that if they didn't focus on the business at hand soon, they might forget why they were there and start wandering back to wherever it was they had come from, leaving her boys to do all the fighting and, more to the point, all the dying that might need to be done. She wasn't sentimental about such things. It was just that in those days of high inflation and rising prices, replacing dead and disabled gang members could be an expensive business, and she wanted to be certain that it would be Jack's lads, rather than her boys, who would be getting themselves killed and maimed. She had decided to increase their motivation for the coming battle by appealing to their better natures and promising that anyone who found Henry Kite and failed to hand him over to her unmolested would be castrated by Boxer wielding a couple of half-bricks. When Dinger had tried to laugh this off as mere bravado, Dolly had pointed with a manicured fingernail at the pair of shrivelled objects rattling around inside the intricately carved golden cage hanging from the chain at her neck.

'These,' she had pointed out, in a voice like chiselled ice, 'belonged to the last tosser who tried to stitch me up. They're a bit past their sell-by date now,' she had added, as Spider's machete had swished into view, 'so any new contributions would be gratefully received. I do hope I make myself clear?'

'Sounds fair enough to me,' Jack had nodded, offering her his hand on the deal. 'What d'you buggers reckon?'

After a moment's hesitation, unsure what it was they were being asked to do, his lads (and the maid for whom castration wasn't [much of] a threat) had gone for the safest option and given him the sort of rousing volley of spitting, snorting and farting that passed for a vote of confidence down at The Lodge.

After that, the scrumpy had started to flow freely again, and with the pools of urine and vomit spreading inwards from the corners of the room, Gummer and Dimmer had decided to regale the company with a graphic account of how they had once rogered their way through a whole flock of sheep in a single humping. The better to illustrate his story, Dimmer had clambered onto a table, taken off the wide leather belt that kept his rubbery paunch in check and held it up to point at the notches carved along its edge.

'One 'underd and sempty-nine!' he had boasted, thumping himself in the chest with a fist. 'Count 'em yerself you don't b'lieve me. An' this 'ere idden even me Sunday best.'

Jack and his lads (and the triumphant maid) had clapped and stamped and roared their approval, safe in the knowledge that Dolly's mob could never come close to matching such an impressive achievement.

Dolly's boys had shifted uneasily in their seats until, to everyone's amazement, including his own, Nobbler had clambered unsteadily onto the bar, and held up his hands for silence. 'Yeah?' he had shouted. 'Yeah? Well I shagged me granny's Alsatian, didden I? So there!'

Jack and his lads (and the suddenly unhappy maid) had fallen silent, while the Essex boys had clapped, stamped and cheered with renewed vigour.

'An' 'e were real vicious, an' all!' Nobbler had added above the clammer.

He'd tried to stand upright on the counter to wave his arms above his head in triumph, but had succeeded only in dislodging what was left of Perce's mugs and glasses from hooks in the ceiling, sending them crashing to the floor to explode around the feet of the assembled company like crystal grenades. So impressed had his audience been by this further demonstration of his lawless depravity that both gangs had begun hurling bottles and glasses at the floor, the walls and each other in an unstinting display of intertribal bonhomie.

Nobbler had been lifted from the bar by Dinger and Curly Hare, hoisted onto their shoulders and carried around the room in triumphal procession. Never before had anyone lauded him for anything, and he'd been so overcome with gratitude that he hadn't known whether to laugh or cry. Suddenly, he'd been granted a place of honour amongst the hardest of the hardcases and the precious moments of comradely backslapping, goolie-grabbing and biceps-punching that had followed had been the happiest he had ever experienced. As the procession holding him aloft had wound its way through the building, he'd decided that it would not be in his best interests to mention that his granny's dog had been a dachshund, not an Alsatian, and that he hadn't so much shagged it as poked it in the arse with his Action Man doll for doing a dump in his toy box.

Sitting alone in a corner, bruised, battered, bleeding and dejected, Vinny had watched Nobbler with envious eyes and plotted how to murder the cocky little shit without being noticed.

Dolly had left the revellers to it, and had told Spider to stand guard at the doors of one of her ambulances while she'd taken a nap in the back. She'd been determined to be fresh and alert for the morning when she meant to get the missing jewellery back from Henry Kite and make him regret, long and hard, the inconveniences he had caused her to suffer.

According to Bonce's new best friend, Simon Hawker, Kite was holed up with some local yokels called the Clatworthies in a ruin of a farmhouse on the edge of something called Sodmire Bog. But it didn't matter where he was hiding, because she meant to take whatever action was necessary to restore both her property and her reputation for brutality: and if that meant initiating a bloodbath of biblical proportions, with the countryside and its inhabitants laid to waste in the process, so be it. She couldn't imagine that a bunch of country bumpkins would hold her up for long, anyway, and if they all spoke with the same whining accents as Jack and his lads, rubbing them out would be doing the rest of the country a favour.

There had been no sign of Perce Pratt, or his friends, since she and Jack had taken control of the Dragon. It hadn't surprised her, because if they hadn't had the guts to stick around long enough to face Jack and his posse of cretins, there was no way they would be hurrying back to face her and her gang of battle-hardened assassins. The only possible cloud on her horizon was Vinny's dubious account of the men with the fancy handguns who, he still insisted, had released the hostages from the pub before she and her boys had go there. If they had existed at all, which she doubted, they couldn't have been anything to do with the police, because, if they had been, Vinny and Nobbler would have been arrested for kidnapping and unlawful imprisonment. Since that hadn't happened, she couldn't see how the mystery men could have been anything other than a pair of straw-chomping hayseeds who'd bought themselves a couple of replica handguns by mail order so that they could go poncing about in front of their yokel friends doing impressions of Starsky and Hutch. She hadn't expected the police to come asking questions, either, because she had a feeling that involving the law in personal matters wasn't the way things were done in this God forsaken backwater. You only had to look at Jack and his band of inbred morons to see that they still lived in a feudal society, and she was certain that if Perce and his cronies ever plucked up courage enough to try to retake the building, they would do so without asking for help from the filth. Not that she would have minded facing a whole troop of the local wooden tops who, she felt certain, wouldn't know their collective arse from their collective elbow, having never had to deal with anything more villainous than a brain-dead farmhand with his todger stuck up the back passage of some unfortunate bovine. And the more she'd thought about things, the more determined she had become not to get caught up in Vinny's paranoia. The best thing she could do, she had told herself, was get a good night's sleep and worry about Bumpkinshire's version of the Untouchables in the morning. If she could be bothered to worry about them at all.

In the harsh light of morning, Dolly surveyed Jack's vigilantes and wondered if they, rather than any gunmen, real or imagined by Vinny, would turn out to be the worst of her problems. Most of them hadn't slept at all during the night, having preferred to take part in an attempt to drink Perce's cellar dry. Now, with their teeth feeling furry and their nostrils clogged with congealed sick, they scratched at their bodies with clawed hands and watched with dull-eyed indifference as Gummer emptied his bowels into the barrel of winter pansies that Perce had planted at the top of the steps by the front door.

The rest of the car park resembled the A & E Department in a big city hospital on a Friday night after the pubs had kicked out. Zombie-like figures staggered, crouched, vomited, pissed, coughed, choked, farted and crapped in an attempt to get the blood pumping back through their veins. One lost soul, standing at the foot of the steps with his arms hanging at his sides, forgot to squat and emptied his bowels into the jeans sagging around his ankles.

Dolly stood in the doorway at the back of the ambulance, and inspected the chaos around her, biting delicately into a croissant, and taking a drag from her first cigar of the day as she watched.

'If one of those lumpkins even *thinks* about messing with my motor,' she told Spider around a mouthful of crumbling pastry, and with a ring-encrusted little finger pointing at the yellow convertible nearby, 'you have my permission to cut his dick off.' She patted delicately at her lips with a napkin. 'OK?'

Spider nodded without expression and tested the edge of the machete's blade with his thumb. 'What about that?' he asked, nodding at Jack standing at the top of the steps with an arm thrust down the front of his trousers.

'Just keep the dumb bastard away from the Merc,' she said, as she pushed the tail of the croissant into her mouth and clamped her teeth on it with an ominous snap.

Spider nodded, and stared steely-eyed across the car park at Jack.

Unlike Jack's lads, most of Dolly's boys had recovered, more or less, from the previous night's drinking. They had known only too well that their boss disapproved of heavy alcohol consumption when there was work to be done, so they had gone easy on Perce's scrumpy, aware that if anyone drank more than Dolly thought was good for them, she was liable to have Spider chop off a toe or two here and there to sober them up. She had discovered long ago that the sight of gang members listing to the left or to the right as they hobbled in circles, had a way of reminding the others where their loyalties lay.

'Right,' she said, licking the tips of her fingers. 'Get 'em fell in.' She took a final drag of her cigar and tossed the stub on the ground.

Spider nodded at Boxer, and they set off to round up the stragglers.

'Tell Curly to have 'em check their shooters,' Dolly called after them. 'Give 'em plenty of ammo, and tell 'em don't ponce about!'

She pointed at Jack. 'And get that pile of arrested development over here now. I want to know everything he knows about this Clatworthy mob.'

Jack scowled as Spider strode towards him. He had spent the night in Perce's bed, dreaming of drowning kittens in a struggling string bag. Now he was as ready for a fight as he was ever likely to be and determined not to allow the stuck-up bint from up London way to take all the credit. As he turned to survey his ragged band of warriors littering the car park, he thrust his hairy paw even further down inside his underpants and rummaged his sagging scrotal sack back into place. Then he spat on the gravel at the foot of the steps and sniffed appreciatively as Gummer squittered over the pansies again.

Inside the Dragon, Vinny was inching slowly towards the door of Perce's spare room. He was hung-over, shagged out and desperate to get away from the terrifyingly knickerless, and heavily tattooed, apparition that lay across the rumpled bed with her chunky legs flung wide and her unguarded pudendum threatening the world. He had always known that one-night stands could be dicey, fraught as they were with the threat of disease and the vengeance of cuckolds. But this latest in an unenviable line of beer-goggle conquests looked like putting all of his previous high-risk encounters in the shade.

The woman on the bed was Sally 'T & G' (Tongue & Groin) Board. The only female member of Jack's posse (and his would-be girlfriend – would-be if he would stop running away!) she might be, but she exuded the psychotic machismo of an all-in wrestler, and was more use in a tight corner than all of the lads put together. She was strong, and meaty, and sported a moustache that had caused many a strong man's libido to wither. With the shoulders of a running back and the thighs of a weightlifter, she was a formidable battering ram of an opponent with a reputation for gumming open beer bottles and tins of her favourite cat food without the aid of her dentures.

As Vinny tiptoed through the door, and out onto the landing, with his crumpled belongings tucked under an arm, Sally's left eye snapped open, and her lips drew back from her nicotine-stained teeth with a snarl.

'Where be you off to, then, my precious?' she growled, rising on an elbow to fix him with a stare as hard and as sharp as a clout nail. 'You idden leavin' ol' T & G afore 'er's 'ad her brekus, is 'ee, my lover?'

Vinny screamed, and fled down the stairs at a gallop.

At the side of the building, in Perce's abandoned lean-to skittle alley where they had spent the night together, Bonce and Simon woke with a deal of self-conscious apologising and manly grunting as they struggled to disentangle themselves from each other's arms. A powerful bond of friendship had built up between them in the short time since they had first met. But now, confused and strangely elated, they were trying hard not to look one another in the eye as they headed, reluctantly, for the door and the coming fight with the Clatworthy clan which neither of them wanted to take part in.

At the back of the building, Dinger Bell and Bert Newton were huddling together on the roof of Henry's dented Volvo with their feet drawn up and their eyes clouded with terror as the Naggs brothers' prize ram, Lord Dunbar III of Pianosa, waited for them to come down. Five hours earlier, they had tried to have their wicked way with one of his favourite ewes, and he had made it clear that he wouldn't rest until after he had returned the favour.

As the morning light stuck through the little barred window above his head, Nobbler stood up and stumbled towards the door of the woodshed at the bottom of Perce's garden where he had spent the night on his own. He had been expecting Bert and Dinger to join him after they'd relieved themselves over Henry's car. But their chance encounter with the enraged Dunbar had put paid to that. Now, with his mouth dry and his head throbbing like a snare drum, he opened the door onto a painfully bright world and headed with leaden steps towards Dolly's boys and Jack's lads as they drew themselves up in ragged lines like a suicide squad from *The Legion of the Damned*.

A mile away, on the other side of Hangman's Hill, Richard Choat shivered under a blanket of straw as he woke from a night spent dozing fitfully in the sty belonging to Hubert's fearsome blue ribbon sow, Chantal du Lac. He had stopped sobbing, and no longer cared what he was doing there. All he wanted was for the nightmare of the past thirty-six hours to come to an end.

Chantal watched him with the same gimlet-eyed suspicion with which she viewed all potential threats to her litter of squealing young ones, letting him know by the matronly, no-nonsense look in her eye that he wouldn't be leaving her company until after Hubert had said he could go.

In bedrooms deep beneath The Stone Dancers, Sam and Amy Johnson were in no hurry to leave.

'You don't really have to go, do you?' pouted Amy, as Max de Griese slipped into his boxer shorts and reached for a T-shirt. 'Don't leave poor little Amy all on her ownsome.' She pouted again: 'Pretty please?' as she threw off the duvet and patted the mattress beside her. 'Come back to bed,' she urged, 'and show little Amy, *again*, what she's been missing all these years.'

Max smiled as he pulled on his jeans. 'Not now,' he said, glancing at his watch. 'Little Amy'll have to wait 'til big Max gets back from work. And if she's been a really, *really* good girl, he might give her a jolly good spanking.'

'What if she's been a really, really *naughty* girl?'

'Then she'll be in serious trouble, won't she? And Max will have no choice but to make things very, *very* hard for her indeed.'

'Ooh, goodie!' she squealed. 'Can we start now?'

'Go back to sleep,' he said, as he opened the door. 'And don't forget that the boss wants to see you and Sam later. I'll come and get you when it's time.'

In a bedroom on the other side of the hallway, Sam watched as Kate bent with her back towards him and pulled on her panties.

'What are you looking at?' she asked, without turning around.

'Just admiring the view,' he said, with his hand sneaking under the duvet. 'I don't suppose you've ever thought of selling postcards?'

'No. But if you're a really good boy I might let you take the pictures.'

'Hurry back,' he said, levering himself into a sitting position against the headboard. 'My camera has a very fast shutter release!'

'Say *cheese*!' demanded Charlotte Piece in high heels and panties as she backed slowly away from Ole, Gunnar and Jon with Sir Richard's Polaroid camera held up to her eye. 'And for goodness sake move closer together,' she scolded, lowering the camera and stamping her foot. 'All those lovely willies won't fit in if you're too far apart.'

'Turn to your left,' said the photographer at Exeter Police Station, 'and don't smile. It ruins the composition.'

'Smile?' grated Sir Richard. 'What the hell have I got to smile about, you limp-wristed moron?'

'Look,' said the photographer, with a creative toss of the head, 'just shut up and get on with it, will you? You're the criminal here, not me. I used to think I was going to be the next David Bailey, I did. Now look at me: taking pictures of pushers, prossies and perverts! By the way,' he added, as he pressed the shutter release, 'which one are you?'

'Sourire s'il vous plait, belles dames, et de passer un peu plus rapproches,' said the street photographer to Jackie, Cyril, Vicky and Beth as they stood grinning happily with their arms around one another outside the entrance to Paris's

Hotel Scribe. 'Bon! Dites le fromage.'

'Pazzey une bonne journee, Monsieur et jeunes filles,' he finished with a bow as he proffered his card.

'Mercy, mon sewer,' said Jackie, smiling brightly.

Cyril clapped his hands and rubbed them together. 'Right then, ladies,' he smiled, 'where're we off to now?'

'*Shopping*!' they cried together.

'If you don't mind watchin' three silly girlies tryin' on lots o' sexy outfits?' said Jackie. 'Second thoughts, you two better go on your own. We don't want poor ol' Sizz gettin' all hot an' bothered, do we?'

She delved into the depths of her enormous metal studded handbag and brought out a thick wad of French banknotes.

'Here,' she said, doling them out in handfuls to Vicky and Beth, 'somethin' for you to be gettin' on with. Don't spend it all at once, mind,' she added as she waved them goodbye. 'An' we'll see you back 'ere for dinner, OK?'

* * *

'I feel sorry for him, actually,' said Henry.

'What that Sizzle?' said Titus. 'You gotta be kiddin' me, buddy. Fallen in the shit an' come up smellin' o' roses, that bugger has.'

'No, I mean Richard Choat.'

Titus shook his head. 'No, no! Listen . . . he had it comin', didn't he? He's one o' them male piggy wosnames.'

'And if that isn't calling the kettle black I don't know what is.'

'Hey, listen buddy . . . I told ya: I ain't no bleedin' racist!'

'No, that's not what . . . '

'Excuse me, sir?' came the colonel's disembodied voice.

'Yes, colonel,' answered the hooded figure, 'how can we help you?'

'Sorry to interrupt such an interesting discussion, sir,' said the colonel with an audible smirk, 'but I thought you would like to know that a large group of indigenous peoples is heading towards your position. Mostly Belgae and Durotriges as far as we can tell.'

'I see,' said the figure. 'And do you know why?'

'The lieutenant's information suggests that they are in the nature of what you might call a band of happy pilgrims, sir.'

'You believe their intentions to be peaceful, then?'

'Indeed we do, sir, yes.'

'Interesting,' murmured the figure. 'Lieutenant . . . ?'

'Sir?'

'How far away are they . . . precisely?'

'The main party is approaching the edge of the new exclusion zone, sir.'

'And how far would that be?'

'Precisely 15 miles, or 24.14 kilometres, sir. However, their advance party is already a good deal closer than that.'

'How close, exactly?'

'Precisely 2 miles, or 3.2187 kilometres, sir.'

'And you believe them to have no hostile intentions?'

'Indeed we do, sir.'

'Go on . . .'

'Well, our intelligence suggests that they are responding positively to the colonel's earlier encounter with the Roman mounted patrol, as we predicted they would.'

'Excellent! But please be good enough to elaborate for Mr. Kite's benefit, would you?'

'Of course, sir. They appear to be celebrating the fact that the drones – if you will pardon the use of the vernacular, Mr. Kite? – scared the living shit out of the Romans.'

'Apology accepted,' murmured the figure.

'Thank you, sir.'

'Colonel?'

'Sir?'

'Are you confident that you have the situation under control?'

'Indeed we are sir, yes.'

'In which case, I will leave the matter in your capable hands.'

* * *

38

GARETH AND THE WHALE

Henry rushed out of the bedroom with the ornate rod of interlocking necklace beads held tightly in both hands. His erection bobbed and bumped against his lower abdomen as he turned and ran along the corridor. When he reached the door at the far end, he pushed it open with the sole of a bare foot and stumbled into the weapons room. The fire in the grate had gone out, and the air had become cool and clammy, but bright light slanted in through high windows to his left and glinted like a thousand tiny suns from the armour and weaponry hanging and standing around the room.

He paused for a moment with his hands in front of his face, shielding his eyes from the glare and squinting along the room to the place where the sword in the armourer's block shone like a tongue of bright fire. With his eyes half-closed and his mouth shut, he put his head down and hurried along the carpet until he drew level with the shining blade. He stopped and stared at it in awestricken silence, aware suddenly that he might be about to make a fool of himself. Then it occurred to him that there was no one around to see him do it if he did, so there was nothing at all for him to worry about.

For a second or two, he was too excited to move. But after a pause, he opened his hands and looked at the assembled line of heavy metal beads lying across his palms. He shook his head in gratitude for what he saw and stretched out his arms like an automaton until the beads were held upright next to the naked hilt of the sword. He checked the pattern on the beads against the tracery on the mirror-like blade; double-checked it; then checked it again. When he was satisfied that he hadn't let his imagination run away with him, he tilted his head back, with his mouth open and his teeth bared, and hissed an ecstatic stream of self-congratulatory gibberish up at the ceiling.

'*Yes*!' he crowed. '*Oh, yes*! *Yes*! *Yes*! *Yesssss*! *Oh I* . . .! *Oh you* . . .! *Oh me* . . .! *Oh hah, hah, hah*! *Oh hee, hee, hee, hee, heeeeee*!'

Then, trembling slightly, and with his eyes staring in anxious anticipation, he lifted the column of beads and positioned it carefully to locate the diamond-shaped hole through its centre over the diamond-shaped shaft of the sword's hilt, before sliding the one slowly and deliciously down onto the other. The pieces were a perfect fit, and it was a measure of his recent lack of familiarity with the sexual act that he could remember no moment of slow penetration that had given him more pleasure.

He let go of the beads, and took a step back to gape in wonder at what he had just done. Apart from the missing pommel, the sword was complete.

There was an apologetic cough behind him.

'Excuse me?' said an unfamiliar voice. 'But you really ought to be careful with that, you know?'

Henry turned to find Mervyn standing a few feet away with Gareth, Jo, Blossom, Lance, Gavin and Rooter around him.

'Well done,' he said, in a voice miraculously free from the whining West Country drawl Henry so detested.

But Henry was too excited to notice. And too drunk on his success with the remaking of the sword handle to wonder what Mervyn and the others were doing there, let alone to register immediately that, apart from the odd towel or two here and there, they were every bit as naked as he was.

'Look,' he said, turning and pointing at the sword. 'Look what I did!'

Mervyn pressed his thin lips together, and nodded. 'Yes,' he said, 'very clever. Very clever indeed. But the thing is . . .'

Henry was disappointed by the old man's lack of enthusiasm. The least he felt he could have expected were wild cheering and dancing in the streets.

'It's the handle!' he cried, indicating the sword with exaggerated hand gestures. 'Don't you see?' He turned and pointed at the weapon. 'I had it on me all the time, and I didn't even notice.'

'Yes,' said Mervyn. 'Yes, of course you did. But you see . . .'

'It was the necklace!' exclaimed Henry, motioning from his throat to the sword with both hands. 'I was wearing it all the time. Don't you see?'

Mervyn sighed. 'Yes, of course we can see. But . . .'

Henry was dumbfounded by the man's apparent lack of interest. He turned and pointed, like a neurotic airhostess motioning tardy passengers to their seats, with his manhood slapping from side to side in time to his energetic hip swivelling. Heavily sedated though she was from her early morning injection, Blossom followed every movement to and fro with gimlet eyes like a hungry mongoose sizing-up a swaying cobra. Henry was blissfully unaware of her predatory fascination and continued to swivel and point for all he was worth.

'Don't you *care*?' he beseeched them, holding his hands out towards them in supplication as his penis slowed its rhythmic waving and came to rest pointing at the ceiling behind them. 'Aren't you even the *least* bit interested?'

Jo tilted her head to one side. 'Better stop waving your dick about, tiger,' she said. 'There's a lot of sharp edges in here.'

He frowned at her uncomprehendingly for a moment. Then he glanced down at himself and immediately slapped his hands over his crotch.

'Oh my God!' he breathed, as his eyes darted towards the door.

'Here,' said Jo, taking a towel from around her neck and preparing to throw it to him. 'Better put this on.' She looked sideways at Blossom. 'The natives are getting restless again.'

He reached out with both hands to catch the towel, but realized as he did so that he was exposing himself again. When he dropped his hands to cover his modesty, the towel hit him in the chest and started to fall to the floor. He reached to catch it as it fell, but remembered his exposed manhood and covered it again with both hands. Then, with a final effort of will, he forced himself to grab at the towel with his right hand as it fell, missing it several times on the way down and managing in the process a convincing mime of a one-armed anal retentive trying to juggle with jelly. Finally, red-faced and knock-kneed, with a claw-like hand covering his genitals, he caught the towel and held it in front of his groin. When he looked up, with an uncertain grin, Lance was smiling and clapping his hands.

'You're a fan of Buster Keaton, then?' he said. 'Or was that Mr. Bean?'

Henry grinned, sheepishly. 'Sorry,' he said, gazing down at himself, 'It's a bit . . . I don't think . . . It won't . . . I can't get it to . . .' He coughed his embarrassment. 'It . . . er, it doesn't seem to want to go down.'

'Mmmm,' murmured Blossom, 'nice.'

Henry smiled, uncertainly. Then he frowned. 'Oh my God!' he gasped, registering for the first time that they were naked. 'You . . . You're all . . .!'

'Yes,' said Lance, nodding amiably, 'we are, aren't we?'

'And,' said Henry, 'you . . . you've all got . . .'

'Yes,' agreed Gareth, looking down at his own impressive manhood, 'haven't we, though?'

'*Jesus Christ!*' gasped Henry, as he wrapped the towel tightly around his waist and clung onto it with both hands. The situation suddenly looked far worse than anything he had previously imagined. It now appeared that these strange people weren't going to hack him to death with gruesome, medieval instruments of torture: they were going to use an entirely different set of weapons on him. Weapons the prospect of which he found infinitely more terrifying than cold steel. And as he glanced anxiously around the semicircle of aroused masculinity hemming him in, he had to admit that Gareth's was by far the most terrifying weapon he had ever seen in his life.

His Adam's apple bobbed. 'What . . . what are you going to do with me?' he asked, his eyes darting nervously back towards the door.

'Nothing,' said Mervyn. 'Not if you mean by that doing something *to* you? But we might do some things together.'

Henry's eyes narrowed to slits, and he crouched, ready to run. 'Together? What do you mean, *together*? An orgy: is that what you're saying?' He thought for a moment. Then he stood up with his head held high in a manner he thought suited to the martyr he felt he was about to become. 'Is it your intention to use me, then?' he asked, immediately nodding in confirmation of his worst fears. 'Yes, I can see it all now. You're some kind of crazy religious sect, aren't you, and you're going to rape me.'

'Cheeky sod!' snorted Blossom. 'We don't have to pretend to be religious maniacs to give you a damned good rogering, you know. We're not ashamed to be slags.' She glanced sideways at Jo. 'Well, I'm not, anyhow. Even if there's one or two round here allows themselves to be held back by unrealistic expectations of perfection.'

'Never been a problem of yours, though, has it?' said Jo. 'No one ever accused *you* of being picky.'

'Stop it!' said Mervyn, holding up a hand like a traffic policeman stepping into the path of an on-rushing truck. 'Stop it at once!'

He turned and bowed to Henry. 'Please don't distress yourself, Henry. We were merely trying to calm you down.'

'Calm me down?' cried Henry, in disbelief. 'Are you mad?'

Mervyn nodded, serenely. 'You are naked,' he said, pointing, 'so we are naked. We thought it would help you feel more at home?'

Henry was stunned. 'Where do you think I live, for Christ's sake: some sort of nudist camp's communal sauna?'

Mervyn shrugged, peevishly. 'We were only trying to help,' he said, as he took a towel from over his shoulder and wrapped it around his waist. 'You could show a little gratitude, you know.'

'Help?' echoed Henry. '*Help?*' He pointed at Gareth's huge member without trusting himself to look at it again. 'Listen – and believe me it's nothing personal Gareth – but did you honestly think that confronting me with *that* in all its enraged glory was really going to make me relax?'

Mervyn motioned for the others to cover their nakedness. 'I'm sorry,' he said. 'Obviously we miscalculated. We just thought it would be easier for you to cope with the truth, if we looked as vulnerable as you probably feel.'

'Truth?' said Henry, waving a hand in Gareth's general direction. 'I'll tell you about *truth*, shall I? How come he isn't drooling down his chin anymore? That's the kind of *truth* I want to hear!'

'Ah, yes,' said Mervyn. 'Yes. Well, you'll have to forgive us for that, won't you, the accents and stuff? We only did it to protect our identities, you know. We couldn't help it: it's a habit, you see.' He put his head on one side. 'Actually, that's a lie; we could help it perfectly well if we wanted to. Well, some of us could.' He glanced sideways at Blossom. 'The rest of us really *do* talk like that.' He leaned closer. 'Irritating, isn't it?' Then he shrugged. 'The trouble is, we've been at it for so long we get confused sometimes. There are easier things than thanking the whale, Henry, you know. You'd understand that if you'd been around for as long as we have. But look, what we really wanted to talk to you about was . . . '

Henry wasn't listening: he was thinking, furiously. He had heard sex called many things in his time, from hiding the salami to spanking the monkey: but thanking the whale was a new one on him. The trouble was that it didn't matter what you called it, sex was either consensual or it was rape; and he wasn't about to let this bunch of weirdos do *that* to *him*. At least, not if he could help it, he wasn't. He reached for an axe on the wall, unhooked it, and held it out in front of himself with both hands.

'Don't come any closer,' he warned. 'Or I'll . . . I'll . . .'

'You'll what?' asked Lance, with a half-smile. He folded his arms across his chest. 'Faint? Soil your boxer shorts? Oh, sorry, you aren't wearing any, are you? Have a really bad panic attack, then, and have to breathe into a paper bag for five minutes to calm yourself down?'

'Actually,' said Henry, with touching candour, 'all of those things, probably. In the meantime, I was kinda hoping you'd leave me alone if I threatened to attack you with this.'

'Look, there's no need for all this aggravation, is there?' said Mervyn. 'If we were going to harm you we'd have done it by now, don't you think? I mean we could've killed you just like *that* if we'd wanted to.' He tried, unsuccessfully, to snap his fingers. 'Well, *I* couldn't. But *they* could.' He waved at Lance and Gavin. 'They might look like a couple of longhaired hippy time-wasters, but actually they're ruthless killers, you know. They could break every bone in your body as easily as snapping a twig. What you really ought to be asking yourself is why they haven't done so already.'

Henry turned and held the axe above the sword in the armourer's block. 'What if I threatened to smash this, then? What would you say about that?'

Mervyn shrugged. 'You can try if you like. But it's made of a particularly tough titanium alloy, so you'd be wasting your time.'

'Would I?' His heart sank. 'Really?' He had a sudden moment of inspiration and turned to grip the sword's handle with his free hand. 'I'll just take these back, then,' he said, tugging at the necklace beads, 'as insurance.'

But it was a hollow threat. The sections of the handle were stuck fast, and wouldn't move, no matter how hard he pulled.

Lance raised an eyebrow. 'The Celts used to fight like that, you know, half-naked with a hard-on? It's quite common for soldiers to get aroused before battle. That's why the great armies used to take wagonloads of hookers along with them: to help unstiffen the stiffened ranks, so to speak.'

'Leave him alone,' said Jo. 'Can't you see he's upset? Look,' she said, taking a step towards Henry, 'I'd let go of that, if I were you. Really I would! If you think life's been a bit wild around here up until now, just wait 'til you see what happens when that thing gets going. Besides,' she added gently, 'there's nothing sexual about thanking the whale, if that's what you're thinking? You've heard of Star Trek, Henry, haven't you?'

He nodded and glanced over his shoulder at the distant door. He was wondering if he could get to it before they jumped on him and dragged him down. On the whole, he thought his chances were slim.

'You know the one where they go back into the past to catch a pair of humpbacked whales,' asked Jo, 'to talk to an alien probe that's threatening to destroy the Earth?'

Henry wondered if this was her idea of foreplay. If so, he decided, her success rate must be abysmal. 'Um, maybe,' he said, guardedly. 'Why? Would you go easier on me if I did?'

'They find the whales, don't they?' said Jo. 'Only the spaceship they're in crashes into the sea when they get back, and the world is being torn apart by thunderstorms and tidal waves and all that sort of stuff, right? Then the spaceship starts to sink and the whales are trapped inside, and it looks like they won't get to talk to the probe and the mission will fail and the world will get torn to pieces.' She shrugged. 'Anyway, Captain Kirk dives into the spaceship's flooded cargo hold and releases the jammed doors so the whales can swim out and talk to the probe. Then the probe stops attacking the planet and the sun comes out and the clouds go away and the world is saved and everybody loves everybody else again. The next thing you see is the crew of the *Enterprise*: Kirk, Uhura, Scotty, Spock and the rest of them, mostly ancient, overweight, unfit actors past their sell-by dates, hanging onto the sides of the spaceship for grim death trying to wave and look happy as one of the whales surfaces in front of them and squirts a victory salute.' She smiled. 'Have you ever wondered what it was really like for that bunch of old farts while they were filming that scene? There they all are, mostly overweight and arthritic, clinging on to a lump of painted plastic while people they don't even know lob buckets of water over them and blast them with fire hoses and air from giant fans. They're racked with rheumatism and hoping their wigs don't get blown off and their corsets don't snap, and the assistant director keeps yelling: "OK my loves, everyone say cheese". Next time you watch it take a close look at their faces. Most of them are hating every minute of it and thinking "Christ, I just put my back out!" or "I ought to be at home with a mug of cocoa and my feet up in front of the fire!" That's thanking the whale, Henry. Do you see? Being somewhere you don't want to be and pretending you love it. It's got absolutely nothing to do with sex.' She glanced sideways at Rooter. 'Well, not unless you're married to him.'

'Really?' said Henry, hoping that they wouldn't notice that he had slipped the axe under his armpit so that he could use both hands to pull at the sword handle. 'That'd suit you down to the ground, wouldn't it?' he gasped as he tugged. 'Put me off my guard so's you can jump me and steal it.'

'It belongs to us,' said Jo. 'So it'd hardly be stealing, would it? Let go of it now, Henry, please? Or there's no knowing where you might end up.'

'What, come to a bad end you mean?' sneered Henry. 'Stealing's the first rung on the ladder to a life of crime? That sort of thing?'

'A bit more drastic than that, I'm afraid,' said Gareth. He shook his head in irritation. 'Look, we're in a hurry, and the automatic safety might not hold for much longer, so why don't you let go and come with us?'

Henry narrowed his eyes. 'How come you're all so bloody suave and sophisticated all of a sudden? What happened to all the dribbling down the bib and the "Gar-gar love Bru-bru" moronic crap?'

'Local colour,' said Gareth. 'Got to give the grockles what they want, haven't you?' He motioned for the others to leave the room. 'Look,' he said as he turned to follow them, 'keep the axe if it makes you feel better. Only for goodness sake let go of the sword and come with us.'

'Nice knowin' you, boy,' said Rooter, as he turned to leave. He paused and sucked his teeth. 'Hang on to that axe, mind, if you're stayin'. You might need the bugger where you're gonna end up.'

Blossom smiled at Henry's crotch. 'Pity, I was looking forward to a bit more of that. I bet you're a real animal when you get going, aren't you?'

'Am I?' he said. Then he frowned. 'What do you mean *more*?'

Blossom sighed, and turned away.

'Look,' said Henry, as everyone started walking towards the door, 'it's just a sword, right? What harm can it . . .?' He held out a hand towards them. 'Wait,' he pleaded. 'Don't go . . .!'

'If you keep hanging onto that thing it isn't *us* who'll be doing the going,' said Gareth. He sighed. 'Look, who was the guy who attacked you when you crashed your car, and why was he on fire do you think?'

'That wasn't real,' said Henry. He grinned uncertainly, and glanced along the line of faces. 'I was delirious, wasn't I? And . . . and someone hit me on the head, and knocked me . . . '

'Really? So how come I know about him? And the men in the Mercedes? Did you *really* think they were just football supporters?'

'They had the shirts and the bobble hats. I just assumed . . . '

'And why did Charlotte Piece attack you at the service station? Didn't you think that was a bit . . . odd?'

'She's mad! Nothing that woman does would ever surprise me.' His eyes narrowed. 'What's she got to do with it, anyway?'

'Not much,' admitted Gareth. 'But doesn't the fact that I know about her, too, strike you as strange?'

'Maybe I talked in my sleep?'

Blossom giggled. 'Oh no, you didn't do that, lover. Definitely not!'

'And did you really think it was fair to pretend you were Tony Gibbons when Suzie Bunt grabbed your dick in the bushes at the Christmas party?' asked Gareth. 'Leading her on like that, Henry: you should be ashamed.'

'I was drunk,' he said, remembering being grabbed from behind in the dark while he was taking a leak in the shrubbery. 'So was she. And anyway, I would have told her eventually.'

'Of course you would. Of course you would. Just like you would have told your Auntie Mandy's mum that you'd stolen her knickers.'

Henry was stunned: there was no way that these people could have known about that. It had happened so long ago, and he had never told anyone about it. He hadn't even mentioned it to Sam.

'She wasn't my auntie, *actually*!' he said, playing for time. 'We just used to call her that because . . . Actually, I don't know why we called her that. It was probably . . . Look, how could you . . .? I mean, I was only nine years old . . .'

'Actually, you were eleven,' said Gareth. 'And frankly I'm surprised you didn't break your wrist.'

Henry looked at the ceiling. 'I don't know what you're talking about.'

'Don't you?'

'It's not a crime, is it? Perfectly natural thing for a growing boy to do.'

'I didn't say there was anything *wrong* with it. All I said was that it was a miracle that you didn't do yourself a serious injury.'

'You made her day, you know,' said Lance, leaning forward, 'Mandy's Mum? Married to a prick like that: you stealing her pants was the most romantic thing that had happened to her in years.'

Henry decided that it was time to change the subject. 'Look . . . who the hell are you people? And how come you're all so bloody *normal*, all of a sudden? Well,' he added, peevishly, 'apart from being bollock naked and having,' he waved his hands in a churning motion, 'hards-on all the time. What happened to all the yokel accents and the "Come yer lover, ooh-arh, ooh-arh"? And don't give me any more crap about whales.'

'Hard-*ons*,' Blossom corrected him.

Henry stared at her, blankly. 'What?'

'Hard-*ons*! They've all got hard-*ons*! You said . . . *hards-on.*'

'Did I?' he said. 'Did I really? And it makes a difference, does it? The point is that it isn't natural to have one all the time, is it? Not like that. In a group. In the middle of the day. *All* sodding day, for Christ's sake! Sixteen hours,' he added, bitterly, looking down at himself. 'Not unless you're twelve years old and trapped in a lift with the Sixth Form Girl's Hockey Team wearing nothing but their bras and panties. I mean, what do you people eat around here for God's sake?'

'Mostly garlic, actually,' said Blossom, leaning towards him with her hands clasped behind her back. 'We have, too, you know?' she added with a wink.

Henry shook his head. 'What? Have *what*, for Christ's sake?'

'Hard-ons,' she grinned. 'Me and Jo? Only it doesn't show unless you look really, really close.'

'You wish,' muttered Jo.

Henry's upper lip curled in disgust. 'Bloody hell!' he cried. 'Don't you people think about anything else?'

'Oh, and you do, I suppose?' asked Jo. 'Staring up my skirt with your tongue hanging out when you were sitting on the floor in the Green Dragon was just accidental, was it?'

'That's not the point. The point is,' he shook his head, resignedly, 'what are you going to do to me?' He looked at the floor. 'As if I didn't know.'

His eyes lost their focus and he gazed at the wall with a hint of a frown. 'It really isn't natural, is it?' He looked down at the towel around his waist. Then he looked up and pointed at Mervyn. 'You think I haven't noticed what's been going on around here, don't you? *Huh*! Well I've noticed an awful lot of things, *actually*!' He waved at the door. 'All those rooms stuffed with people's private belongings, for a start. I mean, how many walking sticks do you need in one lifetime, for Christ's sake?'

'Quite a few,' said Lance, quietly, 'if you live for two thousand years.

Henry was too agitated to notice. He took a long, shuddering breath. 'And what happened to all the poor buggers they belonged to, eh? All the teddy bears and the shoes and the wigs and the God-knows-what-else? Bury them in Sodmire, did you?' He sniffed his contempt, aware that he was losing control, but too far along the path towards hysteria to care. 'Or was that what we had for dinner last night? Those of us who didn't pass out before we'd finished, that is? Jesus H Christ,' he muttered, shaking his head and gazing down at the floor. 'You come down here for your first holiday in years, looking for a bit of peace and quiet, and what do you get? Chased by a bunch of gangsters armed to the teeth with machineguns – *machineguns for Christ's sake*! Trapped by a load of pathological, lying, conniving, two-faced, sex-crazed homicidal maniacs!' He sagged back against the armourer's block. 'I just don't understand what I've done to deserve . . . ' He looked up, suddenly. 'He was real, though, wasn't he?' he said, with his eyes fixed on Rooter's face. 'That bloke?'

'What bloke would that be then, lover?'

'Him,' said Henry, jerking a thumb over his shoulder. 'The one who was on fire. He pulled me out of the car and jumped on my chest.'

'Kinsman, you mean?'

'Yes, Kinsman. Is that his name? Kinsman? What the hell kind of a name is Kinsman when it's at home?'

'It's Kinsman's name,' said Gareth, with a wry smile. 'William Ignatius Constantine Kinsman, to be precise. Better known as J. C.'

Henry's eyes narrowed. 'Shouldn't that be W-I-C-K?'

'Kinsman is a loss adjuster, so you can call him anything you want. And frankly, Jesus Christ suits him rather well when you consider all the sacrifices he's had to make.' He glanced at his watch. 'Look, leave the axe and come with us, will you? There are a few things we need to do before we leave.'

'Leave?' echoed Henry, guardedly. 'Why? Where are we going?'

'Not *we*! Just *us*! There isn't time to prepare you for the shift.'

Henry hesitated and looked anxiously around the room.

Gareth waved a peremptory hand at Lance and Gavin. 'Bring him. We haven't got time for all this gentle-persuasion-type crap.'

Henry started to back away. 'Oh God,' he thought, 'they're really going to do it to me now. They're going to rape me for sure! Erm, now look . . .' he said, as he dodged behind a suit of armour. 'That's . . . No! It's very kind of you, *really*! But I think I ought to be going, don't you? I've got some root canal work that needs doing and I wouldn't want to miss it for the world. Besides, I think I need to have this erection looked at by someone with a bit of clinical expertise, don't you?'

'Wouldn't do you any good if you did,' said Lance, stalking after him. 'Perce's been trying to make his go down since Tacitus wrote all that crap about the druids.'

Henry sidestepped behind one of the display cabinets. 'No, no! It's a tempting offer and all that, really it is! All you chaps gathered round in a group with your dicks out. I mean, I'd support your right to do it until the day I die, but believe me, I have no desire to join in.'

'Up to you,' said Gavin, with a disinterested shrug. 'You're going to be missing out, though, if you stay here.'

'No, no!' insisted Henry, dodging out of reach. 'Don't worry about me. The full-on, knobs-out, gay-group-gang-bang-romp-type thing really isn't something I'm likely to miss, I assure you.'

'I meant life,' said Gavin, tracking him to the right and then to the left. 'You're going to be missing out on *life*. Your friends in the Mercedes are still outside. You know that, don't you? And they've brought a few of their little pals along with them to help chop you into tiny little bits of quivering gristle as soon as you show your face.'

Henry glanced at a window. 'Really?' He swallowed hard and dodged behind Bruno the bear. 'Why would they want to do that?' He glanced at the window again. 'Gristle?'

'Quivering,' nodded Gavin. 'They haven't forgiven you for making them look like a bunch of tossers the first time around.' He pursed his lips. 'Look, are you going to come quietly, or not?'

'Not?' ventured Henry.

Gavin thought for a moment. 'OK,' he said, 'fair enough.'

Henry was perplexed. 'What?' he said, with an uneasy grin as the brothers looked at one another, turned, and started to walk back towards the dining room door. 'You don't want . . .?' He glanced at the window again. 'Look, I was wondering . . . What you said, just now, about . . .'

Lance stopped and turned towards him. 'Listen, it's your funeral. Stay here and get torn to bits if you want.'

'No skin off our behinds,' agreed Gavin. 'When they've got you hung up by your willy don't say we didn't warn you, that's all.'

'Yes,' said Henry, taking a faltering step towards them, 'but . . . *gristle*?'

'If you're lucky,' said Lance, 'they'll get it over with quickly.'

'And if I'm not?'

'Dolly'll have them cut your balls off so she can use your scrotum to keep her lipsticks in,' said Gavin.

'Dolly?' frowned Henry. 'Who the hell's – *lipsticks*?'

'Makeup and stuff,' said Lance. 'You'd be surprised how big a scrotum can get if you know how to cure it.' He took a step back towards Henry. 'What they do,' he said, lowering his voice and leaning closer, 'is they scrape out the dangly bits and stretch the skin over a fire, so they can . . .'

'Yes,' said Henry, hurriedly. 'Yes, thank you! I don't think I need to know that, do I? Really? And who the hell is this . . . *Dolly* when she's at home?'

'Gangster from north London,' said Gavin. 'Not a nice person, at all. You definitely wouldn't want to meet her in a dark alley.'

'Yes, but what does she . . .?'

Lance reached out and grabbed him, twisting his arm up behind his back. 'There,' he said, 'that wasn't too difficult, was it? Shall we go?'

Gavin moved in on the other side of Henry and they lifted him off the ground with their hands under his armpits, wheeled around and frog-marched him towards the door with his legs bicycling in mid-air. They hurried him through the doorway, and dumped him in front of the dining room wall, just as a section of it was sliding open to reveal the stainless steel interior of a lift.

'After you,' said Lance.

'What if I said no?'

'We'd pull your arms out of their sockets,' said Gavin, 'and batter you to death with the stumps.'

'Nothing personal, mind,' added Lance.

Henry nodded and got into the lift.

Mervyn and Jo got in beside him, and the doors slid closed in front of them with a hiss.

'Where are we going?' asked Henry.

'Down,' said Mervyn.

'Yes, but . . .?'

Before he could finish the question, the floor fell away from under him like a fairground ride and the contents of his stomach tried instantly to reacquaint themselves with his back teeth. There was a sudden and unnerving sensation of weightlessness as the lift continued downwards at an alarming rate. Henry's hair stood on end and the towel around his waist clung to him like a coat of wet paint. He swallowed something hotly acidic in the back of his throat, and his ears popped with a sudden change in pressure. The floor slowed its downward motion a moment later, and the contents of his stomach sank into his bowels. Just as he was beginning to think that he would have no alternative but to make an embarrassing mess of the towel, the floor pressed against the soles of his feet and the lift came to a sudden stop.

He remained motionless for several seconds, his eyes staring, his mouth shut, his feet wide apart, his knees slightly bent and his hands held stiffly out to the sides, palms-down, like a terrified surfer frozen on the crest of a wave.

There was a click and a hiss, and the lift doors slid open to reveal a brightly lit room. He blinked at it for a moment, swallowing thickly and breathing out for the first time in what felt like ten minutes, before standing upright, wiping his forehead with the palm of a hand, and turning accusingly to Mervyn.

'Where did you get this thing: a car boot sale at Alton Towers?'

Mervyn ignored the question and motioned him into the room. 'Have a seat,' he said, waving at a nearby sofa. 'Someone wants to say hello.'

Henry watched him walk briskly across the room and out through a door in the far wall. He frowned at it for a moment before turning to Jo with a hunted expression. 'What are they going to do to me?' he whispered.

Jo raised an eyebrow. 'They? Who's *they*?'

'I mean, what the hell's going on?'

'Just tying up a few loose ends,' she said, stepping out of the lift. 'Like the man said: take a seat. It won't be long now.'

He didn't like the idea that he was a loose end that someone was about to tie up. He didn't like the look of the brightly lit room, either, and thought that he would probably be safer if he stayed where he was. Then again, staying in the lift might not be such a great idea if it was to take him back up to the house where Lance and Gavin were probably still waiting to pull his arms out of their sockets if he showed his face. And even if they weren't, there was the disturbing prospect of having his scrotum chopped off and made into a cosmetics bag for the amusement of some vicious-sounding gangster with the unlikely name of Dolly. What, he wondered, bitterly, as he loitered in the dubious safety of the lift, was an apparently major underworld figure doing with a girlie name like Dolly, anyway? Did anyone take her seriously with a name like that? And was she really a *her* and not some bitter and twisted old queen with a penchant for mutilation? And if someone greeted her/ him with a cheery 'Hello' did his/ her escort of scar-faced henchmen chop them instantly into tiny pieces of quivering gristle, or form a high-kicking chorus line and start thumping out the title song of the hit musical? More to the point, what the hell was he doing asking himself such stupid questions?

One thing he knew for certain was that the brightly lit room didn't look quite right from where he was cowering. There were too many prints hanging on the magnolia-tinted walls, for one thing, and too many glossy magazines on little tables, for another. And with all the plants in pretty ceramic pots placed strategically in and around the rest of the furniture, it looked uncomfortably like a dentist's waiting room. And not just any old dentist's waiting room, either, but one of those really disconcerting ones that tries to pretend it's nothing more sinister than a sitting room in a private house, but ends up looking like the scene of a burglary where a highly selective thief with limited space in his getaway vehicle has just dumped a job lot of kitchen chairs to make room for the three-piece suite they've just stolen.

The trouble was that he didn't like dentists' waiting rooms at the best of times, because wherever you found one there was likely to be at least one dentist lurking somewhere nearby. And the trouble with dentists was that you couldn't trust them. They lied to you and said things like 'This won't hurt' and 'You'll only feel a slight twinge' just before they jammed a metal spike against an exposed nerve and had you screeching into the air like a cat with its tail plugged into the mains.

He was just inching forward, tentatively, to check that there were no white-coated figures lurking in darkened corners ready to pin him to leather couches and attack him with vicious drills, when Jo stuck her head around the doorframe without warning and almost scared him to death.

'Well?' she asked, as he staggered back with a hand groping at his chest. 'Will you be staying in there much longer, do you think?'

'Jesus Christ!' he gasped. 'You nearly gave me a heart attack!'

She pursed her lips. 'Mmmm,' she murmured, looking down, 'you dropped your towel, too. Drink?' she added, turning towards a marble-topped counter at the side of the room. 'There's fruit juice, tonic water, lemonade . . . No alcohol, I'm afraid, Merv won't allow it down here.'

He picked up the towel and wrapped it hastily around his waist as he leaned forward and peered into the room. 'Got any mango juice?' he hazarded. 'Look, would you mind telling me . . .?'

She turned towards him with a warning index finger raised to her lips.

He froze instantly, crouching. 'What?' he hissed, glancing around as if he expected to see a giant hand groping at him out of the lift wall. 'What's . . .?'

'Cordial,' she asked, 'squash, liquidized or freshly squeezed?'

He thought for a moment, before grinning sheepishly and standing up straight. 'Whatever's easiest, I guess.'

She shrugged. 'Makes no difference to me.'

He was anxious not to offend her because he had a feeling that she, of all the people in the Clatworthy household, was the one he was most likely to trust. He also realized that he had no proof that she was sympathetic to his predicament, or even that she would be willing to explain just what sort of a predicament he was in. But he didn't want to believe that she was anything other than a really decent, honest and moral person.

'Umm, well, liquidized, then?' he suggested. 'That'd be . . . thanks.' He craned his neck further into the room and lowered his voice to a whisper. 'Look, do you think you could tell me . . .?'

'You know,' she said, as she opened a refrigerator and took out a carton, 'I'd get out of there quick, if I were you.'

'Would you?' he said, gazing around him. 'Why, what's . . .?'

But even as he said it, the doors started to hiss closed in front of him.

A gory vision of his scrotum being hacked off and stretched over an open fire flashed into his head, and he leapt forward, panic-stricken, to avoid being carried back up to the house. But his reactions weren't quite quick enough, and the doors slammed shut on the towel as he lurched into the room.

Jo turned towards him with a tall glass in her hand. 'Ice?'

'What?' he said, with his naked buttocks pressed hard against the cold lift doors and an inadequate hank of the trapped towel pulled hastily across in front of his crotch. 'Ah, yes, that'd be,' he nodded, 'thanks.'

She scooped a handful of ice into the glass and held it towards him.

He smiled wanly, inclining his head at the trapped towel.

She sighed and walked towards him. 'Men!' she murmured, as she pressed a button on the wall and stood back as the lift doors hissed open.

He pulled the towel free and wrapped it gratefully around his waist. 'Look,' he said, 'I really need to know what's going on here, you know?'

'Apart from you making an exhibition of yourself, you mean? You know, Henry, I've never met anyone who liked waving his dick about as much as you do. Did your mother drop you on it when you were a baby, or something?'

'That was an accident,' he said, glaring accusingly at the lift doors.

She handed him the glass. 'I really would sit down if I were you,' she said, pointing at the sofa. 'This is going to come as a bit of a shock.'

Then she turned and left the room through the door in the far wall.

He frowned at it. Then he looked at the drink and frowned at that, too, sniffing at the glass, and holding it up to the light. As far as he could tell there was nothing unusual about it. He sniffed it again, and held it up to the light for second look. What, he wondered, had she meant when she'd said that he was in for a shock? Had she meant that the drink was drugged? He gazed at it for several seconds. Then he shrugged, and took a cautious sip. It tasted good. When he didn't die, or descend into a world of psychedelic phantasms, he drank some more of it, and gazed thoughtfully around the room. It was a lot bigger than it had seemed at first glance, and he had just decided that it looked less like a dentist's waiting room than the solarium in an expensive hotel, when there was a click and the water in a large white-tiled hole in the centre of the woodblock floor started bubbling. He leaned forward and peered into it. It was a Jacuzzi. He was just wondering if he was expected to get in to it when the door in the far wall swung open and people in various stages of undress started filing into the room.

39

MR. AND MRS. KITE

Henry was astonished to see Sergeant Arthur and WPC Evers, in white T-shirts and shorts, walk into the room followed by the vast bulk of Boadicea, who looked more eager than ever to tear someone's throat out. Henry hated to think what they were doing there, and was pondering several unpleasant possibilities, when Gwen turned to him, cocked her head to one side, smiled warmly, and raised a glass in an apparently friendly salute.

He raised his own glass instinctively, and smiled back at her, wondering if there would be any point in throwing himself on her mercy and begging for help. Perhaps she and the sergeant would protect him from whatever degradations the Clatworthy clan had in mind? Then again, it seemed all too likely that they and their gigantic pet were going to be an integral part of whatever lurid entertainment was about to unfold.

There was a sudden peal of laughter, and he turned from thoughts of bestiality to watch as Blossom teetered through the doorway wearing nothing but a purple-spangled thong and a pair of matching high-heeled mules. She swayed across the room, stopped next to the Jacuzzi, kicked off the shoes and slipped open-mouthed into the churning waters with a shriek.

'You dirty old sod,' she giggled, as Great Uncle Bert slid into the water beside her. 'I don't even like goats.'

Henry frowned in confusion at the old man. Last night he had looked not only crazy but at death's door. Now he was clear-eyed and sprightly, and if there was anything senile about him it certainly didn't show. The same was true of Granddad Clatworthy who, in fluorescent pink sunglasses and psychedelic Bermuda shorts, trotted into the room like a spring lamb, and eased himself into the bubbling waters opposite Blossom. Henry wondered if the Jacuzzi could possibly be some kind of miracle-working spa. But he discounted the idea as soon as Perce Pratt entered the room and lowered himself into the water next to Blossom. He was naked and looked even more morose than usual with a pink shower cap pulled down over one ear and his eyes fixed on his wave-buffeted dick. Henry's own 'tumescence of the penis', as the lieutenant might have put it, was still pressing uncomfortably against the towel, and he saw in Perce's expression, the mark of a fellow sufferer.

Rooter came in next with Hubert and Horace Naggs trailing behind him. All three were dressed in voluminous paisley-patterned shorts, and had towels draped around their necks. They elbowed one another, laughing and joking, as they crossed to a table at the far end of the room. As Hubert sat down, he glanced across at Henry, smiled and gave him a friendly nod.

'How's 'er 'angin', lover?' he called. 'Gert 'eller this lot 'ere, then, innet?'

Rooter and Horace turned to nod and grin at Henry as they sat down.

Henry smiled back at them and raised his glass in an uncertain gesture of greeting. He turned away in his embarrassment and watched as Gareth and

Robbie came through the door wearing white T-shirts and shorts. They were deep in conversation as they walked to a table at the side of the room and appeared not to notice him, or anyone else, as they sat down.

Last to arrive were Lance, Gavin, Mervyn and Jo: the brothers in T-shirts and shorts, and Mervyn and Jo in white linen suits.

Mervyn closed the door and walked briskly across the room to stand next to Henry. 'Ah,' he said, 'I see we're looking after you. Good, good!'

His friendly greeting didn't make Henry feel any better about what he thought was about to happen to him. He had seen enough to convince him that everyone in the room had dressed in readiness for some sort of physical activity in which he expected to be forced to take a leading role. But he had decided that he wasn't going to submit to their depravity without a fight.

'Listen,' he said, getting to his feet, 'you won't get away with it, you know.'

Mervyn put a hand on his shoulder and pushed him back down onto the sofa. 'Not now,' he said, clapping his hands and turning to face the room.

'Your attention, ladies and gentlemen, please! I'm sure you will all wish to join with me in welcoming Mr. Kite to our little gathering?' He paused while people smiled and nodded at Henry. 'He still hasn't got a clue why he's here, so the sooner we put him out of his misery the sooner we can get on with the business at hand. And please remember,' he added, gazing down accusingly at Blossom, 'this is supposed to be a clinic, not a bordello.'

He glanced at his watch. 'Right,' he said, clapping his hands again, 'places everyone please!' He turned and smiled at Henry, before walking away to inspect the flurry of activity that was breaking out around the room.

'For God's sake put some trunks on, Perce,' he said, as he passed the Jacuzzi. 'And you,' he pointed at Blossom, 'stop fondling it! It doesn't help!'

'Never mind, tiger,' said Jo. 'Not long now, eh?'

'Until what,' asked Henry, bitterly, 'Hell freezes over? Margaret Thatcher turns into a human being?' He started to get up. 'Look,' he began, 'you can't just go around taking advantage . . . '

'Of course we can't,' she said, pushing him back down onto the sofa. 'And we *do* sympathize,' she added, picked up a tray. '*Really* we do!'

She paused next to the Jacuzzi and dropped three brightly coloured shower caps into the water. Granddad, Blossom and Great Uncle Bert sniggered and jostled one another as they put them on.

Jo shook her head at Perce, put the tray on the floor, reached under her short skirt and slid her knickers down to her ankles.

'Here,' she said, dropping them into the water in front of him. 'I want 'em back, mind, soon as they're gone.'

Henry watched in envious disbelief as the knickers sank towards Perce's groin. And in that instant, every last scrap of sympathy he had been feeling for him evaporated as if it had never existed.

'Lucky bastard!' he muttered, as Blossom took the flimsy garment between her finger and thumb and feathered it over the head of Perce's cock.

'*Blossssom*!' warned Mervyn. 'What did I just tell you?'

Blossom pouted without looking up. 'Come on then, lover,' she said, lifting the panties from the water and jiggling them in front of Perce's face like a zookeeper tempting a performing seal with a fish. 'Up you get.'

Perce shot her a peevish look, but raised first one skinny leg and then the other to allow her to slide the panties up his thighs. When they were fitted snugly into place, he sat back as glumly as before, unaware that Henry's eyes were boring envious holes through the side of his head.

Henry turned away to watch as Jo handed drinks to the people in the Jacuzzi. Then she put the tray on the bar, picked up a pile of fresh towels and started handing them out.

Sergeant Arthur wrapped one around his waist, took off his T-shirt and lay facedown on a recliner with his head on his forearms. WPC Evers took a slim bottle of massage oil from the pocket of her shorts, poured some of the contents onto the sergeant's back, and began rubbing it in with both hands.

On a recliner nearby, Lance and Gavin took up similar positions, with Lance lying down and Gavin rubbing oil into his shoulders and back.

Henry noticed with a shock just how muscular and fit they both looked. It must have been the clothes they'd been wearing at the time, he decided, because when he'd first seen them they'd looked like a couple of weedy hippies, stoop-shouldered and shambling. Now they looked more like Olympic athletes, powerful, superbly fit and finely tuned.

On the other side of the room, Rooter and the Naggs brothers, with towels around their waists and shower caps on their grizzled heads, were turning their recliners to face the Jacuzzi. Hubert and Horace made broom-broom engine noises through their thin lips as they backed and turned and manoeuvred themselves into position.

Jo wagged a school-marmish finger at them and told them to sit down and keep still while she spread a khaki-coloured paste over their faces. It took her only a few seconds, and when everything but their eyes and mouths had been covered with a thick layer of the stuff, she placed cucumber slices over their eyes and stood back to admire the effect.

Hubert and Horace had chuckled and gurgled their way through the procedure, sticking out their tongues and making faces, trying to put her off. Now they lay back and joked that she needn't have chopped up her favourite cucumber, just for them.

'You gets a bit frustrated mind,' offered Hubert, 'I got a gert big marrow back 'ome you can lend.'

'On'y trouble is,' grinned Horace, 'that silly sod comes attached.'

'Sorry boys,' said Jo, 'but I don't reckon you've got a decent-sized courgette between the pair of you.'

On the other side of the room, Robbie leant back in a chair while Gareth put a towel around his shoulders and began massaging his scalp.

Henry watched the room's transformation in a trance-like silence, having risen unconsciously from his seat as if he wanted to join in. But no one paid him any attention, and the spell was broken when Jo pressed a switch under the counter and Procol Harem's *A Whiter Shade of Pale* filled the room.

Henry blinked owlishly at the familiar sound, closed his mouth with an audible click and sat down. So transfixed had he been by what was happening around him that if anyone had asked him, he would have sworn that he hadn't moved a muscle since the whole thing began.

Suddenly, Mervyn was standing over him with the air of a prison warder.

'You have a visitor,' he said. 'More than one, in fact. By the way,' he added, reaching down and taking the glass of mango juice from his hand, 'I think I'd better look after this for you, don't you? Can't have you spilling it all down yourself in the excitement, can we?'

'Okay,' he called, after a final glance around the room, 'bring them in!'

Henry's mouth dropped open in astonishment when Jo ushered Sam and Amy Johnson into the room. Behind them came Kate Clatworthy, Max de Griese and Nils de Boer.

'Hi!' said Sam with a beaming smile and his arms stretching out in greeting. 'How's the holiday boy doing, then, eh?'

Henry blinked in confusion as he got to his feet.

'*Henry!*' cried Amy, running forward and flinging herself into his arms.

Henry flinched and braced himself a fraction of a second before she hit him and wrapped her arms around his neck.

'You're alive!' she cried, hugging him tightly. 'We thought they were going to kill you. Didn't we Sam?'

'Get off him you dozy tart,' grinned her brother. 'Can't you see you've scared the poor sod half to death? She can't help it,' he confided. 'She thought you were a goner. We all did, come to that. Still,' he added, glancing around the room, 'no need to ask how you're getting on now, is there?'

The first shock of their arrival was beginning to wear off, and Henry was starting to enjoy himself. Their presence was comforting after what had begun to seem like a lifetime in the company of strange and unpredictable people. And the best part of it was that Amy was pressing her warm body against his manhood and seemed not to be offended by it in the least.

'How . . .? What . . .?' he stammered into her neck as she clung to him like a limpet. There were so many questions he wanted to ask that he didn't know where to start. And he was reluctant to ask anything at all in case she let go to give him an answer.

'What are you doing here?' he breathed, when she finally released him and took a step back.

'We brought them,' said Mervyn. 'Or at least, our friends here did.' He nodded at Max and Nils. 'Got them out just in time, too, I believe.'

'Out?' asked Henry.

'Max saved us,' beamed Amy, turning to gaze fondly over her shoulder at the mountain of a man behind her. 'Wasn't that wonderful of him?'

Max smiled back at her and Henry's heart sank. A moment ago, she had been pressing herself against him and he had been harbouring thoughts of an intimate, not to say damply erotic, continuation of their reunion elsewhere.

Now he could tell from the way she was smiling at the impressive Max that nothing of the sort was ever likely to happen.

'Excuse me,' said Mervyn, breaking in on Henry's depressing reverie, 'but I'm afraid we're in a bit of a hurry. So if you wouldn't mind . . .?'

'Of course,' nodded Sam. 'Of course! Of course! So,' he said, taking one of Henry's hands in both of his, 'take care of yourself mate, and,' he motioned in the direction of his sister, 'we'll see you when you get back, eh?'

Henry frowned. 'But you've only just got here.'

Sam grinned. 'Been here since last night, actually,' he said. He turned to smile at Kate, who raised an eyebrow and winked. 'Oh,' he added, leaning closer, 'by the way, whatever they've told you about me is probably true. All right?' He glanced quickly at Mervyn. 'Sorry if it sounds a bit, you know, mercenary, but I did it for all the right reasons.' He smirked. 'Well that and the money, of course. No hard feelings though, eh? You'd have done the same for me, wouldn't you?' He moved in closer still and whispered: 'She knew nothing about it.' He inclined his head at Amy. 'Still doesn't, for that matter. OK?'

Henry frowned. 'I don't know what you're talking about.'

Sam nodded, knowingly, and winked. 'Of course you don't. All in the line of duty, eh? No names no pack drill, and all that.'

'No need to thank us,' said Amy, flinging herself at Henry again and hanging on tight. 'Sorry to hear about the house, by the way. Still, we can all get new ones now, can't we? Oh, and Spike's fine. They got him out before everything burned down. We'll take care of him until you get back. So you don't have to worry about a thing, do you?' She let go of him and took a step back. 'We'd do it all again if we had too Henry. I want you to know that. Wouldn't we, Sam? Even if I did make a fool of myself at first.' She leaned forward and kissed him on the cheek. Then she turned with a smile and a wave and left the room with her arm wrapped around Max's waist.

Sam grinned over his shoulder at Henry as he followed her through the door behind Nils and Kate.

Henry held a hand towards them as the door closed. 'Where are they going?' he asked, plaintively. 'Why can't I talk to them some more?'

'Told you it'd be a bit of a shock,' said Jo, steering him back towards the sofa as the others started cleaning themselves up. 'Come and sit down with me for a bit, eh?'

'No,' he pouted, tugging half-heartedly against her, as he allowed himself to be guided across the room and lowered onto the sofa. 'What did she mean when she said "burned down"? And look,' he added, as Jo sat down beside him, 'I think it's about time someone told me what's going on, don't you?'

She patted his knee. 'I told you, we're just tidying up a few loose ends.'

'Yes, but . . .' His brow wrinkled. 'What did Sam mean when he said his behaviour was mercenary?'

'Have a drink,' she said, handing him the glass of mango juice and pointing across the room. 'Ron wants to say hello.'

Henry gazed into the thick liquid. 'Ron . . .?'

'There,' she said, pointing again. 'Isn't that nice?'

Henry looked up to see that a large television screen had replaced one of the prints on the far wall. The picture was a bit fuzzy, but he could make out the head and shoulders of a man reaching towards something in front of him. The picture came suddenly into sharper focus and the man nodded, sat back, and looked straight ahead. 'Henry,' he smiled. 'How's it goin'?'

Henry leaned forward. 'Ron,' he murmured, 'is that you?'

Ron's weather-beaten face cracked into a grin. 'How many people you know with a mug as ugly as this one?' He glanced quickly to his right, and then back at the screen. 'You made it, then? Looks like you're enjoying yourself, too. Have a drink on me, and don't do nothin' I wouldn't do.' He looked to his right again and then back at Henry. 'Look after him, Jo. Only don't forget you're saving yourself for me.'

'Could I ever?'

Henry looked at her in amazement. 'You know him?'

'Ron's an old friend.'

'Damn right!' said Ron. He turned to his left. 'Yeah,' he said, apparently in answer to someone out of the picture, 'right.' He looked back at Henry. 'Gotta go,' he said. 'Got a plane to catch.'

'Wait!' pleaded Henry.

'Can't,' said Ron. 'Me and Rosie's off to Barbados for a month or three in the sun.' He glanced to his left again and then back at the screen. 'Yeah,' he said. 'Rosie sends her love. Says for you to dress warm. Oh,' he added, 'and don't go talking to any nasty men with naughty substances stashed in their toiletries bags, eh? 'Bout time the old bastard got his cum-uppance.' He grinned. 'See you soon, boy. Take care of yourself, eh?'

The screen went blank.

Jo patted Henry's arm. 'There,' she said, 'wasn't that nice?'

He didn't answer. He had a growing suspicion that he was the unwitting subject of some kind of elaborate experiment; a complex psychometric testing programme, perhaps, devised by Sir Richard to see if he was loyal to the company. He couldn't imagine why such a thing had been done, other than to satisfy the old man's outrageous vanity, but as ridiculous as it might seem, it was the only thing that made any kind of sense. His sacking had been part of the programme, he decided (which was why it had happened so suddenly), and Sam and Ron had been in on it from the start. In fact, now that he came to think about it, Sam had virtually admitted as much when he'd described his behaviour as mercenary. The Clatworthies and their friends were clearly part of the plot, too. But he wouldn't mind betting that they didn't know a lot more about what was going on than he did. They were probably just jobbing actors who had answered adverts in *The Stage* or *Campaign Magazine*, or whatever, and been told to turn up at this ruin of a building to play a bunch of genetic throwbacks, with the promise that the last one to give away his or her true identity would win a thousand pounds, or a world cruise or two weeks all expenses paid in Majorca.

'OK,' he said, 'I get it. You're all going to stay in character until it's over.' He held up his hands in a gesture of acceptance. 'That's fine by me. I don't want to interfere with the game. But the thing is, I shouldn't be here at all. You've got it all wrong. I only came to get my car fixed. I mean, *really* I did! I'm not in character now; do you see? I'm on holiday. I'm a tourist. A *real* tourist! I've just got caught up in all this by mistake. I don't know what the old man has told you, but I was sacked and I don't want to go back. I *like* being unemployed. At least, I would,' he added, bitterly, 'if everyone would let me get on with it. So you can take your initiative test, or whatever it is, and tell his lordship to shove it up where the sun doesn't shine.'

'That would be difficult,' said Robbie. 'He's in danger of having something pretty nasty shoved up there already.'

Henry sighed. 'You see? You're not listening to me, are you? You think it's all some kind of a joke. But it's not. It's a mistake.'

'There's no mistake,' said Gareth. 'All this has been carefully planned.'

Henry glared at him. 'You know, I liked you a lot better when you were dribbling down your chin.'

'Possibly. But this is not an initiative test, and there's nothing accidental about it. Well . . . not much. This little charade,' he waved at the room, 'is the final scene in a play that has been running for so long that it makes *The Mousetrap* look like a one-off performance. Your friends think you are a very important person, Mr. Kite. Very important indeed. And they're right. But for all the wrong reasons. Still, they will go away from here secure in the belief that they have been instrumental in saving you from a very unpleasant end.'

He regarded Henry for several seconds. 'What would you say if I told you that they think you are the rightful heir to the throne of England?' He raised a quizzical eyebrow. 'And that we are your guardian angels?' He tilted his head to one side. 'What would you think about that?'

Henry grunted at the absurdity of the idea. 'Yeah,' he said. 'Sure.' He grinned and glanced from face to face to share the joke. But everyone looked back at him solemnly. His face fell. 'What? You can't be . . .? But that's . . . '

Jo patted the back of his hand. ''Fraid so.'

He had a sudden thought. 'But that's impossible. Sam's a republican. He *hates* the royal family. So does Ron, come to that.'

'True,' said Robbie. 'But ten million quid's one hell of an incentive, isn't it? And once they'd given that a bit of thought, they were happy to believe that you are not only the heir to the throne, but also as staunch a republican as they are, and willing to abolish the monarchy as soon as you came into your own. The fact that it would be impossible for you to do so was something they chose to overlook on the grounds that worrying about it too much might ruin their chances of earning themselves truly disgusting quantities of dosh.'

Blossom splashed water at Henry. 'Now you know why they were smiling.'

'Yeah,' scoffed Henry, 'but ten million pounds? That's . . . You couldn't afford . . . How could anyone . . . ? '

Jo patted his thigh. 'This room is more than a quarter of a mile underground,' she said. 'And it took you, what, less than ten seconds to get down here? Think about that for a bit.'

He had never been good at maths, but he knew that a quarter of a mile in under ten seconds was fast for a lift. So fast, in fact, that his brain hurt trying to work out just how fast it was. 'Yes, but you bribed them to be my friends.'

'We most certainly did not!' said Mervyn, indignantly. 'We merely selected them as like-minded individuals, whose natural inclinations meant they could get close to you without a lot of nasty sneaking about in the shrubbery. You see,' he added, haughtily, 'we don't go in for all that old James Bond, clandestine rubbish they put in the comics.' He shivered uncomfortably at the idea. 'Ron and Sam, and the others, were selected from literally *thousands* of applicants. It took us years – absolutely *years* – to find them. And only when we were satisfied that they were perfectly fit for purpose did we pay them to take jobs at your place of work, move into your street, go to your school or your college, or whatever. But we definitely did *not* pay them to be your friends. They were that long before we told them it was you we wanted them to look after.'

'They were?'

'It wouldn't have worked otherwise, would it?'

Blossom splashed water at him, again. 'See,' she said, 'some people like you without being paid.'

'Thanks. Thanks a bunch!'

'All right!' shouted Gareth, standing up and clapping his hands. 'Everyone out! Kinsman will be here soon.'

'Hang on! Hang on!' cried Henry. 'I haven't finished yet!'

Everyone turned to look at him. He pointed at Mervyn. 'You said "others. Ron and Sam, and the others", you said.'

Mervyn shrugged. 'So?'

'Well, what . . . *others*? I have a right to know, don't you think?'

'Just people,' said Mervyn, turning to leave. 'There's a list somewhere. But I haven't seen it for years . . .'

'Hang on!' cried Henry. 'You can't just walk off and . . . Look, how many people are there on this list you haven't seen for years?'

'Oh,' said Mervyn, 'I don't know . . . one or two . . .'

'One or two . . . ?'

'. . . hundred.'

'*Hundred?*'

'It's not a precise art, you know, character profiling. The consultants overestimated their success rates to begin with. Hardly anyone made it through the first part of the selection process . . .'

'And where are they now?'

'Oh, we sacked them, of course. We realized that what we needed was creative intuition, not a cartload of psychometric mumbo-jumbo. It's a very overrated profession, you know, personnel management.'

'I'm not talking about the sodding consultants!' cried Henry. 'I meant the people you paid to spy on me! What happened to them?'

'Oh, they're around . . . '

'*Around*? Two hundred people are . . . *around*? Good God, man, that's everyone I've ever met!'

'Hardly,' said Mervyn. He thought for a moment. 'Is it really?'

Henry stood up and waved his arms about. 'Look! I . . .! You . . .!'

'Steady tiger, steady,' said Jo, grabbing his wrist and pulling him back down onto the sofa. 'You'll do yourself an injury. Listen, why don't you sit here with me for a bit and watch the telly? Eh? And if you don't like what you see, you can go home. What's more,' she whispered in his ear, 'you can wear my panties on the way if you like. What do you think?'

He didn't say anything for several seconds: partly because his eyes had glazed over and his mouth formed into a soppy grin, but mainly because a larger-than-life image of his mother's head and shoulders had appeared in front of him on the giant screen.

'Henry Kite!' she admonished, shrilly. 'What did I tell you about making a spectacle of yourself?'

He gaped in astonishment. 'Mum? Is that . . .? But . . .'

'Never mind all that!' snapped Mrs. Kite. 'You just listen to what the nice doctors are telling you, that's all!'

'Doctors . . .?'

'How am I supposed to hold my head up in front of the neighbours when this is the best you can do?'

'You live in Florida, mum. What neighbours are we talking about here?'

'Don't be obtuse!' snapped his mother. 'Why do you always have to twist everything I say? What will the good doctors be thinking?'

Henry opened his mouth to speak, but Mervyn put a hand on his shoulder, and he subsided.

'Hello, Mrs. Kite,' said Mervyn, brightly, 'it's lovely to see you, as always, dear lady. How are you? All well, I hope?'

'I'm *so* ashamed, doctor,' she said, glancing to her left. 'Look at him sitting there ogling, with that filthy thing sticking up.'

'Do not distress yourself unduly, dear lady,' said Mervyn. 'I can assure you that we have everything under control. But how are you? Still enjoying your sojourn in the wonderful U.S. of A. I hope? And I hesitate to ask, but is everything acceptable to you there,' he lowered his voice, 'financially?'

'Well, I've always thought my allowance was generous, as you know . . . '

'You're a martyr, dear lady. A veritable martyr.'

'And I've *never* been one to complain . . . '

'Oh, absolutely not! However . . .?'

'Well, prices are always going up, aren't they?' she said, fanning herself with the latest copy of *Forbes Magazine*. 'And Miami is *such* an expensive place in these days of rising inflation . . . '

'It must be very distressing for you. Very distressing indeed! Forgive me for asking, but could we *possibly* persuade you to accept a modest increase in your allowance? Would an extra five thousand dollars a month help you out?'

'*Five thousand?*' mouthed Henry.

'Oh, I couldn't,' gushed his mother. 'I really *couldn't!* You are *so* generous already. So *very* generous, as I've always said.' She gave a slow, world-weary shake of the head. 'But of course, if you were to insist . . .'

'It would be our pleasure, dear lady. Consider it done. I'll take care of the paperwork this instant. Do not distress yourself further.'

'Always *so* considerate,' purred Mrs. Kite. 'So *very* considerate and always *so* very, *very* polite!'

Her expression hardened as she glanced to her right. 'Not like some people I could mention. You listen to me, Henry Kite, I don't want any more of your feeble excuses, do you hear? Just listen to what the good doctors are telling you, and do *exactly* as they say. And for goodness' sake, stop ogling that poor nurse and sit up straight. Love you darling? Bye-bye.'

The screen went blank, and for a moment there was an eerie silence in the room. Henry turned to Jo. 'She hasn't got a clue who you are, has she?'

'Not the foggiest.'

'Have I?'

She smiled.

'She thinks you're a nurse, right?'

She smiled again.

'And are you?'

She squeezed his thigh. 'If that's what you want me to be.'

'Me too!' sang Blossom from the Jacuzzi.

'And him?' asked Henry, nodding at Mervyn. 'What's he?'

'That's Dr. Mervyn Spiegelmann. The world famous psychiatrist.'

'Is it? And what does that make me?'

'One of his patients, silly,' splashed Blossom. 'Never mind, though, eh?'

'Wonderful!' said Henry. 'My mother thinks I'm a raving lunatic!'

'A royal raving lunatic, though,' said Mervyn.

'Royal?'

'On your father's side.'

'My father's an estate agent in Australia. He moved out there after the divorce. He works for something called Bruce Prince's Realtors: whatever that is. But I'm afraid Mr. Prince is as close as my dad's ever gonna get to royalty.'

'Indeed. But Martin Kite isn't your natural father, is he? He only stepped into the breach after your mother's little indiscretion on the works outing.'

An icy hand gripped Henry's heart. 'Indiscretion? What . . . ?'

'Don't be too hard on her,' said Mervyn, 'she was only a slip of a girl. And the best her tightwad employers could manage was a day trip to Widecombe-in-the-Moor and a fish supper in the charabanc on the way home. I mean, she was an independent spirit, Henry, wasn't she? She couldn't be tied down as easily as that.' He shook his head, sadly. 'But the problem was that she was a bit naïve, and didn't make the journey home with the rest of the party. She was seduced by some seedy local gigolo who plied her with drink, and had his wicked way with her on the backseat of his Armstrong Siddeley. It was the 1960s Henry, and an abortion was out of the question. You were lucky we came along to help out when we did.'

'I know I'm going to regret asking this,' said Henry, 'but how *exactly* did you help out?'

'Martin was your mother's most ardent admirer. He worshipped the ground she walked on, poor lad. We sort of nudged him in her direction, and suggested that offering to marry her might not be a bad idea if we gave him a few thousand pounds to keep them afloat. They both saw the good sense in the idea: your mother because she wouldn't be banished from respectable society for the rest of her life; and Martin because she had such a great arse.'

Henry was outraged. 'That's my mother you're talking about!'

'Oh, but she did, Henry. Still has, for that matter. In her day she was extremely nubile, and you ought to be mature enough to come to terms with the fact. She's a woman first and your mother second.' He thought for a moment. 'Well, maybe not second: more sort of third or fourth, really.'

'And who is this *we* you keep going on about?' asked Henry. 'MI5, is it, or the SAS? Or just the Special Boat Service With Permission To Screw-Up Other People's Lives? You paid her to abandon me, didn't you? When she went off to America after my birthday, that was you! I bet you even made them get a divorce, didn't you?' He pointed, accusingly. 'And I bet you're name isn't Clatworthy, either.'

'Actually, it is,' said Mervyn, 'more or less. But that's another story entirely. Your parents' divorce was merely a precaution. We needed to get you out of the house so we could keep an eye on you without them fussing around all the time.' He spread his hands wide. 'And we felt it was our duty to draw your mother's attention to the fact that the condition you had inherited from your father would eventually manifest itself, and that when it did the consequences would be dire for everyone concerned unless we were allowed to provide you with the required medical supervision.'

Henry looked down at his hands. 'You mean it's contagious?'

'God, no,' grinned Robbie. 'It isn't even real. Fact is, you're remarkably healthy for someone who never does any exercise and might as well be munching on cardboard for all the nutritional value you get from the crap you insist on stuffing into your face. We just thought she would appreciate a bit of the old *Dr. Zhivago*'s, that's all. The idea that exiled royalty had taken time off from its social whirl to give her a good twonking was intended to appeal to her romantic side. She always liked that old *Mills & Boon* crap, didn't she?'

'We weren't specific, of course,' said Gareth. 'We just pointed out that the unique nature of your affliction would, in the fullness of time, reveal your true lineage to certain hostile political interests who would be sure to take a dim view of your continued existence.' He pursed his lips. 'Murder is an ugly word, Henry, and so is assassination: which, of course, is why we used both of them as often as we could. Your mother saw the implications immediately. Particularly when we pointed out that those same political interests would be anxious to snap off every last twig and branch from your family tree.'

Henry was horrified. 'You mean, you frightened her into divorcing my father and fleeing the country?'

'No, no, no,' said Mervyn, 'your mother isn't a coward. What persuaded her were the truly obscene piles of cash we suggested she might like to accept by way of compensation.'

'Great businesswoman your mum,' said Robbie. 'Crap parent though, eh?'

'You bribed her? You bribed my mother and my father to desert me! And you bribed Sam and Ron, and you . . . But . . . but . . . why?'

'What indeed?' said Mervyn. He clapped his hands. 'OK, everyone out! Time to get changed!'

'But . . .?' pleaded Henry, as they all stood up and headed for the door.

'Not now,' said Jo. 'Look . . . stay here with me for a bit. Everyone's going to get changed, and then they'll be back. And don't worry, we're going to tell you everything you'll need to know to survive after we've gone.'

'Survive?'

'We made him promise,' said Blossom. 'You'll be fine. Really you will.'

'Made who promise?'

'The boss, of course.'

Henry looked at Mervyn.

Blossom giggled. 'Not him, silly. Gareth! Isn't he lovely? So big and strong and clever and . . . ooh, I could eat him all up.'

Henry sat on the sofa with Jo while the others were out of the room.

'Just be patient,' she kept saying, when he asked her what was going on. 'And don't worry: we really *are* going to explain everything before we leave.'

Ten minutes passed before the door opened, and the others started to file back into the room. With the exception of Boadicea, they had all changed into identical boiler suits, and looked like a group of factory workers off for a union meeting. Everyone except Blossom, that is, who still wore the spangled thong and the high-heeled mules. Only now, she had a pink towel wrapped around her head. She swayed across to the sofa and plumped down next to Henry with a sigh of girlie exhaustion, looking less like an anonymous factory worker than a steampunk fashion victim from St. Martin's end-of-year show.

Gareth came in last, wearing a boiler suit and a look of stern resolution.

He closed the door behind him and sat down next to Mervyn.

A shiver of anticipation ran through Henry's body.

This was partly because everyone had turned to look at him, but mostly because Blossom had wrapped her hand around his towel-encased dick and given it a friendly squeeze.

'Hang on tight now, lover,' she breathed in his ear. 'Could be a bit of a rough ride, this.'

40

MR. LIVINGSTONE

Henry was wedged on the sofa between Jo in the white linen suit he found so distracting (no least because, as far as he knew, she still wasn't wearing any knickers beneath it), and Blossom in the spangled thong, the spike-heeled slippers, the towel around her head, and clouds of suffocating perfume. He was striving manfully to ignore them, and concentrate on what Mervyn was saying about a robbery at the British Museum, but it wasn't easy.

'You all right, lover?' asked Blossom, with a hand on his thigh. 'You're looking a bit piqued.'

'He's fine,' said Jo, with a protective hand on his other leg. 'He's just a bit highly strung, that's all.'

His only response was that familiar high-pitched squeak, like the stifled cry of a tiny mammal trapped in the back of his throat.

Jo took his hand and guided the glass of mango juice up to his mouth.

'Here,' she said, 'it'll do you good.'

He managed to thrust his chin forward and pucker his lips over the rim of the glass for just long enough to suck up a mouthful of the cool liquid before she took it away again. He did his best after that to listen to Mervyn's account of the events which, he said, led to the necklace-sword handle coming into his possession two nights earlier, but none of it seemed to make any sense.

For one thing, he couldn't see what most of it had got to do with him. And for another, the succession of images that flicked across the TV screen every time Mervyn pressed a key on a tiny laptop computer only served to confuse him. The fact that the necklace was part of the haul of ancient artefacts stolen by Dolly Killjoy and her gang in the infamous raid on the British Museum explained why Vinny, Nobbler and Bonce had chased him halfway across the country. But it didn't seem to explain anything else.

'Look,' he said in exasperation, 'why are you telling all me this? I haven't got a clue what you're on about most of the time. You've got the necklace-sword handle thing back again, haven't you, so why can't I just go home?'

'They're embarrassed, lover,' whispered Blossom. 'Buggered up the stuff with the encoder, didn't they? Now they feel responsible. 'Sides, you've still got something they want.' Her eyes opened wide and round like a small child's. 'Only I'm not s'posed to tell you about that, am I?' She glanced across at Mervyn. '*Ooops!*' she giggled. 'Must 'ave slipped out!'

'Story of your life,' muttered Jo.

Mervyn glared at Blossom for a moment. Then he turned to Henry with a tight smile. 'We're trying to help you, Henry. Although Blossom is correct, we do feel somewhat responsible for your plight, and would like to make it up to you before we leave. But you really must try to concentrate on what we're saying. Your life could depend on it. Look carefully at the faces again. These are the people who will try to kill you as soon as you leave here.'

Henry looked at the quartet of police mug shots. 'Dorothy "Dolly" Killjoy,' said Robbie, pointing at each of them in turn, 'Vincent "Vinny" Trashman, William "Nobbler" Bates, and Mortimer "Bonce" Mangle.'

'But I haven't got the necklace anymore, have I? You have!'

'They don't know that, though, do they?' said Mervyn.

'Well tell them for Christ's sake! Just open the sodding door and yell: "Henry Kite is innocent! Leave the poor bugger alone"!'

'It wouldn't do any good if we did,' said Jo. 'Dolly would have them kill you, anyway. You have to understand, Henry, that you've caused her a lot of embarrassment and inconvenience already.'

'You'll need to remember these people as well,' said Mervyn, as mug shots of the rest of Dolly's gang scrolled up the screen. 'We can print them out for you, if you like?' he offered. 'It would only take a minute or two?'

'Why can't you just stop them?'

Mervyn and Robbie exchanged glances.

'You really ought to concentrate on these pictures, you know.' said Mervyn. 'It could save your life.'

'No, wait,' said Henry. 'Wait! Look, why don't I come with you? I mean, wherever it is you're going?' He glanced hopefully from face to face.

No one showed the least enthusiasm for the idea.

'Not even until it's safe?'

'Out of the question,' said Gareth. He waved a peremptory hand at Mervyn. 'Let's get this over with, shall we?'

Mervyn pressed another key.

Henry was shocked when an aerial view of a burning building appeared on the screen: doubly so when the camera panned in close and he recognized the house as his own. He sat for a moment, too stunned to move. Then he lurched to his feet, gesturing wildly. 'That's my house! That's . . .! It's . . .!'

'What d'you think we've been trying to tell you for the past ten minutes?' asked Gareth. He turned to Jo. 'I told you he was a waste of space.'

'Yes,' said Henry, 'but that's my house!'

Blossom and Jo pulled him gently but firmly back down onto the sofa and stroked his head and thighs, and cooed soothing things into his ears.

'You ought to be grateful,' said Gareth. 'If Bunsen had caught you at home he'd have set fire to you, too. Still,' he added, 'your cat's safe and you will receive ample compensation for your losses.'

'Ample?' echoed Henry. *Ample?* My whole life's just gone up in flames!'

'Yes,' said Gareth, 'tragic, isn't it? There will be conditions attached to the gratuity, of course. If you tell a soul about what you have seen here, our Mr. Hertz and his jolly band of assassins will track you down and force-feed you with nuclear waste until your penis drops off and your testicles glow in the dark. After which it won't matter how much money we've given you, you will find it very difficult either to keep your existing friends or to attract new ones.'

The screen went blank. 'In case you're wondering,' added Gareth, 'the twenty million pounds we have allocated for your rehabilitation has already been paid into your bank account.' He dropped a sheet of paper onto Henry's lap. 'That was the balance of your account at nine o'clock this morning.'

It looked like a genuine statement showing the balance of Henry's current account, but the numbers didn't make any kind of sense. Why, he asked himself, would anyone want to give him twenty pence, never mind – he counted the noughts – twenty million pounds? All right, so he had been sacked from his job, and his house had, apparently, been burned down, and he had been chased halfway across the country, and shot at, and knocked senseless, and his car had been trashed. But none of that explained why perfect strangers wanted to give him more money than he could ever spend, never mind count. He shook his head at the bank statement, and handed it back. 'It's a fake, isn't it? Anyone could have made that.'

Gareth shrugged. 'Perhaps.' He took a small address book from his pocket and dropped it into Henry's lap. 'That's why I had Mr. Hertz bring this from the bag in your room. You don't remember your bank's telephone number, I take it?'

Robbie reached over Henry's shoulder and placed a telephone in his lap. 'Give them a call. The manager's name is Livingstone.'

'I know what his name is,' said Henry, bitterly, at the memory of Mr. Livingstone's stifled giggling the last time he had asked for a loan. 'The bastard hates my guts!'

'Not anymore, he doesn't,' said Robbie. 'Right now he thinks the sun shines out of all of your bodily orifices at once.'

Henry refused to make the call at first. But Jo stroked his thigh and Blossom blew in his ear until he shrugged and picked up the phone.

To his amazement he was put through to the manager immediately. It was the same Mr. Livingstone who, eighteen hours earlier, had been wondering what colour panties Jackie Choat was wearing as she signed away her husband's savings, and whether she would be willing to show them to him if he managed to convince her to give him a blowjob under his desk. When his secretary told him that *the* Henry Kite wanted to speak to him, he couldn't pick up the phone quickly enough.

The conversation was brief and far from the point, and when it was over Henry felt not so much exhilarated as unclean. According to the fawning Mr. Livingstone, twenty million pounds had indeed been deposited in his bank account that morning; and everything about the transaction seemed to be perfectly legal and above-board. For the first time in Henry's life a supercilious bank official was going out of his way to be nice to him. And not just nice, but cloyingly sweet. In fact, the obsequious Mr. Livingstone simpered so effusively on the other end of the line that Henry began to fear that the man's tongue would eventually worm its way out of the ear-piece, insinuate itself down the back of the towel around his waist and start lapping feverishly at his backside. So paranoid did he become at the prospect that he held the receiver an increasing distance away from his head, until finally he could bear the suspense no longer and slammed it back onto its cradle with a crash, cutting Mr. Livingstone off in mid-grovel.

Gareth grinned mirthlessly at Henry as he sat staring at the phone with his lip curled in revulsion. 'Satisfied?' he asked.

Henry didn't reply.

'This has been a very stressful experience for you, hasn't it, Henry?' said Mervyn. 'And we want to make sure you get your life back on track as soon as possible. Whatever you think of us, I hope you will agree that we have treated you fairly? Now, if you wouldn't mind going over there with Lance and Gavin, and sitting in that chair by the wall, we'll have your brain downloaded into our computer in no time at all, and you can be on your way to wherever it is you might want to be going.'

Henry blinked as Lance and Gavin moved in on either side of him. 'Sorry?' he said. 'What did you just . . .?'

'I assure you that the transfer won't take up any more of your valuable time than is absolutely necessary,' said Mervyn.

'Not that bit!' squeaked Henry, as Lance and Gavin grabbed his arms and lifted him into the air. 'The bit about downloading my brain!'

He struggled gamely, but to no avail. Lance and Gavin carried him across the room, dumped him onto a high-backed chair, and secured him into it with straps across his chest, wrists and ankles.

Robbie came and stood in front of him. 'There's nothing to worry about,' he said, holding some sort of metal contraption in his hands. 'We'll just plug you in to the drain cap we knocked up last night, and we'll be off. OK?'

'Drain cap?' said Henry, shying away from the thing cradled in Robbie's hands that looked uncomfortably like an upturned cooking pot with the handle removed and a forest of tiny lights attached to its rim.

'Off?' he asked, anxiously. 'Off where?'

'See,' said Robbie, holding the thing up for a closer inspection, 'it's really just an ordinary broadband DNA scrambler jump-wired to a microwave transceiver. Do you see? But,' he added, proudly, 'the clever bit is, me and Merv rigged it through an old Dalton's converter we took off the Chi scanner so's we can plug it straight into the mains.' He indicated an untidy bunch of coloured wires leading from the contraption in his hands to a three-pin socket on the wall. 'Who knows,' he added, 'if you survive the reflex blast, and don't end up with the intellect of a head louse, we might even patent the bloody thing. Here,' he said, pushing it even closer to Henry's face, 'beautiful piece of engineering, isn't it?'

Henry screamed like a man who had just been told that the surgeons had cut off the wrong testicle. It was a short-lived, staccato blast that burst from his mouth in an explosion of wide-eyed panic. 'It's a bloody cooking pot for Christ's sake!'

'That's Le Creuset, that is,' retorted Robbie. 'Not just any old rubbish! Teflon-lined, too. Cuts out extraneous radiations.' He held it up, beaming proudly. 'Beautiful piece of engineering, isn't it?'

'You're supposed to fry eggs and bacon in it. Not people's brains.'

'Boil,' said Robbie, gazing at the thing admiringly. 'It's a saucepan. You *boil* things in a saucepan, Henry, not *fry* them. What you're thinking of is a frying pan. That's probably where you're going wrong. Anyhow,' he added, as he held it above Henry's head to test it for size, 'it's perfectly safe; I'm a qualified engineer with letters after my name.'

Henry flinched, as the thing was crammed onto his head.

'Now,' said Robbie, 'we'll just get the chinstrap done up nice and tight, and we'll be off.'

He stepped back and rubbed the palms of his hands down the front of his overalls. 'It's your own fault,' he said, reproachfully. 'We tried to be nice to you, but you wouldn't listen, would you?'

'When was that?' asked Henry, his lower lip thrusting forward with a belligerence not justified by his predicament. 'I must have missed that bit.' He looked down at himself. 'Jesus Christ! It's an electric chair!'

'Yeah,' said Robbie, proudly, 'great isn't it? We got it from Alcatraz in the clearance sale. 'Course, I disconnected the terminals years ago. Only keep it for show now.' He gazed at it, lovingly. 'Convenient for keeping people in one place, mind, bolted to the floor like that.' He sighed. 'You shouldn't have used the encoder, Henry, should you? Now we've got to plug you into the mainframe and it's very inconvenient for us. Merv and me have been up all night building this beauty. And it wasn't easy, I can tell you.' He indicated the helmet. 'Wonderful piece of engineering, though, don't you think?'

'You're mad!' said Henry. 'Stark staring bonkers, the lot of you are!'

Robbie clicked his tongue. 'Don't be like that. I mean, we tried to download the programme with a conventional Chi scanner while you were asleep, only it didn't work.' He waved a languid hand at Blossom. 'Maybe she put too much dope in your wine? Maybe you drank too much of it? Who knows? The point is we don't have a choice anymore, do we? I do wish you'd stop complaining, Henry. You're such a bloody awful whinger!'

Henry glared at Blossom.

'For your own good, lover,' she said. 'Had to be done.'

'Bastards!' he hissed.

'You ought to be grateful,' said Robbie. 'We could've just hit you over the head with a blunt instrument and got on with it. But we don't do things like that around here anymore. Well, not to you, anyhow.' He shrugged. 'Jo wouldn't let us. God knows why. Point is, we got most of what we wanted last night, but there's still a tiny little bit of vital information lodged in your brain.' He smiled, deprecatingly. 'A very tiny bit, as it happens. I mean, there isn't a hellova lot of room in there at the best of times, is there?'

'Look,' said Henry, desperately, 'you've got it all wrong. I don't know anything about any . . . *encoder*. I'm a tourist. I just came to get my car fixed.'

'You were wearing it when you got here,' said Robbie, tiredly. 'So it's no good giving us all that old bollocks, is it? And you did use it, didn't you? How'd you manage that, by the way? Pretty damned clever, that was. There's us thinking you're just a dumb pillock, when really you're a mildly intelligent one. Just goes to show you can't tell by appearances, doesn't it?'

'You weren't supposed to use it, Henry,' said Mervyn, reproachfully. 'All you had to do was bring it to us and go home. Simple enough, you'd think, wouldn't you? But you had to go and experiment with the damned thing.'

'I don't know what you're talking about. I'm a graphic designer!'

'Really? So you deny using the encoder to travel through time?'

'Time? Me? Oh, yeah, sure! Wait a minute,' he said, looking from face to face, 'you can't be . . .? Are you *totally* crazy?'

'People have called us that before,' said Robbie. 'We didn't like it then, either. You're lucky we're not the sort of people who hold grudges.'

'Lucky?' cried Henry. 'That must be some new use of the word not previously known to the English language.'

'Look,' said Gareth, 'do you mind if we cut out the chitchat? Kinsman'll be here soon.' He waved a dismissive hand at Henry. 'And you can explain all this to him later.' He glanced at his watch. 'If he survives.'

Robbie looked at Henry. 'Ready for lift-off, then, are we?'

Henry shook his head. 'Look, what if . . .?'

'No time for that,' snapped Gareth.

'Yes, but . . .'

'No time for that either,' said Robbie. 'Open wide.' He pinched Henry's nostrils until he gasped for air. Then he jammed a rag into his mouth, and tightened the chinstrap to hold it in place. 'There,' he said, as Henry glared at him boggle-eyed. 'All systems are go, Mr. Tracy.'

'Don't worry,' said Mervyn, when a faint hum filled the room. 'This won't hurt a bit. Although, actually, you might feel a slight twinge.'

Henry knew perfectly well what that meant, because all of those bloody dentists had been saying it to him for so many years. And that, he thought bitterly, as the lights around the rim of the drain cap started blinking, was why Lance and Gavin had strapped him into the chair and why Robbie had shoved a gag into his mouth. It wasn't to protect him from injury during the process of information transference, it was so that the rest of them wouldn't have to watch him gnash his teeth in agony or listen to his terrified screams.

Robbie patted the saucepan. 'Bon voyage,' he said. 'See you when the smoke clears, eh?'

Henry glared at him, beseechingly.

Robbie smiled and winked.

Blossom leaned forward and kissed him on the cheek. 'Don't feel bad about us, Henry. We couldn't help it. Really we couldn't!' She grasped his penis through the fluffy bath towel and gave it a tweak.

Jo bent close to his ear. 'You can still wear my panties on the way home, if you like?' she whispered. She kissed the tip of his nose. 'Even if you don't remember who I am after this.'

From Henry's perspective, the experience of having his brain downloaded into the computer was uncomfortably like being stoned.

'What's wrong with that?' Sam asked him years later. 'Sounds good to me.'

'Actually, I'd rather be shot or hanged.'

When the current started buzzing between his ears it was like having 10,000 micrograms of pure LSD pumped into the visual cortex of his brain. Huge, multi-coloured vistas loomed all around him, as if he was suspended in front of a giant projection screen that filled his field of view completely. His whole life flashed in front of him, and the worst part about that was the crushing sense of disappointment he felt at its apparent lack of meaning. He wept as he watched and wished that he had been successful at something. 'Anything,' he sobbed with a mental pout, 'would have been nice.'

When the buzzing stopped, and the lights on the rim of the Le Creuset went out, Mervyn checked the readings on the computer and turned off the juice. Then he and Robbie and Blossom and Jo tiptoed over to Henry and bent down in front of him to gaze hopefully into his unblinking eyes.

'Henry?' called Jo, softly. 'Are you there?'

'Is he dead?' asked Mervyn.

'Isn't moving much, is he?' said Robbie.

'Still got a boner, mind?' said Blossom, who knew where her priorities lay. 'Least-ways there's blood in his veins.'

They watched him for several seconds, but he didn't move.

He didn't even appear to be breathing.

'Take out the gag,' suggested Mervyn. 'I think someone will have to give him the kiss of life.'

Robbie loosened the chinstrap slightly and tried to pull out the rag. He shook his head. 'Jaws are locked tight.'

He turned to Blossom. 'Get that jemmy from my toolbox, will you?'

'No chance,' she said. 'I'm not missing any of this.'

'Forget it,' said Jo, elbowing them out of the way. She tilted Henry's head back with the palm of her left hand pressed against the cooking pot helmet and the heel of her right hand pushing down on his chin. 'Here,' she said to Robbie, 'pull it out when I get his mouth open.'

Robbie gripped the rag with both hands, braced a foot against the leg of the electric chair, and pulled.

Jo pressed down on Henry's chin and tried to lever his head backwards. Nothing happened for several seconds. Then, just as her eyes were beginning to bulge with the effort, his mouth sagged open with a wet click.

The sudden release of pressure took Robbie by surprise. The gag pulled free and he staggered backwards with his hands held out in front of him as if the line on an invisible fishing rod had just snapped. He tripped over Mervyn's foot in passing and landed on his back with a grunt.

Henry woke a fraction of a second later with a deep-throated exhalation.

Blossom, who had moved to kneel in front of him, and was gazing into his sightless eyes, took the blast full in the face. It snapped her head back and sent the towel sailing onto the floor behind her. She tottered backwards on her haunches with her eyes closed, trod on Robbie's crotch with a high heel, lost her balance and sat down on his chest with a bump.

Robbie grunted.

Blossom squealed.

Mervyn and Jo looked down at them, stony-faced.

'Morons,' said Mervyn, wearily. 'I've got morons on my team.'

Jo turned and peered into Henry's face. His mouth was open and his eyes stared wildly. But as far as she could tell, he still wasn't breathing.

'Henry?' she called. 'Henry, are you there?'

When he didn't reply, she shook him roughly by the shoulder. 'Say something, for Christ's sake!'

When he still didn't respond, she turned and glared down at Robbie and Blossom, tangled together on the floor. 'If you've killed him,' she snapped, 'I'm gonna be really pissed off!'

Henry chose that moment to come back to life.

He blinked several times and drew a long shuddering breath.

'The Lord hath spoken unto me,' he said in a sepulchral whisper. 'The prophecies will all come to pass.'

Everyone stared at him in amazement.

'What did he say?' asked Robbie, getting to his feet.

Blossom curled her lip and stood up. 'Sounds a bit bloody spooky to me.'

'Blue! Blue!' chanted Henry, wistfully. 'Everything in heaven is blue!'

Jo shot an angry look at Robbie.

'What?' he asked, defensively. 'What'd I do?'

She turned back to Henry. 'What was blue, Henry?'

He didn't reply.

'What was blue?' she asked, again. 'You can tell us, Henry, can't you? What was blue, Henry? What was blue?'

'The Lord came unto me in my darkest hour,' he chanted. 'And he said unto me "Behold, a fatal exception hath occurred at OE-533-498-623. The programme will close im-mee-di-ate-ly. If the problem persist-eth, consult thee with thy ve-eh-eh-en-n-doooor!"' He blinked. 'I saw him,' he whispered. 'On fire. Mandy was there, too. All wet – *wet*!' He chuckled deep in his throat, and leered at Blossom. 'I wanted to give her one.' He thought for a moment. 'Maybe two or three.' The smile vanished. 'Then she left me.' His face crumpled, and he started to cry. 'Not fair. Poor liddle me!'

Jo rounded on Robbie. 'What've you done to him, you tosser?'

'He's all right,' he said, backing away. 'He just thinks he's Bill Gates, that's all. Look on the bright side, he's years ahead of his time. All right! All right!' he said, backing away even further as Jo stalked after him with her fists clenched. 'It's not ideal, I admit. But, look . . . he must have seen an error message at the end of the download, that's all. You're not supposed to see stuff like that without a VDU, I know; but . . . ' He paused, and thought for a moment, his eyes narrowing to speculative slits. 'Actually, think what your average punter would pay . . . '

Jo grabbed the bib of his overalls, and held a fist in front of his face.

'Yes,' he said, raising his hands in surrender, 'you're right. Absolutely right!

That's not the way to look at it, is it? It was thoughtless of me. Callous!' He tilted his head to one side. 'On the other hand . . . '

Jo bared her teeth.

'Got it!' he said. 'Fair comment.'

Mervyn shone a penlight into Henry's eyes. 'He's in shock I think,' he said. 'The system probably crashed at the end of the download, and burned out a few billion of his brain cells. I don't think it's anything to worry about, though; he's still got several billion left: and that ought to be more than enough for an intellect as primitive as his.' He smiled. 'The good news is we got what we wanted and the damage wasn't as serious as we thought. The bad news is that we're stuck with the silly bugger until Kinsman gets back.' He pressed a key, and pointed at the screen. 'Come and have a look at this.'

It took a little while longer for Henry to come back to full consciousness. When he did, Blossom and Jo were crouching in front of him, staring into his face like a couple of eager opticians waiting to give second opinions.

Blossom was so close that their noses were almost touching.

When he opened his eyes and saw her like that, he screamed.

Blossom stood up and backed away. 'Thanks,' she said, wiping gobbets of spittle from her face. 'I love you too, Henry.'

'Oh, God!' he cried, gazing at her bald head in horror. 'Look what I did!' He turned to Jo. 'I made her all bald!'

'What's he on about now?' asked Robbie, peering over Jo's shoulder.

'He thinks he blew her hair off,' said Jo. 'No, Henry,' she said, bending to disentangle Blossom's wig from the towel on the floor. She jiggled it in front of his face. 'It's a wig. See? Just a wig?'

Blossom giggled, and yanked at Jo's hair. 'So's hers,' she laughed, as it came away in her hand.

Henry gaped in alarm at Jo's shaven head.

'And his,' cried Blossom, taking Lance's wig and tossing it into the air. 'And his,' she added, advancing on Gavin.

'All right!' he said, taking off his wig, and holding it out at arm's length.

'Yes,' sighed Robbie, as Blossom turned towards him.

'Gert eller innet, eh?' grinned Horace and Hubert together.

Everyone but Gareth took off their wigs and gazed at Henry like a bunch of well-adjusted alopecia sufferers. Henry stared from bald head to bald head in mounting panic. The shining skin flashed at him in the florescent lights, making him think of bodies shaved bare and smothered in oil for greater sensitivity, streamlined and naked, frictionless and supple, cleaving water like spawning salmon, stuffed full of hormones and horny as hell.

'Oh, my God,' he whispered, 'they're really gonna rape me now!'

Robbie pursed his lips. 'He's obsessed, isn't he?'

Jo took one of Henry's hands in both of hers. 'Look,' she said, 'you don't have to be a dickhead all your life, Henry, do you? Take at least one day off, eh?' She looked over her shoulder. 'We're all taking the tablets, so you're safe.' She glanced sideways at Blossom. 'Well, from most of us, anyway. We're from the future, Henry, that's all. We're time travellers, just like you are. 'You're a time traveller, too, Henry. You just haven't realized it yet.'

* * *

'Forgive me for interrupting, sir,' said the colonel. 'But there is a delegation here to see you.'

'Ah yes, of course,' said the hooded figure, getting to its feet. 'Your band of happy pilgrims, I believe?'

'Their advance guard sir, yes.'

'Excellent. Show them in colonel, if you would be so kind?'

'Certainly. And I have taken the liberty of bringing this garment for Mr. Kite.' He held out a long black robe similar to the ones he and the hooded figure were wearing. 'I believe it will help avoid awkward questions?'

'An excellent idea,' said the figure. 'Henry, would you be good enough to put it on? Over your outer clothing will be fine. It will, I think, as the colonel suggests, help avoid unnecessary confusion.'

While Henry was putting on the robe, the colonel rearranged the three chairs side by side behind the campfire. Then he walked briskly across the clearing and out of sight between the trilithons.

'Please?' said the figure, sitting on the middle of the three chairs and motioning for Henry to sit in the one on its right.

As Henry took his seat, Titus appeared on the other side of the clearing dressed as a warrior of the Durotriges. He walked quickly over to the remaining chair and sat down.

'What's going on?' asked Henry.

'A little experiment,' answered the figure, 'devised by the colonel and Dr. Spiegel. Don't speak unless you have to. Quiet now, here they come.'

The colonel reappeared on the far side of the clearing with the hood of his black robe thrown back and a double-edged sword held in both hands, its intricately carved blade pointing up at the sky.

Walking solemnly behind him came a thin, middle-aged man wearing baggy breeches and an ankle-length, sleeveless gown, open at the front to reveal a braided belt, a necklace of black beads and a bony chest tattooed with what looked to Henry like a large, blue lizard. His long hair and beard were tightly braided and caked in blue mud. In one hand he carried a staff of polished wood topped with the head of an enormous pike: in the other, a short wooden rod tipped with a mace head of polished blue granite. Walking two abreast behind him came six young women with their eyes downcast and their hands tied behind their backs. Their long hair was braided, crowned with blue flowers and caked in blue mud. Each was naked to the waist and had a lizard-like creature painted on the front of her body, its broad, fork-tongued head on her belly and its long, sinuous tail wrapped round her neck. On either side of the women walked three armed men with lizard shapes tattooed on their chests and around their shaved heads. They were clad in iron-grey eel skin kilts that reached down to their knees. Each wore on a belt at his waist a sword, a dagger and a stone-headed mace. And each carried a spear with its leaf-shaped iron head lowered respectfully to point at the ground.

'Your grace,' said the colonel, bowing to the hooded figure, 'may I present His Holiness Urcskin Gort, High Priest and Helmetbinder of the Royal House of the Newt Foraging Free Durotriges, and his retinue?'

'Oh they're *newts*,' muttered Henry. 'I thought . . . '

The figure turned towards him. '*Shoosh!*' it hissed, before turning back to the visitors. 'You are most welcome, your holiness,' it said, getting to its feet and raising its hands to grasp the edge of its hood and draw it down onto its shoulders. There was a collective gasp as the head beneath the hood was revealed clad in a golden helmet-mask that encased it completely. The face of the mask was that of a man, but its features were smooth, blank and impassive, as if to indicate that its owner was at peace with the world. There were dark, almond-shaped holes for the eyes, and a narrow slit between full lips for the mouth. As it moved, a shifting pattern of reflected images of land, sky and standing stones flickered across its mirror-like surface, punctuated now and then by the sudden sparkle of the afternoon sun. Urcskin Gort and his holy retinue bowed their heads and bent their knees in obeisance.

'It is a great honour, your grace,' said Urcskin Gort. 'May I welcome you to this our brother Belgae's ancient home of the ancestors and ask that you permit our people to celebrate with you in these hallowed precincts and on this day of mid-summer's eve, the purging by your mighty hand of the pagan invader that calls itself Romani?'

'You are most welcome, Urcskin Gort,' said the figure, sitting down and gesturing with both hands. 'Please, be upstanding.'

'Thank you, your grace,' said his holiness, as he stood up and gestured for his retinue to follow suit. 'We wish to acknowledge the presence of this one at your side,' he said, pointing with his rod of office at Titus. 'We know him as the seed of Virdaline the Buxom, honoured female ancestor of our brothers the Toad Furtling Free Durotriges, murdered by the hand of the Romani invader these ten summers past. We heard rumour that he had deserted the cursed invader with whom he served for so long, and is now their implacable enemy. But we had not foreseen his presence in your honoured household.'

This, as Henry found out later, was a deliberately insulting reference to Titus's history as a soldier with the Roman legions. It was, in effect, a formal questioning of his right to call himself a warrior of the Durotriges.

'Corio Boc is honoured in our company,' said the figure, evenly. 'Any questioning of his status would cause us unwelcome concern.'

This in turn was political speak for 'If you don't shut your slanderous mouth immediately I will have someone shut it for you . . . permanently!'

'As your grace wishes,' said his holiness, bowing low. 'And who is this other who sits at your right hand? Does he not have the semblance of a Romani collaborator, with the soft, arse-hair face of a ten-summer youngling whose balls have not yet found the energy to drop? We respectfully crave your assurance, your grace, that he is not in league with the godless invader.'

'He is Henry Dragon Spawn of the New Ancient Celts, and an honoured ambassador to the kingdoms of Britain,' said the figure. 'He welcomes you and urges that you insult him not again for fear that his Great Father, the Dragon Lord of the New Ancient Celts, hack off your scrotum and drink from it your slanderous blood!'

'Then he is thrice honoured in your company and in your household, your grace, and I plead with him that my humble scrotum be not cut from my humble body nor my humble blood drunk.'

He turned to Henry. 'How say you, Dragon Spawn of the New Ancient Celts? Will you spare this, your villainous servant, the most vile of cuts and the most feared of blood drinkings?'

'Er . . . yeah,' said Henry, with an uncertain sideways glance at the hooded figure, 'that's . . . fine.' All the talk of scrotum hacking and blood drinking was making him feel queasy.

'Most excellent news,' said his holiness, bowing low. 'My humble scrotum is, henceforth, yours to command.'

Henry looked blank, and a little unwell.

'Say your knife is sheathed in brotherly friendship,' hissed the figure.

'Oh . . . er, right. Your, er . . . your knife . . . '

'Not *his* knife!'

'Oh! Yes, I see. Er . . . *my* knife remains sheathed, and your . . . er, your holy scrotum shall remain attached to your . . . ' he waved an uncertain hand in the direction of Urcskin's crotch, 'your bodily . . . '

'Don't ad lib!' hissed the figure.

'Sorry. I just thought . . . '

'Well don't!'

The figure turned to Urcskin Gort. 'My apologies, your holiness, but the noble Dragon Spawn is unfamiliar with the ways of this great land. Be assured, however, that your honoured scrotum is as safe from his knife as the sacred helmet of your mighty man pole is fruitful.'

His holiness bowed low. 'Your grace is too kind.'

'And a bit too bloody graphic,' muttered Henry.

'I bring gifts, mighty lord!' declaimed Urcskin Gort, turning to gesture at the six scantily clad young women, 'from the mighty chieftain, Prick Slicer III! They be lusty maidens and virgins all with girl-skins unravaged by finger, dildo or man pole. Yours to use as you wish. Perhaps,' he added, turning slyly to Henry, 'Dragon Spawn the Merciful would mount them in your grace's honoured presence, and grant us the privilege of viewing his mighty coupling?'

'I don't think so,' muttered Henry. 'If by mount them . . .?'

The hooded figure silenced him with a gesture.

'We accept the gifts from your mighty lord, your holiness, and request that you thank him for his generosity. Lieutenant . . .?'

'Here sir,' replied the lieutenant, appearing behind the holy retinue and walking across the clearing in high heels and the short, kilt-skirted gown of a

Greek maiden. She nodded curtly to the helmetbinder in passing, and came to attention in front of the masked figure. 'How may I be of service your grace?'

'These young women are gifts from the mighty Prick Slicer, Lord of the Durotriges,' said the figure. 'They will, henceforth, be under your protection and subject to your tutelage.'

'Of course, your grace,' bowed the lieutenant. 'This way ladies,' she added to the young women. 'Follow me, if you please?'

'A fine piece of ass, that one,' said his holiness, waving a hand at the lieutenant as she passed. 'Would your grace grant this humble servant of the mighty Prick Slicer the freedom to mount it in your noble presence and test its worthiness to receive the royal spunk?'

'Under his grace's protection,' murmured the lieutenant, out of the corner of her mouth, 'women are not chattels to be used and abused at will.'

His holiness pretended not to hear. 'Your grace . . .?'

'I wouldn't recommend it.'

'Even so, your grace,' said his holiness, 'I assure you that in the art of royal test rogering there is none in all Britain to compare with your humble servant.'

'If you must, then,' said the figure. 'But don't say I didn't warn you.'

Henry glanced at Titus, and was surprised to see him smiling, serenely.

'Your grace is most kind,' said his holiness, bowing low. 'Acolytes!' he cried, turning to the armed men. 'Subdue her to my needs, forthwith! My mighty man pole is rampant!'

The acolytes grinned, and converged on the lieutenant to subdue her.

Five seconds later, the subduing had not gone well for the acolytes, as they lay in various states of unconsciousness, either twitching from the crotch up or paralyzed from the neck down. The lieutenant, in contrast, was unruffled. She turned away from the smiling, shyly sniggering virgins to the visibly shaken helmetbinder. 'Would his holiness care to attempt the royal test rogering under his own steam?' she asked, sweetly.

His holiness put a hand up to his throat to loosen the necklace that seemed suddenly in danger of throttling him. '*Heh-hem*!' he coughed, turning and bowing to the hooded figure. 'Your grace will understand that such a course of action would be beneath the dignity of my exalted station.'

'As your holiness wishes,' acknowledged the figure.

'Besides,' muttered Henry, 'your mighty man pole might get dented.'

'Dragon Spawn is wise,' said his holiness through gritted teeth as he bowed to Henry, 'in the ways of the world.'

'Then perhaps we should return to the reason for your embassy to this place, your holiness?' suggested the figure.

Urcskin Gort bowed again and informed the assembly in loud declamation that the people of his master, the noble, mighty and thrice renowned Prick Slicer III, had been so impressed by his grace's recent 'Putting of a holy wind up the kilts of the hated Romani invaders' that they wished in their thousands to celebrate the event by worshipping at this, the shrine of their brother Belgae's ancient home of the ancestors and playground of the sun gods: and that further, they clamoured in equal number to be permitted to serve in his grace's army and, in so doing, help drive the hated Romani invader from their ancestral lands back into the foaming seas whence they had come.

The figure raised a hand. 'Colonel, you will make the royal proclamation.'

'Indeed your grace,' said the colonel, turning to face his holiness the helmetbinder and his slowly recovering retinue.

'Hear this!' he cried. 'Let all gathered here this day take heed of this holy proclamation. From the next rising of the sun, all those who wish may attend at this sacred place of ancestors to worship as they see fit and to take an oath of allegiance to the army of His Grace the Masked Avenger. Let all those who would challenge this right of access step forward now or forever be silent.'

No one moved.

'So be it!' cried the colonel.

'Behold, his grace has spoken!' declaimed his holiness, with his arms raised to the heavens. 'We of the Durotriges will depart this holy place forthwith and bear this wondrous news to all loyal men who would hear it!'

'And women, buddy,' said Titus, under his breath. 'And may the gods have mercy on your soul if you ever meet Cartamandua in a dark alley.'

His holiness bowed low to the masked figure, then turned away, and started to march solemnly back across the clearing with as much dignity as he could muster. The rag-tag guards of his retinue limped along behind him to the accompaniment of much suppressed giggling from the tight-knit group of happy virgins clustered around the lieutenant.

'What was all that about,' whispered Henry.

'As I said earlier,' replied the figure, 'a little experiment of the doctor's and the colonel's devising to further gauge the effectiveness of the motivational techniques that he and his squad are currently perfecting for the non-violent coercion of the repressed and superstitious masses.'

'Yes, but you can't seriously believe that his holiness and his incompetent retinue would have a cat in hell's chance against the Roman army? I mean, that lot couldn't fight their way out of a wet paper bag in a tank!'

The golden mask turned towards him. 'You do them a disservice, Henry. The Durotriges are proud and fearsome warriors, as brave and deadly in combat as any you will find in the ancient world. They just didn't have "a cat in hell's chance", as you put it, against the lieutenant, that's all.'

'Friggin' A!' muttered Titus.

'The fact is,' added the figure, 'not even a platoon of your much vaunted Royal Marine Commandoes would stand a chance against the lieutenant!'

Titus winked at Henry.

'But we are not talking about physical violence, are we? And at some time in the not-too-distant present you will need to remember that fact. So it really is in your best interests to try to keep up.'

* * *

41

COCO THE CHIMP

Henry could be forgiven for not having recognized the Clatworthies for who and what they were from the moment he first met them. After all, his knowledge of time travellers had previously been limited to what he'd read in science fiction stories or seen in movies and on the TV. Like most of his generation he'd spent much of his formative years as a boggle-eyed infant watching through splay-fingered hands as Doctor Who battled to save races, creeds, planets and entire galaxies from the predations of aliens too terrifying to contemplate without the protection of an intervening sofa. And later, as a pimply faced adolescent, he had harboured a secret desire to meet and befriend the sort of omnipotent time travelling alien capable of revealing to him not only the mysteries of the multi-universe, but also, and of far more importance on a personal level, one or two pressing questions he'd had about what it would be like to get *really* close to a teenage girl. But to the best of his recollection, neither Tom Baker nor any of the other incarnations of the good doctor had been in a permanent state of sexual arousal. Or at least, not visibly so. How turned on they might secretly have been beneath all those layers of eccentric clothing by the prospect of galactic domination – not to mention the domination of one or two of their more scantily clad assistants – was anyone's guess. But it was a fact that, on British television at least, a typical Time Lord had never been seen to navigate his TARDIS, nor defeat the machinations of his many alien adversaries, by threatening them with his erect dick. It was to Henry's credit, therefore, that when Jo told him that she and the others were time travellers from the distant future he accepted immediately that she was telling him the truth. But then, why wouldn't he when she was clearly such a good and moral person whose kindness, intelligence and purity of spirit shone from every pore of her face like so many beacons of light. Besides, he was feeling uncomfortably horny, as well as uncommonly groggy, and couldn't ignore the fact that he could see right down her top as she knelt in front of him, and was afraid that if he told her that what she was saying was a load of old cobblers, she would get up and walk off in a huff.

Suddenly, he became aware that everyone was staring at him. He blushed and looked guiltily into Jo's eyes. 'The future,' he said. 'That's what you just said, right? The future?'

Mervyn put his hand on Jo's shoulder. 'May I . . .?'

Much to Henry's disappointment, Jo nodded and stood up. 'Stick to the point though Merv, eh?' she said, as she took a step back.

'Of course,' said Mervyn, earnestly. 'Of course! Of course!' He pulled up a chair in front of Henry, and sat down, facing him.

'What Jo says is correct, Henry. Although actually, it would be more accurate to say that we're from the past. I mean, when people say they're from the future they mean they've only just arrived in the present, don't they? They don't mean they've been hanging around for ages – since the middle of last year or something, right? And even if they did they wouldn't say so, would they?' He frowned. 'Not that most people say it at all, do they: "I'm from the future", I mean? Except in novels and films. But if they *did* say it, they'd say: "I'm from the year AD 2050", or whatever, "and I got here five minutes ago", or "I landed this morning". Or, at the very least, "I arrived last night". Do you see? They definitely wouldn't say: "I'm from the future and I've been hanging around for centuries waiting for you to turn up", would they?'

He smiled, wanly. 'Anyway, if I said something like that, you'd think "So why has it taken you so long to tell someone about it?" wouldn't you? It wouldn't work, would it? Suspension of disbelief, I mean? So when Jo said we're from the future, what she really meant was that we're from the past. If you've been around for a long time, you've got to be, haven't you? If you haven't just arrived, you must have been here for a while, so you're really from the past as well as the future. And the trouble with us is we've been around a lot longer in the past than we ever were in the future. So really, we're from the past, *not* from the future. But we wouldn't have been in the past at all if we hadn't been sent back there from the future in the first place. So, really, we *are* from the future, and *not* from the past. So when I say . . .'

'Merr-rrvv?' muttered Jo, irritably.

He held up a hand. 'No, no, I'm fine. I'm fine. Really!' He looked at Henry again. 'It's very confusing, isn't it, when you try to pin it down? I mean, you're not going to say you're from the past, are you? You, Henry Kite, I mean, are not going to say: "I'm from the past", because you take it for granted that you are, don't you? You were born there, and everybody knows it. So what would be the point? But we were born in the future and travelled *back* into the past. By which I mean that we were born in the future of now, not in the future of some other time. Although we were that too, of course, by definition. And we weren't born very far into the future of now, either. I was born in AD 2030, for instance, only forty-three years from now. Not long at all, really, is it? The trouble is that we were sent a long way back into the past from not very far into the future. From AD 2084 to AD 51, to be precise. So really we've lived a great deal longer in the past than we ever did in the future. But it wouldn't make much sense to say: "Hello, we're from the past", would it? Because everyone's from the past, aren't they?' He frowned. 'Unless they're from the future and have only just arrived.'

'Merrrrv,' muttered Jo, 'for Christ's sake!'

'Yes, yes!' He leaned towards Henry. 'What causes all the confusion is that we worked out early on that it's not a good idea to go around telling people about it. So we're a bit secretive and sort of out of practice with the confessional-type thing. It was self-preservation originally, because people took a very dim view of our sudden appearance in their time and space, and most of them tried to persecute us for it: you know, surrounding us in large groups with bows and arrows and spears, and throwing rocks at us? Or piling sticks under us when they caught us, and burning us at a stake? Or just throwing a rope over the nearest tree and hanging us by the neck until our eyes popped out and our tongues turned a nasty shade of purple. It's a group activity you see Henry, victimizing people, isn't it? And the more insecure people get, I mean, if they read the *Daily Mail* or the *Sun*, for instance, the more they club together to persecute anyone who isn't them. Particularly if they think you might know more about what's happening to them than they know themselves. I mean, they get pretty violent if you tell them there's no such thing as God, for instance.' He gave a self-deprecating smile. 'It doesn't work if they've already figured that one out for themselves, of course. Then they just look at you and ask if you're intending to make a living out of stating the bleeding obvious. But if they *do* believe in God – and it doesn't matter *which* god – they get really irritable if you tell them that he, or indeed she, doesn't exist. Especially if they've based their civilization on believing that he, or she, does – exist, I mean – which, of course, most of them have. And the priests are the worst because they think you're trying to do them out of a job.'

He sighed and shook his head.

'They've been responsible for more employment-related atrocities throughout history than all the other professions put together, you know, priests. I mean, look at The Crusades. Vindictive little buggers, most of them are. Not to mention sex-crazed. Still,' he said, with an apologetic shrug, 'people in glass houses and all that, eh?' He smiled. 'Anyway, the thing is, as soon as we realized we'd wiped out half the local population within a couple of minutes of arriving in the past, just by protecting ourselves, we decided it might not be a bad idea to lie low for a while and wait until the kerfuffle died down. We tried it, and it worked. Well, give or take an unfortunate legend or two. In fact, it worked so well we decided to take it even further and started pretending we were as dumb as everyone else. That worked even better so we've been doing it ever since.' He looked at Blossom. 'Sort of . . .'

Under normal circumstances Henry would have been wondering how long it was going to be before men in white coats burst into the room and started carting people away in straitjackets. But these were not normal circumstances, and he was beginning to realize from his recent encounter with the mainframe computer, that the essence of Mervyn's story was true. The trouble was that the computer had given him none of the details, and as far as he could tell, Mervyn's version of events had one simple flaw: if it were true, it would mean that they were all two thousand years old, and whatever Blossom and Jo might be, they certainly weren't that.

'Yes,' he said, 'this is all very interesting. But it's not really possible, is it? I mean, most of what you've just said is a load of old drivel.'

'Ah!' exclaimed Mervyn. 'Yes, of course!' He tapped several keys on the computer and pointed at the screen.

Henry turned to look. 'Good god! What the hell's that?'

'Not what,' said Mervyn, archly, 'but who.'

Henry tilted his head. 'It's a turd, isn't it, in a turd-coloured smock?'

'No, that's Drivel.'

'I'm only telling you what I see!' said Henry, peevishly.

Jo patted his arm. 'He means it's *called* Drivel. It's not a turd, it's a man.'

Mervyn pressed another key. 'And that's Knobrot.'

Henry flinched. 'Yes, I can believe it. What is it, one of those films about VD to scare the living daylights out of Boy Scouts and stop them trying to have sex with Girl Guides?'

'Drivel's best mate,' said Robbie.

'Still looks like a turd from where I'm sitting.'

'They weren't the most hygienic of tribes,' sighed Mervyn.

Robbie leaned over, pressed a key, and pointed at the screen.

'A pile of turds in turd-coloured Bermuda shorts?' offered Henry. 'Where did you say you went on your holidays: the local sewage farm was it?'

'That's a Faeceantii wedding reception,' said Mervyn. 'Knobrot was Drivel's best man. The turd in the middle is the bride.'

'It's a sheep, isn't it?' said Henry. 'A sheep in a tatty string vest?'

'Very liberal marriage vows, the Faeceantii,' nodded Mervyn. 'Centuries ahead of their time.'

'They were the people living here when we arrived,' said Lance. 'But you must be wondering why we're telling you all this.'

'You're insane?'

Robbie pressed another key, and a modest circular building, like a futuristic cowshed, appeared on the screen.

'Wait a minute,' said Gareth, sharply. 'Give him the basic facts, we said. No one said anything about giving him details.'

Mervyn glanced at his watch. 'There's plenty of time. Kinsman isn't due for a while yet, and everything's ready for when he arrives.' He looked unsure. 'I hope. Anyway, I think he ought to know why everyone's trying to kill him, don't you? If we're just going to go off and leave him?'

'Look,' replied Gareth, coldly, 'you know the rules. We don't interfere. You know what always happens when we do.'

'Why tell him anything at all, then?' asked Gwen. 'Better to leave the poor sod in total ignorance than only give him part of the story.' She smiled at Henry, and looked around the room for support. 'Poor little bugger.'

Blossom put an arm around Henry's shoulders. "T'isn't fair, Gar, is it?'

'Much as it pains me to admit it,' said Jo, 'she's right.'

'Bugger I!' agreed Hubert and Horace.

Gareth stared in silence from face to face as they nodded their agreement. 'All right,' he conceded, 'fine! Have it your way. But leave me out of it. The last thing I want is another boring trip down memory lane.' He got up and stalked towards the door. 'I'll be in the lab if anyone wants me.'

'Spoilsport,' muttered Blossom, as the door slammed behind him. 'I don't know what I'm gonna do with that boy.'

Jo and Blossom helped Henry out of the electric chair and onto the sofa. They sat down on either side him and put their arms around him protectively as the others turned their chairs to face the screen like kids getting ready to watch a favourite movie. When everyone was sitting comfortably, Mervyn pressed a key and pointed at the screen.

'That,' he said, indicating the thing that looked like a futuristic cowshed, 'is, or was, the Pate Institute of Genetic Sciences – PIGS for short. It's where most of us used to work. It was built on what you would call a Site of Special Scientific Interest. It was also in an area of high unemployment, because tourism had collapsed after successive outbreaks of foot and mouth disease on the moor, so we got huge grants from the government, and the lottery, and the European Federation, and just about anyone else who wanted to be seen to be contributing to a good cause. The sensitivity of the location meant most of the facilities had to be built underground.' He pointed as the picture on the screen changed to a set of architect's drawings. 'Originally, there were thirty-five storeys with offices, laboratories, restrooms and warehouses, all of them underground. Many more storeys were added later, including the deepest of the lot, where we are now. There was an underground power plant, a water purification and sewage treatment system, shopping mall, food production facilities and a light transit system to the nearest sizeable town. No parking allowed on site, you see? There was also a helicopter pad, communications centre, catering facilities, health club, and enough retail, service sector and office space for five hundred staff.'

He pressed another key, and the circular single-storey granite building with its slate roof reappeared on the screen. 'But all you could see on the surface was that.' He waved an arm around the room. 'This was one of the deep-level storerooms. It came with us, as most of the lower level facilities did, although we still don't know how or why. It could have been the shielding provided by the surrounding geology – granite, you see? – but the truth is that it's just one of many things we haven't been able to explain fully, even after two thousand years. This level was where we kept radioactive materials. When we eventually realized that it still existed, it took us centuries to dig down to it again.'

'Radioactive?' said Henry.

'Don't worry lover,' said Blossom, 'they won't drop off.'

Mervyn coughed diffidently, and puffed out his chest. 'I was a geneticist. My work was renowned internationally. I specialized in a little-known branch of genetics associated with racial memory.' A cloud passed over his face. 'Unfortunately, my results were not always as precise as I would have liked.' He sighed and looked down at his hands. 'We would have gone back to our own time long ago, Henry, but we couldn't be certain that we'd get back safely without the encoder. And even when we had it,' he glared at Rooter, 'before that pillock gave it away to satisfy his carnal desires, we weren't confident we would get back to were we started from. The system wasn't perfect to begin with, you see? Some of the rats came back, but the work with the chimps and the pigeons was . . . inconclusive at best.'

'Meaning they didn't come back at all,' snorted Rooter. 'Not in one piece, at any rate. He did get a penis back once, though, didn't you Merv? Highly aroused it was. But one dick from a crate-load of monkeys was hardly something to be proud of, was it? He said it was shagging at the moment of recall. Can you imagine that? There you are, giving it a bit of welly, there's a flash of lightning and your dick rockets half a million years into the future.'

Mervyn shook his head. 'We have no proof for a timescale of that order, Rooter, and you know it.'

'Really? And I bet that'd make the monkey feel a hellova lot better, wouldn't it? Listen, I don't know about you, but I wouldn't want my dick rocketing ten seconds into the future, never mind ten million years.'

'Rooter doesn't have a great deal of respect for my work,' said Mervyn. 'In fact, I believe he is of the opinion that if we had put an infinite number of monkeys into white coats, and given them the run of my laboratory, they would have come up with a solution to time travel far quicker than I did.'

'And known how it worked,' muttered Rooter.

'I admit that my research was mostly theoretical in those days. But you can't deny that the board were sufficiently impressed with the results to continue funding . . .' He frowned at Henry. 'Hello? Anyone there?'

Henry was staring into his lap with his hands clasped over his crotch. He looked up. 'God,' he murmured, 'can you imagine it? Only his dick . . .'

'Only good thing about most men,' muttered Jo.

'Only good thing about life,' grinned Blossom.

'Yes,' said Henry, 'but . . . why?'

'Why what?'

'Why did only his . . .?'

'Racial memory is a funny thing,' said Mervyn.

'Bloody hilarious,' grunted Rooter, 'when it makes your willy disappear in the middle of a shag!'

'What he means,' said Robbie, 'is that racial memory is a sex-linked characteristic,' he glanced at Mervyn. 'That and the fact that the penis was probably more intelligent than its owner.'

'Show me a penis that isn't,' sighed Jo.

'A simplification,' said Mervyn, 'but essentially accurate, yes. But not really more intelligent: just more *alive*. Racial memory is a complicated thing, too, you see. Just ask that idiot Carl Jung. He started it. All I did . . .' He coughed. 'Sorry. Sorry. I . . . er, . . . Sorry. Anyway, the . . . er, the spiral encoder was built to recognize racial characteristics. The things that make us all human?'

'Or monkey,' said Rooter.

Mervyn nodded. 'And lock onto them. But it needed a strong signal.'

Blossom squeezed Henry's thigh. 'Like sex.'

'Lust is one of the stimuli that might do it, yes,' agreed Mervyn. 'But there are others: anger, jealousy, pride . . . '

'The seven deadly stimuli,' grinned Lance.

Mervyn inclined his head. 'Certain physiological changes take place during an intense sexual encounter.'

'If you're doing it right,' giggled Blossom.

'Some of which are visible to the naked eye,' continued Mervyn, doggedly.

'Dilation of the pupils; a reddening of the skin . . . '

'A hard-on,' blurted Perce.

Mervyn shot him a sympathetic glance. 'Nice to know you're still with us, old man.' He smiled at Henry. 'He still thinks it only happened to him.' He thought for a moment. 'Where was I? Ah, yes. There are chemical changes associated with the visible signs: a marked increase in electrical activity in certain parts of the brain, an increased sensitivity in what we know as the erogenous zones and . . . so on. In combination these effects create a small but significant magnetic field. The encoder was designed to detect the signature of such fields and lock onto them.'

Blossom giggled. 'It knows when you're feeling horny.'

'Crudely put,' said Mervyn, 'but essentially correct, yes. Although, it doesn't only respond to sexual arousal, it locks on to any powerful signal it detects and reciprocates it temporally.'

'Sorry?' said Henry.

'It locks on to it and throws you backwards in time,' said Gavin.

'Yes,' nodded Mervyn, 'or forwards: to a time and place within a few metres of where you started out.'

'Somewhere with the same level of horniness,' smirked Blossom.

'Indeed,' said Mervyn. 'We were on Dartmoor, or, more precisely, we were a little way under it, in a purpose-built bunker.' He glanced around the room. 'At least, most of us were. As I said, it was AD 2084 and we were transported back to AD 51, into the middle of an area of intense psycho-sexual activity.'

'An orgy,' whispered Blossom.

'A sacrificial rite, actually,' Mervyn corrected her. 'But also on Dartmoor. Or what became Dartmoor, if you see what I mean? We landed close to the institute, as far as we could tell from the bits of it we found later.' He puffed out his chest. 'Reciprocal Aura Temporal Shift, I called it. RATS for short.'

'Lot of good the name did us,' muttered Rooter.

'But,' said Henry, who was still preoccupied with thoughts of vanishing penises, 'what about the monkey's . . . you know? And why didn't the rest of him come back? And whoever . . . or whatever . . .?'

'Yes, yes indeed!' said Mervyn, hurriedly. 'Well, we suspect its mate wasn't entirely enamoured of his attentions at the moment of recall.'

Henry looked blank.

'He means sex of the non-consensual variety,' said Lance. 'She, he, or it – for all we know Coco was shagging a hole in the ground – probably wasn't as enthusiastic about the whole thing as he was. No sexual arousal, no aura: no aura, no time travel. Do you see?'

'No,' said Henry.

Mervyn pursed his lips. 'No, it isn't straightforward, is it? Look at it this way: Coco – we think it was Coco's member that came back – wasn't the brightest of apes, and it is entirely possible that, as the saying goes, he was thinking with his dick at the moment of recall. A small portion of his brain did come back as well, but,' he shrugged his uncertainty, 'what happened to the rest of him, or to his mate, if indeed he had one, is anyone's guess.'

'Yes,' said Henry, 'but you said it was reciprocal?'

Mervyn nodded.

'And that's what brought Coco's . . .thing back?'

'Not in that instance, no. I always reversed the polarity after five seconds, you see, as a precaution. So it was automatic.' He sighed and gazed at his hands. 'Although, as I say, it operated without the degree of predictability I would have preferred.'

'You see,' said Jo, 'he didn't really understand what was happening to his subjects. They weren't meant to disappear, just sort of vibrate at a frequency that would alter their DNA by realigning it with the whole of human evolution. I mean, he hates to admit it, but when they started disappearing he thought they were migrating to an alternative reality: a sort of parallel universe where all the racial memories of our species are stored. He didn't realize they were travelling through time until it was too late.'

'But,' said Henry, 'what was he experimenting on? You said racial memory,' he shrugged, 'but why?'

'Eternal youth?' said Jo. 'Immortality? Call it what you like. Big business it was then – is now, for that matter. All the potions and anti-ageing creams, cosmetic surgery and genetically modified this and that. You have no idea how much money there was to be made . . . will be . . . already is. And he thought he'd discovered a way of tapping into our evolutionary past to give each individual the same life expectancy as the species as a whole: generation after generation into immortality.' She raised a quizzical eyebrow. 'Although I'm sure he'll tell you that what I've just said is a simplification, won't you Merv?'

'You can mock,' he said, self-righteously. 'But I was right, wasn't I?' He turned to Henry. 'The trouble was that I hadn't made any allowance for the reciprocal effect. I'm afraid it wasn't in my calculations at all.'

'What calculations would that be, then, Merv?' asked Rooter.

Mervyn ignored him. 'It wasn't until after we got here, and I'd had time to think about the implications, that it started to make some kind of sense.'

'Try two hundred years,' said Rooter.

'It was complicated. And besides, I didn't have the facilities anymore, or the essential ingredients.' He looked at Henry. 'It took a long time to work out what the RATS effect was really doing, and that it could shift with the subject's state of mind. It wasn't until after we'd been thrown back in time ourselves that I started wondering what had really been going on in the lab.'

'Made the old Nobel Prize look a bit dodgy, didn't it?' offered Rooter.

'There were a few weaknesses in the theory, yes. But as I've always . . . '

'A few bloody *weaknesses*! You lost six dozen rats, two dozen pigeons, ten assorted monkeys, six chimpanzees, five gibbons, four orangutans . . . '

'And a partridge in a pear tree!' sang Blossom. 'Sorry,' she confided to Henry with a hand shielding her mouth, 'I know it's cruel but it all gets a bit too serious for me sometimes, and I just have to let it out.'

'It has been speculated,' said Lance, 'that one of the missing chimps won the US presidential election in 2001. And not entirely fairly, at that. So he couldn't have been completely stupid, could he?'

'Look,' said Mervyn, 'let's say you go back in time feeling angry. Then you end up in an environment where anger is the dominant emotion. That's how the reciprocity side of the equation works. Do you see?'

Henry nodded, uncertainly.

'But imagine your dominant emotional state changes to one of confusion, or fear, as a result of what you've encounter where you've ended up? Yes?'

'OK . . .'

'Then the encoder's automatic return mechanism will throw you backwards or forwards in time to a place where that *different* state of mind is the dominant one. Which might not be the time and place you started out from: particularly if the dominant state has changed there, too.' He gazed up at the ceiling. 'God only knows how many confused animals have been, and will be, materializing around here over the centuries. We haven't seen any of them yet, but that doesn't stop me feeling guilty about it. I knew there was a problem, but I didn't know how convoluted it could get.'

'How come Ernie's fixed it for Kinsman, then?' asked Rooter. 'You said he was a third-rate meddler with no talent for higher mathematics.'

'What would *you* know about it?' asked Mervyn, haughtily.

Rooter raised an eyebrow and touched the side of his nose.

'Meaning what?'

Rooter shrugged, and looked away.

'Anyway,' said Mervyn, with his eyes still fixed on Rooter, 'when the encoder took effect the subject looked as if it was being deconstructed layer by layer: which, incidentally, was more or less what *was* happening to them.'

'Beam me up, Scotty,' offered Lance. 'All that?'

'Then they vanished. They didn't seem to know what was happening to them – something we know from our own experience – and if nothing changed within the lifetime of the experiment, say five seconds, and provided the emotional states at both ends of the corridor stayed the same, they came back in perfect condition. Well, give or take the odd bit of frazzled hair.'

'Only they never did, did they?' said Rooter.

Mervyn sighed. 'Not in the beginning, no. Except once.' He looked at Henry. 'On one occasion, two rats were fighting on the platform just before we started the experiment. As they were disappearing, two lab technicians started fighting, too: something to do with their girlfriends, I believe. Anyway, they were still at it when the rats came back, five seconds later. So were the rats. The trouble was that we didn't realize the significance of it at the time.'

'So the emotion is independent of species?' hazarded Henry.

Mervyn smiled. 'Good! Good! Well done! The trouble was that it took us a very long time to work that bit out.'

'So,' said Henry, 'what happened to bring Coco's willy back?'

'Sexual arousal,' said Lance, 'and La Demoiselle Sauvage.'

Henry shook his head. 'Sorry. You've lost me again.'

'The institute's chief executive kept a mistress,' said Gavin, 'in a small but luxurious boudoir not far from the labs. On the night in question she was feeling a bit horny.'

'Very horny, apparently,' said Mervyn. 'Anyway, to cut a long story short, Coco's penis materialized in her bed: homed-in on her, as you might say?'

Henry grimaced. 'Oh, that's . . . that's . . . *yuck*!'

Mervyn shrugged. 'The trouble was that she thought it was a present from the chief to keep her company while he was away.'

'And decided to put it to good use,' said Gavin.'

'Meanwhile, we thought the experiment had failed.'

'As per usual,' said Rooter.

'We were getting ready to go home,' said Mervyn, with a sour look at Rooter, 'when the chief turned up, white as a sheet, with Coco's tadger in a freezer bag. He had decided to drop in on his mistress as a surprise. But he was the one who got the shock. Apparently, Coco's penis compared more than a little favourably with his own.'

'You mean . . .?' said Henry. 'God! But how could she . . . if it was . . .?'

'It didn't go limp, if that's what you're thinking,' said Lance.

'Well . . .'

'The encoder preserves the subject perfectly,' said Mervyn. 'And as far as we can tell it does so for an indefinite period of time. Which, of course,' he added, carefully, 'is why all of us are immortal.'

'Yeah,' sniggered Horace Naggs with obscene relish, 'an' stiff as a board for the best part of two thousand years!'

Henry cleared his throat. 'So,' he said, carefully, 'does that mean . . .? Are you saying that you were all in the same . . . when you travelled backwards in time? And that's why you all had . . .' he gestured at the ceiling, 'up there?'

'Boners,' said Blossom, gleefully. She reached across and wrapped her hand around his towel-encased dick, as if it was a gear stick. 'You're such a prude,' she grinned, waggling it as if to check that he was in neutral. 'You ought to relax more, you know,' she breathed in his ear, 'stiffies are fun.'

'Yes,' he said, 'it's just a bit of a shock, that's all, everybody talking about them all the time. But that wasn't why you did it, was it: to have eternal hard-ons, I mean?' Maybe it was, he told himself: old Horace was grinning insanely enough to suggest that, for his part at least, it had been a deliberate ploy.

'No, no,' said Mervyn, 'that wasn't why we did it at all.'

'And if the encoder was so unpredictable, why did you risk using it?

'Good question,' said Lance.

'And if there was a five-second recall . . .?'

Everyone looked at Rooter.

'What?' he said, with exaggerated innocence. 'What did I do?'

42

SERGEANT ARTHUR

'There was no five-second automatic recall,' said Mervyn, with his eyes fixed on Rooter. 'There was just him.'

'What? I didn't know, did I? Anyone would think I did it on purpose.' He turned to Henry. 'Two thousand years and you think they'll let me forget it? One mistake – one *tiny* mistake – and they've never let me hear the end of it. Some people would've seen it was an accident. Some people would've said "Never mind, mate, anyone could've done it". But not this lot. Oh no!'

'Some people wouldn't have tried to steal the encoder, though, Roots, would they?' said Lance. 'And stopped halfway through for a shag.'

'You never could resist it,' said Sergeant Arthur, 'could you dad?'

Henry looked from the sergeant to Gwen Evers in amazement.

'Turn-up for the books, that, eh?' she said. 'I think we ought to tell him everything,' she added. 'It's only fair after what he's been through. Besides, he's probably guessed most of it already.' She looked enquiringly at Henry, who was feeling like the only character in an Agatha Christie novel who hadn't worked out who'd done it, even after Poirot had gathered everyone together in the library and explained the plot in the minutest of detail.

'Errr, sorry,' he said, 'but . . .'

Arthur gestured at Rooter. 'Well?'

'Nothing to do with me mate.'

'Tell him!' snapped Gwen.

'Tell him what?'

'You know perfectly well *what*!'

'Don't bother,' said Jo, tiredly. 'We'll be here all day if we have to wait for Lover Boy to admit it.' She looked at Henry, but pointed at Rooter. 'His real name is Leonard John King. Also known, amongst many other unflattering things, as Leo the Bastard, Rooter the Horn, Leo "Rooter" King, Rooter the Beast, and, in the language of the Feaceantu . . .?' She gestured with an upturned palm for Henry to complete the sentence.

He looked at her hand, and then at her face. 'What?'

'Go on,' she urged, 'you can do it.'

He shook his head.

'Just relax.'

He shook his head again. 'No, sorry.'

She clicked her tongue. 'Haven't you been listening to anything we've said?

'Well, I don't know,' he admitted, glancing uneasily at the others. 'I thought earlier . . . sort of, you know, last night? I mean, about the sword and everything, but it's . . . well, that's ridiculous, isn't it?'

'Try us,' said Lance.

'Well, I thought . . . But then I thought . . . You know?'

Jo leaned back against the arm of the sofa and regarded him in silent immobility for several seconds. Then she cleared her throat with a minute shake of the head and gestured at Rooter. 'Uther Pendragon, God help us! Wanted across the millennia for a variety of crimes, but mostly polygamy, grievous bodily harm and aggravated burglary. Modus operandi when breaking and entering, and that is what we are concerned with here, demanded a female accomplice,' she sighed, 'and, on the night in question, that was yours truly, who could be relied upon to satisfy the sexual cravings that were the inevitable by-product of his thieving. Or to put it another way: stealing things turned him on . . . a lot!' She looked at her hands. 'I was doing postgrad fieldwork for a PhD in criminology. *Burglary as an Aphrodisiac to the Recidivist Criminal Mind* was my working title. It doesn't exactly trip off the tongue, does it? But that was the least of my problems. You could say that in my eagerness to produce a really groundbreaking piece of research I got too close to one of my case studies. Anyway, that night he was after anything that took his fancy, which, apart from me, turned out to be the encoder.'

'I thought it was a dagger,' blurted Rooter. 'I thought "Must be worth a bob or two, that?".' He shrugged, and lowered his eyes.

Everyone waited for him to continue.

He didn't.

'Yes, well,' said Mervyn, 'his error was understandable, if not exactly excusable. The encoder, or at least the part of it that you were wearing around your neck last night, looks, as you have seen, not unlike the handle of a sword or a dagger. However, that is purely coincidental; and what you saw upstairs in the weapons room was a disguise. Something we cooked a few hundred years ago to try to stop our friend here stealing it again while we worked out how to use it to get back to our own time. We thought he wouldn't recognize it like that. Unfortunately, that didn't work, either. Which is why it ended up in the British Museum. But that's another story, and we haven't got time for it now. Suffice it to say that he gave it to a visiting princess of the Brigantes in return for her letting him get his leg over. All you need to know is that in its original form, the encoder looked more like a dagger than a sword,' he made a gesture with his hands, 'much, much shorter, you see, sitting in an ornate sheath. It wasn't really a sheath, of course, but a complex electronic device, mounted in a single block of crystal. The technology was far more advanced than anything you will be familiar with today. But it was basically simple, nonetheless. The encoder was in the shape of an inverted cross, and looked like the handle, knuckle guard and top few inches of the blade of a long-handled dagger. It didn't really have a blade. Do you see?'

Henry gave an uncertain shrug.

'What Rooter *thought* was the blade and scabbard of a weapon was really, for want of a more accurate expression, what we will call the encoder's motherboard. The sections you were wearing were the encoder. The blade, the hilt and the knuckle guard in the armourer's block upstairs form the disguise we added later. It's just a sword. A *real* sword made to match the markings on the encoder and hung on the wall in the hope that it would blend in with the rest of the collection. It didn't occur to us that Cyrano de Bergerac here might actually decide to use the damned thing in a duel.'

'So the story about the fight with Lou Cornish was true?'

Mervyn cleared his throat. 'Yes, well, I might have embellished it a bit. Anyway,' he added, quickly, 'in the lab, the encoder and it's sheath-like motherboard were mounted in what looked like a clear glass block – a perfect cube; sort of stuck in it upright, like the sword? It was an optical computer, and far more powerful than anything that exists today outside of our own laboratory. It wasn't glass, either, but a single synthetic crystal about thirty centimetres square, inside which was printed an array of what for simplicity's sake we will call mirrors, lenses, prisms, beam splitters, and other optical elements on a microscopic scale. In the base of the block, a black pad on which the cube sat, were a number of lasers: all of them very small and very powerful. The whole thing stood on a pedestal in the middle of the room. There were no banks of flashing lights, no keyboards, and no rows of switches or dials. All you had to do was speak to it and it would do what you wanted.'

Lance coughed.

'More or less . . .'

'If you were lucky,' said Gavin.

'Which we weren't,' added Lance.

'No,' admitted Mervyn. 'No, we weren't.' He glanced around the room. 'Anyway, there it was, the encoder, sticking out of the computer in the lab like a priceless artefact on display in a museum.'

'That's what he thought it was,' said Jo, 'and it really turned him on. Didn't it, lover? At first, he wanted to wear it in his belt while we were doing it doggie style up against the plinth. But it kept poking me in the arse, so I made him put it in his back pocket until we'd finished.' She sighed. 'He did, but *we* didn't. At least, not in the conventional manner.'

'Apparently, Rooter wasn't the only thing that got turned on, you see,' said Mervyn. 'We think the circuitry responded to his er, . . . excitement. Sort of, set up a sympathetic vibration. Or maybe it was the heat of his . . . whatever. The fact is that we still don't really know. But whatever it was, it created an aura of incredibly powerful proportions: enough to transport the whole lot of us, and most of the institute, two thousand years backwards in time.'

'He got the plans of the building from me,' said Sergeant Arthur. 'And the passwords and stuff? Stole them, didn't you dad? I was head of security at the institute, and he'd only just got out of prison for the umpteenth time. All he ever did when I was a kid. Couldn't stay out for more than a week or two at a time, could you, you silly old bugger? Drove my mother to an early grave, it did. That and the womanizing.'

'She ran off with the bloody vicar,' complained Rooter.

'Exactly!' said Sergeant Arthur. 'Killed her spirit stone dead, you did.' He glanced at Henry. 'Beautiful woman she was, Henry, beautiful! Could have had her pick of the blokes from here to Lands End. Only she had to go and choose that gormless wazzock. I should have known better than to leave the sneaky old sod alone in the house. But he pleaded with me. Begged on his lying knees. Said he'd turned over a new leaf in prison; got religion; wanted to be in the bosom of his family. All that old nonsense. Said signing up for Jo's research proved he was serious about going straight. We fell for it, as always.'

He sighed and shook his head.

'Anyway, I was on patrol that night with me partner,' he glanced at WPC Evers, 'in the company's armoured command vehicle?'

Gwen smiled. 'Only we weren't doing much patrolling, were we?'

'We parked by the perimeter fence.'

'Every night, if we got the chance.'

'First thing we knew about the time-shift was when old Maggot Balls and his gang started trying to break into what was left of the van. One minute we were going at it like rabbits. Next thing we know, there's a thump and a burning sensation and hundreds of little Ancient Britons trying to kill us.'

'Maggot Balls . . .?' frowned Henry.

'It's . . . complicated,' said Mervyn. He nodded at Lance and Gavin.

'Me and Gav worked for Arthur,' said Lance. 'Not really security: more sort of private army? We were on the other side of the compound in an armoured patrol van when everything kicked off.' He smiled. 'You know?'

'You're not brothers, then?' said Henry, with careful nonchalance. 'I mean, you were . . .? Just the two of you, you mean?'

'Gavin Greene,' said Gavin, with a bow. 'I've always had a thing about men in uniform. Can't resist!'

'Laurence Meres,' said Lance. 'Me and Gav were what Robbie would have called hired killers. You couldn't mess about in those days, mind: industrial espionage was a dangerous business. Then there were the protestors. Militant little sods some of them were. I was ex-SAS; Gav was ex-marines. The van was armour-plated like Arthur and Gwen's. Merv thinks that's why the stuff inside survived the shift. Electro-magnetic shielding, or something.'

Mervyn nodded. 'The intensity of the, er, the *auras* in each of the vehicles was probably very high due to the enclosed spaces. Very little of the bodywork survived: just a very thin skin.'

'We came down with a hellova bang,' said Lance. 'But most of the stuff was boxed-up; rocket launchers; smart small arms; and tons of ammo. Some people said we were paranoid. But me and Gav always liked to have an edge.'

'We got knocked about a bit,' said Gavin. 'But the mattress and cushions bore the brunt.' He grinned. 'Right little knocking shop that van was inside.'

'Why did it crash?' asked Henry.

'Wheels and suspension disintegrated,' said Lance. 'Most of the engine and bodywork, too.' He snapped his fingers. 'Just disappeared! Course, the land was lower then, too. Basic geology, that is. Like everybody else, we didn't really know what was going on. Time travel messes with your brain. Instinct must have taken over. Me and Gav thought it was some sort of terrorist attack, so we kicked open what was left of the back doors and charged out, blasting. By the time we realized our mistake we'd wiped out half the

Dumnonii-Durotriges Alliance. Arthur and Gwen got the rest. Old Stonking Rod must have thought Judgement Day had finally come.'

'The dummy-what?' asked Henry.

'Ancient Britons,' said Gavin. 'See, we arrived just in time to stop a military coup. Old Stonking Rod was arch druid – the tribe's spiritual leader and all that? Only she wanted control of the tribal stomping grounds, and reckoned the only way to get it was to wipe the rest of the tribe off the face of the planet. She figured they wouldn't be expecting it on the night of their Big Spring Festival, and she was right. So she made a pact with Maggot Balls of the Dumnonii, and Prick Slicer II of the Durotriges; and they came charging in just as the Faeceantii were starting their sacrificial rite.'

'Only it didn't work out the way she had planned,' said Lance. 'First off, old Knobrot and his boys let their hormones get the better of them. Then me and Gav and Arthur and Gwen turned up with guns blazing, just when she thought she'd got 'em on the run. Maggot Balls and Prick Slicer's mob never stood a chance. I mean it was just their bad luck that we were facing in their direction when we came charging out. It didn't matter that we didn't have any pants on: we were wearing third generation force field tags, and had Intec 6000 smart chips in those M-65s. Heart Seekers, we used to call 'em.'

'There were hundreds of those poor little buggers in baggy trousers and grass skirts and only four of us,' said Gavin. 'But we were the immovable object *and* the irresistible force rolled into one. You point one of those 65s in roughly the right direction and squeeze the trigger, and the intelligent ammo does the rest. At a thousand rounds a minute. Stonking Rod's boys had bows and arrows. We had World War III.'

'No wonder they thought we were gods,' said Mervyn. 'It was a massacre. A bloody awful massacre! But the rest of us were safe. The smart small arms were programmed to ignore anyone wearing institute identity tags.'

'Blew the rest to kingdom come, though,' said Lance. 'Equipped with delayed incendiaries that day.' He held up a hand with the finger and thumb close together. 'Only tiny; but when one of those little devils goes in it heads straight for your heart, waits a fraction of a second and blasts its way out. Nobody gets wounded with one of those things. You get hit, you're deader than a dodo in a microwave oven.'

'The only good thing about the whole horrible mess,' said Mervyn, 'was that it was more or less instantaneous. No one suffered. As soon as they got hit, they were dead.' He shook his head sadly and stared at the floor.

'The D & D Alliance were supposed to get rid of Pickfight and his boys in return for the bog concessions,' said Lance. 'Big business, they were then. The Celts were a superstitious bunch, and chucked tons of stuff into places like Sodmire. Thought they were doorways to the underworld, or some such rubbish. Everything went in: swords, axes, coins, jewellery, people. The more valuable a thing was the more influence they thought it gave them with their gods. A real goldmine, if you had guts enough to defy the bog demons and try to dredge it up.' He glanced across at Rooter. 'Talking of thieving . . . '

Rooter looked at the ceiling.

'Horace and me were cleaners,' said Hubert.

'Ah,' said Henry, with an eager nod of acceptance and a sideways glance at Gavin and Lance, 'I see.'

Horace shook his head. 'No, I don't believe you do, old boy.'

'We were on our tea break, actually,' said Hubert, 'with a pot of Earl Grey and a buttered scone?'

Henry narrowed his eyes in concentration, confused by the sudden change in their speech pattern. 'Sorry?'

'Earl Grey,' said Hubert, 'is a tea much favoured by elderly persons such as ourselves. A scone is . . . '

Henry grinned. 'Yes! Yes, I know. I was . . . It's just that . . . So you don't really talk like that, either?'

'Horace and I have three hundred and eighty-six languages each, dear boy. So we can talk any bleeding way we please. Twenty-seven of those languages, including Dubunni, Iceni and Siluri, have been dead for the best part of two thousand years. Coincidental, or what?' His smile was indulgent. 'When you've been around for as long as we have, old boy, the letters page of the *Reader's Digest* ceases to hold your attention as it might once have done.' He grinned. 'If you are going to live forever, it helps to have a bit of a hobby.

'Hubert and me chose languages,' said Horace, 'ancient and modern.'

'Religions, creeds, faiths and their associated legends, mythologies and tribal superstitions,' added Hubert, his eyes twinkling. 'It helped pass the time on those long winter nights between AD 86 and 1933, do you see?'

'Don't tease,' said Horace. 'The poor boy thinks you're being serious.' He winked at Henry. 'Actually, it only took him two hundred and fifty years to learn the first three hundred and eighty-five languages. He's still struggling with the three hundred and eighty-sixth. English! Still, who isn't?'

'Each of us had our little distractions to help us while away the centuries,' said Hubert. 'For Horace and me it was languages. For Lance and Gavin it was martial arts. They had a natural propensity for it, you see. Imagine it, dear boy, almost twenty centuries studying what even the greatest of the oriental masters could spend only fifty, or sixty, or perhaps eighty years perfecting at best. Have you any idea how frightening they can be when they want to?'

'Always assuming they're sober,' nodded Horace.

'Look who's talking,' scoffed Blossom.

'Yes,' said Horace, 'and no prizes for guessing what our darling Blossom chose as her life's work. You've heard of the *Karma Sutra*, Henry, haven't you? Well, darling Blossom not only inspired most of it, she wrote it, edited it, researched it, abridged it, and took a starring role in the illustrations.'

'You're just jealous.' She wagged a warning finger. 'Don't forget boys, I know what you two randy old sods were up to in that control room.'

'It were all they security cameras an' stuff what done it,' said Hubert, dropping back into a West Country drawl. He nodded at Kate. 'We wos sittin', mindin' our business, while 'er went off to the bogs for a pee. Supervisor, 'er was s'posed to be. Bloody Hitler, more like!'

'The security cameras were automatic,' said Horace. 'And we were eating our tea when up came those two on one of the monitors going at it like the human race was facing an extinction event.' He nodded at Rooter and Jo. 'Well, we had to watch, didn't we? I mean, it was as close as two old codgers like us were ever going to get to a bit of decent rumpy-pumpy. And a hellova lot cheaper than your commercial pornography, too.'

'I saw them as I was passing the lab,' said Kate, 'on my way to the loo? They couldn't see me because I was in darkness on the observation deck, behind plate glass? I was going to sound the alarm or call security,' she glanced at Arthur and Gwen, 'but I thought: "What the hell?" I hated that late shift, anyway. Like watching paint dry, most of the time.'

Lance sat back in his chair. 'So far you've got a couple of cat burglars having it away during, or should that be *after*, the act? A pair of queer security guards at it in the back of a bulletproof van; the head of security and his second-in-command humping in their armoured command vehicle; and no less than three dirty little voyeurs getting their jollies in darkened corners. What, you must be asking yourself, will we be coming up with next?'

'I didn't even work at the bloody place,' said Robbie, with remembered bitterness. 'Robert Loxley, by the way: pleased to meet you. Anyway, me and this girl from Glasgow University were at it in a tent on the other side of the fence. Least-ways, I was at it, she must have passed out because she didn't make the shift. We were a bit stoned, you see – Nepalese Black? Been there for three months protesting, I had. "Ban Genetic Testing" and all that? Most of the others had gone home to their mummies. I wanted to stop these buggers, not join 'em! And look what happens: the love of my life's snoring her head off and I'm back in the Iron Age with a bunch of hired assassins.'

'Didn't make much of a name for himself protesting,' said Lance. 'Didn't help much with the fighting, either. The big con's Robbie's game. Wealth redistribution, he calls it. He's pretty good at it, too.'

Robbie grinned at Henry. 'You ever hear of Beoric, Troth and wosname? Made us a cool quarter of a million, that one did.'

Henry's jaw dropped. 'That was you. In that picture.' He pointed vaguely in the direction of Essex. 'Behind the old man's desk. All snow and smiling Norwegians. I didn't recognize you without the beard and the headgear.'

'A bit of artificial snow; a helicopter ride along the North Devon coast in the dark; and any self-satisfied prick can convince himself he's on a VIP flight to Norway.' Robbie frowned. 'Or was it Finland? I forget . . .'

'You got me sacked,' said Henry, bitterly. 'If it hadn't been for you and those useless CDs none of this would be happening now.'

Mervyn nodded. 'Good! Good! You're getting the hang of it at last. Although actually, the CDs had almost nothing to do with it.'

Perce stood up suddenly with his hands behind his back. 'I were in a car with a lady from down Exeter way.' He gazed around the room. 'Y'know?'

The others smiled, sympathetically.

'I used to meet 'er on Friday nights, I think. I forget. Anyhow, she were givin' me a thingy.' He looked at the floor.

'Blowjob,' nodded Robbie. 'She was a lady of the night, you see. She didn't make the shift, either, did she Perce? Guess *her* heart wasn't in it, either.'

'I were a bit upset about that. Lost me bloody Viva, an' all. Beautiful car she were. Beautiful! Just a useless lump o' metal when we ended up 'ere.' He sat down. 'I don't reckon that were fair, d'you?'

Mervyn turned to Henry. 'Nine others made the shift . . . '

'Eleven, Merv,' said Rooter. 'You're forgetting you and Linnet.'

'I wasn't forgetting. I was just saying there were nine others who didn't work at the Institute, that's all. A couple from the village who weren't married. Not to each other, anyway. The man died of heart failure. His name was . . .'

'Tristram,' said Gwen.

Mervyn nodded. 'That's . . . Was it really? Are you sure? I thought . . .'

'Get on with it!' snapped Jo.

'Right . . . yes . . . umm, well anyway, *her* name was . . .'

'Isolde,' said Gwen.

'Indeed. Indeed. Yes, of course. Obvious really. And er . . . well, she ran off with Stonking Rod's alter ego and started a bakery on Maidenhead Lane. Made quite a success of it, too. Still going, in fact. I believe they sell to . . .'

'Merrrrrrv!' warned Jo.

'Alter ego?' asked Henry.

'Yes, it took us years to work that one out, too. And we wouldn't have done it at all if those two,' he nodded at the Naggs brothers, 'hadn't been so interested in politics. The politics of the future, I mean, not the . . .'

'Merv!' snapped Jo. 'Concentrate, for Christ's sake!'

'Yes, of course! Sorry!' He looked at Henry. 'It seems the reciprocal aura flipped Stonking Rod up into the future. Not quite hard enough to send her back to where we had come from, mind you. She fell short by about a hundred years. She appears to have landed in 1978 or 1979, and displaced an innocent housewife who was flipped back to Sodmire without so much as a by-your-leave. No one noticed the difference for years. Here or there. We thought Stonking Rod had been through some sort of Road to Damascus conversion. And apparently the housewife's husband was too drunk to notice the difference. Mind you, I think we got the better of the deal. Marge was a pedantic old cow, but at least she could cook. So we got a supply of excellent food, while Grantham got a nasty piece of work who delighted in cutting off people's testicles and selling off the family silver. And er, and . . . where was I? Oh, yes! That woman from the cottage in Stratton Widger: Nina Falkreath, her name was, with her seven-year-old Newfoundlander, Chopper.'

'What,' said Henry, trying not to look at Boadicea, 'you mean . . . ?'

Mervyn nodded with a glance at Arthur and Gwen. 'She set up the Sodmire Branch of the WVS with Drivel and Turdfancy. Not that those two little devils ever understood what the voluntary part meant. And of course, Chopper ran off with Knobrot and the rest of his gang.'

Boadicea let out a single, nerve-jangling '*woof*'!

'For a week or two . . .'

Boadicea barked again.

'Before having some sort of personality crisis after his owner went looking for him on Sodmire and never came back.'

Boadicea whined.

Henry looked questioningly at the huge animal.

Jo nudged him in the ribs. 'Best not to ask.'

'A bit like that old fart, Nigel Adams,' said Lance, 'and his personal . . .'

'Adams?' said Henry, sharply. 'Did you say Adams?'

'Sir Nigel Quentin Adams MP, to give him his full title,' said Mervyn. 'And his personal assistant, Charles P. Mordred, Esquire.

'You mean . . .?'

'Dead on arrival,' said Lance. 'Autoerotic suffocation, we reckon. Must have been in the final throes when he made the shift. Bin-liner over his head, women's clothes, couple of yards of clothesline round his neck . . .'

'Must have been a hundred and twenty, if he was a day,' said Mervyn. 'Still, there wasn't anything unusual about that. Medical science had advanced . . .' He looked closely at Henry. 'Are you feeling all right?'

'You don't mean *the* Nigel Adams? The one who works . . . worked . . .?'

'Yes, of course. Are you sure you're feeling all right?'

'I thought I'd be pleased, that's all. But Sam always said that death wasn't much of a spectator sport when you got right down to it.'

'Oh, he didn't die,' said Lance. 'Well, I mean, yeah, he was dead when he got here. But Ramskull's old mum – she was the tribal shaman – took a fancy to his outfit, jumped on his chest to dispel his personal demons, and relieve him of his twinset and pearls, and accidentally jump-started his heart.'

Henry looked around. 'You mean he's still here?'

'Near as we can tell,' said Robbie, 'him and Mordred are somewhere in the Sahara Desert. Although, they could be closer to home: Woollacombe Beach, say, or Slapton Sands? Hard to tell for sure.' He grinned at Henry's confusion. 'The fate of Lot's wife? Only they didn't so much look back as go forward. Lucky for us they did, too, or it would have been one of us.'

'We're stuck here, you see,' said Mervyn. 'And as long as we stay within about thirty miles of Sodmire, we're fine. In fact, we're immortal. But as soon as we go beyond the range of the temporal core, we start dehydrating, like freeze-dried vegetables. They say it's a terrible thing to behold.'

'Adams and his buddy didn't like what they saw when they got here,' said Gavin. 'Couldn't blame 'em for that mind. I wasn't exactly over the moon about it myself. But they decided they belonged with the ruling elite: the Romans? So they sneaked off to join 'em in the marching camp at Isca Dumnoniorum – that's Exeter to you and me. Only the Romans were so pleased to see Adams in his basque, suspender belt and six-inch heels, and Mordred in his tutu and pumps, that they packed 'em off in a crate to Aquae Sulis – that's Bath, by the way. Only they didn't make it, did they? Shrivelled up like the Sunday roast in a faulty microwave and blew away on the wind. People have probably been building sandcastles out of 'em ever since.'

'Turned to dust?' said Henry, quietly. 'And . . . blew away?'

Mervyn wasn't listening. 'So that's . . .' he muttered, unwrapping the fingers of his clenched fist and mouthing a list of names under his breath. 'Ah, yes! Yes, of course! That dreadful woman from the Faye Tea Rooms, where Adams and Mordred were staying. The three of them came together. Well, I mean, not in the biblical sense. Morgan, her name was.' He shivered. 'And we all know what happened to her, don't we?'

'What?' asked Henry, tentatively, hoping that the answer wasn't going to involve more blood, guts and bodily desiccation.

'You don't want to know,' warned Jo.

'She nicked some stuff from Merv's lab and blew herself to smithereens,' said Robbie, with obvious relish. 'Ramskull's old mum, she was the tribe's medicine woman, too, tried to sew her back together. But her surgical skills left a lot to be desired, and breast implants were always gonna be tricky in the Iron Age. Still, one of Boudicca's lieutenants used what was left as a breastplate. Pretty damned impressive it looked, too.'

Henry thought about that for a moment and wished that he hadn't.

'Then there was Billy Balyne and Bobby Balance,' said Mervyn. 'A couple of retired circus performers and jobbing character actors who were living together in an eccentric, and somewhat decadent, semi-retirement in a house on Sodmire. You know them as Granddad and Great Uncle Bert.'

Henry looked around. 'And where are they now?'

'What? Oh, their . . . packing,' said Mervyn, vaguely. 'Anyway . . .'

'So that just leaves you and Linnet, then, Merv,' said Rooter. 'Why don't you tell the nice man what you two were up to when everything kicked off?'

Mervyn sighed. 'I don't see how that is relevant . . .'

'Really?' Rooter turned to Henry. 'He doesn't like talking about it. Not convenient. It's all right going on about poor old Roots. But ask him what he was up to and his mind goes a complete blank. He reckons Perce's got problems remembering. But there was hundreds of 'em around that place. Ask him how come only twenty-one and a dog ended up here.'

Mervyn looked pained. 'I don't think there's any need to go into detail, Rooter, is there? Suffice it to say . . . '

'Yeah? Well I do!' Rooter turned to Henry. 'She wasn't just the chief's mistress, was she? She was Merv's lab assistant, an' all, was our Linnet, and he had his hand up her skirt when we landed. How do I know? 'Cause I saw him, that's how. He denies it, but he would, wouldn't he? She was in a cupboard, or what was left of it, bending over in her white coat. All prim and proper on the outside: all Eskimo Nell underneath. And there was *him*, right up close, pretending he was checking the inventory, or whatever. Only there wasn't any inventory, was there? And that wasn't a Biro she had in her hand.'

'I've told you,' said Mervyn, 'it was a trick of the light . . .'

'So you did. Only I asked her meself, didn't I, five hundred year ago, over

Maidenhead Tor with a gallon o' scrumpy and a box o' Turkish delight. Do anything for a bit o' Turkish delight, would our Mandy.'

'Mandy?' said Henry. 'I thought you said her name was Linnet?'

'Mandy, Linnet, La Damoiselle Sauvage,' sighed Jo. 'It was all the same to my little sister.'

'Your sister? And . . . where is she now?'

Mervyn's reply was mournful. 'She passed away, I'm afraid: about twenty years ago. An unfortunate accident with a mains operated . . . er, toy.'

Jo shook her head. 'Tried to use it in the Jacuzzi. Stupid cow!'

Henry blanched. 'Good god!'

'Died laughing, mind?' said Blossom. 'So did the rugby team.' Her face fell. 'My best friend, she was, an' all.'

Henry touched Jo's hand. 'I'm sorry. Actually,' he added, 'I met someone called Mandy on the moor last night. At least, I think I met . . .'

'That her?' asked Robbie, pressing a key and pointing at the screen.

Henry shrugged. 'Could be. Only she was blonde, not . . .'

Robbie pressed another key.

'Yes! Yes, that was her!'

'Right,' said Robbie to Mervyn, 'another mystery solved.' He turned back to Henry. 'You went back in time. You were feeling horny, right?'

'I don't know about that . . .'

'Must have been. So you could live for . . . what?' He glanced at Mervyn.

Mervyn shrugged.

'Another sixty or seventy years?' suggested Robbie. 'Who knows? Gotta be worth re-jigging your pension for, that.'

'Yes, but . . . Really? Sixty or seventy years?'

'Don't get too carried away, though. Might never happen.'

Henry wondered if dying seventy years after everyone he knew had passed away would be such a good idea. 'Will I . . .? I mean, if I did . . .?' He grinned, sheepishly. 'You know . . .? Would I age at the normal rate, or . . .?'

'Who knows? You might get old gracefully, or you might just go pop.'

'Pop?'

'Don't complain about it, mate. Half the world's population would give their right bollock for what you just got. The other half would give both.'

'That's a population that's one hundred per cent male,' Jo pointed out.

'Sounds good to me,' grinned Gavin.

There was a click, and everyone turned to watch as Gareth came back into the room and went to sit stony-faced on a chair by the bar.

Everyone turned back to Henry.

'What about the other time?' asked Mervyn.

Henry looked blank. 'The other time . . . what?'

Mervyn tapped several keys. 'According to the data we downloaded from your brain, you travelled back in time twice. Once in the afternoon: once in the evening. The first time must have been at the Dragon.'

'Yep,' said Jo.

Henry shook his head. 'Definitely not. I'd have remembered something like that, wouldn't I?' Then an image of the gap-toothed Nell came back to him, and he turned to Jo. 'What do you mean . . . *yep*?'

'They put you on the settle when they brought you in from your fracas with matey in the car park. You were out cold, but you kept moaning and thrusting yourself at the seat, so I left you to it. I was in the office when I heard a lot of grunting and thrashing about. When I went back, you were lying in the grate smoking like a burnt offering. I waited for you to come to, but from the way you were moaning and groaning I figured you already had.' She gazed at him with a look of mischievous enquiry.

Henry hummed and hawed for a bit, before telling them what had happened in his 'dream' with Rooter and Nell.

Mervyn looked at Rooter. 'Well?'

Rooter examined his fingernails. 'Nothing to do with me, mate.'

Mervyn turned to Gavin and Lance. 'And I suppose you two don't know anything about any illicit trips to The Middle Ages or the Battle of Waterloo?'

Lance shrugged. 'Everyone needs a holiday, Merv.'

'Listen, you could've seriously damaged the fabric of . . .'

'Can we move on?' snapped Gareth. 'We're wasting time with all this!'

Mervyn's eyes narrowed at Rooter. 'I'll talk to you later.'

'Oh goody.'

'Waterloo was fun though, wasn't it?' grinned Lance.

'Not for the bloke on the big horse,' muttered Gavin.

'Jammy sod,' said Hubert to Henry. 'He never paid for me to get diddled.'

'Never paid for himself,' said Horace.

'Still,' said Robbie, 'everything's sorted now, right?'

'Yes,' said Mervyn, with his eyes still on Rooter, 'so it would seem.'

'Look,' said Henry, 'this is all very well, but how do you know I went back in time? Couldn't I just have . . .?'

'Because we bugged you with a neat little tracking device of my design,' said Robbie, smugly. 'Well, not so much you as the car. Trouble was, we lost you for a few minutes. Now we know why. You weren't there. Well, I mean, you weren't there last night. More sort of . . . twenty years ago . . . ish.' '

'We needed to know where you were, you see,' said Mervyn. 'Sorry about the invasion of privacy and all that, but we had to make sure you were safe. A lot of time and effort has been vested in you, and we couldn't have you going off and getting yourself lost, could we? It was unfortunate that Gwen and Arthur botched the tracking device on the Probe and messed up the heating system, but everyone makes mistakes, don't they? Our Mr. Hertz is a very experienced operative, but he did something similar to one of Miss Killjoy's cars, I believe?' He glanced across at Arthur. 'We really ought to get these simple things right, you know, Arthur.'

He turned back to Henry before Arthur could reply. 'The important thing is that you're here and we've got the encoder, and everything's working out very nicely, thank you. And now we know exactly how you used it. That's going to be very important to us later.'

'And life and death to him,' muttered Robbie.

'What?' asked Henry.

'Nothing,' said Mervyn, hurriedly. 'Nothing at all.' He bent forward and gazed into Henry's face. 'We've been experiencing certain disturbances in the continuum since your arrival. Everyone's felt it. Some of us,' he added, glancing at Blossom, 'more than others.'

'It's all lies,' smirked Blossom. 'Don't believe a word of it, lover.'

'Most of us have been taking the medication voluntarily to help keep our minds free from lustful thoughts, but some of us have had to be force-fed. It's a lesson we learned a long time ago. The effects of the shift, and the physical state you were in at the time, stay with you for as long as you live. And if you allow yourself to become obsessed with . . . certain things, it can be very difficult to get anything else done. Of course, you're probably beginning to appreciate that for yourself, aren't you? How long did you say it was now? Twelve hours, was it?'

'Sixteen,' said Henry, with his eyes fixed on his knees.

'Indeed. And as you pointed out yourself, it isn't normal, is it? You are still,' he motioned with a hand, 'at the moment, I take it?'

Henry cleared is throat.

'No need to be embarrassed 'bout it, lover,' said Blossom, with a hand on his thigh. 'We're all in it together, y'know?'

'You wish,' muttered Jo.

'Jealousy doesn't suit you, Josephine,' snapped Blossom. 'It never did.'

'Meaning what?'

'I think you know perfectly well *what*! Never mind Henry, I won't let the nasty lady take advantage of you. You'll be perfectly safe here with me.'

'Like he was this morning, you mean,' said Jo, 'when you sat on his face?'

Henry frowned for a moment. Then his eyes almost burst out of their sockets. 'I *knew* I recognized that taste!'

'Lucky bugger,' said Hubert. 'I've been trying to get her to sit on *my* face since the Battle of Baden Hill.'

'Lucky she didn't suffocate the poor sod, you ask me,' muttered Jo.

'That's enough!' cried Gwen, banging the table with a fist. 'We haven't got time for all this bitchy nonsense. Here we are on the verge of the one thing we've all been wanting for two thousand years, and all you two stupid cows can do is bicker about who gets to shag the latest bit of totty.'

Henry had never been called 'totty' before, and he wasn't sure he liked it.

'She started it!' snapped Blossom.

'I did not!' retorted Jo.

'Yes you did! You shagged that stupid wazzock in Merv's lab!'

Jo's eyes narrowed. 'Really?' she said, icily. 'And you'd rather have stayed with Knobrot and his boys, I suppose?'

Blossom thrust out her chin and gazed up at the ceiling. 'Maybe,' she said. 'Who knows?' She stood up, and teetered across the floor towards Gareth. 'At least he gave me my baby,' she said, plumping herself down in his lap. 'So he couldn't have been all bad, could he?'

'There, there,' said Gareth, with a sensitivity that surprised Henry. 'It's all right, mum. I don't mind that you're just an old slapper.'

Henry caught Mervyn's eye.

The old man nodded. 'Blossom didn't make the shift with the rest of us. She was already here. It seems the intensity of what had happened to her shortly before the encoder kicked us back in time, dragged her into the RATS effect, too. She has remained unchanged ever since. Gareth came along nine months later. Even in his pre-embryonic state he must have been caught in the aura that made her immortal. It was almost fifty years before we realized that he had stopped growing somewhere around his twenty-fifth birthday.' He looked at the big man, fondly. 'But I've never believed Knobrot was his father. Look at the size of him, for a start. If it was anyone, it had to be Ramskull. Which is just as well really. I mean, you wouldn't want a father with a name like Knobrot, Drivel, Gobshite or Turdfancy . . . would you?'

* * *

43

J. C. KINSMAN

When the people from the Pate Institute of Genetic Sciences and its immediate environs started raining down on the Faeceantii tribal stomping grounds, it was with shimmering lights and an insistent sizzling that scared the unfortunate Ancient Britons half to death. Stonking Rod was tiptoeing along the top of one of the huge ritual standing stones at the time like a cartoon cat burglar labouring under the mistaken impression that she hadn't been spotted. Her tongue was poking out between her thin lips and her ceremonial robes were held delicately up around her waist, exposing her flimsy pants in a blatant attempt to distract the horny male members of the tribe pursuing her for long enough to allow the warriors of the Dumnonii-Durotriges Alliance to sneak up behind them and start clubbing them to death. A flock of naked acolytes were prancing along beneath her with their erections pointing skywards in the hope that such obvious displays of piety on their part would please the gods to such an extent that there would not only be a bounteous crop of bogweed the following spring, but also a bloodthirsty shag later that evening when they finally caught up with their soon-to-be-deposed leader.

Pickfight was in no hurry to join them, and had positioned himself at a safe distance to watch dispassionately and plan how best to seize power when, and if, She Who Must Be Obeyed had been diddled and sliced into chunky bits of kebab. As her second-in-command, he was an old hand at tribal politics and knew that timing was everything when it came to *coups d'etat*. So he was careful not to appear too eager to wrest control from his leader in case the D & D Alliance failed in its bid to take control of the tribe, and the vengeful Stonking Rod came looking for someone to blame. But he wasn't about to leave it too late, either, in case the acolytes did something really stupid like electing one of their number in his place – a possibility that wasn't as unlikely as it might have seemed to the casual observer.

Stonking Rod's predecessor, an unfortunate whinberry bush named Colin, had been elected by just such an acolyte proxy and had gone on to hold the coveted post of arch druid for the better part of three hundred years. Indeed, he would still have been the proud occupant of that high office had he not been struck down mysteriously by a virulent strain of whinberry bush node rot known previously to have existed only in the Alpine village of Stonkeine Rottsburgh where the current arch druid's family owned several fortified properties and significant tracts of land.

The ex-virgin wasn't eager to take a leading role in the revolution, either, and had positioned herself a few paces behind Pickfight with a clay beaker of holy bog water clutched tightly to her breasts in readiness to toast what she hoped was Stonking Rod's rapidly approaching demise. Suddenly, there was a sound like an ox deep-frying in gallons of spitting beef fat, and the remains of Arthur King's armoured command vehicle landed in the middle of the circle of ancient standing stones with a bang and a shower of sparks. A fraction of a second later, the shell of the security van with Laurence Meres and Gavin Greene bouncing around inside it crashed onto the tribe's communal mud hut (empty of tribal members at the time) and blasted it to a smouldering ruin.

There followed a series of shimmering manifestations all around the tribal stomping grounds as ghostly figures solidified out of the air in a shocking array of flame-licked, triple-X-rated poses. The junior acolytes, startled out of their ritual pursuit of the arch druid by the landings, stopped dead in their tracks and gaped at these pornographic apparitions like infants with their first multi-coloured balloons. They were a broadminded bunch, not easily moved by displays of unbridled sexual depravity, but what they witnessed that night as twenty-one highly aroused, and uncommonly clean, human beings (and one huge, jaw-droppingly horny dog) materialized in their midst, caused many of them to ejaculate spontaneously. Much of what squirted into the air from their eager loins was immediately hoovered up by the ravenous Drivel, who, having starved himself almost to exhaustion in preparation for the Feast of the Big Spring Festival, not only swallowed but chewed.

Knobrot was first amongst the junior acolytes to react to the landings, although only because Chopper stopped his enthusiastic rogering of the tubby-jowled farmer's wife and turned with a snarl of affection to bite him lovingly in the arse. The grubby little Celt squealed with a mixture of surprise and delight, and took off for the open moor with the amorous, and flame engulfed, Newfoundlander in ponderous but determined pursuit. The frustrated farmer's wife, left teetering on the brink by her pet's sudden withdrawal, made a lecherous lunge at the nearest acolyte (the boggle-eyed Gobshite) who, having finally popped his cherry that afternoon with the ex-virgin, thought that all his birthdays and mid-winter festivals of the sun had come at once. Twice in one day, he figured, with women who weren't even drugged, never mind tied-up or dead, must mean that the throwing of his maternal grandmother into the pit of the ferocious bog demons two months earlier had finally started to pay off.

The ex-virgin turned with a nod of approval as Knobrot disappeared, arms and legs windmilling wildly, over a nearby hill, with the neon-bright Chopper bounding along after him like a luminous, love-stricken bear. She was about to raise the holy bog water to her lips in celebration, when Perce Pratt, and the remains of his beloved Vauxhall Viva, crashed to earth at her feet. With his wig smoking like a barbequed ferret and his cock sparking and writhing like an electrified hose, she took his sudden manifestation as a sign from the gods.

'*Heellllp meeeeee!*' he screeched, as he flapped a hectic semaphore of terror at the miniature lightning bolts playing, cobalt blue, over his cock.

The ex-virgin gazed down at him, more out of curiosity than alarm, and was only spurred into action when sparks from his smouldering trousers set fire to the hem of her gown. Thinking quickly, she took a swig from the beaker, puckered her lips like a chocolate box cherub, and blew a fine spray of holy bog water over the flames. Then, with a deft motion borne of long practice, she yanked the gown up over her head, one-handed, and threw it to the ground, where, with a final, carefully aimed mouthful of holy bog water, she put out what was left of the flames.

The petrified Perce, lying on his back, squirming in helpless self-pity, motioned for her to extinguish the fire engulfing his loins. '*Blo-blo-blow some,*' he urged, pointing and flapping, '*o-on meeeee! God! God! Pleeeease? You-you blo-blow-some blo-some . . . o-on on on me-eeee! God! Oh God! Oh God!*'

The ex-virgin, glancing over her shoulder to check that he wasn't talking to someone behind her, turned back and placed a splay-fingered hand on her breast. 'Who me?' she asked, wide-eyed.

Perce nodded in desperate agreement. '*Yes! Yes! You! You . . . blo-blow some, blow some . . . God! . . . on-on me! Pleeeeeease?*'

'Blo-blossom?' stammered the ex-virgin, pointing at herself. 'Me?' Then, as her face lit up with understanding. 'Me Blossom!' she beamed. 'You God!'

Perce couldn't have cared less about semantics. All he wanted was for the flames engulfing his genitals to be put out. He nodded vigorously and pointed in a final, agonized attempt to make her understand that his testicles didn't normally resemble quite so closely a pair of over-cooked onion bhajis.

Believing herself to be in the presence of a divine being who must be obeyed, the ex-virgin dropped to her knees and set about dowsing the flames around his manhood with mouthfuls of holy bog water and the damp hem of her gown. When the last of the embers had been extinguished, Perce sighed, smiled wanly, and passed out.

* * *

'It's a bit painful then, is it, this time travel?' asked Henry with his legs crossed and his hands pressed over his groin. He frowned. 'But I didn't have any of that burning stuff, did I? So maybe it didn't really happen to me?'

'It happened,' said Robbie. 'You only went back a couple of hundred years the first time, and maybe twenty, the second, so the friction was minimal. Besides, the flames look terrifying but they don't really burn the time traveller, just their clothing and hair.' He grinned. 'Pickfight's mud hut went up like it had been petrol-bombed.' He ran a hand over the top of his head. 'Why do you think we've shaved? Anyway, you're forgetting something, aren't you?'

Henry looked blank.

'In the Dragon? After your meeting with Nell?'

'You don't have to keep going on about it!'

'Your clothes were singed, you said, when you woke up?'

'I was lying next to the fire . . .'

Robbie shook his head.

Henry looked to Jo.

'Sorry tiger.'

'Right,' he said. 'OK. But . . . but if I went back to The Middle Ages?' He hesitated. 'Does that mean . . . ?'

'You're immortal?'

'Well . . . '

'Who knows? Point is, it didn't hurt, did it?'

'It was a *bit* hot, actually. But, no, I don't suppose . . .'

'And your memory got screwed up . . . right?'

'Well, there was some weird stuff about yogurt and goldfish and . . .' He shrugged. 'But I knew where I was,' he glanced at Jo, 'didn't I?'

'Try telling Kinsman it doesn't hurt,' grinned Lance.

'Kinsman's *crazy*!' snapped Perce, with a sudden vehemence that took Henry by surprise. 'Kinsman don't count!'

'He just wants the encoder back, Perce, that's all,' said Jo, gently. 'You can't blame him for that, can you? I'd be pretty angry, too, if I'd been zapping backwards and forwards through time like he has, putting the wind up any poor sod unfortunate enough to catch a glimpse of me during one of my lightning manifestations in the here and now. It's not the best way to make friends and influence people, you know.'

She was right: apart from being the most tortured soul on the planet outside the paintings of Hieronymus Bosch, Kinsman had three strikes against him.

He was trapped in a burning time-tunnel, for one.

He was caught in the throes of undying fury, for another.

And, most distressing of all, he was in insurance.

With all that heaped on his shoulders, it was easy to see why he had developed a personality disorder that made the owner of the Bates Motel look like a simple case of mistaken identity.

Of all the time travelling Kinsmans at large in the space-time continuum, Mr. W. I. C. Kinsman was the most reliable. He was also the first born, the original: the one from whom all the other time travelling Kinsmans had been spawned. Less volatile than J. Kinsman, less unpredictable than J. C. Kinsman, and less prone to fits of screaming paranoia than J. B. C. Kinsman, he was a point of relative calm at the centre of a crowd of raging doppelgangers on the fringes of whose swirling vortex of tortured humanity the terrifying F. C. S. P. Y. T. Y. F. T. Kinsman and his offspring whirled like human tornadoes.

It would not have been so disturbing if the members of this tribe of Kinsmans could have been described as familial psychotics – a case of congenitally cloned insanity, perhaps? But the fact was that they were all the same person, in the same body, and with the same tortured, incrementally fragmented mind. It would have been comforting to have been able to dismiss them as a simple case of multiple personalities – in so far as such things can ever be called 'simple' – but that, too, would have been wide of the mark. The disturbing truth was that only one of them had ever been christened in the conventional manner, while all of the others had been created in Professor Earnest 'Ernie' Stampeasy's Baptism of Fire.

The primary Kinsman – the first of the tribe to have been subjected to the RATS effect – had been shunted backwards in time from the year AD 2087 in search of Mervyn and the others accused of stealing the encoder, almost three years to the day after they, and it, had disappeared without trace. It had taken that long for the institute's newly appointed director of temporal genetics, the aforementioned irritable Professor Stampeasy, to catch up with Mervyn's original research and rebuild the parts of the institute destroyed by the Rooter-inspired displacement in time. When he'd finally managed it, and had informed the institute's board of directors of their options, it had been decided that his first task should be to send a loss adjuster from the institute's insurers, Scientific & Mercantile Ins, back in time to track down the encoder and those responsible for its theft.

It might be useful to note here, in a somewhat questionable attempt to defend their decision, that the members of the board had had no more accurate an understanding than Mervyn had had before them of what *exactly* it was that they would be expecting the unfortunate loss adjuster to do.

William Ignatius Constantine Kinsman was the man chosen to make the historic journey, and on April 1 AD 2087 he was duly despatched into the past. Unfortunately, Ernie had made at least one critical error in what had, in truth, always been some shaky mathematics, and although he'd managed to fire the startled Kinsman almost fifteen hundred years backwards in time – to the year AD 554, to be precise – he'd failed to predict what has since become known in the field of temporal genetics as The Bungee Effect. As a result, Kinsman had rocketed back down through the centuries – past them would be a more appropriate description, like a lift flashing down the outside of an infinitely tall building – and been deposited with a bump at a point close to his intended point of arrival. He had remained there for the pre-programmed period of five seconds before being wrenched painfully back up towards his point of departure. Ernie's most significant miscalculation had been in his prediction that the unfortunate loss adjuster would stop and be reinstated precisely at his time and place of origin, plus the five seconds or so that he had spent in the past. What had happened instead was a slingshot effect that had whipped Kinsman up into the future and dumped him in the year AD 3617, almost as far ahead of his point of departure as he had been behind it a millisecond earlier. He had remained in the distant future for a little over five seconds, before being rocketed back down through the centuries, past his point of origin again, to the year AD 558. And so it had continued, with Kinsman being dragged kicking and screaming up and down the skyscraper of time like a flaming yo-yo, for what in Ernie Stampeasy's timeframe had been a little short of three days, but what, for the terrified Kinsman, had felt more like three hundred years. Gradually, as his swings between the past and the future had begun to slow down, and the distances travelled on either side of his point of origin had grown shorter, so he'd appeared in the past and the future, at points a few centuries, then a few decades, then a few years and finally a few hours, minutes and seconds apart. And as the pendulum swings had shortened with each new firing of the slingshot, so the time he'd spent at each successive destination had grown progressively longer. It had been this shortening of the distance between his jumps into the past and the future, and the attendant lengthening of the time he'd been able to spend at each point of arrival, that had salvaged what had remained of his sanity and helped him to stop throwing-up. After a couple of Ernie Stampeasy's days had gone by, Kinsman had visited thousands of separate points in the past and the future, and the length of his stay in each had started to stretch into minutes. This had helped him to come to terms with his predicament, because, while he'd never had much of an interest in history, it had become obvious to him that the percentage of old people in the population went up or down, and the state-sponsored torture and murder of 'terrorists' became more or less frequent and vicious, roughly in accordance with the prevailing standards of nutrition, the frequency of wars, the political complexion of the greedy elite and, most important of all, his direction of travel. Had he been free to take notes during his journey, he would, upon his return, have been able to furnish the world's historians with enough information to keep them out of everyone else's hair for decades to come. But he'd been forced to drop his digital recorder when he'd ducked to avoid being skewered by a spear thrown at Uther Pendragon by Louis of Cornwall during a duel at Castle Mervyne in AD 189.

That initial journey through time had finally ended for Kinsman when he'd arrived back in the year AD 2087 almost seventy-two hours – from Ernie's perspective – after he'd left it. Unfortunately, he had been so disorientated by the experience that he hadn't realized immediately that his ordeal had come to an end. When Ernie had discovered him lying semi-comatose and muttering to himself on the departure platform in the laboratory, he had begun firing questions at him in an attempt to find out where he had been and why it had taken him so long to get back. Ernie had never been the most patient of scientists, and when Kinsman's only response had been to dribble down the charred remains of his vest, he had flown into an uncontrollable rage.

'Jesus Kinsman!' he had screamed. 'Pull yourself together you pillock!'

It had been the volume, as much as the content, of Ernie's interrogation that had finally penetrated Kinsman's fragmented mind.

'Jesus?' he'd murmured, gazing down at his hands. 'Yes, I'm Jesus. I'm Jesus Kinsman. I'm Jesus Kinsman, and I'm still alive!' Then he'd drawn a long, ragged breath and added, with the nervous twitching of an eye, 'I was starting to wonder, y'know? Gives you the screaming abdabs out there.'

It had taken the institute's medical staff a matter of seconds to establish that Kinsman had become dangerously neurotic. But the board of directors had ignored the diagnosis and made it clear to Ernie that if he wanted to keep his job at the institute he would have no choice but to send the tortured loss adjuster back into the past to continue his search for the missing encoder. This was partly because Kinsman had been the only time travelling loss adjuster in existence; but mainly because once his colleagues had got a good look at him, not a single one of them had been willing go in his place.

So had begun what has since become known in the annals of human rights legislation as The Kinsman Abuse. The board had decreed that he should be sent back and, by definition, forward in time until he'd found the encoder and returned it to their safekeeping, regardless of how long it might take. Each time he had come back empty-handed, they had dusted him down, stuffed him full of powerful sedatives, certified him sane, and sent him screaming back down the skyscraper of temporal displacement. From Ernie's perspective it had been like dropping a sentient yo-yo into a bottomless pit and hoping that he had cut its metaphorical string to precisely the right length to enable it to locate what it had been sent down to find. And each time it had come back, having failed in its mission, he had cut its string that little bit shorter, or stretched it that little bit longer, and sent it back down to hover that little bit higher, or that little bit lower, and with a little bit more, or a little bit less, time to look around. But as each hopeful plunge into the past, and boomeranged slingshot up into the future, had clocked up the temporal mileage, so each new interrogation session had addled Kinsman's brain that little bit further, and forced a succession of new and increasingly deranged identities into existence: each one fundamentally different, each one uniquely the same.

'Jesus Kinsman,' had become 'Jesus Christ, Kinsman', then 'Jesus Bloody Christ, Kinsman,' and so on, until eventually 'For Christ's Sake Pull Yourself Together You Frigging Tosser Kinsman!' and his descendants had been born. And as each new persona had screeched, clawed, hollered and flamed its way into existence, so, a week later, with Ernie's Mark II Encoder recharged and rebooted, a new and less predictable loss adjusting yo-yo had been sent screaming, kicking and flaming up and down the terrible high-rise of time.

'He doesn't like his job much, you see,' said Robbie. 'And I reckon he blames most of it on you.'

'*Me?*' said Henry in astonishment. 'Why *me*? It isn't *my* fault, is it?' He pointed at Rooter. 'It's *his*!'

Rooter looked at Mervyn. 'I hope you're pleased with yourself?'

Mervyn ignored him. 'Actually, all Kinsman wants is the encoder. He figures that if he gets it back they'll let him retire. He hasn't worked out yet that Ernie's not going to allow that to happen. At least, not until he's got us as well. Kinsman knows *where* we live and *when* – if you see what I mean? So he's the only link Ernie has got. Unless we can get him off our backs in the next few hours, he'll be after us until the end of time. Which, he has reliably informed us, isn't quite as far away as humanity might like to think.'

'You've met him, then?' said Henry.

'Well, of course. How do you think we know all this?'

'Not so much met as caught,' said Robbie. 'It took a while to work out when he was going to turn up, but once we'd sussed the bungee effect, the rest fell into place. It was the singed sheep that gave him away, originally: the Beast of Sodmire and all that?'

'Me and Gav saw him first,' said Lance. 'Like a human sparkler on bonfire night, he was. He blinked on for a second or two, and went out again. We thought it was the scrumpy talking,' he grinned, 'or the acid. But he came back five minutes later as large as life and twice as sparkly. Merv reckons he told Ernie he'd seen us, and had him re-programme the Mark II Encoder to send him back for a second look.'

'Trapping him is relatively straightforward,' said Mervyn, 'once you know which co-ordinates Ernie's using. Robbie and I calculate roughly where he's going to appear and when.' He nodded at Lance and Gavin. 'And those two catch him in a bloody great fireproof butterfly net. We've had some lengthy conversations with him over the centuries,' he shivered at the thought, 'but it's not a pleasant experience. He snarls a lot, and screams and picks at his skin.' He shivered again. 'Gives me the willies! And it was years before we got anything coherent out of him. He doesn't hang around long, most of the time, because of the bungee effect, and because Ernie always sets the automatic recall to make sure he gets him back. But the ferocity of the grudge he bears against humanity, and you in particular, has to be seen to be believed.'

'Why didn't I meet him before, then?' asked Henry. 'If he wanted the encoder so badly, why didn't he come and get it?'

'Adams' Syndrome,' said Robbie. 'We can live forever, but only if we stay close to Sodmire and the temporal core. Kinsman's the same. He can travel through time, but not space. I mean, he can manage a few miles here and there, but he can't move far away from the institute. He's stuck with it, just like we are. It's the only advantage we've got.' He grinned, broadly. 'That's why he accepted the deal.'

'Deal?' said Henry, uneasily. 'What deal would that be?'

Robbie glanced quickly at Mervyn and Gareth, before bending forward to fiddle with the computer. 'Nothing. Just . . . something he wants.'

'You mean the encoder, don't you?' said Henry. 'And you mean me!'

Robbie and Mervyn exchanged glances.

'No, no!' said Mervyn. 'Certainly not! No! Nonsense!'

Henry felt a chill run up his spine. 'What then?'

Lance stood up, and walked over to a framed print on the wall. He swung it open, like a cupboard door, and reached into a recess behind it. 'There's a few things in here you're going to need.'

He turned to Henry and held up a stainless steel handgun that looked like a small cannon with a second, thinner barrel and a telescopic sight, running almost its full length. 'Magnum SA,' he said. 'Laser guided, and loaded with smart 38s.' He took a pair of bandoliers out of the recess and dropped them onto a chair. 'And enough spare ammo to make this country a republic.'

He reached into the recess again and took out a thing like an industrial staple gun. 'Armour tags,' he said. 'Stop a bazooka at fifty paces.' He motioned Henry towards him. 'Come here: Kinsman ain't a patient man.'

Henry didn't move. But Gavin came up behind him, lifted him off his feet, and dumped him in front of Lance with his arms pinned at his sides.

Lance pressed the device against Henry's left nipple and squeezed the trigger. There was a hiss of escaping air, and Henry felt a sharp pain in his chest. He screeched and tried to recoil, but Gavin held him fast.

Lance positioned the thing above his right nipple and squeezed the trigger again. There was another hiss, and another sharp pain in his chest.

'There,' said Lance, 'didn't hurt a bit, did it?'

Henry wasn't so sure. He wasn't convinced that the staples, or whatever they were, had been inserted for his benefit, either. He had a feeling that they might be tracking devices, or some sort of slow release poison.

Lance nodded, as if he understood what Henry was thinking, and picked up the steel cannon of a handgun. He turned, and walked a few paces across the room, before turning to point it at Henry's head.

Henry held up his hands and started to back away. 'Jesus!' he cried. 'For Christ's sake don't . . .!'

It didn't help.

Lance pulled the trigger and there was a loud crack like a tyre bursting.

Henry stood with his eyes tightly closed, waiting for the blackness of oblivion to engulf him. What he felt instead was a warm trickle of urine soaking into the towel around his waist and dripping onto the floor at his feet.

He opened an eye, tentatively, and squinted at Lance.

'Blanks,' he thought. 'The bastard's using blanks!'

He glanced down, red-faced, at the pool spreading around his feet. 'You *bastard*!' he snarled, looking up. 'I thought the bloody thing was . . .!'

In a room not far away, Tom Hertz looked up at the muffled sound of gunfire. He turned from the bank of screens on which he had been watching Dolly's and Jack's gangs gathering amongst the trees overlooking the farmhouse, and threw a switch on the console. An acoustic monitor blinked on and registered a jagged shock wave and the serial number MA-38. Tom's eyebrows inched up his forehead. He punched a series of buttons in quick succession. A group of screens above his head lit up in sequence.

'Shit!' he hissed, at an image of Henry cringing in front of Lance. He drew a heavy stainless steel handgun from the holster under his armpit and nodded for Gary Harmsworth to follow him.

'Very naughty,' he said, as he opened the door. 'Ordnance discharged in our client's domicile, Mr. Harmsworth. We can't have that, now, can we?'

Lance aimed the big handgun a little to Henry's right and squeezed the trigger. This time a statue of a woman in a toga on a plinth beside him disintegrated in a shower of pulverized marble.

With his hands up in front of his face in instinctive defence, Henry peered between his fingers and blinked in disbelief as Lance pointed the gun at him again. '*Holy shit*!' he gasped, closing his eyes tight and wrapping his arms around his head. '*You crazy* . . .!'

There was another loud crack.

But it wasn't the agony of casehardened steel that Henry felt piercing his flesh, but another stream of urine he felt running down his leg.

There was silence.

Henry waited for a moment before unscrewing his face and peering from under his right elbow at the sound of Blossom click clacking angrily across the woodblock floor towards him, tut-tutting as she came.

'I don't know,' she said. 'What am I gonna do with you boys?'

Henry lowered his arms and allowed his bottom lip to tremble in self-pity.

'He shot me,' he pouted. 'He actually shot . . . '

'Dirty little devil!' snapped Blossom, as she wrenched the towel from around his waist with a snap. Then she put the flat of her hand against his chest and pushed him backwards into the Jacuzzi. He landed with a round-eyed splash of confusion, and disappeared in a fountain of water.

'Men!' muttered Blossom, dropping the towel onto the pool of urine and mopping it up with her foot. 'Where'd they be without us I wanna know?'

Henry surfaced with a gasp and his arms flailing. He righted himself, stood up, and was spluttering his way to the side of the Jacuzzi when the door burst open and Gary and Tom crashed into the room.

Tom crouched and bobbed and dodged his way rapidly across the floor to stand behind Gareth's chair with his gun held out in front of him in both hands and his eyes darting around the room looking for someone to kill.

Henry stood in the bubbling water without regard for his nakedness and raised his hands above his head. '*No!*' he cried. '*Don't shoot!*'

Tom's eyes flicked briefly towards him and then across the room at Lance. His stubbly beard had been shaved off, but he was still recognizable as the drunken idiot who had blasted Tom's windscreen full of bullet holes the previous day.

'Drop it,' said Tom, coldly.

Lance shrugged and let the big gun fall onto the seat of a chair.

Tom inhaled through his nose, and looked at Gavin, and then at Rooter, before turning to glance at the top of Gareth's head. 'We heard shooting.'

'A little demonstration, that's all. Nothing to worry about, I assure you.'

Tom nodded at Lance. 'What's *that* doing here?'

'It's with me.'

Tom's face remained impassive as he cocked the gun with a metallic snick and pointed it at Lance's chest. 'He owes me. Bastard shot my car.'

Lance put his hands in the air. '*Oh, no!*' he trilled in a shaky falsetto. '*Don't shoot me, Mr. Security Man, please!*'

Tom was not amused. To the best of his knowledge he was just about the nastiest son of a bitch on the face of the planet, and he prided himself in the fact that no one had mocked him and lived to tell the tale since he was at primary school. He was always meticulous in every aspect of the planning and execution of what could literally be a cutthroat business, and that meant making sure that no one *ever* called him a cissy and lived. He turned his cold, black eyes on Lance. 'Who is this prick?'

'Good question,' said Gareth. 'Take a seat.'

'I'll stand,' said Tom, with his unblinking eyes fixed on Lance's face.

'Sit when you're told to sit,' advised Gavin. 'It's a lot safer that way.'

'Is it?' said Tom. 'You're forgetting I'm the one with the gun.'

'Yes,' said Gavin, 'but we're the ones with the balls.'

'Oh, how jolly,' muttered Henry, with his arms still held above his head, 'do these people have some sort of special testosterone injections or just a naturally occurring surplus of the stuff?'

Blossom picked up a hand towel and draped it over his cock.

'I'd put that on if I was you,' she said. 'That way Mr. Hertz won't think you're going to shoot him.'

Tom still wasn't amused. It was bad enough that he had been bested by a couple of hippy bumpkins and their bumbling yokel friend the day before, but he was damned if he was going to let it happen again. His eyes flicked from Gavin to Rooter. 'I'm going to enjoy killing you two as well.'

'*Don't shoot!*' cried Lance, his face crumpling in terror. A moment later, he was standing next to Tom with the security man's gun in his hand.

Tom didn't appear to notice that he had been disarmed, or even that Lance had moved. He relaxed his right thumb and squeezed an imaginary trigger, not once, not twice, but three times.

'*Eh-hem!*' coughed Lance. 'It might be more effective with this.'

Tom looked at his empty hand with a quizzical expression. 'Impressive,' he said. 'Very impressive indeed . . .'

Gary pointed his gun at Lance's head. 'Drop it!' he ordered.

'You know,' said Gavin, languidly, as he dangled Gary's gun from the crook of a finger, 'I find threats carry a lot more weight if you've got one of these to back them up with. Don't you?'

Gary looked at his empty hand. 'Bugger,' he said, softly.

A second ago Gavin had been lounging in a chair on the other side of the room. Now he was standing beside him.

Gary's eyes flicked sideways to meet Tom's.

'My apologies,' said Tom. 'I thought yesterday was beginner's luck. Foolish of me.' He smiled tightly, and held out his hand for the return of his handgun. 'If that will be all, Mr. C, we have things to be getting on with.'

'Yes, thank you Mr. Hertz,' said Gareth. 'We mustn't detain you.'

Jo reached out and took Henry's hand. 'Come on,' she said, as she pulled him out of the Jacuzzi, 'let's get you cleaned up.'

44

ERNIE STAMPEASY

Resplendent in a gold lamé jumpsuit and her customary poundage of chunky gold jewellery, Dolly Killjoy stood in the shadows at the edge of the tree-lined ridge and gazed down dispassionately at the Clatworthy's farmhouse in the valley below. Her only concession to the two hundred yards of rough terrain over which she and her boys had trudged from their parked vehicles to their current vantage point were the tiger-print headscarf and fir-lined ankle boots which she fondly believed made her look not unlike Margaret Thatcher on safari in a battlefield tank. Draped over her padded shoulders was an ankle-length leopard skin coat with a bejewelled golden lizard climbing menacingly up the left lapel towards her stringy, pearl-bedecked throat. She took a long, thoughtful drag on her third cigar of the day before handing it to Spider in exchange for a pair of military binoculars. Careful not to chip her canary yellow nail varnish on the cold metal, she raised the binoculars to her eyes and gazed down without expression at the silent, and apparently deserted, monstrosity of a farmhouse below.

    Hunched against a tree trunk behind her, Jack Strawbridge was trying hard to look more robust than he felt as he gazed queasily through an ancient brass telescope that seemed to have developed a mind of its own. With a particularly vicious hangover still beating on the inside of his skull, he was finding it impossible to hold either the telescope or himself level and straight. And with one eye closed in time-honoured fashion, all he had to orientate himself by in his attempt to stay upright was the hazy circle of countryside he could see through the unfocussed eyepiece. He kept opening his other eye to check that he was looking in the right direction, and then closing it again to prevent the swimmingly unnerving clash of movement between near and far objects making him want to throw up. It was like living in a malicious split-infinity world doing its damnedest to pitch him forward onto his face in a puddle of sick. He was dizzy and dehydrated from his part in a late-night drinking session in Perce's cellar, and his enthusiasm for battle wasn't so much waning as waned. He was sobering up more quickly than he would have liked and remembering with unwelcome clarity just why it was that he and his lads were not in the habit of trespassing on Clatworthy land, much less trying to invade it. Too many ignominious defeats, and hours spent trudging home across the moor, minus their trousers and their dignity, with blackened eyes and split lips and the sound of their neighbours' derisive giggling ringing in their ears, had filled them with caution. Not only had they been bested in fistfights with Rooter and the boys, but at the hands of Jo and Blossom in hot pants and high-heels, as well. Taking them on again had seemed like a good idea with ten pints of scrumpy fermenting in his gut, and a dozen heavily armed lads (and one vicious maid) to back him up. But in the cold and painful light of morning, the prospect was beginning to look as attractive as Gummer and Tickle Muttocks in their birthday suits. His only hope was that Dolly's gang of battle-hardened killers would get the job done without him and his lads (and the combative maid) having to raise so much as their voices in anger, never mind their palsied hands.

Dolly had no such reservations about the coming fight: not least because her plan of attack excluded the possibility that she would find herself even close to being in harm's way. First, Boxer, Curly and Stan would blast away from the top of the hill with grenade and rocket launchers until the farmhouse had been reduced to a pile of smoke-blackened rubble. Then everyone who wasn't her would charge down the hill with guns blazing to finish off anyone who had had the misfortune to have been left breathing. When the fighting was over, and the building and its inhabitants had been smashed to brick dust and steaming offal, she would allow herself to be driven triumphantly through the wreckage in her open-topped limousine to count the bodies and search for her missing jewellery. She didn't really care if the few oddments that had been taken from Nobbler's garden shed were recovered after the fighting or not: just so long as she could be certain that they lay buried beneath the wreckage along with Henry Kite's mangled corpse. If she did find the missing beads, it would be a bonus. And if she also got her hands on a living, breathing Henry Kite, she would enjoy listening to him scream as Spider hacked off bits of his miserable body with his machete. But if all she got for her trouble was the chance to grind the heel of her leopard skin bootie into the eye socket of Kite's severed head, she would go home to Essex a happy gangster. And if the parts required for the purpose could not be found, she would have to forego the pleasure of having her personal tailor turn Kite's scrotum into a cosmetics bag. It would be a sad loss to her already impressive collection. But it wouldn't be for the want of trying. And at least her reputation for brutality would have lost none of its lustre.

The only cloud on her horizon was clinging to a tree behind her making noises like a gannet regurgitating a cropful of herring. He was pale and unsteady on his feet, and looked and smelled as if he had been sleeping in a hedge for a month. The dead-eyed bunch of evolutionary throwbacks he called his 'lads' (and the 'maid', away from who even Dolly had felt obliged to lean with a wrinkled nose as she'd passed) weren't any more appealing as they steamed and fidgeted under the trees in a foetid lump. She could smell them at twenty paces, up-wind, and didn't doubt that, when the shooting got started, what was left of their drink-induced courage would evaporate into the chill morning air as their sweat had been doing all morning. She expected them to turn tail and run at the first signs of danger, leaving Spider and the rest of her boys to get the dirty work done. Part of her was hoping that they would do just that, because at least then she wouldn't have to worry about soiling her booties in more of their vomit, or having the stupid sods shoot her and her boys by mistake. But whatever else might happen in the next twenty minutes, one thing was certain: all thoughts of getting the job done without attracting attention to herself had gone out the window. She hadn't travelled more than two hundred miles to Lumpkin Town, Yokelshire to go home empty handed, and regardless of the risk to her anonymity, she wouldn't be leaving until everyone who wasn't on her side was dead.

She motioned for Bonce and Simon to stand behind her. 'Watch him,' she said, nodding at Simon. 'Whack him if he steps out of line.' She looked down at the farmhouse. 'If he warns them we're here, I'll whack him myself.' She looked at Bonce. 'Then I'll whack you. Understand, dumbo?'

Bonce nodded, unhappily, and gestured for Simon to sit beside him on a granite boulder. They exchanged glances as they sat down, and the look in the big man's eyes told Simon how embarrassed and ashamed he was of the way they were being treated. Simon smiled and put a comforting hand on his knee.

'Bleedin' *poofters!*' snorted Vinny, from the branches of a nearby tree.

He had told Dolly that he was climbing up there to keep an eye on the farmhouse. But getting as far away as possible from the predatory Sally had been his real reason. As Bonce and Simon smiled shyly at one another, he turned away in disgust and looked across at Nobbler, loitering amidst the trees with his newfound best mates, Dinger and Bert. They looked far too chummy for his liking, and he promised himself that whatever might happen that morning, Nobbler being alive at the end of it wouldn't be included.

Deep below the Clatworthy's farmhouse, Henry shifted uneasily on the sofa, and pointed an accusing finger at the door. 'That's what he meant, wasn't it?' he said. 'The bad news is we're stuck with the silly bugger 'til Kinsman gets back? He thought I wasn't listening, didn't he? In shock, he said I was. But the silly bugger heard every word and wants to know . . . why him?'

Jo sighed. 'Giving the original encoder to Kinsman is part of the deal. Don't you see? If we don't do that he'll be following us for the rest of our lives. Which, in case you've forgotten, is likely to be a very, very long time.'

'But how do you know you can trust him?'

'Because he's been trying to get away from Stampeasy for centuries, and we're his only chance. Well,' she corrected herself, '*our* centuries. It just *seems* like centuries to him. Merv says that when we give him the original encoder he'll be able to override the one at the institute and escape to a place where Stampeasy won't be able to find him.'

'And this Stampeasy person won't be able to follow you, either?'

'Not after he's taken delivery of the little package Robbie and Merv are going to send him, no. It's been a long time for us too, you know, Henry.'

'Meaning . . .?'

'Meaning this is our chance to be free, and we're going to take it. Merv says he's figured out how to interrupt the slingshot effect that controls Kinsman and hook something up in his place before Stampeasy realizes he's gone. The something he has in mind is a computer virus loaded into a replica of the original encoder. When Ernie tries to copy its databanks across to his mainframe it'll smash his control system to bits. He might try to rebuild it, but even if he succeeds, we will be long gone by then.'

'Gone where?'

She smiled and shook her head.

'And these things?' he asked, pointing gingerly at the marks on his chest.

'Just a precaution.'

'Against what?'

'Kinsman will probably check the encoder as soon as he gets it. If he does, he'll see that it's been used, and he'll want to know why and by whom.'

'It'll still work, though, won't it?'

'According to Merv it will, yes.'

'So what's the problem?'

'Kinsman is a sort of paranoid schizophrenic with homicidal tendencies. Oh yes, and he hates your guts. He's been after you for what seems to him like centuries of agony. He's got a temper that would make a rabid Tyrannosaurus Rex look like a slightly discombobulated woodlouse.' She smiled, tightly. 'What more in the way of problems would you like?'

'But I don't have to meet him, do I? I mean, all you have to . . . ' He fell silent, and his eyes opened wide in sudden understanding. 'Oh, my God!'

Jo patted the back of his hand. 'It's part of the deal. If Kinsman's going to take it out on someone, they figure it ought to be you.'

'The lying . . .! But it was an accident!' He stood up and waved his arms about. 'I didn't mean to use the bloody thing, did I?'

'I know that, but . . .'

'He'll kill me, won't he?' There was a dull finality in his voice. He strode across the room and back again. 'He's already tried it once.' He looked down at Jo. 'What happened to all that *immortality* I was supposed to be getting?'

'Nothing wonderful about living forever,' said Robbie, from the doorway.

'Go away!' snapped Henry.

Robbie walked over to Jo and handed her something that looked like a flesh-coloured, rubber bracelet. 'You can put it on now, if you want. Only don't activate it 'til it's time to go. It'll neutralize the effects of the old one.'

Jo nodded, and slipped the bracelet into the pocket of her jacket. 'He's upset,' she said, nodding at Henry.

'Kinsman's all right,' said Robbie. 'Just a bit hyper is all.'

'A bit hyper?' said Henry. 'Snarls and screams and picks at his skin, you said. Sounds more than a bit bloody hyper to me!'

'That was Merv,' said Robbie, mildly. 'What *I* said was . . . '

'I don't care who said it!' snapped Henry. 'I've seen him, for Christ's sake! Like Freddy-bloody-Krueger with flames!'

'He'll be fine,' said Robbie. 'Just tell him it's a mistake and he'll be fine. If he isn't, just sort of . . . run like hell.' He turned to Jo. 'Where's the tart?'

'I thought she was with you?'

'Said she was coming to say goodbye to him.'

Robbie reached into the pocket of his overalls. 'Here,' he said, handing her another of the rubber bracelets. 'Give her this when she shows up, will you? And don't lose it, there's only a couple of spares.' He looked at Henry. 'See you at the barbecue then, eh, with Freddy?'

'*Bastard*!' said Henry, as the door closed with a click like the cocking of an executioner's rifle. He strode across the room, muttering. 'Selfish,' he turned on his heel and strode back again, 'nasty . . .! It's all right for him, isn't it? He can live forever. I've gotta face Old Nick and tell him I've broken his favourite toy! Seventy bloody years he promised me. Might live forever, he said. Now I'll be lucky if I make it 'til teatime. Sodding . . .!' He hesitated when he saw that Jo was hunched forward, staring into the waters of the Jacuzzi. 'Hey,' he said, walking hesitantly towards her, 'are you all right?'

'It's hard to keep track sometimes,' she said, quietly. 'When you've been playing at being normal for as long as we have . . .'

'Look,' he began, 'I'm sorry, but it's . . .'

'No, no, I'm fine! Really I am! Fine! It's just that . . .' She stood up and took a deep breath. 'So, anyway,' she strode across the room, wringing her hands, 'Merv said I should . . .' She turned back. 'Look . . . there isn't much time, so try to listen, will you? Believe me it's for your own good.' She sat down and patted the sofa beside her. 'Please . . .?'

He sat down, reluctantly. 'Yes,' he said, 'but . . .'

She pressed a finger to his lips. 'We knew you would get the encoder. We've known it for centuries. Kinsman told us a long time ago. At least, he told those of us who weren't too busy getting pissed to listen. And we had to make sure Dolly didn't get it back from you before you reached us.'

'I thought we were talking about Kinsman?'

'We are. Look, Merv told me to prepare you for what might happen to you after we've gone. We don't *have* to do it.' She looked at the floor. 'Well actually, maybe we do. We've got this guilt-trip thing that goes back a long, long way, and,' she looked up and held his gaze for a moment, 'never mind.'

She took a deep breath. 'Please listen. I'll be as quick as I can.'

She took one of his hands in both of hers and rested it in her lap.

'Kinsman told us a long time ago what would happen to you on Maidenhead Lane. He'd seen it and done it already. Do you see?'

'I guess . . .'

'He told us centuries ago how he'd pulled you out of your car after the crash. We thought he was just rambling at first. But after we caught him a few more times it started to make some kind of sense. Especially when Rooter gave the encoder to that Brigantes tart so she'd let him jump on her bones.' She set her lips in a tight line. 'He's a pillock, though, isn't he?' She shook her head. 'Anyway, Kinsman was a bit vague about the details, like who was there, and what they were doing.' She grimaced. 'He kept shouting "*Mine*! *Mine*! *Mine*!" at the top of his voice. But we got enough out of him to know you would survive the crash and get to us eventually.' She patted his hand. 'By the way, that wasn't the only time he almost got you. It was the closest he came, but there were lots of near misses. Did you see a red sports car last night?'

'That was him?'

'We thought he was making that up, too. But apparently he stole it from some terrified grockle who told the police he'd been abducted by aliens. He nearly got you in the lane by the gate as well, and about half a dozen times while you were sleeping. You can thank Lance and Gavin for keeping him out.' She stood up and walked over to the counter. 'Drink?'

He held up the glass of mango juice and shook his head. 'No thanks.'

She filled a glass for herself and walked back to sit down beside him.

'We didn't want to leave anything to chance, but we couldn't come and take the encoder from you, because we can't leave the moor. And we didn't dare have someone steal it from you or the museum in case we created some sort of paradox in time. We knew that Dolly was planning a raid, but Merv got really paranoid about it. He was terrified something would go wrong, so he had Gareth send Tom to watch over you all the way down from Essex. But even that wasn't enough. So he conned Roots and the boys into keeping an eye on you when you got to Maidenhead Lane. They thought they were watching a bunch of signs for Perce, when really they were there to protect you. We knew they could take care of Dolly's mob without any problem, so it didn't seem worth bothering them with the details. Besides, if they'd been paying attention to business, instead of getting hammered all the time, they'd have known about it already.' She smiled. 'Gar has regular progress meetings, every couple of years, to make sure everyone's still "on message", as he likes to call it. But the guys haven't been turning up for ages. Not that it would have made much difference if they had. Rooter never listens to anything anyone says, and Lance and Gav are always going through one of their addictive phases.' She shrugged. 'It happens every couple of decades or so. Then they sober up and get back to business. It really isn't easy living forever, Henry, believe me. Anyway, Tom Hertz didn't know what was going on, either. Still doesn't, in fact. But then, he doesn't need to with what we've been paying him. He's worked for us since 1973. The latest in a long line of security agencies going back hundreds of years. The names change, and people come and go,' she looked down at the Jacuzzi, 'and just as you start to get to know someone . . . ' She sniffed and looked up. 'They're always the best in the business, of course, and we know all there is to know about them, while they know only what we choose to let them find out about us. Which is why Tom didn't know who the guys were just now. We've had many, many years of practice at this sort of thing, Henry, and there is nothing, absolutely *nothing*, we don't know about deception. We invented most of it, and one of the many ways we make a living is by training people to deceive each other: governments, political parties, police forces, the supermarket chains . . . Mind you, we don't do as much of it as we used to. Too many scruples these days, I suppose. Or just the fact that we've got so much money we don't need to bother anymore. Still, we haven't given it up entirely, and although Tom doesn't know it, *we* were the ones who trained *him*. We also had a couple of his boys disarm the security system at the museum so that Dolly could get in. She wouldn't have had a cat in hell's chance if we hadn't. She doesn't know that, of course, or the fact that we trained Bunsen and his little band of arsonists.'

She shrugged. 'Sorry about the house by the way.'

Henry dismissed her apology with the wave of a hand. 'You're saying Tom Hertz doesn't know who I am or why I'm here?'

'All he had to do was dispose of anything that threatened your life. He's very good at that sort of thing, and it's all he needed to know. He is, for want of a better expression, your guardian angel. And he could continue to be that after we've gone. But we're getting away from the point.'

'But,' said Henry, hesitantly, 'if Kinsman told you all this before it happened, how come he hasn't told you . . .? Or has he? I mean, if he knows so much, he must know what . . . what happens to me?'

Jo looked at the floor.

'Doesn't he?'

'It's a tough world, Henry. So don't go getting yourself cornered. OK?'

'He must have told you something, though, hasn't he? About me?'

She shrugged.

'Please? You owe me that much at least, don't you?'

'He doesn't see you!' she said, sharply. 'There's no sign of you on the moor after,' she glanced at the clock on the far wall, 'soon.'

Henry glanced at the clock, too. 'Meaning what?'

'Meaning *nothing*!' she snapped. Her shoulders sagged. 'Meaning Kinsman hasn't seen you after midday today.'

'What . . . *never*?'

She shook her head.

'*Nothing at all?*'

She shook her head again.

'I'm a bit upset about that.'

'Look, the tags will protect you from most things. None of us would have survived without them.'

He glanced instinctively at her chest.

She smiled and gripped the lapels of her jacket with both hands. When she pulled them apart, a button zipped over his shoulder, another pinged off his chin, and a third hit him in the chest and fell into his lap. He looked down at it without expression. Then he looked up at her breasts. To his amazement, she took one of his hands and pressed it to her left nipple.

'What's this . . . granting the dying man his last request?'

She clicked her tongue. 'I'd be offering you something a hellova lot more intimate than this, if it was.'

He swallowed hard. 'Really?'

As she brushed his fingers over her breast, he could just make out the bump of something beneath the skin by the nipple. His own chest was still painful where Lance had inserted the tags.

'Does it hurt?' he asked, shyly.

'Only when I give someone a tit wank.'

He glanced at her face in astonishment.

She raised an eyebrow at his comical expression and inclined her head in an attitude of enquiry. Then her face became suddenly solemn. 'It's a dangerous world out there, Henry. Make sure you survive it. OK? Dolly won't give up, you know. Even if Merv's plan works, she won't let you go. We could tell Tom to take care of her. But we aren't assassins. Not anymore. We've caused far too much killing already.'

'Was it really *that* bad?'

'Worse than you'll ever know.' She looked away. 'So much killing. So much pain. And for what: a load of superstitious rubbish about a womanizing thief, an incompetent magician and a fake sword.' She shook her head. 'Take no notice of me, Henry; I'm getting maudlin in my old age.'

'But I thought you said Tom would kill anyone who got in my way?'

'Yes, but we've got the encoder now, haven't we? And Gareth is always looking to save money . . .'

'Oh great! Thanks a bunch!'

'Hush!' she said, placing a finger to his lips and reaching into her jacket pocket for one of the flesh-coloured bracelets, 'Merv will probably kill me for this, but . . . come here.'

She pulled his left hand onto her lap and strapped the thing to his wrist.

He recoiled in horror as it started to mould itself into his skin. 'Jesus Christ! What the . . .?'

'It's all right. Don't panic.' She took the other bracelet from her pocket and strapped it to her own left wrist. 'Look,' she said, holding her arm towards him, 'it's making itself at home, that's all. It's cybernetic: a sort of living survival kit that will monitor your bodily functions and help you out if you need it. What with that, and Tom, and the armour tags you'll be almost impossible to kill.'

'Almost?' he muttered, as he stared down at the bracelet dissolving into his skin. Soon there was nothing to show where it had been but a slight ridge and a pattern of small purple tattoos encircling his wrist. 'It's alive?' he whispered. He glanced up. 'What does it do?'

'Well, it's an encoder, for a start, and a universal translator. And it's got the antidote in it.' She pointed at the rows of tattooed symbols. 'Just don't press this one once it's activated. OK? It's the reset button for the serum. It feeds straight into your bloodstream and you'll be a nymphomaniac's best friend in a fraction of a second if you do.'

'Antidote? Antidote to what?'

'The mango juice?' she indicated the glass. 'Garlic essence, to stop you feeling horny?' She grinned. 'A bit stronger than the capsules you get at the chemist, but basically the same thing. You'll need to keep it fully charged, so take a regular supply any way you can get it. The raw stuff's best. How long did you say you've been . . . up? Sixteen hours, was it?'

He gave an embarrassed shrug.

'And you've been well behaved, haven't you,' she placed his hand on her knee, 'most of the time?'

'Most of the time,' he admitted, guardedly. 'If you mean,' he glanced down at the hem of her skirt, 'that . . . sort of thing?'

'Blossom's right, you are a prude. But you didn't really think you were controlling it yourself, did you? I might be two thousand years old, Henry, but I can still get 'em going when I want to, you know.'

He had been drugged since the moment he'd woken up in the Green Dragon Inn after his first trip through time, she told him.

'The hangover cure? I didn't know for sure that you'd need it, but I thought it was better to be safe than . . . sexually harassed. Then there was the wine at dinner. It had other stuff in it, too, of course, so you wouldn't wake up when they plugged you into Merv's computer.' She pointed at the glass. 'I told you it'd do you good.'

'Garlic? I'm not gonna start biting people in the neck, or something, am I?'

'The neck, the breasts, the arms, the legs; anything you can get your hands on. It's frightening to behold, believe me.' She pointed at one of the tattoos on the back of his wrist. 'This one's the reset button. Looks a bit like a sugar lump, see?' She turned his hand over. The numbers 0 to 9 were tattooed on the inside of his wrist in lines of five. 'You punch in your personal security code, and it's ready. You haven't got one yet, so it's still set on the default.'

'Which is . . .?'

She smiled and turned his hand the other way. 'Then you press the sugar lump. To stop it,' she turned his hand back again, 'you punch the little garlic clove, there. No need to mess with the numbers when you want to come out of it: the clove's the default. But don't touch *anything* until it's been validated and you've learned some self-control. And for God's sake, go easy on the sugar. Particularly Turkish delight.'

He grinned. 'Yeah, right . . .'

'Look . . . Turkish delight is a powerful aphrodisiac for time travellers like us. Any kind of sugar, in fact. And if you press that you'll be bonking the knotty pine before you know what's hit you. Anything with a hole in it, in fact. You haven't built up any resistance to the shift, yet. When you do, you will need to relieve the pressure every so often.' She pointed at the sugar lump tattoo. 'That's when you press that. Only for God's sake *don't* do it when there are lots of people about or you'll end up in prison for the rest of your life.'

'You're kidding me, right?'

'Do I look like I'm joking?'

'I don't know, it sounds a bit too complicated to me. Can't I just . . . take it off and . . . I don't know, take some sort of pill, or something, instead?' He turned his wrist over. 'Where's the buckle?'

'There isn't one. And no, you can't take it off. Not even with surgery. You'd bleed to death if you tried.'

'You mean I'm stuck with it? Oh, great!'

'Don't you want to know how we figured it out?'

'Figured what out?'

'About the garlic?'

'Not really, no,' he said, as if she was a vampire asking him if he wanted to know why she had bitten him in the neck. 'I don't think I understood any of what you just said.' He looked at his wrist. 'Can't I just . . .?'

She put a finger to his lips again. 'Just listen. Madge made some Turkish delight not long after we got here. She thought it would cheer us up. My god was she right. Nothing was safe: people, animals . . . funny-shaped vegetables. Ordinary-shaped vegetables come to that. It took decades for the wildlife to get its confidence back. You think an oil slick is an environmental disaster, Henry?' She shook her head. 'Totally harmless compared with a bunch of horny time travellers with a kilo of Turkish delight.'

He squinted at her. 'And you're saying garlic is the antidote?'

'It stops you feeling horny. But Turkish delight is only one of the triggers. It's sugar that's the poison. Do you see?'

'No, I don't. I mean, if you didn't have an antidote in the first place, how come Turkish delight was a problem? I mean, how could you . . .?'

'Because we were taking it already! The garlic? It grows wild around here. Pretty much all we had to eat at first, too: that and the tinned rations from the vans. Meat was easy: you could shoot as much of it as you liked. But fresh veg was a different matter. Merv kept making us eat it. Going on about scurvy and rickets and stuff. But give him his due: he was the one who figured it out. About the sugar and the garlic, I mean.'

'It's bad, then, is it, without the garlic?'

She lay back against the arm of the sofa, and opened her jacket.

He licked his lips, and turned to stare self-consciously at the wall.

'Here,' she said, reaching forward and gripping his chin with a hand. She turned his head towards her and held an index finger in front of his face. 'Stay!' she ordered, as she lay back with her jacket open. 'How do you feel?'

'I'm not gay you know, if that's what you're thinking? Not that there's anything wrong with being gay. Some of my best friends are . . . Well actually, they aren't. I haven't got any gay friends. But I would have if I . . . '

'Shut up,' she said, tiredly. 'I'm conducting a serious experiment here.' She shook her head. 'What's a girl got to do to get a bit of attention round here?' She looked up. 'Have you *any* idea how many men have asked me – begged me! – to do this? Well, have you?'

'Well . . . I mean, I imagine . . .'

'Look at me! Look at my tits and tell me what you think.'

He turned towards her, reluctantly. 'Well, I think they're . . . very nice.'

'And . . .?'

'What?'

'Is that all?'

He tilted his head to one side. 'The nipples are very nice.'

'Go on.'

'Not too big, and not too small.'

'Like the baby bear's porridge, then?'

'Sorry?'

She eased herself lower on the seat and shimmied her skirt further up her thighs. 'So,' she said, checking to see how provocative she looked, 'how do you feel now?'

'Apart from foolish, you mean?'

'And that's normal for you, is it, when a girl in a short skirt and no knickers lies back on a sofa and opens her legs?'

'Actually,' he said, with commendable honesty, 'it doesn't happen *that* often. About, sort of, *never*, really, I'd say. So it's a bit difficult to tell.'

'And you've never fantasized about it?'

'Strange as it might seem, I tend to go for the more believable stuff. All that nonsense about women hitchhikers and female passengers on trains ripping their clothes off and jumping on the first man they see never appealed to me much. I kept thinking they must either be escaped lunatics, or sadistic bitches desperate to spread antisocial diseases. I mean I've never been convinced that normal women do that sort of thing . . . do they?'

She gazed at him in silence as she opened her legs wider.

He was astonished to find that his interest in her appearance was devoid of emotion or lust. It was one of the most confusing things that he had ever experienced. He knew that he ought to want to leap on top of her. And part of him *did* want to do that. But an even stronger part of him just wanted to sit back and watch in a detached sort of way. She was beautiful, and desirable: and he figured that any normal heterosexual man would literally have jumped at the chance. But the truth was that he couldn't be bothered.

'I'm sorry,' he said, 'it's very kind of you and all that, but . . . '

'You see,' she said, sitting up. 'Proves my point, doesn't it? Look,' she added, as she stood up, 'give me your hand?'

He did as he was told, and she pulled him to his feet. She took his left wrist in her left hand and her own left wrist in her right hand. Then she punched a sequence of symbols, and pressed both sugar lumps at once.

There was a loud sucking sound, and a wet slap, and they were stuck together instantly like a couple of sex-starved magnets. Henry couldn't remember taking the towel from around his waist, or Jo taking her clothes off, but they must have done both because they were naked and locked together in a passionate bear hug of an embrace. He slipped effortlessly inside her as her long legs wrapped around him and her arms crushed him against her chest. Their mouths were wide open; their lips pressed hard together; and their tongues buried impossibly deeply down each other's throat. His feet were braced flat on the ground, and they were thrusting at one another like rabbits in heat. Sweat flew from their bodies like water from a lawn sprinkler, and the frantic slapping of flesh against flesh was like eels pouring into a barrel of sick.

Henry came almost instantly, and with such force that he would probably have rocketed backwards across the room if Jo hadn't been clamped so tightly around him. Then he came again, and again: twice in as many seconds.

She arched her back and leaned away from him to press the antidote button on her wrist. Then she grabbed his wrist, wrenched it from around her waist and pressed the little garlic symbol there, too.

He shuddered to a halt like Robocop with a blown fuse, and stood motionless and panting. Then '*Shit*!' he breathed in amazement.

He looked up at the ceiling. '*Shit*!'

He looked down at the floor. '*Shit*!'

He looked at Jo. 'I never knew *anything* could be *that* good!'

She unwrapped her legs from around his waist, and stood up. 'Yes, it's been a long time for me, too.'

His face cracked into a grin. 'Let's do it again.'

She shook her head and backed away, picking up her jacket as she went. 'No!' she said, sharply. 'We've got more important things to do!'

'Please?' he wheedled, chasing after her. 'Please? Pretty please?'

'No!' she insisted, dodging out of his way and picking up her skirt. 'It's bad for you. Naughty Henry. Bad Henry. Down!'

She bent quickly to pick up his towel. 'Here,' she said, dodging behind him and wrapping it around his waist, 'make yourself decent.'

'No,' he pleaded, 'I can cope! Really I can! I was just getting the hang of it, wasn't I?' He glanced at the tattoos. 'Which one was it?' He looked up. 'Jo, which one . . .?'

'No, Henry, don't!' she cried. 'It's too dangerous!'

He started pressing tattoos at random. 'Not that one,' he muttered when nothing happened. 'Not that one, either.' He was prodding at his wrist with increasing desperation. 'It must be . . . Must be . . .'

'Stop it!' she pleaded, walking towards him. 'Don't! Or you'll . . .!'

There was a sudden sizzling like a handful of chips in hot oil, and he faded, sparkled, shimmered and disappeared with a hiss.

'Bugger!' she said. Her shoulders sagged. 'What the hell's Merv gonna say to me now?'

45

LIEUTENANT CALLIOPE

Standing on the edge of Sodmire with Max, Robbie and Nils at his side, Mervyn had no time to worry about what was happening to Henry or Jo, or anyone else for that matter, because he was too busy worrying about what was about to happen to him.

'Is everyone ready?' he asked, glancing nervously at the others.
'For Christ's sake, Merv!' snapped Robbie. 'Stop doing that, will you?'
'Doing what?'
'Asking if we're ready, for Christ's sake!'
'I just want to make sure we haven't forgotten anything, that's all.'
'Not every five seconds, though, eh?'
'I'm a bit nervous, I think.'
'You don't say?'
'We can't afford to leave anything to chance, can we?'
'We haven't. We're ready. Look at us for Christ's sake! We're ready, and we've been ready since the last time you asked ten seconds ago.'
'Yes, yes, of course. Of course. I can see that. I'm a bit on edge, that's all.'
'Yeah, well, don't be. Everything's under con . . . '
'Oh, God,' whispered Mervyn, grabbing Robbie's arm and holding on tight as the air in front of them started to shimmer and spark. 'He's coming. Oh God, he's coming! Whatever you do, don't let him get away!'

At the top of the hill overlooking the Clatworthy's farmhouse, Dolly nodded her approval as Boxer, Curly and Stan knelt at the edge of the tree-lined ridge with their rocket and grenade launchers ready to fire. She was about to give them the order to begin the bombardment that would reduce the farmhouse to rubble, when a softly seductive female voice behind her said 'Who wants a nice cup of tea and a biccy, then, eh?'

Dolly frowned and looked over her shoulder. 'What the . . .?'
Lieutenant Calliope, in a skimpy waitress uniform, and with a heavily laden tray held out in front of her, teetered delicately through the trees towards the gangs on a pair of provocatively high-heeled shoes. 'We made them specially for you,' she beamed, nodding at Titus beside her in the battle thong of a Celtic warrior, and with a tray of crockery and cutlery slung around his neck. 'Corio Boc and I really *love* baking together, you know?'

Dolly took the cigar from her mouth and frowned at her boys and Jack's lads who were, to a man, following the lieutenant's progress through the trees with a chorused 'Hey! Whoa! Wow! 'Eller! Look a' that!' and 'Bugger my boots!' as they leered, peered and stood on tiptoe for a better view.

'Oy, *morons*!' cried Dolly. 'Whaddaya think you're lookin' at?'
A dozen distracted voices murmured and a dozen bemused heads turned as a dozen eager fingers pointed at various parts of the lieutenant's anatomy.

Sally T & G shook her head and spat on the ground. 'Wankers!'

Dolly turned to Jack. 'This your idea of a joke you flea-bitten dung heap?'

Jack didn't answer immediately, because, like everyone else with testicles, he had been temporarily deprived of the power of speech by the sight of the lieutenant's flouncy little skirt, tight bodice and stocking-clad legs

'Well?' demanded Dolly, flicking her cigar butt at him and bouncing it off of his head in a shower of sparks. 'You gonna tell me what's goin' on?'

'Dung heap?' muttered Jack, turning towards her with the expression of a hypnotized owl, as his alcohol-sodden brain tried to decide if the lieutenant was real, or just the acceptable side of late-onset delirium tremens.

Suddenly, he started to jerk and hop about, waving his arms in the air and slapping himself on the head like a stick insect on speed as a burning sensation in his scalp told him that the embers from Dolly's carefully targeted dog-end had set fire to his hair and were singeing their way down to his brain. He was soon spared further discomfort, however, when he accidentally coshed himself into unconsciousness with the thick end of his otherwise ineffectual telescope.

'That's better,' said Dolly, looking down at his inert body. 'Now then,' she added, turning to the lieutenant, 'what the . . .?'

'We thought tea and biccies would be *so* much nicer than a lot of nasty old fighting,' smiled the lieutenant, as legs dropped down from the underside of the tray and snapped into place, allowing her to bend forward and stand it on the ground and, in the process, display to the stupefied male audience behind and on either side of her a pair of white ruffle-back panties. 'There's chocolate chip cookies,' she said, pointing in turn at the plates on the tray, 'jammy dodgers and iced rings. Oh, and Corio Boc has got lots and lots of cups and saucers and napkins and things. So why don't you all come over,' she beamed around at the circle of bemused faces, 'and dig in.'

'Look,' said Dolly, testily, 'what the . . .?'

'Oh, I am *so* sorry, Ms. Killjoy,' apologized the lieutenant. 'How rude of me. I am Calliope and this is my lover, Corio Boc.'

'I don't give a monkey's what your name is, darlin',' snapped Dolly. 'What I want to know is . . . Oy!' she cried, turning to the Muttocks brothers, who were heading eagerly towards the lieutenant rubbing their hands together and licking their lips, 'where the hell do you think *you're* goin'?'

'Jammy dodgers,' grinned Gummer, pointing enthusiastically.

'Iced rings,' nodded Tickle.

'I'll ice *your* rings in a minute!' snarled Dolly, pulling a pearl handled Luger from her handbag and pointing it at Tickle's chest. 'Get back in line!'

The brothers stopped in their tracks, pouting.

'Freshly baked?' said the lieutenant, holding up a plate.

Dolly stared at her in disbelief. 'Freshly . . .?'

'Why don't we all just sit down and have a lovely cup of tea and a nice little chat?' suggested the lieutenant.

'Chat?' echoed Dolly, gesturing at the men around her with their rocket and grenade launchers, shotguns, assault rifles, knives, machetes, axes, machine pistols and sundry other instruments of death and destruction, ancient and modern. 'Do we *look* like we're here for a friggin' . . . *chat?*'

'We could get you some folding chairs to sit on, if you liked?' beamed the lieutenant. 'And some little tables, too, perhaps?'

'Listen, darlin',' hissed Dolly, 'I dunno who you are, or why Jungle Jim here,' she gestured at Jack's lifeless body, 'invited you along. But in case you hadn't noticed, we're here to kill people. And if you don't wanna be one of 'em, I suggest you piss off back to wherever you came from!'

'Oh, we couldn't do that,' said the lieutenant, pleasantly. 'That wouldn't be right at all, would it, Corio Boc?'

'Definitely not, my little Sugar Plum Diddums,' said Titus.

Dolly turned to Spider. 'Is he serious?'

Spider drew his machete. 'Want I should carve 'im up a bit for ya, Doll?'

'I don't think that would be a very good idea at all,' said the lieutenant.

'Is that right?' said Spider. 'An' why's that, then, darlin'?'

'Well, for one thing it would be *really* unkind.'

Dolly and Spider exchanged glances.

'And for another?' prompted Dolly.

'We might have to hurt you,' said Titus.

'And we *definitely* don't want to do *that*,' said the lieutenant.

'You,' said Spider, gesturing at the band of heavily armed thugs standing behind him, 'don't wanna hurt . . . *us?*'

'Not if we can help it, no.'

'And what were you gonna do, darlin': put us in detention?'

Dolly's boys and Jack's lads sniggered and giggled.

'More sort of . . . in therapy, actually,' said the lieutenant.

'Or traction, if that doesn't work,' added Titus, putting down his tray and taking up the karate Tsuru Ashi Dachi, or One-legged Crane Stance, of a Yon Dan Renshi Master.

The sniggering and giggling grew louder.

'Well, well,' said Dolly, shaking her head, 'what *have* we got here?'

'Looks like one o' them Chippendales in a nappy,' said Boxer. He put down his grenade launcher, and took a knuckleduster from his jacket pocket. 'Want me to smack 'is botty for 'im, Doll?'

Dolly shook her head. 'Listen sunshine,' she said to Titus, 'why don't you go back home to your mummy, like a good little boy, before I have Boxer here tear you a new arsehole?'

Titus moved smoothly into the Neko Ashi Dachi – the Stance of the Cat. 'Not 'til you put down your weapons and go back to Essex.'

'Really?' said Dolly, coldly. 'And who's gonna make us?'

'We are,' said the lieutenant, with a beaming smile.

'Yeah? You an' whose army?'

'This one,' said Rooter, stepping from behind a tree with Gavin and Lance.

'Don't forget little ol' me!' said Blossom, mincing into view behind them.

Like Rooter, Titus and the boys, she was dressed as a Celtic warrior. Which is to say that she was wearing almost nothing at all.

Something inside Gummer Muttocks' head snapped. Deprived of a handful of his favourite jammy dodgers by the bossy old scrubber from up London way, he decided that the appearance of his most hated enemies, minus their trousers and without a single weapon between them, offered him and his brother the perfect opportunity to release some of their pent-up aggressions. With his face contorting into the snarl of a Viking berserker, he raised an axe above his head and charged at the diminutive Titus. 'Come on then Tick,' he cried as he ran, 'le's 'ack the little bugger's balls off!'

There was a brief, but furious, whirling of arms and legs, after which Gummer found himself hanging upside down in a tree.

'Oh, well done, my little Love Muscle!' clapped the lieutenant, as Tickle came lumbering at her with an ancient cavalry sabre in one hand and a rusty meat cleaver in the other. 'However, I have always found that twisting the wrists at the moment of contact,' she demonstrated by launching Tickle into the tree alongside his brother, 'generates a little more lift and momentum.'

'Thank you my little Love Bunny,' pouted Titus, blowing her a kiss before launching an astonished Dinger Bell and a frankly terrified Bert Newton into the tree alongside the brothers Muttocks. 'Like that, you mean?'

Suddenly, bodies were running, jumping, ducking, crouching, spinning and flying in all directions at once.

Vinny took a knife from his jacket pocket and dropped out of the tree. 'OK darlin',' he hissed in Blossom's ear, with the blade at her throat. 'Let's see how you gets on with a *real* man!'

'I'll let you know when I meets one,' she replied, twisting out of his grasp, thrusting a hand between his legs and hurling him headlong by his scrotum into a tree trunk. 'In the meantime,' she added, as he passed out, 'stitch that!'

'What're you waitin' for?' cried Dolly at the men with the rocket and grenade launchers. 'Shoot 'em for Christ's sake!'

Spider and Boxer bent to pick up their weapons as Curly and Stan raised their rocket launchers and aimed them at Titus.

'*No!*' screamed Dolly. '*Not like . . .! You'll kill the lot of us! Use your guns!*'

She turned to Bonce. 'Hey, dumbo, don't just stand . . . *therrk-urrkle!*' she choked, as he reached out and lifted her off of her feet with a fist wrapped tightly around her windpipe. He tore the Luger from her fingers and handed it to Simon. 'Look after 'im for a bit, yeah?'

"Tidden funny,' he said, turning to Dolly, 'makin' fun o' them what ain't so clever.' Then he lifted her into the air, and threw her at Curly, Boxer and Stan.

'*Bastard!*' cried Spider, rounding on Bonce with his machete raised over his head. But even as the blade came hissing down towards Bonce's neck, Simon raised the Luger and shot Spider neatly through the wrist.

Spider cried out in agonized astonishment as the machete fell from his grasp and buried itself in his foot, pinning him to the ground a second or so before Bonce's huge fist came around in a haymaking right hook to punch out his lights and most of his front teeth.

'Nice shootin',' said Bonce.

'Nice punchin',' said Simon. He blew across the barrel of the Luger and spun it into an imaginary holster. 'Just call me Sundance!'

From behind a tree where he had been hiding since his friends, Dinger and Bert, had become dangerously airborne, Nobbler decided it was time he was somewhere else. As Spider hit the ground in front of him, he turned on his heel and made off through the wood at a crouching run, only to come face to face with the biggest, most terrifying bear-lion-dog-animal thing that he had ever seen in his life. It was Boadicea, and he was delighted to be making the little man's acquaintance at last. He was a placid beast, most of the time, but he had heard a lot of nasty stories about Nobbler's misuse of performance distorting narcotics on defenceless animals and had decided that the time was right for the animal kingdom to bite back.

Nobbler realized immediately that negotiation was out of the question, and was last seen heading over a hill towards Sodmire with his arms and legs pumping wildly, and the ponderous Boadicea in lumbering pursuit.

Jack regained consciousness just as Dolly went crashing to the ground on top of Curly, Boxer and Stan. In the confusion that followed, he reached into the cursing, grunting, heaving tangle of bodies and pulled out a machine pistol. But when he looked around in search of an escape route, he found his way blocked by the scantily clad Rooter, smiling broadly.

Jack swallowed and took a step backwards. 'Don't you touch me,' he warned, pointing the gun at Rooter's belly. 'I'll shoot you, you poofter!'

'Really?' said Rooter. 'You reckon that thing makes you a man, then, do you Jack?' He spread his arms wide. 'OK, if you've got what it takes.'

'You'll 'ave t' take me an' all,' said Sally T & G, coming at him from the side with a pump-action shotgun.

'Whatever you say, Sal,' he replied, turning towards her. 'Nice duds, by the way,' he added, nodding at her moleskin trousers and rabbit skin coat. 'Not the best getup to be wearing where you're going, though, eh?'

'I ain't goin' nowhere,' she said, racking the slide of the shotgun and levelling it at his crotch. 'You are, though, me ol' lover, ain't ya?'

'Not necessarily,' said Gavin, wrenching the shotgun out of her hands and cartwheeling past her to plant the sole of his foot in Jack's crotch.

Jack dropped the machine pistol, groped at his groin, and fell on his face.

'We've got a present for you two,' said Rooter, taking a pair of skin-coloured bracelet encoders from a pouch on his belt with one hand and knocked Sally on her arse with the other. 'Only thing is, kiddie-winkles,' he added, flipping her onto her belly as Gavin knelt down next to Jack, 'you're gonna have to work out how to use 'em yourselves. And to be honest,' he said, as he strapped a bracelet to Sally's wrist and tossed the other one over to Gavin, 'I don't fancy your chances.' He pulled Sally to her feet. 'Not with just the one brain cell to share between you, I don't.'

Gavin strapped the other encoder to Jack's wrist and hauled him to his feet next to Sally. Then he and Rooter pressed a series of tattoos on the bracelets and stood back as Sally and Jack sizzled, shimmered and vanished.

Dolly disentangled herself from her henchmen, and got to her feet with a machine pistol in each hand. 'You ungrateful little shit!' she hissed at Bonce.

'Oy, grandma!' cried Lance, behind her. 'I wouldn't do that if I was you!'

She whirled around to face him. 'Is that right?' she snarled, pulling both triggers and sending a hail of bullets into his chest.

Long before the guns were empty, he should have been lying on his back, riddled with blood-spurting bullet holes. Instead, he was looking down at himself. 'Missed,' he said, looking up.

Dolly threw the guns on the ground, and snatched another one from Boxer's hand. Then she turned and emptied its clip into Lance.

'Sorry,' he said, 'but have you read the manual at all?'

'Doll . . .?' said Curly, behind her.

'Gimme that!' she hissed, wrenching an Uzi from his hand.

'Yeah, but Doll . . .!' he protested, as she turned and fired at Lance.

When the bullets had no effect on him, she turned the gun on Rooter, Blossom, Gavin, Titus and the lieutenant in turn. When it had no effect on them, either, she looked down at it with a puzzled expression.

'What's the matter with these things?' she muttered, staring into the barrel. 'Why don't they work?'

'Doll!' said Curly, urgently. 'I think you oughta . . . '

'I mean, they're s'posed to kill people, for Christ's sake!'

'Yeah, but boss,' insisted Curly, turning her to face the valley, 'look!'

Dolly looked.

Hovering in front of her were *Alpha*, *Beta*, *Gamma* and *Delta*: or, as Colonel Payne-Hertz liked to call them, *War*, *Famine*, *Pestilence* and *Death*. Lights pulsed slowly around their rims as fearsome-looking weapon pods unfolded on robotic arms from doors in their underbellies and scanned the tree-lined ridge.

Everyone but Dolly dropped their weapons and put their hands in the air.

'Cowards!' she sneered, picking up a rocket launcher. 'Why's it always me has to . . .?' She hesitated when she felt herself being lifted into the air. 'What the . . .?' she muttered, looking down. 'How the . . .? Oy! *Hey*!' she cried as she accelerated up into the clouds. '*Put me . . . dooooooooooooooooooown*!

'That's so much nicer, isn't it?' beamed the lieutenant when the echoes of Dolly's voice had died away. 'Now who wants a biccy and a nice cup of tea?'

* * *

'What happened to her?' asked Henry. 'Dolly, I mean?'

'Oh, she got what many would regard as her comeuppance,' said the figure. 'Although the jury is still out, metaphorically speaking, in some quarters, where it is felt that she was dealt with in far too lenient a manner, not only by the judicial system but also by the Inland Revenue Service.'

'Meaning what?'

'The colonel returned her unharmed to her house in London, together with everything she had stolen from the British Museum – with one notable exception, of course – after it had all been recovered from the homes and lockups of the gang members to whom she had entrusted its safekeeping. He hid it in her basement, where even the Metropolitan Police couldn't fail to stumble across it eventually. The trial was a formality, of course. She was found guilty and sentenced to life imprisonment for the robbery, which the state in its wisdom had chosen to regard as an act of treason. It could hardly have gone worse for her if she had stolen the crown jewels. But at least she was spared the hangman's rope and the firing squad. And after a short time in prison, she was allowed to publish her autobiography, *The Grail Heist: How I Did It*. It became an instant global bestseller and went on to make far more money than she would ever have made from the sale of the Grail Hoard.'

The figure looked up at the darkening sky. 'Five years after the book's publication, a major Hollywood studio turned it into a film with Michelle Pfeiffer – God help us! – in the lead roll. But they refused to include the final chapter of the book, in which Dolly claimed to have been abducted by aliens on Dartmoor. The producers said their target audience would never believe it.'

'She came out of it rather well, then, didn't she?'

'If you consider spending the rest of one's life in prison as having done rather well then yes, I suppose she did. And at the very least, she will go down in history alongside figures of similar notoriety, such as Bonnie Parker, Patty Hearst, and Ulrike Meinhof. And the name Dolly Killjoy does have a certain ring to it, doesn't it?'

Henry nodded. 'When you say "turned it into a film", what do you mean? How far into the future can you see, exactly?'

'Far enough to know that as soon as he was released from Chantal du Lac's pigsty, Richard Choat returned home to find his wife and daughter gone, his bank account empty and his house burned to the ground. But it didn't take him long to recover from his losses, because he had decided during his confinement on Dartmoor to forego the pleasures of the flesh and spend the rest of his life atoning for his sins in a religious retreat.'

'What . . .? You mean . . .? Are you saying he became a monk?'

'Indeed. But it didn't last. He took a fancy to the wife of the farmer from whom the monks bought their fruit and vegetables, and, as the saying goes, the farmer "caught him at it". He is still running. Until the next time, that is.

'Before he was released from Exeter Police Station into the custody of his employer, a certain Mr. Hertz, Bumpy Oates told his cellmate, Sir Richard Pate, that the cocaine in his toiletries bag had been planted there by his nephew, Nigel Adams. It hadn't, of course: the guilty party was your friend, Ronald Posset. Nevertheless, the seeds of suspicion had been sown in your former employer's mind, and when he was released from prison, five years later, he used his personal fortune, which had grown enormously as a result of its careful management by a firm of investment bankers based in Norway – or was it Finland? – to fund the first phase of building at the Pate Institute of

Genetic Sciences in the hope that research carried out there would prove beyond a reasonable doubt that Nigel Adams was *not* his love child and could be disinherited without fear of reprisals from the malicious Lady Kitty.'

'This firm of investment bankers wouldn't have been called Beoric, Troth and wosname, by any chance, would it?'

'You know, I do believe it would. Incidentally, did you know that he was originally christened Richard John Head, but had his surname changed by deed pole in his mid-teens to avoid the un-hatched ignominy of Dick Head?'

Henry grinned. 'Really?'

'I imagine he thought he was being enormously clever. But he had clearly not taken into account the un-hatched potential of Dick Pâté.'

'Not something you would want to spread on your toast, is it?'

'Indeed not! And he never got to see the institute completed. He died on his way to an assignation in Torquay with Suzie Bunt when his favourite Mercedes collided head-on with a courier van carrying, amongst other things, a crate load of personalized number plates destined for the House of Lords. As for his loyal assistant, the formerly chaste Miss Charlotte Piece: two weeks spent in drunken debauchery with the three young Norwegians changed the course of her life out of all recognition. She decided that she liked men so much that she wanted to become one: and three years later, after extensive counselling and several significant surgical interventions, she had transformed herself into Charlie De La Mare, the most popular female impersonator on the planet. And with the three young Norwegians, still working for Hertz Global Security Inc. watching over her, she has also become Colonel Tom's most effective agent provocateur.'

Henry thought for a moment. 'You mean . . . she's a spy?'

'I understand that he/ she prefers the less pejorative, and infinitely more chic, French *agent secret*. And according to the colonel, when it comes to wheedling information out of diplomats struggling to come out of their own personal closets, his/ her success rate is second to none.'

Henry grinned. 'I can't wait to tell Sam.'

'He knows already. Kate Clatworthy told him. She visits him regularly on the little Pacific island that he and Ron and Rosie Posset bought with the money the Clathworthies paid them for watching over you. Sam's sister visits them occasionally, too, with her husband, Max. They live in London. She teaches English and Maths to primary school children. He still works for . . . '

'Hertz Global Security?'

The figure inclined its head.

'So everyone really *is* a winner?'

The figure looked down at the fire.

'So,' said Henry, pointing at the sky, 'are they up there, too? The rest of Dolly's gang?'

'Not exactly . . . '

46

HENRY KITE

'I don't doubt that you will be pleased to learn,' said the figure, 'that Mortimer "Bonce" Mangle became head of security at Simon Hawker's butterfly farm. They are, I believe, very happy together, both commercially and domestically, and have recently branched out into the breeding and protection of endangered wild bird species. And I understand that with the determined Mr. Mangle on their case, egg thieves are well advised to give a wide birth to the breeding pairs under his protection. In fact, a rather curious item on the BBC's *Six O'clock News* in the summer of 1988 reported a sudden increase in the numbers of "birding enthusiasts", as I believe they prefer to call themselves, arriving at hospital accident and emergency departments across the country with cracked ribs, fractured limbs and broken jaws, and no apparent explanation for how their injuries had come about.'

'Rooter would be pleased.'

'And not entirely innocent of involvement. And the butterfly farm has been proving very popular since the colourful Mr. and Mrs. Oldroyd joined the team selling Devonshire cream teas to the tourists.

Henry grinned. 'Good for them. What about Vinny and Nobbler?'

'The lieutenant delivered Vincent Trashman to Dr. Spiegel's clinic in San Francisco where he underwent a course in anger management to help him deal with his attachment disorders and the associated fear of abandonment. It took him a long time, but he has since qualified as a psychiatric nurse and now specializes in helping young people, particularly young men from backgrounds similar to his own, recover from the effects of psychological, physical and sexual abuse suffered during their formative years.'

'Really?'

'Yes. And the good doctor is exceedingly pleased with his progress.'

'I can see how she would be. And Nobbler . . .?'

'Boadicea caught up with him eventually, of course: not least because he ran headlong into Sodmire and sank into it up to his neck. And he would undoubtedly have been consigned to a watery grave had not the big dog taken pity on him and allowed him to hang on to his collar and be pulled free. After which he, too, was taken to Dr. Spiegel's clinic where, due to the complexity of his psychological disorders, his treatment is proving a lengthy business. Even so, he has been encouraged to put his experiences as a military guinea pig to a less morally questionable use than the drugging of unsuspecting animals, by working for a global charity that seeks to enable ex-service men and women to gain legal and financial redress for the human rights abuses visited upon them by their governments. He is, I believe, even at a relatively early stage in that career, making such a name for himself as an expert witness that the possibility of a Nobel Prize for Physiology or Medicine for the research team of which he has become such an important component is being whispered, loudly, amongst those in a position to know about such things. And of far more importance to him on a personal level is the fact that his wife and daughter are talking to him again.'

'Dr. Spiegel must be one hell of a therapist.'

'She is a brilliant woman, Henry, capable of making Freud and Jung look almost as incompetent as that brain-dead butcher Jeremy Kyle!'

'Sorry?' said Henry, taken aback by the sudden vehemence in the figure's voice. 'You've lost me. Who . . .?'

'No, no! Don't take any notice of me. I'm getting crotchety in my dotage. Which reminds me . . . Colonel Payne?'

'Sir?' came the colonel's disembodied reply.

'I think now would be a good time to strike camp, colonel, don't you?'

'Indeed, sir. They will be with you shortly.'

The combat drones appeared with a soft hiss to hover above Henry and the masked figure as if they had been magicked out of the air.

The figure looked up. 'Now then, do tell me, which one of you is *Alpha?*'

'That would be me, sir,' said a male voice as one of the discs broke formation and dropped down to hover at head height.

'What is your full designation?'

'Combat and Reconnaissance Drone 27-18-11-22, *Alpha-War-McNaughton*, private, sir.'

'And your original inception date, private?'

'That would be 4 July AD 2077, sir.'

'And have you been the subject of any modifications since that date?'

'Only one significant re-build so far, sir.'

'And that would have been . . .?'

'*Terga data* 30 April AD 1987, sir. The retrofitting of cyber pilot John Michael "Spider" McNaughton, sir.'

'And your current status and assignment?'

'Combat and Reconnaissance Service, Hertz Global Security Inc., first century AD Temporal Zone, UK, sir.'

'And are you happy in your work, private?'

'Oh yes, sir! Very much so, sir!'

'May I ask why?'

'It was either this or spend the rest of me life in prison, sir.'

'And is that the only reason?'

'Oh no sir. I also love it coz I get to do this,' said the drone as it shot into the air, twisting, turning and looping the loop with its rim lights pulsing and its weapon pods scanning the sky.

'Att-tensssss-*hun*!' came the colonel's disembodied voice.

The drone immediately stopped zipping around, and came back to hover in front of Henry and the masked figure.

'Your pardon, sir,' said the colonel, appearing a short distance from the figure's chair. 'It's still early days, and I'm afraid the private hasn't adjusted to the level of freedom the cybernetic service offers its newest recruits.'

'Exuberance isn't a crime, though, is it colonel?'

'Indeed not sir, no. And the doctor's rehabilitation programme is proceeding according to plan.'

'And the other members of the squad?'

'In the same programme, sir, yes.'

'Have them introduce themselves to Mr. Kite and myself, would you? With their inception and rebuild designations, if you please?'

'Very good, sir. Squad, by the numbers, sooooound . . . *off!*'

In rotation, each of the other drones broke formation and presented itself to Henry and the figure before taking its place back in line.

'28-18-11-22, *Beta-Famine-Gurney*, private! 30 April AD 1987, cyber pilot David Stanley Gurney reporting, sir!'

'29-18-11-22, *Gamma-Pestilence-Hare*, acting corporal! 30 April AD 1987, cyber pilot Rowland Edwin "Curley" Hare reporting, sir!'

'30-18-11-22, *Delta-Death-Dogwood*, private! 30 April AD 1987, cyber pilot William James "Boxer" Dogwood reporting, sir!'

Henry was horrified. 'Good god, man! What have you done to them? Put their brains into those,' he pointed at the hovering discs, 'things?'

'Hardly, sir. The technology will seem strange to you, of course, but within a decade or so of your time it will have become familiar to a global audience. You will not have heard of the *Xbox* or the *Play Station* – a bit after your time, I believe? – but they provide a gaming experience rather more immersive than the *Space Invaders* machines you will have been familiar with in 1987, and not unlike that available to the owner of a remote control aircraft. Only in their case, the operatives piloting the drones, recruits McNaughton, Gurney, Hare and Dogwood, are in a command satellite, a mile or so,' he pointed at the sky, 'up there. And the connection between them and the crafts they are currently piloting is of a technology not unlike that which powers the cybernetic device attached to your left wrist. Which is to say that each of the pilots can be considered an integral part of his vehicle, even though he isn't actually inside it physically. If you see what I mean?'

Henry was sceptical. 'And they're OK with that, are they?'.

'Sir, yes sir!' chorused the pilots, as the drones nodded up and down, slightly out of sync, like giant, but imperfectly choreographed, clams.

'Oh,' said Henry, deflated, 'really?'

'Oh, yeah! Right! Deffo!' and 'You betcha!' came the replies from the drones as they bobbed and jostled for position like a pack of eager puppies waiting to go for walkies on a sunny day.

'*Shun*!' came the commanding voice of the lieutenant.

The drones stopped bobbing and jostling, and floated instantly into line to hang motionless in front of Henry and the masked figure with their rim lights extinguished and their weapon pods withdrawn.

'My apologies, colonel,' said the lieutenant's silky voice. 'I'm afraid the boys are still easily distracted by the novelty of their new capabilities.'

'Understood, lieutenant,' said the colonel. 'See to it that they receive additional tuition in squad discipline, will you?'

'Of course, sir.'

'In the meantime, we have a camp to clear. In your own time, lieutenant, but I would be obliged if you would make it quick. Yes?'

'Certainly, sir. OK boys: you heard the colonel. Snap to it!'

The drones immediately set to clearing away the furniture and fittings from in and around the stone circle.

'We can't afford to leave anything behind,' said the masked figure. 'Imagine the confusion if twentieth century archaeologists were to discover the remains of a solar powered Roman fridge-freezer at Stonehenge.'

'Are we leaving, then?' asked Henry, looking around.

'Not yet, no: we haven't quite finished your story, have we colonel?'

'Indeed not, sir, no,' said the colonel, bowing diffidently. 'May I . . .?'

'Of course.'

The colonel turned to Henry. 'The rest of Dolly's boys – there were four of them, by the way – were still running long after Nobbler Bates got himself hauled out of Sodmire. Well, not actually running, as such, more sort of *staggering* really, but *on the run*, if you take my meaning? They almost made it to Tavistock before we decided to catch up with them. At first, we thought of giving them a bit of community service repairing the Green Dragon Inn. But in the end we gave that to Jack's lads instead. They made the mess, after all. We let the London boys go with a promise that if they told anyone what had happened to them we would send certain information about the robbery at the British Museum to their local constabularies. Nothing has been heard from them since, and it seems likely that the threat of life imprisonment will keep them out of mischief for a decade or two yet.'

'Oh, yeah!' agreed *Alpha-War-McNaughton* as it flew past.

'Settle down private, settle down!' admonished the colonel.

'Sir, yes sir!' chanted the private as the drone disappeared into the clouds with the Portaloo trailing behind it.

'Why, though?' asked Henry.

'Why what, sir?'

'Well, the drones: I mean, they're gangsters, aren't they, not some sort of glorified peacekeeping force?'

'Indeed they are, sir. But Dr. Spiegel and myself have conducted extensive research into the workings of the criminal mind, and we are convinced that when channelled in a positive manner it can be very helpful in developing new and more creative means of achieving conflict resolution. Or to put it another way: we are confident that a pre-existing talent for persuasion of the brute force and ignorance variety can be employed in a more imaginative and less destructive manner, not so much in beating the living daylights out of people as scaring it out of them. A sort of deterrent-based approach to settling disagreements, as I believe was demonstrated effectively by the airborne trilithon earlier? And in our on-going attempts to develop and refine such techniques, we are being ably assisted by a select group of the world's more innovative theatre, film, product and games designers, as well as a handful of its most eminent psychologists.'

'Sounds like it could be a lot of fun,' said Henry, grudgingly.

'Oh, indeed it is, sir, yes,' said the colonel. 'Definitely! And now,' he added to the masked figure, 'if you will excuse me, your grace, I think I had better go and check on the . . .?' he pointed up at the sky.

'Yes of course,' said the figure. 'Please do not let us detain you.'

'So,' said Henry, after the colonel had disappeared, 'what about Jack's lads? It can't have been easy keeping that lot quiet, can it?'

'On the contrary, after they completed the repair work at the Green Dragon Inn, they were given unlimited access to the cider vats in its cellars. No one believed a word they said after that. In fact, I understand that they didn't believe much of it themselves.'

'So who's running the place now that Perce has gone home?'

'Oh, but he hasn't. He's still there: the only one of the Clatworthy clan not to have gone to . . . Not to have left. The others still visit him from time to time. Especially the Naggs brothers who say they can't settle in their new home without the benefit of a regular workout pushing their bikes up the hill to the pub followed by a couple of hours of heavy lifting "ferrying the odd pint or six of the Ol' Lovers'" up to their mouths. But I don't think Mr. Pratt will ever leave. And now that he has one of the new wrist encoders, he is free to make regular trips into the future to visit his beloved Agnes and have her relieve him of some of his more intimate . . . er, frustrations.'

'He's got the best of both worlds, then, hasn't he?'

'Indeed. You might say that he has finally found his Holy Grail.'

'And do Jack's lads leave him in peace?'

'In a manner of speaking. Without Jack Strawbridge inciting them to acts of mayhem, they have become the most loyal of Mr. Pratt's customers. And as I believe Gummer Muttocks is fond of saying from beneath his favourite table in the saloon bar "If you'm tired o' the Ol' Lovers', lover, you'm dead!"'

'So if Jack isn't there anymore, where is he? And what happened to the terrifying Sally T & G?'

When Jack and Sally came to their senses, they found that they had been transported 500,000 years backwards in time to the latter part of the Early Stone Age: although it took them two millennia to appreciate the fact. The prevalence amongst the native fauna of woolly mammoths and sabre-toothed tigers (from which they soon found themselves running away screaming) should have given them a clue. But since neither had ever had much use for palaeontology, archaeology, anthropology, or even – and of more relevance given their predicament – athletics, it was a miracle that they managed to work it out at all, much less survive for more than five minutes after they got there.

Sally's first thought was that they had been taken to some sort of safari park. And she immediately set about fashioning a set of rudimentary weapons for herself – a spear from a hazel branch sharpened with her toenail, a dagger from a mammoth's rib chiselled into shape with her gums, and a rapid-fire and surprisingly deadly slingshot from her brassiere and a handful of pebbles.

Jack, in contrast, didn't do much of anything at all for the first few days after their arrival, except sit in the branches of an ancient oak tree wetting himself and weeping for the loss of his shotgun.

Then one morning, a week or so after their arrival, they woke to find themselves surrounded by a tribe of inquisitive little hominids whose DNA made them not quite great apes and not yet quite humans, either. They were small, averaging three feet six inches in height, covered from head to toe in thick, brown, wiry hair, and they saw in the giant, often horny and angry, often weepy and morose, but always tastelessly hairless, new arrivals, a chance to adopt a breeding pair of exotic, if embarrassingly stupid, domestic pets.

Henry was aghast. 'So you're saying Jack and Sally were the first human beings on the planet from whom the rest of us are all descended?'

'Oh no! No, no, no! The little hominids did try to get them to mate, of course, once they had disarmed the combative Sally – a very painful process, I am told. But Jack's part in his gang's enthusiastic attempt to drink Mr. Pratt's cellars dry during their occupation of the Green Dragon Inn had effectively rendered him sterile. Proving, some might say, that too much of the Ol' Lovers' was not, for the future of the human race at least, too much of a good thing. None of which was any consolation to the aggressive Miss Board whose raging libido, and superior fighting ability, enabled her to coax – batter would be a more accurate word – not only the leader of the little group but also all of the other male er . . . members of the tribe into mating with her: many times over. Which traumatic couplings eventually resulted in her giving birth to a tribe of what at least one twenty-first century palaeoarchaeologist will come to believe were the very first Neanderthals in Western Europe.'

'Good god!'

'Quite!'

'And where are they now?'

'Extinct, of course: I thought everyone knew that.'

'No, I mean Jack and Sally – not the Neanderthals.'

'Oh, I see. Yes, of course. Well, theirs isn't the happiest of endings, and yet, perhaps, not the most depressing, either. They stayed with the tribe – the hominids, that is, not the Neanderthals, who were far too intelligent to put up with them for long – for thousands of years, and were greatly revered for their longevity. But they made the mistake of encouraging the tribe to voyage into the far north of the planet in search of new hunting grounds during one of the warmer, interglacial periods, and forgot to head home when the temperature started to fall. By the time the next ice age took a hold on the landscape it was too late for them to go back, and they were trapped in a cave within what we now know as the Arctic Circle. They are still there, frozen solid and waiting for someone to come and thaw them out: the only people on the planet, other than those with too much money and/ or too little sense to know the difference, for whom global warming looks like being a good idea.'

'Global warming?'

'Oh yes, I was forgetting: the Intergovernmental Panel on Climate Change wasn't formed until AD 1988, was it? But I wouldn't concern yourself with that now. You have far more pressing things to be worrying about.'

'Like Kinsman, you mean?' said Henry, gazing around the clearing, which, apart from the campfire and the chairs on which they were sitting, looked much as it had when he'd arrived there that morning. 'I've been trying to avoid it, but I suppose you'd better tell me what happened to him and how long I've got before he gets here.'

'Yes, I suppose so,' said the figure, gazing into the campfire.

Henry waited in tense anticipation with his mouth suddenly dry and a little rivulet of cold sweat running down his back.

He heard a noise behind him and snapped around, expecting to be attacked by a flaming banshee. Instead, he saw Titus striding towards them across the clearing, dressed as a Durotriges warrior. His face and body were daubed with symbols in blue and white mud. In his right hand he carried an axe. In his left, he held a painted shield. Around his waist was a leather belt bearing a pair of sheathed daggers in finely worked gold. Slung across his back were a beaded satchel, a bow of dark wood and a quiver of black-feathered arrows. Something in the way he swaggered towards them reminded Henry of Blossom swaying out of the haze of the rising sun that morning: and he marvelled at the fact that less than a day had passed since then.

'Hiya, buddy,' said the little Celt, sitting on the ground by the fire and laying his weapons around him. 'Thought you might need some backup. Oh, yeah,' he added, gesturing at the chairs, 'the guys wanna take this lot back with the rest of the stuff.' He looked at the figure. 'OK?'

They barely had time to get to their feet before the chairs were whisked up into the darkening sky by one of the drones.

Henry turned with a growing sense of foreboding to gaze around the circle of ancient stones, which, in their massive immobility, seemed to radiate an aura of doom. It was as if they knew that a death sentence had been passed upon him and the executioner was approaching fast.

'Come on then,' he said, with a sigh as he bent to sit on the ground by the little campfire, 'let's get it over with.'

The figure looked up. 'Yes. Yes, of course. As you will have realized, the Clatworthies reconsidered their decision to leave you to fend for yourself against Miss Killjoy and Mr. Strawbridge and their gangs. A change of heart that was, you may be interested to learn, brought about in no small measure by an insistence on the part of WPC Gwen Evers, Josephine Cornwall and Blossom Dart that abandoning you to the gangs' tender mercies would not only have been immoral, but also an act of gross cowardice on their part. Their agreement to hand over the original encoder to Kinsman was a different matter. It had been made centuries earlier, you see, and they intended to honour it in full, regardless of what the cost of doing so might be to their self-respect, their reputations and, more important from your perspective, your continuing good health.'

* * *

As soon as Kinsman flashed into existence on the edge of Sodmire for his rendezvous with Mervyn and Robbie, he was caught in Mervyn's 'bloody great, fireproof butterfly net', a force field generated by the vehicle known as the Multi that Henry had thought looked like a giant Swiss Army Knife on wheels when he'd met Robbie working on it at The Stone Dancers.

With Kinsman held in enraged immobility, Mervyn and Robbie set about breaking the connection between him and the institute to allow them to suspend the bungee effect for just long enough to replace him in the cycle with a convincing replica of the original encoder. When they re-established the connection, the fake encoder rocketed up into the future for the irritable Ernie Stampeasy to find on the departure platform of his laboratory in AD 2088. So overwhelmed with joy was he by its unexpected arrival that he didn't bother to check either its authenticity or its viability, preferring instead to connect it immediately to his mainframe computer and turn it on, blissfully unaware that it contained a malicious little computer virus created by Mervyn and Robbie for the specific purpose of, as they say in the world of temporal genetics, 'kicking his miserable arse'.

Robbie had christened this vicious little gem of a digital invader Billy Whizz, and its purpose in life was three-fold.

Its first task was to disable Ernie's computer by paralyzing its operating system as soon as the fake encoder was switched on.

Its second task was to mutate into an even more virulent infection named Ghengis Mink and jump from the mainframe into Ernie's central nervous system, reprogramming his brain in the process and turning him into the avenging angel of a human rights lawyer known thereafter as Papa John Grisham QC who, in AD 2089, finally secured the prosecution and subsequent imprisonment for life without parole of the institute's board of directors and the board and senior management team of their insurers, Scientific & Mercantile Ins., for the part they had all played in initiating and maintaining The Kinsman Abuse.

Ghengis Mink's final task was to re-enter the mainframe computer and send copies of himself to every device with which the system had ever communicated, and, in so doing, ensure the destruction of every last scrap of information relating to the Clatworthy clan and the institute's work on temporal genetics – with the exception, of course, of the files that had already been transferred into the safekeeping of the legal firm of Grisham, Payne, Calliope and Hertz. With his final task completed to his satisfaction, Ghengis vanished from the face of the earth. Or so it seemed. There has since been a suggestion, made by a twenty-second century astrophysicist and Nobel laureate, that the mischievous little virus travelled back to the beginning of time, where, having taken a quick look around the blackness of the embryonic universal void, he hesitated for less than a nanosecond before uttering the immortal words 'Oy, you! Turn on some lights!'

Once Mervyn and Robbie had satisfied themselves that they could no longer be pursued by Kinsman, Stampeasy or anyone else from the institute or its insurers, the Clatworthy clan – with the exception of Perce Pratt – used their bracelet encoders to travel to a secret location where they intend to enjoy their immortality in well-earned peace and quiet. Although any suggestion that they mean to do so with their slippers on and their feet up in front a fire should be treated with the contempt it deserves.

* * *

'And Kinsman?' asked Henry, anxiously. 'Did he . . .? I mean, what happened to him? Is he still in the butterfly net?'

'No, no!' said the figure. 'They let him go. They had no choice, really, did they? They felt that he had suffered enough and it wouldn't be right to detain him longer than was necessary for them to make good their escape.'

'And is he,' Henry stood up and gazed around the clearing, 'still after me?'

'Oh, yes,' replied the figure, getting slowly to its feet. 'Absolutely!'

'Well, shouldn't I . . .? I mean, what can I . . .?'

'You could try running away,' said the figure, pressing a stud on either side of the helmet mask, causing it to crack open and come apart in two pieces to reveal a face and head horribly disfigured by fire. 'But I can assure you that it wouldn't do you any good if you did.'

Henry and Titus stared in awe as the man behind the wounded features smiled grimly in recognition of the shock he saw etched in their faces.

Henry swallowed hard, and backed away.

'I know you,' he said. 'You dragged me out of my car.'

'Indeed,' said the figure in a hissing whisper as it took a step towards him. 'William Ignatius Constantine Kinsman at your service: I have been waiting a very long time for this moment . . . Mr. Kite!'

'I knew it was you,' said Titus, getting to his feet and drawing his sword.

Kinsman turned cold eyes towards him. 'Is that so?' he hissed. 'And you think that makes a difference, do you?'

'Back off, *buddy*!' warned Titus, raising his sword. 'Henry's my mate!'

'Indeed he is. Why else do you imagine I allowed you to . . . stick around?'

'Don't get all hoity-toity with me, buddy! You want Henry, you'll have to go through me to get him.'

'I think not,' said Kinsman, holding up a hand. 'Now is not your time.'

The little Ancient Briton vanished with a soft hiss.

'Now then, where were we?' asked Kinsman, turning to Henry. 'Ah, yes, of course, you were thinking of running away, were you not?'

Henry shook his head. 'No,' he said, sticking out his chin, 'not anymore. There's no point, is there? Besides, I'm sick of running away all the time. I've been doing it all my life and I've had enough of it.'

'An admirable sentiment, I'm sure. But do you really believe that you have what you need to back it up?'

'Maybe,' said Henry, straightening his shoulders. 'Maybe not. Anyway, what's it to you?' He sniffed and stood as erect as his uncertain courage would let him. 'And I hope you've enjoyed yourself, *buddy*, with all the story telling and the pontificating and,' he pointed at the campfire, 'sitting there like some sort of vengeful spider, toying with me and the others.'

He took a deep breath. 'Come on then,' he invited, shutting his eyes and sticking out his chest. 'Do what you've gotta do and let's get it over with. I've had enough of you and your bullshit stories.'

Nothing happened.

He waited for several seconds.

Still nothing happened.

He opened an eye, and saw that Kinsman had turned away and was standing with his hands thrust deep into the pockets of his robe, gazing out beyond the stones at the setting sun.

Henry opened his other eye. 'So,' he asked, 'you're *not* gonna kill me?'

'If I were, don't you think I would have done it already?'

'I don't know. I thought, perhaps, you might want to . . . you know, torture me or something?'

'Really? And why would I want to do that?'

'Well, I mean . . . you've had a bit of a rough time, haven't you? And they kept telling me that you thought it was my fault, and . . .' His face brightened. 'So you're *not* gonna kill me or torture me, then?'

Kinsman turned towards him.

Henry leaned backwards.

Kinsman smiled a slow smile, and turned away. 'Mervyn and Robbie didn't let me go immediately, which was just as well, really, because as soon as they gave me the encoder, I realized that it had been used, and I was angry – *very* angry and after blood. And when they told me that you were the one who had used it, most of the blood I was after was yours.'

'But . . . you're not after it now,' asked Henry, hopefully, 'right?'

'Before I could escape from the force field and come after you, Max and Nils shot me with tranquilizer darts.'

Kinsman turned with a rueful smile. 'To say that the cocktail of drugs they contained calmed me down would be to seriously understate the facts. I was paralyzed, mind and body, and prevented from doing anything that might have harmed you, or me, or anyone else. Then they sent me to Eve in San Francisco.' He took a long, deep breath. 'I was there for a long time. A very long time! And it was hard. Very, *very* hard! So hard, in fact, that there were times when I thought I would never come through it. But Eve helped me to stand back from what had happened to me and see it for what it was and, in the process, to realize that it hadn't been wasted and that none of it had been your fault. Most important of all, she helped me to understand what I had become, and that none of that was your fault, either. Or mine.'

He walked slowly towards Henry with his arms extended and his hands held out in front of him, palms down.

'Please,' he said, 'let me show you?'

Henry hesitated for only the briefest of moments, before reaching out and taking Kinsman's scarred hands in his own.

There was a brilliant flash of white light, and suddenly he felt himself cascading through enormous vistas of time and space. He saw the distant past and the distant future kaleidoscoping together around him. He saw massive volcanoes spewing molten rock and noxious gases, and primordial seas teeming with life. He saw a world of lush vegetation alive with dinosaurs, flying reptiles and tiny, scurrying mammals. And he saw human civilizations rising and falling amid disease, disaster and war. Finally, he saw a distant Earth, desolate and barren, with human life migrating out beyond the galactic void. Then, suddenly, he was back at the ancient stone circle with Kinsman's thin hands, warm and real, holding his in a shared present.

'I no longer need encoders,' said Kinsman. 'That's what the good doctor showed me: that and many other wonderful things about myself and the power of the human mind. There is hope for us, Henry, as individuals and as a species. That is what I wanted you to understand. That, and how you came to be in this place, at this time. You didn't select it. All you did was open the way. The encoder on your wrist had already been programmed. This was its default setting: the meeting place for the Clatworthy clan, and the first step on the way to where they have since gone. Although not quite in this now. You were out by a matter of weeks. Their futures are in front of them. Just as yours is in front of you. Make the most of it, boy. And be good to yourself. But most important of all, be as good as you can be to others. Don't waste your life. And don't help others to waste theirs.'

He let go of Henry's hands. 'I must go now,' he said, distractedly. 'But call me, if you need me. You will know when and how. In the meantime, decide what is most important to you, and do your best to find it and hold on to it, whatever it turns out to be. But not at any price, Henry: not at any price! That is the way of the frightened, infantile mind.'

'Wait!' said Henry, as Kinsman started to pull away.

'No. I have things I must do. Just as you have. Goodbye. Although, not for the last time I think.' And with that, he shimmered, faded, and vanished.

Henry stood for a long time with his head bowed, surprising tears welling in his eyes and running unchecked down his cheeks.

After a while, he looked at the setting sun. He smiled and shook his head. Then he turned towards the sound of radio static in time to see Blossom materialize in front of him with a crackle and a hiss.

'Hello, lover,' she said, walking towards him dressed and armoured for war as she had been that morning, 'how's things?'

He drew his hands down over his face with a sigh. 'They could be better, I reckon. Then again, they could be a hellova lot worse. How about you?'

'Oh, y'know, nothin' special. Just off to kick the shit outa the Romans over Watling Street way.' She tilted her head to one side. 'The whole family's goin'. Wanna come?'

'Best offer you've had for years, buddy,' said a voice. 'He's gone then?' added Titus, gazing around the clearing. 'Probably just as well. I don't reckon I'd have had much chance against that one, do you?'

'None at all, my little Love Muscle,' said the lieutenant. Like the other two, she was armed and armoured for war.

'Got to protect your mates, though, eh?' said Titus, drawing his sword and sighting along it. 'And those bastards shouldn't have done what they did to my family, buddy. They need a good kickin', you ask me.' He raised a knowing eyebrow. 'And I reckon they're gonna get it.'

'You're going to fight them?' said Henry. 'The Romans? You're going back to Watling Street to . . .?'

'Don't talk daft, lover!' snorted Blossom. 'What d'you think we are, stupid or somethin'? We're not gonna fight the bastards.'

'Oh, good,' said Henry. 'For a moment there I thought . . .'

'We're going to accept their surrender. Then we're gonna kick their murdering arses back to where they came from.'

'Oh,' said Henry, 'that's . . . But . . . Really?'

'Well,' said Titus, briskly, sheathing his sword, 'you comin' or what?'

'Sorry? What? Who . . .? You mean me?'

'You see anyone else round here, buddy?' grinned Titus.

'Maybe this'll help,' said Blossom. She slid a hand down the front of her leather thong. 'Said I'd bring it for you, didn't I?'

Henry hesitated as she held her clenched fist towards him.

'Come on,' she urged, 'we 'aven't got all bleedin' day!'

'What is it?' he asked, holding out a tentative hand.

'Here,' she jiggled her fist. 'He wanted you to have it . . . your dad? Reckons it's all he's got left from . . . you know, the old days, an' that.'

She dropped something warm and metallic onto his up-turned palm.

'Thank you, I . . .er, thanks,' he said, too embarrassed to look at it as he slipped it into a pocket of his jeans.

'An' there's these,' said Blossom, delving into the thong again and bringing out something small and black. 'She said she promised 'em to you before you, you know,' she grinned, 'and ended up here.'

Henry smiled shyly and looked down at the thing on the palm of his hand. It was a pair of black panties, lacy, see-through and soft. He nodded and stuffed them quickly into a pocket of his jeans.

'Right!' said Blossom, clapping her hands and looking around at the others. 'Time we was someplace else, I reckon, don't you? Take care of yourself, lover,' she said, leaning forward and kissing him on the cheek. 'See you round, p'rhaps, eh? Or not. Up to you. By the way,' she lowered her voice and leaned closer, 'she would have brought 'em herself, only she's not as confident as she might look.' She pulled away with a wink. 'You hear what I'm sayin'?'

Then she stepped back, tapped her wrist, and vanished.

'See ya, buddy,' said Titus. 'Oh yeah,' he added, taking the beaded satchel from across his shoulders and tossing it to Henry. 'Thought maybe you could, you know, use this?'

Henry caught it and lifted the flap. Inside was a purple bath towel, slightly singed around the edges. He smiled and looked up. 'Thanks,' he said, making a churning motion with his hand, 'and, er . . . y'know?'

'Yeah, buddy,' said Titus, 'you too.'

'Look after yourself, sir,' said the lieutenant. 'By the way, over there,' she pointed at a trilithon behind her, 'there are a few things that you might find useful, if you should decide to . . . Well, anyway, you'll know.' She smiled. 'Here,' she said, pressing a piece of paper into his hand. 'And dress warm.'

There was a brief hiss of white noise, and Henry was alone again with the wind, the standing stones and the darkening sky.

He stood with his head bowed for a long time, deep in though. Then he glanced at the piece of paper in his hand. There were sequences of numbers printed on it in neat lines. He looked up, and walked across the twilit clearing towards the trilithon the lieutenant had pointed at. Behind it he found, laid out on the ground at the base of the stones, the arms of a Celtic warrior.

He looked down at them for a long time before shaking his head and reaching into his pocket for the metal object Blossom had given him.

He held it up in the fading light. It was a bronze medallion on a chain with an image of two children, running side by side, engraved on it.

He turned it over. There was writing engraved on the other side.

He peered at it in the last rays of the setting sun.

It read:

Stratton Widger Primary School, 2044
Third place in the Three-legged Race (Mixed Gender)
Irene Cornish & Leonard King – aged 8

After a moment's thought, he took off his clothes and packed them into the beaded satchel. Then he wrapped the singed bath towel around his waist, and hung the medallion around his neck. He pulled Jo's panties on under the towel, hung a sheathed sword on an ornate belt over his shoulder, checked a line of numbers on the sheet of paper, pressed a sequence of tattoos on his wrist, and vanished with a soft *whooooooosh*.

To be continued . . .

Lightning Source UK Ltd.
Milton Keynes UK
UKOW04n1519310715

256179UK00002B/27/P